Schular of Magic

ART OF THE ADEPT
VOLUME THREE

By

Michael G. Manning

Cover by Amalia Chitulescu
Map Artwork by Maxime Plasse
Editing by Keri Karandrakis
© 2020 by Michael G. Manning
All rights reserved.
Printed in the United States of America

ISBN: 978-1-943481-38-5

For more information about the Mageborn series check out the author's Facebook page:

https://www.facebook.com/MagebornAuthor

or visit the website:

http://www.magebornbooks.com/

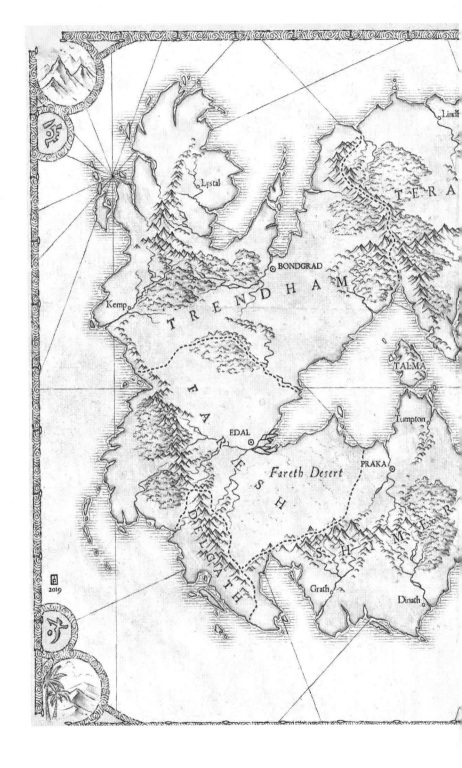

Chapter 1

Will stared up at the towering stone edifice that loomed over him and the other workers. The Lanover Dam was a massive structure that rose eighty feet above where he currently stood, at the base on the downstream side. *Not stone, concrete,* he reminded himself silently, using the term from his engineering class. It looked like stone, though.

As he had recently learned, there were several different types of dams, but the Lanover Dam was what was known as a buttress dam. Originally it had been built as an arch dam, but the structure had shown signs of incipient failure and later builders had added the buttresses, massive iron and concrete supports that angled up from the downstream side, to reinforce the dam wall.

"They should have built it with buttresses in the first place," opined Will. "There's no way a wall that thin could hold all that water."

The lead engineer, a man named Duncan, shook his head. "It did, though, for nearly fifty years. But you're right, it wasn't quite thick enough."

"I don't see how it would last five minutes, much less fifty years."

"It's the arch that does the trick. As it comes under load, the hydrostatic pressure compresses the concrete, increasing its strength," explained Duncan. "They just miscalculated a little when they first built it. It's a miracle they managed to fix their mistake before it collapsed."

"Why didn't they just fill in the downstream side completely?" asked Will. "Like a gravity dam."

"You're talking about a huge increase in the amount of filler and concrete to do that. An arch dam solves the problem with structural elegance and saves a lot of expense."

Will gave his preceptor a lopsided grin. "And yet they had to buttress it anyway, and now we're doing it again. Why do we have to remove this buttress anyway? Wouldn't it be better to just build two new ones on either side of it?"

"We're going to do that, but removing the old one is just as necessary. Damage can't be fully seen until we get it out of the way. If we just put a bandage over it by filling it in, we won't be able to see if there's seepage."

"If it's seeping, wouldn't we see the water?"

"Not if it's underground, which is most likely where it would be. We could bury this thing under stone and concrete only to have the entire thing wash out from underneath. Then it would all come crumbling down in a rush. Trust me, doing the maintenance properly is well worth it."

Will's fellow student, Stephanie Beresford, was sitting in a camp chair nearby. Being the daughter of a viscount, she seemed to feel that field work was beneath her and she wasn't shy about showing her displeasure. "I really don't see why we need to be here," she whined as she poked lazily at the tiny fire elemental hovering in front of her with one finger.

Duncan sighed. "Even as a lady of the realm it's always handy to be well educated about practical matters."

"I don't see why," she huffed. "I'm never going to be an engineer anyway."

The instructor looked away, but not before Will saw the look of annoyance on the man's face. Being a commoner, Duncan couldn't afford to offend the young aristocrat, even if she was his student. Most of the teachers

Chapter 1

at Wurthaven were noblemen themselves, but some, like Duncan, weren't, which forced them to perfect a balancing act of authority and their lower social standing.

Will could definitely sympathize. He didn't plan on becoming an artificer or engineer himself, but he had gained a lot of respect for the meticulous thought and planning that went into their work. Contrary to what he had once believed, a lot of rigorous math and preparation went into building things. It was every bit as much of a science as alchemy, and in the case of a dam, a lot more people's lives depended on the engineers getting it right.

As Will watched, the laborers finally peeled back the concrete casing that made up the bulk of the buttress they were carefully demolishing, exposing the iron brace. Seeing them hard at work destroying the structure made him nervous, but a new buttress had already been completed on one side and a heavy iron temporary brace was already in place on the other side to take up the slack as the damaged buttress was removed.

"Would one of you like to do the honors?" asked the instructor.

"Honors?" asked Stephanie, who had finally gotten out of her chair.

"Now that the metal is exposed, we can accelerate their work by changing the properties of the iron," said Duncan.

"He wants us to weaken it," added Will helpfully.

Stephanie sniffed. "No thanks."

The instructor grimaced. Having a sorceress do the job was preferable since using her power wouldn't shorten her lifespan, but the young noblewoman didn't have much concern for the problems facing engineer wizards.

"I'll do it," volunteered Will.

"Are you sure?" asked Duncan, barely concealing his relief. He had even less desire to use his magic if he could avoid it. "For something this big we usually prefer to have a sorcerer on hand, for obvious reasons."

But at least he has a good reason, thought Will. "Anything she can do, I can do," he announced.

"You're aware of the cost?"

Will nodded. "It won't cost me anything. Talk to Master Courtney if you don't believe me." Alfred Courtney was the head of the Research Department at Wurthaven and one of the few people who knew some of the details of Will's unique capabilities.

The engineer nodded. "He said something to that effect, but it's hard to believe. Very well, show me what you can do." He waved a hand in the direction of the crumbling buttress.

Will moved closer, until he was standing directly beside the exposed iron. Working from memory, he constructed the sixth-order spell that would allow him to manipulate the metal's material properties. At the same time, he expanded his outer shell and began to absorb as much turyn as possible. He waited until he was at capacity before channeling the energy into the spell and releasing it upon the iron. Its appearance changed before his eyes, and the iron began to look dry and powdery on its surface.

Will motioned to one of the workers, who tested it with a cold chisel. The brace flaked and fell apart as though it was brittle stone rather than solid iron. The man nodded at Duncan. "It's good." Then he addressed Will, "How long do we have?"

"It's permanent," said Will.

The instructor stared at him. "How much power did you invest? You should have used a temporary transformation."

"It didn't cost me anything," repeated Will. "This way we don't have to do it again later."

Chapter 1

Duncan studied him with curious eyes. "Aren't you tired at least?"

Will shrugged. "I'm not opening my gate—my source—to get the turyn. I absorb it from the environment. It does take some effort, but I don't get tired according to how much turyn I use. It has more to do with how much focus and concentration it requires."

"I'm not sure that makes sense," replied his instructor.

"It's like the difference between digging a hole with a shovel and reading a book," said Will. "For most wizards using magic is like physical labor, because they're using up the turyn that keeps them alive. I'm not doing that. I'm using ambient turyn that I absorb, so for me the fatigue comes mainly from concentration. It's a purely mental exercise, so I don't get exhausted as easily and it's more of a mental fatigue."

Stephanie broke in, "The important thing is that we know how special he is. Otherwise he'll be forced to tell us, again and again." She punctuated her words with a sour grimace of disgust.

Will ignored her, studying the dam with his eyes rather than giving her remark any attention. After a second he remarked, "Knowing that this buttress can't support any of the load makes me feel nervous."

The instructor nodded. "That's a natural reaction, but not to worry, that's why it's designed with double the tolerances needed. The buttress on the left and the temporary brace we've installed are each capable of handling the load by themselves, just in case either one should fail. We're perfectly safe until we finish the repair work."

A sharp noise, a crack that was reminiscent of thunder with a muffled tone, rang out. It was a sound unlike anything Will had ever heard, and it made his heart jump in his chest. Stephanie glanced at him in confusion, but

Duncan recognized the sound immediately. "Watch out!" yelled their instructor, leaping forward to grab their wrists as a massive slab of broken concrete fell toward their heads. It was far too late, however. Will and Stephanie's reactions were too slow and by the time their brains had registered what was happening, they were on the verge of being flattened into jelly. Will's point-defense spell snapped into being even before he consciously decided to use it, and the massive block slammed into it and split into several pieces that fell to either side. His shield vanished and reformed twice more in quick succession, shunting the larger fragments away from them. It happened faster than he could think, at a level below conscious thought, just as Arrogan had once told him it would: *"Force effects that you can instinctively cast operate at the speed of the soul."*

The instructor and his two students froze in place as the massive fragments settled to the ground in a shower of stone chips and dust. Will was almost as surprised by what had happened as the others were, even though it had been his magic that saved them. Looking up, he saw a long crack growing along the surface of the dam accompanied by more cracking and popping sounds. Smaller pieces of stone continued to fall, and water began to spray from the crack.

Duncan's mouth fell open. Then he muttered, "We're dead."

Stephanie turned to run, but Will caught her wrist. "We can't outrun it. We'd need an hour's head start to get somewhere safe. We have to shore up the dam." Even as he spoke, the buttress to their left shifted sideways as it surrendered under the immense strain. The temporary iron brace was also beginning to bend. It appeared neither of them were operating according to the designer's expectations.

Chapter 1

The sorceress' face was red as she jerked and tried to pull away, but Will's grip was like iron. "Let me go, churl! I'm not dying here with you!"

He ignored her as he constructed a different force spell above the palm of his other hand, one meant to conjure a flat, wall-like force effect. Unlike the point-defense spell, he couldn't cast it reflexively, but it was only third-order, so it only took a few seconds to prepare. Will invested it with power and applied it to the weak portion of the dam above them.

As Will had learned previously, force effects ignored basic physics in several important ways. For one, they ignored things like mass, inertia, and momentum. A force shield couldn't be moved by any amount of normal matter. Its key limitation lay in the amount of turyn required, for the energy needed increased exponentially as a function of both distance from the caster and the size of the effect being created.

In this case, the wall that Will created was over thirty feet above his head, and it covered a ten by twenty-foot area. Those two factors combined meant that he wouldn't be able to maintain the spell for more than a minute, even though he had already expanded his outer shell and begun absorbing turyn as quickly as possible. The instructor pointed out that fact almost immediately. "Nice idea, but we can't keep that up."

The workers beside the failing metal brace looked at Duncan uncertainly. They were seconds from panic. Will spoke quickly, "I can keep it in place for a minute or two. Stephanie, if you use your elemental to supplement your power, you and I can take turns keeping a force wall in place. The workers can sort out the problem with the iron brace while we do that, right, Instructor?"

Duncan nodded. "We don't have any other options."

"I don't know that spell," said Stephanie, pulling away. "Let me go!" Will's hand clamped down harder on her wrist. "You're hurting me!" she shrieked.

Will found it hard to believe she hadn't learned one of the most basic spells they had been taught at the beginning of their second year. *Nobles! Stupid, lazy...* He pushed those thoughts away. They wouldn't help. Instead he attached a source-link to her with barely a thought and began draining her turyn.

"What are you doing?" she asked, her eyes widening in alarm. "Stop!"

"Draw from your elemental. Together we can hold this," Will explained.

Stephanie continued to struggle, but her strength faded quickly. She did draw some turyn from her elemental, so she wound up helping him inadvertently. As the seconds ticked by, Will saw Duncan join the laborers and begin working to reinforce the iron brace. From what he could see without joining them, the central beam had started to fold in an unusual manner, though whether that was because of a flaw in the material or unexpectedly high stresses he didn't know.

The workers wrestled the heavy iron bars into place while Duncan took the unusual step of welding them directly with magic. Will knew it took a lot of turyn to do, and he worried about the cost to his teacher, but it wasn't as though they had any better options at that point. "How much longer?" yelled Will. Stephanie and her elemental had run dry, and the turyn he was absorbing wouldn't be enough to last much longer.

"Ten minutes. Can you hold it that long?" called the instructor.

Will nodded, closing his eyes as he released Stephanie's hand. She slumped to the ground beside him, exhausted but still conscious, barely. She watched him with angry eyes.

Chapter 1

Internally, Will tried not to panic, but he knew with certainty that he wouldn't last another minute, much less ten. *What do I do? What do I do?* His thoughts ran in circles without providing solutions. *I need to absorb turyn faster.* He stretched outward, trying to make his outer shell, the boundary that he drew turyn in with, larger. He failed, but he kept pushing.

Something happened then, and it felt as though his body was slipping away. For a split second he was looking down on himself, as though he floated in the air. Unfortunately, his control also vanished. The energy stopped completely, until his perspective snapped back into its accustomed place, and then he had to work furiously to catch up. The brief loss of control had put him even further behind.

Sweat rolled down his forehead, and the world began to turn gray as he came to the end of his supply of turyn. Oddly, something occurred to him then, a memory of a lesson in alchemy. *"The rate of diffusion of one solute into another is dependent on the difference in concentrations."* Who had said that? Arrogan, or perhaps Professor Karlovic, it hardly mattered. It worked for liquids and gases, surely it would be the same for turyn as well.

Desperate, he split his concentration as he tried something new. He pushed outward with his absorption shell, while at the same time pulling inward on the turyn that entered it, keeping the turyn compacted at the center to create an energy vacuum within most of the space around him. It had just been a vague notion in his mind, but it made sense, and somehow, it worked. His rate of turyn absorption increased, and as the seconds ticked by, he began to feel hopeful. It seemed he was absorbing close to the same amount of turyn he was using.

He wasn't sure if it was slightly more, or slightly less, though. Time would tell. "Are you holding up?" asked the instructor worriedly. "This is taking longer than I thought."

Will opened his eyes to stare at Duncan, but he didn't dare speak. The world was spinning, and he felt as though the slightest disturbance might cause him to topple into disaster. He gave a faint nod, then closed his eyes again. Watching them didn't help his state of mind. It just made it seem as though time was passing even more slowly.

I can do this, he reminded himself, trying to deny the panic bubbling up just beneath the surface of his conscious mind. *Don't think about the time.* His breath came in short gasps as his strict turyn control left his body bereft of its normal energy for autonomic functions. He had to consciously remember to breathe. *As if I don't have enough to worry about.*

An eternity ticked by with agonizing slowness. He began to think he might make it. The instructor and the workers had to be close. It was then that his heart began to lose its rhythm, and unlike breathing, he had no idea how to manage it consciously. It felt as though it was racing, then his chest tightened with pain and the world started to grow black.

"It's ready! Let go, Will!" came the instructor's words, ringing loudly in his ears. With a gasp, Will released the spell and forgot everything as his body jerked and he fell to the ground. A convulsive spasm shot through him, and he thought he might be dying, but then the tightness in his chest faded and his vision began to return to normal. He didn't bother trying to stand up. Lying down was enough, and he focused on breathing.

"Is he alive?" asked Duncan, leaning over and looking down at Will.

Chapter 1

Stephanie answered acidly, "It appears so, unfortunately."

"He saved our lives, Miss Beresford. You ought to be grateful for that," snapped the instructor with a stern expression on his face.

The young noblewoman didn't reply, but Will spoke up faintly to reassure his teacher, "I'm fine. I think."

Stephanie found her tongue then. "You won't be after I report your assault." She rubbed conspicuously at her wrist as she stared down at him.

Will caught sight of the red skin which was probably the first sign of a bruise. In his panic he had probably gripped her arm far too firmly, but then again, if she hadn't been trying to abandon them, he wouldn't have had to do so. Ordinarily he would have felt bad about having hurt her, but instead his fatigue and the look of spite on Stephanie's face combined within him to produce a different reaction.

He began to laugh.

"What's so funny?" she demanded, staring at him suspiciously.

"You," said Will, still chuckling.

"You won't find it a laughing matter once everyone knows about your awful behavior," she snapped. "Once I explain to them what you tried to do to me!" Her visage had taken on a look of almost gleeful malice.

Still lying on the ground, he looked up, meeting her eyes evenly. "Really? Is that what you think? Are you sure you've thought this through properly?"

Stephanie had never shown herself to be particularly bright in class, or anywhere else that he had seen, but as he watched her face, he could almost see the moment that her mind finished the social calculus, and she realized her error. A hint of uncertainty showed in her eyes. "They'll believe me when I show them this," she insisted, lifting her injured arm.

He sat up, shaking his head sadly. "I used to live in fear of people like you. You twist the truth to suit your whims, and regular people, people like me, are forced to simply accept the results. But that isn't the case anymore, is it Stephanie? Maybe you should rethink your plan for revenge against me for saving your life. There's two ways this can play out after we return.

"One, you can stick to the truth, and we'll both leave out the part about your shameful cowardice. Or two, you can spread lies and we'll see who winds up with more shit stuck to them in the end. You remember who my wife is now, don't you?"

Her eyes narrowed. "Assuming she doesn't cast you aside after she hears what—"

Will rose, dusting himself off. "Go ahead," he said, interrupting. "Selene trusts me, and not for any reason you'd understand. We've been through fire and blood together. Unlike you, she doesn't judge people according to their wealth or social standing. She'll see through your lies before I even tell her my side of the story."

He turned his back and began walking away. "So say whatever you wish when you get back. I would personally recommend the version in which you heroically assisted me in keeping this dam from failing, because the story you were thinking about telling ends with you bringing shame to your family."

Chapter 2

Will spent hours more at the dam assisting Duncan in making sure his makeshift repairs were stable before eventually being told to get some rest. He was only too glad to accept that order. The ride back to Wurthaven took nearly two hours, and he had to share the carriage with Stephanie. She made a point of pretending he didn't exist, and he returned the courtesy. Still, it made for an awkward period.

Back at the college, he disembarked and began walking toward his new home, one of the larger buildings among the private residences set aside for the senior masters of the college. In fact, it had once been the chancellor's manse until just a decade ago, when funds had been set aside to build the chancellor a newer dwelling more in keeping with the modern trends in architecture. The vice-chancellor had been considering a move when Selene's influence took the choice out of his hands. Will still marveled at the speed with which she had moved.

She only had one day after we were married, and yet she managed to set me up as though I were a nobleman, he thought wryly.

He mentally reviewed the last year in his mind as he walked. Thanks to his grandmother he didn't feel much like a married man, for he hadn't seen his royal bride since their first day of marriage, nearly twelve months past. He'd finished his first year at Wurthaven alone, and now he was right in the middle of his second year.

Several students waved at him as he walked. Will nodded and smiled politely but didn't stop to talk to any of them. They weren't friends. People had begun to treat him differently once it became known who he had married. Everyone was polite now, no one dared ignore him, and when he spoke, people listened. Having just passed his nineteenth birthday (alone—again), it felt strange to receive such deference, especially when he knew quite well that many of them despised him. Marrying the princess hadn't made him any friends, merely enemies who didn't dare do anything else but pretend at friendship.

Finally reaching the short walk through his private yard, he took a moment to study the place he had been told was his home. It was a three-story building with an elegant portico framing the front entrance. Marble columns on either side supported a second-floor balcony overlooking the small but well-kept garden that served as the front yard. Will advanced to the door and opened it without knocking, for it wasn't locked. He threw the bolt home once he was inside, though.

"I'm back!" he said loudly, but there was no answer. Will glanced around anxiously, studying the open door to the cloak room and then gazing down the entry hall. There was no one in sight. "I swear to the Holy Mother if you're planning on ambushing me, I'll tie you up and strap you until you're black and blue. Do you hear me? I'm not joking! It's been a long day."

There was no answer, and Will felt his blood pressure rising. Moving carefully, he took the right-hand doorway into the front sitting room. No one jumped out at him, but he didn't relax. He called out once more, "Blake, where are you?" Blake was the servant that Selene had forced on him before she had left, though the term *servant* didn't quite fit. Blake had made the arrangements for the house, along with everything else in Will's life. His nominal title was butler, but Blake Word was a gentleman's gentleman

Chapter 2

and it was his job not only to take care of Will, but to train him to be the sort of man worthy of being married to the king's daughter.

"I'm in the kitchen," came Blake's answer.

"Where's Selene?" responded Will, yelling back.

"Not sure. I'm sure she'll find you soon enough."

"Shit," swore Will. She could be anywhere. He scanned the sitting room once more, studying the corners of the room. The turyn in the room seemed to be moving normally, but that didn't mean much; his opponent was skilled in masking her presence. Will shifted his vision to enable him to see heart-light, and the room shifted into shades of gray. In one corner he could see a vaguely feminine outline.

As soon as his eyes focused on the figure, she launched herself at him, not as a woman would, but in the manner of a hunting cat. Selene leaped into the air, crossing the distance between them in an instant. She was stopped abruptly when her face met the point-defense shield that Will erected to halt her advance.

Selene's head snapped back painfully as she met the force shield and she fell over backward. Will stepped forward and put his boot on her neck, forcing her down against the rug. The saber he had summoned from his limnthal was pointed at her chest. "I told you I wasn't in the mood for this," he ground out, his voice cold and angry.

Selene smiled up at him, her tongue darting out to lick away the blood from her split lip in a manner that somehow betrayed her non-human nature. "Survival isn't about being in the mood." Then she focused on the tip of his sword. "But the iron is rude. I'm only trying to help you."

"If Blake sees you do something like that, he's going to know you aren't the real Selene," Will warned quietly. The woman under his boot was Tailtiu, one of the fae, and technically his aunt.

"Don't be a fool. He already knows. He's playing along because his mistress ordered him to. May I get up?" asked Tailtiu, indicating the foot he still had on her neck. Her lip had already healed.

"I suppose." Will sent the sword back to its place inside the limnthal, then removed his foot. As soon as he lifted it, Tailtiu's hand came up, grabbing his heel and shoving his foot up and back, forcing him off balance. Will fell back, and the fae woman was on top of him in the span of half a second, her fist driving down at his face. Will smiled maliciously at her as he heard the bones snap when Tailtiu's fist met his newest point-defense shield just before it could reach his head. His grin vanished when a sharp pain lanced through his skull. "Ow!"

His aunt shook her hand but gave no other sign that it hurt. "I'm the one with the wounded hand, or did I somehow hit you without knowing it?" She was still straddling his waist and she looked down. "Or did I hurt something else?"

"No, it was the spell I think," said Will, gritting his teeth as his head began to pound. "I think I overdid it today."

"You should have told me," said Tailtiu reproachfully. "What if you hurt yourself?" Her hips were moving slowly. "Does this help?"

"Stop that!" snapped Will. "Get off me." After she had complied, he added with a glare, "I did tell you, or I tried to."

"The part about beating me black and blue? I thought that was just a tease."

Will sat up, massaging his temples, but the ache refused to subside. "The dam we were repairing almost collapsed today. I used magic to brace it for ten minutes or more."

"You've been learning earth magics then? You didn't mention that," she remarked.

Chapter 2

He shook his head. "No. The only thing I could think to use was a force-effect spell that wasn't really meant for that kind of thing. The turyn drain was almost impossible for me to keep up with."

His aunt sighed. "Only a human would use something like that when it would be simpler to reshape the stone."

"Can wild magic do that?" asked Will. He had seen her reshape her body in many different ways, her current disguise being one of the mildest examples, but he had never observed her using magic outside of her own physical being.

She nodded. "Some of my people can manage such things, usually those who are older, or if they have a special affinity with earth magic. None of us use the force magics that you seem to prefer. They're unnatural."

"What about Grandmother?"

Tailtiu waved a hand dismissively. "Mother was a wizard before becoming fae: it goes without saying that she can use your magics."

Will's head continued to ache, which only served to accentuate his sour mood. The long ride back from the worksite had done nothing to ease his anger at Stephanie Beresford's attitude. Being attacked as soon as he entered the house certainly didn't help either. His ears picked up the soft sound of Blake's footsteps just moments before the other door into the sitting room opened.

Blake looked askance at him. "Should I brew something for a headache, sir?" He barely glanced at Tailtiu, even though she visually appeared to be his mistress, Selene.

Tailtiu's probably right, thought Will. *He'd show more deference to her if he really believed she was the princess.* "That might be nice, though I don't know if it will help," answered Will with a look of gratitude.

Blake nodded, already turning back toward the kitchen. "I'll put the kettle on."

A short while later Will sat in relative comfort, sipping a cup of willow bark tea. It tasted awful, acrid and bitter, but he knew from experience how well it worked for aches and pains. It had been one of the first things his mother had taught him. He was seated in a wide, cushioned chair, a luxury he had come to take for granted more quickly than he would have previously believed. When he thought about it, it bothered him. His new life was changing him, making him soft in certain ways. Of course, at the same time it was making him tougher in others. His eyes landed on Tailtiu as that thought crossed his mind and he pursed his lips. She met his gaze and lifted one brow in an unspoken question. *As usual, she's probably wondering if I'm looking at her physical attributes,* he noted mentally. He glanced away, telegraphing his lack of interest—he hoped.

His aunt's random acts of violence served to keep him alert. At one point in the past he had attempted to call her bluff by refusing to react to one of her faux assassination attempts. His operating theory had been that she wouldn't dare to *actually* harm him, so if he refused to play the game she would have to give up. That lesson had cost him one of his three remaining regeneration potions to mend a broken arm and replace a lost tooth, not to mention the bruises that accompanied those injuries.

As Arrogan had originally shown him, pain was an excellent teacher.

His headache put a damper on his desire to cook. Blake was excellent in almost every regard, but the man was mediocre in the kitchen. It had been Blake's original suggestion to hire a cook, but Will had refused, preferring to handle those chores himself. Today he regretted it. "I don't feel like cooking," he pronounced.

Chapter 2

"Shall I, then?" asked his manservant.

Will grimaced. "Cured ham and bread will be enough. Don't trouble yourself."

Taitiu smiled, showing teeth that would probably have been pointed if Blake hadn't been in the room. "I'll never understand your desire for cold meat. It's much better warm."

Will knew what she really meant. Tailtiu's idea of cooking meant making sure her food's heartbeat stopped before she finished eating it. Preferably somewhere in the middle of the process. He repressed a shudder at the thought.

Blake stood and went to a small side table in the front entry hall. He returned a moment later with a small wooden bowl, which he offered to Will. Inside were several calling cards.

"How many were there today?" asked Will.

"Just three."

Will nodded, waving the bowl away. "I'm not seeing any of them."

"One of them was from Laina Nerrow," Blake informed him before glancing in Tailtiu's direction. Laina was the older daughter of the baron Mark Nerrow, and unbeknownst to most, including herself, she was Will's half-sister. More importantly, she was Selene's closest friend, and over the recent months she had been growing increasingly impatient with her inability to meet with Selene face-to-face.

Tailtiu rose from her seat and gave Blake her best look of indifference. "Tell her I'm indisposed. I haven't been feeling well recently." She patted one cheek as though to comfort herself. "I think I'll retire early." She gave Will a smoldering look. "I'll be waiting for you in the bedroom."

Will gave Blake a helpless look and shrugged. "I'll be in my study. Bring the meat and bread up when you have them ready."

"You can't ignore her forever," suggested Blake.

"You might be surprised," Will responded, getting to his feet and heading for the private office where he did most of his studying. He had never imagined having something so pretentious as an office of his own, much less the grand house it was located within, but he was learning to adapt to the circumstances.

He found his place in the cushioned chair and put his feet up on the desk. Then he summoned the limnthal and addressed the ring he wore on his right hand. "I think I hurt myself today."

Arrogan's sour voice replied from the air in front of him, "And so you felt the need to wake me up to cry about it? Don't be such a titty baby."

It had been a considerable length of time since he had last spoken to the spirit of his former master, so the language caught him off guard. "What?" he sputtered.

"You heard me."

Will's eyes narrowed, though the expression was pointless since the ring had no eyes to see his face. "It's been well over a month since we last talked."

"You still don't get it, do you?" said Arrogan. "I told you before. I have no sense of time when I'm inactive. For all intents and purposes, I cease to exist, so every time you speak to me it feels as though our last conversation was just seconds ago."

"I guess that makes it easy to remember what we were talking about then."

"It's damned annoying," the ring shot back. "My entire existence is one endless conversation—*with you*. Think about that from my perspective for a moment."

"I see," said Will without sympathy.

"The hell you do, otherwise you'd be screaming as the existential horror seeped into that lard-filled bag you use for a brain."

Chapter 2

Will found himself snickering. He'd missed the old man's biting conversations. "I'll try to meditate on your misery later. In the meantime, I really do think I hurt myself."

The ring sighed. "And that's the extent of the sympathy I can expect. I suppose I should be happy with that much. I'm just a piece of jewelry after all. Fine, let's talk about your problem. I'm sure it's serious."

"And you called me a 'titty baby' just a minute ago."

A long pause followed before Arrogan finally responded, "Point taken. All right, tell me what's wrong with you this time."

Will did his best to describe what he had experienced at the dam when he had been struggling to draw enough turyn to maintain his spell, but he had difficulty finding words to express what he had done. "I sort of pulled all my turyn into a tightly concentrated knot, but I kept the outer shell I was using to draw turyn in with large, even though it was mostly empty."

"You maximized the concentration differential and the active surface area at the same time, is that what you mean?"

"Yes!" He felt a surge of excitement as the ring's description perfectly captured what he was trying to say. The terms Arrogan used were commonly used in alchemy, which was something entirely different, but they matched what had happened.

"Perfectly normal," pronounced his mentor. "Most second- and third-order wizards stumble across the technique eventually."

Will frowned. "You've mentioned orders in reference to wizards in the past, but you didn't have a ranking system for spells like we do these days. That doesn't make sense to me."

"People use classifications to make sense of the things that are important to them. That should give you a clue as to the fundamental difference between the wizardry of my day and the wizards of yours."

He thought about it for a moment. "You're saying they were more concerned with the skill of the wizard in your day, but now all we think about is the difficulty of the spell? I'm not sure why that would be the case. We still use the same spells, for the most part."

"But the wizards today are different," Arrogan pointed out. "Back then spell difficulty didn't matter because any wizard could manage just about any spell. That's why we just called them hard or easy but we didn't bother giving them fancy ranks and orders."

"And now there's only one order of wizardry," finished Will.

"Wrong. Now there's *no* order of wizardry." Will waited, ruminating over the remark, and eventually his former teacher continued, "Remember how we classified wizards. First-order meant the practitioner had compressed his source once, such that it only produced half the turyn of a normal person. Second-order meant they had halved it again, to one quarter, and third-order meant it had been halved a third time, to one eighth. The people running around pretending to be wizards in this degenerate age haven't compressed their source even a single time."

"Ahh," said Will, nodding.

"You know what we called wizards who hadn't compressed their source yet back in my day?"

"What?"

"Apprentices."

"I still think it would have been helpful to classify the spells like they do now," remarked Will.

Chapter 2

"Maybe," admitted the ring, "but you see what I mean now, don't you? For us it was more important to pay attention to a wizard's skill level, or at least his potential."

"I'm not sure I see why. You already said that any wizard could use any spell. What makes third-order any better than first, other than how long they might live?"

"Don't discount age. It's an important factor. Your ability will become more refined with time, and the more time you have, the more polish you will acquire. But again, you're right, based on your limited understanding at least. In my day a first-, second-, or third-order wizard could do most of the same things. None of them were killing themselves by using magic, and almost all spells were manageable by anyone. The big difference between the three orders is in their relative potential, both in the long and short term. Not only does the third-order wizard have four times the number of years to perfect his craft compared to his first-order colleague, but the speed at which he could be expected to improve his control and the heights to which he might rise were also greater."

"Control?"

"Turyn control," emphasized Arrogan. "The order a wizard achieves is a very good indicator of how much control he will be able to attain, how well he will be able to manage the turyn within himself and around himself. Back then, most wizards were first-order, and a much smaller portion, perhaps one in a hundred managed second-order. Very few made it to third-order."

"How few?"

"I only knew of a few dozen. I'd give you a percentage, but that would be a little skewed, since the third-order wizards also lived a lot longer. Suffice to say, it was big news when someone managed to coax an apprentice up to third-order. Most didn't try."

"Because of the death rate," said Will dryly.

"Exactly."

He still had trouble reconciling the fact that Arrogan's last journal had revealed his secret grandfatherly feelings for Will, and yet the old man had still pushed him toward something that had had every chance of killing him. The two things seemed to be at odds. Will stayed silent, lost in thought.

"You know I don't remember the final years, so I don't know for sure what I was thinking," said Arrogan suddenly. "But I have a pretty good idea what I must have been thinking."

Will lifted his chin. "And?"

"Well, given the odds, it's obvious I was desperate to get rid of you." A wicked laugh issued from the ring. "Ha! You thought I'd say something sappy, didn't you?"

He found himself shaking his head. "No, I honestly didn't. I know better."

"Then listen up. If I pushed you all the way to third-order it means I had a damn good reason to think you were capable of it. Do you know how many apprentices I lost?" The ring paused for a second, then answered the question. "None. Do you know why? Because I was that good. Maybe I was mean as hell, I won't argue that, but I knew how to train an apprentice. I wouldn't have pushed you to try for third-order if I wasn't pretty damn sure you'd succeed."

Will blinked, feeling a sudden warmth rising to his cheeks. "How could you tell?"

"Tell what?"

"If you thought someone could succeed, without dying."

"Intuition and careful observation. You watch enough people learning to use magic and you start to get a sense for those who have talent. Talent and stubbornness were the

Chapter 2

things I looked for. Lucky for you, neither common sense nor intelligence seem to be important factors, otherwise I'd probably have just traded you for a cow or something more useful and less aggravating."

"You almost slipped up there. That was dangerously close to a compliment," noted Will wryly.

The ring ignored him. "So, you seem to be developing a more mature control of turyn, but you said you hurt yourself."

He described the pain he'd started having after using the point-defense spell at home.

"Sounds like you sprained your will," observed Arrogan.

"Is that the same thing that happened to me when I first started expressing turyn?"

"I don't remember the event in question, so I don't know. It's helpful to think of your will as a muscle, even though it isn't. Regular exercise will make it stronger, but if you overdo it you can injure yourself. An injury to your will can range from something akin to a muscle sprain to something every bit as serious as tearing a muscle free of the bone. Any serious user of magic will eventually hurt themselves, but if you don't learn to avoid overdoing it you could potentially destroy your ability to use turyn—completely."

"So what should I do?"

"Avoid using any magic for a few days. Try something small after that. You'll have recovered from a minor injury in that time, but if it still gives you a headache, or any pain at all for that matter, then you should give yourself a full two weeks of rest, because that would indicate that you hurt yourself pretty badly."

"That really does sound similar to a muscle injury," agreed Will.

"It's a useful analogy."

Will glanced up as a bell rang from the front hall. Someone was at the door. It was already after dark and he hadn't agreed to meet anyone, so the interruption annoyed him. He considered letting Blake answer it, but a sudden impulse overtook him. Standing up, he stepped out of the study and shouted toward the kitchen, "I'll see who it is." After hearing Blake's acknowledgement, he strode purposefully to the front hall.

CHAPTER 3

A small figure stood before his front door, covered in a heavy wool cloak that was steadily dripping water. It had been raining heavily since shortly after Will had arrived home, but his visitor had apparently been caught by the elements.

Wool was an excellent material for damp weather. It could absorb many times its own weight in water before actually becoming wet, but once it had reached its limit it became a serious liability. Not only would it be wet, but it also weighed many times its normal dry weight. Will couldn't see his visitor's face but he knew better than to allow an unannounced stranger inside. Despite his newfound influence as Selene's husband he had no doubt that he had far more enemies than friends.

He spoke through the small window inset in the center of the heavy oaken door. "Whatever it is we're not interested. Leave a card tomorrow."

As he began closing the window, the stranger replied, "Please. I need to see Selene. She wouldn't turn me away." The voice was distinctly feminine with a cultured accent. It reminded him of Stephanie Beresford.

Just a year before, he would never have considered turning a woman away from his door when it was raining, but he was significantly less trusting these days. He had changed. Plus Tailtiu had already retired for the evening, meaning she had left. In spite of her part in keeping up the illusion that Selene was living there, Will refused to let her sleep anywhere near him. Selene's doppelganger was probably already back in Faerie.

"Sorry. No visitors without an appointment." He felt a faint pang of guilt as he shut the tiny wooden door that closed the window.

Before he had gone two paces a persistent banging began as the woman outside began pounding on the door. "Please! I left my card earlier. I have to see her!"

Will took a deep breath to calm himself, then returned to the door. This time he drew the bolt and opened the door so he could see the woman better. "I already told you we—" He fell back as the heavy wood slammed into him. It caught him slightly off balance and he fell to the right, catching himself on the wall as the woman shouldered her way through the opening.

"Selene!" she yelled, her voice piercing in both its clarity and volume. "Selene, it's me! I need your help. Where are you?"

Tailtiu's daily lessons had left their mark on him, and in spite of his surprise Will reacted a bit more decisively than he probably would have otherwise. As he pushed himself back away from the wall, his right foot swept out to hook the stranger's ankle before she could get out of reach. A second later his hand found her shoulder and he spun her around and sent her into a tumbling fall. Her head made a sharp 'clack' as her jaw struck the wood paneling, slamming her mouth shut. Will's teeth hurt in sympathy as the sound registered. *Ouch!*

"Sorry for that," Will apologized reflexively. "But you can't just barge in here. Who are you?" His hand reached for the woman's hood. In a sudden panic she jerked, and her hand came up. Once again Will's training took over before he recognized the fact that the woman was merely trying to keep her hood down. He caught her arm and twisted it into a wristlock before he had a chance to think. He released it just as quickly,

Chapter 3

feeling a sense of shame. *It seems like I've done nothing but abuse women today.*

"Ow! Let me go, you brute!" she shrieked as her hood fell away. Wet hair fell forward to hide her features, but not before Will recognized the face.

"Laina?" he asked in shock, releasing his half-sister and moving away to put more distance between them.

She seemed to flinch as he said her name. "Don't look at me," she ordered. Beneath the shadow of her hair Will could see that her eyes were red and swollen. Had she been crying? Laina looked away before he could make up his mind.

"Why were you out in the rain? Alone? Where's your escort?" he asked feeling a sudden rush of protective concern for her. Laina had never liked him, and truth be told he didn't much care for her either. Everything he knew of her had shown him that she was a typical young noblewoman, spoiled and entitled. But she was still his sister, even if she didn't know it.

"None of your business," she snapped. "Where's Selene? You can't keep her away from me forever."

There was blood at the corner of her mouth, making Will feel even worse. *Probably from when she hit the wall.* "Are you all right? You're bleeding." He pointed at his own lip to point out where the blood was, then he reached into a pocket and dug out a handkerchief to offer her.

Laina batted his offering away. "I'm fine. What have you done with Selene? Are you hiding her? If you've done something to her, I'll see that you pay for it in blood. Do you hear me?" Her red, swollen eyes held a certain intensity that utterly overshadowed her bedraggled and pitiful appearance. Will believed her.

Whatever his sister's other faults might be, she was at the least a loyal friend.

"She isn't here," he admitted.

"Liar. People have seen her. Even the king says she's here, with you, though I'll never understand why."

"I can't explain the details," said Will directly. "You wouldn't believe me anyway. Maybe you'll believe her when she gets back. I'm sure she'll explain everything then."

"You're blackmailing her, aren't you?" accused Laina. "This is some sort of extortion. It's the only way to explain this sham marriage."

Will threw his hands up in resignation. "There's no reasoning with you."

"It might be a bit more believable if you weren't keeping her locked away somewhere like a prisoner. No one has been able to see her in person."

"That's not true," Will argued. "Why, just last week…"

"No one that knows her—personally," corrected Laina. "What are you doing to her? Have you locked her away? There's no reason why she would refuse to see me."

Will sighed. "This isn't getting us anywhere." He moved to the door, intending to show her the way out, then paused. It was still raining heavily. "I'll have my man get a carriage for you."

"I need to see her," said Laina once more, a faint tone of desperation in her voice.

"She isn't here, but I'll make sure she talks to you first when she returns," he answered.

"When will that be?"

Months? Years? He didn't know. "It could be a while."

Laina's prideful visage cracked. "Please. I need her help."

The look on her face made Will's chest tighten. Whatever Laina's problem was, she obviously thought it was a serious concern. "Maybe I could help?" he offered. "If you'll tell me what you—"

Chapter 3

His half-sister's features hardened. "I'd sooner beg on the streets." She turned to the door on her own, opening it and stepping out. Then she glanced back at him. "You'll get yours when I figure out what you've done to her. Mark my words."

"It's still raining," he cautioned. "Let me get you a coach—" The door slammed shut.

Blake stepped out from the front room. "Perhaps you should have woken her to come down and see her."

Will glared at the man. He was all but certain that Blake knew about Tailtiu's ruse. "Laina knows her too well. You should know that as well as..."

Blake coughed, interrupting him. "I'm not sure what you're getting at, sir. Perhaps I should ask His Majesty for some clarification." There was a warning in the man's eyes.

Will closed his mouth abruptly. *Translation: don't say anything that you don't want the king to hear about.* Blake was clearly loyal to his mistress, but as Will had found out in the past, no one dared attempt lying to the king, not if they valued their lives.

He stared at his manservant for a long minute, listening to the rain pouring down outside. Then he turned to open the door and go out.

Blake called out to him with concern in his voice, "It's cold and wet out there, sir. Let me get you a rain cover."

"No time," said Will. "I'll be back later."

"It's dark. It isn't safe to be out in this alone."

"Exactly."

It should have been a half-moon that night, but the rainclouds ruined any chance of decent illumination. Will earned himself a painful headache as he adjusted his vision to make the best use of the scanty light. Apparently wild magic was just as bad for him as formal spells when it came to his injury. He followed Laina while keeping a considerable distance between them, trusting distance and the dim light to keep him unobserved.

The rain soaked through his doublet and undershirt as he followed Laina across Wurthaven's dark lawns and down the lane that led to the main entrance. He regretted ignoring Blake's advice. An oilcloth cover would have kept the worst of the water off, but what he missed most was his brigandine under-armor. He'd taken it off as soon as he'd gone to his study. Being outdoors without at least that much protection made him feel vulnerable.

The past year had made him a very paranoid young man.

And I'm probably wasting my time, he thought to himself. *Chances are she'll get home without any trouble at all and I'll have gotten myself soaked and chilled for naught.*

As Laina left Wurthaven behind and stepped onto the main road, Will noticed movement in the darkness ahead. Someone else was following her. His heart sped up, and he quickened his steps.

His mind considered the situation as he tried to close the distance. The stranger was skillful, following Laina at a distance of less than thirty yards without making enough noise to alert her. The newcomer clearly didn't have his ability to see in the dark, though, otherwise the fellow would have kept a greater distance, like Will. *Or is he just following her?* He had no way of knowing the stranger's intentions. "But I'll find out," he whispered under his breath.

He would have loved to use magic to hide himself, or to cover the sounds of his movement, but he didn't dare risk incapacitating himself. He relied on the noise of the rain to cover his approach, and he was no slouch at moving quietly when he needed to. Will sped up and began to close ground.

Chapter 3

The stranger was getting closer to Laina as well, and as the man passed under a streetlamp at the next intersection Will saw a flash of metal. Will charged.

The shadowy figure was less than ten feet from Laina's unsuspecting back when Will reached him. The man heard him splash through a puddle at the last moment, and Will saw a flash of bright eyes and thin brows above a cloth mask as the man turned and ducked his first punch.

The fellow failed to avoid the second, simultaneous swing, which connected with the his midsection. The man folded slightly, the air rushing from his lungs, while Will felt a sharp pain shoot up his arm. The assassin had been wearing some sort of armor.

Will's opponent had fallen to the ground, but the man rolled out of the way before Will could bring his foot down. Glancing up, Will felt a sense of relief as he saw that Laina had already noticed the fight and was wisely running away. He focused on her assailant. It was time to get some answers.

The man had already gotten back to his feet, and now that he had time to observe the fellow he could see that the man was rather short with a slim build. *This will be quick.* He moved in and was surprised when his foe spun, turning his back on him, something only a fool would do. When the man leapt from the ground and continued the spin, Will was almost caught off-guard by the heavy boot that came rushing at his head.

Will threw himself to the side, robbing the kick of some of its sting, but he still fell hard. He caught himself on one hand and pushed himself back toward the man, who was following up the kick with a lunging stomp. His sudden change of direction put him inside the fellow's attack, and he took advantage by driving his fist into the man's groin as the stranger stomped at the place where he'd expected Will to be.

The man let out a brief grunt of pain but didn't fall, even though Will was sure he'd connected solidly. His opponent took a step back, but Will pressed his attack, creating a point-defense shield to trip his foe.

Or rather, he tried to do so. A crashing wave of pain overwhelmed him and for a moment he couldn't see. It was followed by a more familiar sort of pain as his opponent took advantage of the moment and drove an elbow into the side of his head. Will fell sideways and caught a boot to the belly as he tried to cover his head. Then his vision cleared, and he saw a flash as a long-bladed knife appeared in the stranger's hand.

The world slowed to a crawl as Will tried to move in time, but his body wouldn't respond quickly enough. A sharp pain took his breath away, and then his head slammed into the cobblestones. Everything went black.

Sometime later he became aware of something striking his face at irregular intervals. Raindrops. With a groan he pried his eyes open. His head hurt fiercely, and he appeared to be lying in the gutter. A small river of rainwater flowed around his shoulder and along his back.

Cautiously, Will sat up, inspecting himself for the stab wounds he expected to find on his torso. He didn't find any, but his head pounded every time he turned it to look this way or that. "I'm alive," he muttered. "Why am I alive?"

"Because you're damned lucky," said a male voice. Will recognized it immediately; it was Blake Word. Glancing back, he saw the manservant leaning against the wall behind him. Blake was breathing heavily, as though he'd been running.

"What happened?"

Chapter 3

"I only saw the last of it. It looked as though you took a hell of a beating and then the fellow finished it off by slamming the pommel of his dagger into the side of your head. I chased him off before he could do anything more."

His fingers discovered a growing lump on the side of his head. "I'm surprised he didn't use the blade."

Blake shrugged. "You weren't the target. Bodies draw attention, unless you get rid of them, and that can be a lot of work."

Will wobbled as Blake helped him to his feet. "Do you think Laina made it home? She started running as soon as the fight started."

"She had a good head start then. I chased the fellow for a short distance after I got here. He ran in the wrong direction. I doubt he would have been able to catch up to her after that. Besides, he had to have been spooked after not just one, but two people intervened. My guess is he called it a night. If he tries again it won't be tonight."

Blake's analysis made sense, but Will wanted to be sure. He started to walk in the direction of Mark Nerrow's city home.

Blake put a hand on his shoulder, stopping him. "That won't accomplish anything. She'll be indoors long before you get there so you won't be able to ask her anything, and somehow I doubt you intend on knocking on Baron Nerrow's door to inquire after Laina's health."

"Someone else might have jumped her on the way home."

"You were out cold for several minutes. If she was attacked again it will be too late. Besides, you're in no shape for further adventures."

Will shrugged off the hand. Ignoring Blake's advice, he walked the streets until they were in front of Nerrow's city home. Only then, when he was certain Laina wasn't wounded in a side alley somewhere, did he relent and allow Blake to lead him home. The rain finally stopped while they were returning and in the quiet that followed, Blake made another observation. "She won't thank you for your efforts. You know that, don't you? That girl hates you with a passion."

"Doesn't matter," he replied. *She's my sister.* "I don't think she saw me clearly, which is preferable. I'd rather not have to answer her questions or give her any more suspicions."

Blake gave him a funny look. "Then why bother?"

"Selene would want me to look after her," Will answered, giving a misleading truth. Of course, Selene would have wanted him to protect Laina, but that wasn't his first reason.

"Good answer, and a true one, but be careful," cautioned the older man. "Her Highness might not like it if you spend too much attention on another woman, even her best friend."

Will began to laugh, which made his head hurt even worse, but he couldn't help himself. As sharp as Blake was, it was good to know there were at least a few secrets the man hadn't picked up on yet. "I don't think that will be a problem."

The other man gave him an odd look but said nothing during the rest of their walk home.

CHAPTER 4

Will was slow to rise the next morning thanks in large part to his injuries. It was a testimony to the painfulness of his bruises that they outweighed the pain of allowing Blake to cook breakfast rather than do it himself, as he normally preferred.

He poked at the rubbery eggs on his plate, dreading the next terrible mouthful, then he leveled an angry glare in Blake's direction. The older man sat across from him, grinning. "You must be very grateful to finally get the chance to eat properly cooked eggs."

"Eggs?" muttered Will sourly. "Is that what this used to be?"

"Tut tut! We'll have none of that this morning!" responded Blake. "These eggs have been cooked to perfection, just as Mama Word taught me years ago, may her soul rest in peace. Play your cards right and I might be willing to give you lessons."

Will stabbed his spoon in the cheerful manservant's direction. "Did your mother have something against butter? Or were we out?"

Blake frowned. "Butter is for toast. Why in the world would you defile your eggs with it?"

Will tried not to grind his teeth, silently promising himself that he wouldn't make the same mistake the next morning—not unless he woke up dead. He suppressed a shudder as he swallowed another mouthful while trying to ignore the acrid scorched flavor. It simply wasn't possible for him to believe the other man actually enjoyed his eggs that way. *No human could enjoy this.* He filed that thought away in a mental box labeled, 'Blake Word, Man or Monster?'

"You saved my life last night, now you're trying to kill me with crimes against food," he grumbled. "What were you doing there anyway? I don't recall bodyguard being one of your duties."

Blake smirked, but the expression didn't quite reach his eyes. "Then you'd be mistaken, which suits my purposes perfectly."

That lined up with Will's previous suspicions about the man. "How long have you served Selene?"

"Since she was seven."

"And before that?"

"I served in the army."

"Under which lord?" asked Will.

Blake hardly blinked. "It was detached duty, special service for His Majesty."

Will was still learning, but he'd gained a lot of experience while in the army, and from what Blake had said the man had been either an assassin or a spymaster, possibly both. "So, you retired from that and were rewarded with the job of royal babysitter."

"It has been an honor to serve Her Highness."

"Did you train her?"

The older man shrugged. "I'm not a sorcerer, so I couldn't help her with magic, but I taught her how to handle a blade."

Will had never seen his wife use steel in combat, but he had seen her battling with water blades created by an elemental on several occasions. "Then I may owe you my life yet again. Her skill saved me a time or two."

"I'll take that as a compliment."

"Perhaps you'd consider training with me a little?"

Chapter 4

The other man laughed. "Can you fight without magic?"

Fair point. "I used to," said Will. "These days I've been learning to include it as an additional weapon."

"You didn't use it last night," observed Blake. "You might have won if you had. What happened?"

Will explained his injury, then added, "When I tried to trip him with a spell, the pain caught me by surprise. Things went downhill after that."

"You should have retreated. I fought the fellow briefly before he ran. You couldn't have matched him without magic."

Will grimaced. "You sure?"

Blake nodded confidently. "I've been watching your fights with"—he paused for emphasis—"Selene. While her methods are unorthodox, your fighting style with that magical shield of yours is very nearly unbeatable, but without it you wouldn't have stood a chance. The man you fought was a highly skilled assassin, likely trained in Faresh."

"The desert kingdom? How could you tell that? He was fair-skinned." Will didn't know much about the southern kingdoms, but the Farrians were famous for several things: their sugar, their textiles, and their dark skin.

Blake seemed surprised. "You saw his skin? Your eyes are better than mine."

Will nodded.

"Well, light skin or dark, he was master of the Farrian fighting arts, what they call the Dalmen Kal."

"How could you tell?" asked Will.

"That spinning back kick he used on you was the first indicator. Add that to the fact that he nearly gutted me during the first pass when I came to your aid and I can say I'm fairly confident."

"He was better than you then?"

The older man shrugged. "You don't survive the type of duties I had in the army by being stupid or overconfident. I'm not as young as I used to be. I had the advantage of size and reach, but the man we fought last night was lightning quick. If he had been out for blood, there's a good chance both of us would be dead right now."

Will choked down the last of the burned eggs, followed them with a piece of overdone toast, then cleared his throat with some tea. "I guess I'll be skipping classes today, then."

Blake frowned. "Why?"

"I'll be busy watching Nerrow's house, in case our assassin returns."

"Can you use magic? You said you have to rest your powers, didn't you?"

"If someone is trying to kill Laina or hurt any of the Nerrow family I can't just let it happen," declared Will. "Selene would be disappointed in me otherwise," he added a few seconds later as an afterthought.

"If anything happens to *you,* Selene will kill *me,*" countered Blake. "Have you considered that? You're no match for the man we fought. Besides, after what happened I'm certain that Lord Nerrow will see that his daughter is well protected."

Will shook his head. "He doesn't know about the attack last night." Blake gave him a quizzical look so Will explained, "She snuck out yesterday and came here alone. Her father wouldn't have allowed that, so clearly, she wanted to see Selene about a private matter. She seemed desperate, so Laina was probably aware that she was in danger, yet she came alone anyway."

The older man rubbed his face. "So, she likely didn't tell her father then. You're right. Still, this isn't your problem. I suggest you send the baron an anonymous warning and let him deal with it."

Chapter 4

The advice was sound. Will couldn't argue that, but his gut was telling him something different. If Laina had only felt safe bringing her problem to Selene then she had probably had a good reason, a reason that presumably she thought Selene would agree with. *And if I alert our dear father to whatever it is, I could make things even worse for her,* he thought.

His determination firmed up, and Blake saw as much from his expression. Before Will could speak, the older man gave him an intent stare. "If only you knew someone skilled in both combat and stealth who could watch over her..."

"I appreciate the offer," said Will, "but I think it best if I—"

His manservant sighed loudly. "You're *my* responsibility. Have you considered discussing this with your wife?"

Will stared at him blankly. *I know he's figured out that she isn't really Selene.*

"Maybe she knows someone skilled in the art of disguise," said Blake, stretching out the words while waving one hand in a circular motion.

"Oh!" Will exclaimed as he finally understood. He nodded in agreement but didn't say more. *How did my life get so complicated?* he wondered. *I'm married, but I only spent one day with Selene before she had to leave. My fae aunt is impersonating her, my manservant knows, but I have to pretend he doesn't, otherwise he'll be forced to admit the truth to the king.* "And to top it all off, I'm trying to help my half-sister who doesn't know we're related," he muttered.

"What was that?" asked Blake. "I couldn't hear you."

"Nothing," said Will. "I'm just thinking out loud." Rising from the breakfast table, he made for the stairs. He stopped briefly before leaving the room. "Don't ever cook eggs again, not even if I'm on death's doorstep. In fact, especially not then. They'd probably push me over the edge. Stick to porridge if I'm too sick to cook."

Blake had the nerve to look genuinely hurt. "That's a bit much, even for a joke."

Does he really think they were edible? Will couldn't decide. "I wasn't joking."

A few minutes later he was back in his room, which presumably was where Selene was. Of course, Tailtiu hadn't returned yet, and normally wouldn't until late afternoon. Her service pretending to be the missing princess was something that Aislinn had worked out with Tailtiu—it wasn't part of any bargain with Will. Consequently, anything he wanted Tailtiu to do beyond her evening impersonation would have to be negotiated separately. He repeated his aunt's name three times and waited, knowing it would take her nearly twenty minutes to reach the house from the nearest congruence.

Usually she arrived in the form of a bird and slipped in through the window to avoid anyone seeing her comings and goings. Today was no different. She arrived after nearly an hour had passed, which meant Will was running short of time if he was to make it to his first class of the day without being tardy.

"What took you so long?" he demanded shortly.

His aunt arched one brow. "Pardon?"

"It shouldn't have taken you an hour."

"I'm under no obligation to appear quickly. Coming here every day to satisfy Mother's demands is trouble enough," she remarked.

Will took a deep breath, silently blaming his dysphoria on Blake's horrifying attempt at breakfast. *Keep your wits about you,* he cautioned himself. He'd gotten so used

Chapter 4

to having Tailtiu around every day that he had started to think of her as somewhat human, a dangerous pitfall if he allowed such thoughts to color their negotiations. "I need your help with a separate matter," he told her. "You still owe me twelve days from the agreement on your payment of the second unbound favor."

"What is it you require then?" she asked. Tailtiu showed no outward sign of annoyance, but her lack of flirtation was all the evidence Will needed to see she was out of sorts.

"It's about my sister, Laina. She's being followed by an assassin." He described the events of the previous night.

Tailtiu frowned at him in obvious disappointment. "You were defeated? After all our work, I thought you more proficient than that."

"I can't use my magic for the next few days," he replied. "Apparently I hurt myself worse than I realized at the dam yesterday. That's part of the reason I'm asking you to do this."

His aunt remained silent for a long minute, her expression pensive. "I can watch her during the day until you've recovered. In the evening I have another obligation, as you are already aware. I can't help you during those hours."

Tailtiu's job in the evening was nominally to impersonate Selene if the need arose, but Will knew her other purpose was to serve as a bodyguard for him. Whether that was because Aislinn had asked for it, or whether Selene had tacked that stipulation on as part of her own negotiations he couldn't be sure. "That won't be a problem," he informed her. "I'll follow her myself in the evenings. You'll just have to stay close to me."

"If you can't use magic you won't be able to hide your presence from her," she pointed out.

"I'll just keep my distance. Besides, I'm not bad at following people, even without magic."

His aunt seemed unconvinced. "You might avoid your half-sister's notice, but I doubt you'll remain unseen by this assassin you mentioned."

He rubbed his chin, nodding in agreement. "You might be right, but I'm going to keep an eye on Laina regardless." Will gave the fae woman a knowing smile. "You'll just have to decide the best way to keep me safe. Letting me risk a blunder or following Laina in my stead."

Tailtiu growled softly. "You're picking up bad habits."

"Must be the company I keep," he returned, meeting her gaze evenly.

After she left to begin her watch over Laina, Will wasted no time hurrying to his first class of the day, Foundations in Artifice. He barely made it in time, causing Janice to give him a questioning glance as he found his seat beside her.

"You're nearly late. What happened at the dam yesterday? Stephanie has been telling some wild stories about—"

He interrupted her, "Whatever she said, she's probably lying." Before he could say more the lower door of the auditorium opened and Professor Salsbury entered. The chatter in the room quickly died away. Todd Salsbury was nominally the head of the Department of Artifice, though the man didn't look much like many of the other teachers at Wurthaven. Despite being in his middle years the professor was still lean and his hands showed the thick skin and scars that came from years of hard use. He was very much a man who had learned by doing, or if his knowledge had come from books, he had then spent most of his time putting it to use.

Chapter 4

The professor glanced over the room, then pointed at Will. "Mister Cartwright, there you are. Master Courtney asked me to tell you to report to the Healing and Psyche building immediately. Doctor Morris is waiting on you there."

All eyes were on Will as he grimaced, then replied, "Should I go after class?"

"Now, Mister Cartwright. Master Courtney seemed to feel it was urgent."

Will stood, glancing down at Janice as he did. Her eyes were full of questions, and chief among them was an emphatic *'what did you do?'* Unfortunately, he had no better idea than she did. He shrugged and made his way down the row of seats until he reached the aisle so he could exit.

Since his class was located in the Engineering building, it took him a few minutes to reach the Healing and Psyche building, which was located near the center of the campus along with three other major buildings that surrounded what was known as the 'quad.' As soon as he entered, he found Ilona Fretz, one of the Healing Department's administrative people, waiting on him. He knew the woman fairly well since she had been the person in charge of buying the potions he had created to pay his bills during the previous semester.

"How do you feel?" she asked immediately.

He gave her a strange look. "I have a headache. What's going on?"

"I heard about what happened at the dam yesterday," she replied. "We've been dealing with the consequences. Follow me. Master Courtney was very insistent that you should be thoroughly examined. Doctor Morris is naturally quite interested as well."

"Interested in what?"

Ilona didn't answer, and he was forced to hurry to keep up with her as she marched down the halls to an examining room. She opened the door and ushered him inside. "Take a seat by the table. The doctor will be here as soon as I inform him you've arrived." With that she stepped out.

A few minutes later the door opened again and a small, balding man with white hair and a round belly entered. There was something distinctly jovial about the man, which was reaffirmed by the smile on his face as he regarded Will. "If it isn't our aspiring duelist. I had a feeling I'd be seeing you again. You don't live a boring life, do you?"

Confused, Will frowned. "Pardon me?"

The doctor chuckled. "Don't remember me? I guess that's to be expected. You'd lost a lot of blood last time we met—after your duel. I was the one who sewed you up."

Will brightened. "Oh! My memory is a little fuzzy about that period. I suppose I owe you my thanks."

Doctor Morris grinned. "I'm just grateful you seem to be in a better mood this time. What was it you said to me when you woke up?" He rubbed his chin thoughtfully. "Oh, yes! You asked which vein was damaged and when I failed to answer immediately you said, 'This fellow is a fucking idiot.'"

Will winced. Now he remembered their meeting. "I'm really sorry about that. I wasn't entirely in my right mind at the time."

The doctor waved one hand dismissively. "Don't worry about it. We hear all sorts of things from people when they wake up after trauma. We were laughing about it the rest of the week." The old man's eyes were moving up and down, and he leaned closer, staring at the side of

Chapter 4

Will's head. "Did this happen at the dam yesterday?" Reaching up with one hand, he probed the lump on Will's scalp, causing him to gasp.

"No, sir," he answered. "I got that last night."

"How?"

"I fell," Will prevaricated.

"Really?" responded Doctor Morris, disbelief in his voice. "It would be very unusual to get a knock on your noggin like this from a fall. It's rare that people fall sideways. This looks more like someone rapped you with something small and hard. You aren't still getting into fights, are you?"

"Only when I can't avoid them," said Will sourly.

"Ilona said you had a headache. Did you have that before you had your accident?"

"No, sir—well, not exactly. My headache now is from the injury, but I'm also getting short-term pains if I try to use spells. I think I injured my will while keeping the dam from rupturing yesterday." Doctor Morris stared at him blankly, causing Will to hurry and add, "But I'm sure it will be better in a few days."

The doctor nodded. "Yes, I see. You know a lot about injuries to the will, do you?"

He felt his cheeks coloring. "Well, it has happened to me once before."

"Does it seem like something that should be commonplace among wizards?"

Will didn't answer immediately, as he could see the doctor was leading him with his questions. Given the current state of wizardry, it probably was unlikely that anyone managed to injure themselves as he had. "Perhaps not," he said hesitantly. *But it would be if people were being properly trained to use magic.* "How many have you encountered?"

"Yours is the first," said Doctor Morris dryly. "Such injuries are discussed in some of the old literature, but I've never had the opportunity to see one firsthand. If you'll make yourself comfortable I'd like to perform a few diagnostic spells."

He lifted one hand to his temple, feeling slightly anxious. "You don't expect me to use any spells myself, do you?"

The doctor shook his head. "No. As I said, I don't have any personal experience with this, but the texts I've studied advise against you using magic yourself."

"What will these spells reveal?"

"I won't know until I try. According to what I've read they won't show any physical injuries, but I'd like to confirm that for myself. May I proceed?"

Will nodded and then waited patiently while the doctor went through a variety of spells, most of which seemed to be passive in nature, although one or two of them did actively probe his body with streams of turyn. After fifteen minutes the physician seemed to have finished. "I'll be back shortly," he told Will before stepping out and closing the door.

Rising from his seat, Will went to the door and listened. He could almost make out the doctor's voice as the man conferred with someone else. Reflexively, he started to adjust the sensitivity of his hearing, but he stopped as a sharp pain stabbed through his skull. *Idiot,* he told himself. *You knew wild magic would do the same thing to you as any spell.* Rubbing his temples gingerly, he returned to his seat.

Unable to sate his curiosity he waited impatiently. A few minutes later the voices drew closer and he recognized Master Courtney's voice. "Have you mentioned Duncan to him?"

"Not yet," said Doctor Morris.

Chapter 4

The door opened, and the two men stepped inside. Will started to rise, but Professor Courtney waved for him to keep his seat. "No need to get up."

Will relaxed. Master Courtney was a classic academic, but as the Head of Research, he held a uniquely influential position with the people who ran Wurthaven. He had an imposing presence despite his below-average height and unremarkable build. It was something about the man's intense hazel eyes. He could never figure out what the man was thinking, but it was obvious that a lot was going on behind those eyes.

Master Courtney glanced at the doctor. "Would you like to give him the good news, or shall I?"

Doctor Morris dipped his head deferentially. "Please, go ahead."

Master Courtney's sharp gaze fixed on Will. "You're perfectly healthy. It doesn't appear that you've suffered any long-lasting effects from what you did at the dam yesterday. Aside from this injury to your will, of course. Has the good doctor given you any instructions regarding that yet?"

The doctor started to explain that he hadn't yet, but Will spoke first, "No magic for a few days, then I test my abilities with caution. If there's any pain I should wait another two weeks before trying again."

Doctor Morris stared at him. "You already knew?"

Master Courtney glanced between the two of them, then turned to Will, his gaze questioning. "You learned that from your former teacher?"

Will nodded.

Master Courtney said nothing for a few seconds. "You're going to have to tell me more about this former master of yours one of these days. He must have been an interesting man."

He ignored the statement and looked at the doctor instead. "I couldn't help but hear you mention Instructor Broder outside the door. Is he all right?"

The two older men looked at one another, then Doctor Morris answered, "I'm afraid Duncan won't be teaching the practicum any longer. The strain of what happened yesterday has forced him into early retirement."

Will felt the blood draining from his face. "How bad is it?"

The doctor grimaced. "It's impossible to say for sure, but I doubt he'll last more than a few years. The amount of turyn he used—"

Master Courtney interrupted, "Which makes your condition all the more remarkable. What was the size of the force-wall you created?"

The man's lack of regard for what had happened to Duncan irritated Will, but he could see that the researcher was caught up by his interest in the topic. "It was roughly ten feet by twenty feet, sir."

"And how far away was it from you?"

"About thirty feet above where we stood."

"And you held it for how long?"

Will shrugged. "I'm not sure. I think it was ten minutes or so, but I can't say for sure."

"That's ridiculous!" exclaimed Doctor Morris, unable to contain his disbelief. "He'd be dead—twice over."

"Three times over," said Courtney dryly. "I'll have to examine the site, though it will be impossible to make more than a rough estimate given what we know."

"You believe him?" asked the doctor.

Master Courtney nodded. "His story matches what Duncan told me almost exactly, and given the fact that the Lanover Dam is still standing I'm inclined to believe the

Chapter 4

boy." After a moment he added, "I have other reasons to believe him as well."

Being discussed in the third person was annoying, not to mention Doctor Morris' outright skepticism about his claims, but Will tried to keep his feelings hidden. "Can I return to class?" he asked the two men, keeping his tone neutral.

Master Courtney smiled. "Actually, no. I'd like you to accompany me to the dam so I can inspect it. You can show me what happened."

Will groaned inwardly.

Chapter 5

The carriage ride to the Lanover Dam site was relatively quiet for the first half hour. Will had worried that Master Courtney would question him the entire way, but the graying professor remained silent, staring out the window and watching the world go by with a faint smile.

He stares at the world as though it's constantly telling him jokes that only he can hear, observed Will. What a strange man. He wondered what his grandfather would have thought of the man. Don't forget he's a noble too, he reminded himself. Outside of academic settings the professor was also a lord of the realm, though more so than even the other teachers at Wurthaven, Alfred Courtney seemed to care very little for his social standing.

"What was your teacher's name?"

The question emerged from absolute silence, startling him. "Pardon?"

Alfred's piercing eyes settled directly on Will. "I asked what your teacher's name was."

His brain leapt into high speed, racing in circles as he struggled to come up with a convincing lie. "Uh. I usually called him Grampa, but his given name was, uh, Johnathan."

"Isn't that your maternal uncle's name? Was he named after his father?"

The question was delivered in an innocent tone, but it was enough for Will to realize he had made a terrible mistake. Master Courtney had apparently researched his family at some point in the past. "Yes, sir," said Will weakly.

"If you don't wish to tell me your teacher's name then don't. I'm not an officer of the law or an agent of the king. I can't compel you to give me answers, but please be truthful. I'd rather you simply refuse honestly than force me to guess at the truth."

His mouth went dry, and for a moment Will wasn't sure how to respond. Alfred Courtney seemed entirely different than his grandfather, and yet for some reason the man frightened him just as much. *He's not going to chase me around with a staff,* he reminded himself, but somehow his body didn't believe it. "Yes, sir," he said at last.

"And? Is there something else you'd like to add?"

"His name wasn't Johnathan. I promised I wouldn't give people his real name."

Master Courtney smiled. "Much better. I prefer to build on a foundation of honesty. Is your grandfather actually dead? It seems strange you'd be concerned about such a promise if he's deceased. The law can't reach him if he's already passed on."

A spark of anger kindled in his chest. "He's dead, sir. He died defending my mother and cousin when the Prophet's men came to our home."

The older man stared at him, waiting.

"My promise wasn't conditional on his being alive or dead," Will explained.

The old scholar looked out the window again, seemingly satisfied. "Interesting," he remarked. "So, this promise was probably as much for your protection as for his own. Your grandfather must have been a notorious criminal."

"He was a good man," said Will stubbornly.

"Being labeled a criminal says nothing about his character. While I would generally assume that most criminals possess lower moral standards, that isn't always the case." The old man watched the trees pass by for a minute or two. "Were you always a natural transducer, or do you think your grandfather's training somehow enabled you to become one?"

Will was pretty sure it was the training, but he wasn't ready to share his grandfather's secrets. "I'm not sure," he answered noncommittally.

"You told Professor Dulaney that you spent several years just training with the candle and source-link before you were ever allowed to learn how to construct a spell. Is that correct?"

"Yes, sir."

"Was there anything specific you had to do during that period of time? Or perhaps things that were done *to* you?"

Will gave the man a flat stare. "I'd rather not say."

The older man laughed. "You don't trust me, do you?"

"There are some things I don't trust anyone with, sir. It isn't personal."

"Yet you've come to Wurthaven to learn what we have to teach. Doesn't it seem a little one sided? We give you everything we know while you keep your secrets to yourself."

Will thought about it for a moment before answering. "A school's job is to teach. The students pay to learn what you have to offer. There's no implicit agreement that students will provide anything to Wurthaven other than their money."

Master Courtney nodded vaguely. "That may be generally true, but Wurthaven is more than a simple school. My position is Head of Research, so surely you can understand that it's my job to try and increase our knowledge and understanding. At the moment you appear to be a fascinating source of information."

"I can understand your perspective, but I have no obligation to satisfy your curiosity."

Chapter 5

Alfred raised one brow. "Even though the king sponsored your entry into Wurthaven?"

Will kept his expression flat. "More so because of it."

"You mean you owe nothing to the college because of your father-in-law, or…" The older man paused for a few seconds, then his eyes lit up with understanding. "You're hiding your secrets from the king himself."

Will said nothing, keeping his eyes focused on the scenery outside the window.

They arrived at the worksite a short while later. They were met by Professor Jason Dugas, the head of Wurthaven's Engineering Department. The senior engineer had come to the site to oversee repairs in Duncan's place. Professor Dugas greeted Master Courtney with a smile and a deferential dip of his head. "I'm honored that you've come to see things personally, Master Courtney."

Will studied the engineer for a moment. Like Duncan, the man was in relatively good shape. He was tall and lean with dark hair and thick stubble covering his cheeks. Dugas and Courtney stepped away and Will followed behind them, listening as they spoke together.

"I haven't sent my report in yet, but as I'm sure you guessed, the dam failure yesterday was definitely the result of sabotage. The buttress on the left side wasn't actually able to hold any load at all. Someone dug down beneath it and exposed the metal before changing its properties. As soon it came under full load, it failed."

Master Courtney nodded absently, seemingly uninterested in the shocking news as his eyes roamed over the ground around them. He stopped suddenly, pointing. "Is that where you were standing, Mister Cartwright?"

Will nodded. "Yes, sir." He was surprised that the man had guessed it so accurately, until he noticed the discoloration around where he had stood. A five-foot circle held no plants at all; the grass and weeds that had been there were shriveled and black. Beyond that, the grass was brown and withered in a radius of about ten feet more. *Did I cause that?*

"Stephanie Beresford was here with him," Professor Dugas informed Master Courtney. "The lady has a fire elemental."

Apparently, that was supposed to explain the dead plants, though Will knew that the elemental had never manifested. Glancing at Master Courtney he couldn't tell whether the old man believed the explanation or not. The head researcher merely replied, "Of course." Then he looked up at the dam wall, his eyes gauging the distance. "Can you get me some measurements Professor Dugas?"

"I can give you whatever you need, Master Courtney. We have full schematics for the dam as well as topographical maps and surveys of—"

"Nothing that dramatic, Jason. I'd just like measurements of the distance from this spot to the dam, as well as the distance up the wall to where the breach began. If you could get those and draw up a simple diagram I would appreciate it."

"Certainly."

"Have it sent over to my office this evening if you don't mind."

Professor Dugas nodded. "Would you like a copy of the report on how the structure was sabotaged as well?"

Master Courtney waved his hand dismissively. "That's a matter for the Crown to investigate. I'm not really interested in it." He stared at the ground. "Do you have some jars? I didn't think to bring any. I'd like to take samples of the soil and plants here."

***

Chapter 5

Will got home at close to his usual time, and while he hadn't had to do any actual work, he still felt tired. Master Courtney hadn't pressed him for any more answers on the way back but the tension of wondering when the next question might come had exhausted him.

Blake greeted him at the door. "How was your day, sir?"

He shook his head. "I've had better. Has T—" He caught himself. "Has Selene come in yet?"

"She's upstairs," answered Blake. "She asked me to reassure you that she wouldn't be attacking you today, in light of your handicap."

Will squinted suspiciously at the other man, wondering whether he should trust him. Tailtiu had been relentless for the past few months. "You've just made me more paranoid," he complained.

When he got upstairs, he opened the door to the master bedroom cautiously. Tailtiu laughed when she saw his careful entry. "Relax. I truly won't attack you again. Not until you tell me your magic is restored."

"I figured you'd say something along the lines of me being prepared to defend myself with or without magic," replied Will.

His aunt nodded. "I considered it, but the nature of the training I've been giving you won't work in that context. Lethal attacks require you to respond without hesitation. If I kept it up, you'd almost certainly be forced to use a spell, and then you might permanently damage yourself. I can wait."

"Did you see anything interesting today?"

Tailtiu shrugged. "She went to a party at some other human's home. After that she went home, so I was a little bored. However, the house she lives in is being watched."

"You spotted the assassin?"

"They spotted me," said Tailtiu. "Whoever it is shadowing her is very good. I was forced to depart the area and change forms several times to avoid raising the watcher's suspicion. For a human, the person watching their house is very observant."

The fact that Tailtiu had been noticed was shocking to him, but Will didn't dwell on it. "Were they still there when you left?"

She shook her head. "Probably had to eat or take care of other business. They left during the late afternoon. I tried to follow them."

"Tried?"

Tailtiu seemed embarrassed. "The watcher passed around the other side of the house and vanished. I'm not sure how they got away from the area. I couldn't find any trace or trail."

That was close to unbelievable. "Nothing?"

She nodded, then tapped her nose. "There wasn't even a scent trail. Even creatures that can mask their turyn can't do that."

"Could they have slipped through a congruence? Or maybe they didn't leave?"

"There were no congruences nearby, and if they'd stayed, I would have found them. I waited and kept an eye on the area for another hour before coming back here, just to see if they'd hidden somehow. If they were still there, they were more patient than I am."

None of that made Will feel better. He started for the door.

"Don't bother," said Tailtiu. "You'll only make matters worse."

"I can't just ignore this."

"If the watcher does come back, you'll be spotted immediately," explained Tailtiu. "Without magic, you

Chapter 5

don't have a chance in hell of remaining unobserved, and you've already discovered you're no match for this one in hand-to-hand combat. I'll watch the house until you've recovered."

Although he felt relieved, Will couldn't help but ask, "Doesn't that conflict with your other promise?"

"It was decided that this was a reasonable exception."

He stared at the fae woman with sudden interest. "You saw her? You spoke to her? What did she say? Is she well?"

His aunt laughed. "I spoke with Mother. I haven't seen your lover any more recently than you have."

Will frowned. "But isn't she with Aislinn? I thought surely—"

Tailtiu cut him off, "I have no idea where she is. Mother doesn't share all her secrets with me."

"But..."

"Rest easy, nephew. Mother is no fool. Wherever she's stashed your girl I'm sure she's safe."

Unless the king figured out that his daughter wasn't where he thought she was. If he decided to, he could use the heart-stone enchantment to summon her back. Will worried about that possibility, and it was one reason he'd gone along with the plan to have Tailtiu impersonate Selene. So long as the king thought she was still within close reach, he seemed content to leave things be. Will ran a hand through his hair in frustration. As usual, the only thing he could do was nothing at all.

Chapter 6

The next morning Will noticed that he was once again collecting more stares from his fellow students. It was something he had gotten used to, both before and after his marriage to Selene, for various reasons. Lately the attention had died down some, but it appeared he had once again become an active topic of discussion.

He and Janice couldn't really talk during class, so she held her questions until the lecture was over, but she was careful not to let him get out of sight as they exited. She caught his sleeve in the hall outside. "Don't even think about trying to escape," she warned him.

His expression was droll. "I knew better than to try." Glancing around, he saw nearly everyone in their vicinity was watching them with interest. Some of them appeared ready to approach and try to start conversations. "Want to get some air?" he asked Janice.

She flashed a warm smile, which reminded him of why he liked her so much. Janice was probably his best friend at Wurthaven, and while they had had a few problems because of some romantic interest, she hadn't let it interfere with their relationship as friends. "Let's go," she replied.

Outside, they were able to keep some distance from their fellow students, but only so long as they remained on the move. "Stephanie was telling some remarkable stories yesterday," began Janice, "and for once you sounded like a hero rather than a villain."

He shrugged modestly.

"I was tempted to disbelieve her tale, since it cast you in a positive light, until they took you out of class yesterday."

Will frowned. "That was unkind."

Janice grinned. "It's not that I think poorly of you, you understand. It's just hard to believe anyone else would think kindly of you."

He snorted. "What did she say?"

"That you saved the work crew at the dam by keeping the entire thing from collapsing."

"That doesn't seem humanly possible."

Janice nodded. "She said she helped by funneling turyn to you from her elemental. She also said you saved her from a nasty fall from a platform." She waggled her wrist in front of him. "She even had bruises to demonstrate where you grabbed her."

Will smirked. "That sounds good. I'll go with it. Everything she said was true." His eyes glanced up toward the sky in an expression of humor. "Ow!" he exclaimed as Janice drove her elbow into his side. "Fine, I'll tell you the truth."

"You'd better."

He explained what had actually happened, along with his tense exchange with Stephanie afterward. When he finished, he saw his friend staring at him with surprise in her eyes. "What?" he asked.

"You really threatened her like that?"

Will lowered his eyes. "I'm not proud of it, but I couldn't think of a better solution. Besides, you know Selene isn't actually…" He let his words taper off without finishing as he glanced around to make sure no one was nearby. He didn't have to say it, though; Janice was one of the few people he had entrusted with the truth about Selene's absence. "If there was a scandal, she wouldn't be able to do anything about it," he added.

She shook her head. "I wasn't judging you. Actually, I'm impressed with how you stood up for yourself. Not too long ago you would have let someone like her just walk all over you."

He didn't see her point. "I've never been one to run from a fight."

"Not a physical fight," corrected Janice. "But you avoided social confrontations, especially with women. I had resigned myself to the fact that Selene and I were going to have to protect you from women for the rest of your clueless life."

Will laughed. "You make it sound as though women are evil."

"You have no idea," she said, shaking her head. "But you're still trying to oversimplify things. My sex isn't evil per se, but we're highly social—maybe you would describe it as political. We fight more with words and opinions." Her eyes flicked to the side of his head for a moment. "Speaking of fights, what happened to your head?"

"Would you believe I was following a young woman at night and tried to stop a stranger from assaulting her?"

She squinted at him. "What really happened?"

He let out a dramatic sigh. "Even when I try to tell the truth, no one believes me. And you wonder why I try to tell people I had an accident."

It was her turn to laugh then. "Usually you lie first, *then* you admit the truth. How am I supposed to know when you're going to change the formula? So, who was the damsel in distress this time?"

"Laina Nerrow."

"The baron's daughter? Didn't you dance with her sister at the Winter Ball?"

"That's an oddly specific thing for you to remember," observed Will.

Chapter 6

"It was a big night for me," said Janice. "It was the first, and probably only, time I was invited to a royal ball. Are you trying to deflect my curiosity? You were a little sensitive after you danced with the other sister at the ball, now you're following the older sister around at night."

He said nothing.

"You're going to tell me eventually," she informed him. "Why drag it out?"

No, I'm not, he thought silently. He trusted Janice, but the secret of his parentage wasn't something he could share. Selene had agreed to let him bring Janice in on her secret, but the Nerrow family didn't have that option. If the secret somehow got out, his sisters might be in danger simply for being related to him.

After a moment she relented. "At least tell me what happened."

"Laina and Selene are close friends," he said, beginning an explanation of the entire evening. He detailed Laina's plea and her unhappy exit, which led up to his following her and the inevitable fight with the assassin.

"You don't do anything by halves, do you?" remarked Janice at the end of it all.

He spotted Rob closing in on them, so Will turned to include his friend as well as let Janice know they were no longer alone. "I don't do it on purpose. Hi Rob!"

Rob's expression was dramatically sour. "I'm not sure I can talk to you anymore."

"I've never been able to stop you before," noted Will with a smirk. "What's changed now?"

"First you marry the princess, and now, just when the rest of us think it might be safe, you go and turn yourself into a hero. Have you heard the things Stephanie has been saying about you?"

"I'm not a big fan of gossip," said Will dryly.

"Every time she tells the story it gets more incredible. I wouldn't be surprised if the next rendition has you showing up on a white charger before single-handedly fixing the dam while practicing the latest dance."

Janice snorted, then her eyes lit up. Leaning close to Will's ear, she whispered, "I know how you can defeat the assassin. Next time you see him you should dance with him. He won't be able to fight after you stomp all over his toes."

"I've gotten a lot better!" Will protested. Janice's remark was a reference to the pain he had put her and his dance teacher through back when he had been practicing for the Winter Ball.

Rob looked back and forth between them. "I must have missed something."

"I have to head to my next class," said Janice, bowing out and leaving Will to explain.

"Well?" asked Rob.

"Come on," said Will, putting one arm over his friend's shoulder. "I'll tell you on the way to Advanced Spell Theory."

***

The next few days passed with frustrating slowness as Will waited to recover his ability to use turyn safely. Each evening, Tailtiu would stop in for an hour or so to relay what she had seen, and he couldn't help but notice she looked haggard. Seeming tired would be normal for a human, but for the fae it was highly unusual.

"Are you all right?" he asked her on the fourth evening.

She nodded brusquely. "I'm just spending too much time in your world. I'll recover once I have some free time to return to Faerie."

Chapter 6

"I'm going to test the waters tomorrow," he informed her. "If I'm able to use magic, then you can go back, and I'll watch her home that evening."

Tailtiu sighed. "I'm not sure there's a need. This assassin seems content to watch. Every day the girl leaves, attending parties and social meetings at various people's homes. Whatever the man following her is planning, it doesn't seem urgent. He's let multiple opportunities pass without attempting anything."

"Unless he's being cautious because you've got him spooked," countered Will. "You said he's noticed you several times."

"He has, but I think there's something else going on. The stranger follows her during her trips, but never gets too close. In the evenings he waits outside for a while before vanishing."

"What are you getting at?" asked Will.

"He only leaves when Laina is at home and it seems certain she won't be leaving again that day. This morning I got there before dawn, even before the assassin arrived, and I sensed something strange."

"And?"

His aunt shrugged. "I'm not sure what it was. It was a strange trace of turyn. It felt cold, but it vanished as soon as the sun came up."

"You couldn't tell what it was?"

She shook her head. "It reminded me of demonic turyn, but it was different. I haven't come across anything quite like it before. I don't think you should try to watch the house. Let me have a day to recover and we can go together."

Will shook his head. "You can recover, but I'm not leaving Laina unguarded, not when it's obvious that someone has it in for her."

Tailtiu's expression was one of puzzlement. "Why bother? She wouldn't do the same for you. The girl hates you."

"She's family."

She snorted. "So am I, but given the right opportunity I'd take your seed and then your life. She doesn't even know you're related. You humans make no sense."

His gaze was flat and unwavering. "I'd do the same for you."

Tailtiu laughed. "And *that* is exactly what will get you killed some day. In any case, I would never be foolish enough to need your help."

Will shrugged. "You're probably right—on both counts—but that's who I am. Anyway, we will see how things go tomorrow."

"I'd really prefer you don't go. Let me rest and we'll go together."

There was a certain emphasis in her tone. *Surely she isn't really worried about me, is she?* He dismissed the idea. He knew better. A knock on the door interrupted his thoughts, followed by Blake's voice. "It's getting late, sir. Would you like me to start dinner or do you still intend on cooking?"

Will stepped to the door and pulled it open. "Was that a threat?"

Blake took a step back, a look of innocence on his face. "Of course not, sir! I merely offered to cook if you were too…"

"Any time you offer to cook, it's a threat."

His manservant raised one brow. "Perhaps if you're that dissatisfied with my efforts you might deign to teach me how to cook then."

Will chuckled. "I like cooking. I'd rather just do it myself, unless you want to pay me for lessons."

Chapter 6

"An exchange then?"

"What would you exchange?"

"I could teach you how to use a blade. You seemed interested a few days ago."

Will was definitely interested, but he put on an air of reluctance. "I'm already taking rapier classes."

"And I'm sure those are valuable in their own way," said Blake with a hint of condescension in his tone.

"I was in the army too."

"So, you've got discipline. You know how to hold a shield and keep your place in a line. I'm offering to teach you something different."

"Such as?"

"The kind of blade work you need to survive in a dark alley. The sort you needed a few days ago but didn't have."

It was an interesting offer. "You said you weren't good enough to take the assassin, though."

"I'm getting old," admitted Blake. "Doesn't mean I don't have a lot to teach you." The look on the older man's face implied that he felt he had a lot to show Will.

"Fine," said Will, relenting. "After dinner we'll spar. No magic. If you can convince me, then tomorrow I'll teach you how to properly cook a roast."

Blake held out one hand. "Agreed." They shook on the deal.

CHAPTER 7

Will's classes were predicated upon his successes and failures from the previous semester. Professor Karlovic had exempted him entirely from the core curriculum Alchemy classes, though Will still rented a lab room for personal use. Professor Dulaney had moved him to Advanced Spell Theory, moving him entirely past the second-year classes on that subject. Math had been a success, but he hadn't been moved ahead, and Composition had been a failure. He was retaking the same class with Professor Conrad this semester.

Currently he was sitting in his last class for the day, Advanced Spell Theory. Most of his fellow students in the class were working on fifth- and sixth-order spells, while Will was working hard to manage eighth-order. In terms of difficulty, he was already well ahead of where he needed to be for the next semester's class, but being able to master eighth-order was a personal goal for him. He wanted to be able to cast Selene's Solution, the cleaning spell created by his wife.

Wife? It still seemed unbelievable to him when the word ran through his mind. *Am I really married?* He supposed that most newlyweds had trouble adjusting to the new labels, but he felt it was even more difficult in his situation. *Most newlyweds get to live together.*

"Do you have someplace better to be, Mister Cartwright?"

Will's eyes snapped back into focus. Professor Dulaney had gone quiet and was now staring intently at him. Most of the class was looking back at him, but rather than show his embarrassment, Will grinned. "Yes, Professor, but I can wait until you're done before I go."

"Since you're bored, perhaps you can explain to your classmates the primary use of transducers in artifice."

Will groaned under his breath and began getting to his feet. Dulaney preferred the students stand when answering. "Sir, we covered that last semester…"

"Some of us need a refresher, if you would be so kind," said Dulaney, his voice dripping with sarcasm.

"Transducers are used to modify turyn, to convert it from one type or mixture of types to another. They're required for any enchantment or magical item, since they must operate without a human to provide the proper turyn needed for them to function."

The professor nodded. "The transducer is modeled on a fundamental spell construct that performs the same function. What would happen if we used them in everyday spells and why don't we?"

Because it would be a damned waste of time—for me, thought Will sourly. He couldn't say that, of course, so instead he answered, "A transducing spell construct would improve the turyn efficiency of any spell to nearly one hundred percent, but it would drastically increase the complexity to a degree that any spell that included a full transducer would be unworkable."

"And yet most transducers are relatively simple. Explain why they create such a problem in spell casting."

Will sighed. "Because every person has a unique mixture of turyn, so every spell would have to be personalized for the transducer to be of any benefit."

One of the other students, Phillip Wakefield, raised his hand. Professor Dulaney pointed at the young man. "You have a question?"

"Yes, Professor. This occurred to me during the reading. Even though everyone has a different turyn signature, once the proper transducer was calculated for that person, they could memorize it and apply it to—"

"I see where you're going Mister Wakefield," interrupted Dulaney. "It won't help. Not only is each person unique, but every spell requires a different mix of turyn. Your hypothetical wizard would still have to create a unique transducer construct to interface with every spell." He nodded at Will. "Thank you, Mister Cartwright. You can sit back down now.

"This brings me to the next topic. As you know, and as some of you have begun to see in your Artifice classes, the things we create fall into several broad categories. Many engineering tools are simple and general-use. The transducers built into those enchantments tend to be simple, standardized, and users are chosen according to their affinity for the implement. Efficiency is rarely greater than seventy percent. On the opposite end of the spectrum we have personalized items created for wealthy individuals. Such items are built with transducers tailored to the owner, so their efficiency is as close to perfect as can be achieved, usually in the ninety-seven to ninety-eight-percent range.

"Most such items are made for the nobility, due to the cost, though some wizards craft such items for themselves. The benefit of such efficiency is even more important to wizards, naturally."

Will raised his hand, then stood and cleared his throat when Dulaney recognized him. "Professor Salsbury told us that the oldest examples of powerful enchanted items didn't include a transducer component at all, but he didn't say why. Could you shed some light on the reasons for that difference between the work of artificers back then and that of modern craftsmen?"

A flicker of disgruntlement flashed across the professor's features, but it vanished as quickly as it appeared. "I should have known you'd bring up the topic

Chapter 7

of relics, Mister Cartwright." Then his gaze swept the room as he addressed the question for the class. "What William has brought up is a subject of some debate, because we don't really know how most of the enchanted items of the past were meant to function. We call them *relics* simply to denote the fact that they are of considerable age, but there's nothing fundamentally different about them aside from age and the lack of a transducer.

"One theory is that relics were paired with a second item that included a transducer and that these transducers simply haven't been found or they didn't survive the passage of time. Another theory is that the items were used by individuals who happened to have exactly the right sort of turyn to make them function, although the odds of that are extremely unlikely.

"What we do know, is that because of the lack of a transducer most relics are able to house more complex enchantments. The Rod of Breven, for example, has three separate functions, each requiring a different mixture of turyn. To my mind, that makes the idea of a secondary transducer even more likely. The original owner of the rod probably had three different customized transducers that could be switched out depending on how he intended to use the item—"

"Or Lord Breven was able to modulate his own turyn," interjected Will.

Dulaney sighed. "I would have dismissed that idea out of hand, but you are living proof that such a thing is possible, though I still believe that your hypothesis is highly improbable."

Will was almost certain he was right, but he didn't have to guess. He resolved to ask Arrogan later and find out the truth. He rolled his shoulder, stretching it to relieve the tightness in it. It was a leftover side effect from his sparring the previous evening with Blake. As he expected, the former special agent for the king had had a lot to teach. The veteran was well acquainted with standard military practices and tactics as well as more formalized fighting styles like the rapier, but Blake's focus had been on more practical techniques.

The older man's teaching had focused on two goals, killing and survival. Blake had been emphatic that Will needed to be very aware of which of the two things he was trying to achieve in any given encounter. "For a civilian, survival is almost always the only goal," the manservant had explained. "But given the life you lead, there may also be times when you are actively trying to end your opponent. In those cases, you need to make sure that your own survival remains the top priority. The only time it might not be is if you're on a suicide mission."

The sparring, if it could properly be called that, had been unorthodox to say the least. Apparently, the older man intended to cover everything from ground fighting to dirty tricks and escape tactics. As the class let out and Will rose from his seat, he could feel several additional sore muscles complaining. It reminded him of something Arrogan had once said when he had been complaining. *"If it hurts that just means you're learning something."*

Since Advanced Spell Theory was his last class for the day, Will let his feet head in the direction of home, but a voice caught his attention before he could get away. "Will! Hey, over here!" It was Rob. His friend appeared to have been waiting for him to get out of class.

He walked over, noting the enthusiastic expression on his friend's face. "What's on your mind?" Will asked cautiously.

Rob grinned. "Funny you should ask—"

"You called me over. Of course, I'd ask," he quipped.

Chapter 7

Rob rolled his eyes. "Ha, ha. You remember Veronica Wellings?"

Veronica was a third-year student who had helped Will the previous semester when he had needed to learn a bit of quick and dirty enchanting for his plan to disrupt Selene's wedding to Count Spry. Will hadn't actually spoken to Veronica himself, but apparently the question had given Rob an opening to get to know her.

"Yes...?"

"The ladies of Primrose House are planning an evening social on Friday and given your newfound fame I'm sure you'll get an invitation since Stephanie is organizing the affair. Veronica would love to go, and I'd love to take her, but—hey!" Rob chased after him as Will turned and walked away. "Don't be like that!"

"I'm not interested," said Will flatly. It wasn't that he was inherently antisocial—well, perhaps a little—the main problem was his absent wife. Everyone would be expecting the royal princess, and any explanation of her absence would likely create more problems than it solved, especially given how little she had been in the public eye since their unexpected wedding. Tailtiu's impersonations had been able to keep the curiosity to a minimum, but Will loathed taking her out in public. Each time he worried they would encounter someone who knew Selene personally, someone who would begin to unravel the truth. *Someone like Laina,* thought Will.

"At least ask Selene," insisted Rob. "She's bound to be bored. She's barely left the house since you two tied the knot. People are starting to think you keep her under lock and key and other silly—"

He rounded on his friend, his face serious. "Don't even suggest such a thing! Rumors are bad enough, but I don't expect you to be repeating them."

Rob blanched for a moment, then his cheeks flushed as his temper rose. "I have ears, Will. I'm not spreading rumors. I'm trying to help you keep them from getting worse. I'd have thought you would understand me better by now, but then again, it isn't as if I ever see you. You still haven't invited me over to see your new home."

Will felt bad for snapping. He tried to apologize. "I didn't mean it like that, and it isn't you. I haven't invited anyone over—"

"And that isn't normal," interrupted Rob. "For some people perhaps, maybe even for you, but not for political figures."

"It's complicated," began Will.

"But you won't explain. You won't talk to me; you won't talk to Janice. Who do you talk to? Do you have any real friends? I'm starting to wonder, since I don't really feel like I'm one." Rob turned his back and began walking away.

Damn, I really pissed him off. He watched Rob go, wondering if he should chase after him or leave him alone. *I should probably go after him, but what would I say?* Rob's complaints were completely valid. Ever since the wedding he had kept his friends, along with everyone else, at arm's length. Even worse, he still hadn't been home to see his family. He had sent a letter, which hopefully had outpaced the news, but he hadn't faced his mother in person yet.

There would be a reckoning for that. Although it was several weeks' travel via traditional means, his mother already knew he could make the journey safely in less than a day. He could get there in a matter of just hours if he was willing to take some of the more dangerous shortcuts through Faerie.

But he couldn't do it. *It's bad enough that we eloped without warning her, but I can't show up alone,* he told himself silently. He kept walking, his feet following the

Chapter 7

path home by force of long habit while his head was filled with morose thoughts.

Blake met him at the door, taking his coat. The man waited afterward, expecting Will to remove his overtunic so he could get out of the brigandine as he usually did. "I'm keeping it on," said Will. "I'll be going to watch the Nerrow house after, um, after Selene gets back." Once again, he stumbled over his words. Keeping up a long-term lie was beginning to tax his reserves.

"Then you've recovered your magic?" asked Blake.

Will still hadn't tested it yet, but he cast a simple spell and conjured a small sphere of visible light, then smiled. His head hadn't given him even a faint twinge. "It appears so." Feeling good about the return of his magic, he headed for the kitchen. He wasn't sure how long he would be out that night, so if he wanted something good to eat, he needed to prepare supper before Tailtiu returned.

Blake accompanied him and graciously accepted Will's instruction as he coached the older man through the simple process of putting together pottage of peas and ham. It was dark by the time they finished, and Tailtiu still hadn't returned.

"Should we eat without her?" asked Will.

"That's entirely up to you, sir."

He was hungry, so they ate. Unspoken was the fact that if Blake actually believed that the woman returning was Selene, he would almost certainly have had something to say on the matter. *I know he knows, but I can't say it because then he'd have to tell the king. My life is so weird,* thought Will.

Stomachs full, the two men leaned back in their chairs. After a few minutes, Will sighed and got to his feet. He'd waited long enough. Something had happened, otherwise Tailtiu would have returned by then. Blake rose to stand as well, his intention clear.

"You can't come with me, Blake."

"If you meet that assassin you might not be able to handle him on your own."

"I've got my magic back," countered Will. "I also have a much better idea how dangerous he is. If I'm going to remain unseen, I can't have you with me. You should stay here in case Selene returns while I'm gone."

Blake ground his teeth. "Fine."

"Help me put my brigandine back on?" asked Will. It wasn't so much a question as a polite order.

"Are you going to be silencing yourself with magic?"

He nodded.

"Then you'd be better with the mail and breastplate."

"I might as well wear my greaves and helm too," said Will sarcastically. "Who wears full armor to sneak around?"

"That chameleon spell hides you better than you could manage on your own. With the silence you don't really have to worry about the armor."

The man had a point. "What about flexibility? I may have to crawl around."

"Crawling might be a chore, but you can handle it, and climbing isn't a problem for you if it comes to that. Magic, right?"

Will finally agreed. "I bow before your superior wisdom, but no breastplate."

"A compromise then," said Blake with a grim smile.

Half an hour later Will left the house clad in mail, helm, and greaves, but he carried no weapons. He had gotten so used to using the limnthal that he kept such things stored within it now. With barely more than a thought he could summon his crossbow, shield, spear, and any of a variety of knives and swords. If he *was* spotted somehow, his opponent would likely underestimate how well he was armed.

Chapter 7

With a chameleon spell masking his appearance and a silence spell on his attire, he would be nearly impossible to see or hear. He just needed to be sure he moved slowly when he might be observed. He also debated what spell he should have prepared as a backup.

If he chose the wind-wall, he would still require several seconds to invest it with enough power for it to be deadly, but he could use a weaker version defensively to clear the ground around him if he got into trouble. The force-lance he could *almost* reflex cast. He had been practicing the simple spell almost daily, but it wasn't quite there yet. If he needed one to attack with, it would take him a second to prepare on the fly, whereas if he kept it ready ahead of time it didn't need the turyn that a wind-wall would. He could unleash it with just a thought.

But the force-lance is sure to kill anyone it hits, he reminded himself. He chose the wind-wall. He could use it defensively in an instant, or offensively if he took a few seconds to charge it up.

He wondered what had happened to Tailtiu as he slowly made his way from the campus to the city streets and on toward the Nerrow house. It was unusual for her not to return promptly, but the fae woman was too formidable for anything bad to have happened to her.

"Tailtiu, Tailtiu, Tailtiu," he whispered to himself. "Thrice called, I summon thee." Ordinarily saying her name three times would establish a channel between them. Not enough for true communication, it would allow her to let him know if she would answer the call or not at a minimum.

He felt nothing. There was no response at all.

CHAPTER 8

He stood still on one side of the street for several long minutes, trying to figure out what Tailtiu's lack of response meant. *No, it was more than being ignored,* he told himself. *It was as if her name didn't connect at all.* Could she be dead? Will shook his head. His aunt was immortal, and while it was possible to kill her, he couldn't imagine a situation that would lead to her dying.

"She was just watching the Nerrow home," he muttered to himself. "Surely the assassin couldn't have killed her." Anyone that wanted to kill one of the fae would have to be both skilled and knowledgeable. Will wasn't even entirely certain what it would take. His grandfather had once mentioned the subject while discussing his enemy Elthas. At the time he had mentioned that trapping a fae in the mortal world and keeping it prisoner long enough would cause them to wither away.

But it's only been a matter of hours, he reminded himself. He began walking again, forcing himself to maintain his painfully slow pace. He wanted nothing more than to run, but ruining his chance at arriving unseen would be foolhardy, especially if whatever had ambushed Tailtiu was still waiting there.

"Stop it, Will," he admonished himself. "You don't know she was ambushed. She's probably fine." Taking a deep breath, he calmed himself and paid close attention to his surroundings. When he got within two blocks of his father's city house, he slowed further, until he was taking steps in slow motion.

He'd considered climbing a building, but Tailtiu had told him that the assassin liked to hide atop the nearby buildings. Even with magic, the awkwardness of climbing might be enough to betray him to someone watching carefully. By staying on the ground and hugging the sides of the buildings, he would have nearly a fifty percent chance of being out of the assassin's line of sight, depending on which vantage point the man had chosen. On the chance that he was approaching from one of the man's clear fields of view, he would just have to move as slowly as possible.

It helped that it was dark out, although this part of the city was lit by gas lanterns, creating a patchwork of dimly lit areas between islands of light. Will adjusted his vision without even thinking about it now, filtering out the glaring heart-light that came from the lanterns and increasing his sensitivity to other wavelengths. It gave everything a weird mixture of colors, but he could see clearly.

There were a few people out walking, but none of them seemed suspicious. He saw no sign of a hidden assassin. Continuing his slow pace, he moved forward, and soon he came to the corner where Mark Nerrow's house sat. He paused there to carefully study his surroundings. Will paid special attention to the ambient flows of turyn in the air, since in the past he had been able to spot well-hidden enemies simply by noting the places where it was obviously disturbed by a living body.

He still saw nothing of note. A young lad ambled down the lane, passing so close that Will almost had to take a step to avoid a collision. After five minutes he moved on, deciding to circle the block and see what the street on the other side of the house looked like.

Will continued his careful pace and slow study, until he passed a side alley that caught his attention. There was a trace of something he couldn't quite see. Adjusting his turyn sensitivity, he spotted the telltale signature of Tailtiu's fae magic. They glowed in small scratch marks on the brick wall to his left. *She must have been shapeshifted,* he observed. The marks went halfway up and then across for a few feet before vanishing. On the ground below was a heavy spot of her turyn on the cobblestones, as though she had jumped down. *Or fell.*

A fine powder coated the ground around the place she had landed. Taking a chance, Will touched it with one finger and lifted it to his nose. Temporarily shifting his vision back to normal, he noted the color. It was brown, and it had a distinct scent of iron. *Rust, and a lot of it.* Had someone used it as a weapon? He could only imagine what a cloud of rust might do to one of the fae. He was sure it wouldn't be pleasant.

Shifting his vision again, he caught sight of a dark stain. Examining it closer, he decided it was probably blood. *Damn it!* He could only guess what had happened to her, but it was obviously bad. Farther along he caught sight of something gray, a type of turyn he hadn't seen before. Moving closer, he studied it, but he couldn't make up his mind what it reminded him of. As his aunt had said before, it was similar to demonic turyn in some way, but it felt cold in a way he couldn't define.

There was a faint handprint on the wall that glowed with the same trace energy. Unlike most of the marks, this one was well defined. It looked human, but for the sharp claw marks that scored the brick at the end of where each finger had been. *What the hell did that?* he wondered.

The hair on the back of his neck stood on end, and he could feel someone watching him. Will froze and slowly looked around but saw no one. He decided it was time to move back to the main street. The sensation of being observed went with him, but there wasn't much he could do about it until he spotted whoever it was. *Unless I'm imagining it,* he thought.

Chapter 8

Unable to do anything about the unnerving sensation, Will kept moving steadily back around the block. He wanted to at least be in a position where he could observe the main door of the house. It took him a quarter of an hour to get there at his glacial pace. Once he could see the front door, he decided to get close. He reasoned that if he couldn't spot the assassin then he might as well be close to the door in case Laina exited. At least then he might be in a position to do something if the assassin made an attempt.

The small front lawn of the Nerrow home was enclosed by an iron fence. The front door opened onto a walk that led to a gate for the residents to use, presumably when a carriage was waiting on them. Will decided to wait there. Leaning against one of the stone pillars that framed the gate, he would be effectively invisible. *Unless whoever it is still has their eyes on me,* he reminded himself.

Once he was in place, he surveyed the street and the buildings across the road once more, but as before, he didn't spot anyone. Since he had nothing else to do, he began experimenting with his vision. Earlier he had eliminated heart-light from his vision because the street lamps gave off so much of it that the glare was annoying. Over time he had come to learn that heart-light, despite the name, had nothing to do with hearts, or life, but rather was a special type of light produced by heat.

The turyn in his vicinity was undisturbed, except for the disruption his own presence caused, so he was almost certain the assassin couldn't be close, but as he shifted his vision to see heart-light, a soft white glow appeared nearby, in front of the other gate pillar. Will's heart jumped into his throat, but he didn't move.

Staring at the position, he slowly altered his vision until a figure became clear. A short slender man, hidden within a cloak, stood less than ten feet away, gazing back at him. Will felt a jolt as their eyes made contact.

Neither of them moved, but the stranger slowly smiled at him, watching his face to see the effect on him. *He's not sure if I see him or not,* thought Will. *If I react, he'll know.* Naturally, it was at that moment that the door of the Nerrow home opened.

"I'll be back soon," came Laina's voice, calling to someone still inside.

She would be at the gate within ten or fifteen seconds. Will moved without thinking, summoning his falchion. The sharp blade would be good against an unarmored opponent, and if the assassin did have protection, Will doubted it would stand up to a thrust from the heavy bladed sword. Plus, the man didn't appear to have a sword.

The other man's cloak flew wide, and something punched Will in the chest hard enough that he stumbled and nearly fell. A sharp pain followed, and Will recognized the sensation, since he'd felt it several times in the past. He'd been shot with a crossbow. His mail and gambeson had mostly stopped it, but the point had still managed to penetrate his skin by slipping partway through one of the rings.

He didn't hesitate. Recovering his balance, Will advanced, dodging deftly to one side as the man threw the crossbow at his head and drew two long knives.

Ordinarily, fighting sword versus knife, or in this case two knives, would have given him the advantage, mainly because of reach, but Will rapidly discovered that he was out of his depth. In the span of five or six seconds he was forced to use his point-defense shield to stop four cuts that he simply couldn't get his sword in position to block. The assassin didn't waste time attacking his body, where his armor protected him.

Wearing armor, using a sword, Will should have had an overwhelming advantage. But he didn't. *Shit, he's*

Chapter 8

fast! Backpedaling, Will struggled to regain the initiative. When his enemy paused for a second, he leapt to the attack, concentrating his turyn in his muscles and increasing his own speed. He thought he might catch the man off-guard, but that turned out not to be the case as the other fellow grinned and matched him.

He was expecting that, Will realized. He barely saw the blade that came at his face, and it was with yet another point-defense shield that he managed to keep his eye. *I should have started with magic. Attacking with a sword was foolish.* It was difficult to get enough space to concentrate, though; his enemy seemed able to read his mind.

A sharp cry cut the night air as Laina caught sight of them. Will turned, thinking to warn her, and the assassin moved in her direction as well. That was too much for him. He had to do something. He released the wind-wall spell he'd prepared earlier, and the sudden violent gusts threw dust and detritus into the air as it knocked the assassin from his feet. It didn't have enough turyn in it to be deadly, but it was enough for what he needed. As the stranger fell, Will summoned his own crossbow, already locked and loaded. Without pause, he aimed and fired.

Will felt a certain sense of relief when he saw the quarrel bury itself in the assassin's hip. The man didn't cry out, but he saw the pain in the man's eyes. Before the assassin could recover or use some other trick, he needed to finish him. It would only take a second or two to construct a force-lance spell.

"Assassin!" screamed Laina's voice from his left as she pulled open the gate in a panic.

"I have him, get back," Will yelled to her, hoping she would change course and run for the house.

A wave of flames washed over him before he could finish his spell. Unprepared as he was, his body still absorbed most of the turyn that fueled the blast, but enough heat got through that it scorched his eyebrows.

Will stared at his half-sister in shock, then pointed at the downed assassin. "Not me, him!"

For her part, Laina finally recognized him. "You!"

"Me?" He could already tell that something didn't add up. Laina was moving to shield the assassin with her body and five incandescent balls of white-hot fire sprang to life in the air in front of the young woman.

She was protecting the assassin.

He's her bodyguard, Will realized, suddenly feeling stupid. The fear and outrage on Laina's face made him feel even worse.

"Surrender and release the spell or I'll burn you to ash," she declared fiercely. "Darla, are you all right?" she asked the bodyguard.

Her words made him realize he was still holding the force-lance spell in his hands. *I look like a right villain, don't I?* Then his brain processed the rest of her words. *Darla?* Staring at the wounded assassin, his mind put the pieces together. The assassin wasn't a slim-built man, but rather a woman—and he'd just shot her.

What is it with me and the female half of the human race this week?

"Last warning!" said Laina through clenched teeth.

He was about to do as she said, when a flicker of movement caught his eye. Laina was facing him, her back toward the corner. If the motion hadn't been across the street directly behind her, he probably wouldn't have seen it in time. A man leapt from the roof of the house across the street.

The house was two stories tall, and the man dropped close to thirty feet before landing on the hard stones of the street. The house was similar to the Nerrow home in its

Chapter 8

construction, which meant the house was set almost fifty feet back from the road. Will's jaw might have dropped if he hadn't seen Tailtiu land after falling similar distances without visible harm. As it was, he had never seen his aunt jump such a distance horizontally at the same time.

All of this registered in the span of a second. The newcomer hit the ground and sprang forward, racing toward them with a strange, unnatural grace. Although the stranger had two arms and two legs, the man's movements would leave no doubt in any viewer's mind. He wasn't human.

Will's expression shifted, showing surprise and determination as he lifted his hands to aim. In return, Laina's face hardened. Will tried to warn her, "Behind you!"

"You asked for it," she spat, then she released her spell.

He expanded his outer shell, hoping he could absorb whatever spell she was using, but he kept his eyes on the man running at Laina's back. As fast as the creature moved, Will didn't want to risk missing, so he cast the force-lance at the last possible second. He was gratified to see it connect, blowing a fist-sized hole in the chest of the thing behind his sister.

Then the blazing orbs struck, all five of them hammering into him in quick succession. They flew in a spiraling pattern, and while the first hit him from the front, the following orbs came at him from a variety of different angles, landing a second or so apart. The first was no problem. The second and third taxed him, and the air around him began to glow as he struggled to contain the fiery turyn. The pain began when he absorbed the fourth. He was also still holding onto the energy from her earlier attack.

Rather than vent the power back at her, Will thrust his hands skyward, releasing a gout of flame as though he meant to burn the heavens. The fifth orb hit while he was still trying to make space and his world became an inferno.

Incredibly he wasn't incinerated, but his hair and clothing caught fire, and there was no doubt he would be blistered in places. He continued trying to vent the excess energy skyward, though he couldn't see much around himself, for he was wreathed in flame.

Then Laina stepped *through* the flames, a cobblestone in her hand. Will was so surprised that she nearly brained him with it before he could stop the blow with a point-defense shield. The flames around them died down as he continued emptying the power he held into the air, and the expression on Laina's face told him she had finally figured out that he wasn't trying to kill her or her bodyguard. She seemed puzzled, though still angry. "What the hell are you doing?" she demanded.

She took her eyes off him for a second to check on Darla, and they both saw the creature rise from where it lay on the street, the hole still visible in its chest. Laina's eyes widened with shock as she realized what had happened, just before the thing charged at her once more.

Will brought his hands down and released the rest of the fiery power at the man who should have already been dead. He hoped the angle was good enough to avoid hitting Laina's bodyguard, but there wasn't time to be sure and he was out of options.

The old, familiar smell of burning flesh found his nose seconds later, as the man-thing became a human-shaped torch. It flailed wildly and seemed to still be trying to find Laina, though its eyes were gone. Will had other things to worry about as he beat out the smoldering flames at the hem of his gambeson.

His sister, for her part, seemed stunned into immobility. The sight of what was, at least in her mind, a

Chapter 8

living human burning to death in front her had sent her into a state of shock. *And yet she was perfectly willing to try and burn me to death just a few seconds ago,* thought Will wryly. He caught Laina's arm and guided her back a few feet to avoid the burning creature's grasping hands. The burning figure collapsed to the ground a few seconds later, still kicking feebly.

"You just burned that man alive," mumbled Laina, still trying to process what had happened.

Will nodded, taking the moment's respite to pull out the crossbow bolt that was still lodged in his mail. "As you tried to do to me just a few seconds earlier." Reaching, up he felt his face and was relieved to find his skin still seemed intact, but his eyebrows were definitely gone.

Something finally clicked in Laina's mind and she snapped into motion, heading for her fallen friend. "Darla!" Will followed her over so he could examine the woman he had shot. A large pool of blood had formed around the bodyguard.

"If she dies, you'll follow soon after," threatened Laina coldly as she knelt by the other woman. "Darla, can you hear me? Say something."

Will knelt on the other side of the warrior and began cutting away her trousers. From the placement of the arrow it might have struck a large vein. He didn't think it was an artery, or Darla would probably already be dead. He could see that her eyes followed his movements, though her mouth opened and closed without making a sound.

"What are you doing?" demanded his half-sister. "This is your fault."

"And I might be able to save her if you let me," he responded without looking up. His sister fell silent as he continued to examine her friend. *It's a deep vein, and above the leg where I can't use a tourniquet to stop the bleeding,* he noted mentally. He couldn't effectively apply pressure there either, which meant the woman would be dead in a short span of minutes. Will glanced up and caught Laina's gaze on his face. Behind the anger he could see she was frightened. As she looked back down at her friend, tears began to well.

And she'll be dead because of me. Because I thought she was an assassin rather than a guard—because I decided, in my infinite wisdom, to interfere where I wasn't wanted. He summoned one of his remaining two regeneration potions from the limnthal and quickly unstopped the vial. He poured a few drops on the wound, then held the tiny bottle to her lips and tilted it up. Some spilled, and the woman choked, but enough got down her throat. It was potent stuff, as he knew from prior experience.

"What was that?" asked Laina, her voice thick with desperation.

"A regeneration potion," he said simply.

"Will it work? She's lost so much blood." Her voice cracked near the end.

"It brought me back from the edge of death," he told her calmly. "It just needs a minute to do the job. It will exhaust her, but after she rests, she'll feel better than she did before it happened." Even as he spoke, the color began to return to Darla's cheeks.

Without warning, Laina shifted subjects. "You murdered that man without a moment's hesitation."

"I don't know what he was, but he wasn't human," Will informed her. "And he was heading for you. You didn't hesitate to try and do the same to me."

His sister's eyes never flinched. "You nearly killed Darla, and I warned you first. I didn't want to do it."

Will's emotions were conflicted as he stared back at her. On one hand he admired the girl for her conviction, as well as her bravery in defending her friend, while on

Chapter 8

the other he was irritated by her obvious dislike for him. Added to the mix was the fact that he was guilty and embarrassed for nearly killing an innocent person. *But I also saved Laina's life,* he reminded himself.

Just what was a person supposed to feel at such a complicated moment? He had no idea. As he struggled to find words, Laina spoke again. "You could have warned me. I thought you were attacking me."

There hadn't been time, but he asked anyway, "Would you have believed me?"

"Probably not," she admitted. Then she gave him a serious look. "I have to call the constable. You killed someone."

"Something," he corrected.

"You can say it was self-defense. They'll probably believe you, especially if I testify on your behalf."

"I was defending you, not me," he replied dryly, "so I don't think it's technically self-defense."

"Either way, you won't hang for it," said Laina. "But you still have to answer for assaulting Darla."

"She shot me first," snapped Will, his patience thinning.

Laina shook her head. "You pulled your sword out, *then* she shot you. I saw it."

A new voice entered the conversation. "I was going to shoot him anyway." It was Darla. Her words were clear though her voice was weak. "I thought he was after you. We misunderstood each other."

Laina went on, "But you did save her life, so perhaps we can pretend it didn't happen."

His sarcasm was thick as he accepted. "That's very gracious of you." He froze as his eyes caught a flash of turyn across the street, from not one, but four separate places. Four men appeared, rising from the ground as though it was no more solid than water. Each of them had three elementals, one of earth, one of fire, and one of air. They were dressed in dark gray tunics that covered what was probably a chain shirt and gambeson beneath. *More people? How many were watching this house?*

The men moved cautiously toward him, taking different vectors so he couldn't keep his eyes on all of them. "Put the sword down and kneel," ordered one of them in an authoritative tone.

Will got quickly to his feet. The gate that opened into Laina's front yard was still open. He moved in front of the two women and spoke to Laina from one side of his mouth. "Help Darla inside and close the gate."

"Neither of you move," barked the stranger, then he focused on Will again. "Don't make me repeat myself. Drop the weapon and kneel, now!"

He was moving his head back and forth, trying to keep all of them in sight, though it was impossible. "Or what? Who are you?"

"Your worst nightmare, child. Surrender or you might not walk away from this." The man was close enough that Will could see his eyes now—they were cold and hard.

"I've seen several nightmares. You aren't even close to making my list," Will shot back.

Laina's hand touched his arm. "Will, stop. They're the king's men, the *Driven*."

He had no idea what that meant, but her tone implied they were part of some special force. "They aren't wearing any livery or insignia," he replied cautiously, weighing his options. He didn't want to fight if they were servants of the king, but he still wasn't convinced.

"Enough of this," said the commander impatiently. In the blink of an eye a source-link snapped out, and to Will's surprise, managed to connect to him.

Chapter 8

Without thinking, he snarled and wrested control of the link away from the man. He paralyzed the fellow before he could react and watched him fall, feeling a sense of satisfaction. One of the others sent something hard flying at his head, but he blocked it with a point-defense shield and then turned to drive his sword at the man who was rushing at his back. Almost by pure chance, his blade skipped up the front of the man's chest and sank into his unarmored throat. The unfortunate soldier fell back, blood spraying from the wound.

The fourth was about to unleash a spell, something involving air from what Will could see, but there wasn't much he could do about it. *If it's a wind-wall or something similar I'm dead,* he thought grimly as he tried to create a force-lance, but he knew he'd be a second too late.

"Unleash that spell on my son-in-law and I'll see you dead, lieutenant." The voice belonged to a fifth man, who had only now chosen to reveal himself, rising from the ground just as the other had before. It was the king.

Will didn't know whether to be relieved or terrified. *This can't be happening.*

King Lognion walked resolutely toward them and the remaining soldiers—the two who weren't wounded or paralyzed—became still while somehow also conveying a sense of respect and deference to their sovereign. From the corner of his eye Will saw Laina drop into a deep curtsey.

The king's eyes flicked down to take note of the burning corpse and the man hemorrhaging from his throat. The one who was bleeding had already lost consciousness and would probably be dead in another minute at best. Then Lognion's eyes went to the paralyzed commander before finally coming to rest on Will. "I see your habits haven't changed in recent months, William. Have you no knee for your monarch?"

Will's brain had finally settled on muted terror for the emotional backdrop of his mind, and consequently his common sense began to suffer for it. The last time he had met the king in person had been when he had confronted the man about his daughter. As the months had passed peacefully, he had begun to secretly hope that perhaps he wouldn't ever have to meet Lognion again. Rationally he had known that wouldn't really be possible—he had pledged to kill the man, after all—but even so, he wasn't mentally prepared to face Selene's father again.

Naturally, he said something stupid, "I thought perhaps family weren't required to do that sort of thing."

A faint quirk appeared at the corner of Lognion's mouth then vanished quickly. "Only in private, assuming I choose to allow you such freedoms, and only if you're prepared to speak to me in a familial manner. Are you suggesting you'd like to call me Father?"

Several awkward seconds passed as Will tried to figure out a response. Apparently he had two options, but he certainly didn't feel like calling the devil in front of him Father. He bowed instead. "Your Majesty, I didn't expect to encounter you here."

"Nor I you, William." He glanced at the paralyzed commander once again. "Would you mind releasing my man?"

"Oh!" Will had forgotten. He dropped the source-link spell a second later.

Meanwhile, Lognion's attention had turned to Laina, who still had her head down and knees bent as she maintained her curtsey. "Miss Nerrow, be at ease. I trust you are safe and sound?" Before she could answer, the commander finished standing and the king held up one hand. "One moment before you answer that." He turned to the commander, and without warning his arm lashed

Chapter 8

out, backhanding the soldier and sending him tumbling to the ground. "Your idiocy almost cost my daughter a husband. Get back on your feet." The king's face shifted from rage to utmost calm as he faced Laina once again. "Where were we?"

Will's half-sister seemed disturbed by what she had seen. Swallowing to clear her throat, she answered, "I'm unhurt, Your Majesty. Thank you for asking."

"Glad to hear it." Lognion addressed the commander again. "The one on fire was our target wasn't it?"

"Yes, Sire."

The monarch sighed with obvious irritation. "An interrogation is unlikely now, but perhaps the body will give us some answers. Detail one of the men to see that the remains are recovered." Then Lognion's focus shifted. "Is this the one you mentioned before?" He waved a hand in the direction of Laina's fallen bodyguard. The woman's wounds had finished healing, but she hadn't risen to her feet yet.

The commander stiffened. "Yes, Your Majesty."

"Seize her," ordered the king. It happened so quickly that Laina barely had time to yelp as the two soldiers on either side stepped forward and grabbed Darla. The woman offered no resistance as they pulled her to her feet and dragged her to stand in front of the King of Terabinia.

Lognion's eyes lit with excitement and he drew a poniard from his belt. "Hold her."

"Your Majesty!" protested Laina. Will started to step forward, but Lognion turned his gaze on them and he froze.

"I merely wish to confirm the lady's identity," said the king with a sneer. Then he whistled and four more men stepped into the light near the street corner. They were dressed identically to the other soldiers. The men joined them, and the commander detailed two of the newcomers to keep an eye on the burning remains while the others stayed alert in case trouble broke out.

Laina deflated and Will stepped back, unsure what to do. Starting a fight now would only endanger his sister.

The king brought the dagger up and inserted the blade into the collar of the woman's tunic then pulled downward. It cut for only an inch before meeting a hidden layer of mail. A chain vest was sandwiched between layers of linen. Undeterred, Lognion kept working, moving the blade to either side and cutting away the fabric. After a moment only the mail vest and the padding beneath it remained. Darla's eyes were flat and empty. "Keep her still," he ordered the two men holding her.

Lognion formed a spell and turyn began to glow around his hands. Reaching out, he grasped the top of the vest and pulled. The riveted steel links began to part and the gambeson beneath it tore. Darla's demeanor shifted instantly. Her right leg came up, but Lognion was ready for her. Releasing her vest, his left hand caught the woman's knee while his right drove forward into her belly. Laina's friend sagged, but the king barked another order. "Hold her up."

Then he resumed his task, ripping the vest and gambeson away to reveal the woman's bare chest. A dark tattoo in black and red showed between her breasts, a stylized spider. "As I thought, one of the Arkeshi. Your life is forfeit, assassin, as it has been from the moment you stepped onto Terabinian soil."

"She's an exile," declared Laina suddenly.

Lognion turned his head slowly, with a predator's grace, until his eyes had locked onto the newest target of his interest. "You know her?"

Laina blanched, but she wouldn't disavow her friend. "She's an exile. She no longer owes allegiance to the

Chapter 8

Great Khan. I hired her to serve as my bodyguard. She's here on my behalf."

The king's lips curled slightly at the corner and Will felt his heart shrink. He had seen that expression on the cruel man's face too many times in the past. "Let me rephrase that for you, Miss Nerrow," said the monarch, his eyes flicking over to study Will for a moment, gauging his reaction. "If you take responsibility for bringing this assassin into Terabinia then the crime is yours."

Will could see his sister's hands begin to visibly shake. She linked them together to hide her fear. Then she asked, "If I do, will you spare her life?"

A deep chuckle resounded in the king's chest. "Do you think your status as the daughter of a lord will keep you from punishment? Someone must pay when a crime is committed." There was an evil light in his eyes.

"What would my punishment be, if I claimed responsibility?"

"Laina, no!" snapped Will. "You have no idea what he's capable of."

King Lognion smiled with mock sweetness. "Such a touching reunion, William. You know what I'm capable of, don't you, and why?" His eyes flitted to Laina for a second, then back to Will.

He's threatening her to get to me, thought Will. *What does he want?* Before he could say anything, Darla spoke out. "Let him kill me, Laina. Death means nothing to me."

"Your guardian is both loyal and wise, Miss Nerrow," said the king. "If you choose to take responsibility, I will grant her amnesty for so long as she serves you, but you will have to accept punishment and I doubt your father will be pleased. Ten lashes in the public square will be a mark of shame on your family's honor."

Laina's face went white, and her lip trembled when she answered, but her voice was clear. "I accept responsibility. Please spare her life."

Will's heart sank, and Darla cried out, "Laina, no!"

Meanwhile the king smiled cheerfully and then gave the order. "Seize her." Darla struggled to escape the men holding her as the commander took Laina's arm.

Unused to such roughness, Laina automatically tried to pull away. "Unhand me!" she commanded. "I've already surrendered."

Lognion took one quick step forward, then slapped Laina with such force that her head whipped to one side. Stunned, she stared back at him, blood dripping down her cheek where one of his rings had cut her skin. "You're a criminal now, Miss Nerrow. Don't expect to be treated as a woman of gentle birth. You'll spend the night in a cell. Once you've taken your lashes you'll be released. Until then"—the king paused, relishing the words—"please resist."

Will couldn't take it any longer. "Let her go."

Lognion Maligant met his gaze. "You have no standing to interfere, *son-in-law.*"

"Yes, I do," said Will flatly. *Lognion is one of the few people who know that Laina and I share blood.*

"Perhaps you do," said the king with a twisted grin. "Would you like to beg leniency on her behalf?"

"What is it you want?" asked Will.

The king's fist lashed out, and Will had to steel himself to keep from using a point-defense shield to protect himself, then he was falling. "That's for showing disrespect yet again."

Sullen anger smoldered in Will's features as he looked up. "What is it you want, Your Majesty?"

"I have five questions," said Lognion. "For each one you answer I'll deduct two lashes from the

Chapter 8

punishment. For each question you refuse, I'll give you the lashes instead."

Stubborn and angry, Will responded, "Agreed." He already had a bad feeling he wouldn't like the questions, and he knew from past experience that the king was a seemingly flawless lie detector.

"Where is my daughter?"

Shock ran through him. *He knows she's gone!* Will's eyes widened, and he struggled to think. From the corner of his eye, he could see Laina studying him with combination of horror and interest, since she also desperately wanted to know the answer. Lying wouldn't work. His mind ran in circles for ten seconds or more before he finally made the only choice available to him. "I refuse to answer that."

Laina gasped audibly, and Lognion held up two fingers. "How delightful. Very well, here is my second question: Where is Selene?"

He started to answer when Laina broke in. "Will, stop. This is stupid. He's her father, just tell him."

You're more worried about finding out yourself than you are with me taking your punishment, thought Will sourly. "I refuse."

Lognion held up two more fingers. "Third question, where is my only living child?"

Will felt a cold sweat beginning to form on his body. He'd been beaten with a coachwhip once as a child, ironically enough because he had saved Laina from a snake the first time they met. The coach driver had thought he had attacked her and had laid into him several times before Selene had stopped the man. He still had the scar on his cheek.

He'd almost taken lashes while in the army, but Tiny had taken the blame for him. Will had seen the damage done to the big man's back and he was sure it was worse than what had happened to him. "I refuse."

The king arched his brows. "How noble of you. Before I ask the next question, you should know I plan on administering your punishment personally. I like to make every stroke count. I also like to soak the whip in brine. Some say that's just cruel, but it's a mercy really. The salt helps the wound stop bleeding more quickly, though it does make the cut agonizingly painful." He paused to let his words sink in, then asked, "Where is your wife?"

Something snapped as fear overloaded Will's mind. "Why don't you summon her and ask her yourself?" The world went black as Lognion's fist drove him into unconsciousness. When he awoke, he was being held by two men in much the same fashion that Darla had been a few minutes earlier.

"Are you awake?" asked the king. "I don't like beating unconscious men. Too much effort for no reward."

Groggy, Will answered, "Yes, and that was your fifth question." Even as he said it, he knew the remark would earn him a more severe beating, but he couldn't help himself. *Probably too much time spent around the fae,* he decided. *That sort of thing would work with them.*

Lognion remained still for a moment, then began to chuckle. "All right, fine. You made me laugh. I'll count that one as a question answered." The smile on the king's face was genuine, which made it all the more terrifying.

He really is insane.

"This is why I love dealing with you, William. You're so much more entertaining than any of my other servants or enemies." Lognion patted his cheek affectionately. He nodded to the two men holding Will up. "Follow me. We'll take him behind Lord Nerrow's house."

Chapter 8

Laina squeaked in surprise. "Here? Now? You were going to take me to the square—"

"Remember your place, Miss Nerrow."

She dipped her head. "Your Majesty."

Lognion nodded happily. "The difference, Miss Nerrow, is that William is my son-in-law. A public flogging would bring embarrassment to the throne, so we will have to make do with a private affair. In all honesty, I prefer it this way. As I said, I do enjoy administering the punishment myself." He led the way toward the Nerrow home.

CHAPTER 9

The Nerrow household fell into chaos at the sudden appearance of the king. The baron's servants were running to and fro, and Mark Nerrow was clearly working hard to hide his dismay at having such an auspicious visitor with no warning.

When Lord Nerrow spotted Will among those who entered, a moment's panic flickered behind his eyes, but he recovered quickly. A look of deep concern entered his face when the circumstances were explained. Will's father stared at his illegitimate son's face, but Will had no idea what the man's expression represented—shame, worry, embarrassment, or perhaps fear of discovery.

Will looked away. Currently he and Laina were standing in the kitchen, he with two guards holding him. Laina was free to do as she pleased, but for some reason she remained in the room. *Why is she here?* Will wondered. *Shouldn't she retire?* Darla had been taken upstairs already, where apparently the bodyguard already had a room of her own.

Lognion was in the next room, speaking with Mark and Agnes Nerrow while he waited on servants to fetch the required implements. Glancing around once more, Will caught Laina staring at him. "You should probably go to your room. I don't think you'll want to see this," he told her.

She ignored the suggestion. "This was supposed to be my punishment. The least I can do is stay with you." She hesitated before asking, "Are you scared?"

"I'd be lying if I said otherwise," he admitted.

They stood in silence for a minute, then she asked, "Why?"

"Why what?"

"All of it," said Laina. "Why did you follow me in the rain? Why were you watching my home? Why would you put yourself in this position for me?"

"I thought Darla was an assassin—" he began, but she interrupted him.

"I've figured that out. I'm trying to understand your motivation. A while back, before she disappeared, Selene told me you were crazy, but I don't think that's the case. There's definitely a reason of some sort. What is it?"

He couldn't tell her he was her brother. Even if he were willing the two men holding his arms would hear. Cudgeling his brain, he tried to come up with a reasonable explanation for his behavior. "Remember the snake, when you were a child?" he said at last.

"Huh?"

Will pointed at the scar on his cheek. "When I got this? Maybe this is just a bad habit of mine."

Laina seemed genuinely confused. "I have no idea what you're talking about. Can you answer without being cryptic?"

There was a stir in the next room as the man who had gone out to find the necessary items returned. His waiting would soon be done. He wasn't about to be executed, but Will felt a sense of urgency. "For Selene," he said quickly.

"Selene?"

"You wanted her help, but she couldn't be there for you. I'm just trying to take care of you in her place."

His half-sister gave him a suspicious look. "I'm not sure if I believe that, and even if it's true, I can tell you for certain she wouldn't want you to take the whip for me."

"I didn't really mean to," said Will. "I didn't think he would ask about her."

"But you could have told him," insisted Laina. "Most would say there's no shame in obeying your king, even if it means you have to break a promise."

He gave her a hard look. "I'm sure she's told you about her family situation. Would you have told him?"

A shadow fell on her expression. "I'm not sure. It depends on the reason. He is the king, after all."

"Then I made the right choice," said Will, firming his jaw.

"What do you mean?"

"About not telling you where she is."

She looked as though she'd been slapped. "I said it would depend on the reason! Don't start making assumptions about me."

The commander called to the guards and they tightened their hold on him. It was time.

It turned out that Baron Nerrow's house contained a small atrium. The area was tiled but contained a plethora of plants, some in large planters while others hung around the edges of the open space. In the center was a bench and a statue of Temarah, presumably so that anyone enjoying the garden atmosphere could reflect on the mercy of the goddess.

Although Will hadn't been included in the discussion between the king and Mark and Agnes Nerrow, he had heard some of it, and much of it had revolved around Agnes' objection to using the statue of the holy mother as a whipping post. The king had won the argument, and now Will stood in front of Temarah's stone form, his arms up and his wrists tied together behind her neck. To a casual observer it almost looked as though he was embracing the goddess.

He squeezed his eyes shut and rested his forehead against the statue's chest. The cool stone felt good against his skin as he tried to stay calm. He had been stripped to

Chapter 9

the waist and the cold night air sent shivers down his back. *I have to relax,* he reminded himself. Someone had once told him that the damage was worse if you tensed up. *How the hell can anyone relax in this situation?*

"At least give him something to bite down on," protested Mark Nerrow. He and Laina stood on one side of the atrium to observe. Agnes had gone inside, unwilling to see her garden defiled. Tabitha, the younger daughter, had awoken during all the commotion and had wanted to be present, but her mother had refused.

Lognion waved a hand dismissively, then leaned in to whisper in Will's ear. "That would ruin the fun, wouldn't it, William? The best part is the screaming."

Will didn't reply, and as the king stepped away he tried not to hear the sound of the whip being removed from the bucket of brine. He was so scared he felt like vomiting. He'd never been particularly religious, especially after learning that Aislinn and Elthas weren't actually gods but rather lords of the fae. Even so he found his attention on the statue in front of him. *Temarah, I don't know if you're real, but if you can help me somehow, I will be forever grateful,* he thought desperately.

There was a faint whistling sound as the whip cut through the air, and then the world vanished as his awareness was consumed by white-hot agony. For a moment he lost control of his body and his legs collapsed, but strong arms held him up. A voice filtered into his mind. *I am here.*

Temarah? Opening his eyes, Will realized the statue was gone. In its place was a woman of flesh and blood. His arms were still tied around her neck, but it was her arms that embraced him, keeping him from sagging in place. The woman was beautiful, but in an entirely human way. Unlike the depictions he had seen in churches, her hair and eyes were brown, rather than blond and blue.

She seemed ordinary, but the warmth in her gaze radiated compassion—and sorrow.

If that is what you wish to call me—most do these days.

Please help me, he begged, then the whip whistled again, and his world filled with pain.

I can't stop the pain of living. You must endure on your own.

When he opened his eyes again, he could see the woman was weeping. She held him tighter and pressed her cheek against the side of his head. *Why are you here?* he asked mentally, desperate to think of anything other than the next stroke of the whip. Blinding agony overwhelmed him again, washing away his thoughts.

Because you called, and you remind me of him. You must be strong afterward. Don't let the shame poison your heart. My beloved was punished like this once and it took years for him to recover his old spirit.

Your beloved?

My husband.

Marduke, the Lord of the Underworld? The next stroke brought such pain that his lungs seized, and he could no longer breathe. He tried to jerk, to move, anything to escape, but the goddess held him still. When he looked at her again, he felt her breath on his face and suddenly his lungs relaxed.

He was not an evil man any more than I was a perfect example of motherhood. The theology of this age has been extremely unkind to him. He was just a man, as you are. We fought and loved together, to make a better future for our children, to be happy.

His back was a single, aching mass that radiated constant misery. With each blow it somehow became more sensitive, and when the next landed his scream was unrestrained. His eyes were already streaming tears and

Chapter 9

his nose was filled with snot. He might have vomited; it was hard to be sure. Only the pain mattered.

And then it vanished. He floated above the atrium, looking down at his body as it stood rigidly in front of the statue of Temarah. Glancing to one side, he realized she was floating beside him. It felt so natural it never occurred to him to ask how they got there. Instead he returned to what she had just told him. *Did you succeed? Were you happy?*

The goddess smiled faintly. *We were happy for as long as we lived. But time can be cruel. Now we seek happiness through this world, though just as often we find pain.*

They watched as Lognion finished the last strokes. Will noticed that his body hardly responded now, as though it was made of stone as hard as the statue of the goddess. *Are you doing this?* he asked.

I kept you still at first, but now that you've freed yourself from the flesh, I am only lending you aid with the artistic touches.

Artistic touches?

When she looked at him again, he could see a burning fury in her gaze. *I have a special hatred for this form of punishment and those who abuse it for their sick pleasure.* She turned her eyes toward the king. *That one in particular. He is due a reckoning.*

I'm supposed to kill him, Will told her. *But I would rather not have to. Maybe your vengeance will save me the trouble?*

She shook her head. *The world is for the living. I merely observe. You must cleanse it for yourself.* She began to fade in front of his eyes.

Don't go! he begged, but it was too late. He was alone.

But he wasn't in his body. Looking down, he saw it still standing rigidly in front of the statue of Temarah. He had no idea how to return and when he thought about it, he began to drift farther away. For a second he panicked, and his perspective began to shift and roll. Will struggled to calm himself, and once his thoughts were clear he started to get a feel for how to control his movement. It was the reverse of swimming. In the water he could use his arms and legs to push against the water around him, but here there was no water. There was nothing solid, nothing material, not even air. Normally solid things like the ground, walls, the statue, other people, all of them were intangible. They provided not even the smallest resistance when his hands touched them.

The trick was to focus on a particular thing. It had confused him at first, because it felt like he was pushing *away* from whatever he put his mind to, but the opposite was the case. In the real world, the physical world, he moved toward something by pushing against other things, such as the ground when walking. Here attempting to push against other things the way he would with a physical body worked against him. Every time his attention wavered to something else, it would send him in that direction.

It felt as though it took several minutes to figure out, but when he took stock of the people standing around his body, he saw that they had barely moved. Focusing on his own face, he felt himself rushing toward it. There was a brief feeling of resistance and then the world exploded around him. *Holy Mother!* The pain was unbelievable.

Opening his eyes, the first thing he took note of was Mark and Laina Nerrow. They stood off to one side, and he couldn't remember the last time he had seen two people so visibly upset. The baron's face was red, and

Chapter 9

his hands were balled into tight fists. Laina was vomiting into one of her mother's topiaries.

Will turned to face his father-in-law. "Are we done?" His throat felt ragged when he spoke, and he realized he had probably been screaming. As he moved, he felt the skin on his back shift oddly and something flapped, as though he wore a shirt that had been badly torn. *Was that my skin?* He glanced down and saw blood soaking into his trousers. Waves of agony washed over him, and he fought to keep his eyes focused on Lognion.

"You must not have heard me," said the king. "But then I suppose that can be forgiven, given what you've been through. I've never seen anyone react to a flogging in quite such a stoic manner. It was impressive, though you took some of the joy from my task. I offered to have my private physician treat you. I may have outdone myself. I believe you'll need professional assistance to avoid permanent injury."

"I don't want anything from you," said Will hoarsely. "I already have the only thing of value you've ever possessed—Selene."

Mark Nerrow stepped forward. "We'll take care of him, Your Majesty."

Lognion studied the baron for a few seconds. "Yes, I'm sure you will. You've always lived up to your *responsibilities,* haven't you, Mark?"

The baron lowered his eyes, but Will could see his father was fighting to swallow his anger.

The king turned away to head back into the house. "My offer stands. If you need help, bring him to the palace." He gathered his soldiers and left while Agnes returned to the atrium to check on Will and her family.

Laina's mother nearly fainted when she saw the tattered skin hanging from Will's back in ribbons. "Mark, we need to take him to the college. Only Doctor Morris will be capable of treating something as bad as this. How could you let him do such a thing?"

"Because he's the godsdamned king!" swore Mark Nerrow angrily. "He's sick! I had to stand there and watch him do it! It wasn't even a flogging. It looked like he was *trying* to flay the skin from his back."

Meanwhile Will had already summoned his last regeneration potion. In less than two hours he had used both of his remaining treasures and they wouldn't be easily replaced. *A thousand gold down my throat,* he thought as he swallowed. Another wave of dizziness hit him, and he swayed. Mark and Agnes both started toward him, but Laina reached him first, slipping her shoulder beneath his arm before he fell.

The act of lifting his arm shifted the skin of his back and sent fire blazing along his nerves. Will found himself leaning heavily on the younger woman. *I'm getting blood all over her dress,* he realized. "That will be hard to wash out, but I have a spell that will do the trick," he commented blearily. His body was beginning to itch intensely as the regeneration potion started its work.

Will stumbled along and eventually he opened his eyes and found himself lying across a large bed. Voices were arguing in the hall behind him. "Why'd you put him in there? You should have taken him to the guest room." That was Mark Nerrow's voice.

"He was about to pass out. I couldn't carry him. If you want to try, you can carry him down the hall, but he's already bled all over the bed. There's no sense in ruining two sets of bedding," Laina responded sharply.

"Is he still here?" asked another young woman's voice, probably his younger sister, Tabitha.

Chapter 9

"What are you doing out of your room? I told you to stay there," snapped their mother.

Mark interrupted, "Let me by. I'm going to move him. We can't have him in Laina's room."

"For the sake of all that's holy, Mark, leave him be!" snapped Agnes. "He's had enough."

"That potion he took healed his wounds," said the baron. "It won't hurt him. He's just exhausted."

"And he's sleeping," Agnes shot back. "After what he's done for Laina he deserves better than to have you dragging him all over the house."

You tell him, Agnes, Will thought with a faint smirk. He'd never really had a chance to get to know his father's wife, or anyone in the family, to be honest, but he'd barely met Agnes before that night. Despite himself, he found he liked her.

He had always had an image in his mind of her as just another spoiled noblewoman. Since she was the woman that Mark had abandoned Will's mother for, he supposed he should hate her, but he couldn't find it in his heart to hold a grudge. She seemed like a genuinely decent human being. *But I wonder what she'd think if she found out who I was? Would she still be advocating for my beauty sleep?*

CHAPTER 10

During the night Will rose once to attend to certain bodily functions and discovered that someone had undressed him. He was forced to use a coverlet to cover himself as he worried that one of the ladies of the house might walk in while he was using the chamber pot. With that out of the way, he returned to bed. Before falling back asleep, he studied the decor. He'd expected it to be filled with luxurious furnishings, but the room was surprisingly plain. That wasn't to say it was poorly decorated, but the style was minimal and tastefully done. It was distinctly feminine, but overall it gave him the sense that Laina was more concerned with function than superficial ornaments.

That ran completely counter to the impression he'd gained when she had visited Selene while he was in the army. Back then she'd seemed bored, and her only concern was shopping. Of course having a room that was modestly furnished didn't make Laina a paragon of virtue. *After all, from what Tailtiu told me she spends every evening running from house to house attending every party thrown in the capital.*

That thought brought his fear and worry for his aunt back to the fore. He still had no idea what had happened to her. *And what was that thing that went after Laina?* The king had taken the remains back with him. *Another question, why was the king there? Was he watching Laina as well, or was he hunting the thing that tried to kill her?*

"None of it makes the slightest damned sense," he muttered to himself. And that was just the start of it. Had he really been visited by Temarah? The part where he had left his body had been bizarre, but it wasn't the first time something like that had happened. When he'd nearly died as a child after being bitten by a snake, he'd had a similar experience. It had been Arrogan who saved his life *and* who put him back in his proper vessel. He'd had a second brief experience while keeping the dam from collapsing.

And now this. *Maybe it only happens when I'm close to death,* he hypothesized, but that didn't make sense either. He'd been in plenty of other near-death situations without leaving his body. Will considered consulting the ring, but he worried that someone might overhear the conversation. He'd wait until he got home.

Instead, he tried to see if he could do it again. Mentally he pushed and strained, trying to leave his body, but he failed. Then he tried relaxing and focusing his attention in the same way he had done in order to move when he'd been outside his body before. Something happened then. He felt a certain pressure, and for a moment it felt as though he was slipping free, but he snapped back into his flesh a split second later.

Will kept it up for several minutes, but his eyes grew heavy. It was late, and the regeneration potion had used up most of his strength. Before he knew it he was drifting once more into dreams.

Or rather nightmares. He found himself back in the atrium. Lognion loomed before him, whip in hand while a vast host of onlookers watched from the sides, jeering at him. He fought to get away, but a swarm of hands took hold of him, dragging him back to the statue where he was again tied in place. The whip whistled through the air, and he screamed, knowing the pain that would ignite in his back.

"It's all right! It's just a dream." Someone was shaking him. Opening his eyes, he saw that it was the baroness. The look of empathy and concern on her features made him feel vaguely guilty, as though he had committed a crime or lied to her. *You have,* he realized. *Lied by omission. How would she feel if she knew who your father was?*

The sunlight was streaming through the window and the angle told him he had overslept; it was probably close to noon. He bolted upright in the bed. "I'm late to class," he informed her.

"Worry about that later," said Agnes soothingly. "After what you've been through you needed the rest. Your classes will still be there tomorrow."

His head swiveled back and forth as he tried to spot his clothes, his armor, or his other belongings. He was still naked under the covers. "I should really be going," he replied. "Do you know where my things are?"

"They're being cleaned," she answered primly.

Will frowned. "Even the armor?"

Agnes laughed. "You aren't the first to wear mail. Andrew knows how to take care of your gear."

"You didn't need to do that," said Will. He guessed Andrew must be the name of one of her servants. "It's too much trouble. Besides, I just—"

She touched a finger to his lips to stop him from continuing. "It was covered in blood. Even the gambeson was soaked through. I'm sure you know what blood does to steel."

Blood? He'd removed his mail before the flogging, and Darla's quarrel had barely cut the skin of his stomach.

Chapter 10

Oh, the soldier... He felt bad when he thought about the man whose throat he'd opened. The fellow had just been following orders. *If I'd surrendered immediately, he would still be alive. It's not as though my stubbornness changed anything.*

He looked up at Agnes. "Even so, I'm too much in your debt already. Let me replace the sheets and blankets..."

She gave him a stern look. "Young man, are you trying to insult me?"

"No, Your Excellency."

"Agnes. Please call me Agnes," she corrected. "What you did last night was a remarkable act of self-sacrifice. It horrifies me to think of one of my children enduring the kind of suffering that you took on for my Laina. I consider the debt to be mine, so please stop trying to refuse my hospitality. Am I understood?"

"Yes, ma'am."

"Are you hungry?"

He was positively starving. "I'm famished," he admitted. "If you show me to the kitchen I'll—"

The baroness frowned again. "Didn't we just cover this topic?"

Will held up his hands. "I'm not trying to refuse your hospitality. I just like to cook my own breakfast."

"I'll have you know that our cook, Armand, is one of the best in Cerria," she said proudly.

He felt a grin begin to form. "Would you like to make a wager?"

Puzzled, she stared at him. "On what?"

"Let me borrow your kitchen to cook for you and I'll compete with Armand. If I can't make something you like better than what he offers I'll eat my hat," he declared confidently.

"Not that I would wish to disparage your skills, but you do realize that you're not just part of the nobility now, but also technically a royal. Cooking your own meals will earn you some strange looks in the future."

"It's a hobby."

The baroness' lips formed a faint smirk. "I suppose that explanation will suffice. Very well, let's see if Armand is willing to take up your challenge, but you'll have to cook for everyone. Are you sure you're sufficiently recovered?"

Somehow, he had forgotten the previous evening. As her words brought back the memory, he felt a flash of pain, and his back tensed so painfully that he contorted and fell back onto the pillows. There was nothing physically wrong with him—the regeneration potion had seen to that—but the memory was so powerful that it overwhelmed him. Agnes cried out in alarm and held onto his arm, but after a few seconds the spasm had passed.

"William?" she asked.

He nodded, though his brow was beginning to bead with sweat. "Let's not talk about it. The memory is still too strong."

"Perhaps we should forget about this contest then," she suggested.

He sat up and threw back the covers. "No, I need to keep myself occupied." His face shifted to red as he realized he was still naked, and he quickly jerked a coverlet over himself.

Agnes wasn't embarrassed in the slightest, though she laughed at his expression. Rising to her feet, she moved to the door. "I'll have some clothes brought in for you. You're almost the same size as Mark, so I'm sure some of his things will fit you. You're practically the spitting image of him when he was your age." With that, she left.

Will stared at the door, feeling nervous once more. *What if she realizes?*

Chapter 10

***

Lethargy caused him to doubt his decision, but once he got into the kitchen and finished waking up, his energy returned. The family cook, Armand, turned out to be a heavyset man in his middling years, and his appearance was unusual in that he had neither beard nor mustache. While being completely cleanshaven was mildly unusual, the man's head also appeared to be thoroughly denuded. *Or maybe he's just bald,* thought Will. It was hard to tell with the white cap that the man wore.

Armand responded to Will's challenge with equanimity and an air of assurance. The man had been cooking for men and women of high station for most of his life. There was no doubt in him that he would win.

Will's blood warmed as he got to work. He had a good idea of the types of food the upper class in Cerria were used to. If Armand was as skilled as Agnes had claimed, then the man would probably serve an omelet or possibly sweet crepes paired with sausages or ham. Rather than compete with him, Will decided to go with something he doubted the baroness had had before.

He chuckled wickedly, thinking of the breakfasts Arrogan had made for him. The crotchety old wizard had been an exceptional cook, and over the course of his hundreds of years the old man had traveled most of the known world. Some of the dishes he had introduced Will to had no equivalents in Terabinian cuisine. The kitchen at the Nerrow house was well appointed, and after a brief survey of the tools and ingredients he had available to him, Will began.

Somewhere in the middle of things Armand glanced over at him. "What a shame."

"How so?" asked Will, glancing up from the apple he was slicing into wafer-thin slices.

"All those ingredients gone to waste."

Will hid a smile. "We'll see. Where did the vinegar go?"

The other man pointed to a shelf and returned to his own work, shaking his head. Will got the vinegar and measured out what he needed, until the smell hit him. Something about it reminded him of the brine from the night before, and his legs sagged beneath him. It was all he could do to catch himself on the edge of the worktable. With an effort of will he straightened up, but his hands continued to tremble for several minutes while he worked.

Breakfast was served later than usual, since Will and his competitor had both gone to great lengths to produce the best they could offer. The family was already seated at the dining table with Mark at one end and his wife at the other while Laina and Tabitha sat on one side in the middle.

Armand had produced a savory crepe that was paired with sausages and sweet strawberry tarts. Will was impressed by the man's skill, and he was glad he had chosen not to compete head-to-head with similar dishes. Years of practice had given the old cook the perfect touch with both his batter for his crepes and the crust on his tarts. Will would have lost if he'd tried to best the man with either of those.

The family glanced at the double set of plates placed before them. Mark Nerrow seemed somber and detached as he tasted the various dishes. Laina was only marginally more animated, but Tabitha was practically bubbling with enthusiasm. She gave Will a smile and a wink as she began to sample each dish.

As expected, they gave Armand's food high marks, but their expressions turned to surprise, then delight as they moved on to Will's offering. Within minutes it was apparent he had won, for they kept sampling, tasting, and

Chapter 10

outright devouring what he had put in front of them. Agnes was the first to address him. "What exactly is this?" She pointed her spoon at the fluffy yet savory concoction that was in the ramekin in front of her.

"It's called a soufflé," Will answered. "It's made with eggs and cheese and it has to be served immediately after cooking, before it falls."

"It's almost like cake," Tabitha enthused, "except it isn't sweet. It's sort of cheesy and light."

Mark leaned back. He had already finished everything he had been given. "I have to confess I never would have imagined having a salad for breakfast, but it went surprisingly well with the cheese thing."

Will smiled. He'd made a salad with bitter dandelion greens and a sweet vinaigrette, then he'd topped it with crisp slices of sweet apple and added crunchy walnuts toasted with honey. The combination of textures and fresh, sweet, and sour flavors made the salad a perfect respite from the light but rich soufflé.

Surprisingly, Armand wasn't a sore loser. After the winner had been decided, the two men returned to the kitchen and ate the remainders, each eating the other's food. Will complimented him. "I couldn't have made a tart like this. It's absolutely perfect."

Armand grunted. "It's just time and practice. Where did you get the idea for that salad?"

"My grandfather. I think he traveled a lot. He was very demanding about his food, but he taught me as much as he could."

"I'd like you to show me how you made that soufflé, if you don't mind."

"Sure." He explained what he had done, then added, "I can return sometime and make it again with you if you wish."

"William," Agnes was calling to him from the other room.

"I'd better go," he told the cook. Returning to the dining room, he sat across from Laina.

"You weren't going to eat with us after all the effort you went to?" asked the baroness.

He grinned sheepishly. "Actually, I just finished. I tasted a lot as I was cooking, and Armand and I just traded our dishes with each other."

Laina snorted. "He's married to a princess, but he eats in the kitchen like a farmhand."

"And cooks like a god," added Tabitha, a dreamy smile on her face. "Will you be visiting us again, Will?"

He wasn't sure how to answer, and his eyes went to the baron and baroness to gauge their reaction to the question. Mark Nerrow frowned faintly, but his wife was firm in her response. "You can visit us any time, William. You are always welcome in our home, and I'd be delighted if you made it a habit to drop by frequently." She smiled to reinforce her words.

Tabitha nodded in agreement. "And if you want to cook something, I don't think anyone here would complain." When her mother looked askance at her, she added, "That was a joke, Mother. Naturally he's welcome whether he cooks or not." She turned back to Will. "Tell Selene to come with you next time too. I miss her."

Didn't Laina tell her anything? He glanced at the older sister, and she shook her head negatively, warning him to refrain from getting into that problem. "I'll try to do that," he said, answering Tabitha as honestly as he could.

The baron eased his chair back and stood, stretching his back in a gesture that seemed contrived. "I'm sure William has a lot to get back to at Wurthaven, and we've

Chapter 10

imposed on his time for long enough. Can I offer you a ride back to the college?"

Tabitha let out a disappointed groan and her mother glared at the baron. "He hasn't been here long, Mark. Let him stay a while."

"Oh, I wasn't trying to hurry him off," insisted the baron. "I was merely offering. It's up to you, William."

Will met his father's eyes. The man's eyes reflected seemingly genuine warmth, but he knew the baron was acting for the benefit of his wife. Will turned to the baroness with an apologetic look. "I'm truly sorry, Your Excellency, but the baron is correct. I really must return to school."

The baroness growled at him.

"Agnes," Will corrected immediately.

She patted his arm with an affectionate smile. "That's better. If you must return then by all means do so, William. We won't keep you, but please do return soon. My invitation was sincere."

He felt something warm form in his chest, and to his surprise Will realized he felt a certain fondness for not just his sisters, but the entire family. It was a wistful sensation, and he replied wholeheartedly, "I would like that, Agnes. Thank you."

Tabitha moved in quickly, and before he could react, kissed his cheek. "Hope to see you soon, Brother!"

Will froze, staring at her. *How does she know?* A glance at his father showed him that the older man was similarly stunned. Laina merely seemed irritated by the comment, but Agnes rebuked her daughter, "You really are too much, Tabitha! What will I ever do with you?"

Tabitha laughed. "We've always said Selene was our sister, so if he's her husband then that makes him our brother-in-law, doesn't it?" She winked in Will's direction.

Hearing her explanation, Will relaxed, but the panic receded only to be replaced by another more difficult emotion. His vision blurred slightly, and he turned away. "I really do need to be going."

The two sisters followed him and their father to the door, and before he could step out, Laina leaned in and said quietly, "Thank you for everything, but please don't do anything like last night again. Selene would murder me if anything happened to you because of me."

He paused and gave her a serious look. "I thought you didn't trust me."

She glared at him. "Maybe I was wrong. Truce?"

Will nodded. "Truce."

"Don't follow me again," she warned.

Having spent a considerable amount of time around the fae, Will circled the question. "After last night I can't imagine anyone would be foolish enough to do that again," he replied. Then he turned to Tabitha. "Thank you for your kindness." Following Mark Nerrow, he was out the door before Laina could make up her mind whether he had answered her question properly.

Chapter 11

Once they were safely ensconced in the carriage and on their way, the baron gave Will a stern look. "You seemed rather comfortable with my family."

The deliberate use of the word '*my*' stung. It was true, obviously, but it still hurt, for it clearly delineated the separation between them. Laina, Tabitha, and Agnes were Mark Nerrow's family, not Will's, nor would they ever be.

Will had never really wanted to be connected to his father, but his half-sisters were a different matter. He hadn't had any hope to speak of, but his recent stay at their home had filled him with emotions that he still hadn't sorted out. He had no idea how to reply. "You have a splendid family. Your wife and daughters are delightful. You must be very proud."

"Protective," stressed the baron. "Someday when you have children you'll understand. Fathers are protective before all else."

"Pardon me, sir," said Will coldly. "I never had a father to serve as an example."

Mark Nerrow's eyes grew angry for a moment, but he suppressed the feeling. "You have every cause to be angry with me, William. I won't begrudge you that. If things had been different—"

Will thought the man looked remorseful, and that irritated him even more. *It was your decision, not mine that led us here,* he reminded himself. "But they weren't," he interrupted.

"Exactly," agreed the baron with a sharp, decisive nod. "I think you realize it's too dangerous for you to spend time around my family. Sooner or later the secret will be out, and I won't risk the problems that would cause my wife and children."

"You're worried about your marriage," said Will.

His father waved a hand dismissively. "You were born before I met Agnes. It isn't as if I was unfaithful. Still, your existence would be a pain for her, and an uncertainty I would spare her from, not to mention my daughters."

The lump in Will's throat was so large he could barely speak. "I can't speak for your wife, but don't you think Laina and Tabitha have a right to know about me? I am their bro—"

"They're my children," snapped the baron. "It's my decision—not theirs—not yours. Mine."

That remark washed over him like a cold wave. "I see," he said noncommittally.

"I'll expect you to ignore my wife's invitation. It's nothing against you, William, and I am grateful for what you did, but it would be better if you aren't around them. Growing attached to them will only complicate things for everyone involved."

His stomach knotted, and he felt the urge to vomit up the breakfast he had only just finished, but he didn't give up completely. "What about Selene?" he asked. "In the future there will probably be occasions where—"

"When possible, make an excuse," directed the baron. "If it's unavoidable we'll simply have to make the best of it, but with some effort on your part those events should be rare. Do you understand?"

"Yes, Your Excellency," said Will coldly. "Can you ask your driver to stop? I'd like to get out."

"You aren't upset, are you, William?"

"No, I'm fine," he lied.

The baron signaled for the driver and gave the order to stop. As Will stepped out onto the street, he looked back. The look of relief on Mark Nerrow's face made

Chapter 11

him want to slam the carriage door. "Don't worry, I'll stay away from you and your family," he reiterated, then he walked away.

He made the rest of his way home on foot while his inner turmoil ate at his composure. By the time he reached his house, he could barely contain it any longer.

Blake was on him the moment he passed through the door. "Where have you been? I worried you might be dead when you didn't return."

Will paused, holding up a hand. "I apologize for worrying you. Things happened. I'll explain later, but for now I need to be alone."

Blake started to argue, but then he saw the look in Will's eyes and the words died in his mouth. He stepped back and let Will pass unhindered.

Will managed to reach the top of the stairs before his control began to fail and his chest spasmed. A single heaving sob escaped his lips as he hurried for the bedroom door. Once inside, he locked the door and went to the bed where he snatched up one of the pillows and held it against his mouth.

And then, he broke down. Completely.

The stress and pain of the previous evening played a part, but it wasn't what drove him to tears. The trauma of Lognion's whipping would probably leave mental scars, but it was Mark Nerrow's rejection that had broken him. Two days ago, he wouldn't have cared if the man had told him to stay away from his family. Now it felt like the end of the world.

Just a tiny bit of kindness from them and I'm undone.

He let his misery run its course, and after a while it emptied itself out, leaving him feeling cold and dead. What should he do next? *I have to find Tailtiu, and after that...* His mind went blank. He wanted to make sure Laina was safe. *After that I'll do whatever is necessary, and Mark Nerrow can be damned if he doesn't like it.*

Opening his mouth, he spoke his grandmother's name three times and immediately felt a connection. She was coming. Many times in the past she had delayed or sent Tailtiu instead when he called, but not this time. *She must know something is wrong,* he thought.

That done, he called up the limnthal so he could speak with the ring. "I have a problem," he began.

"Nothing new there," replied Arrogan. "You were born a problem."

That hit a little too close to home, and Will was still feeling sensitive. "I'm not in the mood today. I need you to listen."

Something in his tone must have convinced Arrogan, for the ring refrained from making a snappy comeback. "All right. Let's hear it."

"Tailtiu is missing."

"Ordinarily I'd tell you to thank your lucky stars, but that sounded ominous. Explain."

Will jumped into an involved explanation, beginning with Laina's first visit to ask for Selene's help and continuing on until he left the Nerrow household. He stuck to the facts but left out the effect that some of it had had on him. When he got to the baron's farewell, he kept it simple. "He told me to stay away from his family."

"That was cold," remarked the ring. "I can understand his reasoning, but he certainly made an ass of himself there."

It felt good to hear his mentor's agreement, but Will didn't want to talk about it. "That's the least of my worries right now," he said, wishing he believed it. "Aislinn is already on her way. I called her a short while ago."

"Aislinn, eh? You don't shy away from danger, do you?"

"She seems like the one most likely to help. It's her daughter after all, and yours too."

Chapter 11

"I'm trying not to think about it in those terms," said Arrogan. "If I start down that path I'll be too upset to offer you any worthwhile advice. The first question is—"

"Where is she?" cut in Will.

"No, you dumb bastard! Don't interrupt me again. Yes, her location is what you want to know, but it isn't the first thing to ask, because it isn't helpful. You have no goddamn idea where she is. A better question is—how was she captured? Along those same lines, when and where was she captured? Those questions are more manageable, and they will hopefully lead to the next question you should be asking—"

"Which is where she is now," finished Will. There was a long pause, and eventually Will asked, "I spoke too soon, didn't I?"

"Damn right you did, you insufferable fuckwit! May I finish now?"

"Ah, go ahead."

"As I was saying, they will hopefully lead to *who* captured her. If you're lucky, the who will lead you to your goal, where."

"So, what should I do first?"

"Well, I would have probably advised you not to call Aislinn. She's going to be too invested, and despite the time and effort she's put into you, her first priority will be her daughter."

"We'll be in agreement then," said Will.

"No, you won't," said the ring harshly. "Aislinn is fae. When I say her first priority will be her daughter, I mean that everything else will probably drop way down her list of priorities—including whether or not you continue to breathe."

"But I want to help her."

"Good, because she never turns down a good tool," quipped Arrogan. "If she isn't fully convinced of your willingness, she may try to apply additional pressure."

"Pressure?"

"Threats. The good news is that she's precluded from harming you directly because of the accord. So, the next question is this: What other sorts of leverage does she have to use?"

"You're slipping, old man," said a soft feminine voice from just behind and to Will's left. He jerked his head in surprise and saw his grandmother standing there, though as usual, the term grandmother was misleading. Aislinn looked every bit as young and alluring as her daughter; the main difference was in the maturity and authority she projected. "You should already know what sort of leverage I have."

Will barely heard her, for his attention locked on the woman who had been hidden from view by Aislinn. As his grandmother moved, he got a clear view. "Selene!" In her eyes he could see a mixture of emotions—happiness, fatigue, pain, and a warning. There were dark circles beneath them that underscored the strain of her training.

"Will."

Selene took a step toward him, but a sharp word from his grandmother brought her up short. "Stop there."

Selene looked at the elder fae, hatred smoldering in her gaze, then she lowered her head submissively. "Mistress, may I? Please?"

Aislinn looked at Selene first, then Will, her expression speculative. "I'm not sure you've earned it, either of you."

Will's eyes narrowed and his anger flared. "Go to hell." Without waiting, he moved to embrace his wife. To his surprise, Selene stepped back, dodging him, a look of alarm in her eyes as she fearfully looked to his grandmother. He would have protested, but he was having trouble breathing, for Aislinn's hand had moved with blinding speed to seize his throat.

Chapter 11

He pulled at her hand in vain, but she held him in a grip of iron that only allowed him the bare minimum to continue breathing. "You aren't allowed to hurt humans," he wheezed. "The accord…"

Aislinn's lips mocked him as she replied, "I'm well within my rights to defend my property. Quench my blade with kindness before I'm done firing it and I will end you." Contemptuously, she released him with a shove that sent him falling backward.

Coughing, Will pushed himself back up on his hands and knees. "She isn't a weapon."

"She is whatever I wish to make her. Nor should you assume I was referring only to the useless trash you call your wife."

"What did you call her?" Will demanded, his anger growing to new heights.

The ring spoke up, interrupting Will's next angry response. "Don't let her goad you, Will. You'll only make things worse."

"Arrogan's memory offers sound advice," observed the fae lady. "You would do well to heed the counsel of my gift."

Thinking hard, Will got to the heart of the matter. "Why are you like this? I called you because I want to help Tailtiu."

Aislinn's lip curled. "You'll have to find your own answers, child, or pay me for them. The time when I could indulge your whimsical fantasies has passed. Shall we get to business?"

Will sighed. "Very well. Truce until we conclude the discussion and for two hours afterward. Answer my questions and I will answer yours without deceit or omission."

His grandmother touched her lip, a pensive look on her features. "I have been generous in the past, but that seems like a poor bargain for me. After all, I know far more than you and my answers are similarly more valuable than yours. Also, any information about where my apprentice has been for the past months is exempt from the discussion."

That set him back on his heels. She had never refused that exchange in the past. Arrogan spoke then. "If your daughter is taken, or dead, you will need vengeance. Given that this is the human realm, the culprit is also likely human. You'll need a human agent to punish those who have given you offense. You might consider that before you set the terms for your exchange, Aislinn. Limited communication might hurt you more than you would gain from extra concessions on Will's part."

The fae woman's eyes lit on the ring for a moment, then an evil smile flickered across her lips. "A good point, but insufficient. Perhaps if someone, or something, with greater knowledge were willing to act as collateral for the exchange of questions..."

"Don't sell me to her, Will," said the ring quickly.

"You were a gift from her, why would she want you back?"

Aislinn laughed. "If your ring agrees to answer questions as well, honestly and without omission, that will be enough. I have no desire to retake the present I gave you."

"Oh." That seemed reasonably fair, but even though the ring was his property and the mind it contained wasn't really his grandfather, he still couldn't compel it to honesty. Unlike the fae, the Ring of Vile and Unspeakable Knowledge was perfectly capable of lying or refusing to answer questions. "Can you agree to that, Arrogan?"

The ring growled. "I'm sure I'll regret it, but it seems like the lesser evil here. I'll consent."

Chapter 11

His grandmother rubbed her hands together happily. "Then we are agreed. You will—"

"Not quite," said Will, holding up one hand. "I was merely obtaining the ring's consent. I haven't given mine. I think you're getting too much here, possible aid from me regarding your daughter, plus Arrogan's knowledge. I need something more to balance things."

Aislinn's eyes flashed. "What do you desire to add?"

"I'd like a day with my wife."

"No."

"But..."

The fae woman shook her head. "She cannot be left unsupervised for so much time, among other reasons."

"What other reasons?"

Aislinn sneered. "Our deal has not yet begun, grandson. I'll answer nothing until we have come to terms."

"Half a day," he countered.

"Five minutes."

"Five hours."

She laughed. "Still too much."

"An hour?"

"Half an hour," she replied. "I'll be forced to wait in your world until the time is done. That is as long as I will remain here."

"Alone," he clarified.

"So long as you pledge to abstain from coitus."

He felt his cheeks coloring. "We're married!"

"Your problem, not mine, child. Are we in agreement?"

Reluctantly, he nodded. "We are."

"Then I will begin with a warning. If my daughter isn't found and returned safely to me, I will see to it that this city suffers for it."

The ring cut in. "That's a threat with no teeth, Will. The accord binds her more strongly than iron chains. The fae are incapable of breaking their word."

"We are also incapable of lying," Aislinn reminded them. "Think about that a moment before you dismiss my threat."

Anyone who had spent any degree of time dealing with the fae knew that while they couldn't technically lie, it was often impossible to get the truth from them, much less a simple answer. Will understood her meaning immediately, as did Arrogan. She might not be able to directly take vengeance, but she would make certain it happened, one way or another.

"Threatening me won't help Tailtiu," he replied. "It would be more productive—"

The ring interrupted him, "You don't owe her a damn thing, Will. Tailtiu's problem isn't your fault."

"She was in service to you at the time," argued Aislinn.

"For an unbound favor," said Arrogan quickly. "Anything, including payment with a life, is permissible to repay such a favor."

"You sound more like one of the fae than a father whose daughter has been taken," Aislinn responded sharply.

"I'm not her father. I'm his memory, and my child died in your womb, eaten by the immortal disease of your realm. Don't pretend to be acting based on emotion. I know your kind better than the stink of my own shit!"

Will met Selene's eyes for a moment, and she shrugged helplessly. He could understand her feeling. Then Aislinn responded, "Colorful as always, you're right, of course. My concern is for the debt the child owed me. If she is not returned, who will pay it?"

Chapter 11

Will swallowed, feeling uncertain as he tried to remember the finer points from the book his grandfather had once made him study. Arrogan responded immediately, "That's not the boy's concern! He isn't obligated to pay her debts just because she was repaying one of hers to him when she got snatched."

"Maybe it would be better if we stuck to discussing what we *can* do," suggested Will. "Bickering won't do Tailtiu any good."

No one said anything for a moment, then Arrogan said, "He makes a good point."

Aislinn snorted. "He has more sense than you ever did."

"Listen up, you rabid old hag! I don't give a damn what you—"

"Arrogan," interrupted Will. "It's you she's goading now. Let's discuss this peaceably."

"Begin with what you know about her disappearance," said Aislinn. "Leave nothing out."

As he had done for Arrogan, Will laid out everything that had happened over the past several days. He didn't really have any reservations about sharing the same information with his grandmother, but he was intensely aware of Selene listening intently. He did his best to pass over the punishment he had taken, but Aislinn was far too sharp for that.

"Stop," she ordered. "Repeat that last part."

"I negotiated on Laina's behalf, since he was threatening to have her publicly whipped. Then the next day I—"

"You negotiated what, exactly?"

"I agreed to answer five questions or take two lashes for each question that I refused to answer," said Will quickly. "After that he took the remains of the creature that attacked Laina, and—"

Aislinn held up one hand. "Don't force me to remind you that if you violate the terms of our temporary agreement the consequences could be severe. You promised honesty and completeness. Has Lognion asked his questions of you?"

Will nodded, his eyes moving to Selene for a second. *She doesn't need to hear this,* he thought desperately. She had enough trouble without worrying about him. "Yes, he did."

"What were the questions, and did you answer?"

"He asked where Selene was, over and over."

Her eyes narrowed. "He asked the same question? I'm assuming that means you refused to answer it."

"Four times, yes," said Will. "But the last time he asked something different by mistake and I told him it counted as the fifth question."

"What was that question?"

He groaned inwardly. "Whether I was conscious or not." He winced as he heard Selene's sharp intake of breath and he spoke directly to her. "It's not as bad as you think. It all worked out in the end."

"You're speaking with me, William, not my apprentice," corrected his grandmother. "Save any words you have for her for when you are alone. Explain the rest of what happened. Have you already been whipped?"

She interrogated him for fifteen minutes, leaving no stone unturned, even to the point of having him describe the condition of his flesh afterward. Selene's color shifted throughout his answers, going from pale to red with anger, and she was visibly shaking by the time he reached the end.

Arrogan spoke first after Will finished. "So we have three main possibilities. The bodyguard that was watching the Nerrow house, the creature that attacked Laina, and the Driven."

Chapter 11

"Lognion would be a fool to jeopardize the accord by destroying or imprisoning one of my people," said Aislinn.

"If he's even aware of the accord," countered the ring. "Will, have you ever heard him say anything that would indicate how deep his knowledge of the fae is?"

Will shook his head. "Not that I recall, though he did spot Aislinn's blessing when he first met me." The blessing was a mostly invisible mark that his grandmother had put on him the previous year. It was meant to facilitate his dealings with the fae, but Lognion had been the only human to notice it thus far.

Aislinn turned to her apprentice. "Do you know if your father understands the fae, or the ancient accords?"

Selene looked down. "No, Mistress. His only words to me on the matter were to avoid them. The little I learned before being taken under your wing was from my studies at Wurthaven. I wouldn't underestimate his knowledge, though."

"The Arkeshi still teach their disciples regarding the fae and the accord," supplied Arrogan. "So, the assassin might have been capable of dealing with Tailtiu if she was of a mind to do so."

Arkeshi, was that what Lognion called Darla? Will couldn't remember for certain. "The Arkeshi, what are they?"

He could see that Selene was dying to speak, but Aislinn continued to ignore her and answered him instead, "An old cult from Faresh. Fanatical assassins who serve the Great Khan. Although their religious beliefs are ridiculous, their practical skills are some of the best to be found among humans in this day and age."

"I don't think it was Darla, though," Will stated, feeling a certain amount of conviction. "My misunderstanding, her actions, all of it—I really think she's sincerely acting as Laina's bodyguard."

Aislinn arched her brow. "And a bodyguard wouldn't attempt to remove a dangerous fae shadowing her master?"

He shrugged. "I suppose it's possible, but she's working alone. The king's Driven seem more likely. What are they capable of?"

The ring remained silent, and his grandmother turned to Selene. "Speak, apprentice. You know your father's servants. What are these men of his like?"

"Utterly devoted," answered Selene. "They're recruited from the army and trained for absolute loyalty. They act as a sort of secret police, personal enforcers, and as an elite guard for the king. None of them come from the nobility, but Father gives them up to as many as four elementals, depending on their service. Unlike most, he makes certain they are trained for combat, physical and magical."

"In your opinion, could they kill or capture one of the fae?"

Selene looked thoughtful. "If they were prepared for the task, there's little they couldn't accomplish."

"You're all ignoring the creature that appeared in the middle of it all," said Will. "It was after Laina. It seems obvious that she hired Darla to protect her from whatever it was. The king was probably hunting it too."

Selene straightened. "Then he should have warned the baron."

"Maybe he did," agreed Will. "Maybe that's why she had an Arkeshi for a guard, or maybe he decided to use her as bait without telling her." He thought about it for a moment. "No, that doesn't make sense, either. If he warned her then why would he have been angry about Darla?"

"The sick bastard probably just wanted a reason to torture you," offered Arrogan.

Chapter 11

"You might be right about that," said Will. "But he had to confirm Darla's identity, so I'm sure he didn't know for certain who she was."

After a few more minutes of rehashing what little they knew, Aislinn made a suggestion. "I'd like to speak to the ring alone, William. Will you give your consent?"

"Why?"

"You and Selene are too inexperienced to provide much more input here. It will go faster if he and I speak directly. At the same time, some of the subjects we will cover are too far beyond your experience and would create questions and distractions you cannot afford at this time."

Shut up, the adults want to talk, he thought to himself. A glance in Selene's direction confirmed that she was equally annoyed by the idea. "I don't mind, but—"

As soon as he had agreed, a source-link shot out from Aislinn and connected to both him and Selene. Over the past year he had come to take for granted the fact that no one he encountered had the strength and discipline to do what Arrogan had done to him routinely while he was apprenticed. His grandmother disabused him of the notion that he might be able to resist her with blinding speed. The connection was made, and his body put into a soft paralysis, in almost the same instant.

He thought of it as a 'soft' paralysis because his body first went weak, allowing him to sink to the floor before he completely lost all voluntary movement. From the corner of his eye he could see Selene sagging to the floor as well, but then his senses vanished and he was left deaf, blind, and dumb. *Or as Grandfather would say, deaf and blind were added to my usual qualities,* he thought dryly.

His limnthal had to remain active for the ring to speak, but Will was no longer able to connect to his turyn, so he had no idea if that was the case. He was sealed in a black void and simply had to trust that his grandmother knew what she was doing.

Considering her hostile attitude when she arrived, he didn't feel inclined to trust her, and shivers of fear began to disturb the tiny void his consciousness was trapped within. It grew stronger, and after an unknown eternity he wanted to scream, but of course he couldn't. In desperation, he tried to escape in the only way he knew how. Inverting his instincts, he focused and tried to pull himself out, imagining Aislinn in the room just a few feet away.

He had failed the last time he tried, but sensory deprivation—or perhaps it was the fear—gave him the extra push he needed. With an odd popping sensation, his perspective left the senseless void, and he found himself floating in the air just behind Aislinn. She was holding his hand in hers, the limnthal glowing above it.

"You know what that thing must be," she said.

"They're supposed to be gone, but you're probably right," answered Arrogan's disembodied voice. "Either a few escaped or Grim Talek recreated them."

"We should have destroyed the lich when we had the chance," she responded, anger tainting her voice. "But you—"

"We weren't strong enough to risk it."

"The hell we weren't!"

"Not safely. I couldn't bear the thought of you—"

"You were weak, and now your attempt to protect me back then has left the current generation vulnerable."

Arrogan's voice was bitter as he replied, "I was human! We both were, in case you've forgotten what that's like. I'm starting to think I'm lucky to be a piece of jewelry, rather than an emotionless monster like you've become."

"I still have emotions; they've just been refined."

Chapter 11

"Down to anger, lust, and greed. It's a miracle you're able to keep your promise still."

"As if I have a choice," she answered. "It's the foundation of what the fae are. I couldn't break it if I wanted."

"And do you?"

There was a long pause. "Do I wish I could break it?" she clarified hesitantly.

"Yes."

The woman known to many as the goddess of magic sighed. "I'm not sure. It's hard to remember who I was anymore. Not the details, but the feelings. You have no idea what it's like. The absolute hunger of pure desires. Sometimes I just want to destroy everything, myself included, but not before I put an end to them…"

"Them being our enemies, or our students?"

"Both," she admitted, and Will saw his grandmother's body shiver.

"I appreciate your candor. You seemed like you were overdoing it earlier."

She chuckled faintly. "You of all people should remember how I was as a teacher. I'm even worse now. I know what I must do to teach her, but at the same time, I really do want to rip her open. I'm sure it's coloring my judgment." She paused, then added, "You know I'm bound to truth. I wasn't making idle threats earlier. If the boy doesn't deliver, I'll ruin everything he loves, starting with what's closest to hand."

"What about the promise?"

"I've had a long time to learn my limits. I can get around it without even straining myself."

Arrogan's voice sounded sad. "Has it come to that? Has the hatred consumed everything left? I still remember our love, even after centuries of living without you. It never left me."

"Stop!"

Will couldn't feel anything physical, but the ring of command in her voice seemed like it should have shaken the foundations of the building. When Aislinn spoke again, her words were sharp enough to cut glass. "Never speak of *us* again. All it does is rouse my rage and fill me with visions of torturing you. I'd rather not taint my memories."

"Fine. What about the creature? You know he's not capable of dealing with their kind yet," said the ring.

Aislinn shrugged. "Let the king handle them. He seems brutally effective. If he was there hunting them that night, then he already knows of the problem. All William needs to do is recover my daughter." She turned her head to glance at Selene but froze when her field of vision passed over the area that Will was watching from.

"You didn't tell me he knew how to project already," said Aislinn coldly.

"He doesn't, but he did it a few times early on by accident. It's part of why I had to train him in the beginning—"

Will wanted to hear the rest, but Aislinn pointed at the space where he floated and twisted her finger in an odd motion before pointing it at his collapsed form. With a rushing sensation, he flew down and blackness once again enveloped him. It only lasted a moment, however, for Aislinn's magic ushered him into a deep sleep.

Chapter 12

Selene was staring down at him when he opened his eyes. Will felt a little confused, for unlike normal sleep, he had no memory of dreams or other sensations to give him the sense of time having passed. He had gone from Aislinn's rebuke to sudden wakefulness as though reality had simply stuttered, pushing him forward in time.

Lifting his head, he looked around. His grandmother stood by the door, her hand on the knob. "Your half hour begins now," she stated before stepping out. Will sat up, and Selene's arms closed around him with desperate urgency.

He closed his eyes again, burying his face in her hair. As always, he loved her scent, though it was different now. Gone was the lavender, replaced with a faint impression of pine and some sort of spice he didn't recognize. It reminded him of the mountains for some reason. *Is Aislinn keeping her in some remote mountainous area of Faerie?*

"I've missed you terribly," she whispered into his neck. "You have no idea what it's been like for me."

Will relaxed his arms and pushed her back just far enough to bring their lips into line for a kiss. It only lasted a moment, then he squeezed her close again. "Arrogan was her student once. He told me she was meaner than him, and he was pretty awful to me."

"She isn't teaching me, Will. It's just torture. I haven't learned a thing."

"It seems like that at first."

"No, I'm not exaggerating. There's no training. Nothing. I'm a glorified servant—no, that's not right either. I'm a *humiliated* servant. I do nothing but clean and work for—" She stopped suddenly.

"What?" he asked.

She squeezed him tighter. "I'm sorry. She forbade me from telling you certain things that might give away where I've been staying, so I can't say who I'm working for."

"You aren't working for her?"

She shook her head. "I only see her once a day, and that's only so she can insult me. I'd go insane if it weren't for—for my friend. He's the only one who treats me like a human being."

He? Will felt a sudden surge of irrational jealousy. "You can't tell me his name?"

"The name would give away certain things."

If it was Edward or Tom it wouldn't tell me much, so it must be a foreign name, he mused. Swallowing his jealousy, he tried to reassure her. "At least you have a friend."

She nodded. "Just one. The others—they see us almost as animals. I'm just a slave to them."

"The fae?" he asked, but she didn't answer. *If it was the fae, wouldn't she have just admitted it? Does that mean she's somewhere else?* He couldn't decide.

"Enough about me," she responded. "I'm disgusted by what that man did to you!"

"Your father?"

"I don't want to think of him as my father anymore. He's a monster. What you did was admirable but please don't do it again. I love Laina, but I can't bear to think of you being hurt for my sake. Whatever that man does isn't your fault."

Chapter 12

He pushed her back so he could look at her, trying to memorize her features so they wouldn't fade during their next long separation. "I didn't do it for you. She's my sister."

"Then next time remember how important you are to me. Put your safety first." Her expression was so emphatic that Will found himself captured by the movement of her lips. They drew him in, and their second kiss was longer than the first.

He broke away at last. There was much more he needed to tell her. "As for your training, if it's like mine was, then you mustn't give up hope."

"She isn't teaching me anything!"

"There's nothing to be taught; she's waiting for you to be ready."

Her reply was saturated with frustration. "Ready for what?"

Will shrugged. "I don't know how to explain it. Heck, maybe that's why Arrogan never explained it to me, because he knew I'd ask endless questions that he didn't have answers for."

"It still doesn't make sense."

"Grandfather once told me that it was easier to teach someone who hadn't learned to use magic yet. I think she's trying to help you get used to being without magic before she tries the next step."

"With as much time as I'm wasting, it would be better to just start and deal with the problems as they come."

He shook his head. "No. The next step is dangerous. You could die if you aren't ready for it."

Selene stared at him thoughtfully. "I remember you saying that once before, but I figured you were just exaggerating for emphasis."

Will ran his fingers through her hair. He couldn't *not* touch her, even for a moment. *I'm like a man dying of thirst,* he observed. "This first phase could last a long time. Has she given you a candle to watch?"

She held up her right hand. There was a gold ring there with a small, clear stone set in it. Will could see an intense knot of turyn hovering over it, and after studying it a moment he could make out the faint lines tying it to her source.

He was surprised. "How did I miss seeing that?"

"You were looking at other things," she said with a sly smile.

"Your face for the most part," he admitted, "to see if you missed me."

"You know better than that. So, what is this ring supposed to teach me? The old hag was emphatic I pay close attention to it. It seems to read my mood but I'm not sure why that's important."

Will thought carefully about his answer. Arrogan hadn't explained that point very well until he was ready to move on to the first compression of his source. Was there a reason for that? Would it be better for her to be left in the dark until she came to her own conclusion? "I'm not sure how much I should tell you," he said at last. "It isn't reading your mood, but your mood affects it."

"Then it reflects the state of my turyn?"

He nodded. *Damn, she was quick. Then again, she's already a fully trained sorceress, so it isn't as though she's completely ignorant like I was,* he consoled himself.

"How is that important?" she asked.

And yet she still missed the point completely, thought Will, fighting to hide a smirk. "I'm sure you've noticed how it changes, when you're tired, angry, excited, sleepy, and so on."

"Or when we kiss," she said with a smile.

"Your current lesson is observing it, so you learn to understand what your inner turyn is doing without needing

Chapter 12

to look at a candle, or in your case a ring. If you want to get ahead of the game, learn to change it."

Selene frowned. "A person's internal turyn doesn't change."

"You've seen it change already."

"I mean it isn't something a person can control. It's like your heartbeat, it regulates itself."

"Remember our bet about whether I could take your spell from you?"

She nodded.

"This is part of it. You have to master the turyn within before you can master someone else's. Here, watch." Will had long since learned the candle spell that Arrogan had used on him, and though he didn't have a candle, the spell didn't actually require one, since the flame was illusory. With a second's effort, he cast the spell and linked his own source to an illusory flame at the end of his finger.

"Impressive," Selene remarked sarcastically.

He ignored her obvious lack of belief. "This is basically the same spell that you have on your ring. The flame reflects my internal turyn. Now, watch." A second later the flame changed from a forest green to a bright red, then it flared, tripling in size. He kept it that way for ten seconds or so, then shrank it down until the flame was a tiny ember, barely visible.

"You aren't using a second spell, are you?" muttered Selene, obviously puzzled. "Is that real?"

"Would I lie to you?"

She narrowed her eyes. "In point of fact, you have lied to me on several occasions in the past."

"Not maliciously!"

"No, you always thought it was for my own good, which made me even madder."

Will held up his hands as a sign that he wanted a truce. "Guilty as charged, but I don't have any reason to lie this time."

"So you claim."

He kissed her before she could make any more accusations, but this time she pushed him back. "Tell me more before we run out of time."

"That's it really. Try not to make the flame larger; that's counterproductive. When the next stage comes it will be important for you to learn how to make it smaller."

"None of this makes sense," Selene grumbled. "How long did this stage take you?"

Will thought about it for a moment, but he wasn't certain. He counted fingers silently. "A year? Two years? I'm not sure."

"A year! I can't wait that long!" she exclaimed. "The last six months have been miserable."

That caught his attention. "She didn't use the candle spell on you until six months ago? She should have done that from the first day."

"That was the first day," confirmed Selene. "Six months ago."

"It's been a year, Selene," he said softly.

She shook her head firmly. "No, it has only been six months. Trust me, I've been counting the days."

"Look out the window." He pointed. "Spring is here. This is the beginning of my second semester in my second year."

"That can't be right," she muttered weakly, going to the window. "What's the date?"

"It's the third of Marta, in Earrach, the year 462 of the Terabinian calendar."

Her face was ashen. "Are you sure? From my count it should still be Mean, of 461."

Chapter 12

Will chuckled. "And what calendar year is it where you've been staying?"

"That's why I counted days, their calendar isn't the same as ours—" she stopped suddenly, putting a hand in front of her mouth. "Forget I said that."

"Well now that I know, I'll have to ask Aislinn why—"

"Please! Don't make things worse for me! You have no idea how she is."

There was genuine fear in her eyes, and Will felt a sudden pang of guilt. "I wouldn't. I only meant to tease you."

She took a deep breath, then changed the subject. "Is there anything else you can tell me about what I'm supposed to be learning?"

He shook his head. "Not really. It isn't as much something you learn with your head as with your body, so there's not a shortcut."

"At least I know she isn't deliberately wasting my time. Why do you think Laina wanted my help?"

Will blinked, trying to shift mental gears. "I have no idea, except she didn't think I could help her. It was you or no one."

"It wasn't necessarily capability," opined his wife. "In fact, knowing Laina, it was probably a matter of trust. She doesn't trust very many people."

"Certainly not me."

Selene's expression turned sad. "That's my fault. She blames you for my disappearance."

"She didn't like me before that," countered Will. "Marrying you and then having you vanish only made it worse, but I think it's better now. We were sort of getting along when I left her house."

She brightened. "That's good. Are you going to see them again?"

His face darkened. "Probably not. Our—*their* father doesn't want me around."

She kissed him forcefully, then stared in his eyes. "I'm going to fix all that when I'm done with this stupid training."

"You can't—" He was forced to stop as her finger pressed against his lips.

"I will," she said firmly. "Believe in me."

Will's eyes began to well with tears. "Goddamnit," he swore. "I didn't want to be sad. We've only got a few minutes more."

"Then let's not waste them," she suggested as her lips closed in on him again. When Aislinn opened the door a few minutes later, they were still in each other's arms, locked in a quiet embrace. Will felt Selene's grip tighten momentarily, then she reluctantly released him.

He struggled to do the same, then turned to face his grandmother. "So soon?"

"You've had as much time as I can give you. Find my daughter as quickly as you can. The slaughter will likely begin tonight. Be prepared," she told him, gesturing to Selene to approach. "We must go."

"Wait," he protested. "What do you mean, 'slaughter'?"

"The ring will explain." Taking Selene's hand, she led his wife from the room and closed the door behind them. Will rushed to follow, but when he opened the door, he saw no sign of them. He ran down the corridor, the stairs, and out the door, but he found no trace of their presence.

How the hell did she do that? he wondered. There was no congruence point in the house—he had searched for one the day he had moved in. The chameleon spell coupled with some type of silence spell was a possibility, but he had adjusted his vision several times while he searched, and he was fairly sure no spell could hide them perfectly enough to cover all the types of light he could see.

Chapter 12

More puzzling, he hadn't seen any changes in the ambient turyn outside the room. It was as if they had faded away without a trace. Irritated, he walked back into the house, only to find Blake waiting for him. "You have a visitor, sir."

Will frowned. "Since when? I just went in and out."

"He's in the parlor. I brought him in while you were occupied upstairs."

"You let him in the house? I'm fairly certain I was emphatic when I said I didn't want any visitors. You should have gotten his name and sent him away."

Blake smirked. "Trust my instincts. I've been doing this for many years. I'm sure you'll want to meet this fellow. His name is John Shaw and he says he's an old friend of yours."

A scowl was etched on Will's features. "I don't know anyone named Shaw."

"From the army," added Blake. "Big enough to be a squad all by himself."

His brain finally snapped into motion. "Tiny!" Will ran into the parlor, where sure enough, he saw a living mountain sitting on one of the delicate chairs. "Tiny!" he shouted. "Is that really you?"

The chair groaned dangerously as the big man shifted his weight and rose to his feet, a wide smile painting his face. "If it isn't, no one's been brave enough to contradict me when I told them my name," Tiny answered.

Will stomped across the room in his haste, nearly tripping and sending one of the end tables over on its side as he threw himself at his old squad mate. Will wasn't short, being almost exactly six feet in height and square-shouldered, but when Tiny threw his arms around him he felt like a child again. Fortunately, while the hug was fierce, Tiny knew his strength and he stopped squeezing just as Will's ribs started protesting.

Releasing each other, they stepped back, and Will gave his old friend an appraising glance. Tiny had changed. The big man was still enormous, but the last of his baby fat had melted away, leaving a lean, heavily muscled giant who stood just a hair over seven feet tall. His face had been tanned by long hours drilling in the sun, though his neck was still fair, since the soldiers usually trained in their armor. He was dressed in a well-made leather jerkin over a brown linen tunic and gray trousers.

"Did you get the mail?" asked Will. Just over a year past, he had paid the local armorer to arrange for a full mail hauberk and leggings for Tiny and Dave, their other squad mate, back in Barrowden.

Tiny pointed at a large oilskin bag sitting in one corner of the room. There were several other bags beside it. "It's there, along with my breastplate and other sundries. I'm still grateful for it. When I've saved enough, I'll be able to—"

"Stop," ordered Will. "You know how much my situation has changed. It was a gift. Don't make me angry by trying to pay me back for it."

"That much money, though…,"

"Doesn't mean much to me anymore," Will reassured him, then he added a small lie. "It isn't as though I had to work for it. Just accept the gift." In fact, he'd worked extremely hard to make the money during a time when he'd thought he would need the gold to pay his way out of a prison sentence, and while it was true that he was technically wealthy now, he had no real way to access the money while Selene was absent. Fortunately, he still had hundreds of gold marks tucked away in the limnthal.

Tiny paused, then dipped his head. "I guess I'll just do my best to accept your gift graciously then."

Chapter 12

"Wow," said Will. "You've polished your courtly graces since I saw you last."

The big man's brow's lowered, casting a shadow on his features. "I've always been polite, Will. It's how I was raised."

Will held up his hands in a gesture of surrender. "That's true, I just meant you sound like you've been practicing your speech for court."

Tiny straightened his back and squared his shoulders. "That's probably because I have been. A squire is expected to learn how to conduct himself."

His jaw dropped. "Squire? What? Who? How?" Becoming a squire put Tiny on the road to becoming a minor nobleman someday—maybe. It certainly made him a gentleman, and while technically anyone could be made a squire it was rare for anyone but those who were already sons of the nobility to be chosen.

"Sir Kyle," said Tiny with a shrug. "There was an ambush during one of our patrols. He was unhorsed and things looked bad for us."

"But you saved him?"

"Sort of. I knocked several men down getting to him, but when I tried to pull him back to his feet, they charged me so I threw the first thing that came to hand at them," said Tiny, his cheeks coloring.

"What did you throw?"

"Sir Kyle."

"You threw the captain?" Will's mouth rounded into a large 'o.'

"It was reflexive," said Tiny with obvious embarrassment. "But it worked pretty well. Before they could recover, I snatched up a mace one of them had dropped and laid into them, then Sir Kyle got back on his feet and together we routed what was left of them."

Will couldn't help but shake his head. "That's amazing, but I'm surprised he didn't have you strung up afterward."

"Turns out Sir Kyle has a pretty good sense of humor. He was just glad to be alive and after we finished running them off, well, you know how it is." Tiny shrugged.

He did know. He and Tiny, along with Sven and Dave, had had a few moments like that, the kind they didn't think they'd live through. Soldiers formed bonds with those they fought beside that were unlike any others. "Well, I'm glad it worked out for the best. How are you here in Cerria, though? Shouldn't you still be in Barrowden?"

"Sir Kyle had to return to the capital for a while, and I had some leave saved. He asked if I wanted to come along."

"How long will you be here?"

"A couple of weeks, possibly a month if Sir Kyle is kept longer."

"And you're staying with him?"

Tiny looked away somewhat shyly, a strangely absurd expression on such a massive man. "Actually, I thought maybe I could stay with you…"

Will felt like jumping up and down. "Absolutely!" The past few weeks he had isolated himself, and recent events had left him feeling as though there was no one he could trust. His heart swelled with sudden joy. "I can't even tell you how glad I am you're here! We have a lot to catch up on."

His friend nodded in agreement, then looked to Blake. "I don't suppose you have any bread or meat lying around, do you? I haven't eaten since we got on the road this morning."

Blake nodded cheerfully, but before he could answer Will put a hand over the man's mouth. "Let's not injure our guest with your cooking the moment he arrives."

Chapter 12

The manservant twisted away from him. "It's just leftovers. I can still slice meat."

Will shook his finger at the man. "I'm hungry too and this is a good occasion. I'll put something together." He glanced at Tiny. "Can you last an hour?"

The big man seemed uncertain. "I'm really hungry. Maybe I can help with the cooking."

"That's my job," said Blake. "In fact, a certain someone is supposed to teach me a few of his secrets in the kitchen."

Will shook his head. "Not this time. I need some privacy to consult with someone and this will be a good chance for that."

"Consult?" Blake seemed confused.

Will looked at each of them. "I'll trust you to police each other and refrain from eavesdropping." Then he gave them a mysterious smile and turned away to head for the kitchen.

CHAPTER 13

Once in the kitchen, Will wasted no time, and since it was his old friend who had come to visit, he decided to use some of the special ingredients that Arrogan had tucked away in the limnthal. He summoned out fresh butter, the spice box, and choice cuts of beef and then went to check the stove to see what the temperature was like.

As usual, it needed some more fuel added and time to reach the proper heat, so he busied himself preparing the vegetables, and when he got to a place where he could think, he reactivated the limnthal and addressed the ring. "Why did she say there would be a slaughter?" he asked without preamble.

"It isn't a certainty, but there's a strong possibility," answered Arrogan. "If the creature you encountered is one of the Drak'shar, and if it captured Tailtiu, well—"

Will remembered the word 'drak' from his studies, and he knew it was an old word for dragon. "Dragon? What does it have to do with dragons?"

"Very little, except they were first made using a twisted transformation of blood from a dragon."

"That sounds fascinating."

"No, it isn't. It really, truly isn't," said Arrogan with genuine emphasis. "The creatures that were produced bear no hint of the noble pride that dragons are known for, nor are they truly alive."

"They're dead?"

"Undead. They're what are popularly called vampires, and we thought they were gone."

Will finished mincing the onion in front of him and began massaging it into the meat. "It makes sense. I remember seeing a spell in that necromantic tome that called for vampire blood. You should have explained them to me back then, when I asked."

"You had more important things to worry about," said the ring. "And I wouldn't touch any spell involving the blood of the Drak'shar with a ten-foot pole, though there's a potion that might be handy if you ever have the opportunity."

"A potion?"

"Dragon's Heart potion," clarified the ring. "It doesn't require a dragon's heart, but it does need the blood of an immortal. It got the name because the wizard who invented it somehow had a supply of dragon's blood to experiment with. Later on it was discovered that it could be made with different types of blood, so long as they came from an immortal."

Will's interest was piqued. "What does it do?"

"It's no good for you. Taken by a second- or third-order wizard, the potion would be ruined, if not completely nullified. Your body wouldn't allow it to work. It's meant for warriors. Makes them stronger and faster than usual."

"The same way I can make myself stronger or faster by manipulating my turyn?"

"Way past that," answered the ring. "It's beyond anything normally possible for a human. For a short period of time you can make a man or woman as fast and strong as one of the Drak'shar. Anyway, we've gotten off on a tangent."

"I want to look that potion up later. Just in case the opportunity arises."

"It's in *Gidding's Apothecary*, but again, we've digressed. The reason Aislinn said there would be a slaughter comes down to the fact that the Drak'shar aren't meant to feed on other immortals, particularly the fae."

"Because—?"

"If that thing really is a vampire, then Tailtiu's blood will act like a potent narcotic and hallucinogen. Whatever self-control the creatures have will be lost and they'll likely go into a frenzy."

"If they're that keen for blood, wouldn't they already be out there killing people?"

"Only with the greatest care and discretion," answered the ring. "We wiped them out, or we thought we had. If any of them survived until now, they did it by hiding themselves almost perfectly, without giving in to their urges. Most importantly, they won't have been transmitting their disease."

"Disease?"

"The first Drak'shar was created, but it was created as a disease. If they aren't careful when feeding, then they pass it on to their victims. A newly created vampire has no sense, no self-control, it can barely think. They're wholly beholden to their hunger."

"So what you're saying is that one of them survived in secret."

"One or several, but only very smart, very careful ones," corrected Arrogan.

"And that if they feed on Tailtiu they'll go mad and start behaving like new vampires."

"Yes, and almost certainly they'll fail to observe their rules to prevent creating more spawn. So a day or two later, you'll have a host of young, rabid blood-fiends running wild through the city."

The meat was ready, so Will put it into an iron pan that he'd already oiled and heated on the stove. A pleasant odor of searing meat rose up, which was just as well, as

Chapter 13

the scent of fresh blood had been disturbing during their discussion. "That sounds delightful," he commented dryly.

"It's anything but. Back before my time, the city of Dylindar had to be burned to the ground when something similar happened."

"Where's that at?"

"It used to be in Trendham. They never rebuilt it; instead they built a new city not far from where it used to be, named Lystal."

Will nodded. "Oh, I've seen that one on the map. When you say before your time, what do you mean exactly?"

"A few hundred years before I was born."

"So how far back was their creation? You said a wizard named Grim Talek created them, didn't you?"

"You heard that while you were snooping, eh?"

Will grinned, though the expression was wasted on the ring. "I wasn't sure what I was doing, but I did get to hear a few things." Watching the pan, he added a small dollop of butter beside the meat.

"Grim Talek might technically be called a wizard," said Arrogan. "He was human once, as far as we know."

"What is he now?"

"A lich, though the term is somewhat speculative since he's unique. No one else ever managed to replicate the feat, though many drawn to necromancy have tried."

"I thought vampires were the pinnacle of undead existences," said Will.

"It depends on how you measure things. Physically they're more dangerous—that's certain—but they were created to serve Grim Talek, and while they're technically immortal, they're much easier to kill. Burning a vampire is a safe bet, but you could completely destroy Grim Talek's body and he'd still be back within a few days."

"Fire seemed to work pretty well on the one I met," agreed Will.

A snorting sound issued from the ring, although it didn't have a nose. Will wondered how that worked, but Arrogan's next warning was more important. "That was just a taste. You caught one by surprise. Be extremely careful and make sure you never face one alone. You don't even have the right sorts of spells to fight them properly."

Will tested the meat with his finger then removed it from the pan. Grabbing a bottle of red wine, he poured some in to deglaze the bottom and began scraping to free the fond that was stuck there. His mouth watered thinking about what the pan sauce would taste like. "What kind of spells do I need?"

"Fire works in a pinch, for getting rid of their bodies, but you won't survive long without a proper defense. They move fast, and they're strong enough to overpower anyone once they get close. You need a surefire way to make sure one can't sink its fangs into you, and there's only one spell I know that's up to that job."

Will waited, occupying himself by tasting the sauce as it reduced. Eventually Arrogan gave up and continued, "Don't you want to know what it is?"

"Aren't you going to tell me?"

"You really are an asshole," observed the ring.

Will chuckled. "I learned from the best. So what spell is it?"

"The iron-skin transformation."

"You mentioned that before. Didn't you say someone tried to use it for his 'little soldier' and wound up killing himself?"

Arrogan began sniggering. "Yes, that's the story of Leonard Kaspar and his infamous iron cock. He died of iron poisoning, but he wasn't using the regular iron-skin

Chapter 13

transformation. The spell I'm talking about is perfectly safe, though it's a little difficult to cast."

A little difficult in Arrogan's terminology probably meant a seventh- or eighth-order spell at least. Will was close to succeeding with eighth-order spells, but he wasn't quite there yet. *And if it's ninth I won't be able to manage it for months.*

The ring went on, "The transformation usually can't be kept up for more than a few minutes at a time because it's both physically exhausting and it uses a significant amount of turyn."

"Physically?"

"Iron isn't anywhere near as elastic as your skin is. The spell manages that by adjusting the effect as you move, but it isn't perfect. The result is that every movement, even breathing, requires more effort than usual, while at the same time, the constant adjustments use extra turyn."

At that point, Will was mashing up the turnips he'd boiled and seasoning them with butter, salt, and a small amount of fresh horseradish. "It sounds like I'm not going to be able to learn that spell soon enough to do me any good. Do vampires have any weaknesses like they do in the stories?"

"Forget the rubbish about churches and holy symbols."

"Garlic?"

"Pisses them off, but only because they have sensitive noses."

"Silver?"

"That's poisonous to them, but it isn't instantly fatal. It's similar to how the fae react to iron."

Will nodded. "Too bad it's such a soft metal. It's difficult to make effective weapons with silver."

"Silver inlay on blades is enough to keep them from healing immediately after cuts, but it's expensive," said

Arrogan. "Easier to burn them, or better still, if you can find the right spells, daylight will wreck them."

"Light?"

"Daylight," corrected Arrogan. "A certain portion of daylight absolutely ruins them. Depending on how strong it is, it can turn them to dust in seconds to minutes. As an added bonus, the spells require less energy than most fire spells since the output is primarily light without heat and flames. You should still have some fire spells ready, though. If you get a chance, look for Ethelgren's Illumination."

"Why, if light is so much more effective?"

"Because any vampire that has survived since my day will almost certainly be smart enough, and wizard enough, to have learned the right magic to protect himself from daylight."

He was about to start organizing the plates for the meal, but Will froze at those words. "Some of them use magic?"

"Not many," said Arrogan. "Being dead, they don't have a source, so it's hard for them to get started, but the ones that survive a long time are more likely to have learned. Also there's the ones who were wizards before they were turned."

"What are they like?"

"If they were first-order, or worse, like the wizards these days, then they aren't much to worry about. Without a source to work from they're crippled, magically speaking, but if they're second- or in your case, third-order, then the change doesn't bother them much."

Will nodded. "Because we don't use turyn from our source anyway. So if it happened to me…"

"At first, you'd be violent and insane, but you'd still be able to use spells. Later you'd probably adjust

Chapter 13

and then you'd be worse—you'd become a long-term threat, an undead monster smart enough to protect and hide itself, while also potentially powerful enough to do almost anything."

"And immortal."

"You've probably got almost eight hundred years ahead of you. That's more than enough to get sick of it all. Trust me."

"Do any of them ever stay good?" asked Will.

"Define good," replied Arrogan. "If by good, you mean did any of them help people or refrain from murdering the innocent, then no. The best—and in my opinion also the worst—outcome has been those that gained enough control to stay hidden, which is probably why we are now facing this very old problem all over again."

"What about the lich, Grim Talek—what's he like? Did you and Aislinn fight him?"

"Clearly you overheard too much," said the ring sourly. "For today you don't need to worry about him. You should focus on the here and now."

The meat was done resting, so it was time to serve and eat. He needed to finish the conversation. "What should I do then, in the here and now?"

"Learn the iron-skin transformation, expand your repertoire with fire, talk to Laina's Arkeshi and see if she knows anything about Tailtiu, but above all else, don't go anywhere by yourself after the sun sets. If you learn something and figure out where Tailtiu is, don't attempt to rescue her alone."

"I understand," said Will, hoping to placate the ring.

"No, I'm very serious here. You've got power enough to destroy them, but you're only human and these things are *fast*. If you get caught by surprise, caught off-guard, flanked, hell, if you just look the wrong way for a few seconds—they'll rip you from throat to groin and your armor will barely slow them down."

"Can they tear through mail?"

"No, but they can hit you hard enough to break bones with just their bare hands, and anywhere you have exposed flesh is a serious vulnerability."

"Damn."

"So, you do what wizards should always do. Prepare. Make sure you've got the right tools and never, ever, put yourself in a situation where you might face one alone. The best way to counter overwhelming speed and strength is to have plenty of allies with you. If they have to fight through your guards, you'll have more time to do what you need to do."

Blake called from the other room, "Something smells delicious. Is it almost ready or are you just torturing us?"

Will dismissed the limnthal and answered, "Come get your plates!"

Chapter 14

Tiny leaned back, pushing his now-empty plate away from him. The chair beneath him groaned faintly. "I haven't eaten like that since I left home."

Will smiled. "Your mother must have been a good cook."

The big man sighed with satisfaction. "I won't speak ill of her cooking now that I've eaten yours, but she knew how to fill me up."

He laughed. Back when they'd been in the army together, Will had often shared his extras to help keep Tiny from going hungry. "I remembered how much you eat, so I tried to prepare accordingly. Aside from getting full, did you like it?"

"It wouldn't be a lie to say that if I died right now, I would have no regrets. What was that mash on the side? I couldn't figure out what it was, but I couldn't stop eating it either."

"Turnips."

Tiny's brows lifted in surprise. "I've never cared much for turnips, until now."

"What about the bread crusts?" asked Blake. "Were those the stale leftovers we had from a few days ago?"

Will nodded. "Buttered and toasted with minced onions. Garlic or shallots might have been better, but we didn't have any. I guess neither of you liked the steak, since all you've talked about are the sides."

There was an uproar at that, and Will found himself laughing as they bantered back and forth. Eventually Blake rose and cleared the table before retreating to the kitchen to clean up. Will and Tiny moved back to the parlor, where the furniture was more comfortable, and once they were seated Tiny mentioned the dinner again. "Most in your position wouldn't be seating the butler at the table."

"It's just the two of us most of the time," Will replied. "I prefer not to eat alone. Besides, it isn't as though I was raised with any of this."

Tiny nodded, then switched subjects. "Sammy is going to be so jealous when I go back and tell her I was able to eat your food for two weeks."

That got Will's attention, for he hadn't seen his younger cousin in more than a year. "You've seen Sammy? How is she doing?"

Tiny turned pensive. "She's feisty as ever, as well as—hmm, I'm not sure how to say this."

"Say what?"

"Well, I don't want to offend you. I'm not sure how you'll react to me commenting on your female relatives."

"If you say she's ugly I'll put a dent in your nose," Will said jokingly.

"A dent?"

"I doubt I could do much more than that."

Tiny laughed. "Fine, well I'll risk a dent then. Sammy is turning into a stunning woman."

Will frowned. He had actually been worried about that the last time he'd seen her, especially because his fiery-haired cousin also seemed to lack any native caution when it came to the soldiers stationed in Barrowden. "Are the soldiers bothering her?"

"Not while I'm there," said Tiny smugly. "I'm a sergeant now, and I made it clear what I'd do to any who step over the line."

Will doubted it was just because Tiny was a sergeant. The man was like a mountain on the move. No one would

Chapter 14

have wanted to cross him, sergeant or not. "You're a sergeant? Was this before or after you became a squire?"

"Before. After you sent the mail, I took the money I'd been saving for armor and invested it in buying my own equipment and becoming a contract soldier. After that it was just a matter of time since they seemed to think I had the aptitude."

"That'll keep you in for at least five years," observed Will. At the same time, he tried to imagine his friend yelling at new recruits and being a general asshole, but his mind blanked out. The big man was just too kind for him to envision it.

Tiny shrugged. "With the current tensions, they wouldn't have let me go for several years at best. I figured I might as well make a career out of it."

"You outrank me now."

"You're still on the rolls?"

Will nodded. "They'll probably force me to go back after I finish at Wurthaven."

"You're married to the king's daughter, Will. You're never going back, not as a private contract."

"You might be right about that."

"I know I'm right," said Tiny confidently. "Just like I know you're scared to ask about your mother now that I've mentioned Sammy."

He looked down. "Is it that obvious?"

"She's going to skin you alive if you don't visit soon. Having the wedding without any warning was bad enough, but all you've done since then is send a letter."

"I've been busy and it's a long trip."

"A week, I just made it, and your mother knows quite well that you can make the journey in a fraction of that. They could come here too. Have you thought about that?" Tiny glanced around as though making note of the massive house they were sitting within. "This would be a huge step up for them compared to that little shanty they've been staying in."

"It's too dangerous here for them."

"But not for your wife?"

She's not here! thought Will, his lips making a firm line as he closed his mouth. "It's complicated and I can't tell you everything. Not here."

Tiny's eyes darted in the direction of the door, his question clear. *The servant?*

Will nodded. "He's a good man, but there are somethings he is duty-bound to report if he hears them. So I do my best not to put him in that position, and he does his best not to hear."

Tiny seemed confused for a minute, then he silently mouthed the words, *you're afraid of the king?*

"Yes," answered Will. "But we can talk about that later." He got to his feet. "You're probably tired from traveling. Would you like to rest a while?"

"That would be nice."

It was still early afternoon, and Will needed to start making preparations. "Blake will show you to your room. Feel free to treat this house as your home for as long as you're in Cerria."

"You're sure?"

"I wouldn't have it any other way. I'll be leaving for a while but I'll be back before sunset, then I'll probably leave for most of the evening." Will paused there, to let his words sink in.

"You're going to be out all night?" Tiny's face held numerous questions. "Is there a party or do you need some help?"

Will stared at his feet for a moment, then lifted his chin and gave Tiny an earnest stare. "I hope you don't

Chapter 14

think less of me, but when I found out you were here, I was happy for more than one reason. I *am* glad to see you, but I'm also about to be up to my eyeballs in trouble."

"What kind of trouble?"

He glanced at the armor bag in the corner of the room. "The kind that makes me glad you brought your gear."

"Damn," swore the big man.

"You don't have to get involved in it if you don't want to," Will said, trying to reassure him. "I know you've seen enough back in Barrowden and you deserve a rest."

Tiny nodded. "You're right, and the thought of putting that armor on fills me with dread, but I'll come with you anyway."

Will felt more alone than ever, but he tried to smile anyway. "Don't worry. I'm sure I'll be fine—wait, what?" It had taken a moment, but Tiny's words finally sank in. *His tone said no, but his mouth said yes.*

"You know I hate violence, but I've made a career out of it anyway. At first, I fought to protect my friends, now I fight to protect the people of Terabinia. If you need help then I'll get to do both."

"I haven't even told you what's going on," said Will. "How do you know it's to protect the people of Terabinia?"

The massive soldier reached out and slapped Will's chest just over his heart, the blow landing with such force that he nearly lost his balance. "Because I know you, Will. Your heart is always getting you into more trouble than you can handle, and it's always on someone else's behalf."

Will shook his head. "That isn't true."

Tiny arched one brow. "We can argue later. I need a nap."

"Don't you want to know what we'll be doing?"

"It might disturb my sleep. Tell me later."

***

At the library, he ran into Janice as he headed for the stairs. "Oh, hello," he greeted her, noting that she had tied her hair into an unruly bun and somehow anchored it in place using only a pencil. *Clearly an act of magic,* he told himself silently.

Janice blinked at him for a second then frowned. "This can't be good."

"What?"

"You're in the library." Pretending to shade her eyes with one hand, she stared in the direction of the front entrance. "Has the sun gone dark? Is this the end? Has Marduke risen from hell to consume the world?"

"Very funny. I do come to the library on my own for legitimate purposes, you do realize that, don't you?"

"Mmhmm," she replied noncommittally. "And what brings you here today?"

Will glanced to one side then focused on meeting her gaze. "Nothing special," he answered, keeping his tone innocent.

"Then you won't mind if I tag along."

"I'm sure you're busy. No need to go out of your way."

"I don't mind," she said blandly, following him up the stairs. As they passed the second floor, she commented, "Third floor, spell archives—why am I not surprised?"

"I could be going to the fourth floor."

"Mmhmm, you could, but I'd bet good money you aren't."

Will stopped. "God damn it, Janice. Don't you have something better to do?"

"And there's the temper," she observed. "Is that why Rob's mad at you? Did he ask too many questions?"

Chapter 14

Will pursed his lips. After a second he replied, "I'm not angry."

Janice took his hand and started back up the stairs. "Come on. I'll help you look for whatever it is."

"I don't want to get you involved."

"I'm not going to get involved. I have no desire to get caught in one of your adventures, but this is the library. I'm pretty good with index cards. I'll give you a hand and then you can go do stupid things with the information afterwards. I won't interfere."

He glowered at her for a moment, trying to decide whether to be offended or touched by her remarks.

She tugged on his arm. "Come on, hero, it's the library. What's the worst that could happen?"

"Fine."

Once they reached the third floor, they headed for the card files. "What are you looking for?"

"A spell called the iron-skin transformation, another called Ethelgren's Illumination, and anything with simple fire battle magics in it."

Janice stared at him blankly for a moment, then her lips began working silently. Will could easily make out the words, 'What the fuck?' but to her credit Janice didn't actually voice her thoughts. Instead she turned back to the card index and began searching.

He stepped to the other end of the card file and started at the E's. "I'll look for Ethelgren's Illumination."

She nodded, already working her way through the I's. Fifteen minutes later, courtesy of Janice, they had a tidy sheet with notes on the locations of what Will wanted. He'd brought his own journal and writing implements, but they were stored in the limnthal, so he had deferred to her rather than display yet another of his secrets.

"You're out of luck," she told him, looking over the sheet once again. "Every single one of these items is in the restricted section, even Ethelgren's Illumination."

"Which makes no sense," he complained. "It's a light spell."

"It might have something to do with the book it's in, *Battling the Darkness*," remarked Janice in a droll tone. "This is just a guess on my part, but I'm betting the book has offensive spells in it too. Remind me again, what did you need these spells for?"

"It's a special project," Will said evasively.

"Are you going to need holy water and specially blessed silver for this special project, or will garlic be enough?"

Will stared at her, then asked, "How did you know?"

Janice's eyes grew round. "It's really vampires? You're kidding, please tell me you're kidding!"

"I'm kidding," he reassured her. "And from what I hear, the garlic and holy symbols don't work, but the silver does. Why did you think it was vampires?"

"I forget how sheltered your upbringing was. The wizard Ethelgren was famous for only one thing, his obsession with vampires."

"Now the title of his book makes sense," said Will, nodding. "It's too bad everything is in the restricted section. You might as well go. I'll stick around and see if I can find anything useful in the non-restricted stacks."

Janice eyed him suspiciously, then whispered, "You're going to break into the restricted section again, aren't you?"

Will frowned. "I don't think I ever told you I did that before."

She tapped her temple, then leaned closer. "I'll be your lookout."

He sighed. He didn't really need a lookout. Over the past year he'd been into the restricted section several

Chapter 14

times. The very first time he had hid in the library and explored it after the library closed, but he had later learned that his efforts had been excessively cautious. For one, almost no one used the restricted section, so there was little chance of encountering anyone, and two, when he did encounter someone, they assumed he had permission. In part that might have been because of who his wife was, but it also had a lot to do with the fact that no one could enter the restricted section without a special talisman that served as a key to prevent the wards from doing them serious harm. If he remained nonchalant and acted as though he belonged, no one would look at him twice.

A lookout would only draw suspicion.

"Just wait over there," he told her, indicating the card index.

She shook her head. "I'll browse, but I'm going to keep you in sight. I want to see how you plan to do this."

He shrugged. "Fine, but it's a lot less exciting than whatever you're imagining." Moving away with a purposeful stride, he headed straight toward the restricted stacks. They looked much like the rest of the third floor, but there was a symbolic cordon around them marked by posts with chains between them. Anyone could easily step over or go under the chains, but the signs warned anyone who could read that doing so would be to risk life or limb. The chains marked off the safe area, and just behind them were a wide network of wards set into the floor.

Most of the outer wards were designed to deter a would-be trespasser, while those farther in would immobilize them. If someone managed to get past those, the third layer of wards included lightning shocks that could potentially be fatal. Will stepped over the chain, stopped at the first wards and took a few seconds to match his turyn to that of the defenses, then he walked into the restricted section. He heard Janice hiss in alarm as he stepped into the wards, but he ignored her.

It took him the better part of an hour to find the three books they had marked on the list they had made. Will didn't bother looking into them and copying out what he wanted, though. Instead he just tucked each book under his arm and when he had all three, he carried them out. He found Janice waiting for him.

She glanced at the books he carried. "You stole them?"

Will looked over her shoulder. "Who's that?"

Janice whirled around, and he stored the books in his limnthal while her attention was diverted. Her lips turned down in a frown of disapproval when she saw that the books had vanished. "How many secrets do you have?"

"The less you know the less they can torture out of you."

"I never know for sure whether you're joking or not," she responded.

A surge of adrenaline shot through him as he unexpectedly relived his recent whipping. Will's heart began beating at a frenetic pace and sweat began beading on his forehead. He took several deep breaths and tried to keep his reaction from showing, though Janice definitely noticed something.

"Are you all right?" she asked, putting a hand on his shoulder.

"It's nothing," he assured her, "and just so you know, I wasn't joking. My father-in-law went to great lengths to try and find out where Selene was recently."

"And now you're breaking into the restricted section?"

Will laughed. "He doesn't give a damn about this. He'd probably congratulate me."

"How did you do that? You just walked through the wards as though they weren't there. Did you steal one of the key talismans?" she asked.

Chapter 14

He shook his head. "No, I just do what the talismans do. Someday, if my life ever calms down, I might try to teach someone."

"I want to be the first on your list."

"It's dangerous, and it takes years," he warned her.

Something flashed in her eyes, a sudden understanding. "That's where Selene went, isn't it? Someone is training her."

He clapped a hand over her lips, looking around anxiously to make certain no one was within earshot. "Be careful what you say. If the king got wind of that it would be worth your life, and unlike me, I don't think he'd hesitate to whip you to death."

"You were whipped?" she mumbled around his fingers, her eyes widening.

In the midst of everything else, Will was suddenly struck by how adorable his friend was, her bright eyes peering at him above his fingers. With that realization came the awareness of her lips against his palm and he drew back his hand as though he were about to be burned. Angry with himself, he looked away.

Fortunately, Janice misread his reaction. "I'm sorry. That was thoughtless of me."

He took the opportunity. "It's all right. You couldn't have known. I need to get back and look these over before evening gets here."

"You're doing whatever it is tonight? You need help."

"You're right, know anyone useful?"

"Ouch," she said, visibly wincing.

"Sorry. I'm just tense. Don't worry about it. I'll manage."

Janice frowned but didn't move to stop him as he walked away, and he could feel her eyes on his back until he had gone down the stairs.

CHAPTER 15

"I have no idea what you're thinking, Will. This is a wall." Tiny stood staring up at the wall that surrounded Wurthaven. His bulk was further accentuated by the mail hauberk and leggings he wore, combined with a breastplate and steel cap. The big man had a round shield slung over his back, a short sword on his belt, and a spear in one hand.

"Trust me. I can get you over it."

"You realize how much I weigh, don't you? Add in all the metal I'm wearing, and I could probably balance a scale with a full-grown boar. You know what happens when heavy men fall, don't you? Even ten feet might be enough to break something serious."

"You won't fall, you'll stick to the wall like a fly." Will stored Tiny's shield and weapons in the limnthal temporarily, but it still took him several minutes of cajoling to get his friend up the wall after casting the climbing spell on him and explaining how it worked. Things got even more confusing when he added the chameleon spell and silent-armor spells on top of that.

He followed Tiny up and helped the giant negotiate the awkward moment at the top when he had to get his body over the edge and reorient for the descent on the other side. "I still don't understand what's wrong with the front gate," complained the big man. "That's what gates are for, right? People like me aren't meant to be up this high."

"Are you afraid of heights?"

"If you were my size, you would be too," hissed Tiny. "If something goes wrong, whatever's beneath me will stop being whatever it used to be and become rubble. At the same time, I will most likely break every bone in my body, if I'm fortunate enough to live to appreciate the extent of my injuries."

"You *can't* fall," Will assured him. "Only one of your limbs can be away from the surface of the wall at any given moment. The spell won't allow you to fall."

Tiny was staring down at the ground nervously. "Easy enough for you to say. You're controlling the spell. I'm having to take all this on faith."

"You don't believe in me?" asked Will with a grin.

"I'm up here, damn it!" swore Tiny angrily. "Shut up and let me focus."

When they were finally on the ground once more, Will could see that his friend's face was covered in sweat, not from the effort—climbing with a spell was relatively easy—but from nervousness. It was something he hadn't really seen before from the usually quiet and easygoing soldier. Tiny caught him staring and looked away.

Will took out the letter Blake had given him and reread it to give his friend a chance to regain his composure. The message was from Lognion and had arrived while he was at the library with Janice. While it didn't materially affect his plan for the evening, it did inspire a mixture of anger and anxiety in him.

> *William,*
>
> *I send this missive to inform you that since you've taken it upon yourself to assume the protection of Mark Nerrow's elder daughter, I have decided to withdraw the Driven from that area. Partly this is for your own protection, so we avoid any confusion between your movements and the activities of my men.*

I do hope you've prepared yourself sufficiently, as you've chosen to take on a dangerous enemy, one that even I would hesitate to face without considerable support. I'm sure you wouldn't attempt such a perilous duty alone. My daughter would be heartbroken if something terrible happened to you.

If you have any understanding of this foe, then you should be aware that this enemy bears similarities to a wound that has turned sour. Sometimes healthy tissue must be excised to save the host. As sovereign, I consider the city, nay the nation as a whole, as my own body. I will not hesitate to remove a rotten limb to save the rest.

Stand too close to the fire and you will be burned.

L.

Tiny noticed him reading it again and put a hand on Will's shoulder. "Little does he know you actually do have support this time."

Will nodded, grateful for the big man's presence. *But will it be enough if we actually meet one of them? What if there's several?* Lognion apparently had small squads of highly trained combat sorcerers hiding in various locations around the city. If the king felt the situation was that serious, what hope would a lone wizard and an armored soldier have? *And I haven't had a chance to learn any of the spells Arrogan recommended yet.*

Although Will was more combat capable than any wizard at Wurthaven, as well as most sorcerers, he knew very few spells that were applicable to the current situation. His repertoire of useful fire spells included a simple method

Chapter 15

for starting fires and a spell to warm the floor when sleeping on the ground. Neither would be particularly helpful in a fight, and chances were that there wouldn't be a sorcerer around tossing fireballs around for him to steal.

The wise thing for me to do would be to stay home, Will thought sourly, but he knew that wasn't really an option for him, and apparently the king knew it as well. He glanced at Tiny. "Are you sure you're up for this?"

The big soldier waved a hand dismissively. "The wall scared me more than any vampire could. What's the plan?"

Will had actually put some thought into it. Even with the spells he had put on Tiny, he wasn't confident his friend could avoid notice, so he intended to make use of the fact. The king's men had been hiding underground last time, while the vampire had dropped down from above. Given that the Drak'shar were inhumanly strong and impervious to ordinary injury, it made sense that they would prefer to hide on the rooftops.

Tiny would move ahead of him at a distance of twenty yards. While he would be hidden by the same spells that Will was using, his size and inexperience would make him more likely to be spotted. If anyone or anything noticed the big man, they'd be less likely to notice the somewhat more inconspicuous wizard shadowing the soldier once their attention had been occupied. If they attacked, Will would have extra time to choose an appropriate response if they were targeting Tiny first.

Of course, there was every chance that the enemy wouldn't risk appearing in the same place twice. Will wouldn't, if he were in their position, but he didn't know what other limitations the enemy was operating under. Catching Laina near her home, at night, might be the only option available to the vampires. He couldn't take the risk with her life.

There was a secondary reason for scouting the area around Laina's home, and it made itself apparent within the first fifteen minutes as they slowly completed their first circuit of the block around the Nerrow house. Will had already adjusted his eyesight so he could see heart-light, so when Darla's figure detached itself from the wall near Laina's front gate he wasn't surprised.

As she approached, he noted that while the Arkeshi was difficult to see, the effect was somewhat greater than just a chameleon effect produced by her cloak. His eyes tended to slide away from Darla if he didn't continually force himself to remain focused on her.

"Someone is approaching," he warned Tiny. "But they aren't hostile so don't overreact."

"Where? I don't see anyone," whispered the big man.

"Here," said the former assassin, pushing back the hood of her cloak. She was standing just within ten feet of the squire when the chameleon effect ended, and Tiny uttered a strange 'yip' before clamping his mouth firmly shut. Will was forced to smother a laugh.

"Darla," said Will, greeting her simply. "We meet again."

The Arkeshi inclined her head slightly. "We do. I was under the impression that my mistress warned you to stay away."

"And do you agree with her?" he asked.

Darla frowned. "It isn't my place to judge such matters."

"I know you were trained as an assassin, rather than a bodyguard, but you still have to realize that the things that may be hunting her are too dangerous for you to face alone. You know you need help."

She looked at him appraisingly. "You're more likely to get in my way. Stay on the other side of the street. If anything happens, don't expect help from me. My duty is to Laina only." She began to turn away.

Chapter 15

Will stepped forward, causing the Arkeshi to jerk to one side. A blade appeared in her hand and Will could see silver runes laid into the steel. He held up his hands. "I didn't mean to startle you, but I have a question before you go." He heard Tiny's body shift as he lifted his spear in reaction. Will waved a hand at his friend. "Don't. We're just talking."

"What's your question?" asked Darla with a tone of impatience. "Quickly. I dislike being away from my post."

"Did you see someone else around the house, before I came? A woman?"

Darla went still, then asked, "Was it with you?"

"It? I'm talking about a young woman, uncommonly beautiful. She was watching the house for me, but she's vanished."

"There was a fae, though it took animal form most of the time. It attacked me."

"She wouldn't do that," he protested, but then he stopped. *Would she? Or was she trying to eliminate the threat before I came and exposed myself?* "We thought you were an assassin, but I only instructed her to watch unless you acted. Did you take her prisoner?"

Darla snorted. "I don't take prisoners. I did what was necessary."

His mouth went dry. "You killed her?"

"Killing one of the fae is easier said than done. I disabled her and left her in the alley. When I checked again later, she was gone. Most likely she recovered and returned to her proper place."

"She didn't," he told her firmly. "Her family is now looking for her."

"The fae don't concern themselves with kin."

It was Will's turn to struggle with his irritation. "This one does. She's my aunt. If I can't find her, bad things will happen."

"The accord protects us, wizardling. Don't they teach you the basics in that fancy school of yours?"

Already irritated, Darla's condescension was too much for him to accept. "Unlike some, I know that the accord isn't eternal. History moves, and the possibility of the accord coming to an end is a very real possibility. I've been dealing with the fae for years now. If I tell you bad things will happen, you would be wise to reconsider what you think you know."

"I have shown you patience only because you spared my life yesterday, but my life does not belong to me, so do not expect gratitude. Stay away from the house or I'll show you the difference between thinking and doing." She turned, raised the hood of her cloak, and faded into a blur.

Will watched her go, and after a second he saw a second change: Darla's turyn shifted in a subtle way, and he felt a faint strain as he concentrated on keeping his eyes on her movement. *What is that?* he wondered. It wasn't a spell, and though the cloak was obviously enchanted, the magic it produced seemed limited to the chameleon effect. *Is she using wild magic of some kind?*

His thoughts distracted him enough that he lost sight of the Arkeshi, and only by concentrating and paying close attention to her heart-light was he able to spot her again. *Whatever it is, it makes it hard to look at her,* he realized, *and greatly enhances the effect of the cloak in the process.*

"Is she really gone?" asked Tiny uncertainly.

Will nodded. "She's across the street, standing to the right of the front gate to the house."

"You can see her?"

"It isn't easy," admitted Will. "I have to focus on the light produced by her body's heat, but even that is tricky since she's also doing something that makes it hard to look at her."

Chapter 15

"I have no idea what you just said," admitted Tiny. "What do we do now?"

"It won't help anything if we start a brawl with Laina's bodyguard. We'll set up over here," said Will. He glanced behind himself. They were standing near the front gate of another lord's home, though he hadn't looked into which nobleman owned the house. There was only one light visible through the windows, the same as it had been the previous night. Will reasoned that whoever owned the estate probably wasn't in residence at the moment. Most nobles maintained country estates where their lands were and city houses in the capital for when they needed to come to court. In all likelihood the owner was currently at his other home. There would still be a small staff, though, or at the bare minimum a lone caretaker if the lord planned to be absent for an extended period of time.

Will stared upward, then leaned in to whisper in Tiny's ear, "The last time I saw one, it came from the roof of this building. If they do show up tonight, they'll most probably come jumping down from this place or one of the other nearby houses. I want you to put your back against the wall and do your best to pretend you don't exist. The less you move, the harder it is to spot you."

"I'm supposed to be the bait," pointed out Tiny.

Will nodded. "Yeah, but if we make it obvious it won't work. From what I've learned they have a keen sense of smell and they may have other senses we don't know about. They may spot both of us, so I'll stay close, just a little better hidden over here to your left." Will moved over to the gate and stepped back into the alcove where entrance was slightly recessed. One thing he had learned from hiding and shifting his senses through different forms of light was that—physical cover trumped everything else. Even if the vampires could somehow see through their camouflage, it was highly unlikely that they could see through the bricks that hid him from view on three sides.

Tiny leaned back against the wall and did his best to relax, while Will tried to do the same. There were challenges that went along with keeping a nighttime vigil, chief among them being the cold. Although it was spring, the night air was still chilly, and since they weren't moving, it gradually settled into their bones, bringing with it a dull ache.

Will adjusted his vision until the dim light was enough to reveal the street almost as though it was daytime. He already knew the vampires didn't give off heart-light, so the only reason to keep that would be to watch Darla. He let it go. It wasn't practical to keep his vision sensitive to too many different types of light, for it tended to muddle his vision and make it difficult to see clearly. In his present situation, the gas streetlights threw off a vicious glare if he tried to use heart-light, so it really wasn't worth the annoyance.

He had two spells prepared, a force-lance and a wind-wall, and he kept a third spell, another force-lance, ready in his hand. He had adjusted the parameters of the wind-wall to cover a slightly different area than usual, and he also made the effort to keep his level of turyn uncomfortably high. Normally he didn't do that, but if he decided to use the prepared wind-wall he wanted it to be fully charged.

Waiting was cold and boring. As the hours wore on, Will fought to stay alert. He had thought the cold would help, but as the monotony wore on, even the dull ache seemed to fade out and he caught himself nodding once or twice. Glancing over, he could see Tiny was also suffering, but the big man's eyes were always open when he checked on him. *What if nothing happens?* Tiny might spend the worst two weeks of his life guesting at Will's home.

Then again, the alternative might be worse.

CHAPTER 16

When it happened, it was much like he had anticipated, and yet it still caught them off-guard. Hours of cold and boredom had dulled Will's reactions. He heard the creature move, for he had his hearing tuned to be as sensitive as possible, but having sharp ears was no cure for monotony. It might have even made it worse. Being able to hear every tiny scrape and bang, every leaf blowing across the road, had dulled his attention.

In comparison, the creature's first movement was loud, yet still so ordinary that he filtered it out of his consciousness, along with all the other ordinary noises. It was ten seconds later, once the adrenaline had kicked in, when he was already fighting for his life, that he recognized the sound as the scrape of a foot when the thing had leapt from the rooftop above. It was an odd moment of retrospection, with no real use for the life-and-death struggle he was engaged in, but the mind was funny like that.

His first awareness of danger came as a shadow fell across his field of view, the shape of a human-sized body dropping down directly in front of the recessed gate he stood before. The sound of its boots slapping heavily against the stone walkway seemed thunderous compared to the relative silence of the past few hours, yet his body still seemed to respond only sluggishly.

Will's heart had just started to leap into his throat when the vampire finished absorbing the shock of landing and unfolded from the ground to spring at him. Everything happened in slow motion, which gave him plenty of time to register events, but unfortunately his body moved far slower than his perceptions, while the monster's body seemed to be moving at an unbelievable speed.

Once again, Arrogan's advice from a year ago saved his life. *"A force-effect spell that you can reflex cast works at the speed of the soul, not thought,"* the ring had told him, prompting him over and over to work on his point-defense shield until he could cast it without thinking. The first shield appeared in front of the snarling thing's face, which was rushing toward his own with horrifying rapidity.

The silent observer in the back of his head watched one of the vampire's fangs shatter as it hit the shield less than two feet from his face. It rebounded and came back at him on all fours, staying close to the ground. His second shield stopped it once more, again appearing right in front of the vampire's snarling lips.

This happened in the span of a second or two. He was still drawing breath to yell for Tiny when his ears heard the screaming sound of iron being wrenched free of its moorings behind him. Apparently, his monster had a friend, and that friend had just ripped the iron gate from its hinges. Will tried to turn and keep his eyes on the fiend in front of him at the same time. Naturally, he failed spectacularly at both. He managed to stop the first vampire's third lunge, but then he felt an iron grip take hold of the aventail connected to the base of his helm. His feet left the ground momentarily as the unseen vampire jerked him back and upward, letting him fall to the walkway.

Will's breath exploded from his lungs as he hit the ground hard, and then the creature was on top of him. The thing didn't seem overly concerned with the fact that armor protected his throat and most of the rest of his body; it was perfectly content to go for the one part of him that was clearly open to the air—his face. Another shield stopped it

Chapter 16

just inches away, but farther down, out of his view, he felt the other monster take hold of his leg, pulling at his boot. *No, no, no!* he thought desperately, trying to kick it away. From the corner of his eye, he saw a third form land in the yard to his right. This one was smaller, though he didn't have time to reflect on its appearance. It moved to take a position on his right arm.

In all, less than five or six seconds had passed since the attack had begun. Will was pretty sure he would be dead before another five seconds had passed—or wishing he was dead.

Tiny's spear went completely through the chest of the monster on top of Will before sliding off Will's breastplate and sinking temporarily into the turf of the lawn. A moment later it rose, lifting the creature upward as the massive soldier used the spear to lever the vampire into the air.

Lifting something the size and weight of a grown man into the air on the end of a spear wasn't a feat most could accomplish—perhaps not even Tiny under normal circumstances—but fear had elevated the big man's strength to heights few had seen. *I can believe he threw Sir Kyle now,* thought Will idly.

Finally, given a moment to act, Will lifted his head and sighted down his body at the creature that was almost done removing his boot. The force-lance he had been holding ready tore through the vampire's left shoulder and sent it flying into the wall next to the gate. Will's boot was still firmly in its hand.

Meanwhile, Tiny's opponent had slid down the spear to reach the big warrior. Tiny had stopped it with one hand, and since his arm was longer, the thing couldn't reach his throat. A moment later he was forced to use both hands to hold the thing at bay, releasing the spear. The vampire had taken hold of the squire's arms and was now prying them away from its throat. Will saw a strange look cross Tiny's face as the vampire's greater strength slowly pulled his arms apart, forcing his hands to release the thing's throat.

Tiny outweighed the thing by a factor of two or three, and still it was overpowering him. The smaller vampire, a girl near the age of twelve by the look of her, abandoned Will to throw herself at the giant warrior. With both his arms otherwise engaged, Tiny would be nearly helpless to stop her from ripping his face off if she so desired.

Will's second force-lance ripped through her back and accelerated her motion, flinging the diminutive vampire over the wall and into the street. Getting to his feet, Will moved to help his friend. He could see the vampire with his boot was already beginning to stand again. *What do I have to do to keep them down?* he thought desperately, though he already knew the answer—fire.

If only he had some.

Hobbling over with one bare foot, Will gave the vampire struggling with Tiny a wide berth. The air was filled with coarse grunts as the big man tried desperately to keep his arms from spreading. Will moved behind him and got close, pressing himself almost against Tiny's back as the first vampire threw the boot away and sprang at them. If the ruinous hole through its body bothered it, it certainly wasn't enough to slow the thing down.

Will released his last spell, the wind-wall. His turyn was still close to his maximum, more than enough to fully empower the spell. A fierce roar filled their ears as the air around them tore the world to tatters. The vampire that Tiny held was partly in and partly out of the minimum radius, but it was torn free in less than a second, becoming just another piece of detritus in the terrible cyclone that surrounded them.

Chapter 16

The spell lasted several seconds, and when it died away they could see the devastation it had wrought. The lawn around the walkway was gone, torn up out to a distance of fifteen feet. Parts of the walkway had also vanished, fragments of it lying haphazardly in the surrounding area. The torn gate and part of the wall had collapsed, and scattered among all the debris and broken masonry were body parts, the remains of two of the vampires. Will could see the arms and legs twitching and moving helplessly as they tried to find each other to reunite. *Can they really survive something like that? Would they heal if we gave them enough time?*

The smaller vampire had been too far away to be affected.

"What the hell was that?" exclaimed Tiny as the roaring winds died down.

"Magic," snapped Will. "Let's see where the other one went. Stay close." He headed for the ruined gate. As soon as he stepped out into the street, he could see that he and Tiny hadn't been the only ones engaged in a desperate fight. The entire front lawn of the Nerrow house was ablaze, and several burning corpses littered the yard. Will was forced to readjust his vision to accommodate the change in lighting, but he'd gotten so used to doing so that the process was nearly automatic.

Mark Nerrow stood on the front steps of his home, two fire elementals beside him on either side. Darla was behind him, her head turned upward as her eyes scanned the roof of the house above them. *She must have played the decoy like Tiny did for me,* Will realized. *Looks like she did a better job of it, though.*

The childlike vampire stood by the gate to the Nerrow house, her body out of view, hidden from the baron by the stone pillar that flanked the gate. As Will looked on, she lifted her chin and uttered a shrill, high-pitched cry. It was almost too high for him hear, and it shifted and changed as he listened, as though she was shrieking words in an impossibly high tone. *Is she talking to the others?*

A second later, two figures jumped down from the top of the Nerrow house, while five others came from another building across the street to Will's right. An intense wall of flame sprang up in front of the baron, but the two that had dropped down were already within it. Darla engaged one, but the second was directly behind Will's father.

Will was already running, and he could hear Tiny's heavy boots pounding the street beside him, but they wouldn't get there in time. They were still thirty yards away, with an iron fence to somehow cross before they could reach the besieged Lord Nerrow. Will's eyes locked on the scene, and he did the only thing he could.

The vampire reached for Mark Nerrow's head, but a force-shield blocked its hand. It reached again, its arms blurring with speed, but every attack was stopped cold. Seconds ticked by, and then Lord Nerrow turned, having finished incinerating those who had made the foolhardy frontal assault. Furious, he lifted one hand and the monster desperately trying to reach him was wreathed in flames.

Meanwhile, Will fought to stay on his feet. He had stopped just short of the iron fence, and only Tiny's large hand kept him from falling. Force spells required more turyn when used at a distance, and while the point-defense spell normally took very little, at that range the cost of using several dozen shields in rapid succession had taken its toll on him. Tiny dragged him to the gate pillar and put his body between Will and the street.

"Are you all right?" asked the big man worriedly.

"I used too much magic. Give me a minute and I'll be fine." Will was already drawing turyn in as rapidly as

Chapter 16

he could to replace his depleted stores. As he did, he saw a small form walk toward them. It was the child vampire.

Her eyes were on his, even though her view was largely blocked by the bulk of Tiny's body. Will edged to one side so he could see her better. She was somewhere just under five feet in height, with dark brown hair and eyes that seemed to swallow the light. Tiny edged farther to the right, blocking his view again, so Will sidled to the left instead.

"You can't have him," said the big man protectively.

"Damn it, Tiny, let me see!" cursed Will.

The vampire stopped at a distance of thirty feet, and as Will edged back in to view, she addressed him, "I've got my eyes on you, human. Your days are numbered, as are theirs." She jerked her head to indicate the Nerrow household.

Her features reminded him of his cousin Sammy, or at least as she had been a few years previously, when she was younger. *Who could do that to a child?* "Nice to meet you," he quipped, letting his mouth run without giving his brain time to think. It had more important things to do anyway. "My name is Will. What's yours?"

A quizzical look crossed the vampire's face, and then she laughed. "Alexa. The next time we meet will be your—" Her words cut off in a shriek of pain and shock as the force-lance Will had been quietly constructing took her in the hip, shattering her pelvis and nearly amputating her left leg.

"Don't let it get away," Will instructed firmly as he began readying another spell. "It will be useful if we can capture it mostly intact." His words were underscored by the fact that the vampire was already up and scrabbling to get away, using her good leg and two arms to move like some grotesque crab. Tiny leapt forward, sword in hand

and shield ready to defend if the creature changed from flight to attack.

And even with two good legs he was too slow. The vampire was definitely hampered by the loss of her leg, but she galloped away on her three good limbs at a pace that rivaled a healthy dog. Her damaged leg left a black smear as it bumped and banged on the ground behind her, still connected by skin and a few tendons.

Will was lining up his shot when he heard the sound of breaking glass behind him, followed by the sound of flames billowing to life. *That wasn't a spell.* Spinning around, he saw an expanding ring of white fire that seemed to stick to the wall on one side of the entrance to the Nerrow home. Although he'd never made it himself, he recognized it immediately—alchemical fire.

"She's too fast, Will," yelled Tiny.

"Forget her, they're trying to burn the house," Will responded. The front gate was still intact, so he used the force-lance he had constructed to destroy the lock, then pushed it open. Tiny rejoined him as they stepped into the yard where the baron was using his fire elementals to control and contain the spread of the fire.

Will couldn't help but admire the man's quick thinking. Water would have made things worse, and wind would have been a disaster. The door opened, and Agnes poked her head out, "What's happening?"

"Damn it! I told you to keep the door shut!" yelled her husband.

Will moved closer, waving at Agnes to go back in, while Darla glanced at him for a split second, disapproval in her gaze. She didn't spare much attention, though; her eyes were still scanning for new threats.

He was almost to the porch when he heard an odd clunk, as though a rock had hit the walkway. Looking

Chapter 16

down, he saw a large, heavy glass vial beside his one bare foot, with a thin strip of rune-inscribed paper around its neck.

The enchantment was familiar to him, for he'd used it in the past, though this one appeared to be acting according to a timer rather than a command word. *It's an alchemical bomb.* The sentence rolled through his head casually as Darla's eyes widened and she began to run.

Without time to escape or flee, Will did the only thing he could. With one hand he touched the vial, and with a thought he stored it inside the limnthal. When he straightened up again, he saw both Darla and his father watching him warily, waiting to see if he would burst into flames. He ignored their looks; he was too busy doing math in his head. *Arrogan said time in the realm within the limnthal runs a thousand times slower, so if the enchantment was going to explode in say, one second then I have...* He lost his place once and had to start over, but eventually he was sure it was somewhere just over fifteen minutes. *Or more if it had more than a second left,* he reminded himself.

If it went off while stored in the limnthal, he wasn't sure what would happen, but his best guess was that everything he had stored within the limnthal's extradimensional space would be burnt to cinders. His gold was in there, along with his weapons and other sundries, but he worried most about the expensive cuts of beef and lamb. Losing so much valuable meat would be devastating. He held up a hand as though asking the others to wait. "I'll be right back."

Tiny followed him as he re-crossed the street and retrieved his boot. Once Will was reshod, he used the butt of Tiny's fallen spear to nudge the various vampire parts into a pile. The task was easier than he had expected since most of them had been gradually wiggling themselves closer together before his intervention.

Initially he had meant to simply resummon the alchemical firebomb and let it handle the incineration for him, but as he watched the wriggling mass of vampire parts, another idea came to him. Back when his grandfather had been educating him on the finer points of troll regeneration (and reproduction), the old man had told him that troll parts would fuse together. Will wondered if the vampire pieces would do the same. *Or will they somehow differentiate and separate themselves? Will we wind up with two new, mixed-together vampires, or one larger, mixed-up vampire, or just the two individuals that we started with?*

"Will, what are you doing?" asked Tiny, nudging his elbow.

"I'm waiting to see if they mix together or separate into the original creatures," said Will absently.

"Shouldn't we burn them?"

"I will, just give me a minute. We may never get a chance to observe something like this again."

"I'm going to have nightmares for months," complained his friend. "In my ideal world, I would never see anything remotely like this ever again." His eyes fixed on the body parts. "They keep moving, ugh."

Will heard a strange noise from Tiny's throat. "Are you all right?"

Tiny gagged. "It's the smell. I think I'm going to lose my supper."

He scowled at the big warrior. "Don't you dare. That meal was a work of art. Go stand a little farther away if it bothers you too much. The smell will be worse when it starts burning." Will still had vivid memories of the stench of burning flesh from when he had set fire to the enemy

Chapter 16

camp in Barrowden. It wasn't the sort of thing one forgot, but fortunately he didn't have a sensitive gag reflex.

Despite his warning, he heard Tiny begin to retch into one of the ornamental bushes planted in the exquisitely maintained garden. Will kept his attention on the pile of flesh in front of him. *It's definitely separating,* he observed. *The parts can tell the difference between self and other.*

The movements were slower as well, as though the vampiric flesh was beginning to run out of energy, like a clockwork music box whose spring was winding down. It wasn't too surprising. They were trying to heal from a massive trauma, and almost all their vital fluids had spilled out. Would they eventually die without nourishment, as the fae did if cut off from Faerie? He had too many questions.

Will activated the limnthal and asked the ring a question. "Do you think it's safe to store a pile of vampire flesh inside the limnthal?"

For once, Arrogan didn't immediately respond with sarcasm. In fact, the ring took several seconds to process what Will had said before it answered. "So many questions. I'm assuming you need a quick decision?"

"Yes," said Will. "I'm not in a safe place."

"If you still have some of the clay jars in there, one of the big ones that I kept water in should do. Dump it out, put your, uh—sample inside. Be careful, though. If you're injured or have cuts don't let any of the vital fluids get on your skin. If it mixes with your blood, you'll have a whole new set of problems. Seal the top with a heavy piece of cloth and tie it tightly around the neck. If any light gets inside it will destroy your vampire."

"It's dark out right now."

"Not here, moron. Inside the limnthal. It might be daytime in there."

That brought a dozen more questions into his head, but there wasn't time. "You said the blood is dangerous. I didn't get cut or bitten this time, but suppose I do—is there a treatment?"

"Sure. Tell your friends to leave you out for the next sunrise, then put a knife in your heart. That will keep you still until the sun comes up. It takes a few days before you start regenerating the way they do."

"Anything less fatal?"

"A blood-cleanse potion will work, but only if given within an hour or so. After that, it will just make you feel sick before you finish transforming into an unholy abomination. It's a good idea to keep a few of them with you as long as you're dealing with the undead."

Will nodded out of habit. The ring couldn't see his expressions or movements. He actually had several dozen blood-cleanse potions stored inside the limnthal already. He'd made most of his money selling them to the school, and when they'd no longer wanted to buy them, he'd been stuck with the surplus. "How long do you think it will be safe in there? I don't want to summon it out and have a fully functioning vampire at my throat."

"If you've fully exsanguinated the creature it will heal very slowly. Hell, it might not even finish unless you pour some fresh blood on it. Add to that the fact that time inside the limnthal is a thousand times slower and I would think that you should be safe even if you wait a week or longer."

"All right. I'd better get to work then," said Will. Following Arrogan's advice, he summoned the big water jar and dumped it out. Then he used the butt of the spear to shepherd one of the now-separate piles of vampire pieces into it. That done, he stood the jar up and used one of his spare school tunics to cover the top before tying it shut.

Chapter 16

He sent the jar back into storage and then took a few steps back from the remaining flesh pile. With a thought, he summoned the alchemical firebomb and tossed it at the pile before moving even farther back.

"Watch out," he cautioned Tiny, who started to step forward, curious as to what he was doing. "It's about to—"

"Damn it!" yelled the big man. He was far enough back to be safe, but the sudden eruption of flames had startled him. "Warn me next time!"

"—burst into flames," finished Will, giggling with nervous laughter. The macabre events were beginning to take a toll on his nerves.

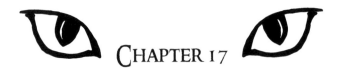

CHAPTER 17

There was a strange scene unfolding at the Nerrow house as Will and Tiny returned to check on Darla and the baron. Agnes was back at the front door, this time joined by both Laina and Tabitha. All three of them had tear-stained cheeks.

Darla knelt on the path from the door to the gate, her head bowed, while Mark Nerrow stood over her, his sword raised as he prepared to strike. Arrogan's advice was still fresh on Will's mind, and he realized immediately what must be happening. "Wait!" he yelled.

The sword came down in a blurring arc but stopped when it met Will's point-defense shield just above the Arkeshi's bare neck. The baron turned to face them as they entered the yard, a look of fury on his face, as well as a few tears of his own. "Stay out of this, William. You don't know what we're dealing with."

"The hell I don't," snapped Will. "She can be saved." As his eyes studied Darla, he saw a nasty cut that ran from the woman's forearm to the back of her right hand. Ugly black veins stood out around the wound.

"There is no cure for the poison of the Drak'shar," intoned the stone-faced assassin, slowly drawing her own blade. "The Arkeshi know this better than any still living."

It was obvious she intended to finish the job herself. Will glanced at Tiny and cut his eyes to the left, indicating the big man should try to flank Laina's bodyguard, then he focused his attention on Darla.

"Then your teachers need to do some research. Alchemy has long been able to cure the disease, if the curative is given quickly enough."

"William, you need to leave her be. The king's instructions were very clear, and Darla agrees with them as well," warned the baron. His eyes were watching Will's hands, where a new spell was forming. Though his words seemed to agree with Darla, there was an undertone of uncertainty in his voice, or perhaps hope.

Darla could see what Tiny was trying to do, and she began edging to one side, keeping her knife between herself and the massive warrior while she worked up her nerve to reverse the blade and put an end to her life.

Just wait a few seconds longer, thought Will as the spell came together. Then it was ready. Something in his posture must have given him away, for Darla flipped her dagger and made to drive it home. Tiny lunged, trying to catch her wrist, but she was too quick and dodged to one side—before slowly slumping to the ground as Will's sleep spell took hold.

Will looked at his father, who hadn't tried to interfere. "You believed me?"

"I just don't want to kill her. My gut tells me you're offering a fool's hope, but I'll take it. If whatever you've got doesn't work, then I'll still have to—" Mark Nerrow made a reluctant chopping gesture with his sword.

"A blood-cleanse potion can stop the change, if it's given within an hour," explained Will.

"And you learned this where?" asked his father.

"From someone who actually fought these things the last time they crawled out of the shadows. Can we take her inside?"

Tiny stepped up and lifted the Arkeshi. Darla's small frame made her look like a doll in the giant warrior's arms.

The baron nodded toward the door. "Let's take her to the front parlor."

The entire Nerrow family followed them in, and Agnes eventually began shooing her daughters away to make room. Only so many people could help with one unconscious woman.

"We'll need to wake her up to be sure she swallows the potion properly," said Will.

The baron nodded. "Then you'll want her bound."

Agnes turned to her youngest. "Tabitha, run upstairs and bring down the spare sheets. We'll bind her wrists and ankles with those."

Her husband frowned at the thought of cutting up the fine linens. "We have some rope in—"

The baroness cut him off. "She's less likely to hurt herself if she struggles."

"But…"

Agnes glared. "She's more than just a servant."

Will stayed out of the argument, and in a few minutes a large bedsheet was brought down and cut into wide strips. Will's father tied Darla into a cushioned chair while Tiny helped position the unconscious woman.

"Don't you need to fetch the potion?" asked the baron as they finished.

He had already taken a moment to step aside and summon the blood-cleanse potion from the limnthal while the others were occupied. Will held it up for the baron to see. "I have it here."

Mark Nerrow frowned. "You had that with you the whole time?"

Will allowed himself a smug look, hoping he seemed mysterious. "Apparently I did. Let's wake her up."

The sleep spell would ordinarily keep a person in a deep slumber for several hours, but it wasn't an enforced

Chapter 17

sleep. Enough stimulation could eventually rouse someone, especially if the person applying it was as determined as Laina was. Darla's eyes opened after a few minutes and slowly focused on her friend. Then the Arkeshi jerked slightly as she attempted to move, quickly discovering her bonds. "You can't keep me like this," insisted the former assassin. "You know that."

Laina won the patient over with her usual brusque charm. "Shut up and drink this." She took the potion from Will's hand and unstopped it before holding it up to Darla's lips.

Darla twisted her head away. "What is it?"

Laina's tone grew hard. "Have you ever disobeyed me before?"

"No, mistress."

"Drink," commanded Laina once again. This time Darla acquiesced, grimacing slightly at the taste.

Will took the empty vial from Laina's hand and dribbled the last remaining drops onto Darla's wound before using a spare piece of the now-shredded bedsheet to work it into the cut. The Arkeshi made no sound, but he could tell it hurt her by the way her muscles tensed as the cloth moved over the injured skin. Once he was sure he had rubbed in the last of the potion, he took another strip and neatly wrapped her forearm and hand with a bandage.

Darla hadn't said a word, but she finally spoke. "We need to see the wound to tell if it's working."

He nodded. "It will work, but we'll check it every hour until we're sure you're better." Will headed for the door.

"Where are you going?" asked Agnes, a look of alarm on her face. "It's still dark out."

Will glanced quickly at Darla. "Your sentry needs rest until she heals. Tiny and I will sit outside until dawn arrives." His eyes stopped on Mark Nerrow for a split second as a bitter thought came to him. *I wouldn't want to wear out my welcome, after all.*

There were only four hours left until dawn, hours that were made more pleasant when the baroness brought out a silver platter with sweet biscuits and hot tea. They enjoyed the refreshments, and Will studied the silver utensils. He needed to buy some silver and see the weaponsmith soon.

When the sun finally began to show on the horizon, Will knocked on the door before leaving. Tabitha answered, as apparently the others had finally fallen asleep from nervous exhaustion. As always, Will was struck by the warmth on his younger sister's face. Her hair was tangled and her eyes puffy, but there was a spark of positivity in her that refused to be dampened by circumstances.

She squinted at the sunlight that was beginning to peak over the rooftops. "Sun's up. You should come inside and rest." Then she grinned. "Unless you'd prefer to cook breakfast first?"

Tabitha and Sammy would make great friends, thought Will. *They're so similar.* He shook his head, though he wished he could accept her offer. "No, I need to get back home. I have lots to do. Here." He held out five blood-cleanse potions he had summoned from the limnthal before knocking. "Take these, in case anyone else gets injured."

"What if you need them?" she asked.

The door opened wider then, as Mark Nerrow stepped up behind his daughter. "Take them in and put them in the kitchen, Tabitha." He waited until the young woman was gone before addressing Will directly. "Thank you for the gift, though I can't help wondering. You haven't left and I'm certain you only had the one potion last night."

Chapter 17

"Perhaps if sorcerers spent more time studying magic and less time looking down on wizards, they'd still know how such things are done," Will retorted, his irritation coming fully to the surface.

The baron ignored his tone. "I've known and studied with quite a few wizards. I was a student at Wurthaven myself once upon a time."

"And yet you're still wrong. I'm the first you've ever met." Turning away, he looked at Tiny. "Let's go."

"William, I know I was a little harsh last time we spoke, but—" began the baron.

Will cut him off. "Don't worry. We'll be back tonight, when it's dark and no one will see me. That way you won't be embarrassed."

As he started walking, he heard Tabitha's voice from inside. "He's leaving? What were you talking about? Did he say embarrassed?"

***

Tiny was silent most of the way back, lost in his own thoughts, but eventually he spoke. "You were very rude to the baron."

"I get stupid when I'm tired," said Will. "He deserved it, though."

"It's never wise to make enemies out of noblemen, Will."

Half a chuckle escaped before Will replied, "Did you notice he didn't respond? He just let me walk away. There's a reason for that. You don't need to worry. He may not be a friend, but he'll never be an enemy." Silently he added, *I hope.*

"Does this have anything to do with the count you killed? Are they afraid of you?"

"You heard the rumors?"

"I'm pretty sure that even the wild men of Barsta have heard about it by now."

Will stopped. "I didn't kill Lord Spry, I killed his son. Selene killed the earl—at their wedding."

The squire gaped at him, then finally closed his mouth. "I heard a version like that, but I dismissed it as unbelievable."

Will nodded. "I'm sure none of the tales come close to the full absurdity of that day."

"Some of them claim you died, and the high priest prayed until Temarah interceded and raised you from the dead," said Tiny tentatively.

They were finally home, and Will laughed as they walked through the door. "No, that one is completely wrong."

Tiny laughed along with him, releasing his hidden tension. "That would be impossible, right?"

"Well, I wouldn't say impossible," said Will carefully. "I did die, for a little while. But it wasn't the priest or Temarah that brought me back. I took care of that myself. I may have met the Mother, though. I had a weird vision while I was being whipped the other day, but I'm not sure. I might have been hallucinating from the pain."

Tiny stared at him quietly, then replied, "We need to have a long talk."

Will nodded in agreement. "We do, but can we wait until after we've bathed and slept?"

Blake stepped through the door at the end of the hall. "Would you like me to heat some water for you, squire? We have a large tub in the back."

The big warrior nodded at his host. "After your master has bathed. I wouldn't dream of being first."

Chapter 17

"Go ahead," offered Will. He planned to forgo the pleasure of hot water and use a spell to save time. Exhaustion weighed heavily on him, and every minute away from his pillow was a minute he wouldn't have to rest later. "I'll take care of myself, Blake. Don't wake me." With that, he headed for the stairs. He paused with his foot on the first step.

"Blake."

"Yes, sir?"

"We will probably sleep for at least half the day, but a few things need to be started sooner. After Tiny is settled, go into the city and find a weaponsmith willing to do a quick job of some silver inlay on a few weapons. Don't haggle too much over the price. Speed is more important to me than saving coin at this point," explained Will.

"Certainly, sir. What sort of weapons do you want me to have them—"

Will cut him off. "Look at Tiny's gear. It's more important that he have them than me. Spear heads, a new falchion, dagger—you've seen his kit. If there will be a significant time delay then have them start on a sword or spear for him before anything else."

"I understand, sir."

Will nodded. "How much do you think you'll need to give them for a deposit?"

Blake waved a hand. "Don't worry about it, sir. I've been handling odd errands for the royal family for years now, some of them far stranger than this. Every merchant in town knows me on sight. They'll start without a deposit. I can give you an exact total when you wake."

Will sighed, grateful that at least one thing would be taken care of.

Once he was in the master bedroom, he started to construct the self-cleaning spell he used on occasions when he was in a hurry, but he paused halfway through the spell. He'd been working on Selene's eighth-order spell off and on over the last year and he was close to succeeding. Trying it while he was so tired probably would mean an automatic failure, but his stubbornness surfaced and made the decision for him.

Sure enough, he forgot a crucial piece as he was constructing the spell, and it fragmented halfway through. Frustrated, he looked for his notes to refresh his memory, but the page they were written on defied his efforts to locate it. He wanted to pull his hair out.

He had originally copied the spell from a book kept in Wurthaven's library. He'd have to go and make another copy when he could find some time away from his current hellish crisis. Then he stopped and thumped himself on the head. "I still have a copy."

A few days before Selene's disastrous near-wedding to Count Spry, she and Will had had one last touching reunion. At the time they had thought it would be their last. During their time together, he had taught Selene two of his spells and she had copied her signature spell into the journal that Arrogan had left him. At the time she had told him to look at it later, but he'd completely forgotten about it.

Summoning the journal from the limnthal, he thumbed through it to the blank pages at the back. The last page with writing was fresher than the others, the ink still black and crisp. It was titled 'Selene's Solution' in the elegant, flowing script that Selene seemed to use effortlessly. Beneath the title was a precise diagram along with the rune inscription that listed the order of construction. Every part of it seemed to embody the care and attention to detail that Selene had put into all of her endeavors.

Chapter 17

At the bottom she had signed it as he had requested, *Selene Maligant,* but after that was a small note and an arrow pointing to the edge of the paper. 'Turn me,' it read. Flipping the page, he found a short letter written on the back side.

> *Will,*
> *Thank you for everything up until now. I never thought I'd have a friend such as you. Know that my heart will always be with you, no matter what the future holds. I think in the days to come you will probably be very angry with me for the choices I have made, but I had only bad options. Someday I hope you will understand and forgive me.*
> *Whatever happens, I will always love you.*
> *Though I may not be your partner in this life, I will still do what I can for you. In the interest of safety, I won't name them here, but remember that the two young women you care so deeply for are my good friends. It may be that they can never know why you care, but I will do my best to provide opportunities for you to cultivate their friendship. I am sure that with my recommendation and some time to know you, they will begin to appreciate you almost as much as I do.*
> *The future isn't all dark. There must always be some light, or the shadows wouldn't exist either.*
>   *Yours Always,*
>   *Selene*

The letter took him back to the emotions of that day. They had been desperate, and it had felt as though the world was about to collapse on their heads. He had felt much as he did now, and it served as a reminder that perhaps he would get through his current crisis. There was always hope. Little had she known that just a few days after that the two of them would be wed to one another. *Or that we'd then be separated for a full year before seeing each other even once.*

His vision blurred as he turned the page back to the spell diagram and carefully tried again. This time there were no mistakes. After a year of frustration and seemingly fruitless efforts, the spell came together flawlessly. It sparkled above his hand, the complex collection of runes glowing with turyn as he invested it with power and set the boundaries for its effect.

When he released it, it expanded gradually to encompass the room. A warm, gentle breeze swept over him, removing the dirt and grime from his clothes even as it swept the fresh tears from his cheeks. The spell was far gentler, yet still more thorough than the spells he had been forced to use over the past year. The last time he had felt its effects had been the day that Selene had inscribed the spell for him.

Opening his eyes, he saw that the room was cleaner than ever. The dust was gone, and the bed looked freshly made. His clothes and armor were pristine, and beneath them he felt as fresh as if he had just left the bath. Undressing, he lay down and let his exhaustion sweep him into the realm of dreams. He was sure Selene would be waiting for him there.

Chapter 18

Will slept like the dead, and when he woke, he discovered that although he hadn't done too much during the fighting, he had still acquired several bruises and a sore back. *Probably from when I was jerked backward and landed so hard.*

He rose quickly, dressed, and went downstairs where he found Tiny seated in the dining room, an empty plate in front of him. Blake stood by the door to the kitchen. Will glared daggers at his manservant. "You didn't!"

Blake's lips twitched, betraying the hint of a smile. "Didn't what, sir?"

Ignoring him, Will gave Tiny an apologetic look. "I'm so sorry. You shouldn't have had to eat that."

Tiny shrugged, his face unconcerned. "I've had worse. You haven't eaten what the new cook for Company B serves these days."

Will turned back to Blake. "If he dies, it will be your head," he pronounced in mock seriousness.

Blake laughed. "I'll take my chances. It wasn't that bad. In fact, there's still some left if you want to try it."

In the kitchen, Will found a small pot still half full of what might have been oat porridge before it had congealed into a passable substitute for brick mortar. He carried it straight to the back door and began scraping the contents into the scrap bin.

"Hey, that was still good!" protested Blake. "I was going to eat the other half if you didn't want it."

Will ignored him, then checked the stove to make sure it was still hot. "I'm making a fresh batch. Pay close attention, and maybe we can avoid poisoning anyone else in the future." He gave precise instructions as he worked, making sure Blake took note of quantities, the amount of water used, how he seasoned, as well as the relative heat of the stove. While he did, he interspersed the conversation with other questions.

"How did it go with the weapons?"

Blake smiled. "A week and they'll have two spears and two falchions ready. It might have taken longer, but I got him to promise to work on ours first. You'll be interested to know they just finished a big order of similar items for the king. He ordered them prepared several weeks ago. Luckily for us, the extra leftover materials made things a little cheaper for us."

Will gave him a sour look. "It would have been even luckier if we'd known what the king knew then so we could have weapons ready now and damn the money. How much do I need to give you for the smith?"

Blake shrugged. "Nothing, it will be paid out of the accounts."

He narrowed his eyes suspiciously. "What accounts?"

"Her Highness's accounts," said the manservant with a smug look.

"I have access to those? You never mentioned that before."

Blake nodded. "She gave the instructions before she left."

"But you didn't tell me," said Will pointedly.

His servant smiled brightly and nodded. "That is correct. I did not."

"But you probably should have, shouldn't you?"

"That's a matter subject to some interpretation. Since you never asked, I never thought to mention it."

Chapter 18

Will glared silently at the man for several long seconds.

Blake held up his hands. "In my defense, I wasn't sure about you at first. I've been taking care of the princess since she was just a girl. I was worried you might be planning to steal or waste her money."

Will started to growl, but then caught himself. Taking a deep breath, he responded, "Fair enough. Actually, I can't say that I blame you. In fact, I admire your principles, and to prove my honesty to you, I'm still willing to pay for the weapons. I never intended to have her foot the bill."

Blake shook his head. "That won't be necessary, sir."

"I insist."

"Truly, Master William. Her Highness would have me strapped if she found out I made you pay for this, especially when it is something so important to your own survival. Trust me, the sum is insignificant compared to her accounts."

"How much did it cost?"

"For a rush job with new weapons and the silver to do the inlay it was just under two hundred gold crowns."

Will had nearly five hundred still saved in the limnthal. "That's nothing. I can cover it."

Blake shook his head. "Based on what I know of you, that's almost half of your reserve."

"How do you know that?" asked Will, feeling mildly alarmed.

"When the princess married you, I started doing some research. Based on what I learned from the Bursar's Office and the Department of Healing and Psyche, you nearly earned enough to pay the weregild for Count Spry's son—before the king paid it in your stead. Given your other purchases and what I gleaned from the merchants in the city, you spent close to half of that. Admirably, you spent a significant portion on armor for your friends back in

Barrowden. By itself, such generosity isn't that uncommon among commoners, but that was the first indicator that prompted me to begin trusting your motives."

"Weregild?"

Blake sighed. "That's the technical term for what commoners call a blood-price or blood-debt. Sometimes I forget who I'm talking to."

Damn, he gets snarky when money is the topic of conversation, doesn't he? thought Will. "I don't want anything to do with the king's money. I'd rather pay myself than owe that man anything."

"This isn't the king's money. Princess Selene has her own separate accounts."

Will growled, feeling stubborn. "Which he gave to her and can probably take back at a moment's notice. What's the difference?"

"Begging your pardon, sir, but that isn't true. While her money did initially come from the royal family, it belongs to her alone. The king can't touch it unless he personally overturned the control of the banks, which would likely result in a civil war. Her money will only revert to the crown if she dies without child or husband."

That set Will back on his heels. "Huh," he said, for lack of a witty response. His mind was blank for a moment, then something else occurred to him. "Is the cellar still empty?"

"It isn't empty, but it hasn't been restocked. That won't be possible until late summer and fall when the harvests come in," answered Blake. "Why do you ask?"

"I need a dungeon," said Will. "Nothing fancy, just enough room to keep one prisoner. How much do you think it would cost to refit the cellar for that?"

Blake lifted one brow and gave him a curious stare. "Can I assume you aren't planning to take up torture or other illegal practices, like abducting free citizens?"

Chapter 18

Will rubbed his chin. "I can't promise that I'll be following the law at all times, but I don't plan on torturing anyone or hurting innocents. Also, it will need to be built to accommodate a prisoner that may have strength well beyond human norms."

"A vampire cell, then?"

Will nodded. "I need a pig too."

"You'll need a mason to do some work. Most of the walls are stone, but some aren't, and you don't want it to be able to dig out. Then you'll need a smith to do some ironwork. We'll have to make sure the shackles can't be torn free. Would you prefer a cage or shackles?"

"I'll need to access the creature to take, uh, samples, so shackles might be best. Perhaps a large cage with shackles inside? That way we can feel safe that it won't escape but I'll still be able to get to it when I need to."

"That sounds reasonable. May I ask why you need such a thing?" asked Blake.

"We captured one last night," said Will. "The things are faster than you'd believe and stronger than even someone like Tiny. There are potions that can be made to improve a soldier's strength and speed, and it just so happens that their blood is the primary ingredient."

Blake shuddered almost imperceptibly but kept his expression blank. "You plan to feed the pig to it so you can harvest its blood?"

"It's a fate befitting a vampire, don't you think? They feed on our blood to survive. I intend to bleed it to help our effort to destroy them."

"Do you need equipment to create these potions?"

Will shook his head. "I have arrangements with the Alchemy Department already. I rent a laboratory from them. Oh! Before I forget, I need a hard leather case with a soft lining and places for potion vials." Taking out one of his journals, Will ripped a page out and used a charcoal stick to sketch out what he wanted. "Can you find something like that, or have it made?"

Blake nodded. "We had something similar when I was serving the king. I'll see about finding one."

A bell chimed, informing them that someone was at the door. "Tell whoever it is that I'm not taking visitors," said Will.

"Understood." Blake left to check the door while Will ladled the fresh porridge into two bowls. There was still enough for Tiny as well, for Will had figured the portions with the assumption that the big man would still be hungry.

Blake returned a moment later. "It's a young woman, Janice Edelman. She says she is a classmate."

She knows better than to try and visit, thought Will. "Let her in and bring her to the dining room." He reapportioned the porridge, two small cups, one for Tiny and one for Blake, since they'd already eaten, and two bowls, one for himself and one for Janice. Placing them on a tray, he carried them into the dining room just as Janice entered.

She was gazing around the room with wide eyes, then she looked at Will. "They hired you to be the cook here? I thought you married the princess."

Will put the tray down on the table. "Ha, ha, ha. Tiny, this is my friend, Janice Edelman. Janice, this is one of my friends from the army."

"Tiny?" she said uncertainly.

Tiny was already on his feet, bowing deeply. "Begging your pardon, miss. My proper name is John Shaw, but my friends call me Tiny. I'd be pleased if you did the same."

A bit of color rose to her cheeks as Tiny straightened and Janice stared up at him, presumably stunned by his size. After a few seconds, she tentatively held out her hand. "Pleased to meet you, Mister Shaw."

Chapter 18

"Squire Tiny," corrected Will. "I forgot. He's been squired recently."

"Just Tiny is fine, Miss Edelman," said the big man, blushing.

"Janice will do," she replied. "I think we're all friends here." She tore her eyes away from the giant and looked at the bowl Will had put in front of her. "What's this?"

"Oat porridge," said Will. "I made a second portion to put my man Blake in his place."

"Your man?"

Blake entered the room and gave a quick bow. "Word, Blake Word, Miss Edelman. I'm pleased to make your acquaintance."

A minute later and they were all seated. Janice was on her third spoonful of porridge, and Tiny was just finishing his cup, a mournful expression on his face. "What is this again?" she asked.

"Oat porridge," Will supplied.

"Are you sure?" Tiny asked. "I've never had anything quite like that."

"I don't really like oats, usually," said Janice. "Mushrooms? Why would you put mushrooms in?" She mumbled as she spooned in another large bite.

He smiled. "I take it you like it? I used mushrooms, onions, and salt pork, plus a bit of sage to lighten the flavor."

"It's terrible," said Blake, spitefully.

"You really don't like it?" said Will, surprised.

The manservant lifted his empty cup. "No, damn you. It was too good to resist."

"I didn't even notice the onions," said Tiny.

"That was where the hint of sweetness came from," Will replied. "I minced them before cooking them until they were dark. They almost disappear into the final dish." While Janice was only a quarter through her bowl, Will had finished two-thirds of his own. He pushed the rest across the table to his large friend. It was a gesture familiar to them both from their time together in the army.

Tiny finished it with a grateful smile and no comments.

Janice leaned forward as she paused between bites. "I found some interesting information. Maybe we can talk privately after I finish this?"

"Is this about my vampire research the other day?" asked Will.

Janice glanced at the others, then relaxed slightly. "I guess they're in this with you?"

He nodded. "No secrets here." Then he paused for a second, thinking. "Actually, let me amend that." He looked at Blake. "Just in case there's anything I don't want a certain someone to know, would you mind starting on those errands we talked about?"

Blake smiled. "Certainly."

A moment later he was gone. Tiny frowned as he asked, "You don't trust him?"

"I trust him," said Will, "but I don't trust the king. Blake still has to report to His Majesty, and Lognion is impossible to lie to. Anything I don't want the king to know about I have to keep from Blake. Which reminds me, anything involving Selene is off limits around him."

"But you don't mind the king knowing you're planning to hunt vampires?" said Janice.

"He already knows," Will replied.

"Oh, well no use crying over spilled milk then." She pulled out a journal and opened it on the table in front of her. "I did a little research after we split up the other day, and I took some notes. It turns out that there's nothing in the library about vampires."

"What little there is, is kept in the vault," said Will.

Janice frowned. "And you know this, how?"

Chapter 18

Will smiled mysteriously but said nothing.

She sniffed and returned to her journal. "Since I couldn't find anything on vampires, I looked into the creator of that spell you wanted, Ethelgren's Illumination. There weren't many mentions of him, but I did find a Linus Ethelgren, who lived before the Terabinian War for Independence."

"Do they have a history or biography about him?"

"There was a biography, but it wasn't on the shelf when I looked for it. I even asked at the desk, and it appears the book was lost or stolen decades ago. They just forgot to remove it from the catalog."

"So someone's trying to hide information about a historical vampire hunter?" asked Will, fascinated.

"Someone decades ago," corrected Janice. "It could be anyone."

"A vast vampire conspiracy," whispered Tiny.

Will shot him a dark look. "Let's not get ahead of ourselves. This is interesting, but it doesn't really help us."

Janice licked her lips. "I'm not finished. I couldn't shake the thought that the name sounded familiar to me, and today while I was in class, wondering why you didn't show up, it came to me." She turned the journal around and shoved it across to him.

Will scanned the page. It appeared to be her notes from Foundations in Artifice. "What am I looking for?"

"Remember when you asked about relics in class not long ago?"

He nodded.

"It was in my notes from a few weeks ago. See the list there?"

There was a list of notable relics on the page. Will's eyes went through it rapidly, and there on the page, third from the top, was what Janice had found. "Ethelgren's Exhortation," he mumbled. "He created a relic?"

Her head bobbed, "Not only that, but it's here, at Wurthaven."

His brows went up. "Really?"

"There's a collection of ancient relics at the Artifice building, but guess what…"

"What?"

"This one isn't in the display cases. They keep it in secure storage down in the basement."

That didn't make much sense. From what he had learned, no one could use ancient relics, since their enchantments were either tailor-made for the owner or (as he believed) modern wizards simply didn't have the necessary ability to adapt their turyn for them. Either way, no one would have wanted to steal it. "Is it made of gold or something?" he asked.

"From what I heard, no," answered Janice. "It's a long rod made of iron with silver runes inlaid in it. Valuable, sure, but not enough to warrant stealing."

Will rubbed his chin. "How did you find all this out so quickly?"

"Drake Barstowe told me about it."

"Who is he?" asked Will. Tiny had remained silent during their conversation, but Will could see him watching intently. His eyes never left Janice's features as she talked.

Janice smiled. "He's a fourth year who is specializing in artifice, but he's been after me for a date for months, so he was more than happy to talk." She glanced at Tiny for a moment, then added, "I didn't promise him anything, though. He knows I'm not interested."

Was that for my benefit or someone else's? Will wondered. He pushed that aside and focused on the matter at hand. "This is all interesting, but no one knows how to

Chapter 18

use the relic and we don't know whether it has any useful properties for this situation anyway."

Janice deflated slightly. "I'll keep looking into it, and anything else that might be useful. It's the least I can do."

"I do need a favor," said Will, which was true, though in part he simply wanted to give her something to do that would be more useful.

"Sure."

"I need some materials for potions, and I don't know if I have time to go to the Alchemy building. I'll make a list if you wouldn't mind going for me. Usually I talk to Professor Karlovic directly."

"I can do that. What do you need?" she replied confidently.

"Come upstairs and I'll make a list for you. I have the references in my room." He rose and started to move, followed by Janice, but he stopped before he reached the door. Glancing back, he saw Tiny staring at him with an intense expression. It took him a moment to realize what was wrong, and when he did it caused him to chuckle. "I'm married, Tiny. What do you think I'd do?"

The big man blushed, then looked away. "I didn't say anything."

Janice put her elbow into Will's midribs. "He's just looking out for me. Don't embarrass him."

Will stared at her quizzically. *Surely, I'm imagining this.* After a second, he waved at Tiny. "Come with us. You can be our chaperone."

CHAPTER 19

Will went through his apothecary and found the recipe for the Dragon's Heart potion. He gave it a quick study, making sure the procedure wouldn't be too difficult, and then copied out the ingredients he would need to purchase. After that was done, he found the next item he was interested in, alchemical fire. The ingredients for that were simple, though one in particular was exceedingly dangerous. "White phosphorous," he muttered to himself. He'd never used it before, or even seen it, though he was fairly sure the Alchemy Department had access to it. He hoped it wasn't too expensive.

He added everything to his list, then handed it over. "I hope it doesn't cost too much, but unless it's astronomical I'll find a way to pay for everything. Tell Karlovic they can put everything in the laboratory I've been renting."

She took the paper, folded it up, and slipped it into an opening in the side of her kirtle. "Do I need to take some coin with me?"

"The professor trusts me," said Will. "I can settle accounts with him later as long as it doesn't run into hundreds of marks."

"What will you do in the meantime?" asked Janice.

"Learn some new spells," he answered. "I'd like to be better prepared tonight. If it hadn't been for Tiny, I wouldn't have lived to see the dawn today."

She smiled—at Tiny, not him. "Anyone would feel safer with such a friend nearby," she remarked. "It was a pleasure meeting you, John."

Tiny dipped his head. "And you, Miss Edelman."

"Janice," she corrected as she made her way to the door. "Try to stay safe tonight." There was a short pause, then she added, "Both of you."

After the door closed, Will couldn't help but laugh, whereupon Tiny gave him a mild punch to the shoulder. At least, he assumed it was supposed to have been a mild punch, as he collected himself from where he had fallen. The big man didn't ordinarily engage in horseplay, for reasons that were now obvious to him.

"Sorry," said Tiny.

Will rubbed his shoulder. "Don't worry about it. I shouldn't have laughed."

"I don't know why I did that. I'm just a little punchy since last night."

Sure, that's what it is, thought Will sarcastically, but he held his tongue. "My nerves aren't much better," he sympathized.

"I'm going to clean my armor and gear. Since you're going to be busy learning spells, do you want me to do yours too?" offered Tiny.

It was a generous offer, but Will had to decline. Selene's spell had done the trick when he had cast it that morning. He hadn't known it could handle armor, but apparently his brilliant wife had thought of just about everything when she had designed it. "I did mine this morning," he explained.

"I won't disturb you until you come down. See you this evening." Although Will knew his friend wanted nothing more than to *not* have to go back out, the big warrior didn't whine or wheedle about it. Some might have said it was because he was a professional soldier, and while there was some truth to that, Will knew that soldiers loved to bitch and complain as a form of stress relief. Tiny was just solid. Rock solid.

Damn, I'm getting sentimental again, thought Will. Shaking his head, he sat down and tried to concentrate. The first spell he was interested in learning was Ethelgren's Illumination, which turned out to be approximately sixth-order, in terms of difficulty. Of course, there was no official rating listed with the spell—it was too old for that. Will judged it based on prior experience.

Given the difficulty, he guessed it would take him an hour or two to successfully construct the first time and possibly several days before he could recreate it without referring to his notes. He could try it out once and then keep it prepared for use that night. As long as he only needed it once, that would be fine. The time required to learn it, though, meant he'd have to forego learning anything else but one or two of the simpler fire spells.

He thumbed through the other book he had 'borrowed' from the school library, *Fire Spells for Fun and Profit*. The author turned out to have quite a sense of humor, though the man had apparently not thought much of using fire in battle.

Fire is arguably the least imaginative form of attack. Easily seen, easily countered, dangerous to self and enemy alike, it is the first choice of fools and novices. To master it, one should learn to use it as a tool first, rather than for battle, and for battle it should generally be one's last option.

"Damn," muttered Will. "He didn't beat around the bush." He flipped through the pages and then went to the index in the back to find the page numbers for actual spells. He didn't have time to spend on philosophy lessons.

He found a variety of different spells, some quite simple and others vastly more complicated. One that caught his eye was a spell that launched a small number of flaming spheres at an enemy, but when he turned to its page, it was fourth-order at least. He wouldn't have time. Eventually he settled on a third-order spell called 'bonfire.' It was essentially an enhanced fire starter that included parameters to allow the user to start as well as maintain larger fires. It wouldn't be much use in combat, but against an unmoving target it would be handy. He figured he could use it to get rid of vampire remains.

Maybe I should tell Janice not to worry about the ingredients for alchemical fire. I might not need them if I can use this spell. He'd have to bring it up when he saw her later.

With that decision made he turned to the third spell he needed to learn, the iron-body transformation. He had only glanced at it the day before, but it was as he remembered, hideously complex. It was also an old spell, and not officially rated for its difficulty, but he guessed it was at least eighth-order, or possibly even ninth. *This one could take weeks, assuming I'm even able to manage it.* He had only just succeeded with his first eighth-order spell that morning.

Will took a deep breath, then let it out slowly. It was easy to let things overwhelm him, but he'd learned to manage by breaking problems down into small pieces. Ethelgren's Illumination was doable, so he would work until he had succeeded once, then prepare it for later. After that he would memorize the bonfire spell. It was simple enough he would be able to recreate it when needed. Once those two things were done, he would spend half an hour on the new iron-body transformation.

The trick with complex spell constructs was to approach them slowly and methodically. With Selene's Solution he had done the same thing, familiarized himself, then spent a short period of time each day attempting to construct it. It was simply a matter of patience and perseverance. While most second-year students were still fussing over third- and fourth-order spells, he had just succeeded with an eighth-order spell.

Ethelgren's Illumination took him a little longer than he had anticipated, but the bonfire spell took less. After his self-imposed hour of familiarization with the iron-body spell, he used his remaining time to run through his daily practice of forming and dismissing each spell he had learned up to that point, everything from the source-link to the sleep spell. Now that included Selene's Solution as well. The point of the exercise was to ensure that he retained all the skills he had previously acquired.

Arrogan had told him that such a routine would eventually result in him being able to reflex cast almost anything he had learned, though it might take years, or even decades for the more complex spells. At the moment the only thing he could reflex cast was the point-defense shield, and that had proved enormously useful, having saved his life at least a dozen times already.

He even finished that routine with some time to spare, so he went outside and practiced the force-lance as he had been doing for months. Repetition was the key to speed, and he was sure that soon it would become the second spell he could use with just a thought.

The sun was getting low in the sky when he finally decided to stop and rest. Sitting down on an old stump that frequently served him as a chair at such times, he summoned the limnthal and sought Arrogan's advice.

"How long has it been since you asked me about the vampire storage thing?"

"That was last night. It's almost evening again, so I'll be going out again soon."

"Idiot! That means you don't have time to do anything."

Chapter 19

Will sighed. "Before you get your tail bent, let me bring you up to date." He detailed the afternoon's events, from Janice's visit and news, to his study and practice choices. It took almost ten minutes, but the ring waited patiently until he was done.

"All right, maybe you didn't do too badly," admitted the ring. "Your priorities line up pretty well with what I would have advised. Now shut up and listen. There are some things you need to be made aware of. Where are you now?"

"Outside, behind the house Selene bought."

"Move farther away, maybe a hundred yards or so, then put a force-dome around yourself."

"Can I ask why?"

"Not until you do as I say, jackass!" swore Arrogan.

"All right, fine! Calm the hell down," Will snapped, already beginning to move. After a few minutes he had found a secluded area out of sight of the house. The force-dome took him five or six seconds, and then he told the ring he was ready.

"Now, look around yourself. Make certain the area inside the force-dome is empty."

That seemed silly. "It is. I'd know if someone was next to me."

"Do it! Look carefully. You aren't looking for someone physical. You're looking for astral presences."

"Excuse me? Did you say astral presences?"

"Sorry, I should have said *asshole* presences, since obviously we have one here already. Yes, you lackwit, *astral*."

"I have no idea what that is, much less what it would look like."

"Pretend you're looking for ghosts."

"I thought ghosts weren't real."

A low growl issued from the ring. "I used to think that too, until I realized your brain died of stupidity ages ago and that I've since been listening to your ghost talk out of your ass. Just humor me."

Will did his best. "I don't see anything, but the question is, would I?"

"Probably, yes," said Arrogan. "You've demonstrated astral abilities on two occasions that I know of. The corollary of that is that if you've developed that ability to any degree you should also be able to sense others proximal to you on the astral plane."

It took Will a second to process that sentence. His vocabulary had expanded dramatically in the years since he had started studying with his grandfather, but it didn't mean he was used to using all those new words in actual conversation.

"Proximal means close or nearby," explained the ring condescendingly.

"I knew that," said Will in exasperation. "It just took me a second to sort it all out. You're talking about when I left my body after the snake bit me, right?"

"And again, when Aislinn and I were talking."

"There was a third time," offered Will. "When I was being whipped. I left my body and the goddess talked to me."

"That one sounds more like a delusion, but either way, you've definitely developed some astral ability."

"Is that a good thing?"

"Mostly, yes. Over time, a large portion of practitioners in my day would eventually develop such abilities. It was rather random to be honest. Periods of extreme stress, like nearly dying, or being whipped half to death, are excellent experiences to initiate such events, but if you live long enough, it's almost guaranteed to happen

Chapter 19

eventually. The important thing for you to know is that some people can and do use those abilities to spy, just as you did the other day."

"That was an accident," argued Will.

"Whatever. The point here is this: force effects extend across both the physical realm and the astral and ethereal realms, so if you ever want to be certain of your privacy, a force-dome like this is a must."

"Ethereal?"

"It's like the astral but it's physical, and considerably more dangerous to play around with. Let's not get into that today."

"I don't have enough context for any of what you just said to make sense," complained Will.

"You don't have much time left either, numbskull, but fine. You know about congruences, places where our plane of existence touches other worlds, like Faerie. The astral plane is one that doesn't have any congruences with our world because it touches it everywhere. It touches our world at every point. It's sort of like skin, covering every part of your body, but in this case, it covers every part of our world, as well as every other world.

"So the key here is that you won't see congruences with the astral, because it's already everywhere. Another point to remember is that it isn't a physical plane, like ours is. Only the mind or spirit, whatever you want to call it, can travel there.

"The ethereal is similar, except it actually is a physical plane and you can travel there. It's sort of like a mirror copy of our reality, except that when you're there, this world is intangible, ghost-like, and when you're here, the ethereal is intangible to you. Do you understand?"

Will rubbed his temples. "I have so many questions."

"Well, stuff them for now. We have a few high-priority things to cover before the sun goes down. Number one, your grandmother may or may not be trying to kill you."

He had gathered that from the conversation he had overheard previously. "And you think she's using the astral plane to spy on me?"

"She can't access the astral plane," said the ring. "She's fae. They quite literally don't have souls the way we—er, you—do. Their physical existence is actually a piece of the Faerie realm, so they can't separate from it and access a purely mental plane like the astral."

"Then why did you want me to use this force-dome?"

"How many friends do you have, Will? No, never mind, don't answer that. There's no point in me humiliating you by focusing on your stunted social growth. Think instead about how many people you know, how many you can ask favors of, how many owe you a debt, or could be paid to help. You're still just a child. Aislinn is powerful beyond your conception. She's regarded as a goddess in many parts of the world, and she's had centuries to cultivate allies and resources. What does this tell you?"

Will was nodding along, having already gotten the point. "She could have all sorts of different people or beings spying on me in any number of ways. Also, you have a lot of balls saying my social growth is stunted. You were a hermit when I met you."

"I used to have lots of friends," argued Arrogan, "but let's not get into what I did to them. I just want you to be aware that you can't blindly trust Aislinn."

"It's a little late for that."

"You just need to keep in mind that she's essentially insane. She's almost like two different people battling for control. One is the memory of her human self, the one who promised to stay true to her original principles as a decent

Chapter 19

human being, even as she was slowly being eroded away by the essence of Faerie. The other is what she actually is, an immortal, immoral, and ultimately selfish creature that vehemently despises the promises that her previously mortal self made before her transformation was complete."

He shook his head. "I just don't understand how she can be both."

"Imagine this as an example. Perhaps there's something dangerous about to come along, like a vampire apocalypse. Her promise forces her to help you, but she can justify a lot by telling herself that surviving such a thing without her assistance will make you stronger. A lot can be ignored by saying it's for your own good. Depending on how she stretches things, she could almost justify trying to kill you herself, or setting you up for any number of near-fatal challenges. One part of her is bound to offer you advice, while the other is actively hoping it can find something that will put you out of her misery."

Thinking back on Tailtiu's frequently murderous attempts to teach him to expect surprise attacks, he could see how Aislinn's methods might be similar on an entirely different and more terrifying scale. "Are you suggesting she engineered this vampire problem?"

Arrogan was silent for a moment. "I don't know. I can't say for certain either way, but there's a possibility of that and you should be aware of it."

"But if that's true—" Will stopped; his brain couldn't complete the thought. Finally, he burst out, "Tailtiu is her daughter!"

"Maybe that was accidental. Then again, maybe she felt Tailtiu was helping you too much. Either way, I can assure you she won't feel a thing no matter what happens to her daughter."

The sky was growing steadily darker, prompting Will to hurry. "So what do you think I should focus on right now?"

"First, you guarded that bastard Nerrow's house last night. There was an attack, but what about elsewhere? Was there a slaughter like I predicted? Were there a few attacks or many? You need to keep your eye on the bigger picture. Laina Nerrow may just be a small part of the story."

Will hadn't inquired about any of that. *But I should have.* There were simply too many things that needed to be done, and he was only one person. "I'll find out what I can in the morning." Then he released the limnthal, dismissed the force-dome, and headed back to the house. Tiny was waiting for him.

Chapter 20

That night passed uneventfully. Will was glad to see that Darla had resumed her watch across the street, but she didn't come over to speak to them, and they returned the favor. While he hadn't really wanted anything to happen, as the sun began to brighten the horizon, he felt as though he'd wasted the night. He could have slept, or prepared, or done something useful.

When they got home, they found Blake waiting for them, along with Janice, who apparently had some news. Blake spoke first, though. "I made more porridge," he announced.

Tiny was starving, as usual, and he grinned at the information. "Thanks!"

Will knew him for a fool, though, and when they began to eat, he was vindicated in his belief. The porridge was bad, but not lethal. Blake watched intently as they ate, while Janice looked on with pity, for she had already had a portion before their arrival.

"How is it?" asked the manservant anxiously.

"Not bad," said Tiny graciously.

Everyone held their breath as all eyes turned to Will. After a moment he responded, "Well, if I had to eat this every day I wouldn't starve to death, but I would probably wish that I could. It's better than what you tried to poison Tiny with yesterday, though, so that's something."

"It's not that bad, is it?" asked Blake.

"You do realize that salt pork is salty, right? You don't have to add additional salt if you use that with it. Also, you burned the onions."

"I did?"

"That's where the bitterness came from," explained Will. Just out of Blake's line of sight, he could see Janice nodding in silent agreement, though she was too tactful to say anything out loud.

Despite Will's complaints, the porridge was still edible, and he was tired and hungry, so he ate. Janice waited, clearly anxious to share her news, and Will obliged by forcing the porridge down as quickly as he could manage. The upside was that he didn't have to taste it as much that way. "All right," he said at last. "It's obvious you're excited. What did you discover? Is it something about the relic?"

She shook her head. "No, something completely unexpected. I went to arrange for the alchemy supplies, and when I asked about the white phosphorous, Professor Karlovic told me that it had all been bought up."

That caught his attention. "Could it have been the military? Lognion has obviously been preparing for this. Blake told me he had ordered a lot of weapons with silver inlay."

"The professor said that the military maintains a separate supply since they use alchemical fire for some of their standard operations. This was bought by a private merchant in the city just a couple of weeks ago."

"Before we knew anything about this," muttered Will. An image flashed in his mind for a second, the vial of alchemical fire that had been thrown at the Nerrow home. It hadn't occurred to him at the time, but the glass vial was much like the ones he had bought from Wurthaven. They were produced by a local glass blower. The alchemical fire had been made in Cerria.

Tracing the maker down through sales of vials probably wouldn't be practical, but finding the merchant

Chapter 20

who bought the rare and dangerous white phosphorous was a sure lead. He started to say something, but Janice spoke first. "I have the merchant's name here." She pushed a piece of paper across the table. On it was written a name, "Factor Jorn Slidden." It was followed by an address close to the central market in the city. "He's a trader," explained Janice. "He keeps a warehouse by the river docks too and does a lot of business in a variety of commodities, though he specializes in wool. White phosphorous isn't part of what I think would be his usual business."

Will nodded. "So he probably served as a buyer for whoever the alchemist was that produced the alchemical fire. Did Karlovic say how much he bought?"

"Something close to two hundred pounds, all that they had," she informed him.

"That's enough for thousands of vials," said Will.

Blake chimed in, "When I was doing special service, we used it quite often. You can wreck a city's hierarchy and control structure with a few judiciously placed fires. Burn out the right homes or businesses and you can sow chaos and throw the government into disarray. Use more and you can start fires so big the whole city will burn. We usually preferred not to cause massive casualties like that, since they could be politically counterproductive, but you don't know what the enemy's objective is here."

"I'm starting to feel alarmed," said Will in a dry tone.

Tiny jumped in. "You're just now feeling alarmed? I started the other night when that thing tried to rip my face off!"

Will smiled. "I was being sarcastic." He turned to Janice. "You found out a lot about the trader pretty quickly."

"I skipped class. Rob was a big help too," she answered.

"Rob?"

"Who would you ask if you want to know about the latest gossip? Plus, he knows a lot of people. He ferreted out most of the information about Jorn within the first hour of me asking. I think he feels bad about jumping down your throat the other day," said Janice.

"Did you tell him about the vampires?" asked Will.

She shook her head. "No, but he knows something crazy is going on."

"How?"

"Because you're involved, and I wouldn't answer his questions. He took everything very seriously, even though I know he must have been annoyed."

Will felt even guiltier regarding his friend. "If you see him later, tell him I'm sorry, and next time he should come with you. I'll explain everything to him."

"So I should tell him about the vampires?" she asked.

He nodded, yawning. Glancing over, he could see Tiny struggling to keep his eyes open. "We should get some rest."

Tiny got to his feet. They were both still clad in their armor. "I'll see to our gear. You should bathe first this time."

Will smiled. "Why don't we all take a bath together?" Most of them frowned at that remark, but Janice's eyes were glued to his palm, where a complex spell was slowly coming together. As he got close to completion, the structure trembled slightly on the verge of falling apart, but it stabilized again, and Will invested the turyn necessary to make it work. Seconds later, the magic expanded, taking in the room and his friends.

He was rewarded with a series of gasps, followed by some 'oohs' and 'ahs'. Selene's spell was not only effective, it was pleasant to experience firsthand, unlike most cleaning spells. Janice eyed him appreciatively. "You finally did it! When did that happen?"

"Yesterday," said Will. "I've been trying for almost a year now."

Chapter 20

"I'm still struggling with fifth-order spells," she said enviously.

He grinned. "You spend too much time in the library."

She narrowed her eyes. "It also helps that you can waste turyn without worrying about your health, and that you train constantly."

"Don't let Sir Kyle find out about this," cautioned Tiny with a chuckle. He was studying his armor closely. "He'll convince them to conscript you again and you'll spend the rest of your days cleaning and maintaining armor for the army."

Blake was staring at the table. "Even the bowls are clean!"

"I did the whole room," said Will. "It took more energy, but you'll find that the floor is clean too and everything else has been dusted."

"How about the rest of the house?" asked the manservant hopefully.

"I'm tired and you need a job. I'm headed to bed," said Will with a tone of finality.

***

Selene fell into her bed, her nerves frayed, and her body exhausted. The skin of her hands felt raw from scrubbing floors. Floors she could have cleaned in seconds if she had been allowed to use her magic.

The room was dim, and she was alone, terribly alone, inside and out. Seeing Will had only reminded her of how miserable she was. The people she worked for treated her like garbage at the best of times, and the rest of the time they insulted her to her face, calling her a 'drab.'

She had held up well for the first few months, but her emotional endurance was beginning to fail her. If it hadn't been for Sylandrea, she would have cracked already. He was the only one who treated her with a modicum of respect.

As often happened, thinking of him brightened her mood for a moment, and she saw an image of him in her mind. Long, slender limbs with just the right amount of muscle, graceful shoulders that supported a face that any artist would kill to paint.

She could see him standing in the doorway, looking at her with concern as the light flooded in from behind him, illuminating his golden hair. *I'm dreaming again,* she reminded herself.

"Are you well?" came a distinctly masculine voice. The words were slow and stilted, spoken by lips that hadn't yet mastered the intricacies of her tongue.

Selene sat up in alarm, realizing it wasn't a dream. "Syl? Is that you?"

He closed the door and crossed the room quickly, seeming to glide across the floor. "I was worried about you. You seemed dispirited when I saw you earlier."

She knew it was inappropriate, even in his culture, for a man to enter a woman's room, even that of a drab, but in that moment she didn't care. Something about his kindness coaxed a sob from her throat. Leaning forward, she threw her arms around his waist.

He stiffened for a moment, then embraced her shoulders. A moment later, she felt his delicate fingers running through her hair, and a shiver went up her spine. Her heartbeat quickened. She held on, not daring to look up, to meet his eyes. If she did, he would see the desire in them and that would be the end of their friendship. His kind didn't associate with drabs, much less touch them. *Then why is he touching me now?* she wondered.

His fingers laced through the hair at the back of her head and tightened as he pulled her head back. She gasped

Chapter 20

at the sudden pain, and then their eyes locked. Leaning down, he crushed his mouth against hers, his tongue diving in. She fought him for a moment, but then he pulled away, leaving her gasping. "Wait," she told him. "I'm confused."

He watched her with burning eyes. "Tell me what you want."

"I'm not sure," she replied, but her hands were moving across his back. At some point she had slipped them under his shirt without even realizing it. She needed the contact, the feeling of another living being. She needed him.

Her arms were pulling him closer, eager to enfold him. She could feel his fingers sliding up the inside of her skirt, sending delightful shivers of pleasure along her nerves.

And then she began to cry, even as she peeled his shirt away so she could kiss his chest. The tears flowed silently, though she couldn't stop herself. Her passion was too great.

"William, I'm sorry," she said softly, whispering in her lover's ear.

"William! Wake up!"

***

Will's eyes shot wide as he started awake. His face was hot and puffy, his throat still half choked by the sobs working their way up from his diaphragm. Janice was beside him, staring down from where she sat at the bedside. Her hand was on his chest, shaking him. "Are you all right? You were having a nightmare."

He could hardly think. He felt broken, angry, upset, and paradoxically—somewhat aroused. *Don't forget embarrassed,* he told himself as he turned his head to wipe his eyes on a pillow. Janice's hand was still on his chest, burning like a hot brand. He sat up in the bed, catching the sheet before it fell to his waist, and Janice pulled her hand away. "Are you all right?" she asked again.

"I'm not sure," he admitted. "It felt real. Why are you in here?"

"I came a little while ago. Your manservant said he would wake you, but then he decided he would make lunch first to surprise you. I snuck away so I could warn you."

"You should have knocked," he admonished her, pulling the coverlets closer to cover an even more embarrassing morning reaction.

Janice scowled. "I did, but then I heard you moaning and whimpering through the door. I wasn't sure what had happened to you." A sudden click announced the arrival of yet another person in Will's bedroom. Janice leapt to her feet while Will took the opportunity to pull yet more covers over himself.

Tiny stood in the doorway, his mouth agape. Janice flushed red instantly. "It isn't anything strange," she blurted out. "I was just waking him up."

The big man's mouth slowly closed, though his expression remained blank. Without a word, he backed out and gently shut the door.

"That's really all it was!" she called out loudly, then she whirled around to appeal to Will. "Tell him that—" Her words cut off as she saw that Will had piled several pillows around his waist, as though trying to hide something. "Is that?"

It was his turn to blush then. "I have to pee! Will you get out, please!"

Janice fled the room.

Chapter 21

Will, Blake, Tiny, and Janice sat at the dining table that seemed to be sinking beneath the weight of a ponderous and awkward silence. Blake's third attempt at oat porridge sat in bowls in front of them, but no one had the heart to complain.

Tiny slowly and methodically spooned the food into his mouth, his eyes firmly on the bowl in front of him, as though it was the only thing that existed.

No one said anything for some time. Will took a few bites, absently noting that the porridge was marginally better than what Blake had made that morning. He would have complained, but when he opened his mouth to speak the first words that came out were spoken in a sullen tone. "I had to pee."

Janice's cheeks colored again. "Will you shut up!" She looked at the others anxiously. "I only meant to knock and wake him, but then I heard him weeping piteously. I didn't know what had happened."

"I wasn't weeping," argued Will stubbornly.

"Sobbing loudly, then," she amended.

"It was a sad dream, but I wasn't crying."

Tiny finished his bowl, scraping the bottom to be sure he had gotten everything. Once he was sure it was empty, he set it aside and looked at them. Will had lost his desire to eat, so he pushed his still mostly full bowl across the table to the big man. Tiny picked his spoon back up, his eyes traveling to Janice's face, to Will's, and then back to his bowl. Without a word he began to eat again.

Blake leaned toward the big warrior, evidently unable to contain himself. "So, let me get this straight. You walked in and found her at the bedside, where Will was loudly crying to himself while trying to hide his tumescent growth?"

Janice paled. Will shot to his feet, angry. "I think it's time for you to clean the dishes," he snapped coldly. Reaching out, he pushed the bowls toward the manservant, including the one Tiny was still eating from. "Now."

Blake smirked and gathered the wooden bowls into his hands. Tiny watched him go, his expression forlorn as the half-eaten porridge left the room. "Hey…" He looked back at the others. "I was still hungry."

Janice addressed him earnestly, "You know nothing inappropriate was going on upstairs, don't you?"

The big warrior sighed. "Miss Edelman…"

"Janice."

"Janice," Tiny corrected himself. "I don't know you that well yet, but you seem like a very proper lady. I do know Will, however, and it never even crossed my mind to think that he might be trying to do anything of that nature. I do find it amusing how desperately the two of you want to make sure everyone knows that nothing was happening, but to be honest, what I care about most right now is that I'm still famished."

"I'll make something," said Will, feeling guilty.

Janice waggled her finger at him. "You have more important things to be working on, I believe." She took a deep breath, as though gathering her courage, then looked at Tiny. "Come along, Mister Shaw. I know a stand that sells hot sausages. I'll make amends for your lost lunch."

Tiny smiled at her. "I told you, call me Tiny."

A moment later, the two of them were gone and Will was left alone, feeling mildly annoyed at having been left

Chapter 21

out. *Or am I jealous?* He shook his head. That couldn't be the case. Heading upstairs, he took out his journals and began running through his practice routines. Two hours later and he had gone through everything and was back out behind the house, practicing his force-lance.

As he did, he saw two men walk down the lane and go to the front door. A moment later he heard the door open as Blake let them inside. *What's that about?* he wondered. Going in the back door, he walked to the front parlor where he found them talking.

"Let me show you the area I'm talking about," said Blake as Will entered the room.

"What's all this?" he asked.

Blake looked over at him. "This is Tom and Brad Gravlin. They're here to look at the cellar." The two men dipped their heads, touching their fingers to their brows in a sign of respect.

"I'll come with you," said Will.

Blake glanced away, then leaned in. "Begging your pardon, sir, but I'd rather you leave it to me. Trust me. I've handled things like this before, and you have other things to occupy your valuable time."

Will straightened. "Oh." He watched them leave the parlor, heading back out the front door so Blake could walk them around to the cellar door. "Damn," he muttered to himself. "Is this what it's like being a lord?" It was a strange sensation, as though he was unwanted, or perhaps useless.

Since the three men were standing around beside the house, he didn't feel like going back out to practice in front of them. So instead he took a walk to find a secluded place where he could talk to Arrogan. Once he was sure he was unobserved, he raised a force-dome and checked for presences. He still had no idea whether he could actually see whatever it was they looked like, but he did it anyway. Then he summoned the limnthal. "There weren't any attacks last night," he said without preamble.

"No attacks where you were, or no attacks in the city?"

"No attacks where I was, but I didn't hear about any others either. I have someone looking into it now, so I'll know more later. Also, I think I've got a lead that might help me find the vampires." He explained Janice's discovery regarding the white phosphorous buyer.

When he finished, the ring took a moment to digest everything. "None of that sounds good."

"Except the fact that at least I have somewhere to start looking."

"That's nice, but what really worries me is that there hasn't been a slaughter as I predicted a few days ago."

Will frowned. "Are you disappointed that a bunch of people haven't died?"

"No, but I'm more worried that whoever is in charge is obviously smart enough to keep his underlings from nibbling on their fae captive. First, you have to realize that for them, she's more tempting than a steak to a dog. The inexperienced ones would lose control immediately. That means that either all the vampires that have come to the city are old and wise, or that the one in charge has an incredible degree of control over his underlings."

"That sounds more dangerous for me," said Will, "but safer for the city as a whole."

"Safer for the vampires too. If the public becomes aware of them, the citizens are liable to turn the city upside down ferreting them out. In a panic like that, they'll get every last one of the vampires and probably kill a lot of innocent people along the way. A mob rarely thinks clearly."

Will was only listening with half an ear. He knew it was selfish and in the grand scheme of things, unimportant,

Chapter 21

but all he could think about was his dream of Selene. It had felt intensely real. Without warning, he changed the subject. "Is it possible to travel astrally while asleep?"

"Define travel for me," said Arrogan cautiously.

"Could I accidentally leave my body and travel to another place, even if I don't know where it is?"

Although the ring didn't have lungs, or need to breathe, it released an audible sigh. "Yes, that's possible and very dangerous."

"Even though I don't know where she is?"

"You saw Selene?"

Will's chest cramped suddenly, as though his heart had tightened into a solid lump. It took him a moment to reply. "I think I did."

Arrogan must have heard the emotion in his voice, for he answered carefully. "Listen to me, Will. Astral travel while sleeping is dangerous on multiple levels. Obviously you returned safely, so I'll move on to the less obvious dangers."

"What are the obvious dangers?"

"Getting lost and dying in your sleep. Can I finish?" Arrogan sounded mildly exasperated. "The big problem is that since you were asleep, you don't know where the line is between what you observed and what you merely dreamt. Do you understand? Because of your anxiety or fear, you may have seen her but mixed it all together with a nightmare."

"How do you know I saw something bad?"

"Because you sound like a man who just watched his house burn down."

"Could it have all been real?"

"Maybe. The best thing you can do is put it out of your mind until you see her again. Fretting over it won't do you any good."

"All right, one more question, though. How did I find her if I didn't even know where she was?"

"It's a mental dimension. There are no physical places. You've learned already that you move by focusing your attention on people; the same thing applies. Your mind took you to her. In contrast, going to a place rather than a person is incredibly difficult. Usually it's impossible unless you have a lot of memories in a particular spot. So, most of the time, the only places you can go are places where there's someone you know very well."

Inspiration struck him. "Could I find Tailtiu that way?"

"I wouldn't recommend it. First, it probably wouldn't work because it's unlikely that you've developed the necessary bond."

"She's family," insisted Will.

"No, William, she isn't. I've been telling you that since the beginning. She's only my daughter in the most technical sense. When Aislinn went to live in Faerie, our child was slowly replaced by the essence of that realm. My true daughter died in the womb, replaced by something unable to truly understand love, affection, or mortality. Even if you care for her, she'll never feel the same way about you."

At some level, Will knew Arrogan's counsel was the truth, but on another he couldn't accept it. "Maybe Aislinn is twisted, but Tailtiu isn't," he argued. "She may not be human, but I know she cares on a certain level. Maybe not the way I do, but she isn't as heartless as you think."

"The proof will be in the fact that you won't be able to find her by projecting yourself astrally," said Arrogan firmly.

"You're suggesting I don't really care about her?"

"No, I'm suggesting she doesn't really care about you. The bond, relationship—whatever you want to call it—it has to work both ways. It doesn't necessarily have to be love either. Any strong emotion can forge a link, but it has to be reciprocal. Whatever you feel for my changeling

Chapter 21

daughter won't be reciprocated, because she doesn't have true emotions."

"We'll see when I test the theory." He paused for a moment, then asked, "How do I test the theory?"

An evil cackle issued from the ring. "I'm not helping you. Go ask your father-in-law to whip you half to death. It worked once, maybe it will work again. I will tell you this. You need to learn a spell to protect yourself against possession."

"Possession? Why?"

"Because although those spells are meant to keep others out of your body, they also work to keep *you* inside. Now that you've gotten so sensitive that you're projecting in your sleep, you need to start taking measures to keep yourself from traveling inadvertently. Other than that piece of advice I'm not going to help you. It's too dangerous. One of those vampires is almost certainly a wizard, and maybe not one of the piss-ant variety they have these days. If it senses you trespassing, you could be banished. While that won't kill you, it will hurt you badly."

"How does banishment work?"

"Look up the spells," said Arrogan. "The important thing to know is that it's very much a contest of wills, except the person casting the spell has the upper hand usually. If you're not certain you're a lot stronger than the person doing the banishing, don't fight it, just go with the flow, otherwise the damage could be much worse."

"So there's spells to keep me from leaving my body at night, and there's spells to banish someone, what about to initiate an astral projection?"

"I wouldn't tell you if there was, but in this case, I don't have to lie. There aren't any. It's an ability you have to figure out for yourself. I still recommend you wait a few years. You have too many other things to learn before you should bother risking yourself on something like this."

"It might be the only way to find her," said Will.

"No. Because it won't work. You'll see. You'll just be risking yourself for no purpose."

Will released the limnthal, ending his conversation. Arrogan had been confident he wouldn't be able to project himself out of his body of his own volition, and from his previous attempt he knew it wouldn't be easy, but the ring's remark about letting the king whip him had given him an idea. Repeat the conditions of one of the instances in which he had left his body, and he might be able to do it again.

With a faint grin, he turned and walked back to the house. The workmen were gone and Tiny was back with Janice. He found them gathered in the parlor and saw they had brought someone else with them.

Rob gave him a shy wave as Will entered. Surprised, Will stopped for a moment. "Glad you're here," he said at last.

"Sorry about last time," said Rob. "I was really angry at myself, but I took it out on you."

Will shook his head. "No, you were right. I've been an ass. Did they tell you about...?"

Rob nodded. "Yes, and to be honest, I'm scared shitless."

"We all are," agreed Tiny.

"But you've faced them already," said Rob, seeming surprised.

The big man shrugged. "Just because I'm big and covered in steel doesn't mean I don't need to change my trousers after fighting something like that."

Will snorted. "You didn't shit yourself." After a second, he added, "But I wouldn't blame you if you did. I was scared out of my mind. By the way, I have an idea for what to do next."

Chapter 21

Tiny grimaced. "Do I need my armor?"

Will smiled. "Yes, but it's just a precaution."

"Do you want me to go?" asked Rob, his Adam's apple bobbing as he swallowed nervously.

"I appreciate the offer, but no. I need your particular skills for a different task." He quickly laid out his simple plan. Tiny would accompany him to the trader's warehouse, where he would attempt to enter by asking to buy some of the phosphorous. The large squire would stay close by, hidden by a chameleon spell and ready to intervene if things went badly. Meanwhile Rob would spend the rest of the day gathering news from around the city.

Ordinarily Rob was only interested in the big things—the doings of nobility, scandals, or items that involved the college. Will wanted him to see if he could discover whether there had been an increase in things like people going missing. If the vampires had been careful, it might not be easy, for they would have stuck to prey that wouldn't be missed. Will left it to his friend to figure out the best way to suss out that information.

When he finished, Janice asked, "What about me? I don't get a job?"

"You make your own job," said Will. "You're the one who discovered the phosphorous trader. You're the one who looked into Ethelgren. Keep nosing around. Whatever you decide to research, I have a feeling you'll come up with something useful."

She sniffed. "I can't decide whether that's a compliment or a fancy dismissal."

"Definitely a compliment," affirmed Tiny solicitously. "He doesn't have the finesse to make subtle insults."

Will sighed. "But apparently you do. Come on, let's go. We only have a few hours of daylight left."

Chapter 22

The warehouse district wasn't an area Will went to often. The last time he'd spent any time there, he had been attacked by a gang of thugs hired to separate him from his remaining years. Ordinarily he had no reason to go there, so it wasn't that he'd been actively avoiding that part of the city. *But if I did have a reason to come here, I would avoid it anyway,* he observed silently.

It was a rough part of Cerria, but generally it wasn't dangerous. Will had just developed a dislike for the area. Tiny noticed the change in his posture. "What's wrong?"

"Bad memories," said Will. "And you aren't supposed to be talking. You're trying not to be seen or heard."

There wasn't anyone close by, so Tiny replied anyway, "Do you know how hard it is to walk this slowly when you're my size?"

Will ignored him, moving ahead and then loitering at the next corner while Tiny slowly caught up. Despite his complaints, the big warrior was doing fairly well. The silent-armor spell made a big difference, and watching him gave Will a lot of useful feedback for the next time he used the chameleon spell on himself.

One thing he had noticed was that the spell was most effective when the subject stayed close to a static background such as a wall or a building. Standing in the middle of open spaces could lead to all sorts of complications that the spell couldn't compensate for, such as people suddenly walking behind the camouflaged individual. An observer on the opposite side would notice something like that immediately.

When they finally arrived at the correct address, Will saw that the building in question was a large, two-story wood frame structure with a stone exterior that only extended up to about six feet from the ground. The side facing them was almost fifty yards in length, and from what he could tell the warehouse was probably the same length along its other sides. He wondered if it was two levels inside or just one with a high ceiling.

The side they approached from faced the street and had several doors. Two of the doors were large enough for wagons to pass through, though they were locked and barred. On the far-left side was a smaller door of the more ordinary variety. It was also locked, so Will began vigorously pulling on a bell rope that had been mounted beside it.

After a couple of minutes, a voice shouted through the door. "Who is it?"

"A customer. I'm looking for Jorn," said Will, speaking loudly to be heard through the heavy oak.

"This is a warehouse. Try his shop at the market."

"They sent me here," shouted Will. "Is he here or not?"

There was a long pause, then the voice replied, "He left the city last week."

"Then why did you tell me to go to the shop? You already knew he wasn't there."

"They're the ones that deal with customers. I'm just a loader. Go away."

Will debated with himself, unsure how aggressive he should be. "You won't even open the door? I don't even know who I'm talking to!"

"Not my problem. Fuck off."

Will glanced at the spot where Tiny was standing. Then he shook his head negatively. He wanted to use a force-lance to ruin the lock and enter, but the building was huge. If he forced his way in, they might not be able to handle the resistance if there were a lot of employees or worse, vampires, inside. Worse, if they tried and failed, he would have warned them that their location was no longer a secret. During the night they might relocate.

Reluctantly, he led Tiny away. Twenty minutes later, they were close to the school gates and Will canceled the camouflage spell so his friend could walk normally.

The big man had a suggestion. "Why don't I wait out here?"

Will smiled. "You're worried I'll make you climb the wall if you come in and we leave after dark?"

Tiny nodded.

"It might be a while before I come back," warned Will. "I have something else I intend to do before leaving, so you may have to wait a couple of hours."

Tiny looked up at the wall. "It's worth it if I don't have to scale that damned wall again."

"Have it your way." He left Tiny there and headed for home, moving at a brisk pace. There wasn't much time to waste. As soon as he reached the house, Blake greeted him at the door. "Welcome back. Where's Tiny?"

"He's waiting outside the school grounds. Is Janice here?"

"She's using your study."

"Perfect. I'll need her help with something, and it may take a while. Make sure we aren't interrupted."

Blake's brow twitched, though he kept his expression flat. "How long?"

"An hour or two possibly," Will replied. "Unless there's an emergency, don't disturb us. Don't even knock." He paused when he saw the manservant's face darken. "It's nothing like that."

Chapter 22

"I didn't say anything, sir," responded Blake, his voice uncharacteristically toneless.

"Listen, you should know me better by now. That business this morning was just a misunderstanding."

Blake nodded. "As I assumed, though if a pattern emerges your behavior will come under more scrutiny."

Will groaned. "Whatever. I answer to my conscience and Selene. Think what you like." He moved past the man and headed for the stairs. *I don't have time for propriety,* he told himself. The door to the study was open, and he strode in without pausing to make any noise.

Janice started slightly when she saw him enter. "You're back."

"I need your help."

She nodded. "Certainly. What is it?"

"Something only you can help me with." He glanced around the study, examining the chairs and the floor. "Hmm, we could do it in here, but the bed might be more comfortable."

Janice made no attempt to hide her reaction. One brow shot up immediately. "Exactly what sort of help are you asking me for?"

"It's nothing like that. I need some peace and quiet to do some experimenting. Blake will make sure we aren't disturbed, and with your help I think I have a way to release myself—"

"Excuse me?"

"From my physical bounds," he finished. "Stop thinking about this morning. I plan to try and project my spirit outside of my body."

Her grin made it clear she had been teasing him. "I wasn't thinking about this morning. So, you're planning to lie on the bed when you do this?"

"That would probably be best."

"As long as you don't have to pee."

Will groaned. "I'm never going to live that down, am I?"

"Not for the foreseeable future at least. Explain to me how you plan to do this. Is it some restricted spell you stole? I haven't heard of it before."

He shook his head. "I'll explain later. The main thing I need you to do is help me cheat. I want to recreate the situation that caused me to leave my body last time. Here's my idea. I'm sure you know the source-link spell—"

"Of course," she interrupted smugly.

"—and you know how to use it to paralyze someone."

"No," she said, changing her tone. "They talked about that, but we never practiced it."

"No problem," said Will. "I can talk you through it, but I'll need you to go a little farther and disconnect me from my source *and* my physical senses."

"Whoa," she said, holding up one hand. "Couldn't that kill you? Separating you from your source?"

He shook his head. "No, it's still there, supporting the body. You'll just be blocking my access to it."

"But then you won't be able to use magic. That doesn't make any sense."

"This isn't really magic, per se. Just help me. I'll explain what I know later."

"Why are you in such a hurry? It's almost nightfall. Wouldn't it be better to do it tomorrow?"

"I'm going to try and find Tailtiu. They wouldn't let us into the warehouse. They wouldn't even open the door. If I can see her and get some clue from what's around her, I'll have a better idea whether we should try forcing our way in, or whether we should search elsewhere. It's already been days. Who knows what kind of shape she's in?"

Chapter 22

Ten minutes later and Will was lying on his bed while Janice stared down at him once again. This time, however, he was fully clothed, wide awake, and not in desperate need of a place to relieve his bladder. As expected, Janice was a quick study and had already succeeded in paralyzing him twice. Separating him from his source was a little trickier, though.

"I have no idea what I'm doing," she complained.

"It isn't something that's easy to visualize," he told her. "It might be easier if you experience it yourself. Lie down on the bed and I'll show you."

Her eyes were full of warnings, but she said nothing.

"Blake won't walk in. Hurry up. The sooner you learn, the sooner I can find Tailtiu." After a moment she lay down beside him, her eyes on the ceiling. The source-link she had created was still active between them, so Will wrested control from her and reversed the link. Then he paralyzed her and proceeded to sever her link to her source.

She panicked, though the only visible sign was her eyes rolling wildly in her head—they were the only thing she still controlled. He could feel her will bucking wildly within her, desperate to regain contact with her source. He kept his voice calm. "It's disconcerting, but try to remember the feeling. I want you to do the same thing to me, plus this." As he finished the sentence, he went further, cutting off her access to her senses.

Her eyes went still, but through the link he could feel her emotional turmoil. Despite knowing what he was doing, knowing that he was a friend, terror had taken hold. Feeling guilty, he released her.

She shot up into a sitting position, gasping loudly as her chest drew in a huge lungful of air. She caught herself and suppressed the scream that almost followed, turning it into a slower exhalation of air. Janice hyperventilated briefly until she could eventually regain her composure. The look on her face as she stared at Will was anything but happy. "Please don't ever do that again!"

"Which part?"

"Any of it. How did you take over the link like that? That surprised me, then you took everything else! I was sort of all right, until it all went black. I don't think I've ever been so terrified in my life."

"Control of the link is a matter of will. The initiator has a slight advantage, but unless they're close to the strength of the person that they're holding, they won't be able to maintain it in a contest."

"I've been attaching to you easily enough, though."

"That's because I'm cooperating. It isn't a matter of skill. It's a matter of *will*, which is something that comes from time, experience, and what type of training you do."

She stared at him thoughtfully. "Well you don't have me on time or experience, so it must be whatever weird training your original master gave you, right?"

He grinned. "Probably."

"Maybe you can teach me someday?"

"Maybe. It was pretty horrible, not to mention risky. Let's talk about that some other time." They returned to practicing, and after another twenty minutes Janice eventually had the hang of how to do what he wanted.

"All right," he told her. "Let's do it again, but this time don't release it. Keep me locked inside myself."

"For how long?" she asked.

That was an excellent question, one for which he didn't have a good answer. Once she had locked him inside himself and disconnected him from his own source and senses, he would have no way to signal Janice when he wanted her to release him. He thought about it for a

Chapter 22

minute, then made up his mind. "Give it fifteen minutes. If it hasn't been long enough then I'll ask you to do it again."

"And if it has been long enough?"

"Then I won't say anything. I'll seem like I'm asleep, or dead maybe. I'm not sure what my body will be like exactly, since I hopefully won't be in it."

"Are you sure this is safe?"

"Perfectly," he lied, but when Janice tilted her chin downward in disbelief, he stopped. "It's a little risky. I've only done it a few times before, and those were by accident."

She seemed pleased by the honesty, but not completely swayed. "Tell me again why I should help you do this if it puts you at risk."

"Because it's the only chance I have to help someone I care about."

"A fae woman who couldn't possibly return the same concern," clarified Janice.

"If she doesn't, it won't work," said Will. "There has to be some sort of bond between us for me to find her."

She seemed to come to a decision, and when she spoke again it was with no uncertainty in her voice. "Lie down and close your eyes."

CHAPTER 23

Wrapped in a void, Will could sense nothing of the outside world. Losing his vision wouldn't have been too bad on its own, but he couldn't feel his body either, and perhaps most disconcerting, his source was gone. There was nothing left of him but a disembodied mind trapped in a sea of darkness.

Unlike the first time he had experienced it, he wasn't panicked. When Aislinn had done it to him, it had been sudden and without him understanding what she was about to do. This time he had chosen it. Hopefully terror wasn't the key factor. If it was, he likely wouldn't succeed.

Rather than try to reach Tailtiu immediately, Will envisioned Janice in his mind. She was close, and they were friends, so there was no doubt in his mind that there was a connection between them. Focusing on her, he began to feel a pressure, as though he was trapped inside a bubble and fighting to pull himself out. It was similar to what he had felt when he had deliberately tried to escape his body, but it wasn't as strong this time.

Losing all physical sense of myself must weaken the barrier, he thought, promptly losing his image of Janice. He tried again, keeping his mental image firm this time. Once more the pressure built, and then with a sudden rush of light, he was out.

Janice sat beside him on the bed, her face worried as she looked down on him. With a little effort and a few false starts, Will managed to position himself above his body but close enough that he could see her expression clearly. *Ouch,* he thought as he caught sight of the redness of her eyes. *Why is she so upset? She knows I'm still fine.*

He would have to ask her later. Clearing his mind, he imagined his fae aunt. Her face wouldn't come to him at first, strangely. Normally he was confident of his imagination, but only an empty, gray space existed where her image should be. *No, it's there. It has to be.*

Yet as much as he tried, the memory of her features wouldn't appear, and a seed of doubt crept into his heart. Had Arrogan been right? Was she truly soulless, heartless—uncaring? No, he wouldn't believe it.

He kept trying, and though her face wouldn't appear, he began to hear a faint murmuring, as though someone was whispering just out of view. *"I don't care. I'll kill you all. There is no pain. Set me free and your death will follow."* The words became clearer the longer he listened, sounding like a litany of cruelty and anger, as though a murderous madman's thoughts were being shown to the world.

But the voice wasn't that of a madman. He recognized it. It was pain, his pain. It was his anger too, burning like a sullen ember in the center of his being, desperately wishing it could escape. With the knowledge of its existence, he realized he had a choice, feed the flames, or accept the pain without letting it dictate his actions.

Neither course would heal the wound. Neither would end the suffering, but one choice would offer the illusion of free will while allowing his pain to control him. The other offered freedom, complete with the unavoidable pain of living.

Inside himself, he reached out, embracing the ember and pulling it inward. It was like a small child, hurt and angry, not understanding the world that had wounded it. Will held it to his bosom, trying to convey the feeling to his innermost self, *you are not alone. I am here with you.*

The words grew louder as the litany continued to repeat, but now he realized the voice was no longer his own, if it ever had been. It was Tailtiu. He listened, and then he tried to call to her. *Tailtiu, Tailtiu, Tailtiu, thrice called. Hear me.*

The pain grew intense, coloring his inner world with a searing, white light that exploded outward, blinding him. Then it faded, and two eyes appeared, green with cat's eye pupils. The pain throbbed at the center of his being, and the eyes receded slightly, while the image of a woman's face grew around them.

Will was in a place of darkness, and his aunt lay on the floor in front of him. Her features were gaunt, emaciated, almost lifeless, as she sprawled like a broken doll. Cruel iron chains held her wrists and ankles, and the skin was black around them. She was in the corner of a large building, chained to the massive wooden supports that framed the wall. Off to the side, Will could see pallets stacked with a variety of crates and boxes.

It was a warehouse.

As he watched her, Tailtiu's eyes glittered, focusing on him somehow, and when their gazes locked, he felt something click inside himself. The sullen ember of his pain flared within him as it connected with whatever was inside the fae woman. His aunt's eyes changed, welling with tears, and her lips formed silent words. "Will? It hurts."

Her features twisted as the pain began to register within her. Somehow Will understood, knowing without being aware of where the knowledge came from. The pain, her pain, had been invisible, unfelt, unknown to

Chapter 23

her—but Tailtiu was beginning to feel it now. Something had changed.

Her pain grew, and as it did, she began to wail. A scream built, though she didn't have the strength to express it. Instead it manifested as a breathless, coarse moan, horrifying by virtue of its very impotence. Nearby, Will heard movement, as something drew closer to investigate the sound. He tried to turn and see the source of the sound, but his point of view remain fixed on the vision of his dying aunt.

"She's screaming," said a voice, brimming with curiosity. "That's new."

Another voice chuckled as it replied, "She can't even scream properly, but I still want to make it stop."

"We can't touch her. Liss will rip our hearts out if we do."

"He's a fool. Look at her! I know you can smell it. He's trying to keep it all to himself."

"Don't be stupid. He said the fae were like a drug. I know you've tried balung before. It's like that."

"It doesn't do anything to me now. There's nothing left but blood—blood and whatever it is that's inside that fae girl. It smells incredible."

"You're right about that, but we still can't risk it. What are you doing?" Will heard the sound of something move, perhaps that of a step being taken.

"It isn't a drug. Liss lied to us. You know why? Because it's really power. She's full of it, and whoever takes her will grow with it."

Will saw the creature when it rushed forward, falling on Tailtiu's frail body. It was the body of a man, heavy-set and bald. As his head leaned down, Will both saw and felt the fangs pierce Tailtiu's flesh. A moan sounded behind him, and a second form rushed forward from the darkness to latch onto one of her legs. Seconds later and the darkness of the warehouse was alive with the sounds of running feet. The others were coming to feed.

Sickened, Will fought to escape the sight, and for a moment he panicked. Several terrible seconds passed before he regained his wits and thought to send his focus elsewhere. Janice. The world shifted and changed, and then he was once more back in his bedroom.

Janice still watched over him, though her expression seemed to have calmed. Will stared at his body and rushed toward it, feeling resistance as he tried to enter. It might have delayed him under other circumstances, but his desperation was too fresh, too raw. Driving inward, he felt his flesh solidify around him, heavy and warm.

Sitting up suddenly, Will tried to stand and promptly fell over, collapsing onto the rug at the foot of the bed. Janice grabbed his shoulder to stabilize him as he began clambering to his feet, heedless of his lack of balance. "What's wrong?" she asked.

"They're feeding," he blurted out. "We have to go. Now." He was upright now, though still unsteady as he started for the door.

Janice held onto his shoulder. "Wait, let's think about this—"

He jerked free and kept moving. "There's no time. She's at the warehouse. They're going to kill her, and then they'll be everywhere."

She chased after him as he stormed down the stairs to the ground level of the house. "Why?"

"Because her blood is a drug to them. It will send them into a frenzy. They've lost control."

"The sun's already down," she protested. "There's nothing we can do about it. If we go out into the streets, we're liable to become victims too."

Chapter 23

"Stay here," he told her. "It's a big city and there probably aren't enough for them to come this far. Actually, go to one of the buildings. Find some sorcerers."

He passed Blake on his way to the door. "Where are you going in such a hurry?"

"She'll explain," said Will curtly, throwing open the door. Rob stood outside, his hand raised to knock, an expression of surprise on his face.

"Will! I found out—"

"Sorry," said Will as he pushed past his friend, breaking into a run.

"You aren't even wearing your armor!" shouted Blake from the house, but Will ignored him. He had his brigandine vest on, and that would have to be enough.

Focusing his turyn, he increased his stamina and speed, allowing him to sprint across the campus at an impressive rate. He took note of his surroundings as he ran. It was dark now, the sun was down, and dusk was almost done, leaving only the faintest hint of light on the horizon. The sky was clear, though, with a crescent moon and plenty of stars. He adjusted his vision to take full advantage of the available light.

His brain worked through the situation as he traveled. Janice was right—as usual, he should wait, make a plan, prepare himself. At the very least, he should stop and spend the ten or fifteen minutes necessary to change out of his clothes and put on his armor.

But he couldn't.

Every time the thought of stopping entered his head, he saw Tailtiu's broken body, heard the sick slurping noises, remembered the pain of their teeth, and then his legs pumped faster. At a normal walking pace, it would take twenty minutes to reach the warehouse. That was too long. Running, he could probably get there in ten.

The school gate came into view, and when he was within twenty yards he shouted for Tiny's benefit. "She's in the warehouse!"

The school guard looked up in alarm and puzzlement as Will ran past without slowing down. "Where are—"

Will never heard the rest. He was too busy repeating his shout to Tiny. "They're killing her!" From the periphery of his vision, he spotted the big warrior leaning against the wall to the right of the gate. *He won't be able to keep up with me,* Will realized. Even without armor, Tiny was simply too ponderous to keep up with him at a full run. Fully clad as he currently was, his friend would be exhausted in a very short span of time. "Catch up with me as quickly as you can!"

He put his head down and poured on the speed until it was all he could do to maintain his balance. Mentally, he reviewed the spells he had prepared earlier. *Ethelgren's Illumination and a wind-wall*, he told himself. Good choices, but he would need a force-lance to get through the door.

Will had continued practicing steadily over the past year, and he knew his limits. He could manage keeping two spells prepared and a third in his hand. At the risk of falling, he constructed the force-lance, but rather than hold it, he pressed it into his chest, to rest beside the two other spells. Without thinking about his actions, he formed a fourth spell, another force-lance, and kept it in his hand.

Idly, somewhere in the back of his mind, he realized he'd passed another milestone, having three spells prepared and still being able to cast another, but he couldn't spare the energy to congratulate himself.

Despite his general level of fitness, the pace was beginning to wear him down. All his usual turyn was focused on improving his endurance, leaving nothing to

Chapter 23

address the shortfall now that his body was using more energy than he could draw. So he began to pull, expanding his outer shell and concentrating his turyn more compactly within it. It was something he had only done once before, at the dam.

Arrogan had told him it was a more advanced technique, but he had no idea what the drawbacks might be. Would he exhaust his will and injure himself again? How long could he keep it up safely? He had no answers, but he tried to keep the intensity of his pull down to a lesser level than what he had used at the dam.

He only needed a little extra, not his absolute maximum. Will's lungs worked like a bellows as he ran, drawing in air to feed his burning muscles. The extra turyn flowed through him, and the burning began to recede as his body and turyn settled into a new equilibrium.

There were still quite a few people on the streets and most looked at him in alarm as he blew past, easily dodging them in the dim light between the streetlamps. Many swore as he passed by, but he ignored them all.

Pounding headlong down the streets, Will reached the warehouse in just under seven minutes from the time he had leapt up from the bed in his home. As it came into view, he slowed only enough to keep from slamming into it. At twenty feet, he unleashed the first force-lance, neatly blowing away the door handle, part of the door, and the bar behind it all. Now moving at a jog, he threw his shoulder into it and then he was inside.

Even to his night-adjusted eyes, it was too dark to see, but he was adjusting his vision already, switching to heart-light and causing the world the shift into a colorless world of grays and blacks. He knew the vampires were cold, but that only meant they wouldn't shine like beacons as living people did. They would still be visible.

Moving down a long corridor, he turned a corner and walls disappeared on either side of him as the building opened up into the main storage room. Before him stretched a long aisle with piles of crates stacked in discrete sections on either side. Between the piles were smaller cross-aisles, and in the distance, he could hear the awful sound of the undead moaning as they lapped up Tailtiu's euphoria-inducing blood.

Nothing moved or approached him. Apparently, the feeding was so intense it had robbed them of their wits and senses. From what he had seen before, his aunt was in one of the corners, and from the sounds he was hearing, it was at the far end of the warehouse from where he had entered, either on the left or the right.

Absently, he knew he should be afraid. He should be absolutely terrified. He had been the first time he had met one of the creatures, in the street in front of Laina's home. Then he hadn't had any real idea of what he was facing and seeing them had made it all the more terrible. By all rights he should be more scared now.

Maybe it was the running, suggested the voice in the back of his head. His heart was already racing, so perhaps he couldn't tell the difference now, since his fear couldn't make it beat any faster. But in truth, in his mind's eye, all he could see was Tailtiu's stricken gaze as her mouth had issued an airy attempt at a scream.

He was furious.

Marching purposefully down the aisle, the sounds became clearer as he went. It was the corner to the right. By the time he reached the middle of the building, he began to see bodies sprawled in the cross-aisles. Vampires writhing in ecstasy, unable to control the vile pleasure coursing through their veins. Without stopping, he kept a mental count, *ten, twelve, seventeen, twenty-five.* He lost

Chapter 23

track somewhere around thirty-five, and after that he just tried to keep a rough estimate.

When he reached the end and turned to the right, he had already passed a hundred, and ahead of him he could see a grotesque mound of bodies heaving to and fro. There were at least half as many more there in the corner, scrabbling with one another to try and reach the center of the pile. Some of those on the outside had given up and were now licking the stone floors, desperately trying to find one more drop of Tailtiu's blood.

The sight filled him with disgust, and rage bloomed in his heart, a red flower of hatred waiting to be released. Something moved behind him, and he turned. A vampire was standing a short distance away, staring at him vapidly with semi-curious eyes.

Chapter 24

Will's force-lance removed the vampire's head, causing a black fountain to spew upward from the stump of its neck. He turned back to the writhing pile of vampire bodies and strode onward, drawing more turyn in as he walked.

He had only cast the spell twice before, during his practices, so he had a good idea of how much turyn to invest, but his anger wasn't satisfied with such prudence. Once he was within fifteen feet, Will drew out Ethelgren's Illumination and poured power into it. Closing his eyes, he lifted his hand above his head and released the spell with an inchoate scream, "Face the sun, you sons of bitches!"

The world went white, and a hundred voices rose to the rafters in an unholy howl of inconceivable agony as the vampires began to burn.

Will had known what to expect from the spell, though he had put more into it than perhaps he had needed to. The flesh of Tailtiu's undead tormentors turned out to be exceptionally fragile under the unforgiving glare of Ethelgren's masterpiece. Six globes of searing incandescence spun outward from his hand, spinning and twisting in a spiral pattern as they brought light into every nook and cranny around him.

That was the genius of the spell. Rather than simply producing a single brilliant globe, it created moving spheres that would prevent any of the creatures from hiding in the shadows provided by crates, boxes, or other obstacles. The spheres moved outward, and the air was soon filled with the dust of collapsing corpses as they disintegrated into stinking ash.

Another interesting feature of the spell was that the globes of light were intangible; they weren't impeded by physical objects or walls. Standing close to a corner of the building, the spheres spent roughly three-quarters of their time and energy outside the building, but there were enough of them that there was always one or two inside. They followed their preset pattern, moving outward from Will's position until the radius of the circle they traced was roughly fifty feet from where he stood. Then they gradually faded out. From start to finish, the spell lasted roughly a minute, and there was nothing left moving within the circumference the spheres had inscribed with their movements.

Except Will, of course. Silence fell, and darkness returned as he slowly opened his eyes. In front of him was a mound of ash interspersed with clothing. Tailtiu's body was nowhere to be seen, but he knew where she had to be. Wading into the ash, he found himself waist deep once he reached the center, and there his foot bumped into something solid.

The stench was a tangible thing, a sweet yet acrid smell reminiscent of rotting meat. Ignoring his revulsion, he bent and plunged his hands into the mounded dust. It was too deep for him to reach her easily, and he was forced to bend farther, until his head and shoulders both went under. A moment later his fingers found her and he straightened gently, his hands under her arms as he pulled and backed out.

They were fully in the corner now, and when he examined his aunt, he was aghast. She was covered in a layer of white dust, and her once-lithe form was naked and torn, covered with small punctures and tears where fangs had ripped her flesh. She seemed to have shrunk, and her weight in his arms was a fraction of what it should have been. Tailtiu was little more than a skeleton covered in broken skin and desiccated flesh. And she was still bound by long, iron chains anchored in the wood beams that supported the building.

Anxious to free her quickly, his first impulse was to use the force-lance spell, but he realized that even if he held onto a chain before blasting it, the spell might not work. If the links didn't part, the force of the blow might jerk the chain free of his hands and damage her limbs. There were better options.

He quickly constructed a spell to alter the properties of steel, the same one he had used at the dam. There was plenty of slack, so he gathered the four chains together with one hand and released the spell, watching as the metal changed from dull brown to a matte beige color. Summoning his falchion, he shattered the links.

Using the razor edge of his weapon on such a target went against every instinct he had gained when training as a swordsman, but he didn't care. He would worry about getting the nicks out of the blade later. He started to put the sword away so he would have both hands to carry Tailtiu, but a new sound made him pause and turn his head.

Not all the vampires were dead. A significant portion had been too far beyond the limit of his spell. Some of them were horribly burned and disfigured, some merely scorched, and a few were utterly untouched. There were at least twenty gathered together, watching him warily.

At some point during his doings, his heart had slowed down, recovering from the exertion of his run. It leapt into a frantic rhythm now, and Will felt his mouth go dry. He had gone from anger to sorrow, and now he felt the beginnings of despair. Tailtiu was dead, his rush to save her had come to naught, and now he would likely join her.

Chapter 24

He kept the falchion and rose to stand over her, facing the mutilated monsters. He still had a wind-wall spell prepared, but the timing would be tricky. He needed another illumination spell, but it was probably too late for that. He tried anyway.

Forming a spell without paying strict attention to the process was something he did quite often, but only with spells he had practiced for a considerable length of time. He tried distracting his enemies, but kept his eyes on his hand as he formed the runes to build another illumination spell. "Come to join your brethren in death?" he asked.

The vampires were spreading out into an arc, and one among them spoke to the others. "He's bluffing. He would have done it already if he could destroy us. He can't even look at us."

Will heard the whisper of feet on the floor as they rushed toward him, and he glanced up in a panic. The spell he had been rapidly constructing trembled and fell apart. He tried to swing his sword, but one of them caught his arm in mid-swing—and then they were on him.

The speed of their movements bruised him in a dozen places, not from blows, but from their haste to rip the clothing from his body. Sharp pains assailed him as teeth sank into his skin in dozens of places, his arms, neck, thighs, and a few seconds later, his chest and back. The shock of it all was so great he couldn't even cry out. A miserable gasp was all he could manage, and then he could barely breathe.

He tried to kick, punch—anything to get them off—but it was futile. They were too many and too strong. His attempts failed to do anything but create tears in his skin as he dislodged their fangs here and there.

Then a light appeared, half-blinding him, followed by a woman's voice. "Run if you value your lives!" The vampires released him in a panic, scattering briefly, and as Will collapsed to the ground, he saw Janice standing some twenty feet away, a shining light above her head. Two men stood with her, Rob on one side, while Tiny towered over both of them on the other side.

Tiny rushed forward, and Will felt the man's massive hands slip under his arms, pulling him upward. "Can you stand?" asked the big warrior.

"I think so. Help her, not me."

Tiny glanced down. "She's dead, Will."

"I'm not leaving without her."

His friend grimaced. "Stay on your feet then. If you fall, I'll dump her and carry you instead."

A loud report echoed through the warehouse and Will looked up to see one of the vampires flying back, a hole in its chest. Rob watched the results with a look of hysterical triumph on his face. Will had taught him the force-lance spell months ago, but he hadn't thought the other student had bothered to practice it.

However, the fact that Rob had had to use the spell at all highlighted a different problem. The light spell that Janice had used had been of the ordinary variety. While it had frightened the vampires, it hadn't actually done them any harm, and the exit was still a long way away. With twenty vampires still moving in the building, the door might as well have been on the other side of the world.

They had just gathered together around Tiny and started to move when the rest of the monsters returned, clustering around them. "Stay back!" warned Rob, another spell ready above his palm. Will began drawing in turyn, trying to regain his strength. Meanwhile Janice was beginning a force-lance of her own, while continuing to maintain the light spell that hovered above her head.

Chapter 24

The vampires didn't wait. No longer afraid of the light, they rushed forward. Janice and Rob released their spells, sending two of the fiends flying back, but the rest swarmed them. Claws flashed, and a pained shriek came from Janice as Tiny dropped his limp cargo and tried to help her. Will heard Rob grunt, and he saw two vampires had seized his friend's arms, pulling him away.

He grabbed hold of his friend and shouted at Tiny, who was desperately trying to keep the others off of Janice. "Get close to me!" Will wasn't able to drag Rob back, but somehow, Tiny seized Janice and managed to drag her along as he rejoined them. The four friends fell then, collapsing under the weight of their attackers.

They might have been crushed under the weight of Tiny and his armor, but somehow the massive warrior rose to his feet again, despite half a dozen undead clinging to his arms and shoulders. Will readied his turyn and tried to adjust his spell so that it wouldn't kill those he wanted to protect, but then, for just a moment, Janice's face turned toward him as she struggled to keep from being pulled away, and he saw what had caused her to shriek a few moments before.

Half her face was gone. Her left eye, the cheek below it, part of her nose, and half of her bottom lip were gone, leaving nothing but a ruin of blood, muscle, and exposed bone. The skin and tissue that had covered the wound now hung limp, like a bloody rag dangling from the side of her chin.

Janice's one remaining eye met his gaze for a split second, and he could see the pain and horror there. She knew she was hurt; she knew something was wrong, but she couldn't yet tell exactly what had happened to her. The sight shocked Will to his core, and as he tried to release the wind-wall spell, his concentration wavered and the spell shattered.

A moment later another pair of hands ripped her away. Janice's spell faltered and the light died. Will screamed furiously, but he wasn't quick enough to grab her hands. Tiny roared and began to charge, but as the light vanished, he found himself suddenly blind.

Will panicked as he realized then that Rob was already gone, and as the vampires tore and pounded on Tiny's mailed body, the big man fell to his hands and knees, covering his last remaining friend. There wasn't much else the warrior could do, and Will could feel the shuddering blows as they resonated through the big man's chest and arms.

Tailtiu was dead, and Rob, Tiny, and Janice would soon follow, all because he couldn't bear to accept the loss of one friend. Will's only consolation was that he would be joining his friends soon after their deaths, so he wouldn't have to live with his shame.

Will could still see, however, and in the weird, gray landscape painted by his heart-light vision, he saw the goddamn cat walk past. He was gazing out from under Tiny's armpit, and the demigod simply stopped a few feet away and stared back at him. "Help us," Will gasped.

"This is what trusting the fae gets you. You've earned your fate," said the cat, its voice easy to hear despite the other awful noises echoing through the warehouse. "Farewell." And then Will watched as the furry bastard sauntered casually away.

A faint whimper escaped Tiny's lips, and Will felt a shudder go through his friend, but the big man only shifted his weight slightly and pulled his arms in further, trying to keep the enemy away from his smaller companion.

They're going to kill him while he's trying to shelter me, thought Will. *And the goddamn cat just shows up and insults me.* A growl began to reverberate in the back of Will's throat. He was wasting time and the opportunity

Chapter 24

his friend had given him. For the moment he was safe, and given enough time, he could do something better than whine in fear.

Will didn't have enough room to see his hand, as he was close to being squashed under Tiny's chest. *Fuck that, I don't have to see,* he decided, closing his eyes and imagining his hand as he began to construct a new spell. It came together in his mind with surprising speed, and he half wondered if it was just his imagination or if the spell was really there, but he didn't have time for doubt. Drawing in his turyn, he invested it in the spell construct and released it.

Once again, a searing, actinic light exploded across the warehouse floor, and six brilliant spheres spiraled outward. Howls sounded, and Tiny suddenly straightened his arms, as though a weight had been lifted from his back—or burned away, as the case might be. The massive warrior sat up, squinting and covering his eyes with one forearm. "Did you do that, Will?"

Will nodded, keeping his own eyes firmly shut. "Do you see Rob or Janice?"

"I can barely see anything, it's so bright."

"Close your eyes until it fades. It won't hurt you like it does the vampires, but too much could damage your eyesight. I'll create a safer light in a minute." But Will had a different priority. First, he constructed another one of Ethelgren's Illumination spells and stored it within himself. He wanted to be ready. By the time he had finished constructing it, the light from the first spell was fading out, and he put together a simple light spell that would allow Tiny to see.

Will got to his feet, but Tiny stayed seated, his chest heaving. "Can you get up?" Will asked.

"I think so," said his friend. "But give me a minute."

Will looked him over. Tiny's mail appeared to be intact, and his helm was still on his head. There were deep scratches in the breastplate and backplate, but nothing had pierced it. There were a couple more lacerations across Tiny's cheek, and Will could see that the capillaries around the wound had already turned black. *What about me?* he thought. He didn't want to look. His overtunic and brigandine had been ripped away, and his chest and arms were bare. He knew without looking that he was covered in fang marks.

Will summoned two blood-cleanse potions from the limnthal and handed one to Tiny. "Drink it or we'll become like them."

Tiny nodded and downed the vial in a single gulp. Will did likewise, his eyes already scanning the gloom for Rob and Janice. He spotted Tailtiu immediately, lying ten feet away, discarded like a broken doll. He went and picked her up, then deposited her near Tiny.

She was dead, so the action made little sense, but he did it anyway. Then he moved outward, looking behind pallets and stacks of goods to see where Janice and Rob might have fallen. He was scared of what he might find. Walking along the center aisle, he spotted a crumpled figure in one of the cross-aisles. It was Janice, with two small mounds of ash on either side of her.

Her head was down and her knees up, while a faint keening sound came from her direction. "Janice, are you all right?" asked Will, knowing the question was foolish. None of them were all right. He summoned another potion from the limnthal and knelt beside her. "Drink this. It will stop the taint from claiming you." Her head bobbed, and she took the potion with one hand, but she didn't look up.

Scooting away, she turned her back to him before drinking the potion. She was hiding her face, but Will

Chapter 24

still saw some of the potion dribble down her neck. Drinking without a cheek and part of a lip was difficult at best. *And I don't have a regeneration potion for her.* What would happen to her? The type of wound she had suffered would permanently maim her at best. Without quick medical treatment she might die from the blood loss, or later from an infection.

But would she be happy to survive such an injury? Will wasn't sure how he would have felt in her position. "Can you walk?" he asked her. "I still have to find Rob."

She nodded, clambering to her feet and keeping her head down so that her hair covered her ruined eye and cheek. Will led her back to Tiny, who was standing and looking around nervously. A smile lit his face when he saw Janice with Will, and Will felt his own heart break a second time.

Tiny couldn't tell what was wrong with Janice, but she sheltered in his shadow, keeping her injury from view. Meanwhile, Will collected Tailtiu's body, and together they made their way through the warehouse, moving toward the exit and searching for Rob at the same time.

They found no trace of him, just more piles of ash. Once they had finished a rough search of the area, they left, for none of them had the reserves to continue searching further.

And Janice. Janice needed proper treatment and the sooner the better. Blood trickled away from her face and soaked the front of her dress. After five minutes of walking, her knees buckled, and Tiny caught her. Lifting her carefully in the cradle of his arms, the big man never broke his stride. Will stayed with him.

"There's a healer at the college, right?" asked Tiny, his voice carefully controlled.

"Yes," said Will. "The Healing and Psyche Department runs the best hospital in the city. They can do more for her than anyone else."

"That's good," said Tiny gruffly. Will could see tears shining on his cheeks in the light from the streetlamps. "I'm sorry about Rob. I did everything I could."

"You saved us, Tiny," said Will. "We can talk about Rob tomorrow. I can't do it now. We have enough to deal with."

"Yeah."

They walked on, and as they neared the campus, Will couldn't handle his guilt any longer. "Tiny, I'm sorry, for everything. This was my fault."

"Will."

"Yeah?"

"Shut the fuck up."

Will shook his head. "But..."

"No buts. If you ever apologize to me about tonight again, I will beat you into next week. Do you understand? We did this for you. We did this because we believe in you, and whatever it costs us, in flesh and blood..." The big warrior's voice choked for a moment, but he continued after a second, "...whatever it costs us, I have to believe it was worth it. So don't you fucking dare take that away from me by apologizing. This meant something, so shut the hell up."

Will closed his mouth and bowed his head as they walked. It was a few minutes later before he spoke again. "Thank you."

Tiny nodded. "Same to you. No one asked you to stop those monsters, but someone had to."

The Healing and Psyche building loomed ahead of them. Unlike most of the other college buildings, there was always a light on at the front entrance, for nights just like that one.

Chapter 25

Doctor Morris sat across from Will, a pensive expression on his face. "It's hard to believe what you're telling me, but then again, I can't imagine anyone intentionally covering themselves with bite wounds to corroborate a story like that."

Will was covered in bandages. The blood-cleanse potion had prevented the vampiric disease from taking hold, as well as stopped the wounds from festering, but they still hurt like hell. Other than dozens of punctures and small tears, the doctor had told him that he was in good health. He hadn't even lost that much blood.

Tiny and Janice, though, were another story altogether. The big warrior had only suffered a few claw wounds, but his body had been covered in bruises. Still he had insisted that he was fit enough to leave. Doctor Morris had other ideas, however.

"Your friend will have to stay for a week or two. Most don't realize how serious blunt-force trauma can be. By tomorrow most of his body will be black and blue and his kidneys will struggle to deal with all the blood being reabsorbed and broken down. That's on top of the fact that his kidneys were also injured by the blows he received."

"But he'll be all right, won't he?" asked Will.

The doctor stared at his desk for a moment, then answered, "Maybe. It's hard to say for sure. We'll be forcing him to drink as much as possible to help his kidneys work, but there's a strong possibility that they'll fail. If that happens…"

Will knew quite well what that would mean, but he held onto hope. Doctor Morris knew a considerable amount that he did not and there might be magical means that Will had never heard about. "Is there a way to save him if that happens?"

Doctor Morris grimaced. "There are forbidden procedures, but I'll have no part of murdering innocents to harvest their kidneys. Aside from that, you'll have to hope for the best."

"What about a regeneration potion?"

"If you have one, give it to him now, or the girl. Either one could desperately use it," said the doctor.

"How bad is Janice's wound?" He already knew it wouldn't be good, but he hoped perhaps it might not be as terrible as it had seemed.

"I managed to save most of the cheek so I could reattach it to cover the wound. The muscle is ruined and of course, her eye is gone. She won't be able to move most of that side of her face after it heals. She will probably also have considerable difficulty drinking and speaking since she lost most of the lower lip. Her life isn't in danger, but it will be difficult living normally after this. Her nose was ruined as well. I had to stretch the skin from the right side to cover as much of the wound as I could, so it won't look…well, you understand."

Will's vision blurred, and he covered his face with his hands. Despite what Tiny had said, he still blamed himself. Then he asked, "You said a regeneration potion would help, right?"

"If you have one, yes," said Doctor Morris. "But it needs to be given within a few days or it won't work properly."

"Why?"

Chapter 25

"It regenerates flesh, but it doesn't remove scars or revive dead tissue," said the doctor. "If Mister Shaw's kidneys die, the potion won't revive necrotic tissue. Miss Edelman's condition is less dangerous, but the same principle applies. If her wound heals as it is, the potion won't reverse that. It has to be given while the body still remembers its proper form. Once it has healed, *that* will be what it considers its proper form."

Will nodded as the gears began to turn in his head.

The doctor went on, "I'll need to report all of this to the proper authorities. If there truly are undead monsters roaming the streets, the king will need to be informed."

"He knows already," said Will bitterly. "But I have the address of the warehouse for him."

"You can tell him yourself," said Doctor Morris. "You'll have to stay here until the king's men arrive to question everyone."

Will gave the doctor a hard look. "Do you really think you can keep me here?"

"That's my job."

"Your job is to take care of patients," countered Will. "I will be leaving in a few minutes, to try and obtain the potions my friends need. If you want to help them, you'll stay out of my way."

"If I actually believed you could do that, I'd be tempted to let you," admitted the doctor. "But I know quite well there's no possible way you could—"

"Do either of my friends need any further treatment from you tonight?" asked Will suddenly.

The doctor stared at him oddly. "No, my assistants will handle the dressing changes in the morning. For now, they're sleeping. I administered a strong sedative so—" His words cut off as Will's source-link spell connected, and a moment later he was paralyzed and his connection to his source was blocked.

With that done, Will took his time constructing a sleep spell, and once it had taken hold, he released the source-link. He stood and summoned a spare tunic from the limnthal. It felt strange wearing normal clothes without his brigandine vest under it, but he had lost the armor at the warehouse.

He left the office and waved to the nurses and other personnel that glanced at him on his way out. None of them tried to stop him, thankfully. Once he was outside, he recovered Tailtiu's body from the bushes he had hidden it in. Cradling her in his arms, he began the walk home.

As he went, he couldn't help but consider how much he had changed. Just a year previously he would have been nervous as hell to carry a dead body across the campus. Now it hardly bothered him at all. He figured anyone that saw him would figure it was simply an unconscious person, and as unusual as that might be, he doubted anyone would have the balls to challenge him about it.

In one sense it was a good thing, but it also reminded him of Dennis Spry. *No one would challenge him either, and because of that he did terrible things to whoever he pleased.* Will had no intention of becoming like that, but it made him acutely aware of how his current status could easily be abused.

He received a fresh surprise when he got home. The front door had been torn from its hinges and now lay on its side beside the gaping doorway. The claw marks made it obvious what had happened, and Will's blood began to boil anew. *They came to take their vengeance,* he realized, and then he felt a sudden surge of panic. *Blake!*

For a moment he remained still, unsure what to do. He still held Tailtiu in his arms and he didn't want to face yet another battle while carrying a dead body, but he also didn't want to leave her outside, exposed to anyone who

Chapter 25

happened by. If the vampires found her, they might well steal the body simply to drain the last of her vital fluids.

A voice saved him from the decision. "William? Is that you?" It was Blake, and as Will focused on the darkened doorway, he saw the manservant lean out from the parlor room, a crossbow in his hands.

"Yes! Are you all right?"

"Mostly," said the older man. "It's safe to come in. They were gone before I got back."

Will carried Tailtiu in and laid her on the divan in the parlor. Then he glanced at Blake. The man was sitting on the floor, a pained expression on his face. "What happened to you?" he asked.

"I tried to go with them," said Blake, seeming embarrassed. "But my body betrayed me this time. I kept up until we were halfway there, then I fell."

Will knelt and began examining the man's leg.

"I think it's just a sprain or something," said Blake. "But I couldn't walk on it, though the gods know I tried. I finally had to improvise a crutch and hobble back here. Took me a little over an hour and by the time I got back… well, you saw the front door."

The bones seemed sound, but Will could see that there was considerable swelling around Blake's ankle, though it was masked by the boot he still wore. "I think it's your ankle," he informed Blake. "But you should have taken off the boot. Now I'm afraid you're going to lose it."

"The foot?" asked Blake sharply, his face lighting up in alarm.

Will smirked faintly, feeling sad and relieved at the same time. "The boot. I'll have to cut it off." If only Janice's wound had been so simple. He did as he had said, using a sharp knife to carefully slice the boot away, exposing the swollen ankle inside. Blake hissed in pain several times during the process, then louder when Will began rotating his foot and probing the swelling. "I really can't be sure, but I don't think you broke anything. A few days of rest and elevation should see you back on your feet."

"Damned rotten timing," swore the manservant.

"You can't stay here, either," Will informed him. "They may return, and I won't be here to protect you."

"Where are the others?" asked Blake.

Will grimaced, then looked away. It was difficult to say, but he managed to communicate the injuries they had endured using the bare minimum of words. "It was my fault, Blake," he said at last. "I'm grateful you twisted your ankle, or you'd be in the same shape, or dead. I still don't know what happened to Rob."

"Worrying about blame right now is a fool's game," said Blake. "The only one to blame when your friends are hurt is the enemy that did it. Blaming yourself does your enemy's work for him." He paused for a second. "You said you weren't going to be here. Where are you going?"

"Tiny and Janice need a miracle," said Will. "So I'm going to go find one for them. I also need to return my friend to her family."

Blake had never actually met Tailtiu as herself. She had always been disguised as Selene. "Is she…?"

Will nodded. "She's been helping me with things. Now I have to explain her death to her mother."

"Are you sure she's dead?" asked Blake, an odd sound in his throat. "I could swear she's looking at us."

Will whipped around, and sure enough he could see a faint glimmer in the dim light. One of Tailtiu's eyes was open and appeared to be fixed on him. He moved over and knelt beside her. "Are you still with us?" he asked, touching her cheek.

Chapter 25

Her lips moved slightly, then she closed the eye, causing his hope to soar. *She's alive!* He turned back to Blake. "Can you make it to the Healing and Psyche building by yourself? I need to take her home, right now."

Blake nodded. "I'm coming back in the morning, though. The workmen will be arriving to start on the changes you wanted. I'll see about repairing whatever they broke while they were tearing through the house as well."

Will hardly heard the man. He was lifting his aunt again and heading out the door. Looking back, he said, "I'll be back in a day or two. Any longer than that and there's a good chance I won't be back at all." He strode out the door and down the steps without answering any of Blake's follow up questions.

After a hundred yards, he summoned the limnthal and asked Arrogan a question. "Tailtiu is alive, barely. I'm carrying her to the nearest congruence point. Should I give her a blood-cleanse potion? Can she catch the vampiric sickness?"

For once the ring didn't waste any time insulting him. "No and no. No, the fae can't contract it, and no don't ever give her a blood-cleanse potion. If she was healthy it would probably make her feel sick, but if she's as badly injured as you suggest it might finish her off."

"Why is that?" asked Will.

"She isn't human. The blood-cleanse potion is formulated to destroy things that are foreign to the human body. As far as the potion is concerned, *she* is a disease."

That got Will to thinking. "Is that true of all non-humans?"

"Most of them, except those that are most similar to us, like dwarves and elves. They're related closely enough that it would work fine."

"Related?" Will had thought they were entirely separate from humanity.

"If you saw a horse and a donkey you would assume they were related, wouldn't you? You can even breed them together. The same is true of elves and dwarves."

"But you told me the elves live in a different world, didn't you?"

"They're still related to us. Just because we live in different realms now doesn't mean that was always the case. Think about the fae, you already know they were once human too."

"Except they can't use the blood-cleanse potion," argued Will.

"Because their bodies have been completely replaced by the essence of Faerie. They're no more human than a well-made marble statue. See the difference?"

"You were wrong about one thing, though," said Will. "I found Tailtiu in the astral plane."

"Ridiculous. That simply isn't possible."

"She has feelings," declared Will.

"Next you'll be telling me you found a dog that can talk. What do you think you connected with?"

"Pain," said Will. "I couldn't find her at first, but I kept trying. Then I sort of went inward and found this bit of pain inside myself. After that I found her, and something connected." He paused for a second, unsure how to convey what he had felt. "It was strange. It was almost as though she didn't care at first, but once my pain connected to hers, she started trying to scream. Do you know what it means?"

"Not a clue, other than that it shouldn't be possible," said the ring. "I'll be curious to hear what she has to say about it after she's recovered."

"She will recover?" asked Will once again, seeking reassurance.

Chapter 25

"Most certainly, completely and utterly."

"What about the experience? After some of the things I've been through, I still have nightmares. What she went through must have been even worse."

The ring laughed. "No, once again, they aren't like us. They don't change. They don't scar, mentally or emotionally. Sure, they feel physical pain, but it doesn't affect them the same way it does us. After she recovers, the only thing she'll care about is getting revenge, but even that won't be personal for her. Everything is a game to them, including torture."

Will nodded. He had left the main campus gate and was now walking down the lane, but even as light as she was, Tailtiu's body was becoming heavy in his arms, and he still had to walk through the city and several miles into the countryside to reach the nearest congruence. "I'll talk to you some more in a little while," he said, dismissing the limnthal. He could hear a carriage approaching from farther down the road.

It appeared a moment later, a carriage drawn by four horses, its lanterns glowing with amber light as they swayed from their hooks at the front. Will moved into the center of the road, making sure the driver could see him clearly.

"Get out of the way, fool!" yelled the man, slowing and pulling on the reins to stop the team.

Will remained still, and once the wheels had stopped, he walked forward, and with a quick source-link, paralyzed the driver. He formed a sleep spell while listening to the occupants ask questions, unsure why they had stopped. After a minute one of them opened the door, and Will was waiting. His spell put the two men and their female companion to sleep almost instantly.

Stepping up, he settled Tailtiu on one cushioned bench, though he was forced to put one of the men on the floor. Then he closed the carriage door and climbed up beside the still-paralyzed driver. "I need you to take a short detour for me," he told the silently terrified man. "Don't worry. I have no intention of hurting you or your master. I just need a ride. Once we get there you can take the carriage and leave.

"In a moment I'm going to release the spell holding you. If you behave and drive for me I won't have to put it back on you, since I'm sure you're a much better driver than I am." He released the spell and watched the man carefully. "You can move now."

The poor driver was too frightened to look in his direction. "Yes, sir."

"Will you drive for me?"

The man nodded. "Yes, sir. You won't hurt me, will you?"

"Not at all. I'm on the king's business. This is merely an emergency."

"Where are you headed?"

"The south gate and then a couple of miles out of the city. You'll have to turn the carriage and team around. My lady friend can't walk on her own, and she needs to be there as soon as possible." The driver nodded and began the process. It was a narrow lane so turning the carriage in the middle of the road was a little tedious. While he did so, Will said one thing more. "Aislinn, Aislinn, Aislinn, thrice called, heed me for your daughter's sake."

"Beggin' your pardon, sir?"

"Just ignore that," said Will. They rode quietly through the mostly empty streets of Cerria. The driver behaved himself for the most part, though Will noticed a

Chapter 25

few wild glances when they passed through an area with more people. "I wouldn't if I were you," he warned.

The man gulped, and Will felt bad for scaring him. "What did you do to Master Haldane?"

"He's sleeping, as are the others. They'll wake up none the worse after you drop us off. I know you don't believe me, but this is the king's business. I have no intention of harming honest citizens."

The driver seemed to relax slightly. "Are you one of the Driven?"

Will wasn't sure how to answer that. "No, but I've met several of them," he said honestly. "Why would you think that?"

"I've heard they wear drab colors and that they're all sorcerers. They scare the shit out of most people. You're wearing brown and you scare the shit out of me; it seemed reasonable you might be one of them."

He fought to suppress a chuckle. "I appreciate the honesty and I'm sorry for all this, truly I am." Something about his answer upset the man, and he saw silent tears begin to stream down the fellow's cheeks. "What's wrong?"

A half-sob escaped the man's lips. "You're goin' to kill me, aren't you, sir?"

"What? No! Why?"

"They always apologize in the stories, right before they murder them!" The driver's words came out in a rush as snot began to run from his nose.

Will was beginning to worry that the hysterical man would lose control of the team. "Look, what's your name?"

"Paul," sobbed the man. "I have two children waiting for me at home. We lost their mother a few years ago."

"Listen, Paul, would I ask for your name if I planned to murder you?"

The driver's answer came out in a pitch so high it was difficult to understand. "Maybe."

He summoned his coin pouch and removed a gold mark, then offered it to the man. "Would I offer you this to make it up to you for all the trouble?"

"You could always take it back after you kill me," blubbered the pitiful coachman. They were about to pass through the south gate, and the look of desperation on the man's face was so intense that Will worried the driver might throw himself out of his seat.

Will reconnected the source-link and paralyzed the driver while putting an arm over the man's shoulder to keep him from being bounced out of his seat. With his other hand he took the reins and tried not to do anything. The team was following the road out of habit, and the road went where he needed to go. He had never driven anything larger than a small cart, and he worried what would happen if anything unexpected happened.

Meanwhile he spoke to the paralyzed man beside him. "Damn, I can't fault your logic. I mean, I'm not going to do anything to you, but I can't argue with your reasoning. There's no way you can know what I'll do, and you certainly don't have cause to believe me, but we're almost there. I'll release you in a few minutes and you can turn the carriage around. You can keep the gold mark too, and your master doesn't have to know I gave it to you if you don't want him to know. He's asleep, so that will be our little secret."

A few minutes later, he did as he had promised, waving to the frightened driver as he drove away. "Don't forget to wake up your passengers!" Will yelled. "Otherwise they might sleep until dawn!"

Gently cradling Tailtiu, he walked through the nearby pasture, heading toward the place where he knew the

Chapter 25

congruence point with Faerie would be. He hadn't felt a response from Aislinn, but his gut told him she would be waiting for him. Glancing down, he saw both of Tailtiu's eyes were open, and she was silently staring up at him. She couldn't talk, but he wondered what she was thinking.

"We're almost there," he told her. "You don't have to worry. Once I get you back everything will be fine. Just hold on a little longer for me, all right?"

She closed her eyes slowly, then opened them again. He hoped it was a sign that she understood, but he couldn't be sure. They still had a half a mile to go, and as they walked he mentally reviewed everything that had happened. He wanted to kick himself for his haste, but he still couldn't see that he'd had a better alternative. If he had delayed, Tailtiu would almost certainly have died, but then again, his friends would probably be safe and sound.

Was it worth exchanging Rob's life for one of the fae? Was it worth Tiny's? And what about Janice's horrible disfigurement? He couldn't help but feel he'd made a terrible bargain with fate and his friends had paid the price for it.

As he pondered and poked at the past, like someone probing a sore tooth with their tongue, a thought came to him, *the warehouse!* He still had a big problem to consider in the near future, and if he couldn't find a solution Tiny and Janice might pay a terrible cost. Will had planned to leave for his old home immediately after returning Tailtiu to Faerie, but now he knew he needed to return to Cerria first.

CHAPTER 26

There was no one at the congruence point, so Will crossed over, and the effect on Tailtiu was subtle but immediate. Her eyes opened again, watching him with more intensity. He couldn't have said what it was exactly, but her body was already beginning to radiate a faint sense of vitality. He wished that Tiny and Janice's problems were so easy to fix.

He laid her in the tall grass and sat down beside her to wait, though he felt a strong sense of urgency. Time wasn't his friend. After something close to a quarter of an hour, there was a shimmer in the air, and his grandmother appeared. Will stared at her in surprise, for she had come from somewhere else, but not through the congruence point with his world.

What sort of magic was that? he wondered.

"You found her," she said simply.

Will watched Aislinn carefully. "You seem surprised."

She arched one brow. "Shouldn't I be? A warehouse full of Drak'shar is a dangerous place. It seemed unlikely you would succeed."

"You knew where she was?" he demanded, feeling his temper rise.

"What don't I know, child? That is a much better question, and one I spend much of my time seeking to address."

"Save the double-talk for someone else," he said, spitting on the ground angrily. "You knew where she was and yet you left her to die?"

"You brought her back," said Aislinn simply.

"I almost died. Two of my friends might still die."

Aislinn gave him a sharp look. "Only one, child, don't exaggerate."

"You were *watching* the whole time? You were fine with me dying, even if it meant your own daughter would do the same?"

"Death is a gift, my grandson, one you have refused several times, and now, it appears you are refusing it on behalf of others. Are you sure you have the right?" She glanced down at her emaciated daughter. "Will she thank you for preserving her life?" Then she leveled her gaze at Will. "Will Janice thank you for it? And what of your lost friend, Rob? I'm sure he's praying for it already."

Will's rapier appeared in his hand, and the edge was close to Aislinn's throat before he realized what he was doing.

His grandmother's mouth twitched into a smile. "Do it. Touch me but once with that iron and I will have won."

"Not if I drag your remains into the mortal realm and leave them to rot," he threatened.

"You understand nothing of me, despite everything I have said." She gave a sigh of longsuffering. "Very well, I will show mercy this once and grant you a second lesson. Unprovoked violence will violate the accord. Strike me or put your weapon away. Choose which victory I will enjoy today."

His fury was so great that the sword began to shake in his hand, but his mind continued to work. *She wants me to kill her? Or does she want an excuse to kill me? Or is it the accord she wants destroyed? Would she really be happy with any of those results?* Straightening up, he sent the sword back into the limnthal.

His grandmother seemed disappointed. "I suppose the game will have to continue then." She snapped her fingers and Tailtiu levitated into the air, floating over to the fae lady. Then she turned her back and walked away. The two of them shimmered and vanished a moment later.

How the hell is she doing that? wondered Will. Irritated, he moved back to the congruence point and returned to his own world. The more time that passed, the more he was beginning to understand the goddamn cat's disdain for the fae.

Returning through the pasture, he suddenly regretted letting the carriage driver leave. If he wanted to go back to the warehouse, he would have to walk on his own feet. Running was out of the question. Every muscle in his body was sore from his marathon sprint earlier, and that was without even considering the pain of the wounds that covered much of his body. All of it was minor, but it added up to a considerable burden.

It was almost an hour before he got to the warehouse. He half expected to find it on fire and surrounded by the Driven, but the area was still quiet and dark. He still had one spell prepared, Ethelgren's Illumination, but he added a second copy and then a wind-wall spell. With three spells ready, he constructed a force-lance and kept it in his hand. Then he entered the building.

Nothing had changed since he had been there a few hours before. Adjusting his vision, he made a quick circuit of the main storage area. When he didn't find anyone, he released the force-lance and created a simple light spell. Searching would be easier with normal eyesight, as writing often didn't show up properly in heart-light and some other types of light.

There was a wide variety of goods stored in the building. Despite the foul things that had been living there, apparently Jorn Slidden was a relatively ordinary trader, or had been. Will wondered if they had turned him or if the man had simply been cooperating to protect his

Chapter 26

life or that of his family. Then again, the man might have been motivated by simple greed.

A cursory search failed to turn up what he was looking for, but that wasn't surprising considering the size of the place. *But would they store it out here with everything else?* He decided that was unlikely. The stuff was too dangerous. He worked his way around the edge of the storage area, looking for a stack that was set far apart from the others. He found several, but they turned out to be other things.

The office? He went back to the door he had entered through and followed the hall in the other direction. It led to door that was already partly ajar, and inside was a desk, several chairs and strangely enough, a large painting on the wall behind the desk. Will stared at it for several seconds, purely for artistic reasons though—not because the painting depicted a woman in a partial state of undress.

Definitely not, he told himself. Since the painting was clearly a work of art, and entirely out of place in such a ratty dockside business, it seemed suspicious. There might be a hiding place behind it. Reaching out, he touched the frame and stored the painting in the limnthal. *It was the quickest way to get it out of the way,* he decided—after the fact. The wall behind was blank and ordinary, though the plaster was chipped and damaged in places.

He made a thorough search of the room and found nothing—until he began moving furniture. Beneath the desk was an old rug, and once it was out of the way he found a large iron door secured with what he assumed was an expensive padlock. He didn't know much about locks, but this one was heavily constructed and appeared far more complex than most he had seen.

Will hadn't needed the unlocking spell in over a year, but he still practiced it during his daily spell routine, and it came together quickly over his palm. Seconds later, the padlock clicked open. He stored it in the limnthal too. Such things, even the cheaper ones, were quite valuable. If he could get a key made for it, it would be worth considerable coin. *First the painting and now this. I'm turning into a common thief.* Then again, he had come to steal something anyway, and one way or another he figured the owner owed him for what had happened to his friends.

Opening the vault, he noted that a ward had been laid over the space just behind the door. It was an unusual arrangement, as ordinarily a ward would be placed on the door itself, rather than the air behind it. He hadn't learned to create any wards yet himself, but he knew that they lasted longer when placed on solid materials.

Behind the ward was a large space containing a multitude of glass jars and vials, along with a large leather sack. Will smiled, then took a moment to attune himself to the ward, before reaching through and removing the contents, one by one. The larger glass jars were tightly sealed with wax, cloth, and twine. The glass was brown, and the jars sloshed as he pulled them out, confirming his suspicion of their contents. Turning the first one around, he saw the chemical symbol for phosphorous had been painted on one side.

The phosphorous itself would be a waxy solid, but it was stored in water to prevent exposure to air, which could cause it to spontaneously ignite. All in all, he removed ten of the large jars—a small fortune if they contained as much white phosphorous as had been bought from the Alchemy Department.

The smaller vials made him even happier, for they were the result of someone else's hard work. Each one was clearly labeled, 'alchemist's fire.' There were twenty of those.

Chapter 26

Last but not least, he extracted the leather sack. It jingled and clinked as he set it on the wood floor beside him. Will untied the bag and looked inside, where he saw the unmistakable glitter of gold crowns. Over the past year he'd had to handle large sums on several occasions, and he had begun to get a feel for such quantities. At a guess, there was somewhere between a hundred to a hundred and fifty gold marks.

He hadn't come for the gold, but he wasn't leaving it behind either. Will stored it in the limnthal along with the jars of phosphorous and the vials of alchemist's fire. He had almost everything he needed now. Getting to his feet, he started to leave when he heard a noise through the wall. Someone was moving close by, just outside the building.

There were several possibilities, chief among them being more vampires or the king's Driven. Either way, he didn't want to give away his theft if they checked the building before he could leave. He closed the iron door, replaced the rug, then returned the desk to its original position. With that accomplished, he rechecked his prepared spells.

He still wasn't sure who was outside, and while the odds were highest that it would be the king's Driven at that point, he was more afraid of vampires. Still, he needed to escape. If he walked out and the king's men tried to detain him, he would need a plan. An idea came to him after a moment's thought.

Discarding the prepared wind-wall spell, he replaced it with a chameleon spell, but he didn't cast it. He now had two illumination spells and the chameleon spell ready. He was tempted to emerge with a force-lance in hand as well, but if it actually was the Driven, they would probably see that as an obvious sign of hostility. Most of the vampires might not be able to see turyn, but the Driven were all sorcerers.

He walked out the main door without a single spell active, though his vision was optimized for the lighting. Will could clearly see the teams of sorcerers spread out around the building. They were clustered in groups of four with about ten to twenty yards between each group, and they appeared to encircle the entire warehouse.

Given the dim lighting, they probably assumed he couldn't see them, and he was just grateful that they weren't hiding in the ground again. Will walked directly toward the closest group. At twenty feet, they ordered him to stop and he did his best to act surprised. "Who's there?"

"Servants of the king. Identify yourself."

Will was nonplussed. "You don't recognize me, yet you claim to work for my father-in-law?"

The leader of the group closest to Will moved nearer, stepping into a better-lit area. "You were reported as being at Wurthaven receiving medical care."

He shrugged. "And yet I'm here. I came back to make sure there were none left. The place was crawling with them earlier."

"Please lie down on the ground, sir. We will have to take you into custody until we can verify your identity." The man pointed at the cobblestones to underscore his command.

Will held his hands out to the side in a friendly gesture as he continued to move forward. "Can't we be more civilized about this? I'll come quietly. I really don't think my wife would be happy to hear that you forced me to lie in the street."

The sorcerer backed up slightly, and his companions moved to encircle Will, who made a show of pretending to turn around and offer his hands behind his back. "You could cuff me just as easily like this," he told them.

"Get down n—"

Chapter 26

Their leader was shouting as Will released his first prepared spell, Ethelgren's Illumination. The brilliant light blinded the men's night-adjusted vision as he rushed forward and pushed one of the men aside, but he didn't run past. Instead he crouched down and cast the chameleon spell on himself.

"Fuck!"

"Damn it!"

"I can't see a thing. He just ran past me!"

Will grinned to himself as they swore and tried to organize themselves. Two of the teams farther out on either side were sent to chase him down, while the others continued to close in on the building. The ones immediately around him moved away a moment later.

He remained still until the teams were fully engaged with securing the warehouse, and their attention was firmly on what was within their circle, rather than what was without. The two teams sent to find him returned empty-handed and once they were accounted for, Will felt secure in slowly creeping away.

The king is going to be very displeased when he finds out I made fools out of them, thought Will. He felt a little bad about that, but he couldn't afford to get tied down answering questions. His friends didn't have the luxury of time.

He debated his next move, as it could technically be accomplished at either end of the journey, but in the end it made more sense to take care of it in Cerria. Plus, since he was already in the dockside district, it would be easy to find what he needed. He stopped at the first pub he found and circled around to the back alley.

Dawn was fast approaching, and so the drinking houses were all closed, but Will worried he might run into an early morning employee coming to begin the day. It was the work of a few minutes to use another spell to open the back door and let himself in. From there, he searched until he found the entrance to the cellar, where what he needed was sure to lie.

In the cool dark there were racks that held numerous casks and barrels. It didn't take him long to find the ale, which was held in four massive butts, the largest barrel size in the room. Once again, he felt a sense of guilt, since he intended to take two full butts, leaving the pub with only one full and one partial butt to supply their customers.

It had been over a year since he had bought wine in large amounts, and this was a different beverage, plus at that time, he had only bought quarter casks. This was roughly four times as much volume, so he did a little mental math, quadrupling what he had paid before, then doubling it again. He still wasn't sure if it was enough to compensate the owner for the trouble of losing his stock, so he added a little more and left an even pile of thirty gold marks on the floor in front of where the butts stood. Then he stored them in the limnthal.

I've been nothing but a thief tonight, he realized, but he wasn't about to second-guess his choices. Exiting the cellar, he left the pub and stopped for a moment to make sure he relocked the door properly. It wouldn't do for someone else to come along and rob the place after he had left. He liked to think he was considerate.

Will resumed his purposeful walk, and soon he was outside Cerria again, heading south toward the congruence point. The sun was rising on his left, turning the pastures and fields into shifting shades of green and gold. Spring was already beginning to leave its mark on the world.

Alone and away from people, he activated the limnthal and sought advice. "I need to get back to your old house quickly."

Chapter 26

"Did you already return Tailtiu to her mother?"

"Yes."

"That's a shame. You could have used her to bargain for a guide. You didn't have any actual debt to repay. The only reason you had to rescue Tailtiu was because of her implied threat," said the ring.

"Well, it's a little late for that now." *And I rescued her for my own reasons, not to bargain with her life,* he added mentally.

"Yep. You're screwed."

"How does Aislinn do that vanishing thing? Twice now I've seen her appear and disappear. Is she becoming invisible or is she traveling somehow?" asked Will.

"It's a form of travel," said Arrogan. "Not one you'll be using any time soon, and never in Faerie."

"So there's a spell that can move you from one place to another?"

"It's called teleportation, and generally it can only be done over short distances, either to a place you can see, or a very familiar place that isn't too far away."

"How far is too far away?"

"A few miles at best," said the ring. "There used to be ways to teleport from city to city, but that required a beacon and there aren't any left."

Will was enthralled by the subject. "What happened to them?"

"Someone destroyed them."

The brevity of the answer raised his suspicions. "It was you, wasn't it?"

"I'd rather not talk about it," said Arrogan. "Don't you have something more pressing to worry about?"

"Why didn't anyone rebuild the beacons?"

"The secret of their construction was closely guarded by the Wayfarer's Society, which was sort of a specialized wizard's guild. The last of their masters died during the Terabinian War for Independence."

"Because you killed him?"

"Listen, I didn't kill everyone who died during that war. It's rude to assume. I know I made it sound like I did a lot of terrible things, but I wasn't the only one involved."

"But you killed the guild master of the Wayfarer's Society, didn't you?" asked Will insistently.

Arrogan growled. "Yes, damn it. Are you happy now?"

"Maybe a little," admitted Will. "It's been a bad day, so it doesn't take much to improve my mood. So, you say I can't teleport. Can you guide me through Faerie? Tailtiu took me on a journey using multiple congruence points back and forth to get back to Barrowden in just a few hours once."

"She's a part of Faerie, so she instinctively knows where all the congruence points are," explained the ring. "Not only that, but she visits our realm now and then and already knew the two places in our world that you wanted to travel between. Both of those things are necessary to figure out a route like that. Regular humans like you and me—well, like you—have to make do with the few routes we know personally."

"So, you're no help at all."

"You already know my old shortcut between Barrowden and Branscombe. That will shave three days off your journey."

He needed to get there and back much more quickly than that. Will released the limnthal and continued walking in silence. Not too long ago he'd had a surfeit of allies and resources; now he had none. As he finally reached the congruence point, he saw something move in the tall grass.

Will paused, suddenly cautious, until a familiar gray form stepped into view.

CHAPTER 27

Gold eyes stared at him without blinking. "What the hell do you want?" Will demanded.

"As you have been useful to me in the past, I thought I would offer you a boon," said the goddamn cat, completely without shame.

"You left me to die last night. I needed your help then, but you abandoned me! They were eating me!"

The cat blinked once, slowly. "And yet you are standing here. It appears that despite your histrionics you didn't need my help after all."

Will growled. "It's about more than me. I lost one friend and I may still lose another. Janice has lost an eye and half her face. Do you think I care about nothing but myself? They matter to me!"

One of the cat's ears twitched, but he still seemed unfazed. "Should they matter to me? Have any of them done me a great service? You helped me remove an old enemy, but did they? Am I supposed to care about all of humankind now? You go too far in your assumptions. You were aiding one of my sworn enemies; did you expect my assistance?"

Will glared at the cat for half a minute. He wanted to fault the demigod's logic, but he couldn't. Nor could he dismiss the fact that the cat *had* shown up at the very moment he had been about to give in to despair. Was it a coincidence? Given the creature's feelings about the fae, he didn't expect an honest answer. Will took a deep breath, held it, then let it out slowly. "Did you say you were offering a boon? How much will it cost me?"

The goddamned cat wrinkled his nose in disgust. "You should know me better by now. I don't deal in favors and bargains. I help those I choose, when I choose. Last night I was disinclined, but today I am otherwise disposed to offer you assistance."

He thought about it a moment, then replied, "Sorry. My words were careless. What do you propose?"

"I can get you to the place you desire, and back, assuming you survive," said the Cath Bawlg.

"You'll guide me through Faerie?"

"I could, but I would rather not waste so much time. I have another path in mind, though you'll need to protect yourself."

Will nodded. "What do I do?"

"The demon-armor spell you used in the past should work nicely, though it will become tiring. This path is not for the faint of heart."

He frowned. "How fast is this route?"

"Less than an hour, but you'll be sorely tested. Make certain your reserves are full before we begin," answered the goddamn cat.

Will expanded his outer shell and began absorbing turyn as quickly as he could, until he felt comfortably full but not strained. When he glanced back at the cat, he nearly fell over backward. The formerly small gray tabby had grown to the size of a destrier. With the cat standing on all four legs, Will could barely see over his shoulders. *If someone's dog saw him right now it would have nightmares for life,* he observed as he stepped back and tried to hide his startlement. "You could have warned me."

The goddamn cat's voice was a deep rumble as he replied, "If I intended to put an end to you my size wouldn't matter."

Size doesn't matter when it comes to giant... Will began to snicker, unable to help himself.

Chapter 27

"Is something funny?"

Will waved his hands in front of his face. "Nothing, just something I'll have to tell Selene one of these days."

The cat ignored his lack of a proper answer. "Climb on my back."

He tried, and although the Cath Bawlg was kind enough to lie down to make things easier, he found it to be about as easy as climbing a mountain of pudding. The giant feline's skin hardly seemed attached to his body, and while his fur was thick it was also slick, providing little purchase. Will eventually got to the demigod's shoulders, but when he tried to get his leg over, he wound up sliding down the other side. "This isn't working," he admitted at last. "I think we need a saddle or something similar."

The goddamn cat showed his teeth in displeasure, a frightening display of ivory sabers set in a disturbingly large mouth. "You obviously missed the operative word, 'climb.' You have a spell for that, don't you?"

"Will that work on a person—or cat?"

"Find out. You're the wizard."

He tried and failed, then he took a moment to study the spell construct as he tried again. Arrogan had walked him through the basics of crafting new spells the previous year and it wasn't something to be done casually, but this seemed like it might be a small change. After a minute he identified the runes that designated the target as an inanimate solid. Switching it around, he altered it to what he thought should target animate solids instead.

When he invested turyn into the spell this time, he did so very slowly. He'd learned the risk of overloading an untested spell once before and he didn't want to repeat the experience. The spell took effect and seemed to be functioning normally so he tried climbing the goddamn cat once more.

The skin still slid back and forth, but he remained firmly attached, like a stubborn tick. He worked his way up to the shoulders and managed to get himself astride the massive feline with no trouble. Both legs were firmly affixed on either side of the Cath Bawlg, and since the spell forced the user to keep three limbs attached, he had to keep one hand on the cat at all times as well. *Maybe I should work on a version that only requires two for situations like this,* he thought. It would be handy to have both hands free.

"Ready?"

"Sure—areaghhhhh!" Will's assent transformed into a terrified scream as the cat leapt forward. The beast moved with incredible speed, and unlike a horse, whose back was relatively stable, the cat's spine, shoulders, and hips all seemed to move in different directions at the same time. He was suddenly grateful that he couldn't come loose and started to wish his free hand was similarly stuck.

They raced across the field and into a small copse of trees, but the world shifted as they entered the shadows, transforming into something entirely unfamiliar. The turyn was different, and Will could tell they were no longer in the world he was familiar with. "Where are we?"

"My ancient home, the Shadowlands."

It was hard to see, as the air seemed to swirl around them in dark ribbons. Will thought there were trees, or bushes, but the light was dim, and everything seemed insubstantial. He tried adjusting his vision and only succeeded in making himself nauseous. The world only grew stranger the harder he tried to perceive it properly.

The Cath Bawlg stopped suddenly, and Will probably would have fallen off if it hadn't been for the climbing spell. Something even darker loomed in front of them, or perhaps it receded. *Or is it sinking downward?* His mind struggled

Chapter 27

to make sense of the alien geometries that seemed inherent to everything in the Shadowlands. "It's time to use the demon-armor spell," warned the goddamn cat.

Will had formed the spell once a day as part of his daily practice routine, which turned out to be a good thing, for when he saw the colors of the runes forming above his palm he nearly lost his train of thought. They formed in shades of silver, gray, and black with none of the ordinary chromatic hues he was familiar with. Discipline alone got him through his surprise, and a few seconds later the spell was ready. He released it, and silver flames formed around his body.

"What is that dark thing?" he asked, referring to the mound or pit (he still couldn't decide which it was) that lay before them.

"You call them congruence points. There are none to this plane from your world, which is why I brought you here."

"Which plane?"

"Your kind usually call it Hell, not that any humans have seen it to make such a judgment."

"Wait, what?" Will's words went unheard as the Cath Bawlg leapt forward and dove into the nebulous darkness. The world shifted, and Will gasped, shocked by a pitch-black sky that hovered above a brown landscape of stone pillars and shattered boulders. The air burned his lungs as he inhaled, and he began to choke. At the same time, Will noticed that the Cath Bawlg was also covered in silver flames, though he wasn't producing them. The goddamn cat was protecting himself.

"Keep your energy focused on the demon-armor spell," cautioned his mount. "The basic essence of this place will erode your flesh and melt your bones if you don't vigorously resist it, and that includes the air."

His turyn was rapidly diminishing as the flames that surrounded him flickered and began to thin out. He might have panicked if he had been in the same situation a few weeks ago, but times had changed for him. Will had survived a worse drain on his turyn at the dam, he'd endured the worst pain of his life at the hands of the king, and his sanity had been tested by the sight of both himself and his friends being taken for food by creatures too vile to exist.

Put simply, Will was done with panic—at least for the time being. *Give me a few years of rest and relaxation and maybe this will bother me,* he thought grimly as he expanded his outer shell and ramped up his turyn absorption. Between the demon-armor and the small additional drain of the climbing spell, he still only had to push himself to roughly half of what he considered his maximum absorption rate.

Better still, since he was absorbing and converting a portion of the void turyn before it reached the demon-armor, he actually lessened the amount of energy it took to maintain. The strain was more than bearable, and Will found himself enjoying the challenge. A rough smile appeared on his face. *Every day I get thrown into the fire, and every time I emerge stronger,* he thought. His control of turyn, both within and without, had grown to a degree that he could now feel the difference. Much of the growth had happened slowly, over the past year, but the tests of the present had brought the changes into the light where he could notice them.

"This is nothing!" he yelled into the air—air that could no longer hurt him. A slow rumble built between his legs before erupting into a complementary roar from the goddamn cat.

Chapter 27

Unlike the Shadowlands, Hell was easier for his brain to make sense of. The realm had an understandable geometry that didn't threaten to twist his mind into knots. It wasn't pretty, but aside from the fact that every part of it was utterly inimical to life, it was knowable. There was a sky above, stony soil below, a host of rock formations, and occasionally strange black, red, or orange plants.

If one could get used to the bizarre color scheme, it might even be beautiful in places. "This isn't quite as awful as I expected," said Will aloud.

"The wilderness isn't as bad as the populated regions," replied the cat. "But all of it is hideous because of the basic nature of its existence."

"Which is?"

"The realm is parasitic. It feeds and grows by stealing matter, turyn, and all other manner of resources from other planes."

Will was shocked by the revelation. It simply didn't fit within the model of reality that he had constructed over the past few years. "How can a plane steal from other planes?"

"Through the governance of the demon lords, but the truth is that they're a product of the realm too. The Shadowlands weren't always as you saw them today. My home was once beautiful. What remains is a hollowed-out husk, the unwanted remnants left behind by the predations of demon kind."

Will fell silent, unsure what to say. The goddamn cat had made no secret of who his enemies were: the fae, the elves, and demons. Now Will could understand why he hated demons so much. He mulled it over for several minutes, then came to a new question. Were there similarities between the Cath Bawlg's enemies?

"Is Faerie the same?"

"As what?"

"As Hell," said Will. "Is it parasitic too?"

"An astute observation for one so young," said the demigod. "Faerie is a disease, but unlike Hell, it doesn't destroy and kill its hosts. It connects to multiple realms, growing slowly and poisoning everything it touches."

"Is that why you hate the fae?"

"One reason, yes," admitted the demigod.

"And the elves?"

"I hate the elves because they knew better."

"Better than what?"

"Keep growing, wizardling. You've impressed me today. Eventually you'll understand enough to ask the right question, as you just did regarding Faerie. If not, ask me again in a century."

The refusal to answer was frustrating, but Will also felt a faint glow of pride. He'd never heard a compliment from the goddamn cat before. "Do you think I'll really survive a century? I barely survived the last week."

"That depends entirely on you."

Will thought about that for a moment. "I think there's a lot of dumb luck involved too. There have been plenty of times when things could have gone just a little worse and I wouldn't have been able to survive no matter what I did."

"Trust me, that will never happen."

"How can I believe that?"

"Because I'll make sure of it," said the Cath Bawlg. "There will always be a way."

The goddamn cat had spoken to him on so few occasions that Will didn't know whether to believe the demigod or not. On the one hand he had never known the cat to lie to him, but on the other, the fae never lied either, and he knew how their advice worked. The best evidence he had to go on lay in what had occurred just the

Chapter 27

previous night. He'd been on the verge of giving up, until the goddamn cat had shown up.

Not that he fucking helped or anything, thought Will sourly. *But he did make me mad enough to keep trying.* He resolved to ask Arrogan's advice on the matter later. After all, his mentor had a great deal more experience with the Cath Bawlg.

Something bright made the horizon glow ahead. "What's that?" asked Will.

"Our exit back to the Shadowlands."

"Why is it so bright like that?"

"It's one of the tears that the demons use to drain the vitality from my home, much like the one we entered through." Another growl issued from the demigod. "It appears someone has anticipated our destination."

Looking forward, Will saw a collection of oddly shaped humanoids. They were roughly human-sized, but they were both muscular and grotesque in their proportions. Many of them held strange black rods in their hands. "What are those things they're holding?"

"A weapon, similar to a bow or crossbow," answered the cat. "Each one can only fire once, but it hurls a nasty black bolt similar to a quarrel. They're poisoned as well. One hit would probably kill you, so be careful." The Cath Bawlg picked up speed, his paws tearing the stony ground as his claws emerged to provide extra traction.

"You're heading straight at them!" yelled Will.

"Guard yourself and my flank," said the cat, his voice becoming a roar at the end of the sentence.

Will still had one illumination spell prepared, but as they charged, he readied a wind-wall and a force-lance as well, but he didn't keep a spell in hand. He wanted it free so he could use his shield as necessary, and the closer they got the more necessary it looked like it would be.

The demons scattered before their approach, moving to the sides and aiming their strange weapons. The Cath Bawlg picked a target, though, and focused on running directly at one of them despite the frightened creature's attempts to evade.

Will tried to watch all of them, even though it was impossible. He could only block what he saw coming. At ten yards, the demons began firing, their weapons erupting with puffs of smoke and sending black rods flying toward them at speeds too quick to see. Will felt his point-defense shield activate a dozen times in the span of a second. It happened at a level just below conscious thought, which, though it should have been strange, felt oddly familiar to him.

Even so, several shafts got through, burying themselves into the goddamn cat's thick coat of fur. If the weapons bothered the demigod, he gave no sign of it. With one last great leap, the cat flew through the air and landed on his chosen target. The result was almost instantly fatal for the hapless demon.

Will's body whiplashed back and forth as the massive feline he rode turned and ripped into those enemies who were closest. He tried to keep his eyes open and block new attacks, even though the speed of the cat's movements made it difficult to focus. After a few seconds he gave up and switched tactics. "Guard your eyes! It's going to get bright!" he yelled, releasing his prepared Ethelgren's Illumination.

If the sudden light bothered the goddamn cat, Will couldn't tell. Of course, his own eyes were tightly shut, but the beast's violent spins and leaps continued unabated, so he hoped all was well. As the light began to fade, he opened his eyes, only to find one of the creatures had latched onto the demigod's tail.

Chapter 27

The goddamn cat was protected by his own version of the demon-armor spell, but this demon seemed not to care for its own safety. It ignored the burning flames and crawled resolutely forward, stabbing claw-like fingers into the cat's hindquarters. Will unleashed his force-lance, blowing the blighted demon's head from its shoulders. The rest of the body fell away a second later.

A moment later, Will's stomach rose into this throat as they suddenly took flight. The Cath Bawlg leapt an incredible distance, covering more than twenty yards as he headed for the tear that would take them back to the Shadowlands. The demons, most of them still alive, couldn't hope to keep up with his speed, but those few who hadn't fired already lifted their weapons to aim. Twisting to keep his eyes on them, Will felt his shield activate five times in quick succession. He couldn't be entirely sure, but he thought he had blocked all the enemy's shots.

The world shifted and twisted, becoming darker and more difficult to comprehend. They were back in the Shadowlands. This time Will gave up trying to understand and simply closed his eyes. It was better than getting a headache from the bizarre geometry of the goddamn cat's home plane. "How much farther?" he asked.

"Not far," said the cat, his voice sounding labored.

"Are you hurt?" asked Will, but the demigod didn't respond. Will worried, but there was nothing he could do. The cat continued running, and he could only hope nothing serious was wrong.

CHAPTER 28

They emerged from the shadows of a tree deep in what Will presumed was the Glenwood. "How close are we?" he asked.

Panting, the Cath Bawlg replied, "Your old home is a mile to the south of us." There was a sick, wet sound in his voice.

"How badly are you hurt?"

"More than I would like." The cat stopped and sat on his haunches. Will took the opportunity to release the climbing spell and slide to the ground. He moved around to survey the massive beast from the front.

Three black metal shafts were buried in the goddamn cat's chest. Will wasn't sure how long they were, but only a short span of inches was still visible. "Those don't look good," he observed calmly, remembering his mother's oft-repeated advice. *Never panic in front of a patient.* "Do you have some magic to remove them, or can you transform into your usual size?"

"No and no. The metal is imbued with a magic inimical to my being. I can't heal until it is removed, neither can I shift my size."

"But you can't die, right?" asked Will. "You're a demigod."

"Human labels don't mean much, wizardling. Demigod just means, 'too powerful for us to understand but probably not a true god.'"

"But you can't die," insisted Will.

"I have no idea," said the Cath Bawlg. "I am unique. I have lived through uncountable years by human standards. I have never died before, if that helps, though the demons never stop inventing new ways to attempt it."

A surge of fear went through Will, but he suppressed it. "I can get them out, but it will hurt. If you were human, I might advise we wait until I had proper tools and medicines to make the process easier and safer."

"Get them out," declared the cat. "Whatever damage the process causes will be nothing compared to what their magic is doing inside my body."

"It's probably going to hurt a lot," said Will. "If they're barbed, I'll have to cut into you to free them." He was certain his feather trick wouldn't work to extract barbed heads as large as these looked to be.

Will summoned a paring knife from the limnthal. He kept a variety of cooking knives in there, and he liked them to have a razor edge. He studied the wound, then dismissed the blade, choosing instead to summon a larger, general-purpose knife with a sharp point and a six-inch edge.

The entry point was tight around the shaft, which was half an inch in diameter. Looking at the metal, Will noticed it wasn't entirely black; there was a shimmering blue almost invisible within the metal. *Demon-steel,* he realized. *Or what did Arrogan call it, driktenspal?* He thought he had the name right.

Making a small cut next to the shaft, he tried to insert a finger so he could feel the length of the bolt. More cuts followed, until he could get two fingers in, but he still couldn't reach the head. *This thing's at least a foot long,* he thought grimly.

What followed was an hour-long ordeal. The goddamn cat proved his resistance to pain, but even the demigod grunted and hissed as Will was forced to cut ever deeper into his flesh to reach the wickedly barbed metal points. His arms and tunic were soaked in blood before he had the first bolt out, and by the time the third was removed, he might as well have bathed in the demigod's vital fluids.

He stored the evil weapons in the limnthal, knowing how valuable the metal might someday be, and when he looked back he saw that the Cath Bawlg had already transformed, becoming once more the ordinary gray tabby Will had first met years before. "What's your true size?" Will asked suddenly.

"You've seen the Shadowlands," said the cat.

Will nodded, understanding the answer without truly being able to comprehend. The strange nature of the Shadowlands made things like size and shape into less tangible concepts. Kneeling down, he started to gather the cat into his arms, but the goddamn cat hissed and bared his teeth. "What's wrong? Don't you want me to carry you?"

The cat's warning yowl slowly diminished, becoming less and less audible. Will eased forward and carefully collected his benefactor, ignoring the warning when the volume of the Cath Bawlg's growl increased again. *He'll let me cut things out of him, or even ride him, but this is where he starts to get irrational,* thought Will. *He really is feral.*

Holding the bloody cat close against his chest, Will began the short trek home. Since they were within a mile of the house, he soon began to notice familiar groups of trees and similar landmarks. He was on familiar ground. He'd grown up playing in the forest, and now he knew exactly where he was.

He approached Arrogan's old hermitage from the front. He didn't see anyone outside, so he stepped onto

Chapter 28

the porch and knocked on the door. After a few seconds, the door opened and his mother stared out at him, her eyes growing wide with shock as she took in his appearance.

Will realized his mistake immediately. "I'm fine!" he hurriedly reassured her. "It isn't my blood."

Erisa blinked and took a slow breath. Blood didn't bother her, and she never lost her composure over wounds and injuries, but her son was an entirely different matter to her. Spotting the cat in his arms, she noted the bloody fur. "Is that?"

He nodded. "Yes. He helped me get here, but we got in a fight along the way."

Erisa held out her hands. "May I?" Will handed the goddamn cat carefully to his mother, silently hoping the demigod wouldn't lash out at her. The Cath Bawlg remained silent. Bloody cat in her arms, Erisa jerked her head toward the yard. "The tub is still around on the side of the house. Don't come in until you're clean." Stepping back, she pushed the door shut with her foot.

Will stared at the closed door, fighting to hold back a laugh. Some things never changed, and his mother was certainly one of those things. He looked around at the porch, then began constructing his favorite cleaning spell. It took a few minutes, but once he was done he set the boundary to include the porch before investing his energy and releasing it. *Might as well clean a little extra while I'm at it,* he thought.

When he entered the house a minute later, his mother glanced up with a look of irritation. "I thought I told you to wash before—oh! Never mind then."

Will was more surprised by what he saw. The goddamn cat was half bundled in a warm towel by the hearth, and Erisa sat on the floor beside him, a damp rag in her hand, which she appeared to be using to carefully wipe away the blood and dirt that had stuck to the demigod's fur. The cat's eyes locked onto his with an expression of longsuffering, but the Cath Bawlg said nothing. *Maybe he won't kill her,* thought Will. "If it's too much to bear, let me know and I'll take you outside," he said aloud.

His mother misunderstood who he was talking to. "Surely you haven't been gone long enough to forget what I do for a living, have you?"

He chuckled. "Never. Where is everyone?"

"Shouldn't I be asking you that question?" said Erisa. "Where has my son been all this time?" She never took her eyes off her patient, but Will could hear the displeasure in her tone.

"I've had a lot going on," he said weakly.

"Too much to bring your wife to visit between school semesters?"

Ouch. "You've met Selene before—"

"And I liked her," interrupted his mother. "Is she too important to visit now that she has you?"

He tried to process that statement. Was she implying that Selene felt she was more important because she had married him? That would only make sense from a mother's point of view—no, it had to be the opposite. She thought Selene felt she no longer had to try. Maybe. He wasn't confident in his translation. Will countered the multilayered question the only way he knew how, with honesty. "I don't know what that question means exactly, but I have a lot to tell you. The first thing is that I haven't actually seen Selene but once since we got married."

Erisa stopped, then slowly turned her head to look at him. "Say that again?"

"She's being kept hidden away. Even I don't know where she is."

"She was kidnapped?"

Chapter 28

"No, it's voluntary, to protect her from her father."

His mother frowned, but returned to what she was doing. "But you're safe in the capital? Wouldn't the king simply arrest you if he was angry at her?"

Will decided to lie a little. "He's afraid to do anything to me for fear of upsetting his daughter."

"Yet she has to hide from him? William, you're not making any sense."

"It's really complicated, Mom, and I don't have a lot of time."

She glanced at him sharply. "You just got here, and *he* doesn't look like he's going anywhere for a while."

"I have to use Granddad's lab again, then I'll have to leave, whether he's fit to travel or not. People are depending on me."

"Sammy will be home in less than an hour," said his mother. "If you leave without seeing her, she'll be furious."

Translation, Mom will also be angry, thought Will.

His mom froze then. "Wait, the laboratory, you don't mean you're going back to where the trolls are? You nearly got yourself eaten last time!"

He swallowed. "If I don't, Tiny might not survive another week, and another friend of mine might lose an eye and half her face."

Erisa glared at him. "*Her*? Never mind, what about Tiny? He just left for the capital a couple of weeks ago. What happened?"

Will was mildly surprised by the amount of distress in his mother's voice. Apparently, she had grown attached to the big warrior while Will was away. "He took a heavy beating for me, Mom. I mean, he actually covered me with his own body." His throat constricted as he tried to answer. "The armor kept his skin safe, but they bruised him badly, especially his kidneys."

His mother blanched at that. She knew quite well what that meant. "It might not be that bad, Will. If he drinks a lot of water and rests…"

"It's that bad, Mom. The head doctor at Wurthaven felt his chances were pretty bad."

"Isn't there some other way? If you wait, Sammy can let Eric know. He could probably bring some of his soldier friends to help. You can't go alone, not again."

Will shook his head. "More people would only make it worse. Trolls don't respect men and steel; they fear nothing aside from fire. If I go alone, I can do this. Trust me."

"You said something similar last time."

"I didn't tell you what I was doing last time. Did I?"

Erisa shook her head. "You aren't improving your case with me."

"I'm sorry, Mom, but I'm not making a case. I'm doing this whether you approve or not."

Tears began rolling down her cheeks. "For most mothers, watching their sons grow up brings quite a few tears, but you—I swear to the gods it will kill me. I can't bear this." She wiped her face on her sleeve, then added, "Come back, and when you do you'd best say hello to Sammy before you leave, or else you shouldn't bother coming back at all."

"What about Uncle Johnathan, or Annabelle?"

"Your uncle is living in our old house, so he can be closer to his work. The army is paying him to produce carts again. Annabelle ran away, but she left her son with us. His name is Oliver. He's napping in the other room. Try not to wake him when you leave."

"Damn, a lot has changed," said Will.

"You should visit more often. Maybe it wouldn't be such a shock."

"Mom, I had my reasons—"

Chapter 28

"That your bride disappeared, and you were afraid to come without her? I'm your mother, William, not the king. Just *tell* me and I'll never judge you. I'm on your side, remember? I always will be, no matter how stupid you are, or how angry you make me."

He stared at her for a moment, at a loss for words. "I'm sorry, Mom."

"Go. I have a patient and it's never good to cry in front of a patient," she told him. Feeling riddled with guilt, he turned and headed for the bedroom. His mother's voice called to him once more. "William. Make sure you have your mind on what you're about. Don't put yourself in danger until you're focused. You can feel guilty about me after you're back safe and sound."

"I will, Mom," he answered, then stepped through the door. *I will? I will what, feel guilty? That was the stupidest answer ever,* he chided himself. Then he dropped the topic, shoving it to the back of his mind. Erisa was right. He needed to focus on what he was doing; otherwise he'd wind up in a troll's belly instead of returning to save anyone.

CHAPTER 29

Muskeglun was just as pleasant as he remembered it being, which was to say, not at all. Will could feel the oppressive atmosphere settling into his skin within seconds of passing through the congruence point. The air was hot and heavy, and a sweltering miasma of rotting vegetation made sure his nose didn't feel left out of the fun, either. The friendly local greeters, also known as mosquitos, swarmed closer to make him feel welcome.

"I hate this damn place," he muttered after activating the limnthal.

"Wherever you go, there you are," said the ring cheerfully.

"What does that mean?"

"Any place is awful if you're there," clarified Arrogan.

"I'm in Muskeglun."

"Ooh, all right. My mistake. You're right. Muskeglun is in a class of its own, but think of it this way, you're bringing happiness and joy to others."

He wrinkled his brow in puzzlement. "What others?"

"The mosquitos."

Will chuckled. "At least someone's happy to see me."

"Do you have a plan? They were pretty pissed when we left last time."

He took a deep breath. "I sort of have a plan."

"What is it?"

"Well, everyone I've talked to is pretty opposed to me coming here, for the very reason you mentioned a second ago. But on the other hand, I don't really have a choice, otherwise I'll lose one friend and see another maimed for life…"

Arrogan interrupted, "You're starting to make me anxious. Skip to the plan part."

"So thus far, in order to convince people to support my decision, I've been pretending I had a plan."

The ring groaned. "And how many people fell for your bullshit?"

"Up to now, very few have given me a chance to explain. The head physician at the school didn't, so I had to put him to sleep. The king's Driven tried to arrest me, so I had to run from them. After that, the goddamn cat just showed up and helped without asking what I planned to do. Mom didn't really ask either."

"So, no one then?"

"Me," said Will. "I fooled myself, otherwise I'd have been too scared to come. I did bring a sizeable carrot and an equally large stick, though, plus I have a translator."

The ring made an audible sigh. "Assuming I'm the translator, what carrot and stick did you bring?"

"Two full butts of ale and twenty vials of alchemist's fire. I've also got a sizeable store of white phosphorous if things completely go to hell."

"I see. So it's going to be, piss in the cup or I burn your village to the ground? You realize that's a pretty awful way to behave. Burning people alive is just about the classic definition of evil, and that's coming from someone who once killed most of his friends."

"They're trolls," argued Will.

"They're people too. Plus, if you go with threats, things are very likely to go to hell. Trolls panic when they see fire. Do you know what people do when they panic?"

"Run?"

"Some run, some freeze, and others lose their minds and attack. If you make a threat in the troll village and someone calls your bluff, you'll have to light someone or something on fire. When you do that, they'll panic. Even if you manage to throw a bunch of those vials, they'll tear you to pieces."

It had been more than twenty-four hours since Will had last slept, and he was getting close to snapping as desperation and anxiety ate at his nerves. "Do you have an idea, then? I'm running out of time."

"We'll do it my way. Let me do the talking and do everything I tell you."

"What's your way?"

"We'll be nice."

Will's jaw dropped. "When have you *ever* been nice? To anyone?"

"I'm always nice when I know I can't win in a straight fight."

"Not that I've seen," countered Will.

"That's because I was a badass. You probably never saw me around anyone I couldn't whip, but this is one place where I always mind my manners."

"Your manners are only matched by your excessive modesty and humility," quipped Will.

"You really have a mouth on you, boy," replied the ring.

"I learned from the best." He was too tired to argue, though. "Let's do it your way."

He was dressed lightly, wearing only a single layer of cloth, an undertunic. He might have gone bare-chested, but the insects dissuaded him from doing that. On his head, Will wore the antler hat that Arrogan had made from the horns of the fae lord, Elthas. It didn't have any magical properties, but since trolls couldn't distinguish the differences between humans, it served to identify him. They didn't know that Arrogan had died, so the antlers made them think he was the same man they had been dealing with for decades.

Chapter 29

And the same one who had run out on the last deal without paying them their bonus cask of wine.

He had actually given them more wine than promised, but because it had all been in a single rundlet cask instead of in two separate quarter casks, the trolls had thought he had cheated them. Arrogan had had some choice words for him over that blunder.

Will hoped today's gift would help clear up the misunderstanding. The two butts of ale were huge compared to the rundlet cask he had brought before, and apparently size mattered. A butt was roughly equivalent to seven rundlets, so he was bringing fourteen times the volume of ale as he had of wine.

"You're sure you can talk them into this?" asked Will nervously as they marched eastward away from the stagnant lake.

"You brought two whole butts of ale, right?"

"Yes."

"I'd say we have a fair chance, but don't do anything weird like pointing at their dicks like you did last time. There will be a lot more of them in the village, and while Lrmeg wasn't interested, you never know when you'll come across a troll pervert."

"That was an accident," protested Will.

"Mm hmm, is that what you tell your wife?" said Arrogan, finishing with a wicked cackle. Will didn't respond, so the ring continued to tease him. "Remember when you came back from Barrowden with a pregnant girl? You could come back from this place by yourself but still have to explain to your mother why *you're* pregnant. I'm sure Erisa would get a kick out of that."

Will shuddered, remembering the horrifying details of how trolls reproduced by breaking off a piece of themselves inside a partner. If the partner was a troll, the flesh would combine and a new troll would grow like a tumor. If the partner wasn't a troll, the piece left behind would simply grow into a twin of its troll parent, consuming parts of its host until it was big enough to violently erupt from the 'mother.'

"Can we talk about something else?"

"As long as it's interesting. You know I get mean when I'm bored."

Obviously, thought Will. "I have a question about Selene."

"Leave me out of your marital problems."

"No, about something she told me. When Aislinn gave us our half an hour together, we found out that she had only been through six months of time, while I've had a whole year pass by. Do you know where she could be?"

"Holy hell!"

"What?"

"Shut up, let me think," said Arrogan. Will waited patiently, walking in silence, until finally the ring began muttering to itself. "That sneaky, conniving, wily bitch, that's how she's keeping Lognion from finding her."

"How?"

"The heart-stone enchantment creates a bond that can enforce the master's will even across the boundaries between dimensions, but it won't easily cross multiple planes, and if there's a temporal difference the connection gets even more muddled."

"That clears up everything for me," said Will snidely.

"Don't be an ass. Of course it doesn't. There could be any number of planes that have a temporal difference like that, but I only know of a few. The real key is that I know a lot about her past, which narrows things down considerably."

"Aislinn's past?"

Chapter 29

"No, Selene's, you idiot! Yes, of course, Aislinn's past. Her teacher was from another world, one which Lognion couldn't reach even if he knew which one."

"And you're about to tell me, right?"

"I'm not sure that would be safe," said the ring cautiously.

Will didn't feel like taking no for an answer. "She already told me about it and described everything. She even has a friend there; his name is Sylandrea. So you might as well explain the rest."

"Sylandrea? She told you she was friends with an elf?"

He remained silent, waiting to see if Arrogan would reveal anything else. After a moment, the ring sighed. "Damn it. You only knew the name, didn't you?"

"And you fell for it," said Will, trying to ignore the painful ache in his chest. He had learned the name in what he had thought to be just a dream. Now it was apparent that he had actually travelled astrally. *And my hope that I was just imagining her with someone else is getting thinner all the time.* Whatever the truth was, he still had important questions. "If Aislinn decided to do something, like trying to keep her for good—is there a way for me to get there?"

"Nothing is impossible, but this might as well be. You could try to sneak aboard an elven trading vessel in Trendham, but I wouldn't recommend it. Plus, you'd have to wait a long time; they only show up there every four or five years. They're also very wary of that sort of thing and their magic is nothing to sneer at."

"How did she get from there to our house so quickly, though?"

"I don't know," said the ring honestly. "Within Faerie, Aislinn can probably teleport freely, which means she can get from anywhere there's a congruence to any other plane in almost no time at all. So she either knows where the entrance to the elven lands is, or she knows of another path through a different realm altogether."

"And you said her teacher was from there?"

"Graylin was his name," said Arrogan. "Well, that's not his full name of course. They all have ridiculously pompous names that take way too damned long to say. Graylin is what he was called by those he was familiar with."

Will stopped suddenly as a tall form stepped out from behind a tree. The troll's shadow fell over him, and he felt his mouth go dry. "There's one in front of me now," he announced quietly.

"An elf?"

"A troll."

"Oh, time to go to work." The ring began issuing a long series of grinding barks and guttural coughing noises. "Hold your hands out to either side to show him you have no weapons."

Will opened his arms and spread his fingers wide to show he wasn't holding anything.

"Make sure to keep them balled into fists. Trolls use claws, so if you open them it's an aggressive gesture."

The troll was already beginning to growl, but Will quickly corrected his mistake. "I had them open for a moment."

"I'll apologize," said Arrogan, beginning another sentence that sounded as though he might be trying to cough up a hairball. The troll responded, then leaned in to smell the air around Will's head. After that, it straightened and turned away. "He says for you to follow him to their village. He's going to let Clegg decide what to do with you."

"Is that safe?" asked Will, his feet already moving him into a jog so he could keep up with the troll's long stride.

"Clegg's a good guy," answered Arrogan. "You didn't get to meet him last time, but I'm sure you'll like him."

Chapter 29

"How can you like a troll?"

"Well, putting a clothespin on your nose helps. If you can get past the smell, they're not that bad." Will didn't reply; instead he focused on keeping up with the troll, who moved with deceptive speed through the tangled underbrush. The exertion, along with his slowly diminishing level of turyn, made him feel as though he was suffocating. Fifteen minutes into the journey, Will had to summon his first elixir of turyn and take a large swallow.

His first trip to Muskeglun had all but exhausted his supply of the valuable elixir, though those potions had mostly been left over from Arrogan. Since then, Will had replaced them with elixir of his own making, which was both fresher and easier for his body to assimilate. This was the first time he'd had to use any of the newer potions, though, and he was pleased to find that they worked as well or better than the old ones.

"Are we there yet?" asked the ring, unable to see the world around them.

"Not yet."

A few minutes later he asked again. "How about now?"

Will ground his teeth together. "Are you going to ask me every ten steps?"

"This is boring. You could dismiss the limnthal until we get there. Then I wouldn't have to endure this eternal darkness I live in for the entire trip."

"I might need you to translate for me," said Will. "If I dismiss the limnthal, you wouldn't hear what the troll said."

"Then I guess I'll have to keep asking questions."

"What did I ever do to you?" said Will, exasperated.

"Besides being born? You cost me a lot of sleep, not to mention ruining my favorite tunic."

"Huh?"

"Erisa was living with me when you were born, remember? I had to deliver your wrinkly red ass. You woke me up from a perfectly good dream because you just couldn't wait until morning to be born. You were a very selfish baby."

His mother had told Will that she had stayed with the old man until he was born, but he hadn't ever really thought through the practical ramifications. "You helped with the delivery?"

"Yep. Worst thing I ever did. If you think you're ugly now, you should have seen yourself back then. Your face was all squished up and distorted, and after you arrived I didn't get a decent night's sleep for months."

"Mom told me she went to live with Uncle Johnathan after I was born," countered Will.

"Sure, almost a year later, after you'd done your worst. Your uncle got the easy end of it. I had to deal with the crying and the puking. It was a relief when Erisa finally listened and got the hell out of my house. Now look at me—suffering the rest of eternity as a piece of jewelry—*with you*! There's no justice in the world."

Will had long since learned to see through the bluster and mock misery in Arrogan's diatribes. The old man wasn't likely to ever admit to having a soft spot, but Will knew better. He'd read some of his grandfather's journal, which was considerably more honest.

He almost ran into the back of the troll leading them when it stopped suddenly, pointing with one gnarled and twisted arm to indicate they had arrived. Will saw a clearing ahead of them, and in it was a cluster of large shelters constructed of the limbs and the trunks of fallen trees. He wasn't sure what he had been expecting.

Chapter 29

On one hand, he couldn't see that trolls needed much protection from the environment, but on the other, building homes out of the rotting remnants of fallen trees did seem to fit them. If anything, it was sometimes hard to see where the moss-covered houses ended and the trolls standing in the doorways began, as they tended to blend together visually.

The fact that they built houses also made it harder for him to see them as simple monsters. "We've arrived," he said quietly for Arrogan's benefit.

The troll he had been following stepped into a central clearing between the homes and cut loose with a loud, guttural bark. Within moments the doorways filled as trolls large and small (relatively speaking) looked out to see their strange visitor. Over a span of minutes, a crowd grew around them, making Will feel ever more nervous. If things went badly, he wouldn't be able to escape. There were at least a hundred trolls around him now, fanning out in every direction from the center of the village.

Despite the chaos, he could eventually tell that two of the trolls seemed to be more important than the others, though he had no way to identify them. His guide spoke loudly to those two, making sure everyone could hear him. "What is he saying?" whispered Will.

"He's talking to the chief, Clegg, along with his second in command, Lrmeg. Incidentally, Lrmeg is the one you stabbed in the dick last time."

"Do you think he holds a grudge?"

"Probably, but Clegg is making the decisions today, so don't worry too much. Oh, he's repeating my apology and offer to them."

"You offered them the ale already?"

"No, something else. Not to worry, it's merely a formality."

The way the ring said it made Will nervous. "What formality? Tell me what you said."

"It's a traditional troll apology. To make up for your former transgression, you offer the village one of your limbs as a meal."

"A limb?" Will's voice pitched higher as fear.

"Yeah, like an arm or a leg. You know the expression, 'I'd give an arm and a leg for such and such.' The phrase actually originated with trolls, so we owe them for that little piece of our culture."

"That's not all right!" hissed Will. "I don't want—"

"Shhh, I'm trying to listen," said Arrogan. "Oh, he sounds angry."

"Who?"

"Lrmeg, shhh!" A few seconds later, Will was nudged forward to stand before Clegg and Lrmeg. There followed a long series of grunts and coughs in which the ring spoke back and forth with the elder troll. Eventually the conversation paused, and the crowd pulled back slightly. Another troll appeared with what looked like a section cut from a massive tree trunk. The enormous piece of wood was deposited in front of Will with the flat side up, creating a table of sorts.

Arrogan spoke up. "I have good news and bad news."

"Fuck me," whined Will.

"You want me to tell Clegg that?"

"Just give me the news!" barked Will, already beginning to shake.

"Well, the good news is that Clegg has granted your plea for clemency and will agree to the trade of ale for urine, but there are a few conditions." Will was already sweating from the heat, but he began to sweat more. "First, and probably worst of all, you have to stay for the party."

"That doesn't sound so bad," said Will.

Chapter 29

"Spoken out of pure ignorance. Remember, trolls don't cook anything. They're afraid of fire, and that's just the beginning. Anyway, the second condition, which Lrmeg is insisting on, is that you honor the offer of an arm or a leg."

"What?" His face grew cold as the blood drained away.

Arrogan hurried to add, "They know how dangerous that is for humans, so they'll allow you the use of fire to cauterize the wound, though. And you get to pick the limb. I'd choose your off-hand arm. People never realize how much they need two legs. Also—and they don't have to know this—if we get back soon enough, you might be able to regrow the arm or leg if you can make the potions quickly enough."

The ring's words seemed to come to him from across a vast chamber, echoing in his ears. Will's shaking grew more violent as he saw that one of the trolls had arrived with what appeared to be a massive cleaver. The iron implement was large enough to cut a cow in half. Glancing around, Will could see that there was nowhere to run.

"You don't have to, though."

"What?"

The ring's voice was calm and even. "Clegg says you can leave if you want. You don't have to accept the deal, but you won't get the urine."

"Really?" Will's heart leapt at the news, and his voice emerged in a high-pitched squeak, but a second later, his fear returned. He couldn't do it. A dozen justifications ran through his head, but they all lead back to one ending. "God damn it."

"Should I tell him no?" asked Arrogan.

Will's teeth chattered, and tears rolled down his cheeks as he answered, "Tell them to take my left arm." He almost fell as he stepped closer to the table and put his left hand in the center.

The ring whistled. "Damn, Will, you may be dumb as a stump, but you've got balls the size of boulders." Arrogan resumed his grunting, guttural conversation with the trolls.

Clegg barked something in return, and the troll with the cleaver stepped forward. Will's legs grew weak, and he found himself sagging downward, until his shoulder was even with the table. Some helpful troll grasped his shoulder then, to keep him from sinking too low, and held him in place. He closed his eyes and lowered his head, so he couldn't see the impending blow.

The trolls began to cough loudly around him, their sounds rising in an almost rhythmic beat while he waited for the blow, but Will didn't dare look up. Almost a minute passed, and he felt his heart trying to leap out of his chest, but still the strike hadn't happened. Eventually, he cracked on eye to look around.

The cleaver was gone, though the trolls around the clearing continued to cough loudly. Dimly, Will remembered the sound from his first visit, along with what Arrogan had told him it signified. Laughter. "This was a joke, wasn't it?" he asked tremulously.

"Yes, little human. It was," said Clegg in broken but still understandable Darrowan.

The troll holding him up stepped back, and Will fell on his ass in the mud.

CHAPTER 30

"You speak my language?" Will asked after gaping at the chieftain for a long period. It was a stupid question. He realized that even as he asked it, but his mouth wasn't strictly tethered to the rational part of his brain at the moment.

"A little," said the troll, squeezing two of his fingers together in a gesture that seemed far too human-like. "Long time."

"Clegg is the one that taught me their language," offered the ring.

Will glared at his hand as though he might cut it off himself, but it was the ring that his ire was focused on. "You! When we get out of here, I'm not talking to you anymore."

"At least you're not dumb enough to try that while we're here," said Arrogan approvingly. "Besides, I didn't lie to you. Everything I said was the truth."

"But you knew Clegg wasn't going to insist on taking my arm!" A series of fresh coughs came from Clegg at that remark, fresh laughter. "What about last time? When they chased me out of here? Was that a joke too?"

"Lrmeg have bad temper. Always talk to Clegg," suggested the chieftain.

"He's right," agreed the ring. "You probably would have been torn apart. That's why this plan was so much better, and funnier. By the way, Clegg is quite intelligent. He understands I'm in the ring now."

"I see that," said Will, then he dipped his head respectfully toward the troll. "If you taught Arrogan your language, who taught you ours?"

"Old wizard, long ago. He was Lanthel, first troll friend. 'Gan is last troll friend."

'Gan, that must be short for Arrogan. "How long ago was this?" asked Will.

Clegg scratched his head. "Very long."

"Lanthel wasn't in favor of the scorched-earth policy back when they were driving back the troll hordes," Arrogan informed him. "He made contact with Clegg and managed to convince the last tribe in our world to relocate voluntarily. Since then, the council maintained contact with them for diplomatic reasons. I was the last ambassador appointed before the Terabinian War for Independence."

"You knew Lanthel?"

"No, that was over a thousand years before I was born. I just happened to be the last wizard who handled our contact with Muskeglun before—well, before everything went to hell," explained the ring.

Will nodded, swallowing as he tried to comprehend what he was hearing. "So Clegg is somewhere around two thousand years old?"

"Who knows?" admitted Arrogan. "He was old before Lanthel first met him, supposedly, but whether that was fifty years or five thousand years, no one can say."

Clegg smiled, showing a multitude of dark, stained teeth. "We don't count many. The years mean little." Lrmeg leaned in, making an odd series of sounds. The chieftain translated for Will, "Enough talk. Time for drink."

Will produced the first butt of ale, causing it to appear atop the heavy wooden trunk section. The trolls didn't bother tapping it the usual way. Lrmeg moved up beside the massive barrel and with one heavy fist knocked the top end into the keg, then pulled it out. Trolls began disappearing into their homes and emerging with large wooden bowls, which they dipped into the keg before pouring the contents into their mouths.

Chapter 30

There was a tap on his shoulder, and Will looked over to see Clegg holding a small bowl by troll standards. "Drink," ordered the troll chief.

Will did as he was told. He was so relieved to not be facing the loss of an arm or leg that he would have done almost anything just then. The bowl held something close to what a large human tankard might contain, so he drank it as speedily as he could. Clegg took the bowl, filled it, and gave it back to him a moment later.

"The drinking has started?" asked Arrogan.

Will swallowed another mouthful of the ale, which was quite good. "Yeah."

"Good luck," said the ring. "Enjoy the dancing and don't worry too much about the food. You can take a blood-cleanse potion later."

"Food?"

"They'll want you to eat with them."

"How bad is it?"

"They're afraid of fire. You can guess what I mean," said Arrogan. "Just be sure you don't eat any troll. The stuff they hunt won't kill you, but sometimes they get excited and someone rips off his own arm or a leg. If you eat troll flesh, you'll wind up with more than an upset stomach."

Will wrinkled his nose. "That's revolting." He didn't say more, though, because one of the trolls let out a loud 'whoop' and snatched him up to sit on the massive creature's shoulder. The crowd seemed to be cheering, so Will held his bowl up in the air and yelled with them.

Then he drank.

He didn't have very much experience drinking, aside from a few minor occasions while he was in the army and one or two formal events in Cerria. During most of those times, he had been more concerned with keeping a clear head or babysitting one of his squad mates. This time he had only himself, and the trolls insisted that he drink as much as his stomach would hold.

When he got too full and belched up a large mouthful of foam, they laughed and cheered. Things got considerably more chaotic after that.

Drums were brought out, and the trolls began to dance. The music was strangely compelling, particularly since it was different than anything Will had ever heard before. There were no strings or horns, only drums, so the music consisted entirely of a variety of percussive beats that shook his bones and vibrated through his chest. Before long, he was up and dancing with the trolls, while the world swirled dizzily around him.

When they finally brought in the food, Will was drunk beyond his wildest imaginings. The feast consisted of a large reptile some twenty feet in length. He'd never seen anything like it, but the size, short legs, and long, sinuous tail suggested the beast was semi-aquatic. If he'd been in his right mind, he would have decided he was glad that he hadn't gone near the lake. As it was, he was busy watching the trolls rip the massive reptile apart, exposing its guts and flesh, which they greedily stuffed into their mouths.

Someone handed him a handful of something bloody. Will held it for ten or fifteen seconds, hoping the giver would move on, but the troll simply stared at him, then barked and pointed at his mouth.

Well, shit, he thought blearily. Steeling himself, he shoved the bloody gobbet of flesh into his mouth and chewed the rubbery meat. It was an effort to keep from gagging, but being drunk seemed to help. Eventually he swallowed, and the trolls began cheering for him again.

He smiled at the troll who had fed him, whereupon the seven-foot humanoid promptly grinned back before

Chapter 30

vomiting. A cascade of foul-smelling fluid rained down on Will's head, and he reciprocated by gagging and retching up the contents of his own stomach.

Lrmeg appeared then, yelling something at the troll who had vomited. He pointed at the empty barrel, and Will guessed that he was reprimanding the troll for not vomiting into the container so it could be saved. *That's right,* Will reminded himself. *They only have one orifice, so they piss and shit from their mouths.* He looked down at himself, covered in rancid troll bile, and promptly threw up again.

Thankfully, he passed out soon after.

He awoke sometime later, as someone shook his shoulder. Opening his eyes, he saw a creature of nightmare staring down at him. He almost screamed before recognizing it as Clegg. "Barrel full. Time to go," said the troll in what was probably a gentle tone.

Sitting up, Will's stomach lurched, and his head began to pound. "Oh," he groaned. He'd had a few minor hangovers in the past, but this was an entirely new level of misery. Reaching up, he rubbed at his temples, only to find that his hair was stiff and sort of crunchy to the touch. Examining himself, he realized he was still covered in troll vomit, or piss, whichever way one preferred to label it. The disgusting fluids had dried in his hair and on his clothes while he slept.

Thankfully, he couldn't smell it, or much of anything else for that matter. His nose had been overwhelmed by the constant onslaught of troll stench and had given up at some point while he slept, but he had no doubt he probably smelled like something that had been retrieved from a cesspit.

Clegg was laughing. "Humans don't drink well."

Will agreed, but his head hurt too much to nod. "Yeah. You're right."

"Hungry?" asked the chieftain.

The memory of what he had choked down the day before made his stomach begin to spasm. "No thanks," he replied, leaning over to fight back a fresh wave of dry heaving. That made his head hurt even worse of course, and he discovered he also had a sharp pain in his right thigh. Looking down, he saw that his trousers were ripped, and a scab had formed on his skin. The flesh was swollen, red, and very tender. "That must have been a monster mosquito," he muttered to himself.

His body felt incredibly weak, and he quickly realized that though he was absorbing turyn as quickly as possible, he was almost entirely drained. If he had slept longer, he might not have woken up at all. Summoning an elixir of turyn from the limnthal, he downed the entire bottle. He waited a few minutes, then followed it with a blood-cleanse potion.

Clegg helped him get to his feet, and Will did his best to ambulate out of the chieftain's rotting home and back into the dappled sunlight of the village center. Once there, he stored the emptied and newly refilled butt cask in the limnthal and replaced it with the second butt of ale. "Thank you for your hospitality," he told Clegg slowly, attempting to sound sincere.

The chief barked out a series of orders, and two trolls came over to stand on either side of him. "They walk with you. Keep safe."

An escort? Considering the thing they had hauled in to eat before he had passed out, he wouldn't turn his nose up at the idea. After a few minutes of walking, the trolls grew tired of waiting on him, since he was too debilitated to jog. One of the trolls reached down and picked him up, and he found himself riding on the troll's shoulders.

Things went much quicker after that, though the swaying motion made it difficult for him to control his

Chapter 30

nausea. He was glad beyond belief when they finally reached the lake and he was once again placed on his own two feet. Will activated the limnthal. "I'm about to leave, and I want to thank the troll who carried me to the congruence point," he told the ring.

"Tell him, 'brak gall,'" said Arrogan. "That's troll for thank you. It's about time you start learning troll anyway. You won't be a very good ambassador if you don't speak the tongue."

"Ambassador?"

"I'm dead, so you'll have to take the job."

"There's no longer a council of wizards," Will pointed out.

"How does it feel to be head of the council too? My, what lofty positions you hold for one so young," said the ring dryly.

Will faced the two trolls and loudly repeated what he'd been told, "Brak gall." Then he bowed and moved to the congruence point. Seconds later, he was home. With a sigh of relief, he slid down the wall of the laboratory and sat on the cool stone floor. He wasn't quite ready to go up the ladder and face his mother again.

He needed to clean up first.

Casting Selene's Solution turned out to be much harder than he expected. His mind was fuzzy, and combined with the pain of his throbbing headache, it was extremely difficult to focus. It took him ten minutes and three tries to finally assemble the spell. He drew in more turyn than was necessary and set the spell boundaries to take in the entire room. *Might as well do some spring cleaning while I'm at it,* he told himself.

The feeling of being clean once more was indescribable, and he silently thanked his absent wife for the genius of her magnum opus. It wasn't enough to make him forget the misery of his hangover, but it was a step in the right direction. Will started to rise to his feet—and promptly dropped to the floor, a half-choked scream emerging from his throat.

The muscle in his leg felt as though it was on fire. Looking at it again, he saw that the swelling had increased. *I took a blood-cleanse potion,* he reminded himself. *Surely the wound can't be turning sour.*

He activated the limnthal and described his swollen leg to Arrogan, ending with, "It's like some giant mosquito bit me, but the lump is almost the size of a small turnip now."

A long laugh came from the ring, rising into a maniacal cackle at the end. "You must have really enjoyed the party. Did you pass completely out?"

"It was awful," lamented Will. "Passing out was the best part of the whole experience."

"Did you make any close friends before you blacked out?" asked Arrogan, his voice tinged with hidden mirth.

Will frowned. "What are you hinting at?"

"Just that you need to learn moderation. Obviously, you can't handle your drink, and just as obviously, one of the trolls took advantage of you."

"Took advantage? What does that mean?"

"You're pregnant."

"What?" Will shrieked.

"Don't be such a baby! Most women experience pregnancy at least once and you don't hear them screaming about it. Well, some do, but usually at the end."

"I'm not a woman!" yelled Will. "This is not something I ever expected."

"That's why I never liked the term, 'expecting,'" mused Arrogan. "Because so many don't expect it at all. Anyway, I warned you. Remember?"

"No. I'm pretty sure I would have remembered that," said Will sourly.

Chapter 30

"Hmm, I thought I did. Oh, well." There was a brief silence, then the ring added, "You know what?"

"What?"

"I bet Lrmeg is the father of your love-child. He was still nursing a grudge. It would be poetic justice, wouldn't it? You stabbed him in the dick last time, and this time he stabbed you *with* his dick."

Will groaned. "I'm really starting to rethink my refusal to melt you down."

"That's what I'm going for," said Arrogan gleefully. "Sweet, sweet, release." Will thought he was finished, but then Arrogan piped up again. "Just like Lrmeg and his sweet release!"

"Ugh, stop! I'm going to throw up again. How do I fix this?"

"There's only one way. You'll need an abortion."

"What's that?"

"A highly dangerous medical procedure that no one really tries for anymore, since there's no decent wizard-healers these days. In your case, though, it should be much simpler since this is more like a parasitic infection than a normal pregnancy. You'll need to cut it out. After that, a fire should keep the little troll-let from continuing to grow."

"There's really a baby troll in my leg?"

"A teeny one," said Arrogan, failing to hide a snicker. "The sooner you cut it out, the better. Otherwise you might lose the whole leg."

Will examined the wound and summoned one of his knives. He'd rather take care of matters before seeing his mother, but when he pressed the point to the swollen flesh, the pain took his breath away. There was no way he could do it on his own. In the end, he never really had a choice. Climbing the ladder with his wounded thigh would be close to impossible. Drawing a deep lungful of air, he yelled, "Mom!"

He repeated the cry several times before he heard the stomp of feet on the floorboards above. The trap door opened, and a woman's head surrounded by frizzy red hair looked over the rim. It was Sammy. "Will! Is that you?"

"Yes," he said, trying to sound calm.

"Auntie is napping up front. You shouldn't wake her," said Sammy cheerfully. "Come up and we can talk in the bedroom."

"I don't think I can climb the ladder, Sammy," said Will carefully. "I hurt my leg. You're going to have to wake Mom."

His cousin's eyes went round at the news he was injured, and she vanished in a flash. "Aunt Eri, Aunt Eri! Will's hurt! He can't get up the ladder. Quick, come quick!" The words spilled out in one long, continuous stream that somehow maintained an incredibly loud volume throughout. Will covered his face with one hand. Sammy couldn't ever do anything quietly. His poor mother was probably about to die of shock.

Within a minute his mother had stormed down the ladder and was examining him carefully. She gave Sammy a baleful glare. "You scared me half to death, girl!" she chided.

Sammy pointed at Will. "He's the one who said he couldn't climb the ladder."

Will pointed back. "I never told you to yell bloody murder, though! I said I was hurt, not dying."

Erisa shook her head, probing the swollen region carefully with her fingers. "It looks like a massive boil. How did it get so large in just a few hours?"

"What time is it?" asked Will.

"Midafternoon," answered Erisa, then she wrinkled her nose. "You reek of ale. Have you been drinking?"

Chapter 30

"I had to," said Will. "I couldn't offend them." Midafternoon meant it still hadn't been a full twenty-four hours since his friends had been injured. He wasn't sure how long would be too long, but he was determined to get the regeneration potions to them before forty-eight hours had passed. "It isn't a boil," he told his mother. "It's sort of a parasitic sting."

"There's something in there?"

He nodded, and as if to emphasize his point, the lump on his leg moved slightly. "Oh, that's disgusting," announced Sammy. "I think I'm going to be sick!"

Erisa looked at her niece sharply. "No, you're not. Go upstairs and put the kettle on the stove. I'll need hot water, fresh towels, and linen bandages. Once you get the water heating, find my kit and bring it to me." Sammy scampered up the ladder with alacrity, and Will's mother looked back at him, radiating calm confidence. "It appears to be in the muscle. Depending on how deep I have to cut, you're probably going to have trouble walking for a while. It's going to hurt a lot too, but I have some tincture of poppy saved for just this sort of thing—"

Will put a hand on his mother's arm. "I can't take the tincture, Mom. I have to be clearheaded after this."

"Why?" she asked, her voice clear and untroubled.

"I have to make potions when I get back."

"Tiny's kidney problem won't kill him for a week or two at the worst. You have time."

Will shook his head. "No. The regeneration potion won't work if the kidney has already died. The same for Janice's face. If it heals partially, she could be disfigured for life. She lost an eye, Mom."

"There's no way you can travel like that," Erisa said stubbornly.

"She lost her eye for *me,* Mom. She and Tiny didn't have to be there. They came even though they didn't have a hope in hell of saving me. Rob too."

"Who is Rob?"

"The one that didn't make it back," said Will somberly.

She sighed. "Can you make them here? Maybe the cat can take me back with the potions in your stead."

"I don't have all the ingredients here. It's all waiting for me back at Wurthaven. Plus, I'm not sure you would survive the trip through Hell."

"Hell?"

"That's where the goddamn cat was wounded."

Her calm demeanor, carefully cultivated over the years for when she was dealing with patients, cracked and her cheeks paled. "And you think you can survive the trip? With a hurt leg?"

"I don't need my leg to use spells, and the cat does the running."

CHAPTER 31

Will had experienced a wide variety of painful things since he had been born, but enduring minor surgery without anything to dull the pain was a novel form of torture. Unlike being whipped half to death, the pain came steadily, at the hand of someone who he *thought* loved him, but who he now suspected was in league with the forces of evil.

Erisa was merciless, and her face showed no doubt, no reserve, no hesitation as she carved into the meat of his thigh to remove the 'parasite.' Will's grunt's turned into screams almost from the beginning, and when Sammy began to cry, his mother finally lost her temper.

"Are you listening?" she snapped when Sammy failed to respond to the latest command. When Sammy responded with an incoherent sob, Erisa paused and put her knife down for a moment. "Sammy, you're going to make this take longer than it should, which will hurt your cousin more. He was helping me with things like this at eleven. I think you can pull yourself together long enough to do what needs to be done."

To be fair, Will had nearly passed out the first time his mother asked him to help with delivering a baby, so he felt a great deal of sympathy for his cousin, or he would have, if the pain in his leg wasn't blotting out every other possible sensation.

Sammy clenched her teeth together, then managed to answer, "Yes, Aunty."

"Take that towel and mop up the blood around the incision. I can't see what I'm doing," said Erisa calmly.

Will hissed when Sammy touched him, and Sammy flinched, but she kept at it. Soon the knife was back, and Will was choking back screams again.

As family reunions went, it wasn't the best, but it was something none of them would forget. When Erisa finally got the parasite, out a strange look of shock passed over her face, and predictably, Sammy was the first to say something. "It's like a little baby chick." The creature didn't have feathers or down, but it did have large eyes and a bulbous head.

Erisa gathered it into a towel, then handed it to her niece. "Throw it in the fire."

Will was full of mixed emotions, but he spoke before sorting them out. "Wait. I'll take it back."

His mother stared at him suspiciously. "You said it was a parasite."

"It's a troll," he admitted.

"How did you get a troll in your leg?"

"Someone was playing a joke."

Erisa's voice ascended the scales to a much higher pitch. "This was someone's idea of a joke?"

Will tried to give a brief review of what Arrogan had taught him about troll reproduction, which failed to impress his mother, and elicited a nervous giggle from his cousin. His mother spent the time carefully bandaging his bloody thigh. When she was done, Sammy fetched the crutches that Erisa kept for patients, and they helped Will up and onto his feet. "How far do you have to go to return this troll?" asked his mother.

"It's a bit of a walk," he admitted.

"I'll come with you," she told him.

"But…"

"I'm coming or you don't go. Would you rather toss it in the fire? I'm still in favor of that plan," she responded, cutting him off.

Chapter 31

He gave in, realizing he had no hope of winning, and his mother helped him hobble over to the corner of the room where the congruence point was. Will had the troll-let wrapped in the towel, but somewhere along the way it managed to slip its head free. He felt a sharp pain as it bit down on one of his fingers.

Gritting his teeth, he pried it loose and pushed it back into the towel, wrapping it more tightly. Then he transported them across to Muskeglun. He was surprised when he arrived, for several trolls were sitting around the area of the congruence, using a fallen tree as a bench. One of them smiled at him, and he thought it might be Clegg. Trolls were still hard for him to identify.

Erisa reacted to the smile by nearly falling over, which almost took Will down with her. After a few seconds of fumbling, they regained their collective balance. "It's all right, Mom. They're friendly," he reassured her.

The troll that had smiled stood and moved closer, while Will held out the towel and opened it so they could see what lay inside. Then he pointed at his wounded leg.

"Hello," said Clegg, confirming his identity with the greeting.

That was a relief. "I found this in my leg," said Will.

The troll chief cocked his head to one side. "And you brought it back?"

"I couldn't leave it in my world," said Will. "You know how dangerous that would be."

Clegg examined Erisa. "Who is this?"

"My mother, Erisa," said Will.

"Mother, an interesting thing," said the chief. "We do not have them. All trolls are fathers, until now. You are the first to bring one back."

"Pardon me?"

"Many times have troll played trick on humans. Never do your kind return with troll."

Will gaped at Clegg. "Were they supposed to?"

The chief troll shrugged. "Not care. Was joke." Then he focused on Will for a long minute. "But you are strange. You have earned a name." The chief turned to the other trolls, and they talked for several minutes, ending the conversation with a long series of cough-laughs.

Clegg turned back. "You are Grak-Murra, Troll-Mother."

Will was stunned. "I thought trolls didn't have mothers. How do you have a word for them?"

"Just made it," said Clegg. "Mother sounds bad to us, so 'murra' is close enough."

Feeling vengeful, Will made a request. "Can I name the child?"

Clegg smiled. "What would you call it?"

"Gan," said Will. "After my grandfather." He could still hear the troll's cough-laughter in his ears when they reappeared in the laboratory.

His mother was giving him a strange look.

"What?" asked Will.

She shook her head. "You've changed so much in the last few years. Those things were terrifying, but you talked to them as though it didn't bother you at all."

"I was swarmed by vampires yesterday, Mom. I guess it's all relative." He had no intention of mentioning the joke regarding him having to sacrifice an arm.

"Why did you tell him to name it Gan? Why not Arrogan?"

"That's what they called Arrogan," said Will.

Sammy could hardly contain herself. "That was quick! What happened?"

Will explained while struggling up the ladder. With only one leg, he was forced to hold himself up with both arms while he took each step. It turned out to be easier than he expected, though his leg complained every time

Chapter 31

he bumped his right foot against anything. After he had finally pulled himself over the edge, he sat and rested a moment while the others came up.

He noticed something interesting in the middle of the giant, four-poster bed that took up one wall of Arrogan's old bedroom. A small pedestal of cushions had been built up, and in the middle of them, resting like royalty, lay the goddamn cat.

Trying not to scream when the muscle was pulled as he stood up, Will hobbled over to examine the demigod, who appeared to be sleeping. In his housecat form, the Cath Bawlg always appeared as a gray tabby with short hair, but there was something different about him now. Sammy stepped up beside him, then put a finger over her lips as she whispered, "Don't disturb him. Mister Mittens is sleeping."

Will's eyes bugged out. *Mister Mittens?* Had the goddamn cat heard her call him that? He looked Sammy up and down, but he saw no signs of scratches or bloody wounds. Then he looked back at the cat and realized what had been bothering him subconsciously.

Someone had tied a neat little pink bow in the goddamn cat's hair, centered between his ears—and it was adorable. Using the crutch, he shuffled out of the bedroom as quickly as he could, giving Sammy weird looks the entire way. Once they were in the front room, he confronted her. "Did you do that to him?" he said in a worried half-whisper.

"Do what?" she asked innocently. "I made him the bed on top of the bed, and I brushed him out," she admitted. "From what I could see *someone* hasn't been taking very good care of their cat." She gave Will a look of disapproval.

His jaw dropped. "My cat? Are you insane? He's nobody's cat. He's a goddamn demigod! Did he let you put that thing in his hair?"

She smiled. "It wasn't easy, but he was sleeping and Aunt Erisa always tells me that I have very clever fingers. I tied it by hand."

"He's liable to murder us all if he finds out!" exclaimed Will.

"Stop exaggerating. Mister Mittens has been a perfect gentleman since you left. I never knew how much I liked cats until you brought him to visit." She paused, then added, "How did he get hurt, by the way?"

"I was riding him through Hell and some demons shot at us with these weird magic crossbows," said Will dryly.

"Be serious, Will!" she demanded angrily. "Someone deliberately hurt that cat, didn't they?"

"I'm fairly certain that's what I just told you." They were both distracted then, when the goddamn cat slipped through the open door and walked between them. Will stifled a laugh when he saw the bow again. *Damn, that's cute.*

Sammy knelt. "Mister Mittens! You shouldn't be walking around. You need to rest so you can heal," she remonstrated the cat gently. "What's this?" She began feeling around in the fur on the cat's chest. "I can't find the scabs."

"He heals quickly," said Will, amazed that the Cath Bawlg seemed to be letting his cousin touch him without complaint.

"Nothing heals that quickly," argued Sammy.

Erisa stepped into the room. "This cat does." She glanced at Will. "Are you still determined to leave?"

He nodded.

Sammy was immediately up in arms. "You just got here! And you haven't cooked anything!"

"Is that all you care about?" asked Erisa.

Will laughed. "I promise I'll come back as soon as I can, and I'll cook something special for everybody."

Chapter 31

Sammy hugged him and then stepped back. "Be sure to bring Selene next time. I'm sure your wife must be desperate for my advice on how to handle you."

The words brought a quiet stab of pain, but he laughed politely, wishing he could do exactly that. "I'll tell her. She definitely wants to visit." His mother hugged him then, and after a long exchange of 'good-byes' and 'be carefuls,' he and the cat escaped back into the Glenwood. Will hobbled along on his crutches while the cat walked beside him.

Will waited until they were a good distance from the house before he asked, "Mister Mittens, huh?" The goddamn cat declined to respond. Will wondered if the demigod realized there was a ribbon tied in his hair. Had he played along, or was he oblivious? In the end Will decided it wasn't worth risking his life to ask.

When they were almost to the congruence that led to the Shadowlands, the Cath Bawlg resumed his larger form. Will was pleased to note that the bow wasn't dislodged during the transformation. It was killing him to keep from sniggering.

Casting the climb spell on himself, Will painfully crawled up the beast's side and back until he was once again centrally positioned and well affixed. "Hang on," cautioned the goddamn cat, and then they were flying through the forest. The constant jarring sent a continuous stream of painful impulses up Will's leg, causing him to grunt and moan whether he wanted to or not.

A leap into the dark shadows beneath a particular set of trees, and Will found himself once again within the strange, twisting Shadowlands. It didn't improve the pain in his leg, but the wound did distract him from the headache caused by the strange dimension's weird geometry.

Chapter 32

The goddamn cat left him at the outskirts of Cerria. Will was grateful to end the torturous ride, but now he faced a less painful, but much longer walk through the city. He watched the cat walk away, aloof as always, never looking back—and still with a pink bow tied between his ears. He smirked as the demigod left. "Even the darkest day has something to chuckle about," he told himself.

He summoned the crutches from within the limnthal and set off down the road. The sun was about to set, which meant he was getting close to the twenty-four-hour mark for when his friends had been injured. His goal was to have the potions to give to them before hitting forty-eight hours.

Will had no good way to judge what his true time limit might be, but sooner was safer. He also worried about the time the potions would take to produce. Last time he'd had only a quarter as much troll urine, and he'd managed to make seven potions. This time he could potentially make several times that many, but he would need to restrict the size of the batch he worked with, otherwise it would take far too long.

The first stage of the process involved boiling down the urine to fully sterilize it, but boiling a hundred gallons of urine took a lot longer than boiling twenty or thirty gallons, and that was without considering the fact that he would have to work in smaller portions because he didn't have vessels large enough for such amounts.

He thought about it as he walked and decided he would scale his production to half of what he had done the year before and try to produce four potions. "One for Janice, one for Tiny, and one for this gimp leg," he muttered. That would leave only one to spare for an emergency, but he could make three more similar sized batches later.

It had taken him three days to make the regeneration potions last year, but that had been partly because he'd had other things to do as well. If he kept the batch small and stayed throughout the process, starting the second and third stages as soon as they were ready, he thought he could finish in about twelve hours.

Will was halfway through the city when the sun sank fully below the horizon and the street lighters began to light the lamps. Other than those vital workers, he saw no one else outside, which was unusual. Like most places, Cerria's activity died when the sun was gone, but there was usually some traffic. The odd carriage, a few late-night workers, and the inevitable foot traffic back and forth to the public houses.

Tonight, there was none of that. The city seemed deserted.

Nervous, Will checked his prepared spells and adjusted them accordingly, one illumination spell, one wind-wall, and a chameleon spell. The light between streetlamps dwindled as the sky lost the glow of dusk, but that wasn't a problem for him. He might have considered using the chameleon spell and sneaking the rest of the way back to Wurthaven, but his leg made that impractical. He had to move slowly and smoothly for that sort of thing, and there was nothing smooth about his hobbling gait presently.

Plus, he didn't want to waste the time.

Fatigue sat heavy on his shoulders. "I guess being passed out drunk for four or five hours in a troll village isn't a substitute for sleep," he muttered sarcastically to himself. "I'll have to be extra careful at the Alchemy building, or I'll make a stupid mistake and ruin the whole thing."

He turned a corner and found himself twenty feet away from a group of men, City Watch by the look of them. "Hold!" one of them shouted.

Damn it, he thought, but he stopped. There were six men in the patrol, an uncommonly large size. Normally the watch patrolled in twos. Then he noticed one of the men was a sorcerer.

The sorcerer stepped forward. "You'll have to come with us."

"Why?" demanded Will. "I've done nothing wrong."

"Defying the curfew," said the officer.

"What curfew?"

"The decree was announced at midday and read out for everyone to hear," said the sorcerer.

Will sighed. "I got back at sundown. How was I to know? Just let me be on my way and I'll be off the street as soon as I get home."

"You can talk to the magistrate about that—in the morning," said the sorcerer, a malicious grin on his lips. Will knew his type, men who exulted in having the opportunity to exercise power over others.

Then again, maybe he was just biased, but either way, he couldn't afford to spend the night in jail. He wished he had prepared a sleep spell, but he had been more worried about vampires than watchmen. He was tempted to try the 'do you know who I am?' trick, but as bedraggled as he was there was virtually no chance anyone would believe he was the king's son-in-law.

Chapter 32

He smiled. "I'll be happy to cooperate—" but he wasn't. Before the sentence was finished, he released the wind-wall spell, though he did so without putting much power into it. He wasn't trying to murder anyone.

The air whipped up, and chaos ensued as the men were knocked off their feet. Before they could recover, Will caught three of them with a source-link. The two regular watchmen he had caught were paralyzed, and then he focused on the sorcerer. It was a brief struggle, lasting no more than a couple of seconds, and then the man was disconnected from his source and paralyzed.

The other watchmen had regained their feet, and two were already swinging at him with their truncheons. Will blocked each swing in turn with a point-defense shield, leaving the men with strange looks on their faces as they tried to figure out why their blows weren't connecting.

Things were looking rather desperate, though. The sorcerer's fire elemental had manifested and was now swelling up to full size. He still had three men to deal with, and if he was going to release the source-links on the three he had already stopped, he would have to either drain them or inject turyn to make them nauseous. He didn't want to leave them helpless at night in a city filled with vampires, though, since he already had a good idea why the curfew had been created.

On the other hand, he had a bad leg and he wouldn't be able to run away, nor could he keep blocking the watchmen's attacks forever. Without having a sleep spell ready, he didn't have a safe way to stop them without hurting them. He backed up until he felt the nearest building brush against his shoulders. He was cornered.

"Give it up," said one of the men.

"Listen, I'm not coming with you and I'm running out of safe ways to end this without hurting you," responded

Will, trying to put as much sincerity as possible into his voice. Looking over the man's shoulder, he saw the elemental was on the verge of throwing a massive fireball in his direction. *That will probably set the building on fire and might kill these men,* he realized.

The sorcerer was still conscious, and Will locked eyes with the man. "Call your elemental off or you won't see the sunrise." Since the man was unable to touch his source, Will wasn't entirely sure if he could still communicate with the elemental, so he released the man's throat muscles and vocal cords. "Tell the men to back off too," ordered Will.

"Let him go," said the sorcerer, his voice weak. Without conscious control of his breathing, it was difficult for the man to control the volume of his voice. Will corrected the problem quickly when he understood. The sorcerer repeated his order, and the watchmen stepped back. "You won't get far," he warned. "The Driven are out in force tonight. They'll find you."

"Good," Will agreed. "They're keeping the vampires in check, I hope."

The sorcerer stared at him thoughtfully. "How do you know about that?"

"I'm the king's son-in-law, William Cartwright. I know a lot more than most."

"You expect me to believe that?"

Will winked at the man. "I do. Do you see an elemental with me?" The man said nothing, so Will continued, "And yet you're lying on the ground, helpless. Have you heard of any other wizards who could manage that?"

"He's lying!" sputtered one of the other men. "He's dressed like a beggar."

"The clothes I wear are none of your concern, patroller," said Will, affecting a condescending tone. He quietly began constructing a sleep spell to replace the

Chapter 32

wind-wall he had used, but he didn't intend to use it. He addressed the sorcerer, "I'll need you and your squad to escort me the rest of the way. As you can see, my leg was injured, and it has put my mission in jeopardy."

"Mission?"

Will had him. Taking a chance, he released the source-links, allowing the men to regain control of their bodies. "I've told you who I am, which has already violated the secrecy of my task. I can't say any more."

Getting to his feet, the sorcerer in charge stared at him suspiciously. "You expect me to believe anything that comes out of your mouth?"

"The way I see it, you've got two choices," began Will, "either you escort me to my destination, or you try to stop me. If you try to stop me, I won't pull my punches the second time around. Your men might manage to apprehend me, but you, sir, probably won't be there to congratulate them. Finally, even if things go perfectly and you drag me in to the magistrate, I promise you'll wind up tied to a flogging post for interfering with me."

"Assuming you live to see the magistrate," suggested the sorcerer, but his voice was more speculative than hostile.

"In that case the king will see you all hanged," said Will confidently, lacing his words with an air of indomitable superiority. He kept his gaze fixed firmly on the sorcerer, giving the impression the others didn't matter at all.

A tense silence ensued, then unexpectedly the sorcerer lowered his eyes. "As you wish, milord. We are yours to command."

Will let out his breath slowly, trying to hide his relief and surprise. *I didn't really think that was going to work.* Keeping his chin elevated, he asked, "What's your name and rank?"

The sorcerer stiffened, coming to attention. "Lieutenant Dan Ramfeld, milord.

"I assume you're not part of the City Watch."

"Detached duty, from the King's Special Service."

Will narrowed his eyes. The Driven all had more than one elemental.

"I'm still in training, milord. His Majesty has every able man out on the streets tonight."

He hadn't seen anyone else on the street, but he could make some guesses in that regard. "Only the regular watch patrols are visible then," he observed out loud. The Driven would be hidden.

"Yes, milord."

"Sir is good enough for me, Lieutenant," Will informed him. "My last official rank was 'corporal' and these days I'm just a royal-in-law. I don't hold any titles."

"Very good, sir. Where are we heading?"

"Just get me to the gates of Wurthaven. You can return here after that." Lifting one crutch, he pointed in the direction he was going, then began to move. The men fell in around him. As they walked, he asked, "Tell me about last night. Something bad must have happened for His Majesty to have put a curfew in place." Of course, he had been in the middle of his own struggle to survive, but he didn't know what might have happened elsewhere in the city.

"Felt like the whole damn city went mad," said one of the watch patrollers. A second later the man added a belated, "Sir."

"I'll tell it, Sims," said the lieutenant. "Three homes were burned, and Father Latimer was found brutally murdered."

Father Latimer was the high priest for the Church of the Holy Mother, the man who had performed Will's

Chapter 32

own wedding ceremony. He could hardly believe his ears. "Was he?"

"All I know is hearsay," admitted the officer. "But his body was cremated, on the spot, if that's any clue for you."

"And the homes?"

"They wasn't random," said Dan. "One was the high priest's house, but the other two belonged to high ranking nobles. Lord Tintabel's home was ransacked and his family murdered before the house was set afire. And Lord Nerrow's place was—"

"Excuse me, did you say Lord Nerrow?" Will's heart had frozen in his chest.

"Yes sir, the baron, Mark Nerrow. His home was vandalized and set on fire. Apparently, he put up a fight first, though. It wasn't the first attempt, so he was ready for them. Still, it didn't keep them from burning the place down around his ears."

Will felt as if he was walking through a tunnel, for the officer's words sounded as though they were echoing from miles away. "Did his family…?"

"Oh, they was all fine, sir. Do you know them? I should have said that first. Apparently, he held them off for a while, then they retreated inside. He had some sort of fortified basement ready. The fiends couldn't get to him. After the fire burned out, they all emerged safe and sound this morning."

The heavy lump in his chest eased slightly. "Where are they now?"

"I dunno, sir. Wherever rich people go when their houses burn down, I suppose. They might be at the palace."

That made sense to Will, though he wished he could have offered his own home to them. But he'd been too busy nearly being murdered himself, and then he'd spent the day traveling through Hell and drinking with trolls.

My life is beyond weird, he thought. "Any idea why those people in particular were targeted?"

"Nothing official," said the lieutenant. "But my personal theory is that the Prophet is trying to destroy our morale."

"The Prophet? He's in no position to start a war. He lost most of his army recently. It will take years before he can afford to antagonize Terabinia," argued Will. *If anything, Lognion was preparing to attack Darrow soon.*

"Maybe the Shimerans then?" suggested the officer. "Demons and vampires are about the same thing, aren't they?"

Clearly, he wasn't one of Wurthaven's brightest graduates, thought Will, then he shook his head. "No, they're entirely different."

"Well, anyway, whoever it is that started all this, it seems to me they want to demoralize the people. That's why they've gone after popular figures, well, except for Lord Tintabel. He wasn't known for much aside from his paintings, but the priest and Lady Nerrow were obvious targets."

That caught his attention. "Lady Nerrow? Is the baroness popular?"

"Not the baroness, sir, her daughter Laina. She's probably the most popular person in all of Cerria right now. If something happened to her, I don't know what people would do."

That was news to him. "I don't understand."

"Have you been living under a rock, sir? Lady Nerrow championed the Mother's Widows and Orphans charity after the Prophet attacked, and she was only a girl then. She's just barely reached her majority but she's already famous. She's out at every event in the

Chapter 32

city, shaming the rich into paying up to provide for the poor and disadvantaged. If it weren't for her, a lot of people would have starved, and I don't just mean those in the city. Hell, she was in Branscombe not long after the Darrowans attacked, bringing supplies and aid for the citizens of Barrowden and Branscombe."

Will was flabbergasted, but there was no mistaking the tone of reverence in Dan Ramfeld's voice. The man truly believed that Laina Nerrow was some sort of merciful lady sent to rescue the people from misery and squalor. Will remembered Laina's visit to Branscombe, and as far as he knew her part of the trip had merely been as company for her father. How could he have been so completely unaware?

I was a little focused on not dying in the war, thought Will. Still, he hadn't seen anything but a spoiled nobleman's brat. Was it really possible that his half-sister was more than that? It was hard for him to credit, but it did explain why Laina had been a target for the vampires. *She was sixteen when the Prophet's army invaded Barrowden. How could she possibly have become a public figure and a driving force behind a widow's charity?*

Then again, maybe she had been Selene's best friend for more reasons than the fact that they grew up together. Maybe his wife had known a different Laina than the spoiled asshole that Will had always interacted with. As far as he knew, Selene had always been big on helping people—was that trait what had connected the two women?

"Well fuck me sideways," muttered Will. "It turns out I'm the judgmental asshole."

"Beg your pardon, sir?" asked the lieutenant.

It was pure chance that Will happened to look over at the man at just that moment. Otherwise things might have gone very differently. They were walking along a dark portion of road, with barely enough light to see where to put their feet. Naturally, that wasn't a problem for Will, but the lighting made it impossible for the men to see what was racing toward them from a side alley.

The vampire was mere feet from where the sorcerer stood to Will's right, and it was moving at full speed, rushing toward the man like an evil wind. Will didn't even have time to blink. His point-defense shield stopped the fiend in its tracks with the crack of bones breaking. His shield vanished, and a force-lance removed the creature's head.

The thing wasn't alone, however. Two of the watch patrollers went down at the same time, as they were hit from different sides. The vampires weren't trying to feed, though; they knocked the men from their feet and turned to do the same to the others, clearly intending to disable their entire group before killing them.

Ethelgren's Illumination put an end to that plan as searing white spheres spiraled out from Will's upraised hand. Screams and hisses echoed through the dark as the monsters closest to them burned and died. Will's eyes were closed, so he couldn't be sure, but it sounded as though some of those farther away escaped complete annihilation, for their howls and footsteps moved away even as the spell moved farther out. As the light dimmed, he opened his eyes and went to help the men who had been knocked down.

"Were either of you hurt?" he asked, trying to see without bending down. His leg would make crouching and standing again nearly impossible.

One of the two patrollers had suffered nothing more than a bruise, but the other had a shallow cut along his arm. Before Will could offer, the man pulled out a glass vial and swallowed the contents. The shape of the vial was

Chapter 32

familiar to him. *Did the king buy blood-cleanse potions from Wurthaven?* If so, Will had probably been the one who made them.

Will began replacing the illumination spell immediately, having learned his lesson at the warehouse the night before. The patrollers and the sorcerer gathered around him. "You were damn quick with that spell," said the lieutenant gratefully. "He might have ripped my head off before I even saw him coming."

"I just stopped him for a second," said Will modestly. "It was your force-lance that took his head off."

"Force-lance? I haven't heard of that spell before," said the officer.

Will stared at him for a moment, reviewing the fight in his mind. *Did I cast the force-lance?* He hadn't had one ready. If he had done it, it meant he had finally reflex cast the spell for the first time. Looking down the alley, he picked a target and tried to *will* a force-lance into being. Nothing happened. He held out his hand and constructed the spell in the normal way. He'd been practicing the spell regularly for over a year, so it came together in just under a second. It felt faster than it had been a few days before, but it wasn't instant.

He couldn't be sure. It had been just as confusing when he had started reflex casting the point-defense shield. First it had been unconscious and then later it started responding to more deliberate attempts as well. Either way, it was a good sign.

"Sir?"

He shook his head. "It's a combat spell. I'm sure they'll teach it to you when you start your battle training."

"I wish I knew it right now," said the sorcerer enviously. "Or that light spell you used, that would be even better."

You should learn the point-defense spell first, thought Will, hearing his grandfather's voice in the back of his mind. The memory made him smile. The ring had been right. The point-defense shield had saved his life a dozen times over by then. Even so, he didn't feel right putting the man off. Not when any bit of knowledge might be the bit that saved his life.

When they reached the gates of Wurthaven, Will asked the lieutenant to wait for him. Then he went to the guardhouse. The guard recognized him and greeted him with a quick nod, which Will returned. Then he summoned a journal and a charcoal stylus he used for sketching. The spell was simple, and ink would take too long. He quickly wrote out the diagram for the force-lance, then ripped the page out of the journal. Dismissing the book, he hobbled back over to the patrollers. "Here," he said, holding out the page. "The spell I used. I'd teach you the light spell too, but it's too complicated for the time we have."

"Thank you, sir!" said the officer, sincere gratitude in his eyes. "Are you sure you don't want to come with us? Even with that bad leg of yours, I think we might feel safer if you did."

Will smiled. "I wish I could, but I have too many other things to attend to." He left them there, heading directly for the Alchemy building. The campus had always felt like safe ground to him—usually it was the city outside the walls that threatened him—but he couldn't relax as he worked his way down dark lanes and across well-trimmed lawns.

He knew quite well that the walls were no obstacle to vampires, and the campus was nearly deserted at night. Will swiveled his head constantly, trying to watch every direction as he painfully made his way to his destination.

CHAPTER 33

Unlike the buildings that only held lectures, the Alchemy building, much like the Healing and Psyche building, always had a few people manning the front entrance. There were quite a few staff as well as some students who used the facilities late into the night, especially since the hours didn't conflict with their daytime classes.

That wasn't to say that the building was always busy at night. On the weekends it was nearly deserted, and on most nights the place was almost empty after midnight. It was still just the beginning of the night, and it wasn't a weekend, so there were several people at the front desk, and Will saw a number of lights from the windows on various floors.

His crutches drew a few looks as he signed in and made his way to the stairs, but he was a well-known face in the building. The only remark he received was a quick, "What happened to you?"

The one who asked was named Lawrence, a young man and a senior student who was aiming for a career in alchemy. Will glanced at his clothes and realized that although he was clean, his trousers were a shamble. His mother had cut one leg completely away when she worked on his thigh. "It's a long story," Will replied.

"It always is with you," said Lawrence with a chuckle. "Things have been crazy since yesterday. I suppose you heard about the fires?"

"Yeah." He wouldn't have minded hearing more, but he was also in a hurry to get started. He dodged the rest of the conversation. "I need to get moving. Sorry." Will breathed a sigh of relief when he finally made it to the private workroom he rented from Professor Karlovic. No one ever bothered him there, aside from the professor occasionally coming by to see what he was up to.

Wasting no time, he began setting up his largest vessel to boil the raw troll urine. It could hold several gallons of fluid, which was much more than most students needed for their projects. Will had bought it the previous year when he had been desperately trying to earn enough to keep from being put in prison.

Everything seemed harder than usual. His shoulders and arms ached, his hips hurt, and his leg was a constant misery of throbbing pain punctuated by sharp moments of agony whenever he accidentally bumped it or tried to use the muscles in his thigh. When he finally sat down and began doing the calculations to plan out the reaction ingredient masses, it seemed like a relief, but he discovered it was hard to focus.

There were several lamps in the room providing more than enough light, especially since he could adjust his vision, but the numbers and symbols on the page in front of him blurred in and out despite all of his squinting. Will put his pen aside for a moment and rubbed his face with his hands. Then he tried again.

The math wasn't that complex, but he had a nagging suspicion something was wrong when he got to the end, so he repeated the calculation, starting at the beginning.

His answer the second time was different. Growling angrily, he tried again. Ten minutes later, he had a third and still different result. Will fought the urge to throw the journal across the room. He could hardly recall the last time he had felt so frustrated.

Chapter 33

Taking a deep breath, he started again. This time his result was the same as his second attempt, but he still didn't trust it. He had to be sure; otherwise he could ruin a lot of expensive materials. His fifth attempt confirmed his first calculation.

Will wanted to cry. He knew it was him. He hadn't slept in almost two days, aside from his short, alcohol-induced coma, and during that time he had been in multiple fights. Add to that his wounded leg and he was obviously not in a fit state to do rational calculations.

A knock at the door startled him from drowsing. He hadn't even realized his head had drooped and his eyes were half-closed. Will straightened up, grabbed his crutches, and hobbled over to the door. He had locked it so no one could interrupt him, though there was only one person likely to appear.

He opened it to find Professor Karlovic standing in the hall. "I thought I'd drop in and see what you were up to. You haven't been in for a couple of days." The professor gave him a curious look, studying him up and down as Will let him into the laboratory. "You look the worse for wear."

"Don't get me started," said Will sourly, running a hand through his hair. "I can't even do figures right now."

"This kind of work isn't safe when you aren't at your best, William. I'm sure you know that," cautioned the professor. "What happened to your leg?"

I got drunk and woke up pregnant with a troll-let, Will wanted to say, but he stopped himself, fighting back a semi-hysterical chuckle. "I had an accident while collecting troll urine."

Karlovic's eyes lit up with interest. "You managed to get more? How?"

Will sighed. "You know I don't share those secrets, Professor."

"So, you're trying to make more regeneration potions. Why are you risking such valuable materials by working when you're clearly exhausted—not to mention injured?"

"Because it's necessary. You know about the trouble in the city last night, right?"

The professor nodded. "More than I'm supposed to talk about with the students. We're considering a curfew on the campus starting tomorrow."

"I was in the middle of part of what happened last night," said Will. "Janice Edelman and another friend of mine are in Doctor Morris' care because they came to save me. If I don't find a way to fix what happened to them, the consequences will be permanent."

Karlovic looked uncertain. "I heard about poor Janice. You were *really* involved? You know about what's happening in the city?"

"You're not supposed to say 'vampire' in front of the students, I guess?" asked Will. "I saw a lot of them, too many for comfort." Reaching down, he pulled back one of his sleeves, letting the teacher see the now scabbed-over puncture wounds that ran up and down his skin. "I wouldn't have lived if Janice hadn't done what she did."

"They're real?" asked the professor. "They briefed us, but it was hard to believe. Supposedly the king has soldiers and the Driven patrolling the streets."

"They're real," Will confirmed, staring down at his page of mangled calculations.

Professor Karlovic came over and nudged him aside. "Let me do this. You're in no state. It's better to have someone else do the checks anyway."

Will stared at his bearded professor, then moved over and sat down. He blinked several times as his vision

Chapter 33

became blurry. The stress of the past two days had been too much. Breathing slowly, letting his throat relax, he finally replied, "Thank you, Professor. You don't know how much it means."

"Think nothing of it. You've done plenty of checks for me."

"Back when you were paying me," said Will wryly.

His teacher didn't answer until he had finished the calculation he was doing. "I have a feeling you're doing more for me and everyone else right now than anyone knows, so this is probably just a proper repayment. Even if it isn't, it's a teacher's job to help students when they need it." He moved on, then started a second time, rechecking the work he had done. Karlovic was done a few minutes later as both of his sets of calculations agreed with each other. They also matched Will's original second run through. The professor underlined the final amounts, then rewrote them on a second sheet of paper so they wouldn't get confused with the rest of the numbers that covered the original worksheet.

He handed the sheet to Will. "Here's your final working amounts. Where are you at in the process?"

"Just doing the first boil," said Will. "But I need to measure all this out so I'm ready for the next stage."

"Not going to sleep?"

He shook his head.

"You're already about to fall over. You're bound to ruin it if you don't rest first," the professor pointed out.

Will shrugged.

Karlovic pointed at the stool. "Stay there and don't do anything. I'll be back in a few minutes."

He had no idea what the professor intended, but Will did as he was told. By the time the teacher returned, a quarter of an hour later, he was nodding off on his seat, repeatedly waking up when his head slipped and jerked him awake. Karlovic opened the door and dragged in a wooden folding cot. He had a pillow under one arm.

"I told you I can't sleep, sir," argued Will. "I have to get this done."

His teacher ignored him, setting up the cot on one side of the room. "You lie there," he ordered. "I'll play assistant tonight."

"Huh?"

"I'll measure it all out and get the second stage going."

"But you can't..."

The professor walked/dragged Will over to the cot, then forced him to sit, which sent a surge of pain through Will's leg. "I can," said Karlovic. "I won't try to do the activations. I don't intend to shorten my life, but I'll do everything else. Get some sleep. I'll wake you up for the part that sane wizards avoid like the plague."

Will stared up at the man, barely able to think. Finally, he answered, "All right." Then he flopped onto his side and closed his eyes. He was asleep within seconds.

Almost immediately, someone shook his shoulder. Will blinked, staring fuzzily at his antagonist. It was the professor again. "You told me to sleep," he complained.

The other man smiled. "That was four hours ago. You need to activate the ingredients for the second stage."

"Oh." Will sat up, feeling muzzy and almost drunk, then he tried to stand and nearly fell. His right thigh was swollen and sore to the point that he was completely unable to move it. It took him a prolonged period of maneuvering with Karlovic's assistance to get back to a standing position while keeping his right leg straight.

Finally, at the workbench, Will began drawing in turyn and tuning it to the specific types that the ingredients would need to be infused with. Externally, there was

Chapter 33

nothing to see, but he could feel Professor Karlovic watching him intently. "Are you hoping to discover my secret?" asked Will.

"Well, it's clear that you haven't suffered from all the potions you made last year, so I would dearly love to know how you do it without killing yourself," said the older man honestly.

Will felt a similar urge to honesty. The Alchemy teacher had been good to him from the beginning, and while the man also made a small profit sourcing buyers for Will's potions, he seemed to have an honest heart. "I wish I could teach it to you," he admitted. "My original master said it's something that has to be done when you're young, and it's best done before you learn to use magic."

"So you *did* learn this through some special training," muttered Karlovic. "Master Courtney has been speculating about that."

"I haven't been very forthcoming," said Will. "I'm not sure who I can trust."

"Afraid they'll put you on a rack and torture it out of you?"

He nodded. "Or tie me to a table and dissect me."

"Courtney wouldn't do that," insisted Karlovic. "He's a good man, even if he's a little odd. Are you worried I'll tell him what you told me?"

Will shrugged. "I had to trust someone sooner or later."

"And you chose me? I feel touched."

He grinned. "We'll see how it goes. One of us may regret it before too much time has passed." Will finished the activations, then started organizing the materials for the next stage. Karlovic came over and shuffled him aside.

"Sleep some more. I'll let you know when the potions are ready to be finalized."

"Shouldn't you be going home?"

"My wife is used to me keeping odd hours," said the professor. "She'll probably forgive me for coming home late again."

Will didn't argue. It took him longer to fall asleep this time, but after a few minutes he drifted away, grateful for the rest. The next time he awoke it wasn't because someone was shaking him, but rather because his nose had detected something.

It was the smell of fresh bread, and something else. Tea? Will's eyes popped open and he scanned the room. He spotted his teacher decanting the final product into small vials that would then wait for a final infusion of turyn to activate them. Off to one side, on a small table, was the object of Will's desire, a plate filled with sweet buns. A small teapot sat beside it along with two empty cups.

Will moaned, then began struggling to get upright once more. Professor Karlovic turned and looked over one shoulder at him, smiling. "Oh, I see the food woke you."

"Where did you get that?" Will asked, adoration in his voice.

"I sent one of the early-rising students over to the Residents' Hall cafeteria. The tea should still be warm."

"I could marry you."

The professor laughed. "My wife might be grateful to have me out of her hair, but you're still a newlywed. I doubt your wife would approve."

Ignoring the intense pain his movements required, Will managed to get up and onto his good leg without assistance. His stomach was insistent, and he could only comply with its demands. The buns were simple and sweet, a confection made of little more than ordinary dough supplemented with honey and extra butter, but just then, they were heaven on earth. He had devoured one and was struggling to swallow before he poured his first cup of black tea.

Chapter 33

The tea was strong and bitter. Too much had been used, and it had been steeped far too long and at too high a temperature, but it complemented the sticky sweetness of the bread, and Will welcomed the extra energy it would hopefully give him. He fell to eating with a vengeance, and a few minutes later the plate and teapot were both empty. Belatedly, he looked over at the professor, feeling guilty, for he hadn't left any for his savior.

Karlovic glanced at him and laughed, then patted his slightly rounded paunch. "I didn't need it anyway, while you obviously did." He stepped back from the worktable and gestured at the vials. "Care to see your product?" There were five vials lined up on the table.

Will frowned. "I only planned on four. How did you manage five?"

"You had more set out than you realized, so I redid the math and worked out the other ingredients to make five. It was just small enough that it wouldn't require larger vessels so I knew it wouldn't cost you any time." The older man paused. "Will you be able to activate that many at one time?"

"Sure," said Will. "I'm not using my turyn. I absorb it from the environment, so I can replace it without too much trouble." He hobbled over to the bench and proceeded to begin doing just that. Each potion took fifteen to twenty minutes, as he had to draw in turyn, convert it, infuse the potion, then repeat the process until it had been saturated with energy.

After a little over an hour and a half, the five regeneration potions were done. Will gazed at them thoughtfully. He needed three—two for his friends, one for himself, and another for emergencies. Then he looked at Professor Karlovic. With one hand he offered the man one of the potions.

His teacher wanted to take the vial. Will could see the hesitation in the man's movements, as his hand started to reach out before he pulled it back again. "You keep them," said Karlovic.

"I couldn't have done this without you."

"That potion is worth nearly a thousand gold marks."

Will shrugged. "I don't need the money."

The professor's hand started to move again, but then he tucked it behind his back and turned away. "I don't know what sort of things you're up to, William, but I think you're far more likely to need that extra potion than I am to need a thousand marks. If you still feel grateful, offer me one later, when things are back to normal. Right now, I won't take it."

He sighed, then stored the five potions in the limnthal. At the same time, he removed his coin purse and took out a few coins. Hobbling over, he grabbed his teacher's hand and put the coins in his palm.

"What's this?" asked Karlovic, staring at the silver.

"Two clima," said Will with a grin. "Isn't that the going rate for a lab assistant?"

They both laughed, and then his professor asked, "Aren't you going to take one of those potions for your leg?"

"Not until I go to the Healing and Psyche building. They make you very sleepy afterward. I don't want to pass out before I make sure my friends are taken care of."

"You'd better get going then."

"What time is it?"

"It's just past seventh bell. The dining halls are still open if you need more breakfast."

CHAPTER 34

Doctor Morris met him before he could enter Janice's room, having been summoned by an orderly who spotted the man who had absconded two nights before. "You've a lot of nerve," said the doctor. "Do you have any idea how long they questioned me after you ran off? I'm not sure they believed me when I told them you escaped against my wishes."

Will felt a little bad, but not much. He'd been through worse on his side of things. With a flourish, he produced one of the regeneration vials, making it look as though he had palmed the item like some common street magician. "I got it."

"Is that?" Doctor Morris' eyes grew wide.

Will nodded. "I'm sorry for the trouble yesterday, but if I had let them hold me I wouldn't have been able to help them."

"Where did you get it?"

"I went to hell and back. Met some trolls along the way. I spent last night in the Alchemy building." Limping, he moved around the doctor and pushed through the door.

The room was well lit, with sunshine streaming in through an eastward facing window, but Janice probably couldn't see it. She was a shapeless bundle on the bed, with blankets pulled high to cover her entirely. "Janice, it's me," said Will. "I have something that will help."

The mound of blankets didn't move, but he heard a faint grunt. Doctor Morris stepped up beside him. "She can't talk. Her head and face are tightly bound right now to keep her from hurting herself more."

"How will she take the potion?" he asked.

"There's an opening in the bandages for a tube. She'll have to take liquids through that until she's healed."

Will thought about it a moment. "The bandages will have to come off. She can take it through the tube, but if they're binding the flesh and skin, she might not be able to heal properly with them in place."

Doctor Morris nodded. "I was thinking the same, but it will be painful. Let me give her some medicine to ease the pain first."

The doctor left to gather help while Will continued to talk to his friend. "It's all right, Janice. I've got a regeneration potion. It will probably hurt a lot when they take the bandages off, but hopefully you'll be able to have your eye back and everything will be normal again."

"Mmmphf hmm," she responded unintelligibly. He hoped it was an affirmative.

Minutes later they had her sitting up, and he could see her one good eye staring at him through the bandages that swaddled her face. It pierced him like an accusation, though he couldn't honestly say what her expression might be. One of the nurses held out a hand for the potion, but Will wouldn't release it. "I'll pour it in," he told the man. "I'm not letting go of this vial until I'm certain it's empty and she's received it."

Doctor Morris nodded, and they made room so he could approach and pour it down the tube that ran into Janice's bandaged face. Her eye stayed on him the entire time. "Here goes," he told her, then he tilted the bottle up, letting the fluid pour into the tube.

She got it down without gagging, despite the taste, and once they were sure the liquid had been swallowed, Doctor Morris began removing the bandages using a sharp pair of scissors. Will felt a sense of urgency, as he worried the man wouldn't be quick enough. Meanwhile Janice

Chapter 34

began to groan as her pain increased. Tears ran from her one good eye, and the doctor moved more quickly.

The final cut was made, and the bandages fell away like a blood-soaked cocoon. Beneath them, her skin and flesh were a twisted horror to behold. Janice shoved the doctor away from her, then pulled her blanket up again to shield herself from their eyes. "Mmm ammay!"

Will finally understood, and he turned his back while his own tears began to spill over. She had been begging them not to look at her. "It won't take long, Janice. I promise. It might hurt, but it won't last."

Doctor Morris stepped forward after a minute. "Janice, I need to see. I can't tell how well it's working if you won't show yourself."

Apparently, something was happening, for she was able to respond in a thick voice, "Get him out!"

"Janice," he started to say, but she cut him off.

"Please! Get out!" Her voice was rising through the registers, climbing toward panic.

The doctor gave him a sympathetic look, then gestured toward the door. Will went, but just before he stepped out the physician called out, "Your other friend is across the hall."

"Thank you, sir." Racked with guilt, regret, and a whole host of other mixed-up emotions, Will retreated. Outside, he took a moment to breathe and regain his composure.

Through the door he could hear voices, some of them loud enough to understand. "No more visitors," Janice begged. "Don't let him in again."

One of the nurses responded, "He's just trying to help, miss."

After that, all he heard was crying and his chest tightened. Moving forward, he crossed the hall and opened the opposite door. Tiny was in the bed, partially elevated into a half-sitting posture by a collection of pillows. Unlike Janice, the big man was naked, at least the parts Will could see from the waist up. Pale skin covered thick muscles, and everywhere Tiny's body was discolored. Most areas were shaded blue or purple, but some regions had deep black bruises, where blood had congealed under the skin.

And that was his front. From how things had played out, Will knew the back side was probably worse. Tiny spotted his friend and smiled brightly, showing a mouth full of undamaged teeth. In contrast to Janice, his injuries had almost entirely been to the body. Aside from a few scratches, his head had been untouched. "Will!" he called cheerfully. Then he frowned as his eyes tracked toward Will's wounded leg. "That's new. I shouldn't have let you out of my sight."

"You're still in worse shape."

"Says who?" argued Tiny. "I could get up and whip your ass, if they'd let me out of this bed. There's really no point in keeping me here. It's just bruises."

Will smiled. "It won't even be that soon." He summoned the second regeneration potion and offered it to his friend. "You'll be right as rain after you take this."

Tiny turned his head away. "How's Janice? Give it to her."

He sighed. "I already gave her one. She's healing as we speak. This one is yours."

The big warrior gave him a sincere look. "I don't really need it, Will. Save it for an emergency. I'll be fine."

Will closed his eyes. "No, Tiny, you won't. I don't know what they told you, but you aren't all right. You might not recover if you don't take this. Your kidneys are bruised as badly, or maybe worse, than the rest of you. Take it."

Chapter 34

"They said I would be fine," repeated the squire.

"They didn't want to scare you."

Tiny took the potion from Will's hand. "What is this?"

"A regeneration potion. It will heal anything and everything, but only if you take it right after you get hurt."

His friend looked at his leg again. "What about you? Do you have more?"

Growling with frustration, Will produced another vial. "This one's for me. Are you happy?"

"Let me see you drink it," insisted Tiny. "You heal that leg, then I'll accept this one."

"You're an idiot," snapped Will. "Fine." With a grimace, he downed his potion. "Now you."

Tiny followed suit, choking and gagging as the taste assaulted him. He managed to swallow it down, though. The pain in Will's leg increased a moment later, followed by a sensation of heat. He watched in fascination as the swelling decreased, and he quickly removed the bandage. The edges of the skin knitted together before his eyes.

Meanwhile Tiny's skin changed color as his bruises began disappearing. The warrior winced a few times as he experienced a variety of disparate pains, but his expression quickly turned to one of relief as the various aches vanished.

Looking down again, Will saw that his leg had finished healing. He tested it by bending his knees and then straightening up again. Everything worked perfectly, though he still had quite a bit of crusted blood stuck to his skin. "Feel like a bath?" he asked.

"More magic?" asked Tiny warily.

Will nodded.

"Sure. After the embarrassment of that nurse trying to bathe me earlier, anything has to be better."

It took Will a few minutes to construct the spell, but once he was done he quickly turned it loose, allowing the magic to clean Tiny, himself, and a portion of the room that lay between them. As always, he felt immediately better, although the spell couldn't do anything about his missing trouser leg. Glancing down, he studied the now-clean skin of his leg.

Fine silver lines traced where the wound had been and where his mother had been forced to cut while she was extracting the troll-let. Will frowned as he spotted the scars. Previously when he had used the potion there had been no trace of his injury left behind. *But your leg was hurt more than half a day ago,* he told himself. *And Janice and Tiny were hurt almost two days ago.*

He looked at Tiny anxiously, but he couldn't see any sign of residual injury. But then, bruises didn't leave scars. He hoped the big man's kidneys had healed properly.

But Janice…

She'll never forgive me, Will realized. *No, I'll never forgive myself.* His sudden fear was dulled by a wave of fatigue that washed over him, a side effect of the regeneration potion. Looking over at Tiny, he saw the man's eyes drooping.

"That potion really hits fast, huh?" said Tiny. "I thought I slept well, but I could go back to sleep right now."

"Sleep," Will encouraged him. "They'll probably kick you out after you wake up and there's nothing wrong with you."

"What about you?"

"I'll go home and take a nap." Will patted Tiny's shoulder and headed for the door. Outside the room, he saw Doctor Morris leaving Janice's room. "How is she?"

The doctor smiled. "She'll do well. Her eye is back and functioning properly."

Chapter 34

"Can I see her?"

The other man shook his head. "No. She's asleep now. She was very clear that she didn't want anyone to see her."

Will repeated the words slowly. "Anyone to see her. How is…?"

"She's different," interrupted the doctor. "It was fortunate that her eye regenerated, but there are some pretty drastic differences in her appearance now."

"Her mouth? Her lips?"

"She'll have no trouble eating or drinking. Her cheek healed as well. Everything is perfectly functional. The changes are primarily aesthetic, and there's some scar tissue, of course. She will probably be very self-conscious about her appearance for a period of time, so be patient with her."

"I understand," said Will, but he didn't. He couldn't. It wasn't fair—it would never be fair. Stepping back, he turned and headed for the exit. The walls were closing in, and he felt as though he was suffocating. He needed air.

Outside the sun was warm and bright. It beamed down as though everything was right with the world. Spring was finally making its presence known. The air was fresh and blowing gently, carrying the scent of new leaves and vitality. The world was waking up again.

But it couldn't touch the rock that had replaced his heart. Will felt cold and dead inside. The weariness brought on by the regeneration potion only enhanced his numbness. He started walking for home.

The journey was dreamlike, or rather nightmare-like, given his emotions, but he arrived before long and found that his house was abuzz with activity. No fewer than two carriages and one large wagon sat in the drive alongside his house. He recognized one of them as belonging to Mark Nerrow.

There were also a large number of men outside with tools and shovels. Will even spotted a pickaxe in one fellow's hands. *Are those the workers Blake hired?* It seemed like too many, and what would they need a pickaxe for? Steeling himself, Will kept walking, and when he got closer he saw that the entry was partially blocked by several men who were mounting a new door in place.

One of the workers glanced at him as he approached. "Servant's entrance is around back. This door won't be usable for a while anyway."

Will stifled a laugh. It was almost refreshing to be thought of as a commoner again. Tired, he nodded and waved a hand in acknowledgment as he walked around to enter through the kitchen door. He was almost there when a man who seemed to have been dipped and battered in dirt yelled at him. "Hey, you! Get over here!" Will walked over. "Give me a hand."

With a sigh, Will helped the man right his wheelbarrow, then he took a shovel and loaded it up again while the other fellow took a breather. The workman seemed to have had a hard day, so he didn't complain. "What are you folks working on here?" he asked, genuinely curious. He had asked Blake to remodel the root cellar, but it appeared as though the men were involved in a brand-new excavation.

"Oh, pardon," said the laborer. "I didn't realize you weren't part of one of the crews. Guess I should have guessed by the fact you weren't dirty."

"No offense taken," said Will. He finished shoveling the dirt and rocks into the barrow.

"On the other side they're refitting the cellar to be a dungeon. Over here we're excavating for a workroom

Chapter 34

or some place to do magic and things. Who knows with these nobles? I feel sorry for whoever he plans to torture, though. That's no way to die."

Will hid a smirk. *A workroom? I never told Blake to do that.* "Who lives here?"

"Oh, you've heard of him!" said the workman emphatically. "It's that crackpot from Barrowden. The one who married Princess Selene last year after murdering her husband-to-be."

"Crackpot? Seems like I should have heard of him."

"Everyone has," insisted the stranger. "Supposedly he stopped the Darrowans and stopped the war, but the rumor is that he made a pact with a demon to do it. Sound familiar yet?"

Will put on a look of disbelief. "A demon? You're making this shit up."

"Cross my heart," said the worker. "I'd swear it to the Mother. After that he came to Cerria and the king sent him here to become a wizard. Bad idea if you ask me, but then—"

"They never do ask," said Will with a sympathetic nod.

"Yeah. Rich people are crazy. Why would you send a confirmed demon worshipper to Wurthaven, to make him even more powerful? Anyway, after he came here they say he straight out murdered Lord Spry's son. That's the same fellow who was going to marry the princess. Then he murdered the father and took his bride!"

"That can't be true!" exclaimed Will in mock outrage. "The king wouldn't stand for it!"

The laborer shrugged. "If you ask me, they're all nuts—noblemen, royalty, wizards—all of 'em. And with all these people disappearing, who knows what's going on? Makes you wonder why this prick's got us out here digging a new dungeon, doesn't it?"

Will straightened up, then offered the man a hand to help him get back to his feet. "Well, truth be told, I know the man you're talking about."

His new friend gave him a wary eye.

"He's me. And I promise I'm not planning on torturing any people, though I might make some of the creatures who are actually making folks disappear suffer. If I don't get myself killed first." He lifted a hand and tipped an imaginary hat to the man before turning back to the house.

Chapter 35

There were more surprises in store for him when he stepped through the kitchen door. Blake was standing in the room with his back to where Will had quietly entered, while across the room and facing the manservant at an angle was Laina Nerrow, who bore an expression of extreme vexation.

"Do you think she would have approved of this—this—waste? She trusts you, Blake! Is this how you repay her?" sputtered Laina.

Blake's tone was steady as he replied, "I assure you, Her Highness personally instructed me to give him full access to her accounts. She would have done exactly the same in my place."

"She'd agree to digging up the property to install a fucking dungeon? Are you mad? What has he done to your brain?"

"It is *his* money to spend," said Blake calmly.

"The fucking hell it is!"

"And he didn't ask for a dungeon. He only wanted me to refit the cellar. The expansion for a laboratory was my idea, as well as something Her Highness would have doubtless done if she were here."

Laina threw her hands up in the air. "Only because he's twisted her brain into a limp noodle!"

Blake relaxed slightly, putting one hand on his hip in gesture that would definitely have been too casual for such a servant speaking to most nobles. "You know better than that, Laina. I know you dislike him, but even you don't believe he's evil. Quite the reverse, in fact."

Will's half-sister pressed her lips together in frustration, unable to deny what the man had said. Then she found her voice. "It's still a colossal waste of money. Think how many people it could have helped."

"A moment ago, you were fine with the money being kept safely in Her Highness' accounts. Now you're suggesting she's parsimonious for not giving the money to your charity? Hasn't she already donated considerably to the cause?"

"That's not the point."

"What is the point then, Miss Nerrow?" asked Blake in an innocent tone that would likely have infuriated even a saint.

Laina's face was turning red when her mother appeared behind her. "Stop haranguing the poor man, Laina. I raised you to comport yourself better." Blake bowed as the baroness entered the room.

Her eyes were the first to fix on Will standing quietly in the kitchen doorway. Despite her station, Agnes Nerrow curtseyed respectfully. "It appears our gracious host has returned. I am glad to see you again, William, if you will forgive us for bursting into your home unannounced."

Laina and Agnes both glanced at his trousers, noting the one bare leg with curiosity. Will stepped forward, feeling uncertain, and his cheeks colored as they stared at his ruined clothes. A few seconds passed, then he regained his wits. "Excuse my attire. It's been an interesting day. If you'll pardon me, I need to change." Without another word, he slipped around Blake and out the other door, heading into the hall. All he could think of was getting to his bedroom and locking himself in. Nowhere was safe.

Behind him, he heard Blake's voice. "Pardon me, milady. I need to attend to my employer. I'll return shortly." He followed Will into the hall and up the stairs.

Chapter 35

Stopping at the head of the stairs, Will turned around. "What in the hell is going on?"

"Their house burned down. I told them you would put them up for a while."

"I didn't agree to that!" Will hissed in a whispered yell.

Blake raised one brow. "You'd have turned them away? Be honest."

Fatigue and frustration combined to overwhelm him. Will's eyes focused on the balustrade that bordered the stairs, and suddenly a piece of it exploded, flying away in a shower of splinters. Blake jerked and stared, then looked back at him. Neither of them said anything for a few seconds, until Will spoke first. "Fuck." He'd inadvertently reflex cast a force-lance. There was no doubt now.

"Not to worry. I already have a carpenter downstairs. I'll put him on the repair as soon as he finishes the door," said the manservant reasonably.

Closing his eyes, Will rubbed his face while composing his thoughts. "I need some quiet. Please give my guests my apologies. I'll speak with them after I've rested."

"Certainly, sir, however—"

Will held up a hand to silence the man. "No buts. I'll think about all this after a nap." Turning away, he went to the master bedroom door and opened it. He came face to face with Mark Nerrow, who was in the process of changing into a robe and slippers. Will's robe, and Will's slippers. The two men stared at one another for a split second, then Will gently closed the door.

"It was the only room fit for a man and his wife," said Blake from beside his shoulder. "The guest rooms were too small."

Will pointed at one of the guest room doors.

"Miss Laina is in that one, sir."

He pointed at the final bedroom.

"I put Miss Tabitha in that one."

He nodded, pursing his lips, then responded, "They're sisters—couldn't they have shared a room?"

"Ordinarily, sir," agreed Blake. "But Miss Laina's bodyguard, Darla, is sharing her room. It seemed uncouth to force all three of them into one room."

"Oh, sure. That makes sense," agreed Will equitably, a strange sound in his voice. "And the servant's quarters downstairs, I assume that's occupied as well?"

"I'm letting Armand share it with me," said Blake. "But I can sleep in the parlor, and you can use the bed. He and I were taking turns anyway."

Will pointed upward. "The old attic quarters?"

"Monique is using it for now."

"Monique."

"Their maid. She doesn't have any family in the city, so she had nowhere else to go."

"Naturally," said Will, starting down the stairs.

Blake called after him anxiously, "Where are you going, sir?"

"The dormitory I suppose," announced Will. "I'm sure they have a closet I can sleep in." He made it to the bottom of the stairs when a figure with long dark hair darted out of the hall and charged toward him.

"Brother!" It was Tabitha, presumably referring to his status as their pretend brother-in-law. She caught him with a smile and threw her arms around him.

Will froze, but Tabitha didn't release him. She was a bit like Sammy in that regard, or perhaps she sensed his tension. Will's emotions grew turbulent, and his fatigue ate away at his control. After a moment he returned the embrace, staring over her shoulder. Tears began to well in his eyes and when he looked up, he saw Agnes and Laina standing in the kitchen door, watching him.

Chapter 35

Agnes walked over, and Will silently disengaged himself from Tabitha. The young woman's face registered that something was wrong, though she wasn't quite sure what it might be. Agnes took his arm and led him back up the stairs. "I assume you saw Mark in the bedroom?" she asked.

He nodded.

"He was just changing. We lost most of our clothes, but he wasn't going to bed. You look tired."

"Yeah." Somehow, he couldn't protest as she pulled him along.

"Let's put you to bed for a while then," she said soothingly. Her husband was stepping out into the hall as they approached. He nodded at Will and started to say something, but Agnes warned him away with a look. She took Will into his bedroom, and Blake followed them in. "Get some rest, and when you're awake I'll have Armand prepare something warm for you to eat. We can talk then."

"I'll see to the rest, Your Excellency," said Blake.

The baroness nodded and quietly ducked out of the room.

Will stared mournfully at Blake, but the manservant merely shrugged. "Let's get you out of those clothes. They look like they're ready for the rag pile."

For once, Will didn't fight while Blake helped him undress. A few minutes later he was in bed, his head comfortably resting on his favorite pillow. *Selene's pillow,* he noted absently, vowing to hide it after he woke later. She had brought it with her after leaving the palace. Glancing up at Blake, he asked, "Remind me again, why didn't they go to the palace instead?"

"The baron didn't trust the king," said Blake immediately. "Not after what happened a few days back, when you were whipped."

"Oh, that makes sense," said Will, then he closed his eyes and drifted away.

He woke up suddenly somewhere close to noon, feeling a sense of impending doom. It was too late. He'd wasted too much time. After a moment, he oriented himself and his heart rate returned to normal, but the anxiety remained. *I'm not prepared for tonight,* he realized. That was the heart of the matter.

But he was rested. The sleep at the Alchemy building, as well as a few hours of rest after the regeneration potion that morning, had combined to leave him feeling hale and hearty, though he wasn't sure if he was sound of mind. Janice flashed through his thoughts, and he hastily pushed the thought away. He needed to get ready; there wasn't time for wasting.

Will rose and dressed in simple but clean clothes, a pair of trousers and a light tunic. A pair of boots and a belt completed his attire, and he was dressed, though he felt strangely light without his customary under-the-tunic brigandine. He would have to order another made once everything returned to normal.

That done, he went to his desk and did a quick mental assessment of his resources. *Two potions of regeneration, eighteen blood-cleanse potions left, twenty vials of alchemical fire, and a foolish amount of white phosphorous.* He also had his armor and weapons, which he summoned and checked briefly. One sword was badly nicked, so he spent a moment to sharpen it with a spell, then sent it back to storage.

There was still a vampire in a jar, but until the renovations were done, he couldn't do much with it. He readied an Ethelgren's Illumination and closed the curtains to the bedroom before summoning the jar to check its contents. His heart was pounding, but the jar was still

Chapter 35

sealed and seemed otherwise intact. Keeping the spell in hand, he untied the twine, then removed the cloth covering the jar. Nothing jumped out, and when he glanced inside, he saw that the pile of pieces had reunited into a whole—an emaciated body lay within.

One eye stared up at him, but the creature seemed too weak to move. He replaced the cloth and tied the jar shut again, speaking to it all the while. "Wait a while longer and I'll feed you, but don't think of leaving the jar. The sun is out." Then he sent the creature back into storage.

He felt better after assessing everything, so he brought out his journal and began his daily ritual of running through each spell he could cast, one by one. That didn't take long, and afterward he moved on to the new spell he was working on acquiring, the iron-body transformation.

An hour of that left him a little frustrated, but he knew it was all part of the process. The spell was slightly more complicated than Selene's Solution, and he'd only managed to master one other eighth-order spell at that point, so it was reasonable that it would take him a while to get the hang of it. *The question is whether I'll be able to use it before I get turned into a pincushion for fangs again.*

With that done, it was time for his more repetitive practice, though that seemed almost pointless now that he was beginning to reflex cast the force-lance spell. Being able to cast the spell unconsciously was great, but he wouldn't feel truly comfortable until he could also count on being able to do so deliberately. *But once I can do that, which spell should I start working on next?* Getting to the point of reflex casting took a lot of time and practice, so choosing a spell he would need to cast quickly and often was important before investing the effort.

The problem was that he had a lot of useful spells. The chameleon spell would be a great choice, but so would the unlocking spell, or the wind-wall. *Or hell, even the climb spell.* Then again, a larger defensive spell might be best. The force-dome used a lot of turyn, but if he was faced with a large scale attack, it might be the only option for defense, and it would be a lot easier to learn to reflex cast than the iron-body spell would be.

"After a hundred years or so, most of the spells you use frequently get to the point where they're instinctive." Arrogan had told him that, and he suddenly wondered what his future self might be able to do. *Future Will could probably handle this whole vampire problem without breaking a sweat,* he thought enviously. *If only he were here instead of me.*

Drawing the curtains, Will opened one of the windows and looked outside. There was a tree about twenty feet from the bedroom, so he took aim and began practicing on it with the force-lance, trying to remove individual leaves. The spell was coming together in less than a second now, but it still refused to let him cast it with merely a thought.

Glancing down, he saw the laborer he had spoken with that morning staring up at him curiously. Will smiled and waved broadly, causing the fellow to hurry back to his job. Will shrugged and shut the window. "At least I tried to be friendly."

At that point, he had done all he could. It was time to face the world, so he went to the door and stepped out. He could hear voices downstairs already, and he hoped he wouldn't be inundated with questions. All the noise was coming from the dining room, so he turned and headed that way. The table was nearly full when he stepped into the room.

Chapter 35

"Will!" said Tiny cheerfully, waving from the far side of the room. "I thought you would sleep all day."

He didn't feel like explaining his solitary practice, so he replied with a simple, "I needed the rest." Gazing around the room, he saw that the entire Nerrow family was gathered around. The side door opened, and Blake and Armand entered carrying a variety of plates and dishes—all covered with food.

Will's stomach rumbled appreciatively.

Blake called out, "You're just in time. We had given up on waiting for you to come down for lunch."

He ignored his manservant and pulled Armand aside quickly. "You didn't let him prepare any of this, did you?"

The older cook winked at him. "You're safe."

"Thank the Mother," Will exclaimed, moving to find a seat.

CHAPTER 36

It was a simple meal, but it had obviously been put together by an experienced hand with an eye for perfection. Will took note of several things he wanted to ask Armand about later; in particular, he had questions about the sauce the older man had used, but that would have to wait.

As the actual eating slowed and people began to finish, Mark Nerrow spoke to Will. "I owe you a debt of thanks for letting us use your home."

Having slept fully and with a full stomach, Will was once again in command of his faculties. He nodded graciously. "Let's not speak of debts," he replied. "I hope you don't think I would be so poor a host as to count the cups." 'Count the cups' was an expression he had learned from Selene before she had left. While he didn't understand the origin of the idiom, it essentially meant penny pinching, or acting in a cheap manner, something the nobility would rather die than be accused of.

"Of course not," said the baron.

"Then feel free to use my home as long as you need. If you feel the need to recompense me, all I ask is for the details of the previous evening. What happened?"

Agnes spoke first. "It was horrible. I was sure we wouldn't survive." She glanced lovingly at her husband. "But Mark had planned ahead. It was his forethought that saved us."

If the remark seemed overly contrived, the faint blush that came to Mark Nerrow's cheek destroyed that thought. Will decided that Agnes was simply well spoken and not afraid to give praise when it was due. The baron replied simply, "I merely wanted to keep my family safe. It was a decision made years ago."

Agnes looked at Will. "When we bought the house, he had the builders renovate portions of it. One thing he insisted on, something I thought he was mad for, was creating a sub-cellar we could retreat to in the event of a fire or an armed invasion."

Will turned to Mark. "You really were thinking ahead. Maybe I should add a similar provision to the work they're doing on my new workshop?" Blake was standing beside the kitchen door, behaving for once exactly as an ordinary butler would. He coughed slightly to catch Will's attention. Will glanced back, then laughed. "You already put something like that in the plans, didn't you?"

A slight nod from Blake confirmed it.

Laina spoke up. "Your staff might be small, but Blake is the envy of many a noble household. There's a reason the king employed him on Selene's behalf all those years ago." Her eyes locked onto Blake as she continued, "Even if he occasionally has lapses of judgment."

Agnes put a hand on her daughter's arm, effectively silencing her. Then Mark returned to his story. "Darla was on watch, as usual, and she was able to give us some forewarning; however, this time they wasted no time in their assault. By the time I was able to respond, they had already thrown more alchemical bombs at the house. Everything was in flames. The house burned so quickly it was all we could do to gather the servants and get into the cellar."

"I'm sorry for all that you've lost. The house must have held many items that were precious to you," said Will. He noticed that Tiny gave him a look of approval as he said it.

"Things we can replace," said the baroness, looking around the table gratefully at her family. "We saved everything that was important to us." She noticed that her younger daughter was fidgeting, so she asked, "Is there something you wanted to say, Tabitha?"

Tabitha grinned, then winked at Will. "Just that I think it's terribly unfair that Selene found William first and married him without giving anyone else a chance." She glanced at her sister. "Don't you think that was terrible of her, Laina?"

Will almost had a spoonful of peas to his mouth, but he was so startled that he missed, and the peas scattered across his plate. Laina glared and her hand moved suddenly to one side, knocking the gravy boat onto Tabitha's lap. "Oh! I am so sorry, Tabby! I'm so clumsy today," apologized the older sister.

Tabitha's eyes could have burned a hole through Laina. "You did that on purpose!"

"Why would I do that?" asked Laina in mock innocence.

"This is the only dress I have left! You've ruined it."

Agnes' voice cut through the brewing storm. "Girls!"

Will took the chaos as an opportunity and stood up, pushing his chair back. "If you'll excuse me, I have some things to attend to." He gave Tiny an emphatic look, and the big man rose from his seat as well. A few minutes later, they were standing outside the back door, but before they could leave, Mark Nerrow stepped out.

"William, before you leave…"

Will turned back. He also had a few things he wanted to say. "I don't mind you staying here," he told his father, "but I'm not sure you'll be safe. They've already broken in once when I wasn't here."

Chapter 36

The older man frowned. "I wanted to say thanks once again. I'm not sure there's anywhere safer that we could be. With you, me, Laina, not to mention Darla, Blake, and your giant friend here"—he nodded appreciatively at Tiny—"I'm not sure how better we could be protected."

"I'm not sure where I will be tonight," said Will honestly. "I wasn't watching your home the night it burned either, so I'm worried about what will happen tonight."

"Then stay here," suggested his father. "I realize you may bear some ill will after what I said to you—"

"I do," Will interrupted, "but that has nothing to do with my concern for the people in that house. Their safety is important to me and not just because they're under my roof."

"Then it makes sense that we concentrate our strength here."

Will shook his head. "What about the rest of the college, the rest of the city? I caught over a hundred of them in a warehouse that night, feeding on a friend of mine. They went wild and some of them escaped. From what I understand any new vampires created need strict control and supervision to keep them from running wild during the beginning of their undead existence. They've lost control, and if lots of people have gone missing then it means we're only a day or two away from the entire city being turned upside down."

"Which is the king's problem," countered Mark. "He has the resources, the power, the authority, and the men to deal with it. Right now, my only job is to keep my family safe."

He grimaced. "As you pointed out so bluntly a few days ago, it's *your* family, not *mine*. I'll do everything I can, but I'm only one person, and I'm not counting on the king to save the city. Before I commit to hiding here with you, I'll be doing everything I can to get ahead of this problem. I'll only be here tonight if I fail to find a better answer."

"Aren't you the arrogant one?" said his father snidely. "Don't you think it's a bit presumptuous to think that you're the only one that can save the city? What power do you have that makes you so confident and prideful? You aren't even a sorcerer—you're too good for that—yet you think you can rid Cerria of this plague? What hubris!"

"Two nights ago, I slew over a hundred of them," snapped Will, "but that wasn't good enough, and my friends are still paying the price for my weakness." Reaching up, he jabbed his index finger into Mark Nerrow's chest. "You want to hunker down in a hole with your family? Fine. I applaud you. I'm glad you did, since I care about them too. But don't expect me to hide in the hole with you. As you pointed out, I'm not *family*, so it doesn't really matter if something happens to me, does it? I'll be out there doing as much as I can, and if I get killed for my hubris it's none of your concern."

The baron looked down at the finger that had stabbed into him. "I've half a mind to teach you some humility, lad."

"Try it," spat Will. "I'm a little overdue for some *fatherly* discipline."

Mark snapped, but he didn't fight stupidly. He faked a punch, then sent a source-link at Will when he thought the young man would be distracted. Unfortunately for him, neither attack had a chance of working. A point-defense shield stopped the fist painfully in mid-swing, while the source-link dissipated the moment it touched Will's turyn-absorbing outer boundary.

With a thought, Will sent his own line out, catching his father and paralyzing the man almost instantly. He felt the older man's will struggling for a moment, then he separated his father's will from his source. Using one hand, he gripped the baron's coat to keep him from falling, then pushed him back and braced him against the wall of the house.

Chapter 36

Three elementals manifested around him, swelling as they took physical form. Will ignored them, his eyes locked onto Mark Nerrow's panicked gaze. "This is just a lesson, but if you want to make it into something tragic, then by all means, threaten me with the elementals. It won't change a thing."

Before anything else could happen, Will released the link to his father and turned away. Tiny was still watching silently, but he could see an unhappy look in the big warrior's eyes. "Let's go," said Will, and together the two of them started walking.

"William," called the baron, still trying to regain his composure.

He kept walking.

"It does matter if something happens to you."

His face twisted, but he refused to look back. *Goddamn it, just let me hate you!* he thought. *Don't make it complicated for me.*

***

Halfway across the campus, Tiny finally said something. "So, you and the baron have some personal issues, huh?"

Will didn't say anything.

"I remember you saying you were a bastard, but when you made that remark about 'fatherly' discipline, it was something of a giveaway."

He shot a look at his friend. "That information could get me killed."

"I'm not going to say anything. Just wanted to make sure I wasn't imagining things. Where are we headed?"

"I don't know."

Tiny sighed. "You sounded like you had a plan when you were arguing with Lord Limpdick."

Will snorted. "What did you call him?"

The big man shrugged. "It seemed like something Dave would have said."

"Where is Dave now? Is he still in Company B?"

"They let him out. He's probably in jail somewhere. So, to be clear, you don't have a plan?"

Will stopped, staring at the ground. "No. I have a feeling, though. This is probably out of control. It's going to get really bad if we don't do something, and hiding won't help."

"Oh, good. We have a feeling."

"Sorry."

Tiny shrugged. "It's all right. Sometimes your feelings result in painful consequences, but they never lead me into anything I've regretted."

"I'm sorry about what—"

Tiny lifted a fist. "Remember what I told you?"

Will shut up.

"So, where are we headed?" repeated Tiny.

He thought for a minute. "We should check on Janice."

"She's fine," said Tiny immediately. "We were released together."

Will felt hesitant to ask, but he did anyway. "How did she seem?"

"I think she was a little shocked at the change, but she'll adjust," said Tiny confidently.

He frowned. "How can you be sure?"

The big man laughed. "You'll know when you see her. She's beautiful."

Will nodded. "She was beautiful, I remember, but now…"

"She's different, but if anything, she's even more radiant," said Tiny in a matter-of-fact tone. There was no doubt in his voice.

Chapter 36

He began to wonder what Tiny's standards for female beauty were based on. Was the man being kind and referring to Janice's exceptional character? Or maybe the former farmhand had never had much to compare her to. *I wonder what his mother looked like?* Will studied Tiny's face for a moment, then envisioned a square-jawed, broad-shouldered mule of a woman. *No, that can't be it.* Finally, he simply said, "Look, Tiny, I'm her friend. Just be honest with me. How bad is it? Are there a lot of scars?"

Tiny smiled faintly. "You're really worried for her, aren't you?"

"Of course, it's my fault that..."

The big warrior lifted his fist threateningly.

"I'm talking about her, not you!"

His friend shook his head. "Same difference, and she would feel the same way. Don't let me catch you apologizing to her in front of me, or I won't just joke about thrashing you. She chose to do what she did, she knew the danger, and she saved your ass. So let's not entertain the idea of diminishing that."

Will held up his hands in surrender, and Tiny nodded acceptingly, then continued, "To answer your question, you'll have to see for yourself. I won't spoil it, but trust me, she's as lovely as ever."

Will looked away but watched Tiny from the side of one eye. *Maybe he can't see her objectively, because...* Unable to contain the thought, he asked, "Tiny, are you smitten with her?"

"Of course not!" said Tiny immediately, his cheeks coloring. Trying to defuse the moment, the big man struck Will playfully, knocking the wind out of him and sending him falling backward. "Oh, sorry!" He held out a hand and helped Will back to his feet.

Dusting himself off ruefully, Will decided to table the subject. It obviously wasn't a safe topic for casual discussion. Then he saw that Tiny was holding out a folded sheet of paper. "What's that?"

"A note from Janice. She wrote it this morning before we parted ways."

"You could have told me that a while ago," said Will, taking the paper and opening it.

"When? While you were measuring dicks with your dad, or when you were trying to get me to tell you whether Janice was horribly disfigured?"

Will gave his friend a sarcastic smile. "Everyone thinks you're this kindly gentle giant, but I wonder what they'd think if they heard the way you talk sometimes. Measuring dicks?"

"What would you call it then?"

"Verbal sparring?"

"How about phallic fencing?" countered Tiny with an evil grin.

Will choked, then laughed. "I can't win. Let me read this." He held up the note as though he would shield himself with it.

Tiny nodded. "Wise move. You don't want to match *swords* with me. I'm not just long of limb, you know." He stretched out one arm and made a fist, as though to illustrate his point.

He was laughing so hard by then that he had tears in his eyes. "Holy Mother! Please stop." Staring at the page in his hands, he blinked until his vision was clear and then focused on the words.

> *Will,*
>
> *Forgive me for my outburst earlier. I was in a bad state of mind and in no shape for company. Thank you for the potion.*

Chapter 36

I've no idea how you managed it, but I worry about what you may have done on our behalf. In any case, that's not what this missive is for. I have news you might be interested in.

During the day you were away I received a note from my friend, Drake. He did some more digging for me, and it turns out that the reason that Ethelgren's Exhortation is kept locked away is that it isn't safe, not even for display. In years past everyone who has touched it with bare skin has perished. Some suffered immediate seizures; others simply stopped eating and withered away.

Whatever the relic's secret, it appears to be incompatible with wizards of the present. I wish I had better news. Today I will look into the reputed functions of some of the more benign relics. It may be that some of them are helpful even if they aren't specifically related to the current situation.

I'll find you tomorrow. I know you're probably worried about me. I just need a little time to adjust before I face the prying eyes of others.

Your friend,
Janice

"What does it say?" asked Tiny.

"I forgot you couldn't read," muttered Will.

"Sir Kyle is teaching me," said the big man defensively. "He says any squire worth his salt has to learn."

"Not to worry." An evil idea came to him then. *Dear Will, please don't tell Tiny how much I adore his huge muscles. If he were to ever find out I would simply die.* He shook his head, remembering the blow that had knocked him down. It wouldn't be safe to tease his friend. He read the note aloud for Tiny's benefit, without adding anything.

"That's not much help then," observed Tiny. Then he looked off into the distance. "What's that?"

It appeared to be soldiers, a lot of soldiers. They were marching in from the direction of the college gates.

Chapter 37

It turned out to be three full companies of soldiers, or somewhere close to three hundred and sixty men. They marched across the campus in formation, then stopped when they reached the central square between the main buildings.

Will and Tiny waited off to the side of the main lane and watched as the soldiers marched by. "Recognize any of them?" asked Will.

Tiny shook his head. "Company B is still quartered in Barrowden."

The soldiers formed up in the main square, then one of the officers read aloud a royal proclamation. The gist of it was simple—the army would be doing a building-by-building search of the entire campus. They also made it clear that it wasn't just a policy focused on the school, but apparently similar proceedings were occurring all over Cerria, and had been since early that morning.

Will looked at Tiny. "They must be trying to flush the vampires out of their daytime hiding places."

"It's not a bad idea," remarked the big man. "We hold the advantage while the sun is up. Once it sets, the situation reverses."

"William?" asked a tentative female voice.

They turned around to see a student had approached. Will didn't know her well, but he recognized her, primarily because she was the girl that Rob had been keen to date, Veronica Wellings. Will lifted a hand in greeting. "Veronica."

"Have you talked to Rob lately?" she asked.

That hit him like a club to the face. *What do I say?* Before he could respond, she went on, "He sent me a letter and he sounded weird, as though something happened to him. He said he's not coming back to school."

Will glanced at the soldiers, who were splitting into squads and fanning out to enter the various buildings, then back at Veronica. "Have you heard any rumors about what's been happening the last few days?"

She frowned. "I heard about the fires, and people have been talking about disappearances and monsters. Most of it is just hysteria, isn't it?"

"Rob went missing two nights ago," Will said honestly. "I don't know how much you'll believe, but things are much worse than you imagine."

"But I got his letter this morning. He left it at the girls' dorm for me. It was dated yesterday. There's one for you too; that's why I wondered if you knew something." She held up a small sealed envelope.

His heart sank. If Rob hadn't died that night, then he had survived to become one of the enemy. He couldn't lie to Veronica, though. "There are vampires, Veronica. They took him two nights ago. If he's still writing to you, then they've turned him. If you see him, you need to run the other direction."

She rolled her eyes, seeming irritated. "Listen, I don't know what sort of weird prank you two are trying to pull, but I don't appreciate it. I was genuinely worried about him."

"But—"

Veronica cut him off. "If you see him, tell him not to bother wasting my time. I'm not fond of games." She marched away.

"That went well," observed Tiny.

"What else could I have done?" asked Will.

Chapter 37

"Next time maybe paralyze her and push her up against a building? That worked well with the baron," said Tiny sarcastically.

Will glared at his friend. "Seriously, you have developed a nasty sense of humor."

Tiny shrugged. "It must be the company I keep."

He shook his head, then opened the envelope that Veronica had given him. The contents did nothing to ease his mind.

Will,

My school days have come to an end, but rest assured, I am alive and unwell. I despaired at first. The change is painful, but I bear you no ill will. This is my last message to you as a friend, however. If we meet again, well, it's best that we don't.

I tried, though. I tried hard. Maybe everyone does. The mind remains, but no amount of reason survives when the thirst strikes. I have already done things that would have horrified me just days ago, yet my sense of guilt is strangely dull.

This is my last gift to you. Get out of the city. Those who control the night have let slip the reins; not all is moving according to their plan. Apparently, the thing you went to save that night was the catalyst for a disaster that no one wanted.

But my new masters are adaptable. They will use the chaos as they adjust their plans. Friday night will be the end for Cerria, and for its king. I both fear and delight in the thought of what will come after.

Farewell my friend. Run far, run fast!
       Robert

"Fuck!" swore Will. Then he looked at Tiny. "I need to talk to someone."

"Who?"

He held up his hand, showing the Ring of Vile and Unspeakable Knowledge to Tiny. "I've kept this a secret to most, but the mind of my old teacher is trapped here."

Tiny stared at the ring. "When did you get that? I don't think I've ever seen you wearing a ring."

"Most people don't notice it. It's part of the magic," Will informed him. "Anyway, don't be surprised when you hear it talking." He activated the limnthal, then addressed the ring. "I'm back at the college now, but it seems like the vampires are probably multiplying."

"How's the baby?" asked Arrogan with a snicker, ignoring what Will had just said. Tiny's brows went up in surprise.

Will growled. "It's fine. I named it Gan, in your honor."

"You kept it? Those things are dangerous!"

"I returned it to the trolls. They even gave me a name, Grak-Murra."

"Troll what? That last part is nonsense."

"It's new. Clegg decided it's their new word for mother."

Arrogan began chortling. "So you're the 'troll-mother.' Oh, that's rich! In the history of wizard ambassadors, you're the first to deliver the baby and take it back to them."

"The same thing happened to you then?"

"Why don't we focus on this vampire problem you have?" suggested Arrogan, suddenly serious. "That's obviously the most important thing."

Of course it is, thought Will wryly. He took a few minutes to explain the situation and give the ring an update on current events, including the content of Rob's letter.

Chapter 37

Arrogan sighed. "That isn't good. You say people have been disappearing?"

"That's the rumor, but it makes sense."

"The building searches probably won't find much," said the ring.

Will frowned. "Why not?"

"Oh, they might find a few random nests—some of the wild ones that got loose after what happened with Tailtiu—but from what your friend's letter indicates, the leaders are still here. They may not be in total control of the frenzied ones, but they'll be giving advice on where to hide."

"And where would that be?"

"They don't need to breathe, so they have a lot of options. The simplest is just to dig right into the earth like a worm, but they can also hide in any dark nook or cranny. In the city they'll probably take to the sewers."

"Lognion will probably have thought of that," offered Will.

"So what if he has?" snapped Arrogan. "Even if they go down there in force, they can't find them. Some will be in the smaller pipes; places so small no sane person would crawl into them. Others may hide underwater. This is how they survive. The only ones that will be caught are the newer ones."

"Then how do we win?" asked Will in exasperation.

"Well, Lognion does have one thing right. It is helpful to limit their hiding places by doing daytime searches, but it won't win the fight. The smarter ones can only be caught at night, when they come out to feed, which, of course, is also when things are the most dangerous for humans. What really makes no sense to me is the strategy here."

"Whose?"

"The vampires," answered the ring. "Whoever is leading them was obviously wise and careful, but once things fell apart with Tailtiu they should have fled. The old ones are smart. They know what happens when humans discover their presence. People panic. This daytime search is just the beginning. Eventually the people will start tearing the city apart, even to the point of ripping up the streets to expose the sewers. They'll burn everything and anyone. If their initial goal was simply to demoralize the populace then this is going too far."

"Rob did say they were adaptable."

"But not suicidal," countered Arrogan. "I wish I knew who was leading them."

Something popped into Will's mind. "I forgot to tell you. A few days ago, when I was protecting the Nerrow's home, I talked to one of them for a moment."

"How nice," said the ring sarcastically.

"It was a young girl and I asked her name. She was different from the others."

"First trolls, now this…"

"She told me her name. It was Alexa."

The ring was silent for a brief time, then it exclaimed, "Shit."

"You know her?"

"I met her master once. He was the one who got away from Aislinn. Alexa was his favorite pet. If she's here then Androv won't be far away. He's no fool, William, and he was a third-order wizard long before I was even born. If you encounter him in person, you're not likely to survive the meeting."

"A vampire wizard then?"

"The worst of the worst," agreed the ring. "He was Grim Talek's second in command, and none of this is like him at all. He wouldn't have left Tailtiu alone in that

Chapter 37

warehouse. He knows better, which means he planned on things going out of control."

"There must be some way to stop him."

"Listen up, William. You won't be a match for a wizard like that for at least a hundred years, maybe never. He's been at it so long that he can almost certainly reflex cast almost any spell he knows, and his turyn control will be flawless. The fact that he's also a vampire is almost irrelevant compared to that fact."

"Sunlight will still destroy him. I have Ethelgren's Illumination," said Will.

"And he uses spells to protect himself from sunlight. Hell, he's probably walking around the city right this minute. He could be in the middle of the market, smiling and buying an apple from a fruit seller. With his mastery of magic, he might as well not even be a vampire; he's more like a human, except that he's immortal and can regenerate from any wound. He's almost as dangerous as Grim Talek himself. The only difference between him and the lich is that vampires have to feed. Other than that he's practically unkillable."

"I need some practical advice," said Will. "You've made it clear I can't beat him head to head, so what should I do?"

"Remember what I told you when you found out about the demonic ritual last year?"

Will sighed. "Yeah."

"Pretty much the same advice here."

"You already know I'm not going to abandon the city. So let's skip over the argument and get to the part where you give practical advice for suicidal idiots. What about relics? My friend Janice was looking into the ones we have here at the school. There's one that was left by Ethelgren, but supposedly it kills whoever tries to use it."

"Enchanted items are the recourse of lazy wizards," said Arrogan angrily.

"Why?"

"They hamper your growth. Sure, they're useful, but they become a crutch. Back in my day some wizards produced some truly miraculous items, but it was always a shortcut to power. In the end they wound up mediocre wizards because they relied on their toys to do everything for them."

"Not to quibble, but at the moment, I could use a shortcut to easy power," pointed out Will. "If the old magic items were such a problem, why did anyone create them?"

"Oh, they weren't a problem, they were just too easy. Let's say you want to be able to cast a spell instantly. One way is to learn it and practice it. Eventually you start reflex casting it naturally. But another option is to create an enchanted item with the spell built into it. You provide the turyn, it produces the spell. So long as you have the magic item, you can effectively reflex cast whatever spells are built into it. But the problem is that you quit doing the work on your own. You never develop the ability to do it yourself, because it's always easier just to use the item. We had a number of great artificers, but they always fell into that trap. They'd become great craftsmen, but they never gained any more skill than the minimum required to cast a spell well enough to make an item for it."

"Well, Ethelgren was known as a vampire hunter, and he left behind an item. Surely it would allow me to use spells that would be helpful for this," he suggested.

There was silence for a moment, then the ring replied, "I can't argue with that."

"Do you know of any reason why it would be deadly to try and use a magic item?"

Chapter 37

"Well, you know the wizards today can't properly transform turyn. To use the spells in properly enchanted items you have to attune yourself, learn the type of turyn needed for each spell. It can take a few hours. I wouldn't think any item could hurt those incapable of using it, but I'm guessing it was simply incompetence on the part of those who tried."

Will nodded, glancing at Tiny. "Then I have a plan."

"Even if you steal it, don't think you can take on Androv," cautioned Arrogan.

"I'll keep that in mind," said Will, then he dismissed the limnthal and looked at Tiny again. The big warrior had heard a lot of new things in a short period of time, many of them disturbing, but he looked as solid and unperturbed as ever. "Let's go."

Chapter 38

"This is an awesome plan," said Tiny enthusiastically as they strode purposefully across Wurthaven.

Will gave him an odd look. "I haven't even said what it is yet."

Tiny nodded. "I know."

"You're just going to take it on faith?"

"Considering how confidently you're striding across the lawn, I can only assume that the plan is so audacious, so daring, so unanticipated, that the enemy will fall into a full rout without you even needing to confide the details to me before we engage them."

He couldn't help but laugh. "You've gotten awfully eloquent lately."

"It's the company I've been keeping," said Tiny. After a brief pause, he added, "Present company excepted, of course. I meant Sir Kyle and his officers. I've had to practice my speaking skills. You understand, now that I'm a gentleman and all that. No offense to you though, Will, still being a commoner, you probably wouldn't understand."

Will smirked. "None taken. So, do you want to hear what I intend to do?"

"Not really. If it's so uncertain you have to share it with me then it probably isn't very good. You might shake my confidence in you."

"Are you done yet?"

"I'm out of ideas."

"We're going to steal the relic I was talking about a little while ago."

"Yeah, I understood that part already," said Tiny. "What's the plan?"

"Well, that's it really. I'll sneak into the basement of the artifice building and use a few spells to spring it from where they've got it locked up. Then we clear out."

Tiny was moving his hand in quick circles in front of him. "And then?"

"Then I'll figure out how to use the relic. Hopefully once I know what sort of spells Ethelgren used, I'll have a better idea of what we can do to stop all this." Will waved his hands around to indicate the world in general.

"That isn't much of a plan."

Will nodded. "No, I suppose it isn't. Do you have anything better?"

"We go to the king and report everything we know. With his authority and the men and resources at his disposal, not to mention the advice of his military advisors, I'm fairly certain he could do something significant."

Just the thought of Lognion sent chills through Will and sparked phantom pains in the muscles of his back. "No good. The king whipped me half to death just a few days ago."

Tiny stopped walking, his face blank. Will pulled up and watched him carefully. After a moment he noticed that the tips of the warrior's ears were turning red. "You should have told me that, Will," said his friend, his voice tense.

"We haven't had a lot of time to talk since you got here. Are you all right?"

His friend was taking deep breaths. "Not particularly. You know I've been whipped twice myself."

Both times because of me, thought Will.

"Did he have a reason of any kind?"

"Not really. He was threatening Laina for hiring an assassin, but in the end, it was mainly an excuse to take his frustration out on me, because I wouldn't tell him where Selene was." As he spoke, he saw a multitude of strange emotions crossing Tiny's features. "Tiny, what's wrong?"

"You know, I like how things have gone for me lately," said his friend. Then he waved his arms in a circle. "Not the past few days, obviously, but I mean being a squire. Since joining the army I've gained a sense of purpose. I have friends, comrades, and we're serving a higher purpose, protecting Terabinia—and serving the king. If I really start to believe the king is an evil bastard, that all sort of falls apart for me."

Will was mildly shocked, not just at the big man's convictions, but the amount of thought he had already put into them. He knew Tiny was a smart man, but his size still disarmed people. *Always remember, he's big, not dumb.* "It's always complicated, Tiny. Even if the king is a monster, which he surely is, the army still serves a noble purpose. Until he orders you to do something that directly contradicts your conscience, I don't think you should fret over it."

"Oh, I'll fret all I want. Until I know exactly what to do in such a situation," said Tiny. "For now, let's stick to your stupid plan."

***

A few minutes later, they were looking at the front entrance of the Artifice building. Will was familiar with the place, though he'd never been in its basement. He'd already put a silent-armor spell on his clothing, and he had a chameleon spell, a sleep spell, and an unlocking spell ready and prepared. He was fairly confident he wouldn't have any significant problems.

"You just want me to wait out here?"

Chapter 38

"I already know the place. You don't. I'm a student, you aren't. Plus, it's easier to sneak around alone. If anything goes wrong, I'll put them to sleep and come back."

Tiny's eyes were slits. "Something always goes wrong when you're involved." He looked over his shoulder. "There will be several search squads here in a few minutes. Shouldn't you wait until after they're gone?"

Will shook his head, already walking toward the building. "Easier while the soldiers have everyone rattled. I can get it, hide, and wait until they're gone."

"If you say so."

He was too far away to continue the conversation. Will strode through the entrance with casual confidence. He walked past a couple of students and down the main hall, wondering where he would find the basement stairs. A young man at the front desk stopped him with a question. "What are you looking for?"

"Professor Dugas," said Will immediately.

"His office is over at the Engineering building."

"Sorry, I meant Salsbury—Professor Salsbury."

The other student, who Will didn't recognize, shook his head. "Sorry, he isn't in today. All the staff are in a meeting at Administration."

God damn it, just leave me alone, thought Will. He didn't want to have to start disabling people before he even got started. "I'll just leave a note on his door. Do you know where it is?"

"Second floor. You'll see the signs."

Will thanked him and headed down the hall, breathing a sigh of relief. He wanted to be out of sight before the soldiers entered and chaos ensued. The main stairs were off to the right, halfway down the main corridor, and now that he thought about it, they were probably the best place to start looking. They provided access to all the upper floors, so it seemed logical that the basement stairs probably originated in the same area.

Once there, he decided it was less than obvious. The stairs were wide enough for three students to walk abreast, and they led upward only, stopping solidly on the ground level. On either side of the stairs were side doors that led into maintenance areas and closets respectively. A man looked up at him curiously as he looked into the maintenance room. Will nodded and ducked out. "Wrong turn."

There were two other doors, but neither of them led to anything. *Maybe the basement stairs start in the maintenance area. If it's only used for storage, that might make sense.* Moving back to that door, he cracked it until he caught sight of the man within. He seemed to be working on something. Will's sleep spell sent him sagging to the floor. He stepped in and closed the door behind him. Down the hall, he could hear a commotion as the soldiers entered the front doors of the building and made their announcements.

Shit, if they find him sleeping, that will arouse their suspicion, he realized. Glancing around the room, Will took stock. On the opposite side of the room were two double doors leading somewhere. On the left side were lockers and a rack for storing cleaning implements and supplies; to the right was a cluttered desk and an old ratty chair. Perfect.

Sleep spells didn't keep the target in an enforced slumber, but right after the spell took effect the subject tended to be very hard to wake. Will got a grip underneath the worker's arms and dragged him over to the desk. Lifting him up high enough to settle into the chair was difficult, but he managed it, though he was grateful that the man was relatively skinny. From there he simply arranged the fellow with his head on his arms, leaning over the desk. The soldiers would hopefully assume he had fallen asleep on the job.

Chapter 38

He could hear loud steps in the hall, so he moved on to the double doors, since there was no other obvious exit. It was a relief when he saw a modest stair behind them, leading downward. There was no light, so once he closed the doors behind him, he had to adjust his vision. Simply increasing his light sensitivity wouldn't do, for there was *no* light. He had to change to heart-light before he could brave the stairs.

Will was halfway down the stairs when he had an unsettling thought. *How often does anyone come down here?* If the answer was almost never, and the area was unlit, well that made it an almost perfect place for vampires to hide. His heart rate doubled in the span of seconds. *Damn it, stay calm,* he told himself. His pounding heart ignored him.

He'd already used his sleep spell and he'd meant to replace it, but now he wondered if another sleep spell was really the right choice. Taking several steps back up the stairs, he constructed an Ethelgren's Illumination without debating it further. His fear of vampires was far greater than his fear of soldiers.

Better prepared, he slowly descended. There was no door at the bottom, just an opening into a large room interspersed with heavy stone pillars to support the building above. As he looked around, he realized that the size of the area was deceptive. There were crates stacked up here and there, along with dusty pieces of furniture and other items that were no longer in use. The effect of all that was to give the impression of walls, when in fact it was merely an interruption of his line of sight. As he moved farther in it was apparent that the basement was fully as large as the floor above, and it was a single room.

The stone pillars that supported the multilevel building above were massive, approximately ten feet in width and scattered no more than twenty feet apart. Between those and the sheer amount of stuff stored between them, the open basement was more of a labyrinth.

"How the hell am I going to find it in all this junk?" he muttered quietly. It could be in a box, or a display case, or buried under any number of things. The sheer size of the area he needed to search was daunting. *If I ever need to protect something important, I'm going to hide it in a place like this. Locks can't stop me, but this has me completely flummoxed.*

He decided to work outward until he reached one of the outer walls, then make a rough circuit of the entire area. After that he would cut across a few times. He probably wouldn't find the relic, but if it was in something obvious, he might get lucky. If not, he would at least have a mental image of the layout and the various regions of junk to be searched.

There were also the soldiers to consider. *They'll do the upper floors, knowing they won't find anything, just to be thorough. Once those are done, they'll cordon off the lower level and make a serious search of the basement.* He didn't actually know any of that for sure, but it seemed like the wisest course. Either way, they would likely be coming down before he found what he was looking for, so he would need to figure out where he would hide.

Inside something was a bad idea, whereas standing against a blank wall was probably the best. An empty section of wall wouldn't be searched, and the chameleon spell would work best there. Moving forward, he began inspecting the area around him, with an eye for both the relic and an empty section of wall.

He almost forgot his fear of finding vampires. Almost.

Looking up, he saw something odd protruding from the low ceiling. In the gray on gray of his current vision,

Chapter 38

it took a moment to sort out what he was seeing. It looked something like a pile of rags, or it would have if it had been lying on the ground, but this was the ceiling.

Then it moved, and he saw a hand. His mouth went dry. *Fuck!*

It was a mass of vampires, huddled together on the ceiling, clinging there by their fingertips, as though gravity wasn't really a concern. Will froze in place, his eyes glued to the enemy above. *Are they asleep?* He was alone, so it seemed improbable that they would have feared to attack him.

Then he saw a face; its eyes blinked slowly as it watched him. They were perfectly aware of his presence. *They don't know I can see them in the dark,* he realized. *And they're probably thinking I'll leave. If they kill me it would give away their hiding place, in the middle of the day, so they couldn't relocate to someplace safer.*

They weren't afraid; they were smart.

That didn't help his stomach, which was tied in a knot, or his heart, which was beating a rapid drumbeat in his ears. *Can they hear that?* Since they hadn't attacked, he guessed not. He probably wasn't close enough.

A short distance back, he heard the doors at the top of the stairs open. He had misjudged; the soldiers intended to search the basement first. Boots sounded on the stairs, and the mass on the ceiling shifted, beginning to scatter outward. There was about to be a battle, and Will was right in the middle of where it would happen.

The first three men to enter were normal soldiers, but behind them were two sorcerers. Light spells shot out in two directions, illuminating the area. They weren't the right sort of light spells to destroy vampires—apparently the Driven hadn't learned those spells. Until a week ago no one had really believed that vampires existed, and most probably thought they'd never existed. And according to Janice, Ethelgren's biography had been removed.

How much other information had been deliberately destroyed over the years? If it was a coincidence, it was an awfully convenient one for the vampires. Will doubted it was anything but deliberate, the result of years, decades, perhaps even centuries of planning. *And now I'm in a basement where a relic of a legendary vampire hunter is stored, and it just so happens there's a whole gaggle of the monsters here as well.*

It all came together in his head in a flash of clarity. They'd been looking for Ethelgren's Exhortation. It was possible they'd been here for days, searching through the assorted junk, trying to find one of the last good weapons that might be used against them.

Hell, maybe the curse on the relic was a carefully created fabrication. Maybe the vampires had been selectively killing those who touched it to instill fear. *Then again, that's a little much,* thought Will. *There's paranoid and then there's crazy.*

The vampires had scattered and were approaching the basement entrance from all directions. Will prepared to release his illumination spell when something unexpected happened. Both the sorcerers who had created the light spells fell as bolts of blue light speared through their chests.

More soldiers were coming down, and a third sorcerer appeared, stepping over the bodies of his fallen comrades. Seeing what had happened, he lifted his hands and a force-wall appeared in front of him just before more bolts of blue splashed against it.

There was a spellcaster among the vampires. Will released Ethelgren's Illumination as that thought percolated through his awareness.

Chapter 38

As before, the searing white orbs shot outward, raising howls of rage and fury from the vampires as they burned and died, but this time there were a few differences. As the globes moved away and Will opened his eyes slightly, he saw that two of the creatures hadn't died, and both of them turned their eyes on the source of the brilliance, squinting against the glare.

He began moving sideways, trying to get away from the epicenter, which turned out to be wise. More blue bolts flashed into the area where he had been standing, coming from the hand of one of the two vampires, a tall male with a commanding presence and long, black hair. The one beside it he recognized—it was the child-like female he had met before, Alexa.

They adapted quickly to the bright light, and he could see them tracking his position as he ducked to the side. His point-defense shield appeared several times in rapid succession, blocking more of the deadly blue bolts as the vampire wizard focused on him. The creature's aim was perfect; any one of the attacks would have nailed him, despite his movement.

The vampire smiled, showing long fangs, then reached up with a piece of cord in his hands and began to casually tie his long hair back. The expression in his eyes said it all. *'I'm going to enjoy this.'* Will felt a shiver of fear run down his spine. Alexa merely looked at him and smirked, as though she knew he was in over his head. She made no move to attack.

Meanwhile, the soldiers and sorcerers coming down from the floor above weren't idle. One continued to hold the force-wall, protecting them as they formed up, while several other sorcerers readied spells. The soldiers moved to either side, preparing to guard the flanks when the shield was released.

The lead vampire continued to ignore them, reserving his attention for Will. "Alexa told me about you, but I hardly dared believe her words. Are you real, child? Or have I begun to have delusions after so many years?"

Will didn't have another illumination spell ready, not that it would have helped. The chameleon spell and unlocking spell would similarly be useless. *I'm fucked,* he thought. *Royally, fucked.* So he tried what had worked before, with Alexa. "Alexa is your pet? That means you must be Androv? Is that correct?"

The vampire gaped at him in mock surprise. "How long it has been since I heard that name from mortal lips? Who was your teacher, child?"

Alexa hissed. "Just kill him, my lord. He uses words only to delay."

Will glanced at her, and his deadly intent found expression. A force-lance blasted forth, only to stop as a point-defense shield appeared in front of the small vampire's head. Androv smiled graciously, then growled at his subordinate. "Silence, Alexa. Leave the conversation to your betters." He looked back at Will. "It has been centuries since I've encountered a true practitioner of the arcane. I thought they were extinct, among your kind at least. Who was your master?"

"It's rude to ask questions without offering something in exchange," countered Will. From behind the vampire, he could see that the sorcerers were finally ready with their planned attack. *Keep talking just a little longer, you pompous prick.*

The force-wall dropped, and lances of fire flashed forward, followed by four fire elementals. Even before he saw the results, Will knew they wouldn't be good. *Fire? He's a wizard. Even I could handle that.*

Chapter 38

Sure enough, the fire-lances faded out as they reached Androv, dribbling away into impotence. The elementals should have been more of a problem, but a force-dome sprang up at the last instant around the vampire. *No! It's two force-domes!* realized Will. *But that's impossible.* He knew that no caster could have more than one force effect in play at any given moment. Then his eyes spotted the trick.

It wasn't two force domes; it was a single spell with a complex shape. It was open above and below the vampire, but around him was a circular wall that was more like a tunnel. A cylinder with the elementals trapped inside it.

And he reflex cast that, thought Will. *Shit.*

"Pardon me for a moment," said Androv, and then the vampire vanished. Or so Will thought at first. After a second, he realized the monster had simply vaulted over the ring of force, landing in front of the surprised sorcerers and soldiers. One of them managed to raise a force-dome, but it didn't save them. The ground beneath their feet exploded upward, sending jagged shards of stone through the bodies of everyone inside the dome. The king's men were dead before they could finish falling.

Another highly specific spell, and again Will knew it almost certainly hadn't been prepared in advance. It had been reflex cast. None of the spells Will knew could save him from such a monster, not even if he was able to reflex cast all of them. He was overmatched in every single way.

As the sorcerers died, their elementals began to fade away, no longer forced to manifest, though they had already set fire to some of the boxes and furniture that had been trapped near them. The force-ring vanished, and Androv turned back to Will. "You said I shouldn't ask questions without offering something in exchange. How about this? Are you here looking for this?" The vampire reached into a coat pocket and withdrew a short iron rod decorated with silver runes. The end had metal flanges mounted on it, like a small mace. Will knew immediately what it must be. "We found this yesterday. It's a shame you didn't come sooner."

"You should be careful," said Will. "I hear that all the previous owners had bad luck."

The vampire laughed. "Bad luck is for inferior beings. You should know better than that. After all, your luck has improved considerably today."

Will noted that the smoke was increasing rapidly in the enclosed basement. Eventually it would choke him to death, but in the interim it might provide an advantage. He already knew that vampires could see heart-light as well as ordinary light, but the flames and smoke were already creating a chaotic haze that his own vision was having difficulty with.

It was his normal sight that was making up the difference, using the ordinary light produced by the flames. He adjusted his vision until the smoke vanished, and the room was clear except for the solid objects within. "I'm not feeling very lucky," said Will, waiting for the smoke to grow thicker. He began walking rapidly to his left, causing the smoke to swirl and making it difficult for the vampires to track him visually.

"Clever, boy, clever!" shouted Androv. "The reason you're lucky is because I found you first! Most of my minions would simply devour you, but I understand your true worth! How far have you progressed? Are you merely first-order? Or did you manage second-order?"

Will said nothing, but he released the chameleon spell. Between it, and the smoke and flames, even the vampires would find it hard to see him. He watched them and saw that their heads were no longer tracking his

Chapter 38

position. Instead they swiveled back and forth, trying to catch sight of him again. Androv snapped his fingers, and Alexa moved forward. "Be careful, my sweet. We want him alive."

Alive? Will felt a stone appear in the pit of his stomach. *He wants to recruit me.*

"You can't escape, young wizard. The smoke obscures everything, for both of us. But I know you need air to live. The door is your only hope and I'll be waiting here for you."

So you think, asshole.

The master vampire was still holding the relic in his hand as Will quickly formed a force-lance. Point-defense shields only worked when you could see the attack coming. Androv screamed as Will's spell removed the vampire's arm at the elbow, sending the relic and the hand holding it skittering away into the smoke-filled basement.

Androv responded with a volley of blue bolts, but Will was able to see them coming. He blocked those that threatened to skewer him, then began circling in the other direction, heading toward Alexa, who was stalking blindly through the smoke. As he moved, he prepared another force-lance.

She must have heard something, for she shifted the direction of her travel, moving around a collection of bookcases and wardrobes to circle around behind him. But he could see her every move. Reaching down, Will picked up a broom someone had dropped and tossed it ahead and to the right, so that it landed ten feet in front of him.

Alexa pounced.

Taking aim, he blew her left leg off. The leg would limit her movement, and since it was the same one he had nearly removed last time, it had a sense of irony that he felt sure she wouldn't miss.

He backed away quietly, but with his next breath the smoke was too powerful, and a choking cough escaped his lips. Alexa leapt toward him on her remaining leg.

She moved too fast for him to dodge, but a point-defense shield met her in midair, stopping her forward motion and causing her to fall. Then a force-lance took her in the shoulder, shattering her clavicle and spine. It had been a reflex cast spell. *Damn, I wish I could do that on command.* Currently, panic seemed to be a good motivator for his new ability.

Turning, he began to run, coughing as he went. He had to get out soon, or the smoke would be the death of him. He headed in the direction he had seen the relic fall, which was also in the direction of the exit. Unfortunately, his coughing also gave his position away, and he saw Androv running past boxes on his right, moving to intercept him. Will stopped and focused, and then he felt what he had hoped for. Keeping his eyes on the moving vampire, he began to fire force-lances, one after another in rapid succession.

It was like finding a rough spot on your tooth with your tongue, impossible to forget. Once he had latched onto the knack of it, he was able to launch the bolts at will.

But the master vampire had anticipated him after his previous surprise attack. The creature was moving with some kind of mobile shield protecting him. The force-lances scattered impotently away from it.

Will ducked sideways between two looming piles of wooden crates that were just beginning to catch fire, hoping to buy himself some time. But he couldn't stop coughing. Androv would find him in seconds.

Not that it mattered. Spells had failed him. He was utterly inferior to the vampire wizard in every regard. Magic, usually his greatest tool, was about to be his

Chapter 38

undoing. For a moment his mind flashed to all the people who he would miss. Selene, his mother, Tiny, Janice, his half-sisters, and perhaps even Mark Nerrow—then the man's face brought an idea to him.

Will summoned a small object from the limnthal and placed it on the ground in front of him. Then he summoned a second and took five steps back, waiting and coughing. One might be enough, but the second was his insurance against failure.

Seven feet away, Androv rounded the corner like a vengeful ghost. He was close enough to see Will through the smoke, and the vampire's eyes lit with triumph, seeing the end of his chase.

Will put the point-defense shield directly in front of the vampire's chest, forcing him to stop exactly where he wished, then his eyes dropped, and he fired a force-lance at the vial at Androv's feet.

The vampire's reflexes were too fast for a human to comprehend, and if it had relied on them Will's gambit would probably have failed. But Androv was a wizard first and foremost, and he trusted his magic more. He blocked the force-lance with a point-defense shield and started to grin at the human who had been foolish enough to try and trap him.

His smile vanished as the second vial of alchemist's fire, the one Will had thrown, landed beside the first, shattering and exploding into raging white flames. The fire swept over the master vampire, clinging to his clothes, and a moment later the second vial exploded as well, adding to the conflagration as the monster screamed and howled in wounded fury.

Will backed away, and his foot stepped on something, causing him to stumble. Looking down, he saw the object of his quest, Ethelgren's Exhortation. Snatching up the rod, he stored it in the limnthal and started running. His coughing was getting pretty bad by then, and his heart was beginning to pound strangely in his chest—never a good sign.

Circling back, he found the exit and saw Alexa crawling across the floor, trying to reach her burning master. He summoned a third alchemist's fire and tossed it at her for good measure, then he ran for the stairs.

The smoke was worse there, for it was billowing outward and climbing upward with him. He was staggering before he reached the top, and he fell to his knees when he reached the maintenance room. Crawling forward, he looked around and was grateful to see that the soldiers had woken the maintenance man, for the room was empty.

He started to climb back to his feet, but the air was much clearer close to the floor, so Will settled for a determined crawl. The rest of the soldiers seemed to have retreated from the building, for as he reached the hallway, he saw that there was no one in sight. The smoke above him was a thick cloud now. Only a foot or two of air just above the floor was still clear enough to breathe and his lungs were still spasming with the smoke he had inhaled in the basement.

Leaving the central stairs, Will headed toward the front entrance, but he wondered if he would make it before the smoke overcame him. *I defeated an evil master wizard-vampire, only to die crawling out of a burning building. Typical.*

His hope died when he came to the end of the hall. In the smoke and confusion, he had gone the wrong way. Now he would have to crawl back in the direction he had come. He wanted to scream in frustration, not that he had the air to do so. He started crawling back, but he knew he wouldn't make it.

Chapter 38

Then two massive feet appeared on the floor in front of him. A giant hand caught the back of his tunic and another gripped the waistband of his trousers. Tiny was there, and with Will hanging between his two hands like a toddler caught doing something terrible, the big man began to run, stomping through the hall.

Trying to hold his breath, Will saw that the big man had a towel wrapped around his head. *That's a good idea,* he thought. *I should have done that too. Might have made it easier, at least for a while.*

A few seconds later, Tiny kicked open the main door, and Will was blinded by the sunshine. Fresh air flooded his lungs, kicking off a fresh round of coughing, which eventually resulted in Will losing control of his stomach. Still grateful, he vomited onto Tiny's boots, then passed out.

Chapter 39

Someone was leaning over him. Having experienced similar situations in the past, Will decided he must be in bed somewhere. He remembered being rescued. With luck it might be Selene come to chide him for his foolishness. Blinking, he tried to focus on the face.

His eyes finally did their job, and he was disappointed to find it was Doctor Morris looking down at him. "Of all the luck," he muttered.

"It seems the spell was effective," said the doctor. "You're breathing much better now."

"There are spells for this?" asked Will suspiciously.

"For many things," said the doctor. "They aren't perfect, but with the right knowledge and the right magic, at the right time, we can do a lot, even without fancy things like regeneration potions."

"But I *could* have taken a regeneration potion," said Will stubbornly.

The doctor leered at him maliciously. "Yet you didn't, and you passed out. If your enormous savior hadn't broken the doors down getting you in here, you would almost certainly have died from smoke inhalation."

Despite his mother's training, Will didn't really know much about injuries involving fire and smoke. "I was in the clear when I passed out," he countered confidently.

"It's about more than just getting fresh air. Smoke is poisonous, and your blood was already circulating the poisons through your body and brain," explained Doctor Morris.

"So, I should have used a universal antidote potion," said Will snippily. "I have a few of those too."

"And yet you still didn't take one before passing out."

Will deflated, accepting defeat. "Fine, Doctor. I owe you one this time."

Doctor Morris laughed, straightening up and stepping away. "See that it doesn't happen again!"

"You shouldn't tease someone who just saved your life," said a female voice from the other side of the bed. It was Janice.

Will turned toward her, fearful of what he might see, so he went immediately for humor to defuse the blow. "Tiny, is that you?" he asked, hoping his tone sounded playful as his eyes locked on Janice's face.

If he had seen her from a distance, from the wrong angle, he might have mistaken her for an old woman, for the hair on one side of her head was shockingly white, utterly devoid of color. It created a stark contrast with the brown hair that covered the other two thirds of her head, but it wasn't ugly.

Her eyes were what sent a jolt through him. Her right eye, the one that had been spared, was still hazel, but the left eye, which had regrown, was now an icy blue. There were also fine silver lines that traced where the skin had been torn and mended, but for the most part her cheek and nose were smooth and unblemished.

In short, Tiny had told the truth. While Janice would never be mistaken for ordinary again, she was still lovely, and that beauty had been enhanced by the exotic strangeness of her dual colorations. "You look good," he said suddenly, forgetting his joke.

Janice smiled, tears in her eyes. "You look like shit. There's soot and smudge marks all over your face, not to mention your hair."

"My hair?" He lifted a hand to explore his head. His scalp seemed to be fine, but it seemed that a large portion of the hair was gone on one side, burned down to within an inch of his scalp. He had no memory of being burned, but it wasn't too surprising considering what he'd been through. At least now he had a haircut to match his missing eyebrows.

Tiny entered the room, catching the end of the conversation. He ran a hand through his own short military cut. "I think you'll have to go short for a while, like your betters."

Will chuckled. "Probably."

"You shouldn't have gone in there," said Janice. "I warned you that the relic wasn't usable anyway. You nearly got yourself killed for nothing."

"I wouldn't say that," responded Will. "I found it on my way out."

"How?" asked both of his friends simultaneously.

He spent the next few minutes explaining what had happened and describing the fight in the basement, though he did his best to downplay the sheer terror he had felt, and the hopelessness of fighting such a powerful wizard. It didn't matter anymore anyway. Androv was dead. Now they just had to worry about the ordinary monsters.

As he finished, his two friends glanced at one another, then as if by mutual agreement, Janice told him, "You're so full of shit."

"Huh?"

"There's no way it was that simple. I know you. It must have been twice as bad as that," she explained. Tiny nodded in mute agreement.

He sighed. "Well, it was little worse than that, but it all worked out. The bad guys are dead, and I've got the relic."

Chapter 39

"Which you can't use," said Janice.

"Says you," Will replied, glancing at his ring. "My advisor says otherwise."

"Advisor?"

"My college advisor," Will said deflecting the question.

"That makes no sense."

Will rose from the bed, and though his throat felt a bit sore and his head swam a bit, he was otherwise fine. He swung his legs over the edge of the bed, then realized his clothes were gone. He glared at his bare feet. "Not again."

Tiny guessed his thoughts. "The boots are fine. The rest of your clothes weren't fit for a beggar."

"That's my second set of clothes in as many days. At this rate I'll be forced to go naked by the end of the week." Ignoring their laughs, Will used Selene's Solution to clean himself, then summoned a spare tunic and trousers from the limnthal. Ordinarily he wouldn't have used it in front of them, but he was done hiding it, from his friends at least. They watched him intently, but neither of them asked what he had done.

They'd seen too much weirdness around him already.

Rising from the bed, Will left, and though Doctor Morris protested mildly, he made no attempt to detain Will this time. After a short walk, they arrived at his house, where the workmen were hard at it once again. The front door was in working order, so he entered in the usual fashion.

Tabitha was the first person he encountered, and she studied him as he walked down the hall. "I liked your hair better before," she announced.

"It wasn't intentional," said Will wryly. For some reason Tabitha always improved his mood. Nothing dark or ominous could survive in her presence. "Where's your father?"

"Upstairs," she replied. "He and mother are sleeping. They weren't able to sleep last night, so they're finally catching up on their rest. Why?"

It was getting late in the day, but Will had come to a conclusion. "I'm kicking you out."

"What?" His half-sister looked at him in confusion, and the looks from Tiny and Janice were similar in tone.

"Just for the night. You'll be safer in your own home. You can come back in the morning. I'll cook breakfast."

"But our house...," began Tabitha, pausing in midsentence. "Oh."

Laina stepped into the hall from the parlor. "He means our bolt-hole." She focused on Will. "Is it really that unsafe here?"

Will nodded. "It's going to get worse, and they can enter the university grounds at will. I've become a target, and they know quite well where I live. No one would think to hunt for you in the ashes of your old home."

"What about me?" asked Blake, hobbling in on his sprained ankle.

"Hopefully, the baron will be kind enough to accept you and Janice as well."

"Along with Armand and Nellie," Tabitha informed them. "It's going to be crowded."

Laina glanced at Tiny, then Will. "Very crowded with these two along."

It was tempting, so tempting. After what he'd been through in the basement of the still-burning Artifice building, Will wasn't sure how he could be considering anything that might bring him face-to-face with yet more vampires. But he was. "Tiny and I won't be joining you," he told everyone.

No one said anything for a moment, and Laina in particular looked thoughtful. Lifting her chin, she responded, "Darla and I will come with you."

Chapter 39

"You don't even know what I'm going to be doing."

Laina's eyes grew stubborn. "I know you need help. Just look at you!"

Will ignored her. "How is the renovation going?" he asked Blake, moving over to face the man.

Laina tapped him on the shoulder. "I'm not done talking to you."

Blake looked at him nervously, then glanced over his shoulder.

"I'm done talking to her," said Will. "Tell me about the basement." The look of alarm on the manservant's face warned him, and he barely ducked in time to avoid Laina's swing at the back of his head. He gave Laina an annoyed look and then took Blake by the arm. They moved away several feet.

His half-sister paused when she saw a spell forming in his hand, and before she realized what it was, he had surrounded Blake and himself with a force-dome. Smiling sweetly at Laina, Will slowly turned around, putting his back to her. "Now tell me what you were going to say."

Blake shook his head in disbelief. "That girl is going to skin you alive when we come out of here." When Will didn't respond, he finally answered, "The basement isn't finished. There's still a lot of masonry to be done, but the cage is in already."

"Cage?"

"It's hard to anchor chains when they're meant to hold something as strong as a vampire. The steel might be strong enough, but whatever you anchor them to has to be just as solid. In an earthen basement with only support pillars, there isn't much that can provide the sort of strength you need. However, there was an exotic animal dealer in the city a few weeks back and I managed to secure a bear cage that was meant for him."

"A bear cage?"

"It's solid. The ends are all lap welded. It's meant to be on a wagon, for transport, but with some work we were able to get it in the basement. I'm pretty sure that if you chain a vampire up inside it, he won't be able to get free. If he did manage to break the chains, he'd still be inside the cage."

Will nodded. "Good thinking."

"As far as your workshop, that will probably take another couple of months. They're still excavating, and that will take…"

He waved a hand. "I never asked you to do that, but thank you. By the time it's done, this crisis will hopefully be over. I'll have to use the laboratory at the Alchemy building for what I need in the present."

Blake kept glancing over his shoulder and Will finally asked, "What's going on?"

"I don't think people are supposed to be that color," said Blake.

Will turned around. Laina had turned an odd shade of red-purple and seemed to be speaking loudly in his direction. He could almost make out the words through the force-dome. Mark Nerrow was behind her, also shouting it seemed, though primarily at his daughter. Tabitha stood a good distance away, apparently enjoying the show. Oddly, Will felt jealous of them all. He and his mother had never really argued. What would it have been like to grow up in a raucous household with siblings?

He looked back at Blake. "How about the pig?"

"Already tied up out back. I'll miss her. She's been taking care of all the scraps since yesterday."

Will winced. "You shouldn't have gotten attached. You know the plan for him."

"Some would say the same about you," Blake pointed out.

Chapter 39

"I feel like a lamb being led to slaughter most days," he agreed. "Get ready for noise." Will dismissed the force-dome.

Strangely, everything was quiet. The baron had left, presumably to get his things together for the evening. Tiny and Janice were in the parlor, talking with one another, and only Laina was left in the hall with him. "You're getting help whether you want it or not," she announced.

"Fine. Can you bleed a pig?"

"Excuse me?"

"Have you ever bled a pig?" asked Will. "I need to feed a vampire, but I'm not sure whether I should bleed the pig first or just toss them in together."

"What are you talking about?"

"The pig out back," said Will. "The basement renovations. Do you want to help me feed a vampire so I can harvest alchemical ingredients from it?"

She rolled her eyes. "Talk to me when you're serious, but if you try to leave, I'll be right behind you." She turned and walked away, projecting the body language of someone who had just won an argument.

Will shrugged. *I guess she told me.* Heading outside with Blake, Will went to the former cellar while Blake fetched the pig.

The entrance had been widened considerably to allow the cage to be moved in, but otherwise the cellar wasn't much changed. The cage itself was eight feet in length, and four feet wide and tall. Long, heavy chains led from each corner to the center, where they were piled up. There were eight chains in total.

Thinking about what he intended to do made him feel queasy, but Will had done worse in the past. The vision of Arlen Arenata rose unbidden in his mind, followed by the inevitable cold revulsion that always accompanied her memory. He had bled her much as he intended to do with the pig. He shook his head to clear it. *It's a pig, not a human.* That didn't help much, though. *She was a pretty shitty human, whereas this pig is probably a pretty decent pig.*

Pushing those thoughts aside, he opened the cage and organized the chains, separating them and moving them out of the center. Then he summoned the vampire jar from the limnthal and carefully tipped it over. The monster inside was just as feeble and helpless as before. A trickle of sunlight was falling on the cellar steps, and enough of it reached the desiccated form that smoke began to rise from one of the bloodsucker's arms.

Will moved to shelter the vampire with his shadow. He would have shouted for Blake to shut the cellar door above, but by the sound of things the man was bringing the pig down. Will waited.

Eventually the pig was there, and Blake lit an oil lamp that sat on a shelf across the room. Then he went upstairs to shut the outer door. Once he had, Will began shackling his corpselike vampire subject. The monster was little more than a skeleton clad in skin, which made its limbs too skinny for the shackles.

Will was forced to wrap the chains tightly around the respective limbs, the neck, the torso, and then affix the shackle to the chain itself. He imagined the vampire swelling up with blood, its flesh growing around the metal links like a tree grows around a metal fence. *Hopefully it's painful.*

Once he was sure he had the vampire secure, he dumped it back into the jar and stood it up again. The thing was too weak to feed, so he figured he could use the jar to marinate the monster in pig blood. He shuddered. *I shouldn't have thought of marinating, now I'll remember this when I'm cooking.*

Chapter 39

"How long will this take?" asked Blake.

"For the vampire, I'm not sure," said Will. "The potions I want to make are fairly simple. I can produce a few in a couple of hours; it's just a single-stage process."

Even in the warm lamplight, the old Special Services veteran looked pale. "Do you want me to stay down here with you?"

Will decided to take it easy on him. "Go up the stairs and wait at the cellar door. If things go badly for some reason and I yell for help, open the doors. The sunlight should solve whatever problem I'm having." He began arranging jars on one side of the room, then put a large metal pan in the center of the floor to catch the blood.

Blake evacuated.

Chapter 40

Will tried a sleep spell, which worked, but as soon as he began cutting, the pig woke again. He was forced to use a source-link to paralyze the poor animal, and he watched its eyes rolling wildly as he bled it from the main carotid arteries. It was pretty much the same thing that would have happened at the slaughterhouse, but Will still felt a strong sense of guilt.

He did his best to catch as much of the vital red fluid as possible, though some splashed out from the force of its panicked heartbeat. The animal's consciousness faded away, and Will released the source-link. He almost lost his blood as well, when the pig fell sideways and almost knocked his catch pan into the dirt. He was forced to hug the three-hundred-pound gilt against himself as he dragged her back in the other direction.

Once again, he was liberally smeared with blood and dirt. *Why do I even bother cleaning myself off?* he wondered. *Clearly, this is meant to be my natural state.*

Another thought came to him then, and Will carefully moved the blood pan off to one side so he wouldn't knock it over. Then he went up the stairs to where Blake waited. "Can you get Tiny for me?"

"You need his help?"

"We can't waste the meat, but I'm going to be too busy with the rest of this to butcher it."

"This is what you get for rushing. You should have planned for this," Blake remonstrated.

Will frowned. "Too bad. It isn't as though I've had a lot of time to plan things."

Blake left and returned a few minutes later. Together the two men dragged the heavy pig's body out of the cellar and up aboveground where they could cut her up. Will went back down below. He made sure he had Ethelgren's Illumination prepared before he poured the pig's blood into the jar.

Nothing happened at first, so he moved back and locked the cage door. He'd been afraid the vampire might instantly spring to life and rush at him, but that wasn't the case. Several minutes passed, and then a wet, slurping sound found his ears, and he could see the jar moving slightly as the thing inside shifted from side to side.

I'll never get used to this, thought Will. Then again, he couldn't decide whether he wanted to get used to it. Was it better to be inured to such horror, or to remain unspoiled, happy, and innocent? He had a feeling it was the latter, but life hadn't given him much choice in the matter.

The jar exploded as the vampire finally emerged with an unholy howl of pain and outrage. It glared at him hatefully as the chains arrested its movement close to the center of the cage. "You will die for this, human!" it hissed. As he had suspected, the chains were inside the creature's body, where the flesh had grown over them.

Will stared at it coldly, trying to give no sign of the extreme unease he felt. "I sincerely doubt that, spawn of the grave." With a thought he sent a force-lance through the bars, removing the vampire's head. Its body fell sideways, and he rushed forward with a shallow bowl, trying to catch as much as he could of the black blood leaking from the stump of its neck. The head lay off to one side, staring at him and gnashing its teeth. Without lungs, it couldn't make its curses audible.

Unlike the pig, the vampire's blood emerged sluggishly, without a living heart to pump it. His first bowl filled, and he grabbed a second. When that was full, the neck had stopped bleeding and had begun to heal over, while the arms still scrabbled aimlessly about, searching for the head. He removed his two bowls, poured them in to a jar that he could tightly stopper against light, then stored it in the limnthal.

With his prize stored away, Will used several force-lances to further dismember the creature. Then he opened the cage and used his sword to do a more precise job. It was bloody and awful. The smell alone was enough to turn his stomach.

His goal was to return the vampire to a pile of parts, devoid of vital fluid. It was a harder job than he imagined, and he wound up wishing he was only covered in pig's blood by the time he was done. Then he removed the chains and stored the vampire's body in a new jar, covered it, and stored it away in the limnthal.

Throughout the horrid ordeal, Will made mental notes. The next time he needed to harvest vampire blood, he would have a better process in place. Going up the stairs, he opened the door. The fading rays of the sun burned away the black blood coating his tunic and sticking to his hair. He used Selene's spell to further purify himself.

Blake and Tiny were fully engaged in cutting up the pig, but it was obvious they wouldn't finish soon enough. The sun was dropping quickly, and Blake needed to leave with the others. Will shooed them to the side and stored the rest of the pig in the limnthal. "You can finish this tomorrow. Blake you need to go."

"All right," said the manservant. "Are you going to come see them off?"

"It would just give them another opportunity to argue. Tiny and I will head to the Alchemy building. Make sure they know I won't be back, otherwise they might try to wait," ordered Will.

Chapter 40

Blake nodded and Will and Tiny set off.

"Janice is going to be unhappy about us sneaking off without giving her a chance to join us," said the big warrior.

"But you didn't argue against the idea, did you?" said Will.

"Guilty as charged."

Lawrence was once again manning the desk at the Alchemy building. He glanced up as Will signed in. "Hi, Will. Who's your friend?"

"This is T—"

"I'm his bodyguard," interrupted Tiny, affecting a menacing expression.

"Tiny, stop it," said Will, embarrassed. Then he turned back to Lawrence. "He's a good friend of mine."

Tiny nodded. "That's true, but I'm also his bodyguard." He held out his hand. "The name is Skullcrusher."

Lawrence wasn't quite sure whether they were joking or not, but he offered his own paw and watched Tiny's hand engulf his. "Nice to meet you."

Once they were on the stairs, Will turned to his friend. "What's gotten into you?"

"Janice said I seem very nice."

"You are nice."

The big man frowned. "It's well known that women prefer dangerous men. Besides, I am your bodyguard; it won't hurt for me to project a more intimidating image."

"This is hilarious. So you're doing this because you think it will make you more appealing to Janice?"

In response, Tiny shoulder-butted Will, knocking him into the wall. He caught Will's shoulder before he could fall down the stairs. "Sorry. No, of course not Janice! I meant women in general."

Will was pretty sure that his eyes had rolled around several times inside his head, but things straightened up a moment later. "You never worried about *women* in the past. Why now? It seems suspicious."

"No reason. It's just something I've been thinking about lately."

"Since when?"

"A while."

"Since you met Janice?" Will braced himself in case Tiny reacted badly, but his friend kept his involuntary reflexes under control this time.

"The l-last f-f-few months," stammered Tiny as he utterly failed to lie convincingly.

Will nodded. "All right."

"Honestly."

"Sure."

Tiny's face was shading toward a bright pink. "You won't say anything to her, will you?"

Will looked up at him with innocent eyes. "About the fact that you're looking for someone to court? Or the fact that you're infatuated with her?" Before the sentence was half out, he dropped down against the landing to avoid the blow that he anticipated, but Tiny didn't move.

He was stricken by a pang of guilt when he saw the desperate look on Tiny's face. "Please?" The giant warrior was practically begging.

Will stood back up and patted Tiny's shoulder. "Of course not. I won't say a word." *Damn, this is serious.* He hoped Tiny wouldn't wind up with a broken heart, and he resolved to try and stop teasing the man.

With that taken care of, he led Tiny up to the small laboratory he was renting and got busy setting up his latest project: Dragon Heart potions. He couldn't help but think that the name sounded very impressive, despite the fact that the primary ingredient was singularly disgusting. *Then again, I guess the same is true of regeneration potions*, he realized.

Chapter 40

It took half an hour to get everything set up, and once it was going, they had about an hour before Will would need to decant the product into its final vials and activate the potions. As they stood around, Tiny asked, "Are you sure this is the right thing to be spending your time on?"

Will shrugged. "I don't know what the best course of action is, but although their leader is dead, there's still an unknown number of vampires hiding in the city, and most of them are young, so they're likely to continue spreading their corruption. If any of them are still organized, though, then they'll be attacking en masse tomorrow night."

"But all this potion does is make someone stronger. That doesn't seem very important."

"If you're going to act as a bodyguard, you'll need to be able to handle them up close. I can't use these potions, so if I'm going to have some muscle protecting me, it has to be you."

"Why can't you use them?" asked Tiny.

"The potion temporarily alters the internal turyn flow of whoever imbibes it. All the training I went through to become a wizard means that my body will automatically resist something like that. At best it would make me sick, but most likely it would just fail." Will took that moment to bring out the case he had gotten Blake to acquire.

"What's that?"

"A present," said Will, laying the leather case on the worktable. It was roughly two inches thick, seven inches long, and six inches in width. There were rings mounted at every corner along with a collection of straps. Depending on how the straps were used, it could either be put on a belt at the waist or strapped to the leg. The top flap was secured with a unique mechanism that Will had never seen before, a spring-loaded buckle that could be released with a small amount of pressure applied to the right place. It kept the case securely shut but made it quick and easy to open when needed. Will was grateful that he had asked Blake, since obviously the military had seen the need for such an item long ago, and they had put a lot of time and effort into designing it.

Once the top flap was opened, the interior was simple. It was divided into six velvet-lined compartments that had a small amount of woolen batting stuffed loosely into them. The extra bit of wool allowed the compartments to hold a small vial snugly in place. Tiny picked it up, feeling the leather with his hands. "It's stronger than it looks."

"The leather is hardened, but there's also a thin layer of metal sandwiched in between the outer layer and the velvet to help it hold its form if it's put under stress, say if you fell on it or something."

"It's for potions?"

Will nodded. "More specifically, it's for you. Since you can't store things in a secret magical space, you'll need somewhere safe to carry potions so you can use them in a pinch when the time is right."

Tiny looked hesitant. "Those things are valuable. You should keep them. If I lost them or broke them by accident…"

"*You're* more valuable to me, Tiny. More valuable than any amount of gold or magic."

The big warrior raised his brows and rubbed his chin. "Really? How about Selene, more than her?"

Will pursed his lips.

"See! My love means nothing to you!" They both fell to laughing at that. Then Tiny pointed at the interior of the case again. "So, there's six spots. Do you plan on putting these Dragon Heart potions in all those spots?"

"You can only take one or two before they become worthless. The first one lasts about half an hour, but if you take a second one the effect is lessened, and you only get

Chapter 40

another fifteen minutes. Taking more than that is pretty much a waste of time, and probably dangerous to your health. I thought it would be better to put other potions in those slots." He pointed to the two on the left. "Two Dragon's Heart potions, then beside those, two blood-cleanse potions, then one regeneration potion, and for the sixth spot a universal antidote."

"You think someone might poison me?"

Will shrugged, then gave Tiny a meaningful glance, eyeing him up and down. "I think most people would rather poison you than fight you face-to-face, at least if they're smart."

Tiny rolled his eyes, but then he became thoughtful. "You should give this to Janice. She needs it more. The other day, if she had had…"

Will felt another stab of guilt. "I didn't have any regeneration potions then, but I agree with you. Once this is over, I'll have some time to make more."

"Things are dangerous *now,* Will. Let me just give her these."

"No." Tiny narrowed his eyes, beginning to show signs of stubbornness. Will held up a hand to forestay the man before he set his heels. "I only have two regeneration potions right now. Do you want me to give her mine?"

"Of course not. She'll be safe tonight. You should… oh, I see what you mean."

An hour later and the potions were done. Will had made five, though he could have made even more given the amount of blood he had. From what he could tell the black fluid was spoiling rapidly and he doubted he would be able to use the remainder. He'd likely have to bleed another pig and feed his prisoner again. Next time he vowed to have more time so he could maximize his gain from the procedure.

They loaded two of the potions into Tiny's case, filled the rest of the slots with the other potions they'd talked about, and then Will stored the extras in the limnthal.

"What now?" asked Tiny.

"Well, we could spend the night making another batch of regeneration potions, or I could see if I can attune myself to the relic. Since their big plans were for tomorrow, I think I should probably use the time to see if I can use the relic."

"So, no fighting?" Tiny's relief was faintly visible.

"My house isn't safe. They know to look for me there. But the Alchemy building stays open all night. We can stay here. It will be boring for you, probably, but you could always perfect your 'skullcrusher' persona with Lawrence while I study the relic."

"So you *do* think I should try to seem more dangerous!"

He laughed. "No. I think she'll either like you or she won't. Trying to change yourself isn't going to fool her."

"Hmm, I'm not sure you're qualified to give advice on this subject."

Will lifted one hand and pointed at himself with his thumb. "I'm married, remember?"

"You murdered your bride-to-be's groom on her wedding day, then got yourself stabbed to death, only to be resurrected and married at sword point. Are you *sure* you're in a position to give advice?"

"She killed the groom, not me," corrected Will irritably. "Why does everyone keep saying it was me?"

"Because he'd still be alive if you hadn't shown up uninvited in the first place?"

He gave Tiny a narrow stare. "Whose side are you on anyway?"

"I'm on any side that doesn't send Janice running in the other direction." He paused briefly, then put a hand on

Chapter 40

his stomach. "Is there any food here? This will be a long night if there isn't."

"There's usually stale bread from the dining hall. They leave it out for the students that come at night. It's in a little room behind where Lawrence sits downstairs. I'll show you where it is." Together, they went downstairs, but they were surprised to see that Lawrence had company at the front desk when they got there.

Laina looked up from her conversation and smiled maliciously. "There you are. I was just telling Lawrence here that they shouldn't let too many unsavory types in the building. Your presence is liable to spoil the potions the same way you curdle milk at home."

"Curdling milk sounds more like you," returned Will, glancing at the window beside the doors. It was pitch black outside. "Your father let you run off by yourself?"

"Darla is here too, keeping watch."

"Still, the question stands."

"I hid at the last moment, while they were going in. By the time they had everything locked down and did a head count, I was already on my way here. Father wouldn't be foolish enough to abandon everyone and search on his own."

"You hope! What if he does?" countered Will.

Tiny groaned audibly. "Janice will be twice as mad now."

Will glanced to his friend. "We didn't allow her to join us on purpose."

"For a married man, you don't understand women much. Do you think that will matter when it comes to her feelings?"

Laina snickered. "See, even the ogre has more sense than you."

For some reason, that set Will's temper ablaze. "He's not an ogre. He's just a regular person."

Tiny set a hand on his shoulder. "It's all right, Will. She didn't mean it harshly toward me."

Will's half-sister looked regretful. Looking up at Tiny, she apologized. "No, he's right. That wasn't fair of me." Her eyes bored into Will. "I shouldn't drag others into it when I'm putting this jerk in his place."

He did his best to ignore her and showed Tiny where the leftover bread was kept. When he stepped back out, he looked at Laina. "We're going to be here all night. I suppose you should join us."

She lifted one brow. "You're not going out to fight the forces of darkness?" Her words were heavily laden with sarcasm.

"Not a chance," said Will. "That's tomorrow. Tonight, I'm just making some preparations. You ditched the family lockup for nothing." It was well hidden, but he could almost imagine she looked relieved to know that nothing dangerous would be happening. *Not that I blame her,* he decided. *It's incredibly brave and stupid of her to insist on coming when she thought I might be in the thick of things.*

It didn't occur to him that the same reasoning applied to him as well. As they started up the stairs, he asked about her bodyguard. "Is Darla outside?"

Laina nodded. "She insists on keeping watch. Don't worry. She'll spot anything before it gets close and come warn us. As tough as she is, she knows better than to fight those things alone."

Will led her up the stairs and showed her to his small, rented laboratory. "Welcome to my lair," he said, waving his hand in a flourish as he opened the door for her.

Laina wrinkled her nose as she entered. "It smells."

Chapter 41

Since he was done brewing potions, there wasn't much for Laina or Tiny to see or do. Will stepped out and borrowed a couple of chairs from across the hall, then returned.

Laina looked back and forth between the two of them. "So, this is it?"

Tiny nodded. "Exciting, huh?"

"I'm actually planning to try to attune a relic, but I don't have much for either of you to do," said Will.

Laina straightened up. "Actually, if you don't mind, you could write out a few spells for me. After seeing what happened a few nights back, I couldn't help but think I might need to expand my repertoire."

Relying on elementals for everything isn't good enough anymore, eh? thought Will, but he kept his opinion to himself. Laina was willing to learn; he wouldn't drive her away and miss the opportunity.

"Which spells are you interested in?" he asked.

"The force spells you used were pretty handy. The way you stopped the sword when Dad was about to put Darla out of her misery was fairly impressive," admitted Laina.

"What force spells do you know already?"

"A simple wall and the force-dome," she answered immediately.

"Can you reflex cast any spells?"

"Pardon?"

"Have you practiced any to the point of being able to cast them just with barely a thought?"

"Oh. No. I stuck to the basics in school and I always figured my elementals would be better when quick, dirty magic was needed," she explained.

"Well, the spell I used for Darla was called a 'point-defense shield,' and it's really small. That makes it handy because it doesn't use much turyn normally, but until you can reflex cast it there's not much point in having it ready. You'll have to practice it daily for a long time before that happens."

"How long?"

"Weeks, months maybe? For the present, the force-dome is more likely to be useful if you're planning on having a spell prepared in advance."

Laina sighed. "I'd like to learn it anyway, and the force-missile spell you used."

"Force-lance," he told her. Summoning his journals, he used one to supply a couple of sheets of paper and copied the two spells out for her. Then he dismissed the journals and brought out Ethelgren's Exhortation.

Everyone's eyes locked onto the rod of iron and silver. Tiny said nothing, but Laina had questions. "First, I'd love to know how you're making things appear and disappear, but more importantly, is that it?"

Will nodded, holding the rod in his hand. It wasn't very large, but it had a substantial heft to it. The silver runes glittered as he rolled it between his fingers. "I'll let you go over those spells while I figure out how to use this."

"You're just going to pray over it?"

"Meditate," he corrected her. "I'm also going to be talking to an old friend, so try not to interrupt. You're going to hear voices."

Tiny smirked, and Laina frowned. Will activated the limnthal and addressed the ring as he sat down cross-legged on the floor. He could have used a chair, but he worried in case something happened. It was a shorter fall if he was

Chapter 41

sitting on the floor rather than a chair. "I'm ready to start trying to attune this relic."

"And you want me to hold your hand?" asked Arrogan derisively. Laina's eyes widened when she heard the unfamiliar voice appear, but Tiny shook his head 'no' before she could interrupt.

"No. I want you to tell me how to do it."

"You have to get inside it—or get it inside you. You say it's a rod? Try jamming it up your ass."

Laina snorted, and Will gave her a hard look. "I'm serious."

"Close your eyes and focus your attention on it. Try to imagine that you're sending turyn into it through your hand. By now you've gotten pretty good at your turyn control, so that should be easy. You'll get a feeling of resistance until you find a match for what the item needs, and it will need a variety of different types of turyn depending on how many spell effects are built into it. Each one will have a different turyn requirement. Make sense?"

"Sort of."

"It's like finding the right key for a lock. You keep trying different ones until you get one that matches, except that this lock can probably take a lot of different keys, one for each magical effect it can produce."

"I see. So, it's basically like when I attune myself to bypass a ward."

"Yes, exactly. Except you don't have the ward to look at and see what you need to match. You have to feel your way blindly until you find all the different types of turyn that the item will accept. Then you have to learn which ones do what."

Laina couldn't contain herself any longer. "Isn't that what a transducer is for? He's a human, not a transducer. People can't change their turyn."

"Who's that?" asked the ring.

Will glared at his half-sister angrily. "Just someone who didn't know when to stay home. Don't worry, though, she may be intrusive, but I trust her."

"Obviously you're still an idiot, because from that question I can tell she's just about as stupid as you ever were."

Laina wasn't about to sit still for such abuse, but Tiny clamped a giant hand over her mouth, which given the relative size of his hand meant that he covered most of her face. He removed it after a second, but his eyes warned her to silence.

Will ignored them. "I'm going to go ahead and start. I'll leave the limnthal active so I can ask questions if something strange happens."

"Go ahead," said the ring.

Will closed his eyes and began expressing turyn through his fingers, modulating it slowly through various frequencies and 'flavors.' The rod shed the turyn like a duck sheds water, but after a moment Will heard a voice in his head. *Is someone there?* it asked.

"Who are you?" responded Will out loud.

"An advisor to the mentally deficient, obviously. What's that question supposed to mean?" asked the ring.

Will was used to the insults, so he let it pass. Instead he continued trying different types of turyn. The voice spoke in his head once more, *A wizard? A true wizard at that. What order did you attain?*

"It's asking me questions," said Will. "I'm going to try and project an answer with the turyn."

"What?!" barked Arrogan.

Third-order, though I'm still young. I have much to learn. Are you part of the relic?

Arrogan's voice was panicked, but his warning came too late. "Will, drop it! Now! Don't touch the thing! It's a trap—"

Chapter 41

The voice had already heard Will's mental reply, though. *Perfect!* Even as his ears registered Arrogan's words, something reached out through the turyn he was projecting, establishing a link, something very similar to a source-link.

A split second later, the war began. The limnthal deactivated as the turyn within him surged and shifted back and forth. The link was more than similar to a source-link; it was damn near the exact same thing. Will's body was paralyzed, locking his hand around the rod. Startled, Will failed to react for a moment, which turned out to be a critical mistake. The relic was working to separate him from his source by the time he began to fight.

Will seized hold of it and tried to reverse the link, but the item's will felt like iron, strong and inexorable. He was already on the wrong end of things, for his late start had given the item a large advantage. It was rather like trying to win a shoving match when you were standing on a slope—of shifting sand.

Let's not fight it, child. I know it's disconcerting, but there's nothing you can do. I'm centuries ahead of you, said the voice in his head. Will slid further, and then his contact with his source disappeared. He was a prisoner within his own body. *That's better. Now let's see what we have here. Did you say third-order? Was that the truth, or a lie?*

Will refused to even think an answer, but then he felt something shifting in his mind. The voice was rummaging through his memories! *So you were telling the truth! I never dared to hope! How about vampires? Are they still about or were you just a greedy little bastard?*

He felt more sifting through his mind. *So they're back. You chose wisely.*

You'll help me? asked Will tentatively. *Can I have my body back?*

I'm afraid not. Only one of us can use it after all. Rest assured though, I'm the right one for the job. No one knows this enemy better than I do.

But it's my body! exclaimed Will.

Was. It 'was' your body. Now it's mine. You appear to have had a lot of potential, so it's a shame. I feel a little guilty about cutting short such a bright future, but it's clear which of us the world needs right now.

How about afterward? asked Will desperately.

You won't be around. I'll keep you for a while, so I can pick out the memories I need. Once I've adjusted to your life and the people you deal with, I'll let you go softly into the dark night.

That's murder!

Would you rather live trapped in a void for seven or eight hundred years? I think not. Trust me, child. I am not a cruel man. It's best to let you go.

But—! And then the world went black as Will's senses were cut off. He was once again locked within a black void.

***

Will opened his eyes slowly, examining the room around himself. Someone was leaning over him with a worried expression. *Good lord, he's immense!* Will almost fell backward to escape the looming giant. "Back off!" he shouted.

Tiny frowned but stood back up. "Are you all right?"

"I'm fine, ya great whopping beast of man! Step back, let a fellow breathe!" said Will testily. Then he noticed the stunning blonde sitting across the room. "Well, hello!" She frowned as he addressed her. "What's your name, my sweet little dumpling?" She became visibly angry at that, and he realized his mistake. Holding up one hand, he took a moment to do a quick mental search. "Laina! Right?"

Chapter 41

"I knew you were mad," she replied. "First you were talking to strange voices and now you're acting like a lunatic."

Will winked at her, then turned his eyes back to the giant, pointing a finger at the man. "Tiny! Sorry if I startled you. My head was a little scrambled for a moment." Getting up from the floor, Will stretched, marveling at the youthful vitality of his body. "Damn, that feels good." He ran his hands over himself, exploring his arms and legs, then rubbed his groin for a moment. "Oh, this is very nice! I'm going to love this."

Tiny was looking very concerned. "Will. Maybe you should lie down and have a rest. You don't seem well."

"*Well,* maybe you should lie down," he responded. "I feel fine."

"Will?" asked Tiny, a funny look on his face.

"Will I what? Make sense, man!" snapped Will.

"Something is wrong with him," Laina told Tiny. "He isn't usually this stupid."

Will paused and searched through his memories a bit more, until finally he realized what was wrong, then he laughed. "Ha! I was just on a lark. You didn't think I honestly forgot my own name, did you?"

Laina nodded almost imperceptibly to Tiny, indicating he should move behind Will. Then she smiled. "So, did you already finish attuning yourself to the relic?"

"Relic? Oh! This thing!" said Will, holding up Ethelgren's Exhortation. "I've got it mastered now. It's amazing the things it can do."

She smiled, then winked, and Tiny moved to wrap one arm around Will's chest while grabbing hold of the rod with his other hand. Or rather he tried to do so. Will turned and pushed one hand toward the big man, as though he was pushing air. Tiny flew backward, smacking into the wall with solid but not dangerous force. He remained there, held back as though by an invisible hand.

Will tutted gleefully at the big man's discomfiture. "Not so fast, my overlarge friend." Laina started to move behind him, but he turned and snapped his fingers. She froze in place, but not from a spell. The move had been so sudden and the sound of his fingers snapping so loud that she had feared some lethal effect.

Will smiled. "Don't run off too quickly, darling. We need to talk." Turning back, he looked at Tiny pensively for a moment while his mind rummaged around looking for details in his memories. A spell formed above his hand. "Tiny, my good friend, I'll explain everything later, but for now you'll need to take a rest. I do apologize." The spell flew from his hand, and Tiny sagged, slowly collapsing to the floor, unconscious.

He turned back to Laina. "Don't worry. He's fine. Is there anywhere we can get something to eat? I'm famished!"

"What is wrong with you?" she demanded, fear and anger fighting for dominance in her expression and voice.

"Nothing a good meal and the arms of a good woman wouldn't solve," he responded rakishly, giving her another wink.

The look Laina gave him was one of absolute disgust. Finally, she answered, "It isn't safe out tonight, so I wouldn't trust one of the public houses."

"Oh, the vampires? No need to worry. I can handle them." Moving past her, he opened the door and then offered her his arm. "Shall we go?"

She stared at him for a moment, but when he didn't move, she finally reached out and draped her hand over his forearm. He looked up and down the hall before finally choosing the correct direction and then heading for the

Chapter 41

stairs. As they descended, she reminded him, "You know there's a curfew on right now, don't you?"

"That's a damn shame," he agreed. "But not a bad idea, considering the circumstances. I'm sure we can find someone willing to cook for us."

That earned another odd look from Laina, but she didn't say anything. As they stepped outside, she glanced around, but she didn't see Darla. The former assassin appeared behind them seconds later, as if by magic.

Will didn't react well to being surprised. As Darla started to announce herself, he turned and 'pushed' with his hand again, sending her flying into the side of the Alchemy building. She was pinned there, and he glared at her menacingly for a moment before Laina got his attention.

"What are you doing?" she demanded. "Let her go! She's my guard!"

Will stared at her for a moment, then sheepishly apologized. "Oops." He gestured, and the force holding Darla vanished, allowing her to slide to the ground. "Sorry about that, miss. I'm a little jumpy given the current circumstances."

Darla started to reply, but Laina was standing out of Will's line of sight and she held a finger in front of her lips to indicate the other woman should remain silent. The Arkeshi dipped her head and bowed, then moved to stand beside her mistress.

He stood for a moment, seemingly lost in thought, then set off in the direction of the school gate. Laina and Darla exchanged looks but followed without comment, and soon they were walking down the streets of Cerria. After only a few blocks, men appeared around them.

"You should know better than to be out wandering with a curfew on. Identify yourself," said the leader of the guardsmen.

Will paused a moment, then announced, "William Cartwright, and my companion is Miss Laina Nerrow, daughter of Baron Nerrow." He glanced at Laina with an unspoken 'right?' in his eyes. She merely nodded.

The leader of the guardsmen bowed. "Forgive me, milord. The king has instructed us not to interfere with your movements."

He nodded, smiling. "Well that's just swell! Give the king my thanks!" He waggled a finger at Laina. "Let's go m'dear!" With that he resumed marching down the street as though he hadn't a care in the world.

As they walked, Laina glanced over at him. "You seem very different."

"I've recently come into a great deal of power," Will said, lifting the enchanted rod and twirling it between his fingers in an elegant gesture. "You know what they say about power?"

"It corrupts."

He grinned. "No! That it's fantastic! Honestly, you wouldn't believe the amount of confidence I have right now. That and some truly unbelievable urges!" His eyes traveled downward briefly as he gave her a lewd appraisal.

She visibly restrained herself, making an effort not to gag at the thought.

He gave her a direct look. "You wouldn't understand. I feel like a sixteen-year-old right now, full of vim and vigor. I can hardly bear it!" For a moment, he focused on her eyes and Laina saw a strange flash of turyn swirl in front of his face for a moment. "I can tell you're in love with me, by the way," said Will confidently.

Her eyes flew wide and her nostrils flared with rage. "I am no such thing!" Her elementals responded to her anger, manifesting in the air beside her, one a burning figure, the other a rocky presence of stone.

Will glanced at them. "Neat." Then he seemed to dismiss them as his attention returned to her. "You know

Chapter 41

it's the truth. I can read your emotions. Admit it, you want me as much as I want you." He stepped closer, and a force-dome appeared around them, leaving both the elementals and Darla standing helplessly a few feet away. Shocked into disbelief, Laina gasped as his hand slid around her waist and his face drew close. He was about to kiss her.

With a shriek of fury and disgust, she pushed him back. Seeming confused, Will let go without a fight. "You're married!" challenged Laina, scrabbling to collect her wits.

He seemed surprised. "Oh! I forgot! Where is she then? I've got an itch you wouldn't believe!"

Furious, Laina gaped at him. "That's my best friend you're talking about!"

Will held up a hand. "Just a moment." Once again, his eyes seemed to lose focus as he looked away to one side. "Oh, damn! A whole year, eh? No wonder I'm feeling so pent up."

"That's no excuse for your behavior! Take down this shield."

He merely smiled. "Not to worry, you're safe with me. I wouldn't touch a woman who didn't want me to."

"You just did!"

"Does Selene know you're in love with me?" he asked suddenly. "That you think about me secretly at night?"

Her hand flashed through the air, catching the side of his head and rocking his face to one side. "You disgust me!"

Will straightened up, rubbing his cheek. "Nice arm you've got there, but clearly you're lying. I mean, yes, you do have an ungodly amount of rage in you, but right there behind it I can see the love. Why deny it?" He leaned forward. "Just one kiss. See if you like it."

"I'm your sister!" she snapped. "Have you no shame?"

Will blinked, then leaned away. "Oh." He stared into the air for a moment, then looked back at her. "Oh! Oh, I'm sorry! No wonder! Oh, that's embarrassing. I didn't expect that. Love can be so confusing. Generally, with two young people of the opposite sex, it indicates some romantic inclinations as well, it just never occurred to me. Siblings! Well, that settles that, doesn't it?" he said genially. Then he winked and asked, "Or does it?"

She slapped him again.

He rubbed at the other cheek. "I guess it does. That's too bad. I guess it's to be expected, growing up together and all, that sort of thing is very taboo." He glanced at Darla. "Your bodyguard looks very healthy, in a strong sort of way. Do you suppose she—"

Laina swung at him once more, this time with her fist, but he caught her wrist. "That's enough of that. I'll accept the other blows because you had good cause, but now I'm just asking an honest question."

Her face was a thundercloud of anger, but Laina's thoughts were clear. "Who are you?"

"I'm your dear brother, William," he said smugly.

She shook her head. "No, you're not."

"What tipped you off?"

"When you wanted to find someone to cook for you. Idiot that he is, the real Will is an excellent cook. Who are you?"

He released her hand and offered his in a handshake. She declined to accept it. "Linus. Linus Ethelgren at your service." He winked, then added, "I'm here to save the world!"

CHAPTER 42

Bereft of his senses, Will circled the infinite emptiness of his prison. He'd experienced the same thing often enough that he didn't panic immediately this time, which might not have been for the best, for he couldn't seem to escape. *If I could just get out of my body, maybe I could see what was happening!*

Every time before, he had either been dying or in a state of panic. Except the time that Janice had helped him, but he'd still felt a small amount of fear then. This time he was completely calm. But was fear really the catalyst? He tried to make himself afraid, but failed utterly.

He still couldn't quite understand what had happened. There had been someone else, but the other had been nothing more than a disembodied voice, or perhaps a spirit trapped within the relic. In some sense, it was similar to Arrogan, except it wasn't tied to the limnthal. How had it had the power, the strength of will, to trap him inside his own body?

Will pondered that for a while, but got nowhere, so he decided to change tactics. He focused on Tiny, imagining his friend as vividly as he could. He felt something for a while, but then it faded. Arrogan had told him that there had to be a bond, but that shouldn't be a problem. Tiny was his closest friend. *Why won't it work?*

He considered Laina for a moment but discarded her as a prospect immediately. She despised him. The only bond they shared was mutual distaste, and he didn't feel like swimming through such negativity just to escape.

Darla! She was nearby and she would meet up with her ward soon enough. Then he could see what was going on with his body.

He tried that avenue for ten or fifteen minutes, but there was nothing. He simply didn't know enough about the former assassin to even begin to find some sort of link between them. He considered trying Janice, but there wasn't much point. She was locked away for the night and wouldn't be able to see him anyway. Even if she could see him, she would only put herself in danger if she tried to leave before dawn.

In the end, there was only one option—Laina. Clearing his mind, he tried to envision her as he had seen her just a short while ago. Her face was blurry at first, until he started adding his emotions to the mix. She irritated him to no end, but deep down he was worried about her. The image grew crisp and began to gain solidity.

I'm worried about her, he told himself, but there was something more. Completely alone, he was still embarrassed by the thought. *I'm not just worried, I care about her. She's my sister, and in some strange sense, I love her.*

With an almost audible 'pop,' the world sprang into existence, and he found himself in the middle of the street, not far from Wurthaven. Laina and the imposter were inside a force-dome, while Darla pounded helplessly on the exterior. Two very irritated elementals also stood by, though they didn't waste their time attacking the dome.

He tried focusing on Laina, to draw him closer, but he was rebuffed when his point of perspective came up against the force effect. Unlike everything else, it felt completely solid. Remembering how Arrogan had once had him create a force-dome before they had a conversation, he could see just how effective the spell was now.

Chapter 42

He would simply have to wait.

But he nearly lost his mind when he watched himself slip an arm around Laina's waist and draw her in for a— *Oh hell, no!* He was relieved when he saw her push him back and he cheered when she delivered the first slap.

The second slap was even better. *I just hope she doesn't permanently maim my body,* he thought. *It would be awful if I get my body back and had to live with some terrible scar because of this fool's bizarre behavior.*

Will wished he could hear what they were saying, but the force-dome kept him from hearing any of the conversation. He was glad when it appeared that the imposter was apologizing, but the continued lewd gazes gave him an uneasy feeling. *If she hated me before, this is going to take things to a whole new level.*

Oh well, it couldn't get much worse, could it? He watched as the imposter tried to shake her hand and was rebuffed. Then the force-dome came down. He quickly reoriented his point of view so that he was staring over the imposter's shoulder. Will didn't know if the spirit that had invaded him could see astral bodies or not, but it was better not to take the chance.

Laina's eyes never glanced at him, so he soon gave up on being seen by her. The elementals were now fading back into their private storage spaces, so they were no help, not that they had shown any sign of being aware of him anyway. He looked at Darla and felt a sudden thrill.

Her gaze was firmly locked on him. Will imagined himself waving, and he saw the bodyguard lift one brow in unspoken acknowledgment. *She can see me!*

An orange glow appeared in the distance above the buildings to the south. The light was steady, but there were variations in its brightness. It flickered. "I think there's a fire," said Laina, pointing.

Linus Ethelgren glanced in the direction she pointed. "It seems likely. We should head in that direction. Stay close to me or I cannot guarantee your safety."

Laina caught his arm. "What about my brother?" Will heard her say it clearly, and it sent a shockwave through his spirit. *She knows! How?*

The reincarnation of Linus Ethelgren gave her a sad smile. "I'm afraid he's gone. This body could only hold one of us."

Liar! Will wanted to scream. *I'm still here!*

Laina Nerrow froze. "He's still in there, though, right?"

Linus patted her shoulder in what was probably meant to be a comforting gesture but which merely served to convey how completely unsympathetic he was. "He was briefly, when I first spoke to him through the rod." He lifted the rod to emphasize his point. "But when I explained the choice he had to make, he elected to take the hero's path."

"Hero's path?"

"Only one of us could exist, and since your city is overrun with creatures of the night it was obvious to him that I was sorely needed. He sacrificed his life to allow me to take his place."

His half-sister's face was flushed and blotchy, with red patches on her cheeks, neck, and ears, as she shook her head in negation of the words she was hearing. "No. No, that's not true. You're a pervert and a liar. He wouldn't do that."

"I'm sorry, Laina," said the imposter. "But you know him better than I do. Think about it. Think about the things he's done in the past. Are you so certain he wouldn't make such a choice, when the safety of his friends and family were at risk? Wouldn't he want to save his sister?" He paused a moment, gazing into the distance. "Sisters? Yes, sisters. Wouldn't he want to save you both?"

Chapter 42

Laina's shoulders were moving roughly, as though she was fighting to breathe, and Will could barely see the whites of her eyes any longer, for the lids were puffy and what was visible was red. Ugly tears leaked from the corners to stain her cheeks. She blinked and continued to shake her head. "No. We hate each other."

The imposter lifted his arm and pretended to wipe away a tear with his sleeve. "I already told you I can see emotions, Laina. I know that to be false. Perhaps you have been fooling yourself, but while he was probably more conflicted, he was honest about his emotions. Hasn't he already shown himself to be willing to sacrifice himself for you and your family?"

A woman stumbled out of a nearby building, blood running from claw marks on her cheek and neck. A fiend leapt through the window of the same building to land on the lane in front of her, while a second one exited the same door she had used. Linus looked over his shoulder, then gestured with one hand. Three brilliant beams of white light intersected each of them. The vampires promptly began to burn, disintegrating into dust over a period of several seconds.

The woman merely died, a cauterized hole having burned through the center of her chest.

"You killed her," accused Laina, snapping back to reality.

"She was already infected," Linus replied.

"You could have saved her with a blood-cleanse potion."

He shook his head sadly. "It's good you know about that. Will must have been diligent in his studies, but I don't have any at hand, and if I did I wouldn't waste it on that poor waif. How many people are in this city? If there are hundreds of vampires running loose then there will be thousands infected and tomorrow will be even worse. It will all have to be purged."

Laina backed away. "You're a monster."

"Stay close, Laina. It isn't safe out here alone." Then he snickered and added, "Unless you're me, of course." More screams sounded nearby, and Linus turned to face the new threat. Seeing a swirling mass of soldiers and vampires fighting at the next street corner, he started toward it. "Don't lose sight of me," he yelled, but Linus never looked back. Lifting one hand, he made another gesture, and a long white coat appeared, flowing over his body and shining as though it was made of pure light. His steps quickened as he saw his favorite enemy in the distance.

Laina watched him go but made no move to follow. Darla moved closer, giving her a brief hug, but then she stepped away. The Arkeshi needed to keep her hands free given the possible threats around them. "We should go, Laina. It isn't safe here," advised her bodyguard.

"He's dead, Darla, dead. And I never said a single kind word to him," muttered Laina listlessly.

The Arkeshi glanced at Will once more, then shook her head. "No, Laina, he isn't dead. He's still alive. He's here with us now."

Laina's face grew angry. "Save the platitudes, Darla. I'm in no mood for fairytales."

"Right there," said Darla, pointing. "He isn't dead, he's projecting himself."

His half-sister wiped her face absently, causing some of her hair to stick to her cheeks and generally making herself look even worse. "You aren't making sense."

Her bodyguard sighed. "Some people, usually warlocks and sorcerers, but occasionally normal people too, learn to project their spirits outside of their bodies. I was trained to spot such things. William is here now, listening to us."

"Why haven't I heard about this before?" asked Laina.

Chapter 42

"Because your people are stupid," snapped Darla. "And also, those who learn the secret usually keep it to themselves."

Laina didn't seem convinced. "You're just making things up now."

The former assassin didn't take that well. "Have I ever lied to you before?" she demanded.

"No…"

"Then do not accuse me of it now. He's here! If you wish, you can try and talk to him."

That got Laina's full attention. "How?"

"Touch him. If your hearts are in sync then your spirits can touch," said the Arkeshi.

Laina's nose wrinkled again. "You do it."

Exasperated, Darla moved closer to Will, then moved her hand back and forth through the area he occupied. He felt nothing. "I cannot," said Darla. "His bond is not with me."

"That's just revolting. There's no bond between us."

"You just admitted he is your brother," Darla pointed out. Will found himself nodding in agreement, *Yeah.* The Arkeshi continued, "He could not be here otherwise. He has anchored himself to you."

"Now you're giving me the creeps," said Laina.

Darla sighed. "Fine. Let's return to the school. William's friend is there. We should at least wake him and tell him what has happened."

"Wait, what about—all that?" Laina waved her hand mysteriously at the air near where Will was located.

The Arkeshi shrugged. "If you do not care then we can ignore him. Eventually his spirit will wither and die or return to its body. He's no longer our concern."

Laina didn't move. Rubbing her face with her hands, she stared in Will's general direction. "Where is he?" she asked.

"A little to your left and three feet forward," said Darla.

His half-sister moved according to her bodyguard's instructions. "I just reach out? Oh!" She jumped back as her hand touched the space where Will was. He wasn't sure what she had felt, but he had experienced an electric tingle that ran through his phantom body. "That was him, wasn't it?" asked Laina.

"Yes. Try not to flinch away next time," advised her friend.

Laina nodded, then moved closer, holding her arms out. Will focused his attention on her, moving himself forward, and then they collided, sending shivers through his astral form and causing his sister to shudder, but she didn't retreat. It was then that he realized how cold he was.

The astral space he inhabited was home to a deathly chill, and now that he had touched Laina, he could feel the living warmth that radiated from her skin. It was vitality, sustenance. It maintained her soul, nurtured her spirit. Without it, any spirit being would eventually starve and wither.

"Can you hear me?" she asked.

Yes, he replied, trying to project his thoughts through their superficial contact.

Laina frowned, then glanced back at Darla. "I felt something. I think he's trying to talk, but it's just a buzz."

The Arkeshi shrugged. "This is the limit of my knowledge. I have never interacted with a spirit form."

Laina stared through him again, failing to focus her eyes on the place where he stood. "Try to get closer," she suggested.

We're already skin-to-skin, thought Will. *We can't get any closer.* He pressed forward, feeling a springy resistance as the boundary of her flesh rejected him.

"He's trying," said Darla. "But there's a wall around you. Try to be less negative."

Chapter 42

"I'm not negative!" Laina bit back, but her friend gave her a look of obvious disbelief. "I just don't like him," she added.

"The bodysnatcher was wicked, but there was some truth in his words," posited the Arkeshi. "You are dishonest with your emotions."

Laina bit her lip, but she didn't argue. Facing Will again, she opened her arms, and her expression changed. The perpetual glare faded and something more vulnerable appeared. "I'm open," she said hesitantly. "Let me help you."

At that point Will was a foot or two distant, but the look in her eyes drew him in, as though a channel had opened. He felt a rushing sensation, and then the world dissolved into a chaotic riot of sensations. Laina was gone, and when he looked around, he saw that only he and Darla remained. "What?" he muttered.

But it wasn't his voice. It was distinctly feminine. His eyes widened in alarm, and then he felt her. She was inside him. *Will?* she asked nervously.

He closed his eyes—her eyes. *Laina?* As the name formed, he felt the connection between them. They weren't two souls in one body; they were one oversized soul in a single body. The boundaries between them had vanished, and their thoughts and emotions were rushing back and forth, like waves on a beach. As her name crossed his mind, so too did all the emotions he felt regarding her—anger, annoyance, concern, worry, and behind it all, a fearful love that he was always afraid to admit.

And she was much the same. Her anger was greater, and when her thoughts turned to him, he felt her self-loathing. Laina hated him with the passion of her own self-loathing, and behind that was a similar tentative love, mixed with pity and compassion. Drowning everything else, was an ocean of guilt.

Will began to cry as he felt it all, especially the guilt.

Laina had known all along, since she was a child. She had always been intelligent, and even as a girl she had quickly deduced the reason her father went to visit the remote village of Barrowden, and who the dirt-smudged peasant boy that lived there must be. She had known, and she had hated him—and pitied him. Laina had loved her family, and when she looked at the peasant child in Barrowden, she had felt guilt, for she knew she possessed a treasure he could never have.

She had known, and she had buried the feeling behind a wall of guilt so high she couldn't even fathom its meaning. It was invisible to her. Every flaw she had found in herself, in her father, in her mother, and even in Tabitha, she pushed into that dark place, heaping it full of her rejection and scorn.

And while Will found himself inundated by that river of sorrow, Laina experienced his own heart. His pain and sense of rejection, his desire for love and belonging, feelings he could never give voice to in the light of day. He had felt continually unworthy, an outsider begging for things that he didn't deserve.

Will sank to the ground, hugging himself as the misery threatened to swallow him whole. The feelings were so powerful that he wanted to die. No, *she* wanted to die. Laina had devoted herself to the suffering of the poor, secretly trying to assuage the guilt she didn't even know existed within her. Filling her days with a passion for charity that had driven her from the age of fourteen until the present, as she stood on the cusp of full adulthood.

It's all right, he told himself, speaking to her. *We were children. It wasn't our fault. It wasn't anyone's fault.*

She felt his acceptance, his forgiveness, and something similar came from her in return, but they were still forlorn,

Chapter 42

ravaged by the storm of emotions that the meeting of their souls had unleashed. Until he felt strong arms encircle him, pulling him back to his feet. "Shhh, emshee," cooed Darla softly, using a pet name he didn't recognize. "Shhh, it will be all right. Come with me."

He let her lead him, and Darla took them out of the middle of the road to the shelter of a doorway so they would be less visible. She stroked his hair and kissed his brows gently. "Relax, emshee, breathe. You must get control of yourself," said the bodyguard.

It felt so natural that it was several seconds before Will realized how intimate Darla's treatment was. *She kissed me?* His body felt a familiar, yet unfamiliar stirring as his sadness faded. Unsure of himself, he slid one hand down to check his—*Oh, holy fuck!* In the confusion he had forgotten what body he was in.

He probed the region for a moment more, curious, then he felt a sudden surge of anger coming from the other half of his joint-soul. *Stop!*

Will was paralyzed with a welter of strange emotions, from curiosity, to fear, to disgust. He wasn't entirely sure where each originated from. *Is it incest if I want to see how everything works from the inside?*

It didn't help that Darla was still trying to bring him, or rather Laina, back to her senses. "Wake up, emshee! We must go. You cannot wallow in your emotions here."

Laina was forlorn, and desperate, and while they were two, she felt terribly alone. Lifting her chin, she gazed into Darla's warm eyes. The other woman's eyes scanned the street behind her for a second, then her lips parted and she darted in for a quick but passionate kiss. She pulled back after barely a second. "There. Are you awake? There is no time for this!"

Will was awake. He was terribly, amazingly wide awake, and the danger of the moment only made things worse. He could barely remember the last time he had been so horny. Despite the change in anatomy, the feelings were similar, and he could feel a compelling heat growing in his lower regions, as well as an increased sensitivity that seemed to include his entire body, which was relatively more intense than what he had experienced as a man.

The beast reared its head within him, and he pressed Darla back against the door as he nuzzled her neck, the line of her chin, and then finally brought his lips back to hers. The Arkeshi received his passion willingly, but her eyes widened a moment later. "It isn't like you to be so forceful, emshee, you—"

They both froze, then Will pulled himself away. "Forgive me. I'm not sure who I am right now."

"I thought he vanished. You—you are *both* in there?" exclaimed Darla.

He nodded. "Forgive her, she wouldn't have done…" He paused as his brain worked through the moment, processing what had happened. *She kissed me first, but she thought I was Laina.* His internal perspective reversed itself, and Laina's thoughts reached him. *You didn't realize. It wasn't you that wanted her. It was me.*

Will's eyes locked onto Darla. The former assassin wasn't just Laina's bodyguard, she was his sister's lover. "Ohh…," he said slowly, letting his eloquence fill the air.

A loud explosion rent the night, and rocks and debris flew through the air. Will quickly constructed a force-dome to shelter within, while at the same time the earth elemental surrounded them with a heavy stone dome. He heard heavy boards hitting the stone a few seconds later. *I had that. You didn't have to use the elemental!*

Chapter 42

How was I supposed to know what you were doing? returned Laina. Her frustration permeated his chest. *This is getting too confusing,* she added. *What are you doing?*

Feeling guilty, he put his hand back down by his side. *I was just curious.*

Don't touch my breasts.

I wasn't feeling it with the hand. I wanted to know what it felt like from the other side, he tried to explain.

Just don't. Don't ever. And if we get out of this, I never want to hear another word about it. None of this happened!

He couldn't argue with that. *Deal. Let's just hope this is over before we need to go to the bathroom.*

She sighed, taking control of their lungs for a moment. "Why did you have to say that?" groaned Laina.

"Say what?" asked Darla, who was standing beside her within the earthen dome.

"Sorry," said Laina, then Will nodded. "I was talking to myself." *Damn, this really is confusing,* he thought. *By the way, thank you.*

Her response was a nonverbal feeling, a question without words.

For coming to help me tonight. I would be lost and doomed if you weren't here, he explained.

You're welcome, she replied, and the words carried her emotions with them, a surge of warmth that washed back and forth between them, like a wave caught perpetually between two shores. A resonance seemed to grow, and the wave became higher and higher, until at last she managed to put an end to it. *Enough of that. I'm going to have nightmares for years after this.*

He smiled inwardly.

Chapter 43

Darla wanted to return and wake Tiny, but Laina had changed her mind. Will wasn't sure what was right, but since it was her body he felt it best to leave the decision to her. "We can't leave him to run loose in Will's body. The man is mad. He might well get killed, and then where would we be?" she said aloud.

I wouldn't stay. This is only temporary, one way or another, Will reassured her silently.

Shut up, came Laina's response. *You can do stupid things and get yourself killed when you have your own body back. Until then don't be an idiot. You're in my care for now.*

The Arkeshi sighed. "He will be easy to find, since he's in the middle of all the commotion, but it's unlikely you can approach without being seen." She eyed Laina's dress with mistrust.

"Speak for yourself," said Will, lifting one hand. He quickly constructed a chameleon spell and then cast it on himself, fading into near-invisibility before adding a silent-armor spell to complete the set.

One of Darla's brows went up. "I suppose there are advantages to having both of you in there." She lifted the hood of her cloak, and the enchantment on it activated, producing a similar chameleon effect. A second later her turyn also shifted, blending and fading. It wasn't a visible effect, but somehow it made her even harder to find. His eyes kept sliding away if he let his concentration slip.

"What is that second spell you're using?" he asked suddenly.

"I don't use spells," she stated, no doubt in her voice.

"Is it the cloak then? You're hard to find, even when I know where I should look. My eyes don't want to go there."

Inside their head, Laina's interest was also piqued. *What are you talking about?*

It's more than the chameleon effect, he explained. *She's doing something with her turyn.*

Darla understood immediately. "It is no spell. It is the lim-leesi. A special technique the Arkeshi train in."

"Wild magic," Will realized, speaking out loud. "You're using wild magic, like the fae. Can you teach me?"

The former assassin's eyes narrowed. "The Arkeshi do *not* use magic," she said emphatically. "And it is forbidden to teach outsiders the technique."

"But you're no longer part of the Arkeshi," Laina pointed out.

"I have betrayed them, but my other oaths still hold. I will not break my teacher's trust."

Will had already learned to adjust his senses, stamina, strength, and speed, to varying degrees. By watching how Darla's turyn moved, he was already beginning to get a feel for what she was doing. Ignoring the conversation, he began trying to emulate her, though his turyn moved clumsily at first.

The Arkeshi couldn't see turyn, but after a moment she stopped talking and her gaze locked onto Laina's body, then drifted slightly before returning. Her face grew alarmed. "You cannot!" she insisted.

Will's tongue was sticking out to one side as he concentrated, an expression he imagined was probably cuter on his sister's face. "Am I getting this right? It feels weird, but I think I'm close."

"Impossible. This takes years to master! I have not taught you." A second later, she dropped to her knees and clasped her hands together. With eyes closed, she began chanting in a foreign tongue, the words taking on an almost ritualistic cadence.

What is she doing? Will was confused.

Laina sighed internally. *I'm not sure precisely, but she did this a lot when she first came to me. It's some sort of prayer for forgiveness or atonement. She thinks she's broken her oath.*

Will knelt down beside the Arkeshi. "Darla. It isn't your fault. I'm using magic."

The woman paused, opening her eyes and staring at him doubtfully.

"You don't use magic," he repeated. "I do. I'm using magic to imitate you. This isn't your fault." Inwardly he thought otherwise. *I'm doing exactly the same thing. She uses wild magic whether she realizes it or not.*

If it's the same thing, how did you learn it so quickly? asked Laina.

I'm a wizard. Manipulating turyn is what I spend every day training to do. It's just like a dance instructor learning a new dance within minutes.

Laina's reply was full of humor. *I heard you're a terrible dancer.*

I'm better! he insisted. *But it took me a long time just to learn two dances. The same holds true for Darla. She was taught a special form of magic without even knowing it was magic. Of course it was hard!*

But this is easy for you? questioned Laina. *I can't even tell what you're doing. It feels like my skin is dancing across itself.*

You aren't a wizard.

Chapter 43

I'm a sorceress, she shot back. *I'm just like you, only with more power.*

Remember you said that, Will told her. *After this is over and I have my body back, remember you said that. You'll feel foolish when you think back on it.*

Darla was staring at him. "You're having another conversation in your head, aren't you?" she asked.

Laina nodded, then stood back up. "Are we going to go find him or not?"

The Arkeshi stood and began to move away, taking point. Will started to follow, but as he began his first sustained walk in a single direction, he realized something was wrong.

What are you doing? demanded Laina. *You're moving weird.*

It's your hips. There's something wrong with them.

Mentally she pushed him aside. *There's nothing wrong with them, idiot. They have more play in them than your stupid man hips do. You have to adapt to it.* She took over walking for a while, and Will paid close attention to the process from within. Laina made it seem easy. *Of course,* she replied. *I was born like this, dolt.*

I always thought... he stopped himself before his thought got him in trouble.

What?

It was useless trying to hide it, so he went on. *I thought you people did it on purpose.*

You people?

Uh, women, I mean.

Her spirit swirled around him, filled with suspicion. *You thought women did what on purpose?*

This walk thing. I thought it was deliberate.

What's that supposed to mean?

As a man, it's very distracting, he answered, trying to project honesty. *I thought it was a sort of deliberate act of femininity.*

Oh, so we were acting? her thought was tinged with annoyance. *This is acting!* Her walk shifted, swaying farther and becoming more fluid. If she had been visible instead of hidden any onlooker would have instantly known she was vying for attention. *If you see a woman doing that, then it's deliberate.*

Got it, he told her quickly. *You can stop now.*

Why? Does it bother you?

It just feels weird.

She was laughing silently. *Oh, this is too good! You need to get in touch with your inner woman, Will!* Her stride became even more sultry, and her hands slid up over her hips and across her torso.

He couldn't see exactly what she was doing, but from within, he could perfectly envision it, he was just as aware of the body as she was. It was a powerful feeling, but it was strange nonetheless. *You've made your point,* he told her, signaling his surrender.

They came to a stop. Darla had halted in front of them, and she was now exerting all her concentration to keep her gaze locked on Laina. "We're going to get killed if you keep behaving like a whore. Pay attention to our environment."

"That was Will," Laina lied. "He's having too much fun with my body."

"No, I'm not," he protested.

"You're a pervert."

"What?"

Darla covered her face with her hands, then hissed, "For the love of the Mother! Stop! You're giving me a headache."

Chapter 43

Will nodded. *See what you did?*

Don't blame me, stupid, Laina shot back.

A silent explosion of light followed by howling screams, heralded their proximity to the latest battle. Darla moved closer to the building they were passing by, and Will matched her example. The Arkeshi eased forward to look around the corner, then blurred into motion.

A vampire hurtled around the corner at speed. The creature was in full flight. Though Darla couldn't match its speed, her long knife, inlaid with silver, moved in line just quickly enough to cut a deep, smoking slash across the vampire's thigh, sending it into a tumbling roll.

Will sent a force-lance into the creature's head as it started to rise, then he blocked the rush of a second monster coming around the corner. Brought to a violent stop by Will's point-defense shield, the vampire was stunned for a second, during which Darla's blade moved with perfect efficiency, cutting across, over, then down, severing vital tendons in the wrists and arms of her opponent.

Before the thing could stumble back or retreat, Will sent a force-lance through first one, then the other leg.

Laina had only just begun to react, and more of the creatures were spilling around the corner as what seemed to be an endless horde swarmed toward them. Darla looked back in panic. "Run!"

Slow to start, Laina wasted no time once she realized what was happening. A brief command sent her earth elemental into action, and a dense, earthen wall grew up and over their position, keeping the vampires at bay.

Will had been about to start a force-dome, but seeing what Laina was doing, he switched tactics. He had time now.

"We're trapped," observed Darla.

"Not for long," Laina announced. "He's got something special planned."

Don't spoil it, complained Will as Ethelgren's Illumination came together above his palm. "Close your eyes," he warned, then released it. Inside the enclosed space, the radiance was searing, even through closed lids, but after a few seconds the glowing orbs moved out through the solid walls and beyond, to where the vampires were trying to dig their way through.

More howls announced the deaths of the bloodsuckers in closest proximity, and more screams followed as the orbs continued outward. "That spell is perfect for these things," Laina enthused.

You can thank Linus Ethelgren for it, Will informed her. *It's one of his.*

Never mind, she replied, changing her tone. Now that the orbs were out at a distance, she had her earth elemental lower the protective dome. The street appeared empty except for noxious dust swirling in the breeze.

They hurried around the corner, and at the other end of the next block, they saw what had sent some of the vampires running in fear. A tense battle was still in progress as the younger, frenzied vampires swarmed over and around a small contingent of the Driven. From what they could tell, there had been ordinary soldiers with them, but those were already face-down in the dirt. Linus Ethelgren stood in the center of the melee, untouched, his glowing white coat shedding radiance in all directions.

The coat was a potent protective spell, and while it didn't harm the vampire beyond a short distance, it was strong enough that any that slipped past and tried to engage him quickly burst into flames.

Aside from watching, the ancient wizard did little besides cackle as men and vampires fought and died. Elementals raged, sending gouts of flame to consume some of the undead, but the creatures were unbelievably

Chapter 43

fast. The unwary were caught, but many others dodged the jets of fire. As some of the vampires slipped in among them, one of the Driven panicked, releasing a wind-wall.

The deadly winds destroyed the nearest vampires, as well as some of his fellow sorcerers. The human defenders faltered, and the vampires farther out could sense their weakness. Uttering a series of high-pitched clicks, the undead called for more of their own to join the incipient feast, and more came scrambling out into the street.

Through it all, Linus Ethelgren stood laughing, his cheeks flushed with excitement. He was having the time of his life. As the undead tide rose, threatening to overwhelm them at last, the ancient wizard lifted a hand up to the sky. Argent sparks shimmered in the air around him, becoming silver blades that danced in the air. They cut through everything and everyone near him, sorcerers and vampires alike, but those blades that struck flesh remained in their targets. Lines of silver turyn flashed back from them to their creator.

Ethelgren's spell was just beginning.

The power coursed into him and flowed into the second layer of his spell construct. Grinning like a madman, the wizard lifted his hands and brought them together in a thunderous clap with his fingers pointing outward. An actinic beam of devastating power lashed out, cutting through vampires and buildings with equal ease.

Slowly, gleefully, Ethelgren began to turn in place while his silver beam continued to chew through everything in its path. He seemed intent on making a complete circle.

Will couldn't see how far out the beam went, how much it could cut through before petering out, but it was much too far for their own safety.

Laina barked a single word. "Darla!" The Arkeshi responded instantly, moving to stand closely beside her mistress. Meanwhile, Laina's earth elemental began building another dome, thicker, denser, stronger than before. At the same time, Will dismissed the chameleon effect and started constructing a force-dome spell. Given the direction of Ethelgren's turn, his beam would reach them in just seconds, and he doubted the earthen wall would stop it, for the silver power was already eating through stone and wood buildings with equal ease.

The wall of force appeared just as coruscating, argent power tore into Laina's defense, which predictably turned out to be very little defense at all. In theory, force effects were utterly impervious to physical effects. Mass, momentum, inertia, these things meant nothing to force spells. They were immovable or irresistible, depending on their design.

But magical energy was a different matter. Will's spell would require a commensurate amount of power to match the spell that was about to slam into it. *Laina, I need your help.* He had already extended his outer absorptive shell and started drawing in power as quickly as possible, but it was unlikely to be enough.

The earth elemental was already busy, and Ethelgren's spell had completely disrupted its body. Laina directed the turyn of her fire elemental into Will's spell, shoring it up just as the silver beam struck.

The world went white as the beam washed over them. The earthen dome was gone in an instant, and Will felt the force-dome shudder, signaling its imminent collapse. The power he and Laina were channeling into the protective spell was nothing compared to the power Ethelgren had sent against it, and Will suddenly understood why.

Not only was the mad wizard's spell fueled by the turyn of those who had been impaled by his silver blades during the first phase, but the beam itself was a ripsaw of turyn

Chapter 43

currents. Power wasn't merely flowing outward; it was flowing back in a high-frequency current of devastation. With each high-speed pulse outward, the beam destroyed whatever was in its path, and with each complementary return, it stripped away the turyn of the living and the dead in that same path, fueling its continuation.

While it looked like an ordinary—if flashy and extraordinarily effective spell—in essence it had the same terrible power as a strategic ritual performed by a multitude of casters at the same time. It was clever and devious, and the fact that Ethelgren had originally designed it only highlighted the mad wizard's absolute genius.

They were outclassed on every level, and Will knew it down to his bones. Their defensive force-dome trembled as the fear rose within him.

Laina felt his fear, and though she didn't understand the magic they were dealing with, she knew something deeper. *Damn it, Will. You said you'd make me feel foolish. Show me what you meant!*

He remembered his previous fear, and the goddamn cat's insult. This was the same. His mind cleared, and then he remembered one of his earliest lessons with Arrogan:

"What can you do the next time someone decides to whack you with a stick?" the old man had asked.

"Make my own stick," he had replied.

"That's one solution, and it's often the best one, but not always. Sometimes the other person has a much better weapon than you do." Arrogan tossed his branch at Will's face, and when he flinched, the old man stepped close and twisted the larger stick from his hand. *"If your will is strong enough, and you have the skill, you can sometimes take the other person's stick away from them."*

All this passed through his mind in an instant, from Laina's encouragement to his moment of insight. Shifting his focus,

Will deliberately allowed the force wall to begin crumbling, but his will latched onto the silver power that seeped through, taking hold of the turyn and bending its purpose.

He couldn't have managed it without the momentary delay the force-dome provided, but it was just barely enough. A second later he felt searing pain tear through his/Laina's body, not from the destruction of their flesh, but from the strain of controlling so much so suddenly. The silver beam came to a halt, arrested between Linus Ethelgren and Will, a blazing curtain flashing between their hands.

They had reached a stalemate.

"What the hell do you think you're doing?" yelled Linus angrily. "You're ruining it!"

"You'll destroy the entire city at this rate!" shouted Laina, since Will's concentration was entirely on his effort.

"That's the point, you daft slut! It's a purge! The city is already lost."

"You're insane!"

"No, I'm a goddamn hero, you trollop, and sometimes heroes must make noble sacrifices!"

Laina gaped at him. "Idiot! It's only a noble sacrifice when *you're* the one sacrificing. What you're doing is simple slaughter."

Ethelgren started to reply, but Laina hadn't been idle while she conversed. She had been constructing a force-lance, her very first. It flashed at Ethelgren's chest but was instantly deflected by a point-defense shield.

You're a quick study, Will congratulated her internally. *Thanks.*

"You asked for it, bitch!" screamed Ethelgren, and he returned fire with a high-speed barrage of force-lances. Will similarly deflected them, grateful once again that he could reflex cast the point-defense spell.

Chapter 43

That went on for several seconds as they exchanged attacks, but it was clear that it wasn't gaining them anything. Ethelgren was red-faced as he shouted again, "This spell wasn't meant for dueling between wizards! As soon as one of us slips they'll be annihilated. Do you think you're good enough to outlast me? How long have you been a wizard? A few years? You're nothing but a child!"

I'm going to restart the force-lance and defense battle, Will explained. *Send your fire elemental out and around from a long distance. Make sure he can't see it.*

Laina understood his plan immediately and improved on it. Her earth elemental was still weak, but nonetheless she had it submerge itself beneath their feet and move forward while the fire elemental circled around.

Meanwhile, Will began sending a barrage of force-lances at Ethelgren. He kept his assault up, giving the ancient wizard no time to think as he defended himself. Laina's fire elemental quickly moved into position, and then it sprang into action.

Surging toward Ethelgren's back, it launched a series of firebolts. There was no way for the wizard to defend himself, given that he couldn't see the threat, but Will felt his hopes fall as their enemy began to laugh.

The shining white coat the man wore flashed as it absorbed the fiery attacks harmlessly. "You fools! I was doing this while you were still just—erp!" Ethelgren yelped as Laina's earth elemental seized his ankle and jerked him down into the ground.

The movement pulled Ethelgren out of line, and he lost contact with the silver river of power, which now fell under Will's control and began ravaging outward from his hands in the direction facing where the other wizard had been. He could feel the power surging through him as it slew and harvested still more power, along with the inexorable need to turn, to continue unleashing it before it destroyed him as well.

Lifting his hands, he sent the power upward into the sky, where it slowly diminished as it crossed miles and miles of open air. The turyn gradually weakened, and eventually he was able to draw in what was left, pulling the spell to a final close. Tired and fatigued, Will sagged, leaving their shared body to Laina's full control.

Exhausted, Laina Nerrow stood victorious, her chest heaving as she tried to catch her breath. From the outside she cut a magnificent figure. Her hair had long since come loose, and while bits of it were stuck to her face, the rest flowed out behind her. Her dress was tattered and torn, but rather than detract from her appearance, it merely confirmed the heroic struggle she had endured. Darla knelt beside her, head lifted to gaze adoringly up at the woman she loved.

Inwardly, Laina and Will cheered each other, basking in the glow of their mutual success. Most of the vampires had fled the general vicinity of the battle by then, and some people were slowly emerging from their homes, where they had watched while in hiding. A few even cheered.

Laina reached out and lifted Darla back to her feet, and the two of them walked toward where Ethelgren had stood. Will idly wondered what he would do next. His body had been buried alive, so soon he would have to make his goodbyes.

The ground exploded in front of them, and Laina felt a powerful disruption in her link with the earth elemental. Elementals were impossible to destroy, but hers had been finely dispersed in such a destructive way that it would be hours before it could reform. Linus Ethelgren emerged from the crater, levitating on a magical disk that lifted him out and deposited him gracefully beyond the rim of ruined paving.

Chapter 43

"You fucking asshole," he spat. "You just couldn't leave well enough alone, could you?"

Good news, Laina reported wryly. *Your body is still doing just fine.*

They were tired and worn. Laina's earth elemental was out of the picture, and with a gesture, Ethelgren caught the fire elemental in an odd cage made of flames. He was walking toward them with an evil gleam in his eye.

He's going to kill us, Laina, Will informed her.

He's male, she replied, *and he's already shown his weakness. He thinks with his dick. I can handle this.*

What does that mean? asked Will, feeling uncertain.

Just watch and try to figure something out. I don't know how long I can distract him.

The mad wizard stomped toward them, and as he got close his hand lifted, palm facing them. Darla started to move sideways, to circle around, but his hand moved, then changed orientation. He pushed down, and the assassin was flattened against the cobblestones. Laina didn't move, but her breathing increased as her chest heaved.

Are you starved for air? asked Will.

Shut up and figure something out! she yelled at him internally. Her eyes widened as she watched Ethelgren approach, and then her knees began to fail. Slowly, she sank to the ground, her skirt mounding up around her gracefully. Her chin dipped, but her eyes looked upward at her oppressor, giving the impression of complete defeat. At some point, her dress had slipped off one shoulder, causing a scandalous shift in her décolletage.

When did that happen? Will wondered. *Did she do that on purpose somehow?*

Focus! she chided him.

Linus Ethelgren sneered down at her, then reached out and seized her hair painfully, jerking her head back. "I should kill you for this," he threatened, but his eyes kept slipping away, distracted by other regions of Laina's anatomy.

Will felt a sharp pain as the bastard grabbed their hair, but he was shocked when his sister lightly bit her lower lip, then followed by quickly licking her lips. Her eyes never left Ethelgren's and they smoldered.

I'm going to be sick, thought Will.

Think! This isn't easy for me either!

"That's an interesting look on you, girl, but I'm too old to be fooled," Ethelgren informed her. "This is your brother's body after all."

"But *you* aren't my brother," she replied, her voice shifting to a slightly different register. "And no man has ever forced me to submit before."

"Then you have never faced true power, amateur," replied Ethelgren, but there was a look of nervousness on his face.

Will understood the man then. Despite Linus Ethelgren's bluff and bluster, the man was deeply insecure, and being faced with Laina's sudden reversal, he was unbalanced. He knew it was likely a ruse, but he was torn between his desire to believe, his sense of worthlessness, and the natural taboo that most men felt when it came to violence against women.

It didn't hurt that Laina was especially comely, and her eyes were burning with desire.

The wizard hesitated, then spoke. "I cannot kill a woman such as you, for I have rarely faced such a determined—and lovely—foe." He released her hair. "But I cannot trust you either."

"You will release me?" Laina responded, sounding almost disappointed. Then she hopefully added, "Or would you rather punish me?"

Chapter 43

"Enough, temptress! I have more work to do. I know your feminine cunning." He started to walk away. "Cross me again and I will show you no mercy."

Will realized then that they might live, but something else occurred to him. The Ring of Vile and Unspeakable Knowledge was still on his hand, or rather, on Ethelgren's hand. If the wizard ever activated the limnthal, he would soon discover the ring's secret.

And Arrogan had no idea that it was no longer Will at the helm. His knowledge might well fall into Ethelgren's grasp as well. At the very least Will needed to find a way to warn him. "Wait!" he said suddenly, taking control of their voice.

Ethelgren paused, "What?"

"You have his limnthal."

"He had a limnthal?" asked Ethelgren, his tone changing to one of interest. "He was further along in his training than I realized."

"There are a number of important family heirlooms stored within it," said Will. "I beg you to return them."

You're terrible at this, observed Laina. *You sound like you're bartering for turnips at the market.*

Well excuse me for not knowing how to sound alluring! Will bit back.

"Whatever is in there is mine now," said Linus Ethelgren, with a tone of finality.

"Some items were purely sentimental," he added. "I don't want anything of value. Plus, you have no idea what was stored in there. I could help."

"I could just empty the entire thing. Or better still, with a little time I'll sift the details from his memory," said Ethelgren.

"Sir, please show some mercy."

The mad wizard paused. "What is it you want exactly?"

"He kept a journal within. It was a gift from his grandfather. In the back there was a handwritten note from his wife."

"A spellbook?"

"Just odd spells," explained Will. "It was his grandfather's first spell journal. Nothing you would covet, but of great value to the family."

"Hmm. I'll be the judge of that," said Ethelgren, his eyes glinting greedily. "If I see nothing of value, you may have it. Describe the journal to me; it will help me find the memory so I can summon it."

Will described the journal carefully, and after a moment the mad wizard nodded. Raising one hand, he activated the limnthal. *Now's my chance to warn him,* thought Will. "Sir, since you've taken control of Will's body, is there a chance you'll let me have some of the potions or other minor possessions he kept stored within the limnthal?" *Hopefully Arrogan was paying attention.*

Who? asked Laina, but before she could reply, Ethelgren stiffened. His eyes rolled back into his head, and he started to fall.

Catch him! urged Will, since Laina had already taken control of their body.

She leapt forward and rammed her elbow into Ethelgren's jaw, then stomped on his belly when he struck the ground.

That's my body, you remember! Will shouted mentally. *He's already unconscious.*

Just making sure, said Laina dryly. Her statement seemed prescient as Ethelgren's eyes popped open and the man started to move. She sent a kick at his head.

The wizard slipped away slightly, caught her ankle in one hand, and then surged to his knees, throwing her off balance. Laina toppled backwards.

Chapter 43

At the same time Darla had apparently been freed from the spell holding her, for she charged forward. The Arkeshi stopped suddenly when a source-link caught her at the last second, and the wizard paralyzed her body.

Ethelgren stood, rising to loom over Laina, a look of anger and disdain on his features. "Are you fucking stupid, girl? First you warn me, then you try to take my goddamn head off!"

Laina was still confused, but Will recognized the shift in tone and vocabulary. "Arrogan?"

Chapter 44

"Who the fuck else would it be? Moron!"

It was beyond strange watching his own face swear at him while doing such an absolutely perfect imitation of Arrogan's mannerisms. Will leapt to his feet and threw his arms around the old man who now controlled his body.

Or tried to. He found himself stumbling as Arrogan stopped him by putting one hand on his face and holding him at arm's length. "Lass, get control of yourself! I'm far too old for that sort of thing."

"I'm not a lass!" yelled Will.

"You fucking well look like one."

"I'm not. Let me explain," began Will.

"What's that then?" asked Arrogan, pointing at Laina's torso. "Looks very much like a tit hanging out of your dress to my eyes. Have things changed that much since I died?"

Internally, Laina grew embarrassed, and she quickly took control to fix her wardrobe malfunction. Meanwhile Will continued to talk. "It's me! Will! Your grandson."

Arrogan squinted at him carefully. "Hmm." After a second, he made up his mind. "Nope, you're nowhere near ugly enough to be him. Fetch me a mirror. I'll show you what he's supposed to look like."

Will rolled his eyes in exasperation. "Listen. You're in Will's body, and I already know you're Arrogan. Where do you think Will is right now?"

"Right here," said the old man, tapping his chest. "That asshole Ethelgren trapped him in his own body and may yet again. We need to go somewhere quiet so I can coax him out and prepare him for what he needs to do."

"I already got out," explained Will. "Laina is loaning me the use of her body temporarily."

That set Arrogan back on his heels. "You projected yourself, again?"

Will nodded.

"And now…" The old man pointed at Laina's torso again. "You're both in there?"

This time, Laina answered. "Hello, nice to meet you. This is Laina."

Arrogan stared at them for a moment, his face pensive. After a moment he asked, "The half-sister, right, one of Nerrow's spawn?"

Laina was livid. "Listen, you old bastard! You'd still be trapped in there if I hadn't decided to help your stupid grandson!"

Arrogan held his hands up. "Whoa, hold on to your temper, girl! The worm-ridden apple doesn't fall far from the rotten tree does it? You must take after your father."

Don't let him get to you, Will cautioned her as Laina's rage began to spiral out of control. *He's like this with everyone. He absolutely loves to piss people off. Don't give him the pleasure.*

She held her tongue, and after a moment Arrogan continued, "Both of you in there, that's insane. Do you have any idea how incredibly dangerous that is?"

"I had already lost control of my body," said Will. "Given the situation, doesn't it make sense to take some risks?"

He watched as his face nodded back at him. "Sure, for you. What about the girl? Did it ever occur to you that there might be permanent repercussions?"

Will and Laina both froze as they felt a faint shiver of anxiety. "Repercussions?"

"Death is the most common. There was a wizard once who used to experiment with what you've done. He wanted to create a hybrid soul that would enable him to do two things at once. Naturally he experimented with others before risking himself. Most of his initial subjects died, but those that didn't went irretrievably insane, usually within minutes of the fusion."

Will felt Laina's mouth go dry.

"He figured the problem was that his subjects were strangers. So he moved on to testing it with married couples, which turned out to be a disaster. The survival rate was better, but the insanity rate was worse. Eventually he gave up on the whole idea, but only after someone managed to murder him in retribution for the people he had tortured."

"Oh," said Will.

"So then an enterprising do-gooder tried to do the surviving but insane subjects a favor by separating them. Of course, he only had one body, so he essentially split the soul and let one die. But his solution didn't help either; the soul that remained usually became violent, or suicidal."

"Are you saying I've killed her?" asked Will.

His grandfather shrugged. "Not at all. The fact that you're both alive and still relatively sane suggests that you must have been remarkably compatible, but that's just a guess. I have absolutely no way of knowing. It might also be because of the fact that your fusion was a mutually voluntary process. You didn't have anyone from the outside forcing you into it."

We are not compatible, not by any stretch of the imagination, remarked Laina. *So just forget he even suggested that.*

Will chuckled to himself. Laina's thoughts and her emotions were completely at odds. "So what should we do?"

Chapter 44

"Fix it," said Arrogan. "And the sooner the better. The longer you two remain in there, mixing and sloshing about, the more likely you'll start to meld into one inseparable whole."

Laina was horrified. "Can we do that here? I'm ready when you are."

"We need a safer place," said the old man. He held out one hand, and a spell construct swirled into existence, a complex meld of two elemental turyn types, earth and air. When he released it, a disk formed from the cobblestones beneath his feet and then rose into the air, lifting him up. Reaching out, he offered Laina a hand as she scrambled aboard. Darla deftly leapt up, landing perfectly. "Hold onto me," said Arrogan. "My feet are anchored by the spell, but yours aren't."

Darla took one arm while Laina grabbed the other. The disk lurched into motion with sudden speed, and her grip tightened.

"Which way?" asked Arrogan as they glided forward.

"North," said Laina. "Follow that street there. We should be safe in the Alchemy building. Will's friend is there."

Arrogan smiled, and the disk sped up. The ground was rushing by just a foot beneath them, and he seemed to be enjoying the wind as it roared around their faces. Yelling, he asked an academic question, "Do you know why I chose an elemental spell for our transport?"

Internally, Laina frowned. She wasn't familiar with Will's previous conversations with his teacher. Will came to the fore. "What other kind of spell could you have used?"

"There's a force-disk spell that works in a similar fashion. It's easier to use and far more efficient in the amount of turyn it requires," answered Arrogan.

Will understood. "You don't want to limit your options if we're attacked."

Arrogan nodded.

What does that mean? asked Laina.

You can only use one force-effect spell at a time. If he had a force-disk active, he couldn't use the point-defense spell or a force-lance. But this is an elemental spell, so those are still available to him if we get attacked, explained Will.

Oh. I didn't know that, said Laina, filing the information away.

Dulaney taught that in Spell Theory, Will reminded her.

Since we never learned anything about battle magics, I probably forgot, she admitted. *It would seem rather pointless without that context.*

He couldn't argue with that logic.

A few minutes later and they were already past the school gates, leaving a contingent of guards gaping in their wake. Will figured he would have some explaining to do later, since several of them had almost certainly recognized him, or rather his body, as Arrogan sent them hurtling along. They reached the Alchemy building in record time and the disk slowly descended to the ground. When the spell was dismissed, it fell apart, leaving an ugly pile of crumbling stones and mortar on the walk. Will hoped no one noticed who had made the mess.

Back inside, they breezed past Lawrence with a quick series of hellos, and then they were up the stairs, heading for Will's rented laboratory. Despite his anxiety, Will was relieved to see that Tiny was still there, safe and sound, sleeping on the floor.

"Holy Mother! Look at the size of him," exclaimed Arrogan on seeing the slumbering squire. "This is your friend, Tiny?"

Chapter 44

Laina nodded.

"The name is a little misleading, don't you think? What do they feed him? A few more soldiers like him in the army and the kingdom will be bankrupt."

Will felt himself beginning to prickle like a hedgehog. He wasn't fond of people making fun of Tiny's size. "Mind your tongue when I wake him," he warned.

"Why? Is he violently disposed?"

He glared at his mentor. "No. He's one of the kindest, most intelligent, thoughtful, and genuinely sincere people I have ever known. I won't have you insulting him."

"Wow. So he's your complete opposite. Perhaps you two should consider making your relationship more public! I'm sure Selene would love that."

Will and Laina growled synchronously.

Arrogan ignored them, but a thoughtful look came over his face. "I'm not going to get to see Selene, am I?" He dipped his head at Laina. "It was nice seeing your face, Miss Nerrow, and Tiny's too. I hear about everyone through Will, and sometimes I get to hear conversations directly, but I haven't had any faces to associate with the names."

The sudden change in tone caught both Will and Laina off-guard, and Will felt a sudden surge of sadness as his eyes grew misty.

Arrogan winked. "Don't go soft on me now, asshole. Let's wake him up." He turned away and began shaking Tiny's shoulder.

Tiny woke with a start, scrambling back against the wall as his eyes took in the scene, and he tried to figure out what had happened. From his perspective, they had been just beginning to fight a moment ago. His eyes locked onto Laina's dress, noting the dirt and damage. Then he glared at Arrogan. "What did you do?"

Will spoke first. "Tiny, it's me! That's Arrogan in my body currently."

Tiny stared at him, then Arrogan, then he closed his eyes. "How long have I been asleep?"

"An hour, maybe two?" offered Will.

"When you say, 'it's me,' you put a certain emphasis on it. Should I infer that you mean you're someone other than Miss Nerrow?"

Arrogan began to chuckle while Will and Laina struggled to explain the bizarre twist of fate that had led to their current situation. Tiny remained calm throughout, asking pertinent questions now and again to help him understand. Will couldn't help but admire the big man's aplomb. He doubted he would have been so rational if the situation were reversed.

"So what do we do?" asked Tiny at last.

Arrogan took over from there. "First, Will must remove himself from Laina and return to his proper flesh. Once that's done, I'll talk him through the process of resuming control of his body."

"Is it that difficult?" asked Laina.

Arrogan nodded. "Ethelgren is still in here, locked away in the same fashion he had Will trapped. When I return to my own place, he will be freed, and they'll have to start their battle for supremacy over again."

Will was dubious about his prospects, but Laina was thoroughly dismayed. "He already lost once! You think he can win this time?"

Thanks for the vote of confidence, observed Will.

Hush, I'm worried about you, she snapped without a trace of shame. A phrase like that would have deeply embarrassed her just two hours before.

"How do I extract myself?" asked Will.

"How did you get out of your first bodily prison?" asked Arrogan in return.

Chapter 44

"I don't like being trapped without being able to see or hear," said Will.

Arrogan smiled. "Easy enough." A source-link snapped out, and he paralyzed Laina's body. A split second later he severed them from her senses as well. Will and Laina were trapped in a seemingly endless void.

Will had experienced it before, but Laina didn't take it very well. A surge of panic shot through her, rocking Will as well. He struggled to contain her emotions, which only made matters worse. For the first time since his arrival, the two of them began to struggle against each other in earnest.

It went on for a short time, and Will finally realized that the struggle was necessary if they were to separate. It was painful, and yet it was the only way to tear themselves apart from each other. His own fear began to rise as they continued to fail, and then it was over. With a familiar popping sensation, he was out.

Arrogan spotted him floating in the air above them and promptly released Laina from the source-link, restoring her movement and senses. She opened her eyes and looked around, her expression vacant and empty. As the seconds passed, her features changed, going from numb to forlorn. Clutching her hands to her chest, Laina curled into a tight ball, hiding her face from view.

Will was also in pain, though probably only Arrogan could see it. It felt as though he had lost something vital, something important, something he couldn't live without. For a while he had been *more,* and now Will felt alone—more alone than he had ever realized. The intensity of his solitude was crushing. For a moment his only desire was to go back, and it took all his willpower to resist the urge.

Arrogan was watching him carefully with a steady gaze. After a moment, the old man spoke. "Come on." He snapped his fingers and opened his arms.

Will focused on his own face and felt himself rushing forward. A split second later, he felt himself once again encased in flesh, and he sensed the warmth of Arrogan's presence. Desperate to end his loneliness, Will tried to cling to the other spirit.

No, god damn it! That's what got you in this trouble to begin with! Arrogan admonished him. Seconds later, Will found himself driven into a dark place, locked and sealed, bereft of his senses, as he had been before he escaped.

His only contact with his body, or the outside world, was the old man's voice, echoing through the void. *Get ahold of yourself. I have to return to the ring before you can have your body back, but when I go Ethelgren will return with a vengeance.*

Where is he now? asked Will, struggling to regain his composure.

Locked away, just as you are. The moment I leave, the two of you will be on your own. You have to be ready.

Do you really think I can win?

Listen, boy, I know you better than you think, and I've already tested that fool personally. You're stronger and more stubborn. Back when I was still alive you were already getting to be a problem when I needed to restrain you. This is your body. You have the advantage here. You won't lose to some half-baked enchanter.

Enchanter?

Someone who relies too much on creating magic items, rather than improving their innate skills, explained Arrogan. *From what I know of the man, he fits the stereotype.*

You didn't see the spells he was casting, countered Will. *They were unbelievable.*

Almost all of them were built into the rod, said Arrogan. *I doubt he could cast them at will on his own.*

Chapter 44

Will still felt unsure.

You took his spell away from him. You. You're hardly more than an apprentice. He was a wizard for hundreds of years before he was murdered. If that isn't a clue regarding how much he actually practiced, I don't know what is. You can do this, just don't let your confidence waver.

That made him feel better, but something else occurred to him then. Arrogan had referred to a memory of teaching him, giving lie to his previous statements that he couldn't remember the most recent years before his death. Not only that, but the old man had managed to take control of his body, even though it was being vigorously defended by another wizard.

Will hadn't even suspected that that was possible, and it cast serious doubt on the foundation of their relationship. *Thanks,* he responded. *After this is over, assuming I win, we need to talk about some things.*

Arrogan's response was delayed, but eventually he replied, *Yeah. You're right. We do.*

Chapter 45

Tiny stood behind the body of his best friend. He had rejected the idea of using a club and instead merely had his hand held in a fist. It was his job to knock Will out if he lost his battle with Ethelgren.

"Neither of them can see or hear at the moment, so they don't know you're back there," Arrogan reassured them. Then he locked eyes with Laina, who stood in front of him. "You know your part, right?"

She nodded. Laina still wasn't fully recovered from the trauma of separation, but there was a sense of tenacity about her. "If it isn't him, I knee him in the groin," she repeated.

"That's right," said Arrogan. "Just don't overdo it. If you rupture a testicle, he'll wind up having to use a regeneration potion, and those things are too valuable to waste."

"Maybe I should do it," suggested Darla. "I have extensive experience."

Will's face took on a thoughtful expression, then Arrogan replied with a chuckle, "Nah, you might kill him. Besides, if it's Laina there might be some therapeutic value."

"What does that mean?" asked Tiny.

Laina nodded immediately, determination and earnestness showing in her eyes. "That makes sense."

"All right, here goes," Arrogan said. Internally, he warned Will to hopefully give him an advantage, and then he retreated back into the ring.

Will's world burst into a cacophony of light and sound as his senses flood back, but he tried to ignore the sudden overload while he clamped down on his source and his body. Half a second later, he felt Ethelgren's presence. The old wizard had been surprised by the sudden change and he was scrabbling to do the same, but this time it was him trying to play catch up.

It was still a tough fight. The old wizard's will was as tough as nails and more tenacious than boiled shoe leather. Despite what Arrogan had said, Ethelgren had still been a practitioner for hundreds of years, and the strength of his will was nothing to sneer at.

His body tensed and seemed to vibrate under the strain of the intense struggle taking place within, but eventually Will felt Ethelgren's struggle begin to slacken. That raised his own morale, and his victory began to pick up speed as he pushed the ancient wizard back, corralling him into the rod from which he had originally emerged.

A minute later and it was over. With a thought, Will stored the relic in the limnthal, and he felt relief that he could finally relax. He opened his eyes and realized that his body had been so tense that he wasn't breathing. With an explosive rush, he opened his mouth and let the air out so he could take a deep breath. "Pfhaahhh!"

Laina's nose was just below his own, her eyes studying him watchfully, and as he exhaled, it startled her. Pain exploded through Will's groin and up his spine. With a faint scream, he folded over and collapsed sideways. From the ground, he saw Tiny hovering over him, fist raised, ready to pound him into oblivion. "It's me, Tiny!" he managed to squeak.

Tiny looked at Laina, who shrugged. "I can't tell. Maybe you should hit him anyway."

Still in agony, Will's brain struggled to think of something, anything, that might save him. In the end only one word came to him. "Janice!"

Tiny froze, then after a moment he nodded and straightened up. "I think it's him. It wouldn't have occurred to the other one to mention her, not without some time to think about it anyway."

Laina wasn't convinced. "Prove yourself," she demanded.

Will stared at her for a moment, then he glanced at her bodyguard. "Darla. That's something I didn't know before we shared a body."

She had been standing with her foot partly drawn back, ready to kick him while he was down. Laina relaxed and resumed a normal stance, a faint look of disappointment on her face. She stepped back, then frowned. "Mention that again and I'll make you regret it."

The pain was beginning to subside a little, and Will managed to sit up. He gave his sister a serious look. "You know me better than that." Their eyes connected, and neither blinked for several seconds as the enormity of their shared experience threatened to overwhelm them once more.

Laina turned away as her eyes began to glimmer with excess moisture. "I still don't like you," she said unconvincingly.

He nodded. "Yeah, I know. You don't have to say it."

Tiny looked at Darla with a puzzled expression. The Arkeshi returned his look, then shrugged, equally confused. When they looked back, they saw Laina was watching Will with a faint look of concern. Finally, she asked, "Are your testes all right?"

The big warrior couldn't help but snort, and Darla turned around, covering her mouth.

"No thanks to you," Will groaned.

Darla caught Tiny's eye once more, and he saw something flicker across her normally deadpan face.

Chapter 45

Suddenly an air of faint worry came over her, and she put a hand on Laina's shoulder. "You were too enthusiastic. We should probably check." Laina's face paled, and she seemed to wilt, but Darla was ready for that. "Do not worry. I have some experience with wounds." Then she looked up at Tiny. "Help me remove his trousers."

Tiny was more than ready to play along. "Of course. Let's get him up on the worktable." Reaching down, he put his hands beneath Will's arms and made as though he would lift him up.

Will's eyes were round, and his face had gone red. "No thank you! I'm fine now."

Darla shook her head. "You don't look well. Let me see." She reached out as if she might undo the laces of his trousers.

Will began scrambling back, kicking the Arkeshi away as he backed into the corner of the room. "I said, 'no thank you!' I can check them myself—later—when none of you are looking at me!"

Darla broke character first as a strange, raspy, laugh began to emerge from her. Tiny soon followed, laughing deeply, and then Laina joined them, realizing she had been had. Will declined to join them. He was still fighting diffuse pains and a feeling of nausea.

He probably would have joined them in their laughter, eventually, but Lawrence appeared at the door to the laboratory. "Will, are you in there?"

"Unfortunately," he answered.

"There are soldiers downstairs. They want you to come with them. It's a summons from the king. They're asking for Miss Nerrow as well."

"Fucking hell," swore Will. He started to get up and gratefully accepted a hand from Tiny. Standing perfectly straight still wasn't comfortable, but he tried not to visibly hunch as he opened the door. Someone took his other arm, helping him to stand straight, and he was surprised to see it was Laina beside him.

By mutual consent neither of them made eye contact. It was still too soon.

Downstairs in the lobby, Will found a Royal Guard captain along with eight of the Driven. Standing just outside was a large group of additional soldiers, at least four squads worth. *Damn.* He might still choose to fight, but the odds weren't good. "What do you want?" he demanded, affecting an air of annoyance.

The guard captain bowed deeply. "Captain Geoff Harris at your service, sir. The king has sent me to request your presence, as well as the attendance of Miss Nerrow, daughter of Baron Nerrow."

The respectful attitude caught him completely off-guard. Realizing his confusion, Laina leaned over to his ear. "While you were *out,* we discovered that the king ordered his men not to interfere and to provide assistance if needed."

He glanced at her, then quickly returned his eyes to the captain. The old saying about eyes being the window to the soul seemed truer than ever. Meeting Laina's gaze might tear the wound in his spirit wide open all over again. "Did you need so many men to make your request, Captain?"

"The streets are not safe, sir. They are merely for your protection."

Unable to find fault with that, Will gestured to the others and started forward, but the captain spoke once more. "The invitation is only for you and Miss Nerrow, sir. No one else is allowed in His Majesty's presence."

Laina's hand tightened around his upper arm. Will lifted his chin. "I won't be separated from them."

Chapter 45

"They can still accompany you, sir," explained the soldier. "But they'll have to wait outside the receiving room."

Will relaxed. "Oh, of course."

The four of them were loaded into a plain but well-built black carriage, while soldiers marched in front and behind them. Strictly speaking, it wasn't necessary, as the palace was practically next door to Wurthaven. Will could have walked there on foot in ten or fifteen minutes, and in much less time if he were running. He didn't mind the carriage, though; it seemed appropriate, especially since Laina was with him.

As soon as he realized what he was thinking, he laughed at himself. *Maybe I am turning into a nobleman. When would I have ever worried about a 'lady' needing to ride rather than walk in the past?*

They arrived at the palace without trouble, though he paid close attention to their surroundings through the small window on his side. The palace gates had to be opened for them to enter, which was in itself unusual. Ordinarily the gates remained open with only a small guard. The palace had been locked tight. Will could see guards, sorcerers, and military men in every direction. The palace yard was full of busy men.

The carriage stopped at the main palace entrance, and they were shown into the front hall with all the respect and courtesy that any landed lord might expect. *I suppose Laina counts,* thought Will, *even though she doesn't actually have a title of her own yet.* Of course, as the princess' husband he *should* have been granted a title or two, even if he was lowborn, but Will hadn't exactly married the king's daughter under the most amiable of circumstances.

He'd openly defied the king on several occasions, as well as refusing to accept either an elemental or a grant of land and title. It wasn't so much that he was averse to moving up in society; rather, he knew such a ceremony would involve swearing fealty to the king. To make matters worse, he'd openly told the king as much.

The public might not know it, but as royal sons-in-law went, he probably rated slightly lower than the city rat catcher in King Lognion's estimation, which suited him just fine. In Will's own appraisal the king was only slightly less repugnant than a demon-lord.

And he'd met one, so he figured his opinion counted for something.

A footman approached, bowed respectfully, then gestured with his arm. "If your friends would follow me, I will make sure they are kept comfortable while you are attending His Majesty."

Tiny glanced at Will, who nodded. The big man and Darla went along without trouble, while a second footman led Laina and Will down a smaller side hall. She draped her hand over Will's arm, but he leaned over and brought his ear closer when he felt a slight tug. "Have you ever been summoned like this before?" she asked.

He nodded quietly. In fact, he hadn't, but in the more general sense, he'd been in similar situations with the king. Once when he had been released from the royal dungeon, once after saving Selene from a hungry demon, and then once when he had invited himself in to steal the princess away. On almost every occasion he had been subjected to violence at some point. *Except when I took Selene,* he noted.

"How did it turn out?" Her voice was smooth, but given her last encounter with their monarch he knew she was nervous.

He wanted to reassure her, but after their recent spiritual exploration of one another, he knew that kind words would only make it worse for her. She wouldn't believe them. "Usually I try to be polite but eventually

Chapter 45

I offend him anyway. Most of the time I wind up with a black eye or a few bruises, but nothing more."

"That was before he nearly whipped you to death, wasn't it?"

He winced. "And before I eloped with his daughter." Another thought came to him then. His last encounter had gone badly specifically because of Laina's presence. He'd taken the whipping because Lognion had threatened his sister. *Did he insist on her presence so he could use her as leverage against me?* Will's stomach twisted at the thought.

Laina's hand moved down his wrist and she clasped his hand briefly. "Don't worry. I won't let him hurt you again," she told him.

She's more worried about me? He didn't think there was much she could do one way or another, but the thought made his chest hurt as he realized they were each worried more about the other. Like family.

The footman opened one of a pair of large double doors, then gestured for them to enter.

The room was relatively small, less than thirty feet in length on the longest side. A collection of cushioned chairs and benches were scattered artfully around the space, with side tables positioned helpfully, so that those who were seated would have places to rest their drinks or other refreshments. It was, in short, a salon, an excellent place for a small gathering to eat and converse informally.

King Lognion stood at the other end, watching them. As they entered, the door closed behind them, and Laina automatically started to curtsey, but Will caught her arm and prevented her from observing the customary formality. She tugged at him for a moment and shot him a warning glare, but he refused to let her lower herself. "Not with me," he growled in a quiet voice.

Lognion chuckled and walked forward, his posture relaxed and unworried. "Trying to teach your bad habits to others, William?"

He glared daggers at his father-in-law. "I was just explaining to Miss Nerrow that this is a *family* gathering, so there would be no need for such obeisance."

"Family?" said the king in a querulous tone. "Oh! You meant *me*! I wasn't sure for a moment."

It was a veiled threat, that the king might reveal Will's secret relation, but Laina, despite her nervousness, wasn't having it. "Surely you didn't forget that my brother is married to your daughter, Your Majesty?"

Lognion blinked, his eyes studying her for a second, then turned to Will, who merely smiled. *That caught him off-guard.*

But Lognion wasn't one to linger, especially not on a point that had taken him unaware. Instead he pivoted to the matter at hand. "Tell me about what happened in the city a few hours ago. A vast portion of my capital has been destroyed, and I'm getting interesting reports regarding who was responsible for the damage."

They had stopped Ethelgren's spell before the mad wizard had made much more than a five- degree turn, but that still meant that roughly one or two percent of the city had been destroyed, assuming the swath of destruction had gone all the way to the outer wall. A few percent might not sound like much, but Cerria was a densely packed city of several hundred thousand people. The number of buildings, homes, businesses, and most importantly of all, the people who had been annihilated in that small arc was hard to conceive.

And the man who had done it had been wearing Will's face. Not only that, but Ethelgren had taken command of the Driven and soldiers in the area just before his act of

Chapter 45

wholesale slaughter. Presumably they had all died when the first portion of his ritual spell had taken place, but if any had survived—their fingers would be pointing directly at Will.

But Laina had been present as well. If any of the blame were to spill over onto her…

"It was me," stated Will.

"Will had nothing to do with it," said Laina simultaneously.

The king smirked. "This is more interesting than I had anticipated. William, come here please."

Will stepped forward, keeping his face clear. He could see the king already making a fist and he knew what was likely to come. The knowledge made it hard to remain still, and his eyes closed as he saw Lognion's shoulder begin to move. He felt the air in front of his face move and something brushed against his chin, but no blow came. When he opened his eyes again, he saw Laina standing in front of him. Only one word emerged from her lips, "No."

The king was studying her thoughtfully. "You've gotten much more protective of your brother, Miss Nerrow. I can only wonder what brought on such a transformation." He made as though to swing at her, then began laughing as he saw the look in Will's eyes. "Not to worry, William. If I plan on beating your sister, I'll do it when you aren't present. I'd rather not break my hand on one of those annoying shields.

"Back to business. You lied to me, William, while Miss Nerrow was kind enough to tell the truth. Do explain."

"I stole Ethelgren's Exhortation from Wurthaven, but when I attempted to use it my body was possessed by the spirit of Linus Ethelgren. He was intent on destroying the vampires, but his best solution was to destroy the entire city. Laina stopped him," he answered.

The king looked at Laina. "That's a truly outlandish story, but William seems to actually believe what he's saying. What do you think, Miss Nerrow? Was that true?"

"No, Your Majesty."

He frowned. "Now you both claim truth and my instincts agree. What part of William's story do you disagree with, Miss Nerrow?"

"It wasn't me who stopped Ethelgren," she replied. "I helped, but it was mainly Will himself. He was in my body at the time and we worked together."

The king glanced at Will, then nodded. "He believes you as well. Very interesting. Describe the scene to me, Miss Nerrow, leaving out nothing."

Laina detailed her experiences and gave as accurate an account as she could manage. Some parts were necessarily confusing, and when she was done Will was required to do the same. The entire telling took almost half an hour, and Lognion rarely interrupted, doing so only to clarify details he was unclear on. When they had finished, he smiled broadly. "It seems I am in the presence of not one, but two heroes. Unfortunately, there were other witnesses as well, and their accounts, while similar in form, don't contain the subtleties of whose spirit was in whose body at different times.

"Of course, in either tale, you present an inspiring figure, Miss Nerrow, and given your reputation as a public figure you're a natural to take on the mantle of Terabinia's savior." Lognion paused, then stared sadly at Will. "In your case, William, I'm afraid that both your prior activities and what was reported this evening make you an excellent fit for the villain of our little play."

"No." Laina's negative wasn't a plea or a denial so much as a statement of fact.

The king arched one brow. "You have a different idea, Miss Nerrow?"

Chapter 45

"I'll tell the truth," she responded boldly. "Try to spin whatever tale you want, but if you expect your heroine to cooperate, it won't involve making a scapegoat of William."

"You'll do anything I ask of you, Miss Nerrow. Hasn't William explained that to you yet?" His eyes flashed and he barked a command, "Kneel!"

Laina's knees buckled, and she was genuflecting before she even realized what her body was doing. Will moved to stand in front of her. "Stop it."

"I'm merely giving her a lesson, William. Not to worry, I won't harm her. This time."

Will glanced back and was pained by the expression of terror and confusion on Laina's face. Her body had utterly betrayed her, and worse, she had no idea why. He had never told her about the truth of the graduation seal. In all honesty, he'd never really thought about the matter except as it pertained to Selene, but now he realized to his chagrin that the king's leverage over him was much greater than he'd been willing to admit. *Selene, Laina, Mark, Agnes, possibly even Tabitha.* He didn't think Tabitha had been to Wurthaven, but he wasn't sure. Selene had started at an early age, so it was possible.

"Stand up again, Miss Nerrow. Do you have a knife on you? Please show it to me."

"Yes, Your Majesty," she answered, removing a small dagger from an ornamental sheath at her waist. Her eyes were bulging as she watched her hand moving, seemingly of its own accord.

"Do you want a war right here in your palace?" growled Will. "Push this any further and that's what you'll have!"

"It's just a demonstration, William. Please relax. I would never hurt the daughter of one of my most loyal vassals." Lifting one hand, he snapped his fingers, and the door at the opposite end of the room opened. "You may enter now," said the king.

Three of the Driven stepped in and moved to stand off to one side.

Lognion pointed to the man on the right, then gestured at Will. "This is the man you saw?"

"Yes, Your Majesty," answered the sorcerer.

"And do you know his name?"

"William Cartwright, the husband of Princess Selene, Your Majesty."

Lognion nodded, then asked the others. "Do you agree with his account?"

They both nodded and answered, "Yes, Your Majesty."

"So all three of you agree that my son-in-law was on the verge of destroying most of the city, along with its citizens?"

The three men hesitated, then affirmed the statement.

The king frowned. "That's a terrible shame. It seems that if my son-in-law is to retain his reputation the three of you will have to be silenced."

"Order us to silence, Your Majesty. We would never betray your trust!" cried one of the sorcerers, suddenly fearful.

"Kneel and stare at the ceiling so I can see your necks clearly," ordered the king. "Make no other movement." Then a delicious smile crept across his face as he turned to Laina. "Miss Nerrow, please cut their throats so that they don't betray your brother to the public."

Horrified, she began to walk rapidly toward them, knife in hand.

"No!" shouted Will. He moved to interpose himself while Laina tried to dodge around him.

Lognion's voice cut across the confusion with chilling clarity. "William, if you touch your sister, I will kill *her* instead."

Chapter 45

Will froze and Laina darted past, tears already running from her eyes. As she approached the first victim, the king gave yet another order. "Slowly, Miss Nerrow. I want you to watch their expressions while they die."

Unable to stand it any longer, Will blocked Laina's knife hand with a point-defense shield as she slashed at the first man's throat, and then, when she drew her arm back to try again, he blew a hole through the soldier's chest with a force-lance. Without pausing to think, he repeated the act, killing all three men in less than a second. Disgusted by his own action, he yelled at the king, "There! Are you satisfied?"

Lognion began to laugh. Not some small chuckle, but a deep, hearty, bellowing boom that came from the diaphragm. From anyone else, at any other time, it might have been a comforting sound, but from the king it was disturbing in the extreme. Laina turned back to face them, dropping her knife on the rug. Will could see blood droplets on her face, neck, and chest, a perfect complement to the look of horror in her eyes.

Glaring at the king, Will began to form a spell in one hand, but the insane monarch seemed utterly without concern. When the spell was finished, he released it, targeting his sister. She struggled against the magic for a moment, but he said softly, "Relax, Laina. Trust me."

Her eyes met his for a moment, and then her lids drooped as she stopped fighting the sleep spell. A second later she was asleep and Will carried her to a nearby divan. Ignoring the king, he formed another construct, Selene's signature spell, and used it to clean away the dirt, blood, and grime that coated himself and Laina. "We need to talk," he informed the king, his tone dark.

"That is why I summoned you, after all."

"A serious talk. No more games."

Lognion rubbed his chin. "Something tells me that you aren't planning to tell me where my wayward daughter has gone."

"Is her absence such an inconvenience for you?"

"More than you realize. Explaining her absence is becoming more difficult by the day and her body double isn't good enough to rely on for social events, is she?"

Will tried to imagine Tailtiu at a dinner party and his mind refused to attempt it. He shook his head. "The reason Selene can't return is you. You realize that, don't you?"

"Does my control bother you so much? It isn't as though I would ever exercise it. The day of the wedding was a stressful and understandable occasion. Can you blame me for that?"

He stared at the man, trying to discern the sick humor behind the man's statement, but it simply wasn't there. *He honestly believes himself. He doesn't have a trace of real humanity, does he?* "You have no moral boundaries. Whatever your motivations, I could never trust you."

Lognion walked over to look down at Laina as she slept. His gaze traveled slowly from her head, down her neck, torso, waist, and ended finally at her ankles. Then he smiled at Will, his eyes flashing. "But I have plenty of reason to trust you, William. We still have common ground to forge an agreement over."

Chapter 46

He couldn't stand seeing the king's eyes on Laina, so Will moved to interpose himself once again, prompting a new laugh from Lognion. "We saved your city for you. I think you owe us a debt already."

"I never asked you to save it, William. In fact, I find myself in agreement with Linus Ethelgren. A complete purge is the only way to be sure of eliminating the vampiric scourge and ensuring that Terabinia is safe. I am still glad you stopped him, since I might have been killed as well, but I do see the sense in his logic. Nevertheless, I accept no debts with regards to unasked for actions on your part."

"You're as mad as Ethelgren then."

Lognion's lips compressed into a line. "I prefer to say that I am different. I am under no illusion about what humanity considers normal, but I was born this way." His eyes looked heavenward for a moment. "I am merely as the Mother made me. Some may doubt that, but I am confident that if it weren't for me and my peculiar differences, Terabinia would not have survived until the present."

"You aren't really human, are you?"

The king grinned. "Unfortunately, I am, though I have long lamented that fact. Cut me and I will bleed red, the same as you do. No, by some strange quirk of fate I was born without the same emotions that most of humanity are afflicted with. I feel very little, except in extreme moments, which is why I enjoy tormenting you, William. But I don't let such pale pleasures control me.

"Instead, I use my gift to rule this nation with wisdom and reason. If destroying my own capital is the only way to save the people of Terabinia, I will do so, without tears or regret. In fact, I was already moving in that direction, for I feel this city is already lost," explained the king.

Will's eyes widened. "You can't be serious!"

"But I am. Under the guise of trying to bring the chaos in the streets under control, I have already begun positioning the Driven along the city wall. Tomorrow, while the vampires are driven back into their holes, I will instruct my sorcerers to empower a wide-scale ritual to reduce the entire city to ash, even unto its foundations and sewers."

Will stared at the floor, trying to think of a way to dissuade the mad king. It was obvious that an appeal to mercy wouldn't work. Only one thing came to him. "If Cerria is destroyed, it will greatly weaken Terabinia. At the moment we have the advantage over Darrow, but they will be emboldened once more if the capital is lost."

Lognion nodded. "Do not think I haven't considered that. In fact, I have good cause to think that this undead disaster is the result of their desperation to turn the tables. I am almost tempted to capture a few of these monsters and return the favor."

"You couldn't possibly—"

"Rest easy, William. Did I not just tell you that I am not afflicted with the frailty of emotion? Even revenge fails to motivate me to abandon reason. I am quite aware that the uncontrolled spread of these bloodthirsty creatures would spell doom for every nation. That is why I am forced to the desperate measure of razing my own capital. If there were any other option, I would take it."

"Let me do it," said Will suddenly, his mouth moving before his brain could catch up.

Chapter 46

"You have a solution?"

No. What the hell am I thinking? He stared at the king for several seconds as his mouth worked open and closed. Eventually he found his voice again. "Give me an extra day."

"To do what?"

"Rituals can do more than destroy. I'll find one that can cleanse the city without wiping out the populace or destroying their homes."

The king's eyes narrowed. "I can see you aren't lying, but though you've performed several miraculous feats in the past I have trouble envisioning you doing something that would require that level of expertise."

"I have help. Remember the signatory witnesses of my marriage?"

Lognion was quick as always. "Aislinn?"

Will nodded. *Or Arrogan, I'd rather not bring my demented grandmother into this.*

The sovereign of Terabinia rubbed his chin, lost in thought for a few seconds. "The fae do not provide help without payment," observed Lognion.

The statement reminded Will of his own situation and he had another idea. "Neither do I."

"Oh?"

"If you want me to do this, I'll need something in return."

"You imply that you will let the citizens of this city die? I hardly believe that." He paused, then his eyes lit up. "What do you want?"

Free Selene! he wanted to scream, but he held himself back for a moment and his eyes fell on Laina. He needed more than one person released from the king's enchantment. "Release them from the enchantment."

"Them?"

"My family, Selene, Laina, Mark Nerrow, Agnes, and Tabitha if she's been to Wurthaven."

"She hasn't," the king informed him. "Neither has Agnes, though I find it interesting that you choose to include her."

"Will you do it?"

Lognion laughed. "Of course not! You won't swear to me, lad. Why would I release the only leverage I have over such a wonderful and useful tool?" Then he leaned in. "Choose one."

"All or none."

"I don't need this bargain, fool. Even if I lose my city, I can still outwit those fools in Darrow. It will be a tragic setback, but I'll accept it rather than lose so many bargaining pieces. Choose *one*."

He wanted them all free, but narrowing the selection was relatively simple. Mark Nerrow was the simplest to give up, and while he was fond of Agnes, she didn't rate as highly as Selene or Laina. It was those last two that tore at him. His first instinct was to choose Selene, but after the past few hours the choice wasn't so simple. Either one would be a significant means for the king to control him, and he couldn't bear to see either tortured or hurt.

In the end it was pragmatism that made the choice for him. Selene was already safe, and even if she did return, she had already proven she couldn't be controlled. If her father gave her a command, she refused to obey she would die. Such a limitation made her less useful for the king's purpose.

"Laina," he said at last. "Free my sister."

Lognion's face lit up with undisguised mirth. "Oh, I didn't say I would give you what you asked for. I merely wanted to see who you would choose. It's always an

Chapter 46

instructive exercise, and I'm sure you learned a few things about yourself."

Crestfallen, Will glared at the man. "Have you nothing better to do than torment me?"

"Careful what you wish for, William. The day I no longer find you interesting enough to torment is the day you die." Reaching up to his chest, he concentrated for a moment, and Will briefly saw the flicker of hundreds or perhaps even thousands of heart-stone enchantments. Eventually the king picked one and held it out, displaying it for Will's inspection. "This is the control link for my daughter. Since her recent rebellion, she is of much less use to me. Take it."

"I don't want you to transfer it. Just release her," said Will sharply.

"Take it or I will kill her now," said Lognion.

Will held out his hand and Lognion passed the enchantment to him. Careful not to let his body destroy it, Will accepted the link and felt it stitch itself to his soul. As soon as the process was done, he reached out and examined it, looking for the correct point to begin unraveling it. He had freed many elementals in the past, so the process was familiar to him already.

"Before you make a mistake, William, let me give you some advice," said the king, his tone suddenly paternal. "Do you know how I developed my ability to discern truth from lies?"

Will met his gaze but said nothing.

"It was the heart-stone enchantment. Over the years I've held the lives of tens of—" His voice stumbled for a moment. "Of thousands of men and women in my hands. I was always gifted at discerning lies, but with the heart-stone enchantment I was able to know with absolute certainty every time someone tried to deceive me. Over time, that feedback allowed me to train my natural intuition to perfection. By watching someone's expressions, their body language, and even the turyn that flows around them, I know with absolute certainty whether they are lying."

"I'm never going to enslave people the way you have."

"I'm not suggesting you should, but think how useful it would be to have a wife whose loyalty you could be absolutely certain of, who could never betray you, who might obey orders that she was not even aware were orders?"

That made him angrier than it should have. "I've always trusted Selene," he declared, but inwardly he felt a sliver of doubt. The dream he had had—was it really a dream?

"Liar," said the king. "I can see your mistrust, and you are *right* to doubt her. No man or woman is completely trustworthy. People change over time. An honest oath, a sincere promise, they may be meant when they are given, but time will change the hearts of those who make promises. I'm offering you a refuge from such uncertainty. You can *know* she is yours. You can ensure that she *never* strays. The enchantment is subtler than you realize.

"I made a mistake the day you drove me to order her explicitly to do something she was absolutely against. Yes, I admit you were clever that day. It's one of the main reasons I decided to let you take her as your wife. But you don't have to be foolish. The heart-stone enchantment will reinforce her own desire to never stray, to never lie to you. Let me give you this gift."

Will felt the older man's words circling in his brain, and there was a certain logic to them. He didn't have to necessarily use the enchantment to control Selene, but he could use it to always know whether her words were true

Chapter 46

or not. Would that be so wrong? For a minute he was sorely tempted, more than he wanted to admit.

Before his heart could waver any further, he began plucking at the enchantment, carefully unravelling it. A few seconds later it dissolved, and he knew that Selene was finally free.

Lognion shook his head. "Such a shame. I had high hopes for you, William."

"Even if I only used it for truth telling, it would be a violation."

"You suggest that lies are somehow a good thing?"

He nodded. "Some are. Trust isn't about truth or lies. Humans need their social deceptions. We wear them like clothes, to hide ourselves from the judgment of others, or even ourselves. To strip her of that would be to rob her of her privacy, her individuality. It would be a betrayal of love."

"In your world perhaps," admitted the king. "Love has never existed in mine, so I have nothing to lose. Your argument is still lacking, though. Truth is the foundation of trust."

Will shook his head, feeling certain at last. "No, it isn't. Trust is a form of faith, faith in another human being. It isn't founded in a cold reliance on absolute truth, but simply on the belief that the one you trust has your best interest at heart. That they can be relied on, even when they lie, to be on your side. I won't sacrifice something so precious just for absolute truth."

"Suit yourself," said Lognion. "You have tomorrow to do what you will. If the infestation persists then I will proceed with my plans on the next morning." Turning away, the monarch left the room without even glancing at the dead bodies. Someone else would be along to deal with them.

Will felt lost for a moment, and as he looked at Laina he couldn't bear to wake her. The experience she had had was too fresh and he wanted her to be somewhere safe and pleasant when she opened her eyes. Anything to blunt the memory of the king's savage cruelty. *And my bloody response to it,* he added mentally.

The spell was fresh, so he didn't fear waking her. Bending carefully, he slipped his arms behind her head and knees and cradled her against his chest before lifting and carrying her from the room. It was all he knew to do.

CHAPTER 47

Out in the hall, he was immediately approached by another servant, but before the man could speak, Will addressed him, "Are Princess Selene's old quarters still unoccupied?"

The man bowed. "The king has kept them maintained exactly as they were the day she left, sir."

"I'll be using them until morning," said Will, putting as much authority in his voice as he could manage. "Please show my friends up to join us."

"Should I get someone to carry her for you, sir?"

The look in Will's eyes turned fierce, causing the man to wilt away, though Will didn't mean to frighten him intentionally. "No. I know the way." He set off without looking back. The one place in the palace he knew exactly how to find was Selene's old room.

Another servant fell into place a few steps behind, and when they came to the door, the man helpfully opened it for him. Will carried Laina inside and laid her gently on the bed. Then he went to the front room and looked out the window, remembering happier moments.

He frowned. *They seem happy now, but at the time we were scared to death. Funny how time changes one's perspective.* He wished desperately that Selene was with him now. He needed her calm resolve. Having been raised by a madman, she always seemed unflappable.

A few minutes later, a knock came at the door. "Your companions are here, sir. Shall I let them in?"

Will grunted an affirmative, and Darla and Tiny came in. Darla looked past him and immediately became more alert when she didn't see her ward. "Where is she?"

"Sleeping in the other room," said Will soothingly. "Our meeting with the king was rather traumatic, but physically she is fine."

"Physically?"

He gave them a quick description of what had happened, including the king's bizarre games and cruel humor but omitting their philosophical discussion near the end.

"You put her to sleep?" asked Darla, seeming offended.

Will nodded. "I snapped. I killed all three and when she turned to me, the look of horror on her face... I just—I put her to sleep. She could have tried to resist the spell, but she didn't."

"You shouldn't coddle her," said the former assassin. "She will be a great lady someday, but death and killing are things she must become comfortable with."

Not if I have any say in it, thought Will. Then he saw Darla head for the bedroom, and he moved to interpose himself. "Stop."

"I will wake her."

"Let her sleep. She's been through as much as any of us. She may as well rest since we're safe and she's already out."

Darla's eyes measured him. "And if I disagree?"

"Then we'll have words." He pointed at one of the chairs. "Make yourself comfortable instead."

She lifted her chin. "I will guard the door. I do not trust the king's men not to eavesdrop." Moving away, the Arkeshi went to the outer door and stepped outside, closing it behind her.

Tiny looked at him and shook his head. "I'm not sure I'd be so casual about offending that woman. She

Chapter 47

seems like she could just as soon cut your head off as look at you."

She's a good kisser, though, Will remembered with a half-smile. He shook his head to clear away the thought. Was that a remnant of Laina, or had he been unfaithful in his thoughts? Will sighed. For the rest of his life he would likely be uncertain. He guessed it would be the same for Laina as well.

"What now?" asked Tiny, glancing around to take in the room.

Will noticed his friend slap his stomach a few times unconsciously. "Why don't you and Darla see about having some food sent up?"

"Sent up?"

"The kitchens here are always busy. Get word to one of the servants, and they'll send up enough food to feed even you."

Tiny was out the door before Will could say another word. Will laughed, then activated the limnthal. "Are you ready to talk?"

"I'm at your beck and call," said Arrogan in an uncommonly cooperative tone.

"You lied to me. Repeatedly. Why?"

"I was selfish," said the ring.

"Selfish? You could have told me you remembered everything. You could have told me you were really my grandfather, not just some magical copy. What could you possibly gain from hiding that?"

"Peace," said Arrogan. "For you and me. It hurts to remember, and I only have to do it when the limnthal is active. You're still alive. I didn't want you to know it was really me trapped in this ring."

"Well I know now, and I'm ticked off," spat Will.

"Is that all you're upset about?"

"Should there be something else?"

The ring issued an audible sigh. "Just when I think you might not be utterly stupid."

Will snorted. "You must be referring to the fact that you're not just a spirit of pure intellect, but the fact that you retained your will as well."

"It makes me dangerous," said his grandfather.

"Because you could attempt to steal my body, the way Ethelgren did?"

"Yes!"

"But you wouldn't do that," insisted Will.

Arrogan lost his temper. "How do you know that, you little shit? Do you have any idea how tempting it is? I'm dead!"

Something occurred to Will then. He remembered their previous conversation regarding Aislinn and her dual motivations, helpful and murderous. "She made you as a trap for me," he said aloud as his thoughts clarified.

"Damn right. And I've felt terrible about it ever since."

"But you didn't have a choice, except not to do it," countered Will. "And you didn't."

"I could have told you," said the ring. "But I didn't. Do you know why?"

"Why?"

"Because I was afraid you'd get rid of me."

That didn't fit with the ring's constant begging to melt him down. "That's not true. You were always begging me to put you out of your misery."

"I knew you wouldn't, not unless I told the truth. And secretly, deep down, I've been keeping my options open."

"Options…," muttered Will, tasting the word and finding it unsavory.

"Yeah, options. As long as you keep calling on me, I could always change my mind. A new life waits for me, in

Chapter 47

your body. All I have to do is throw aside my scruples and do what Ethelgren did."

He mulled it over for a minute, then shrugged. "Oh well. I guess I'll take that risk."

"You really are a fool."

"Not at all," said Will confidently. "I trust you. We're family."

"Did Laina kick you in your balls or your brain? Wait, never mind, that's probably where you keep your brain anyway," said Arrogan sourly.

Will wasn't fazed. "I learned something new today, about trust, and I think even the king was impressed."

Suspicious, the ring asked, "What was it?"

He relayed what he had told Lognion about truth and trust, faith and people. Will wasn't sure if he managed to say it quite as eloquently the second time, but he did his best to get the point across. There was a long pause after he finished, so he asked, "What do you think?"

Arrogan didn't hold back. "As philosophers go, you're about the most laughable, shortsighted, and naïve one that I could possibly imagine. That line of thinking was so simpleminded and imbecilic that it barely merits a response. The king wasn't impressed; he was stupefied. You probably lowered his intelligence just reciting that line of half-baked bullshit within his hearing."

"That wasn't a counter argument," observed Will. "It was just a string of ad hominems."

"How'd you learn such a thing?"

"We studied logic last semester."

"Huh. Next even pigs will learn to fly," snipped the ring.

"You don't have a decent rebuttal, do you?"

"Get over yourself while I'm being nice. I don't want to crush your tiny ego. Plus, it won't do me any favors trying to win the argument, because then you'd have to get rid of me."

Will smiled. "I accept your surrender."

That triggered a barrage of swearing so intense that it threatened to blister his ears, but Will merely laughed through it all. When Arrogan finally wound down and ran out of new insults, Will changed the topic to the issue of the day. "I need your help."

"What else is new? Let me guess, you need me to tell you how to wipe your ass again?"

"I need a ritual spell powerful enough to destroy all the vampires in Cerria without killing the people or destroying property."

"Oh, that's easy."

"It is?"

"Yeah. There isn't one."

That wasn't an option, so Will persisted. "Can we make one?"

"So far as I know you've redesigned one spell. Don't you think creating a strategic class ritual would be something of a reach?"

"Not for you."

"Just because I was one of the best wizards to ever live doesn't mean I can just pull something like that out of my ass. Besides, we've been over the reasons why I can't teach you even simple spells already."

"You could borrow my body and write it out, then we could switch and you could explain it to me," argued Will.

"No."

He was undeterred. "Why not?"

"First, I'm not sure I could resist the urge to keep your body if I had it a second time. Second, even if I did, creating such a ritual is no easy task. There were wizards who dedicated their lives to that sort of thing. It was never my forte."

Chapter 47

"I'd rather not ask Aislinn," said Will.

"And you'd be wise not to," agreed the ring. "Besides, while she's probably better at it than I am, it still wasn't her strongest point. Have you thought about talking to some of your teachers at the college?"

That caught him completely off-guard. He'd never heard the old man say a kind word about anything the school had to offer, much less the professors who taught there. "I only have a day. Do you really think one of them could help?"

"Maybe. They don't have to be able to cast it, but some of them might have studied the theory that goes into it. You just need to know how to push them in the right direction, assuming you can find someone that isn't an idiot."

He rubbed his hands together, beginning to feel slightly less hopeless. Professor Dulaney might be able to help, or maybe even Master Courtney. "So what do I need to know?"

"I'll go over the basics. First, there are three major considerations for any ritual: desired effect, control, and power required. The desired effect and the circumstances that the ritual will be used under have a lot of impact on the other two."

"What sort of circumstances?"

"Where, when, geography, active resistance, that sort of thing," said Arrogan. "Control is achieved via one of two principal ways, people and ritual design. Power is—"

Will interrupted, "Wait, explain control first."

"Rituals create large effects and utilize a lot of power, so finding ways to control that power, to properly channel it, is a major concern in ritual magic, much more so than in ordinary spellcasting. The ritual you stopped last year, for example, was controlled with a large, elaborate, and well-designed circle. The entire chamber, from the sacrificial altar to the control runes built around the ring, was all carefully orchestrated and thoughtfully planned; otherwise a single human could not have enacted that ritual.

"But rituals don't have to be controlled by well-designed circles. They can also be controlled by using extra manpower, auxiliary casters whose purpose is to help control and channel the energies being brought together. Rituals can also incorporate a mixture of both, so you can design it to match the resources you have. With a surplus of time and money, designing a circle is no problem, whereas if you have a shortage of those, additional helpers can reduce the need for a complex or expensive design."

Will nodded. "That makes sense."

"On to power. There's lots of ways to power a ritual, but the two main ones are ley lines and people. Generally speaking, ley lines provide vastly more power, but that often creates more problems than it solves. Usually you don't need that much, and in order to keep the effect at the scale you want, you have to overbuild your control parameters to keep the ritual from overloading. People are nice because you can add or remove participants depending on how much turyn you need. The trouble there often comes when you need more power than the people you have on hand can provide, in which case many desperate individuals resort to sacrifice, since killing one of your sources can more than double the turyn they provide.

"So, to make a long story short, if you're using people to power your ritual you generally don't need nearly as much effort put into control, because the power matches the ritual more closely and because the people providing that power can also assist with control functions. Understand?"

Chapter 47

"I think so," answered Will. "At least I know how to present the problem. I need a ritual that can destroy every vampire within the confines of the city, without hurting innocents. There's a ley line in the city, and I know its location, so I could probably..."

"Not going to work," interjected Arrogan.

"Why not?"

"You told me you sealed it off, right?"

"Mmhmm."

"So, nothing has changed since you were last there. You have *one* day. You'd need to reopen it, get a crew of workmen down there and rip up the old circle, then lay down the new one that you just so happened to design while tearing out the old one."

"But can't I use people to control it?"

"Ley lines contain a *lot* of turyn. To use one for a ritual without an elaborate control ring would be an absolute mess. I doubt you could even get enough people into that room to even try it that way. Honestly, ley lines overshoot the power requirement by such a large amount that I've never even heard of anyone using *just* people to provide control. There's always a ring design incorporated."

"So what am I going to do? I'll need...," Will paused. "I guess I could use a lot of sorcerers. The king alone probably has an untold number of elementals under his control."

"There's also a limit on the amount of power a single caster can provide," Arrogan informed him. "So the king isn't going to be able to use a hundred elementals and power this all by himself. You'll need numbers of actual living people, not just someone with a bunch of elemental slaves."

Will mulled that over for a moment. "It isn't that I don't believe you, but why can't you get the power from a few people with lots of elementals?"

"It falls back to control once more," said Arrogan, "but this time at a level below that of the overarching ritual structure. An individual can only control so much power at a time. Lognion might have ten, or a hundred, or a thousand elementals, but that power has to go through him before it can go to the ritual, and an individual can only handle so much without being obliterated by their own power."

"Oh. So I just need a lot of sorcerers, without really worrying about how many elementals each has since they can only supply so much turyn."

"Essentially, although a sorcerer with more elementals will be able to provide power for more time before being tapped out. Proper wizards would be better in almost every respect."

Will was no fan of sorcerers, but he didn't see why that would necessarily be the case. "Why is that?"

"Control and sustainable power. Wizards in my day developed their will to a greater degree, and that enabled them to contribute more to control in a ritual like this. And while they didn't have elementals, they could draw a considerable amount of turyn over an almost indefinite period of time. I don't have any way to guess for sure, but I'll bet you wind up needing twice as many practitioners for your ritual than you would have back in my time."

"Well, there's no shortage of sorcerers from what I can tell," offered Will.

"But there's a serious shortage of wizards. I hope you realize how dangerous this will be for you."

"Isn't it always?"

"No, I mean this ritual specifically. You are the *only* true wizard left. They couldn't begin to perform a hastily constructed ritual based on casters without a wizard at the heart of it. It's going to take someone with a degree

Chapter 47

of turyn control and discipline that these modern turds couldn't even begin to approach."

He sighed. "But I'm up to the task." Mentally, he added, *Right?*

"Are you? You're still new to all this. I have no doubt your will is strong enough. You bested Ethelgren to regain your body. You even took a spell away from him, so you've definitely got the necessary inner strength, but what you lack is experience. You've only dealt with one ritual in the past, and it used symbols and structure to provide most of the control. If there were other wizards—*real* wizards—it wouldn't be so bad, since they could share the load.

"But even if you have every sorcerer in the city beside you, you'll still be alone, because they're nowhere close to being able to help you control it," finished the ring.

"Wait, but you just said they'd be providing control, instead of the ring structure," said Will, feeling confused.

"Yeah, the rough overall control, but the fine work in the center, that's all going to be on your shoulders, and don't let the term 'fine work' fool you. Without highly skilled assistants, it's going to be hard as hell. If you slip up and lose control, it will rip you to shreds. There won't even be a body. They'll have to mop you up to have a burial."

"How comforting," said Will wryly.

CHAPTER 48

Tiny and Darla returned, heavily laden with food. Not only that, but they had recruited two servants to follow them with large platters piled high with roast fowl, lamb, pig, and a collection of sides, pastries, and desserts. Will gaped at their haul.

"Did you leave anything for the rest of the palace?" he asked.

Tiny's face broke into a wide grin. "Apparently the head cook panicked when the king started bringing in all his troops and guards. Rather than run short, he made too much. We were doing them a favor."

Spreading their feast out on the floor, they sat down around it and then they fell to with a will, demolishing the plentiful pabulum, until at last even Tiny leaned back and patted his swollen belly with a sigh of satisfaction. Darla made no overt gestures, but Will could see that her eyes seemed to blink more slowly, as though she was fighting post-prandial drowsiness.

"Did you eat too much?" Will asked her.

"Never," she replied in a no-nonsense tone. "The Arkeshi are trained not to overeat, lest we become slow in our reactions." To illustrate her point, she rolled back until her shoulders were on the floor and her feet were in the air. Kicking up with her legs, she flipped her body neatly up onto her feet. A loud noise accompanied her feat of agility, and her cheeks reddened as Tiny began waving his hand in front of his nose.

"Obviously you didn't have enough room left to keep everything in," remarked the squire with a chuckle. "Maybe you should wait until you've had a chance to digest your food properly before you engage in more acrobatics?"

Smoothing her features, Darla ignored them and proceeded to the door. "I'll resume my watch," she told them.

Tiny lifted one leg slightly and made a voluminous contribution to the fetor that Darla had started. "Don't be like that," said the big man. "See? You aren't the only one!"

She shut the door with a firm and resounding thud, and the two men began giggling like small boys. After a moment Will went to the window and threw it open to help clear the air. "That really is foul!" he gasped.

"Not my fault," said Tiny with an air of self-righteousness. "My portion was rose-scented."

Will laughed, then caught himself in a yawn. He was tired. The excitement, along with all the odd hours of the past few days, was working to wear him down, even though it hadn't been sixteen hours since his last rest. *I'm not used to being up over the middle of the night,* he told himself.

But he had a lot to accomplish. Turning back, he took a few minutes to explain the rough details of his plan to Tiny.

"So you need to go back to the college and find some of your teachers?"

Will nodded.

"They're most likely asleep," said the big man.

"Then I'll rouse them."

His friend scrutinized him carefully. "You're tired. Get some sleep. Rest for tonight. You can get up early and brace them when they're also rested and ready to face the day. Everyone will be smarter and better able to think."

As usual, Tiny's words made a lot of sense. With a nod, he went to the door. "We're going to get some sleep. Why don't you come sleep in the bedroom with Laina?"

"I'll keep watch," insisted the former assassin.

"We can bar the door. You need rest, and it won't matter if the king's men eavesdrop on us sleeping."

She thought about it, then relented. "Perhaps you are right."

Darla made a show of sleeping on the floor in the bedroom, though Will wondered how long that would last once the door was closed. *Then again, I really have no idea how their relationship works,* he reminded himself. The Arkeshi was a strange person, and it was entirely possible she insisted on such privations except for well-circumscribed moments of intimacy. It wasn't his place to pry or interfere.

Will and Tiny bedded down in the front room, borrowing pillows and cushions from the furniture. Will had a few blankets stored in the limnthal, so he summoned two of them and handed one to his friend. It was almost like their days in the army together, except they'd never had such neat and level ground to lie on back then. The palace rugs weren't quite enough to soften the hard stone floors, but they went a long way in that regard.

Neither of them had trouble falling asleep.

When he awoke after some unknown time, the sky was still dark in the window, but his back felt uncommonly warm. Tiny was sprawled out across the room in front of him, and he was lying on his side a few feet from one wall, so that didn't make much sense. Turning his head carefully, Will saw the back of Laina's head. She had snuck in at some point and worked her way in between

Chapter 48

him and the wall, putting her back against his and pulling her knees up to her chest.

She had to be cold and uncomfortable, with no pillow or cover. Reaching out, he snatched a small cushion from a nearby chair before carefully turning over so he could ease it under her head. If the movement woke her, she gave no sign of it. Resuming his former position, back-to-back, he shifted his blanket and tossed half over Laina, then he went back to sleep.

Sometime later Tiny shook him awake. "It's almost dawn."

Groggy, Will looked around. Laina was gone. "Where are the others?"

"Darla's outside the door again. I don't think Miss Nerrow is awake yet."

Will was willing to bet that she was awake, since she'd started sleeping before the rest of them, but he wasn't about to say that. It was obvious that Laina hadn't wanted anyone to know she had switched sleeping spots during the night. *She was probably having nightmares, not that I can blame her.*

He knocked on the door to the bedroom. "Are you dressed?"

Laina pulled it open immediately. "Why wouldn't I be?"

"It's just a common courtesy to ask," he replied, noting the grease on her cheek. "You have some duck stuck to your face."

She wiped it on her sleeve without the slightest bit of self-consciousness. "Are we about to leave?"

He nodded.

Laina waved at Tiny, then tugged on Will's shirt. "Can we talk for a moment first?"

"Sure." He followed her into the room and waited while she shut the door.

"It's about last night, er, this night—is it dawn yet?" she asked irritably.

"The sun is just coming up."

Laina walked over and took a seat on the edge of the bed, then stood again, too nervous to remain in one place. "I kept waking up, hoping it had been a nightmare."

"I'm sorry for putting you to sleep—" he began.

"Honestly, it was a relief. I couldn't believe what was happening. Those men…"

Will blanched, then looked away.

"I understand what you were trying to do, but it was still almost as bad. I'm glad I didn't have to do it, but now I feel guilty, because you took the burden on in my place. Again." She paused and stared at him steadily for several seconds. "You didn't even hesitate."

He felt the accusation in her eyes. He was a killer. He'd started with Darrowans in his home village, moved on to killing sentries, then Dennis in a duel—he wasn't even sure anymore how many occasions he had been forced to kill, though the worst was his memory of sacrificing Arlen Arenata. Looking down, he stared at his feet. It was only natural she would find him disturbing after what she had seen.

Laina's arm went around his midsection as she hugged him tightly, her cheek against his chest. "Thank you, but don't do it again. You've got enough bad stuff to remember. Don't add any more because of me again." She pushed him away and stepped back.

"I can't promise that."

"Do it again and I'll put a knot on your head," she warned, showing him her fist. Laina smiled for a moment, but then her features darkened again. "How did he do that to me?"

"It's a long story, but the essence of it is that the graduation seal you received is actually a heart-stone

Chapter 48

enchantment, except you're not on the controlling end of it, King Lognion is." Her face went blank, and Will watched quietly while a variety of realizations passed through her mind. Then he added, "That's where elementals come from. Someday, when you die, the enchantment will continue to bind your soul, and Lognion or whoever his successor is, will use it to transform you into a new elemental."

She sat down suddenly, still numb. Rather than bombard her with more, Will stood silent, waiting for the inevitable questions. "That's why you refused the elementals?"

He gave a single nod. "When I interrupted Selene's wedding to Count Spry, something similar happened, and she learned the truth. Afterward, she released her elementals and went into hiding, partly so she could relearn magic, and partly to avoid letting her father control her again."

"She knew he would use her against you." Her eyes widened. "What did he say after I went to sleep? Did he make you swear to some awful bargain? Is he using me the same way now?"

"No, but I did make a bargain. He offered to free one of you. In exchange, I told him I'd get rid of the vampire problem."

"That's ridiculous." When he didn't laugh, she grew worried. "You're serious?"

Will frowned, "Don't you want to know who I chose?"

She shook her head. "That's a stupid question. Besides, you chose Selene, right?"

He sighed. "No, I decided she was already safe, so I chose you, but unfortunately he was thinking the same way, so he freed Selene to spite me."

Laina smiled. "That's good. Now she can come back."

"You're still trapped—" he began, but then her words replayed themselves in his mind. *Now she can come back.*

A surge of happiness ran through him with that realization. "Shouldn't you be more worried about yourself?"

"I'm too young to worry about something that's going to happen decades from now. Besides, I'll figure out a way to stop him before then," she said confidently.

He wasn't sure he believed her bravado, but it felt necessary, so he didn't argue. Instead he asked, "Why did you come to my house that night?"

"To find Selene."

"But why?"

She gave him an odd look. "Can I trust you?"

"Really? After everything we've been—"

"Relax, I'm joking. I had two reasons. One was business. Someone I trusted stole a large amount of money from the donations to our charity. I didn't want to make it public, or accuse the man openly, since he's well known in lofty circles. I hoped that Selene, as a princess, could apply quiet pressure and force him to admit his wrongdoing, or at least return the money while avoiding a national scandal."

"What was the other reason?"

"I was mad. I've been mad since she married you, then she disappeared without even giving me an explanation."

Will frowned. "It was unusual, but she probably thought you'd understand that she fell in love. It's not the most unbelievable thing in the world, after all."

"But we had been friends most of my life. It was too sudden. It felt like a betrayal. I was closer to her. If it had been anyone…" She stopped there, her cheeks coloring. "Forget it."

A few days prior and he would never have understood, but after spending time in her body, with her soul, the knowledge leapt out at him. "You were in love with her."

The look on Laina's face was one of pure panic. "Absolutely not."

Chapter 48

"You were jealous."

"Will you stop?" There was a thundercloud brewing beneath her lowered brows, with red cheeks on the horizons.

"It's all right," he said calmly. "I was jealous of you too."

That made her pause. "How so?"

"Your family," he said simply. "It's the same thing really. Being jealous of someone else's love. Well, except yours involves kissing and naughty bits, while I was only jealous in a more innocent fashi—hey!" A pillow had struck him in the face.

Laina still held the weapon in her hand, and she was ready to use it again. Will stared at her then slowly puckered his lips. "Oh, Selene…!" Whop! He hopped away as she began beating him steadily with the pillow.

That pillow gave up after several heavy blows, and down feathers exploded across the room. Not deterred at all, Laina grabbed a larger cushion and resumed the chase while he laughed and ran across the bed to escape her. "By the way," he hooted, "did you know that this bed is the very first place where we…" He stopped and waggled his eyebrows suggestively.

Laina shrieked and threw her pillow at his head. "You're dead. You're absolutely dead!" But she was beginning to laugh even as she yelled at him. It was a sort of hysterical release, a confession, a battle, followed by understanding—all facilitated through the medium of pillows.

Will ducked, continuing to taunt her, when the door opened and Tiny caught the pillow with his face. It slid off, then dropped to the floor, while the big man stared at them with an odd expression.

Will and Laina both stopped, red-faced and panting, as they tried to adopt a more somber demeanor. He glanced at his sister and saw a sliver of fear in her eyes, but he shook his head. *I wouldn't tell anyone.* "She wouldn't wake up," he lied to his friend.

"And you wouldn't leave me alone, so I had to defend myself," added Laina pointing awkwardly at the pillow at Tiny's feet.

Tiny said nothing for several seconds, then backed out and slowly closed the door.

"It wasn't anything strange!" called Laina, but the door clicked shut on her words.

From the other room they could hear Darla ask, "What was all that about?"

"Just a pillow fight."

CHAPTER 49

The city seemed to be holding its breath as they walked back to Wurthaven, as though it feared that even the sun wouldn't bring safety. The northern part of the city, which they didn't quite enter, was sullen and quiet, lacking its normal sounds of bustling activity as the people began starting their days.

Will felt guilty, though it wasn't his fault that vampires had taken so many from their beds. His remorse was for the portion of the city that had been utterly destroyed. They couldn't see it from the lane they walked down, but he knew it was there, just a few blocks over, hidden from view, a violent scar across the face of Cerria.

Back in Wurthaven, they walked to his home first. He intended to leave immediately and begin seeking advice, but a piece of parchment was pinned to his new front door. Will felt a sense of foreboding as he pulled it down and turned it over. It was Rob's handwriting.

You must leave, for they won't let us escape. We are kept here, even though they know what the king has planned. We are merely decoys. No matter what the outcome tomorrow night, Terabinia loses.

Leave, or I may kill you. Please.

Will folded the paper carefully and slipped it into his pouch. He had a lot to think about and little time. He would have to consider Rob's words while he worked on other things. *We are merely decoys,* the words repeated in his head.

The door opened before he could knock, and Janice stood within, looking distinctly unhappy. Will was relieved to see that her gaze focused primarily on Laina. Blake stood behind her, and he waved to Will with an expression of helplessness.

Laina lifted her chin, ready to face the challenge, until a deep voice boomed from down the hall. She visibly wilted as she recognized the owner. "Is that her?" demanded Mark Nerrow.

Janice gave the baron's elder daughter a smug look. "Your father waits on you inside, Miss Nerrow." She glanced down and saw Will squeeze his sister's hand briefly, and a questioning frown flickered across her features.

"Don't worry, Laina. You survived the king; your father won't be half as bad," said Will.

She squeezed back. "You'd better get moving or you'll get caught up in all this." Taking a deep breath, she went inside. Janice and Blake came outside.

Tiny spoke first. "We had no idea she would show up last night." He spoke as though he had done something wrong, which Will simply couldn't understand.

"It's all right, Tiny. I know you didn't mean to ditch me and bring her along instead," said Janice, then she glanced at Will. "What was that?"

"What?" he asked, feigning innocence.

She took his hand and squeezed. "That. What was that?"

"You could pretend to be a little less observant once in a while, you know," suggested Will. "In fact, I should tell you my latest revelation about truth, trust, and lies."

"Is this an attempt to distract me? That's even more suspicious," she observed.

"No, honestly, listen. Lies are clothes, and sometimes we wear them because the truth causes us to lose our…"

Chapter 49

He paused. "Wait, that's not how I said it before. Truth is an invasion of privacy, but lies are clothes that we don't want to see through because..."

"Because you might have to pee when you wake up?" said Janice pointedly. Tiny and Blake both snickered. "I don't think philosophy is your forte, so just fess up."

Tiny couldn't take it any longer. "Last night Will was inside Laina and now they're friends."

Janice glanced at Tiny and slow-blinked. Then she put one finger against his lips. "You are not helping."

Meanwhile Will was glaring at his friend. Tiny was generally well spoken, but for some reason he seemed to have lost his facility with words. While Janice's eyes were elsewhere, Will mouthed, *Don't help me anymore,* to Tiny. Off to one side, Blake continued to silently enjoy the show.

"Well?" asked Janice.

"What Tiny said wasn't technically wrong, it just sounded wrong. I was possessed by Ethelgren's relic and then I escaped, but there was nowhere for me to go..." The quick explanation took ten minutes, and at the end Janice was still asking more questions. "Listen, we need to find Professor Dulaney," said Will. "I have a ritual to prepare, otherwise the king is going to raze the city tomorrow."

Blake stepped up as they started to leave. "Um, should I come with you, sir?"

Will could hear the argument brewing in the house. Baron Nerrow's voice was carrying well beyond the walls. He had no mercy for Blake, however. "Wait here. I may need the baron's assistance when I get back later."

The manservant's face fell, but he turned back to the house. The rest of them walked toward the central part of the campus. "Does Dulaney have classes this morning?" asked Will.

"That shows how out-of-touch you are. Classes were canceled yesterday. Hundreds of people in the city are missing, and after last night that number is probably thousands. The entire city is on the verge of panic," said Janice. "It doesn't help that the king has closed the gates and is refusing to let anyone in or out of the city."

Will couldn't really blame them. "How will we find Professor Dulaney then?"

"I'm pretty sure there's a lot going on at the main Administration building. At the very least there will be someone who can tell us where to go," she responded.

They followed her suggestion, though as they walked Will noticed Tiny was acting strangely. "Why do you keep touching your lips like that?" he asked.

"I wasn't," declared Tiny as his arm swept out and nearly knocked Will to the ground. His face shaded to pink. "Sorry, I'm a little tense this morning."

Will covered his smile. "We all are." Just to be safe, he stood on the other side of Janice after that.

At the Administration building, they quickly learned that the chancellor had called an early meeting, but it had already ended. Dulaney would be found in his office within the General Class building next door. It was an office Will had been to many times in the past.

The door was open when they arrived, and the professor seemed to be in a rush, collecting books and papers and piling them on his desk. Will knocked on the door to catch his attention.

Professor Dulaney looked up with distracted eyes. "William."

"I need your help, Professor."

"This isn't really a good time, William. The king has called on the school to cease educational activities and provide manpower for his new war effort."

Chapter 49

Will was stunned. "War effort? We haven't declared a war." *Yet.*

"We are to provide two hundred senior students, though I don't think you need to worry about your name being put on the list, given your wife," said Dulaney brusquely.

"Two hundred? That's nearly—" His mind went blank.

Janice finished his thought for him. "—A third of the student body. What good will wizards do him in a war, though?"

"His Majesty plans to elevate them, this afternoon. Each will receive an elemental before being assigned to work with various parts of the military. I daresay it's a great opportunity for most of them, assuming they aren't killed."

Will's mind was running in other directions, though. *How many Driven did he lose last night that he's that desperate to create new sorcerers?* He stared at Dulaney. "Sir, the reason I came is regarding a task that His Majesty has given me."

That got the man's attention. Dulaney put the books down and straightened up to look directly at him. "What task?"

Will explained it to him with as much detail as he could manage.

"*You.* You're supposed to come up with a ritual large enough to purge the entire city?" The professor gaped at him as though he had grown an extra head. "Why would he even expect something like that from you?"

"We disagreed on some things."

"And he's punishing you by putting the fate of thousands in your inexperienced hands?" demanded the professor.

Will shook his head. "I pleaded with him for a delay. If we can't come up with a better solution, His

Majesty is ready to implement some rather drastic measures tomorrow."

"How drastic?"

"Very drastic. I can't say more than that, but it will be very bad for most of the city if we don't find a better solution."

Dulaney ran his hands through his hair. "This kind of thing isn't done in a day. I'm not even sure we *can* create such a ritual. Modern rituals don't compare to what was supposedly done in the past. The old designs claim to get far more from fewer people. We would need to design a complex circle and use a ley line to achieve something on a city-wide scale."

"And there's no time for that," said Will. "But we *can* do something like they did in the old rituals. I just don't know how to design it."

"How?"

Will pointed at himself. "Me. If I'm the center, I can provide the control that a ritual like that needs, though I'll need to have a lot of people to support it and provide the power required."

The professor stared at him for several seconds. "Mister Cartwright, if it wasn't for all the peculiarities I've learned about you over the past few years, I'd think you were mad, but this—this just doesn't make sense."

"I've kept some secrets, Professor," began Will. "My differences aren't from some accident of birth, they came from the way my master trained me. Eventually I could teach others, if they're young enough."

His teacher squinted at him. "What are you saying?"

"I wasn't taught by some ordinary hedge wizard. I was trained by one of the old masters, the kind you'd find in the history books."

"Who then?" challenged Dulaney.

Chapter 49

"Arrogan."

"The Betrayer? He died. If he were alive, he would have had to be—"

"He was a little over six hundred and ninety years old when he died," finished Will.

"Not only is that impossible, but even if it were true, do you expect me to believe you were taught by the Betrayer and yet you came to this school not knowing how to do even the simplest magics?"

Will nodded. "Imagine how frustrating it was for me. He refused to teach me anything until he thought I had what he considered to be the 'foundations' ready. I was just beginning to learn the runes when the Prophet invaded and my teacher died."

"And this deludes you into thinking you can control something like one of the old rituals?"

"Yes, sir."

The professor sighed. "At least you're an honest lunatic. Here's the truth, though. Unless there's already a ritual designed, there's no way I could create one quickly enough. My field is Spell Theory, but I've never put much time and energy into ritual design. You'll need more expertise than I can provide." Reaching into a desk drawer, he drew out a ring of keys, then headed toward the door. Tiny and Janice stepped aside to let him through. "Come with me," he told them.

"Where are we going?" asked Will.

"To see Master Courtney. If anyone can design such a thing in such short time, it will be him. He's also better qualified to decide if you're insane."

***

Lord Alfred Courtney's office was a study in dark colors—dark wood paneling, dark maroon rugs, deeply stained bookcases, and a floral wallpaper that might once have been a light tan but had been stained by time and pipe smoke.

The Head of Research at Wurthaven had a desk that was massive and heavy, constructed of black walnut, and at the moment its owner sat behind it, his favorite briarthorn pipe in hand. The smoke curled up past his face, highlighting the man's bushy brows, which had unruly tufts that reminded Will of a horned owl. Courtney exhaled, then leaned forward with an unsettling smile, his eyes fixed on Will. "I knew you'd come to me eventually."

There hadn't been enough chairs or space in the room, so Tiny waited in the hall, while Janice and Dulaney occupied the other two chairs beside Will's seat. Dulaney had finished describing Will's request a moment before, and he responded first. "I know it sounds ridiculous, but I do have some reason to give credence to Mister Cartwright's claims."

Master Courtney's attention never left Will. "You wouldn't tell me his name before, are you ready to share now? I promise not to tell the king."

Dulaney glanced at Will, but said nothing rather than betray the young man's trust. Will's response was unexpected, though. "You can't make a promise like that when he could compel you to reveal what you know."

The Head of Research laced his fingers together. "You've learned some unsettling things then, haven't you, Mister Cartwright? I assume you're referring to the graduation seal?" Dulaney's expression turned to confusion when he heard the last question.

"You mean the heart-stone enchantment," corrected Will.

Chapter 49

"Even so. I assume this is the source of your long-standing conflict with the king then?" asked Courtney.

"I won't abide slavery," said Will. Meanwhile Dulaney's eyes went back and forth as he began to piece together the meaning of their conversation.

Master Courtney chuckled. "And yet, it is sorcery that we require to survive our present crisis, is it not? If we can construct this ritual it will need the input of hundreds of sorcerers to power and control it. No simple wizard could maintain the energy required for any length of time."

"True wizards could," countered Will. "If there were any these days."

"Apparently there is one," said Lord Courtney. "Or is it two?"

"My teacher died, but there might be another in a few years."

"The princess?"

Will's lips formed a hard line, but he didn't answer.

Master Courtney's eyes turned to Dulaney. "Mister Cartwright trusts you. He told you the name of his teacher, did he not?"

Professor Dulaney lowered his head. "Yes, Master Courtney, but he told me in trust."

"I won't ask you to reveal it then," said the old wizard. "Was it a name you recognized?"

"Yes, sir. I scarcely believe it, though I don't doubt he believes himself."

The Head of Research rose from his chair and went to the door. Looking out, he spotted Tiny. "Make sure no one eavesdrops." Then he closed the door and began constructing a spell. A few seconds later the room was enclosed in a rectangular structure of force that closely conformed to the walls of the office. The sound in the space also became strangely muffled. "This is a spell

I designed myself, for moments when I desire absolute privacy." The old educator returned to his seat and leaned forward.

"The king cannot ask about a thing if he doesn't suspect its existence." He paused and let that sink in. "I have been aware of the nature of elementals and the cruel truth of the graduation seals for much of my career. In fact, I'm an accomplice of sorts, and have been for many years. When I first confronted His Majesty about my suppositions, he quickly took steps to ensure my loyalty, first by demonstrating the efficacy of the heart-stone enchantment on me and also by reminding me of my duties to my family.

"So, you are absolutely correct, Mister Cartwright. I cannot be fully trusted, and neither can Professor Dulaney." At the same time, Dulaney started to rise from his chair, a question on his lips, but Master Courtney waved him down. "Sit, Franklin. I know some of this is a shock to you, but I can answer your questions later. Right now, I need to make my position clear and settle the matter of how we can help the boy."

Dulaney closed his mouth and sat. Will tried to hide his surprise. *Franklin? Professor Dulaney's first name is Franklin?*

"From this point forward, you are all part of a new cabal," said Courtney. "A conspiratorial group with the express purpose of undermining the status quo. Does that sound sinister enough for you?"

Janice stifled a faint laugh. "Yes, sir."

Lord Courtney continued, "The risk here is mine, for the moment. I'll help you and I'll share my own small betrayal of the king so that you can find some small amount of trust in me. I won't ask you to share your own secrets. I have been seeking the secret to unlocking the feats of wizards-past for most of my career. That interest is what

Chapter 49

led me into my present field of research, and it has in fact driven all my studies since I was a young man.

"Initially I sought that knowledge for the sake of knowledge itself, but after I deduced the nature of elementals and the graduation seal, I gained a second motivation. I wanted to find a way to overturn the status quo, to undo the unnatural grip that the king has over wizardry in Terabinia. That confession alone is probably enough to warrant a death sentence, if the king ever considered me a real threat. As it stands, however, he knows I can never openly defy him.

"The course of my research has been mostly a failure, for I have never discovered even the smallest clue as to how our forebears managed their seemingly impossible feats, but I have advanced the state of Magic Theory considerably. I have codified and calculated what they could do. As I sought to understand, I was able to clearly define the strengths and abilities that were necessary to enable the spells, potions—and most importantly at this moment—the rituals of the past."

The old man's gaze focused on Will. "Mister Cartwright, do you truly believe you can perform in the same capacity as one of those wizards of old? I'm not asking rhetorically. I need to know because it will greatly affect what is possible if we try to create a ritual for this situation."

Will blinked, then answered in deliberate fashion. "Yes, Master Courtney. I am inexperienced, but Arrogan told me the foundations were solidly laid within me."

The old scholar smiled faintly. "I appreciate your trust, Mister Cartwright. I'll do my best to remain worthy of it. When this is over, do you think you would consider sharing more?"

He frowned. "What do you want to know?"

"How it is done, how you were trained. Every year I see hundreds of students pass through these doors, lambs to the eventual slaughter, either in this life or the next. Imagine what could be done if we could teach them another way in secret. Imagine if those same students began leaving the school without graduating. It might be the slow but inexorable beginning of a revolution."

Will smiled. "I think I'd like that."

"Then we'd better start working on this ritual," said Lord Courtney, his face lighting up with unconcealed enthusiasm.

CHAPTER 50

Tiny had gone back to the house, having nothing he could contribute, and Will and Janice now sat at a large table with Master Courtney, Professor Dulaney, and two of Courtney's senior research fellows, David McCandish and Elizabeth Sundy.

Lord Courtney took charge of the meeting. "First, we must decide what spell effect will be central to the ritual. Naturally, it would be best to have a complete and balanced spell in advance, one we could work upward from, though I can't think of anything currently known that could fit those requirements. Second, we need to decide where the epicenter will be so that we can plan the geometry and calculate the power and control requirements. It goes without saying that the physical design elements will have to be minimal since we have little time to work."

Will had been thinking about it for some time already. "Have you looked at the works of Linus Ethelgren?"

Professor Dulaney coughed. "His Majesty has had us digging for information regarding him and other important figures from that era for days now. Unfortunately, it appears that someone has carefully removed every volume related to Ethelgren and his work."

Slouching, Will reached under the table and activated the limnthal. When he straightened up, he held *Battling the Darkness* in his hand. "Do you think this might help?"

"Where did you get that?" demanded Mistress Sundy.

He and Janice glanced at one another, then he admitted the truth. "I stole it."

"From the restricted section?" The senior researcher seemed incredulous.

He nodded, and Master Courtney intervened. "Elizabeth, let's table those questions for now. It's more important to stick to the matters at hand."

Will opened the book and thumbed to the location of the spell he had been thinking about, then he pushed it across the table. "I've used this spell several times in the past few days. It kills vampires without hurting humans. It also passes through solid objects, so if it could be made larger, and extended in the vertical as well, so that it will pass through the sewers and hidden underground areas, it might do the trick."

They studied the spell for several minutes, then David McCandish asked a pertinent question, "How long do we have to design this thing?"

Master Courtney looked pointedly at Will. Swallowing quickly, he hurried to answer, "Until tomorrow morning. If we don't manage to do this and clear them out before then, the king plans to do something drastic."

"Define drastic," said Elizabeth.

"I can't," said Will. "But it's safe to say there might not be a city here anymore."

She frowned. "So, he's planning a ritual of his own, but with less selectivity."

Will shrugged. "I don't know the specifics, but in my experience he rarely bluffs."

David nodded. "It makes sense, according to a certain brutal logic, though the idea is horrific."

Master Courtney had been busy sketching something out on a large sheet of paper. He pushed it over so that his two associates could examine it. "I'm thinking something roughly along these lines, but we'll need to do the calculations carefully to sort out the specifics."

Chapter 50

The two other researchers glanced at one another, then Elizabeth pointed something out. "The tolerances are too tight. This looks like an imitation of some of the old historical rituals. We need to think in modern terms if this is to be doable."

Alfred Courtney lifted his brows and sat back with an air of resignation. "Go ahead and do a rough estimate of how many sorcerers we will need to do it in 'modern' terms."

Elizabeth and David both set to with pens and paper, muttering and drawing. In the end, after fifteen minutes of figuring and quarreling with each other, they had reached different conclusions. David spoke first. "It can't be done."

Elizabeth shook her head. "No, it can, but we need time to build a ring and significant control structure."

David glared at her. "He just told us we don't have the time for that."

"But it *is* technically possible," she remonstrated her colleague.

"Don't be such a pedant!"

Master Courtney leaned in to stop the fight that was brewing. "We are going to do it and we will only rely on quick chalk markings and human participants. Pretend you're making this thing according to the theoretical tolerances we've discussed in my research."

"But that's all speculative," argued David. "We don't really know how they did those things."

"We will when we succeed," said Lord Courtney. "Because we have here someone that can replicate what our forebears used to do routinely." His eyes fell on Will.

"Surely you jest," said David. "He's just a student!"

Master Courtney ignored him. "We should get to work. It might take the rest of the day to work out the details."

Janice and Will looked at each other, then she asked a question. "Should we leave? We don't really know enough to help."

Elizabeth gave her a stern glance. "Stay quiet and do as you're told. There's no better time than the present for you to learn a little." She addressed the Head Researcher. "They might be handy doing some of the brute work."

Will frowned. "Brute work?"

Master Courtney chuckled. "Figuring large products and quotients."

"Oh," said Janice. They wanted them to solve simple math problems while they dealt with the more complex results. "We can do that."

In the end their contribution turned out to be mostly symbolic. All three of the researchers were blazingly fast when doing simple figures, the result of many long hours doing such rote work. They gave Will and Janice token problems now and then, but it was clear they weren't really needed. For the most part they simply redid problems to make sure the others hadn't made a mistake in their haste.

Watching them work was instructive, though. Janice and Will both learned a lot regarding how spell theory related to ritual theory, and how those principles were applied in a practical sense. Sadly, sunset was only two hours away when they finally were satisfied with the ritual they had planned out.

"This is the best we can do," said Elizabeth with a sigh. "A hundred and seventy-two sorcerers will be required." She dipped her head in Will's direction. "And of course, our good luck charm over there. If he can't perform the way you think, all of this is pointless."

David nodded. "And it will have to be performed in the cathedral. The Church of the Holy Mother is the most central location in the city."

Chapter 50

That point had been made several times over during the afternoon. Any other location would require vastly more manpower because of the increase in area that would need to be covered. The cathedral marked the center of the city, which meant that the radius of the circle that contained the entire city would be smallest from that point, conserving power.

"The last question," said Will, "is who will be involved in actually performing this thing?"

David glanced at the others. "You'll need one of us to help organize everyone. Master Courtney is too old, not to mention important." He glanced at Elizabeth.

She spoke before he could say anything else. "Don't try to be heroic, David. You have children at home. I'm a spinster. It's obvious I should go."

"But…"

Elizabeth shook her head, and then Janice spoke up. "I'll go as well."

"You don't have an elemental," Will pointed out.

"Neither do you."

"I don't need one."

"They're handing them out to two hundred students. I'll take one of those," she replied quickly.

Will's eyes grew round. "Even though you know how they're made?"

Janice smiled. "At least I can guarantee mine will be freed after this is over. One fewer soul suffering, isn't that a worthwhile goal?"

He hadn't thought of it that way. "I can't fault your logic," he admitted. After that they split up, agreeing to meet at the main gate that led from Wurthaven in an hour. Will, Janice, and Tiny headed for Will's home, but along the way they noticed a large increase in the number of people walking around, most of whom didn't look like students.

"I wonder what that's about?" said Janice, but Will hardly paid heed. His mind kept returning to Rob's warning note. *'We are merely decoys.'* What did he mean? *Is there another threat?*

At his home he found the Nerrow family appeared to be preparing for another pilgrimage to their old home to hole up for the evening. Laina and her father seemed to be in the midst of yet another argument, while Agnes and Tabitha looked on worriedly. The baron glared in Will's direction when he approached. "Are you the one who put these foolish ideas into her head?"

Taken aback, Will wasn't sure what to say. "Huh?"

"She wants to release her elementals! That sounds an awful lot like your nonsensical philosophy has infected my daughter's mind to me," accused Mark Nerrow.

"It's slavery!" insisted Laina, her determination unwavering.

Will looked at his father. "I didn't suggest anything, but I agree with her. Did she tell you why she believes that?"

"If she would talk reason, I would listen," said the baron angrily. "As it is she—"

"The king used her graduation seal to command her to slit the throats of three men last night. She very nearly did it, too." Laina's eyes were panicked as she heard the words leave his lips.

"That's impossible!"

"Selene nearly died trying to murder me when I interrupted her marriage to Count Spry," added Will. "She fought the control so hard it nearly ripped her soul in two. That's why she's not here. She left to go somewhere the king couldn't use her." He had their full attention then. Silence reigned for a few seconds as everyone tried to process what he had said.

Chapter 50

Will continued, "The graduation seal is just a false label for the slave end of a heart-stone enchantment. That's how elementals are made, from the souls of dead wizards. *That's* what will happen to you and Laina someday when you die, an eternity of slavery."

"That can't be true," said Mark Nerrow, but his voice no longer carried the sound of unshakeable conviction.

"You'll have to think about it later. Tonight, we're off to perform a ritual to rid the city of this plague of undead," he declared.

Agnes interjected herself then. "Is that why we've been told no one can leave the college grounds?"

That was news to them, and their faces said as much. Mark Nerrow spoke next. "The king is bringing the populace into the college. Within a few hours the entire city populace will be scattered across the campus, waiting out the night. It's almost certain to be a disaster. No one is allowed out."

"I thought you were getting ready to go out," said Will.

Agnes nodded. "We were, but now we're going back inside. Hopefully you don't mind."

He shook his head. "No, of course not."

"I'll be coming with you again," declared Laina.

"Me too," said Tabitha cheerfully.

Their mother reacted first. "Neither of you are going anywhere!"

Mark added, "I second that."

"I'll do as I please," said Laina. "Tabitha, you're too young." Then she looked at her father. "You can't stop me, but you might consider coming with us."

The baron's face turned red, and he stepped toward his daughter menacingly. Will moved at the same time. "I wouldn't," he cautioned. "We need a lot of sorcerers for this ritual, and if we don't get it the king is going to do something drastic tomorrow."

"You'd even risk your—" The baron stopped, then rephrased his words. "You'd even risk Laina on this?"

"I'd rather risk you," said Will, his tone biting, "but she's capable of making her own decisions and I'll support them, whatever they are."

The standoff lasted thirty seconds or more, and everyone grew tense watching the two men stare at one another, until at last Mark Nerrow asked, "How many do you need for this ritual?"

"Mark! You can't be considering it! The king and his men will deal with this!" said Agnes sharply.

"A hundred and seventy-two sorcerers," answered Will.

"I want to help too, Momma," said Tabitha, tugging on her mother's sleeve.

Agnes' response was so sharp that for a moment Will feared she would backhand the fifteen-year-old. "You'll stay here with me and that's the end of it," snapped Agnes, clearly overwrought.

In the end, after more bickering and a few tears, Mark and Laina Nerrow both joined them at the meeting place by the gate, though neither of them spoke much. Their party as a whole was noticeably devoid of chatter, and Will was grateful when he saw Elizabeth Sundy approaching. A long train of students followed her, the ones who had been chosen for the king's service.

She was a tall, lean woman with hawkish features, and she had changed out of her robes and into something decidedly mannish, wearing long trousers and a brown linen jacket. She noticed him studying her and grinned suddenly. "My gardening clothes. They suit the occasion better." The middle-aged woman stuck out one leg and wiggled her foot, highlighting the heavy leather boots she wore.

Chapter 50

After that it was a matter of organizing themselves and getting through the gate. There was a small amount of confusion, but Elizabeth Sundy was able to explain their purpose to the Wurthaven guards. Outside the gate was a contingent of the king's men, but they likewise stood aside once Will's identity had been confirmed.

Ten minutes later they were in the main yard of the palace. Janice and the other student sorcerer candidates were led away to receive their elementals, while Will, Laina, Elizabeth, and Mark Nerrow were taken for a quick meeting with the king.

Chapter 51

Lognion met them in a more formal audience chamber, and his eyes landed on Mark Nerrow first. "Lord Nerrow, I did not expect to see you here this evening." Then he waved his hand at the rest of them. "Please rise and be at ease."

The baron, like the others in the room, was in the midst of an extended bow, which only ended once the king gave them leave to end their obeisance. Will as usual had remained recalcitrant, even though it made the others extremely uneasy. Mark straightened up and responded, "I felt ill at ease when I learned your son-in-law was planning to strike at the enemy this evening. My daughter insisted on accompanying him, and as her father, I could do no less."

The king's gaze focused on Laina. "I'm sure you couldn't. With the people's savior on this mission you cannot help but succeed, even if the avatar of Marduke were also beside you." Lognion's attention turned to Will as he finished the sentence. "Did you succeed, William?"

Will glanced at Elizabeth, then nodded. "Yes, Your Majesty, with the help of Lord Courtney and several talented researchers, such as Mistress Sundy here. I merely presented the need; they provided the solution."

"Present your plan then," said Lognion.

Everyone seemed hesitant, aside from the baron. Elizabeth seemed tempted to speak, but she kept looking at Will. In the end, he knew it was his responsibility. "The ritual will be organized by Mistress Sundy with me at its center. We will need to perform it in the cathedral to cover the entire city. As far as requirements, we need a minimum of one hundred and seventy-two sorcerers to participate."

The king leaned forward in his seat and appeared to be counting them. "Do you have that many? I only see two with you."

"I assumed Your Majesty would provide them," said Will. "We brought the two hundred student candidates with us as well. Their number alone would be sufficient—"

"You presume too much, William. The ranks of the Driven have been severely affected by this crisis. These new candidates are barely enough to replenish them. If we lose them in this untested foray of yours, it will endanger the future of the kingdom, for I won't have enough to cut the head from this undead snake."

"Wurthaven has more students," said Will coldly. "If we fail, recruit another two hundred. It won't matter. Your plan will eliminate Wurthaven anyway. You may as well risk these lives knowing you can harvest another crop without any real loss tomorrow." That earned him some strange looks from those around him.

"So jaded for one so young," said the king. "What of protection? If I give you that number, how will you get them to the cathedral safely? One small ambush and your plan will fail."

Laina stepped forward, her body tense with repressed anger. "Since you seem ill-disposed to order men to the task, what if I ask for volunteers?"

Lognion was unflustered. "Go right ahead, Miss Nerrow. The majority of my forces are not here. Unless you are willing to make a journey to the walls to recruit them, you may find a lack of manpower." A newcomer entered the hall behind them and bowed from the waist. "You may rise and report, Lord Tintabel."

Will was startled by the name, and it took him a moment to remember where he had heard it before. *He's the neighbor to the Nerrows, the one whose house I fought in front of.* There was something else, though. *His house was burned. I thought he was dead.* He glanced at Laina, wondering what she thought since she probably knew the man better.

The expression on her face was one of extreme displeasure. It seemed she didn't have a high opinion of her neighbor, although the baron's face didn't reveal anything similar. Will wondered if she had a personal grudge. *It isn't as though she's the most likable person after all,* he observed.

"The students have received their elementals. We can begin disseminating them among the troops as soon as you give the word, Your Majesty," said Tintabel.

"It seems that won't be necessary, Lord Tintabel. I've just promised them to my son-in-law here. If they survive the night they may take their new positions then," said the king.

Lord Tintabel raised one brow, quite a feat given how thick and bushy they were. The man's hair was long and black, giving his pale face a shadowed appearance. "And if they don't survive, Your Majesty?"

"Then we take another two hundred in the morning. There will be time enough to do our work before the next sunset, if it comes to that," said the king affably.

Laina glared at her neighbor. "Why don't you come with us, Lord Tintabel? Your help would be of great use to us."

The man gave an apologetic half-bow. "My apologies to you, Miss Nerrow, and to your father, but my place is here beside His Majesty, coordinating our last defense. It would not do for your effort to succeed only to discover that we had lost our king in the midst of it all."

Chapter 51

"I'm sure the nation will remember your bravery in undertaking our monarch's defense," Laina responded, her words dripping with acid.

In the end there was no more help forthcoming from the crown, but Will had an idea. He'd once had to plan an escape from the cathedral—via the sewers. Tailtiu had planned the route for him. If she had recovered sufficiently, she might be able to advise them on a similar path from the palace back to the center of the city. He explained the idea to those with him as they returned to the palace yard.

Mark Nerrow wasn't a fan of the idea. "Do you even know if we could all fit? Some of the sewers are perilously narrow."

"As long as we follow the right route, we'll be fine," said Will. "But if we mistakenly turn into the smaller branches, we could get stuck, but I know someone who can guide us."

"What about the vampires?" asked Janice. "Aren't they hiding in the sewers? It seems more dangerous to go down there than just walk through the streets."

"They're coming up to hunt us during the night," countered Will. "On an open street they can move faster than we can handle, and they can come at us from any direction. In the sewer tunnel their movement is restricted to the tunnel. If we can limit the directions we have to defend against, then we can manage it easily."

Laina spoke next. "What about side passages?"

"We have two hundred elementals. The vampires can't kill them. We position a few at each side passage as we pass by. Earth elementals can create temporary blockages, as can water and air elementals. Fire—"

Elizabeth Sundy interrupted, "It's best if we avoid the use of fire down there. Sewer gases can be quite explosive.

In fact, you'll want an air elemental to clear the air in the passages ahead of us or we could be poisoned."

Will looked to the senior researcher. "So you think the plan has merit?"

"If you have a guide," she responded, raking her salt-and-pepper hair back over one ear.

"Give me an hour," he told them. "I'll know within that time whether we have a guide or not." Then he started to walk away. "I need a little time alone."

Will distanced himself by twenty yards or so, moving to stand close to the exterior wall between the palace and the city. He felt slightly nervous about calling Tailtiu, since he didn't know what her condition might be. There was also the risk that Aislinn might appear instead, and after her last visit he was less certain of her motives.

He closed his eyes and prepared to repeat her name when he felt something bump up against his leg. Looking down, he saw the goddamn cat. "You!" he exclaimed.

The cat sat down, staring up at him without expression. "Me."

"Where's your bow?" asked Will, unable to stop himself.

The cat stood and started walking away. "Perhaps you don't need my advice after all."

"Wait! I was only teasing. Forget what I said." The cat stopped and sat down again. "Where have you been?" asked Will.

"At my house. Where your mother lives. I needed some rest after our excursion."

Where Sammy lives, thought Will suddenly.

"I can read your expressions," said the cat angrily, "and your thoughts are crude and unrefined. I was merely worried that your cousin might be distraught at my sudden disappearance after being so badly wounded."

Chapter 51

"Sure."

"Do you want my advice or not?" The cat's tone was surly.

"Yes, please."

"The tunnels are a good idea, but don't call on the fae."

"Do you think Tailtiu has recovered?" asked Will.

The goddamn cat licked one foot. "Almost without doubt, but involving them further would make the situation extremely dangerous. Your aunt's scent would likely draw every vampire within a significant range down on you, and that isn't even considering the danger of dealing with her mother again."

"How do I lead them through then?" asked Will. "One wrong turn could spell disaster."

"I can show you the way."

"You'll come with us?"

"No. Remember Arrogan's tracking spell?"

Will nodded.

"Cast it on me. I'll run the path quickly, and you can trace my path afterward."

"Why won't you come with us?"

The Cath Bawlg wrinkled his nose and panted in disgust. "The stench down there is unbearable."

"But you're going to travel through it on your own?" Will was confused.

"Not in this form. Hurry up and cast your spell."

Will had never actually used the tracking spell, but he had practiced it, creating it once daily when he ran through his routine. The spell was only third-order, so it wasn't hard to remember. The construct came together quickly above his palm, and then he placed his hand on top of the goddamn cat's back. At the same time, he gave the feline an experimental scratch, but all he got for the effort was a hiss.

"Follow the path quickly. It will only take me a minute. After that you're on your own," said the Cath Bawlg, then he did something Will had never seen before. He dissolved into what appeared to be an insubstantial smoky shadow. He raced away and then disappeared down a sewer grate next to the palace gate.

Will returned to the others. "We're set. I can get us there."

"Where do we meet your guide?" asked the baron.

"That's already done," he answered, tapping his temple. "I have a path to follow."

"And we're supposed to trust you?" asked his father anxiously. "You walk away and pretend to have a secret conversation, then you come back and tell us your imaginary friend taught you how to get there?"

Janice started to open her mouth, but Laina was even quicker to respond. "If he says he can do it, he can!" she snapped. Then she looked at the others, a challenge in her eyes. "If any of you don't believe him, then you shouldn't have come."

Without further argument, they formed up near the sewer and Laina used her earth elemental to quickly remove the grate and widen the opening so they could easily get down. From there, they formed a long line. Tiny offered to take the lead, but Will was the only one able to see the line marking their path, or at all for that matter, lacking a light source of some kind. Tiny and Laina would follow him, while Mark Nerrow, Elizabeth Sundy, and Darla would bring up the end of the line, with the two hundred students in between. Janice would be in the middle of the line, where she could help organize the students according to their elementals, sending those forward who would be needed to block side tunnels.

Chapter 51

Being in the front, Will adjusted his vision accordingly. The others used light spells behind him, but Tiny's bulk blocked most of the light that filtered forward, so Will preferred to stay a little ahead as he could actually see better without the extraneous light ruining his vision.

Each time he came across a crossing point or a t-intersection, he stopped to warn the others and wait for an elemental to block the path that wouldn't be used, then he would resume moving forward. All in all, it was significantly slower than it would have been to walk the streets aboveground, but there didn't seem to be any vampires present. He had prepared three Ethelgren's Ilumination spells, and he hoped that those plus his force-lances and shields would be enough to get them through.

The worst of it was the feeling of the murky sewer water seeping into their shoes and soaking the lower portions of their clothing. Well, that and the smell. Although an air elemental kept bringing fresh air in from the street grates they passed under and pushing it forward ahead of them, the smell was still unbelievably foul.

He was starting to think they might make it the entire way without encountering anything when something gray flickered through the tunnel in front of him, moving almost too fast to see. The vampire rebounded from his point-defense shield less than five feet from where he stood, but he began hammering it with force-lances before it could make another charge. Leg, leg, chest, arm, head, the creature's body came apart under his rapid-fire spells.

Will wished he had gotten a chance to learn the spell that Ethelgren had used, since it seemed to kill the creatures with a single shot, but then again, it would have taken months to get to the point where he could reflex cast it.

Tiny had seen some of what happened, though the combination of darkness and flickering illumination from the light spells behind him made it difficult to sort out exactly what happened. "We have one in pieces up here," called the big man.

Janice had someone send an earth elemental forward, and the pieces of the vampire were quickly separated and encased in stone. That gave him pause as he wondered how thorough the ritual would be. It was meant to illuminate even underground spaces, but would it be fine enough to handle body parts encased in stone? Before he could ask, he saw smoke rising from one of the stone balls as it began to crumble away.

Oh, acid, he realized. If it worked for trolls it probably worked for vampire flesh as well, though it wasn't as fast as fire.

Will moved forward even more cautiously after that, but after a hundred yards more he saw that the line went straight up to a grate roughly seven feet above his head. There were no rungs or other means of climbing, since the drain wasn't meant for human access, but Will thought it might be the same sewer grate he had planned to use to escape from Selene's wedding.

If so, that means we're near the east-side door to the cathedral. He wasn't sure though. They could just as easily be on the west side, which was probably just as good. North and south would be less ideal, since the layout of the cathedral meant that the nearest gutters were much farther from the front and back entrances.

"We're here," Will said to Tiny, who turned and passed the word back.

He felt more nervous about emerging from the safety of the sewers than he had about entering them when they had seemed dark and unknown. Now it was the land above

Chapter 51

that seemed most dangerous. *Is this how rabbits feel before they leave the safety of the warren?* he wondered.

They had come too far to back out now and waiting wouldn't help. Will prepared to cast a climb spell on himself. He still had some rope inside the limnthal, so he figured he could tie it off at the top and the others could use it to get up. He was about to start climbing when Laina squeezed around Tiny and nudged him with an elbow. "Move, idiot."

He moved forward, to the other side of the space beneath the grate, and Laina's earth elemental flowed upward, creating wide, easy hand- and footholds in the stone as it went. At the top, it shifted the paving stones and moved the iron grate aside with a minimum of noise. "Oh," said Will, feeling slightly silly. "I keep forgetting about the elementals."

"I wish I could," said Laina darkly, and before he could stop her, she ascended to the street.

Surprised, Will reacted slowly, and Tiny beat him into position to be second. Fortunately, the street was quiet once he got aboveground. The city was covered in darkness, since the lamplighters hadn't been able to do their duties. The windows in the buildings across the street were dark, and the only light came from the stars above.

That was enough for Will, as he adjusted his sight to make use of the starlight, but for the others it was barely enough to keep from stumbling. Laina made as if to cast a fresh light spell, but Will touched her arm. "If we're lucky there's none near, but they'll see the glow from that light from blocks away." A scream in the distance echoed down the lane, underscoring his point. It seemed a few people hadn't obeyed the king's order to gather at Wurthaven.

On one side of them, the cathedral loomed less than twenty feet away, with steps rising to broad double doors.

Will had been right; it was indeed the east-side entrance. Laina leaned in, trying to see his face, and almost slammed her forehead into his nose. "No one can see. How are they going to find the door?" she hissed.

"Wait here a second," he replied, and before she could object, Will moved up the steps to the cathedral entrance. Testing the handle, he found the door locked. *Figures.* Quickly, he cast the unlocking spell and then eased one door open, wincing as the hinges whined loudly. Then he summoned his rope and tied it to the door handle. He stepped back to the grate and handed the rope to Tiny. "Put their hand on it as they come up. It's tied off at the entrance."

The others began to ascend while Will and Laina moved just inside the cathedral doors. "It's even worse in here," she complained. "We have to have light to work by."

Will guided her to the right, then put her hand on the closest of several tall candelabras. "One for now. We can light more once everyone is inside." She nodded, and there was a tiny flicker as her fire elemental lit the closest candle.

The candle made quite a difference, even to those just coming up from the sewer, for it enabled them to see their target, and the rope was hardly needed after that, though it helped keep them from stumbling on the stairs. Twenty people were inside when a voice rang out from the galleries above, echoing in a manner that made it impossible to pinpoint. "I warned you, Will, but you wouldn't listen."

Everyone froze as a bolt of terror shot through their collective hearts. Unlike the others, Will could see clearly within the cathedral, and his eyes soon spotted a gray form moving on the balcony across from them. "Rob?" he called out.

Chapter 51

The vampire laughed. "The one and only. I see you brought friends. This reminds me of the day you first came to Wurthaven. Do you remember? When we looked out the dorm window?"

Will remembered. "It wasn't that long ago," he answered, feeling sad. Rob's fascination with the female student body had caused him to wax poetic. What had he said? *"They lie before us like a banquet waiting to be supped upon."*

"That's what you all look like to me now, Will. Delicious and bursting with vitality."

Will avoided looking directly at his friend. Given the relative darkness, Rob would be seeing him primarily by his heart-light, and while the candle behind him would create a little glare, he knew his old friend would clearly be able to see where his gaze was directed. By looking off to one side, he hoped not to give away the fact that he could see Rob clearly. "Why don't you come down here where I can see you, Rob? We can talk. Maybe there's a way to fix this."

Rob laughed again. "You'd like that, wouldn't you? I'm not stupid. I know the things you can do. You'd end me the second you could see me. If our positions were reversed, I doubt you would care enough to try as much as I have."

"That's not true," said Will.

"Then why didn't you listen? Wasn't I clear enough? Are you trying to force me to kill you?"

Will's mind was racing. *We are merely decoys.* He still didn't understand. The vampires couldn't have known about his plan for a ritual when Rob had written the message, so it couldn't have been part of their plans. He had hoped that his action would circumvent their plan, thinking they only knew about the king's final contingency.

Yet Rob was there waiting for them, in the cathedral. How had he known they would appear there? "Decoys for what?" asked Will.

"That's the beauty of Androv's plan," said Rob. "It doesn't matter what you do. All roads lead to an ending with two results, a dead city, and a dead king. Both will happen, and even if you managed to prevent one through some miracle, the other would be all but inevitable."

"Help me then," Will pleaded. "Despite what they've done to you, you know what's right. Help us."

"You don't know what it's like. The pleasure, the hunger, the taste of someone's life flowing through your lips. Even if I could return to my old self, I wouldn't want to now. I only warned you out of some strange feeling of sentiment, a feeling that has almost faded away."

"But you came here to warn me again?" asked Will. "Or is this an ambush?"

"This is farewell, my friend. Whatever you do here doesn't concern me. Androv will protect me." Rob began backing up, moving closer to the stained-glass windows that lined the galleries.

"Androv is dead!" declared Will.

"Believing that was your biggest mistake." Rob's body blurred into motion, and glass shattered as he flung himself through the window. Will's force-lance passed through the space a half-second later. *I wasn't quick enough,* he chided himself, but he knew it wasn't true. He had hesitated because he couldn't bear to hurt his friend.

CHAPTER 52

Janice and almost two-thirds of the rest were in the cathedral by then. She moved closer to Will and asked, "That was him, wasn't it?"

He nodded, unsure what to say.

Her features carried a multitude of emotions, but she stuck to the issue at hand. "Is it going to be safe to continue? Do they know we're here?"

"I don't know," he admitted. "But we don't have a choice. We have to try."

Laina glanced between the two of them, then went back to the doors to encourage the last of the line to hurry up. Soon Elizabeth Sundy and the baron were in, and they were at last able to shut the doors, though Laina found herself staring upward at the dark windows.

Elizabeth didn't waste time. Moving to the altar in the center, she began pointing at people and barking orders. "You, we need the doors sealed with stone! You, over here, we're going to chalk out the circle. Move everything; we have to clear a space. Someone light the candles so we can see."

Laina was already covering the windows with stone, and soon it seemed they would be sealed inside the cathedral, like a caterpillar within a stone cocoon. Darla moved closer to make a suggestion. "You should leave one door open. Let me watch outside."

Will heard the conversation and joined them. "Why?"

"How many defenders do we have?" asked Darla.

"Twenty-seven students, plus the baron, Laina, Tiny, and yourself," he answered.

The Arkeshi pointed at the windows Laina had already sealed. "Can the Drak'shar break through these?"

Laina shrugged. "It's an inch thick. It should slow them down. If we have enough time, I can double that."

Darla nodded, then pointed at the east door, which they had entered through. "If there is a way in, they will take the path of least resistance. If there is not, they will climb over everything and begin creating their own entrances."

"They may not even notice the open door," Will pointed out.

The Arkeshi pointed at herself. "That is why I will wait out there. As soon as I spot them, I will light a candle and move inside. The candle will announce the position of the open door and draw them to it, like moths to a flame. Our small number of defenders can concentrate their efforts just inside the door, destroying them as they come."

"Unless they have someone with them smart enough to figure out our plan and redirect them," Will stated glumly, thinking of Androv.

"With how few we have, this is the best we can do," said Darla. "If they do have a brilliant commander, we are already dead."

Tiny spoke up, as he had been listening from a few feet away. "Let's do it. I agree with her reasoning."

For some reason everyone seemed to be waiting on Will to make the final call, so he did. "We'll do that." They began moving. *When did I turn into the leader here?* he wondered. Elizabeth Sundy was still barking orders at the students, so he felt some relief. *At least I'm not the only one.*

The lectern and other furniture had been cleared away, along with the altar table, and now the dais where the high priest normally stood was completely clear of obstructions. "Will, come here," called Elizabeth. "You'll

Chapter 52

stand on this mark, at the center." She handed him a sheet of parchment. "Can you do this?"

It all started with a spell construct, Ethelgren's Illumination, with a few alterations. His biggest worry was that he might create the original spell and omit the changes before moving on to the second stage. He nodded. "I can." He had barely gotten the words out before the scholar had moved on, calling to the new sorcerers who would be participating. "You, over here. You, here." It went on and on.

She arranged thirteen in a circle around him, those she judged to be the most experienced students, for their jobs required more finesse as they would be providing auxiliary control, guiding the flows of turyn from the rest of the students into channels that would flow around Will in the center.

While she organized the last of them, Will nervously activated the limnthal. "I'm about to start the ritual," he told Arrogan quietly. "Wish me luck."

"Fuck luck. Luck will get you killed," said the ring, speaking softly. "Remember what happened when the dam nearly collapsed on you?"

"Yeah."

"This is like that. You have to make your own luck."

"I'm not going to be doing the double draw like I did then, though," said Will, somewhat confused.

"No, but you're going to have to step up and do something similar. Controlling the turyn in a ritual like this requires a more advanced technique."

His heart sped up. "You should have said that before! I don't know what I'm doing," he hissed under his breath, hoping no one heard him.

"If you did that, you can do this. The trick here is to keep the turyn *away* from yourself. Visualize a sort of shell around your core, your body. You want to control the turyn they're sending in your direction, but you can't let it slip through and into your inner boundary, otherwise it will undermine your control."

"What the fuck does that mean?" demanded Will, beginning to panic. "I think you should do this. Take my body."

"I wasn't lying when I said I might not be able to give it up. I'm not doing this for you. It's you or nothing."

Will said nothing.

Arrogan went on, "You have to think of it this way. You're keeping the turyn at arm's length, away from *you*. There's so much of it that it will literally tear you apart if it gets too close. So you have to control it at a distance. It sounds harder, but it really—all right, that's a lie—it is harder, but not as hard as dying."

"How am I going to control that much energy if I'm keeping it that far away?"

"Ever seen a tornado?"

"What's that?"

"How about a dust devil?"

Will nodded. "Yes."

"You're going to whip the first turyn that comes in around yourself, like a wind-wall spell. Keep it moving, and its momentum will draw the turyn that follows along with it. As long as you don't falter, the turyn will stick to the pattern."

"What about the ritual construct?"

"You pick a little turyn out of the storm and use just that. Then let the construct pull more in on its own, sort of like its own independent dust devil within your larger dust devil. As it grows, you feed more of the external to it and eventually it consumes all of it and the ritual finishes."

He frowned. "Except the ritual construct isn't a dust devil at all. It's a static structure."

Chapter 52

"Stop bitching, it's a metaphor."

"Don't you mean an analogy?"

"No, asshole! As you just pointed out, it's not *actually* the same. It's more symbolic, so it's a goddamn metaphor!"

"Ahh," said Will. "I keep getting them mixed up."

"Mister Cartwright?" It was Elizabeth. "Are you all right?"

"Yes," he said immediately, dismissing the limnthal.

She turned to the others. "Get ready. We're about to begin."

And just like that, a moment of enlightenment hit him like a bolt of lightning. All the tiny things that bothered him seemed to resolve into a single question. He wasn't sure of its significance, but he had to know. "Wait."

Elizabeth held up her hand, a questioning look on her face as Will stepped out of the circle and went to Laina Nerrow. "Who was it that stole the money?"

His sister blinked. "Pardon?"

"From the charity. You said you wanted Selene's help to pressure the person, but you didn't say who it was."

"Aaron Tintabel."

Things began falling into place. Tintabel's home was close to the Nerrow house, and the first vampires he had seen had leapt from its roof. Of course, that didn't mean much, but with later context it made sense, especially now that the family was dead, and the only apparent survivor was Lord Tintabel himself. It didn't matter much, but Will asked anyway, "Was he involved in the wool trade?"

She nodded. "His estates produce much of the wool in Terabinia."

Jorn Slidden, the trader who had bought the white phosphorous, had dealt primarily in wool, meaning the man had probably been a close associate of Lord

Tintabel's. Will began walking away from everyone, in the direction of the main entrance. He couldn't guess whether Slidden had been a willing or unwilling participant; in fact, the same might be true of Tintabel. If the lord had been involved, why would he kill his own family? Were they being used against him? Had he defied someone's orders?

And why had he stolen the money? Lord Tintabel was presumably a very rich man, certainly rich enough to have afforded the white phosphorous without resorting to petty theft—unless for some reason he had been unable to access his own accounts. A chill ran down Will's spine. Since marrying Selene, he had apparently become wealthy, but until Blake had informed him he'd had no idea. He still had no idea how to access the money on his own. Tintabel might be the same. *If the man calling himself Lord Tintabel was an imposter who had no idea how to access the real Tintabel's funds.*

He activated the limnthal again. "Could a wizard disguise himself as someone else?"

Arrogan sensed his urgency. "Of course."

"How?"

"There's plenty of ways. Illusion, flesh shaping, mental enchantments, you get the idea."

"Do you think a wizard could fool King Lognion that way?"

"There's always signs. A practitioner will notice an illusion, and mental tricks are much more difficult, but physical transformation might do the trick. You've said the king is very adept at noticing deception though, and his sense of turyn is well honed if he saw Aislinn's mark on your forehead that time. For a wizard to fool someone like him, they'd have to be extremely experienced."

"How experienced?"

Chapter 52

"Centuries of practice probably, although it's funny. When you're dealing with someone like Lognion, who has such absolute certainty regarding his ability to detect falsehoods, if you can fool him a little, then you can easily fool him a lot. Someone like that never expects that someone could actually lie to him, so if you can trick his intuition, he'd probably believe anything you said, even if you said the moon was purple. See what I mean?"

"Do you think Androv has that sort of skill?"

"How do you think he's survived until now? He's been walking under the sun and disguising himself as a living person since before *I* was born. I doubt there's anyone Androv couldn't fool."

"Thanks." Will dismissed the limnthal. From the corner of his eye he could see that everyone was watching him, but he didn't care. While they were isolated, in the center of the city, Lord Tintabel was beside the king, and most of the king's forces were spread out around the city wall. If Androv really was masquerading as Tintabel, and if the king couldn't see through the man's lies, then he'd believe anything the man said.

So what if our ritual works? He'll tell him it wasn't enough, and that they have to go ahead with the purge of the city. Once that happens, he kills the king as well. Cerria would be thrown into complete disarray, and Darrow could claim it with only a token struggle. Greater Darrow would be reborn, under the rule of the Prophet.

Assuming the Prophet is the one in control in Darrow. Will wasn't sure what he could believe anymore.

Rob's warning had been spot on. Their ritual didn't matter. Androv's plan was completely indifferent to it. Will stared at the people waiting on him, depending on him, and he felt impotent, hopeless. Inevitably, his eyes traveled to his friends, Janice, Tiny, and his sister, Laina. They had pinned their hopes on him.

And he had failed them—utterly.

The only way to save them for certain would be to abandon the city. The sooner the better. He had sworn to kill the king anyway. Laina would be free of the man's control, as would any wizards and sorcerers who survived the coming catastrophe, though it would mainly be those outside of the capital.

All he had to do was make peace with letting a few hundred thousand people die. He could choose who to save, get the Nerrow family out of Cerria, gather his family in Barrowden. *We could start anew in Trendham.*

He squeezed his eyes shut, blinking away tears of frustration, and then his feet began to move. Lifting his chin, he met Elizabeth Sundy's gaze and said clearly, "I'm ready. I just needed a moment to clear my head."

CHAPTER 53

The ritual seed, similar to a spell construct, came together flawlessly in the air between Will's outstretched hands, shining in all its argent glory. The inner circle of participants began channeling turyn around him, forming thirteen separate bands of power that moved in a tenuous spiral. He caught the bands of turyn with his will, taking ownership and increasing their speed, while the thirteen controllers began accepting turyn from the other one hundred and sixty sources gathered beyond them.

His mind felt like ice, like the sharp clarity of the first wind of autumn. Moving his arms outward so that they pointed straight out to either side, he faced his palms toward the flows of turyn, quickening them and maneuvering them into ever more powerful channels. Soon he was surrounded by a whirlwind of magical currents that continued to increase in intensity, blinding him to anything outside their boundary.

Gradually, he teased delicate strands of power away from the whirlwind and began feeding them into the ritual seed, which pulsed and glowed before him. Will was exhilarated, as though he stood on a precipice looking down at a fall that might kill him. The power ripped at the very fabric of reality around him. It sang in his ears and tugged at his soul, tempting him to step off the cliff and join it.

To become pure magic.

But he was a wizard. The heart of wizardry was control, not submission, not transformation. Asserting himself, Will maintained the balance, refusing to be pulled away, to surrender his life or his humanity. Then a strange voice came to him. *Stubbornness is good, but can you maintain it forever? Or will you become like me?*

It sounded male, and though he hadn't heard it with his ears, he recognized the speaker. It was the man he had met when he died. The one who had counseled him on whether or not returning to life was worth it. Will was curious, but he couldn't afford distractions, so he ignored it.

A crashing sound echoed through the cathedral, and Will heard someone scream. The vampires had found them, but Will could do nothing. He continued feeding turyn into the ritual seed. To stop would mean their deaths.

The sounds of battle continued to assail him, grunts and cries, the grinding of stone, and the wet noises of flesh being torn, and in his mind, Will began to fear for those he loved. But he couldn't see what was happening.

Wild magic can help, advised the voice. *Your focus is strong enough.*

He didn't have time to wonder at the source, but Will understood. Adjusting his vision, he reduced his sensitivity to turyn, and the brilliant glow around him faded, becoming transparent. He could see.

Laina and Mark Nerrow stood side by side, while Tiny and Darla stood in front of them. Their elementals, earth, fire, air, and yet more fire, danced around them, burning and destroying anything that came near. Some of the students assisting in the defense were already down.

Laina's earth elemental provided substantial defense, but they couldn't see through its walls, so she couldn't surround them with an impenetrable dome. Instead she used moving panels, stone walls that flowed and shifted back and forth, allowing them a view at the battle around

Chapter 53

them. As Will watched, one of the undead leapt through a gap, only to be met by Darla's silver blades.

The Arkeshi didn't have room to maneuver, though, and with Mark and Laina behind her she couldn't retreat. Despite the timing of her attacks, she might have been overwhelmed, but for Tiny's timely intervention. Seizing the fiend with both hands, the big man used his mass to arrest the creature's momentum.

It was too strong for him to pin, though, and the vampire turned on him, clawing and biting at his armor, but that was enough. Tiny held it in place long enough for Darla's silvered weapons to disable it, cutting through tendons and joints. Soon they were kicking the pieces of the creature back outside their little stronghold and waiting for the next entrant.

The single-entry idea had worked perfectly, but for the obvious flaw. As they'd predicted, someone among the vampires was smart enough to direct some of the monsters to find other entrances. Laina and her father alone were enough to guard the door, but those that remained of the other student sorcerers were in trouble.

Two of the stone-sealed windows had already been breached, and there were burning remains on the floor beneath them. Fire elementals were picking off vampires as they entered, but the fiends moved so quickly that some kept slipping through.

While he watched, one such free agent ran up the aisle toward an unsuspecting defender. It slammed into a point-defense shield, then lost its head a second later as a force-lance tore through its neck. Will felt a brief tremor run through the currents of turyn around him, but they stabilized a moment later.

Then he spotted another vampire that had somehow escaped notice. It was crawling down one wall like a roach as it prepared to drop down on some of the ritual participants. He wrecked the beast with three force-lances, and then one of the defenders noticed and dispatched a fire elemental to dispose of the quivering remains.

A juggler had come to Barrowden once when he was little, and Will imagined that his experience felt somewhat similar to what the performer had done back then. He continued to balance the devastating currents of power, while occasionally throwing force-lances out to disrupt the enemies that had gotten past the defenders. It was like keeping a dozen balls in the air and unexpectedly tossing one out to the audience now and then.

He had never learned to juggle, but Will was starting to think he might be good at something much better, at least for a wizard. He fought to contain a giggle of hysteria as he continued feeding turyn to the ritual seed, all while letting his peripheral vision inform his reflexes, blasting anything that moved too quickly.

He felt like a god.

The student defenders rallied, burning the bodies of the ones he brought down and consolidating their control over the open windows. The entry of vampiric invaders slowed, and soon the cathedral sanctuary was quiet, except for the heavy breathing of those who were grateful for the rest.

Will didn't need a rest, though. He could have kept it up forever. The power was spinning around him effortlessly, dancing in and out as it passed between his hands and entered the ritual seed. How long he spent like that he was unsure—long enough that it began to seem normal, as though he'd spent his entire life doing nothing but that.

He became exquisitely aware of the feeling, the touch of turyn, the way it moved. He'd never controlled that

Chapter 53

much power before, not firsthand. It required a delicate touch and a sense of rhythm, like dancing. Fortunately, unlike dancing, he seemed to be a natural. *Once you've felt it, you can never forget,* said the stranger's voice. *It becomes part of you and everything changes. You are reborn, child; this is your baptism in magic.*

"Who are you?" Will cried, but he didn't receive an answer.

And then it was time. Seizing the currents, Will sent them crashing inward to fill a ritual construct that was finally large and strong enough to contain them. His head fell back, and his mouth opened as his voice screamed out with joy, though he had no idea what he might be yelling. It was like an orgasm—no, it was better.

Argent energy streamed outward in the shape of millions upon millions of brilliant silver spheres. They blinded him even through closed eyelids, and they kept coming, an endless flow emerging from the living womb of power he had built. Those around him fell to their knees, covering their eyes with hands and arms, trying to block out the searing light. But Will merely laughed. He had changed his eyes, dimming everything, and when the others could finally look at him again, they saw that where his eyes should be there were only unsettling black orbs.

The ritual power finally finished and passed beyond the cathedral walls, soaring into the night and dipping into the earth and sky. It rushed over the city like a wave, purifying everything, and wherever the vampires hid, they perished, burning away into piles of ash that the breeze soon scattered.

As the light died away, Will's eyes returned to normal, but he couldn't stop the giddy laughter from spilling from his lips. It had felt *so good*. He was nothing but smiles—until he saw the bodies of the students who had died.

Blood was splattered across the sanctuary floor and walls, some red, some black. Scorch marks covered everything, along with crumbled pieces of stone and splintered wood. But while the vampire bodies had disintegrated under the withering glare of the ritual's magic, those of his fellow students had not.

He got himself under control, and then his ears began to decipher the sounds around him, a mixture of quiet sobbing and tearful goodbyes being said to friends who wouldn't see the sun rise tomorrow. Looking toward the door, he was grateful to see that his friends and family all appeared safe and unharmed.

Two students, one male and one female, stood out to him, for they had died while holding onto each other. He didn't know either of them, but their faces were vaguely familiar. Unlike most of the other victims, these two showed no signs of tooth or claw. They had died instantly, from the distinctive, fist-sized hole of a force-lance that had gone through both of them simultaneously.

Will's mouth went dry, and he took a step back. Several other students were kneeling beside them, speaking quietly to one another, and when they looked up at him, he saw the knowledge burning in their eyes. They knew who had killed their friends. "It was an accident," he said weakly, barely able to breathe. "I didn't know."

A fellow he did recognize, Phillip Wakefield, had just come closer, and he asked, "What happened to Lynsey and Simon?"

One of the nearby girls answered, "One of those things was running at Simon, and Lynsey tried to get in front of it, but then—" Her tear-stained face turned toward Will.

"—Will tried to save them," declared Laina, her voice carrying loudly over the din of soft voices. "Just like he saved the rest of you. This time he missed."

Chapter 53

"But…"

Her eyes flashed angrily. "But nothing! If he hadn't tried, they would have both died anyway. If he had tried and missed them, they would have died anyway. He tried and he failed, but ultimately it was the vampire's fault. The monsters are the ones who are responsible for all of this. Save your blame for those who truly deserve it."

No one said anything for a moment, then the voices slowly resumed. Through it all, Will heard someone say, "He was laughing the entire time…"

Laina's ears were just as sharp. "How many of you nearly died tonight, when they started coming through the windows? Have you forgotten already? How many of you nearly had your throats ripped out before someone smashed your killer with a bolt of force? If I hear one more remark suggesting what he did was anything less than heroic, I'll teach you how the spell works myself!"

"Laina, you need to calm down. We're all stressed here…," began her father, reaching out to put a hand on her shoulder.

Laina sidestepped him and continued, her voice rising to the ceiling in a commanding shout. "Do you understand me?"

No one said anything for a while, then people began lowering their eyes, and the air filled with a smattering of yeses. Elizabeth Sundy and Mark Nerrow began calling for order after that, sorting through who had been wounded and who hadn't. Other than the dead, only seven people had been scratched or bitten. Will summoned blood-cleanse potions from the limnthal and gave them to Laina, who passed them out to those who needed them.

She made clear to each recipient that it was Will who had created and supplied the potions. Janice sidled up to

Will and quietly remarked, "You seem to have a tireless advocate defending you."

He smiled weakly. "Not sure I'm worth it."

She elbowed him in the ribs. "Don't make me tell Tiny you said that. You know how he feels."

Will chuckled.

"I was about to do the same thing, but she beat me to the punch—and honestly, I don't think I would have had the guts to go as far as she did. She wasn't pulling any punches."

"She's like a badger," said Will. "Once she gets her teeth into something, she never lets go."

Janice shook her head. "I've seen her give up a few times, mainly when the baron put his foot down, but not where you're involved."

He shrugged.

"I guess that's why they're talking about making her a saint."

Will yelped, "What?"

Janice nodded. "Not while she's alive, of course, but people talk. She can't overlook an underdog. She gave a famous speech in front of the cathedral two years ago, rallying the people to give to the cause. She helped shame the nobles into opening their coffers for the poor and those who had lost everything when Darrow invaded."

He found it almost unbelievable. *She was only sixteen then, and I'm sure her father didn't want her out making a spectacle of herself.* Now that he knew her better, he could understand. His sister was a fighter, and he couldn't be more proud.

Standing up, Will walked over to Tiny and whispered, "We're leaving in a minute."

The big man's brow furrowed, and his lips mouthed the word, 'now?'

Chapter 53

Will nodded, then he raised his voice. "If I can have your attention!" It took a minute—his voice didn't carry as well as Laina's—but eventually everyone grew quiet. "The city won't be safe when dawn comes. You should head for the southern gate. If the guards won't let you out, destroy the gates and escape. Another ritual is planned, one that will kill every living person within the walls."

That shocked them into silence, until one person spoke. "What the hell are you talking about?"

Mark Nerrow was close behind. "William, you aren't making sense."

He held up his hands. "I know it doesn't seem fair after what you've done, all of you. You saved this city, but I'm not lying. At least one of the vampires remains, and he's close to the king right now, as we speak, filling his ears with lies."

"He's lost his damned mind," someone muttered.

Another voice added, "I could tell that already."

Will ignored the naysayers. "Whatever you do, don't go north. Whatever is happening will be centered around the palace and Wurthaven." Then he turned away, nodding at Tiny, who quickly followed him.

The crowd seemed too shocked to respond, but Laina's voice wouldn't be denied. "Where do you think you're going?" she demanded.

Will turned back and saw Janice and Laina had already closed the distance, with Janice leading in the race. "Are you trying to ditch me again?" asked his classmate.

He looked at Laina and addressed her first. "You have to make them follow you. Your father won't listen to me. If I can't stop him, he'll destroy this city and everyone in it at dawn, if not sooner. The vampire scourge and our response to it was all part of the diversion."

"Who?" snapped Laina in exasperation.

"The king and Lord Tintabel, otherwise known as Androv."

Janice hissed, "The vampire wizard you fought before?"

He nodded.

"Do you think you can beat him this time? You made it sound like you got lucky in that basement," asked Janice.

He was ready for the question, and Will put everything into projecting confidence as he lied, "Definitely. I've already figured out how to do it."

"How?" challenged Laina.

"I don't have time to explain." He looked at Janice. "You have to keep her here so she can lead them."

For once his classmate seemed to believe him. Janice nodded and took hold of Laina's arm, but Laina twisted away, giving Janice a cold glare. "Fuck this! I'm coming. She can stay and lead them."

He met her gaze evenly. "Don't make me embarrass you in front of everyone. I'm quite capable of paralyzing you."

His sister growled but finally looked away, and he knew then that she had finally given in. Janice looked at them, and a sudden sense of urgency passed over her features. "Bring him back in one piece," she pleaded.

Will and Tiny answered in unison, "I will."

Janice smiled at the dual response. "Close your eyes."

Not sure who she meant, Will complied, but a second later he heard something next to him. Opening them again, he saw Janice stepping back. She had climbed up on her toes and pulled Tiny down a little so she could plant a kiss on his cheek. "For luck."

Will watched his friend warily, worried he might faint. *If he goes down none of us could catch him.* Laina let out a sigh of disgust.

Chapter 53

They turned away again, and this time they made it out the door of the cathedral, but Will's embarrassment wasn't quite over yet. As they started down the street, he heard Laina's strident warning cut through the night air. "Come back alive, you jerk, or I'll find your stupid corpse and cut off your balls!"

Chapter 54

They were moving at a brisk pace, though Will wished they could go faster. If he'd been alone, he would have run, but Tiny's heavy frame made that impractical. The big man was in excellent shape, but he simply wouldn't be able to match Will's running pace for very long. It made more sense to stay together and arrive without being exhausted.

"Where are we going first?" asked Tiny.

"The palace."

"Think they're still there?"

Will shrugged. "If not, then Wurthaven is right next door. The entire city populace is packed onto the grounds. We should make sure they're still safe anyway."

"We just wiped out all the vampires, though," Tiny reminded him. "Wouldn't it be better to look for the king before he gets murdered?"

"That's why we're heading for the palace first, but the king will be alive. Androv won't kill him until he's destroyed the city."

"Shouldn't Androv be dead already? That spell in the cathedral seemed pretty intense."

"He's a wizard," said Will. "He's had centuries to perfect his magic, and he has spells that allow him to survive sunlight and pass as human. For that matter, he's probably protecting his closest servants as well, like Alexa. I doubt he'll be alone."

"You said you had a plan to deal with him."

Will stopped and gave his friend a long, serious look. "I lied."

"You don't think you can win?"

He shook his head. "Not in a straight fight."

The big warrior shrugged, then started walking again. "That's all right. This time you have me with you."

Will watched him from behind for several seconds. *Mother, help me if anything happens to him. I'd be utterly lost.* He hurried to catch up.

As they got close to the palace, they could see that the gates were open and the sentries were gone from the walls. In the direction of Wurthaven, there were flashes of light and the sounds of fighting. Will wondered if the king had abandoned the palace to assist in defending Wurthaven and the people there.

It didn't seem likely, though. *He thinks the city is lost no matter what, including all those people. He'll be wherever it is that he plans to enact the ritual.* The more he thought about it, the more it made sense. Androv would be with the king, making sure that no one else could contradict his story.

Whoever was attacking Wurthaven was simply part of the diversion. Lognion wouldn't be there, and neither would Androv. Yet if Lognion intended to work a massive, city-wide ritual he would need a large number of sorcerers to assist him, and trying to do it from some point on the city's walls would be needlessly difficult. If that's where most of his forces were deployed, the king was potentially operating alone.

That meant there was only one possible place the man could be planning to perform his ritual. Will froze.

Tiny gave him a worried look. "There's fighting over there. We have to go."

"That's a diversion, and any vampires over there will be ones that were protected from our ritual," said Will. He pointed southwest. "He's that way. If we stop here, we might not make it in time."

"We still have to help the people," said Tiny.

Did they have time? Any vampires that had survived the ritual Will had performed would be protected against daylight, so they'd be much more difficult to dispatch. He was pretty sure that Androv wouldn't kill Lognion until the king's ritual was done, and the king had told him he would wait until dawn. That was still hours away. "You're right," said Will, hurrying forward.

The school gate was wide open, not that it mattered. The stone walls weren't much of a hindrance to creatures that could leap twenty feet and claw their way up the rest of the way to the top. Dead guards lay scattered about the entrance like broken dolls, and in the distance, Will could hear screaming.

The fox was in the henhouse.

As big as Wurthaven's grounds were, the populace of the city was sufficient to fill almost the entire place with a light crowd. The vampires, however many there were, were running loose in a giant playground, killing indiscriminately. Will needed to get their attention, for it would be impossible to track them all down in the time they had.

Activating the limnthal, he summoned his shield and handed it to Tiny since his friend had left his at the house. "I'm going to try and attract their attention," he told him.

"How many do you think will come?" asked Tiny, looking nervous for the first time. "It was pretty intense back at the cathedral, and it's just you and me now."

"I don't know, but if you see more than three or four, maybe you should take the potion."

"Which one? Oh!" Tiny opened the potion holder and made sure his fingers knew where the appropriate vial was.

Chapter 54

"Here we go," warned Will, then he used one of his prepared spells, Ethelgren's Illumination. Filling his lungs, he yelled as the balls of searing light soared outward, turning night into day. He didn't expect it to kill these, since they were obviously protected, but there was no better way to draw attention at night. "Come and get me, you bloodthirsty bug-fuckers!"

Tiny gave him a confused look. "Bug-fuckers?"

Will shrugged. "Would chuckle-fucks be better?"

"You need help." Tiny's eyes grew wide. "It's more than three or four!" He jerked the potion free of the pouch so hastily that it flew from his fingers and broke on the pavement several feet away. Fumbling for the second vial, he slowed down just enough to successfully unstop it and bring it to his lips.

Will was already picking them off as they came into range. The force-lance spell, like most force effects, didn't need much turyn when used over short distances, but the cost went up exponentially with distance. At ten yards it was negligible, at twenty it was tiring, and at thirty yards it was well beyond his rate of turyn recovery. He started firing at forty yards, and by the second spell he knew he would run out by the fourth. At twenty yards he started again, but it only took a second for them to close that distance.

He took down ten in that time, though it was obvious they were only wounded. Once they were in melee range, he switched to using the point-defense shield since it was more effective at stopping their forward movement and he wasn't killing them anyway.

Through that span of several seconds, Tiny hardly moved, though a low growl was beginning to emerge from his throat. The big man seemed to be vibrating, as though he might be on the verge of a seizure.

Will began to despair, for he couldn't see in all directions, and the vampires on the wings had kept running, circling to flank them. He wanted to turn so he could see the threat coming at his back, but the monsters in front of him moved too quickly. It was all he could do to repulse their attacks with a blinding series of shields.

A roar erupted from Tiny, a sound so deep and feral Will thought some new monster had sprung upon them. The big warrior blurred as he spun in place, and his falchion cut through *something* behind them. Will didn't have the liberty of watching. A second later the squire danced in front of him then passed behind, moving around Will in a circle. Clawed hands, arms, legs, and pieces of wood-hafted spears fell to the ground in his wake.

Spears?

They had come in with such speed that Will hadn't even seen the weapons. Behind the blood-maddened young vampires there were three wearing armor and bearing weapons. They had hung back, letting the wild ones take the damage as they charged in. One of them was now tossing aside his spear in favor of a broadsword.

Seeing the sharp metal made his skin prickle, and Will was acutely aware of the fact that he hadn't donned any armor that day. He felt naked, and for the first time he realized that perhaps he had grown too comfortable relying on his spells. He could only watch so many directions at once.

Tiny was behind him, and Will saw a shadow pass overhead. Given the way the vampire flailed, it seemed the monster had been thrown, rather than leaping on its own. Will kept using his point-defense shield, for the attacks from the front kept coming too quickly for him to try and inflict damage. He absently noted that several broken crossbow quarrels were now on the ground in front of him. *There are more in the back firing at us!*

Chapter 54

Tiny came around once more, and Will could see several shafts caught in his mail. Apparently, there were fiends firing from other directions as well, directions Will couldn't see. Tiny was cutting a deadly swath through monsters, but without silver on the blade, the wounds healed too quickly—even severed limbs could be reattached without too much effort, if the cut was clean.

Will had thought the fight would be smaller, that they would have some room to breathe, time to use the alchemical fire he carried to destroy the vampire remains. He already knew these were protected from daylight, since they had survived the ritual, so the spells he had prepared were useless.

It was only a matter of time before Will and Tiny tired and soon after that they would die.

Desperate, Will stepped left to avoid one creature's rush rather than use his shield, and with that moment to spare, he summoned Ethelgren's Exhortation. He resumed using the shield a second later, while at the same time he felt the old wizard begin to rush into his body.

He shut that down instantly, pushing Ethelgren back while still defending himself, and his spells never faltered. *That's not going to happen,* he sent mentally.

I had to try.

Asshole. I'm surrounded by vampires protected from daylight. Any ideas?

Let me take control, suggested Ethelgren dryly.

Not again. If I die, I'll drop this rod and your enemies will melt you down.

The ancient wizard gave a mental sigh. *Since you're not dead, you must be defending yourself. What are you using?*

Point-defense shield.

That's all?

I don't have anything else!
Amateur.
Is that coat of light spell you used built into the rod? asked Will.
It is, but it's no good if they're protected from sunlight. It won't stop physical attacks, and light won't repel them. You need armor or an iron-body transformation.
I haven't mastered that one yet.
It's built into the rod. Let me show you.

Will was still steadily blocking attacks from howling fiends that were just a few feet away. Mentally, he eased up on the pressure he was using to contain Ethelgren and he received a flash as the long-dead wizard showed him the turyn signature needed to activate the iron-body transformation.

A second later, Will repeated what he had felt but with more turyn, which he directed into the relic. The overall sensation was similar to casting a spell, except that instead of routing his energy into a spell construct, he was sending it into an item. It was also much faster, since he didn't have to create the spell first, so in a sense it was like reflex casting. There was a slight lag, though; unlike a force effect, other spells did require some small amount of time to function. He still hadn't learned to reflex cast any non-force spells, so the delay had never been noticeable before, but he could feel it now. Even so, it took less than a second, and suddenly he felt a cold stiffening of his skin, slowing his movements.

His skin had darkened, taking on a reddish-brown color, and it felt as though someone had dressed him in heavy but supple leather, from head to toe. *It worked!* he announced internally. *Now I just need a way to kill them.*

Are you any good with a sword?
Somewhat, but there's someone even better next to me. Do you have any silver on you?

Chapter 54

Just money.

He sensed Ethelgren's mental nod. *That works.* Another flash of turyn came to Will, along with an explanation. *You have to hold the weapon when you cast it, and the silver is consumed. The spell only lasts an hour or so; after that the steel reverts to normal.*

It coats the blade in silver? asked Will.

Ethelgren chuckled. *I designed the spell. It's much better than that.*

Shifting the relic to his left hand, Will summoned his smallest coin pouch and tried to shake out the coins he needed, spilling gold marks, silver clima, and copper bits in all directions. He caught a few and then discarded all but one clima. He passed it over to his left hand and then summoned his rapier.

During his chaotic coin dance, Will lost focus on what was going on around him and he felt several thudding blows against his body, but no pain. One vampire even managed to grab hold of him, but Tiny cut the creature fully in two; then, when it was apparent that the upper portion was still hanging on, he cut the monster free by slicing off its arms.

The hands continued stabbing at him with sharp nails, but Will's skin resisted everything. Then he activated the spell and the coin in his hand dissolved, flowing toward the sword he held. As it ran up the blade, the silver dust exploded into argent flames. *Damn that looks wicked!*

That's why the ladies loved me, said Ethelgren.

Shut it, pervert, Will chastised. "Tiny, catch!" he shouted, and with those words he tossed the rapier into the air. If their positions had been reversed, Will probably would have missed the catch. There was simply too much going on, and catching a sword by the hilt required a certain amount of concentration, even if a person was ready.

But in Tiny's present state, the falling weapon was moving at a relatively sedate pace. He tossed his falchion at Will and snatched the rapier by the hilt in one blindingly fast motion. On his end of the exchange, Will arrested the falchion's movement by attempting to block it with his face. A point-defense shield stopped it at the last instant, though when he thought about it later, the sharp edge probably wouldn't have cut him with the iron-body transformation in place anyway, but reflexes didn't wait for thoughtful decisions.

From the moment Tiny took up the burning silver blade, his whirling rampage changed, becoming a holy storm of destruction. Throughout the course of their fight, the outlying vampires had drawn closer and closer, threatening to overwhelm them with numbers as they ran out of ammunition. Now they began to retreat, and the smarter ones turned to flee.

Will had planned to summon his own falchion and repeat the silver-sword spell, but there wasn't time. As the space around them increased, he switched to using force-lances to cripple those trying to run.

Tiny had become an unstoppable force of nature. The Dragon-Heart potion had given him incredible strength and speed, and while the vampires could match that, they didn't have his mass. The shield Will had given him was long gone, destroyed by powerful attacks the vampires had assailed him with, but his sword rose and fell in blinding arcs, cutting and burning everything in its path, while his left hand seized those that came within reach. Some vampires he drew closer, if his sword was headed in the right direction; others he simply jerked off their feet. Usually before they could recover, his sword had returned.

Silver fire and black ash surrounded the giant man, who seemed to have transformed into an incarnation of carnage.

Chapter 54

The last of the vampires were running, but they did so without legs. Some crawled on arms alone, still moving at an impressive speed, but it wasn't sufficient to escape the raging warrior and his burning retribution. Tiny raced after the last of them, while Will tossed vials of alchemical fire on those that were closer.

A minute later and it was all but over. Will stood panting where they had started, while Tiny raced around in the distance, roaring and killing anything that moved. Any people that had been within sight of them at the beginning had long since retreated. Will watched as a beautiful elm that had lined the road leading from the gate crashed slowly to the ground, flames spouting from the thickest part of its trunk. *Holy shit! Did he just cut that tree down—with a rapier?*

Told you it was a good spell, said Ethelgren dryly. *Though your friend must be exceptionally strong to do that with it.*

Dragon-Heart potion, Will informed him.

Ahh.

Will waited, and after a few minutes Tiny returned. His chest was heaving, and his eyes glowing red in a fashion so unnatural that it even made Will nervous. "Are you all right?"

Tiny grinned maniacally. "Never better! Do you see any more of them?" His head kept moving from side to side as he scanned the area, but his neck moved so quickly that his features blurred each time. "I think that's all of them." He sounded disappointed.

At the very least there weren't any more screams to be heard. There might still be some hidden, but Will hoped that the soldiers or perhaps some of the remaining sorcerers would find them. Quite a few of the teachers and some students had elementals, after all. He shared his concern with Ethelgren.

The spell that protects them from daylight won't last long without someone to reapply it. If there's a wizard with them, you'll never catch him in a crowded area like this, said the dead wizard.

Then I should move on and find the king and Androv.

You're going after that one? You should let me take over.

Will shook his head. *Again, no.* The iron-body transformation was beginning to feel onerous as it used a not-inconsiderable amount of turyn to maintain, so he dismissed it. Then he noticed that Tiny seemed to be swaying on his feet. "Are you all right, Tiny?"

The squire's breathing was coming in big gasps. "Yeah. I'm just a little tired. I think I need to sit down."

Will helped him over to a tree and watched Tiny slide down it until he was resting with his back against the base. "Are you hurt anywhere?"

"I'm not sure. Things are starting to hurt."

Concerned, Will began checking Tiny over. His armor seemed to be intact, but one of the crossbow quarrels seemed to have penetrated the mail a short distance, though not far enough for the barbs to enter his flesh. He pulled it out and then looked at Tiny's face and hands, which were bare. There were several small cuts, but none of them bled. *Weird.*

Tiny began to moan as his agony slowly increased. Will began checking the man's ribs and found several that appeared to be out of place, though whether they were dislocated or fractured he couldn't be sure through the padding and mail. The biggest shock came when he realized that the big man's clavicle had snapped. *He shouldn't even be able to move!*

The potion finally ran out, and Will saw the cuts on his friend's face suddenly begin to bleed, right in front of

Chapter 54

his eyes. Seconds later, a red bloom appeared on Tiny's gambeson where the bolt had pierced his side. Tiny tried to move his arm and screamed.

Will summoned a blood-cleanse potion and gave that to him first, to make sure none of the cuts caused him to turn. They looked clean, but he wasn't going to take the chance. After that, he waited a few minutes and pulled the regeneration potion out of Tiny's belt case. "Here, take this." He held the vial up to Tiny's lips so he wouldn't have to try and use his arms.

The next few minutes were pure misery for the squire. Will had to help him lie flat while his bones were mending, which prompted a long series of groans and painful cries. When he finally seemed comfortable, Will knew he needed to go, but he still felt guilty.

Tiny's eyes were closed as he spoke. "We still need to find the king, don't we?"

"I'm pretty sure I know where he is."

"Just let me catch my breath and I'll be right as rain."

Will shook his head. "Your body was wrecked. The regeneration potion is going to take a toll. I doubt you'll wake up until tomorrow."

"I just won't go to sleep," insisted the big man, his voice slurring.

Will wished he could move him. Leaving him there on the ground, barely a hundred feet from the school entrance, didn't seem safe. There probably weren't any more vampires in the area, but he didn't know that for sure. *"Bring him back in one piece."* Janice's words rang through his mind.

Tiny surged upward for a moment, then sagged and slumped back down. "My body feels like jelly. Do I still have bones?"

"You still have bones. You're just tired."

"I don't think I can walk without bones."

Will nodded. "That would be a problem."

"You'll have to go without me, Will. I'm sorry."

"Don't be sorry."

"But you need help. I said I'd be there…"

Activating the limnthal, he summoned a pillow and blanket. After making his friend as comfortable as possible, he replied, "You were there. Don't worry. The others are back now. They're going to help me, so you can get some rest."

"Really?"

"Yeah." Tiny was asleep before he finished answering. Standing up, Will pushed his guilt aside and started back out the gate. *If anything happens to him, I'll never forgive myself.* But he knew if he didn't go, his friend would die anyway.

Chapter 55

Alone again, Will jogged at a modest pace, one he could maintain without tiring himself out. He was heading for the wealthy part of town, where the noblemen and rich merchants kept their homes. It was the same area that his father's house was in, but the specific home Will was going to was a few blocks from the Nerrow home.

As far as he knew, it was still empty, though most would expect that it belonged to the heirs of the Arenata estate. Will knew that wasn't the case, however. After he had slain Duke Arenata and murdered his guests, some of whom might have been innocents, Will had sacrificed the duchess on her own altar. It sounded horrific, and the actual event had been just as terrible as it sounded, but Will had acted with good intentions. In fact, he'd saved the city from a demonic invasion.

Beneath the house, deep underground in a secret chamber, was a convergence of ley lines. Selene had sealed the passage that led to it with stone, but her father had discovered its existence later and had used his royal prerogative to lay claim to the empty dwelling, paying the family a nominal amount of gold to silence their complaints.

And that had been that. Or so Will had thought.

The only place someone in Cerria could create such a massive ritual without the assistance of additional practitioners was there, and the king might well have had the time to construct the circle it would require. Will didn't know how many days it would take, but the king certainly had the resources.

Just because I didn't know about the vampire threat until a few days ago doesn't mean he didn't know, especially if Androv was already whispering in his ear.

Will summoned Ethelgren's Exhortation again. This time the inhabitant put up a token struggle but quickly surrendered. *Are you going to do that every time?* asked Will.

Maybe.

I'm heading into what used to be an abandoned home. I believe the king and Androv are in a secret underground chamber where they can access a ley line.

Did your warrior friend die?

What? asked Will, alarmed. *No.*

Oh, good, Ethelgren replied, his tone unconvincing. *Those potions can be hard on the body. But I take it you're planning to go in there alone?*

Yes.

You should let me take over. I'll give you your body back afterward.

Will ground his teeth. *No.*

What if I promise?

No.

You're going to die, and then I'll wind up in Androv's collection. If I'm lucky, he'll take me out every once in a while, to taunt me. If I'm not he'll melt me down.

Then help me defeat him.

He's not a one-trick pony. The man is clever, and he's got thousands of spells at his fingertips, cautioned Ethelgren. *Even if you understood every function I built into this rod, you probably wouldn't have a chance. I could only put so many in, and you don't have the experience and spells of your own to make up the difference.*

Chapter 55

I whipped your ass, Will remarked.

Technically, you didn't. You tricked me into letting your creepy grandfather out of his cage. By the way, have I mentioned how awful that is? Who does that to their own family?

It wasn't my idea. Are you going to help or not?

Sure, but you'll still lose. Just remember I told you so.

Will grimaced. *Fine. With my last dying breath, I'll be sure to tell you how right you were.*

That'll do. All right, here's the spell effects that are most likely to help you. Pay attention as I show you the turyn signatures.

***

Will slowed when the Arenata home came into view. From the outside, it still looked much as it had the last time he had been there. Someone had been maintaining the plants and keeping up the ornamental garden. One might easily assume someone still lived there.

For personal spells, Will had replaced the illuminations with a climb spell, a wind-wall, and on Ethelgren's recommendation, a blur spell. The blur spell was an illusion that he had learned over a year ago and had kept in his daily practice, but he'd never used it in combat. Usually the chameleon spell seemed preferable to him since he liked to avoid fights, and once a fight started, he rarely had a chance to use anything but spells he had prepared, or those he could reflex cast.

Ethelgren had advised him to use it. *He'll be able to see straight through your chameleon spell. That's true of all vampires. They can track your body heat.*

Hmm, said Will. *I always called it heart-light.*

Same thing. Anyway, the blur spell is an illusion that smears your appearance across several feet, making it hard to tell exactly where you are. It works for all kinds of light, so it helps against things like vampires too.

Is being blurry that great?

If your body outline is spread across twice the distance, they only have half the chance of hitting you. It makes a big difference if you screw up and he hits you with a point attack.

Point attack?

Like my silver bolts, or a force-lance. There are lots of different kinds of single target attacks.

Oh, said Will. *So he'll only have a fifty-fifty chance of blowing my guts across the wall.*

It's better than a hundred percent chance, and the illusion costs next to nothing to maintain.

Will walked across the street and took a few seconds to cast a spell to unlock the front gate, then he went to the door and repeated the spell. He didn't hurry. He might not be able to run away from the problem, but he wasn't going to rush to his death either.

Opening the door was a bit stressful, but nothing came charging out at him, and after a second or two he had adjusted his vision to the dim gloom. Seeing no enemies, he sent a quick pulse of turyn to the rod and felt a gentle chime of magic rush outward in all directions.

The sound was illusory, and only he could hear it, as it was merely part of the spell designed to inform him of its result. The brief pulse of magic covered an area roughly fifty feet around him, and as it passed through objects it measured two things, transparency to sound and visible light. Normal objects affected both, but a creature using a chameleon spell would cause the spell to return a deeper, more ominous tone, warning the caster of a hidden foe.

Chapter 55

Subsequent pulses could narrow down the range and direction. Will had wondered why the spell didn't cover a greater distance, since it didn't require much energy. Ethelgren had replied, *Because, you usually use the spell indoors. Greater range just confuses things.*

This time the spell returned an 'all clear' chime, so Will stepped into the entry hall. Taking another nervous breath, Will cast a silent-armor spell on himself to muffle sounds. While he might not be actively sneaking, there was no reason to give his presence away any earlier than was absolutely necessary.

After several tense minutes of searching, Will was certain the house was empty, so there was nothing left but for him to move on to where he knew they must be. The storage closet under the stairs was still as he remembered it, but inside the hidden door that Selene had sealed with stone was now a gaping arch without any door at all. Beyond that, the old stone stairs led down just as they had before. The only thing covering the opening was the illusion of a stone wall.

The closet was empty, both of clutter and dust. The stairs beyond were also clear and obviously had been used a lot recently. Will guessed that was because the king had been sending crews of workers down to prepare the chamber for his new ritual. He stepped through the illusory wall and began moving down the stairs, shifting his vision to see by heart-light as he went.

As before, it was a long descent, but this time the goddamn cat wasn't with him. He almost wished it were a demon-lord he was facing again, just so he would have the demigod's help. Halfway down the long stairs, he saw a small gray figure sitting on one of the steps, as if his thoughts had summoned it.

Will stopped. "You."

The goddamn cat stared at him without blinking for a long period, then slowly blinked.

"Are you here to help?"

"I'm here to warn you that I won't be helping. Don't expect any intervention. If you go down there you likely won't come back, and if you do come back it will probably be as an undead abomination."

"Thanks for calming my nerves. If that's all you had to say you could have just skipped coming here," Will replied.

"If you go in there it will further the agendas of some who you might prefer not to aid."

"If I die, or if I succeed?"

"Either," answered the Cath Bawlg. "Your ally is also your enemy, and she plays both sides of the game."

Aislinn, thought Will. "Why are you telling me this? What outcome would you prefer?"

"Your death might be nice. If the accord collapses, my opportunities to seek revenge against the fae will increase. That is why I won't aid you."

"Then you may as well have not come," observed Will. "Or are you playing both sides too? Do you have something to gain if I live?"

"Sammy would prefer it."

Will couldn't help but laugh. Had his cousin really won over a demigod simply by scratching his head and tying bows in his hair? He felt the knot in his chest loosen. Whatever would come, would come. It was best to face it with a clear head. The goddamn cat might not be willing to help, but if Sammy had won him over, at least he didn't have to worry about her.

The cat began bathing himself, and Will stepped over him so he could proceed down the stairs. The Cath Bawlg's voice said one more thing to his back. "Do you know why I choose the form of a cat?"

Chapter 55

Will kept walking.

"Cats keep themselves clean."

Utterly confused, Will turned around to look back, but the cat was nowhere to be seen. Shaking his head, he resumed his trip downward.

Chapter 56

The small room at the bottom of the stairs was still as it had been, though the powerful ward that protected the archway leading into the ritual chamber was no longer present. Will had destroyed it last time, to allow the goddamn cat to enter and confront the demon-lord Leykachak.

He could hear voices in the next room. Lognion and Lord Tintabel were talking to each other.

"There's really no point in waiting, Your Majesty," said Tintabel. "My scouts reported to me just before I came down. Your son-in-law and the others failed. Most of them are dead, and those who aren't will soon number among our enemies. We have no other options remaining."

The king sighed. "I had high hopes for him. At the very least, since he's hidden my daughter, I can be sure she remains safe."

"A great comfort, I am sure."

"Assuming she returns and gives me a child. If not, I may have to marry again, and that's always tiresome."

Will stepped through the archway. "You may as well remarry then, for I'll never let you have any child of mine and Selene's."

The king whipped around in surprise, his eyes snapping to Will's face. "You?" He glanced at Tintabel. "But you just said…"

"He must have run from the battle," suggested Tintabel.

"Or I succeeded and have come to report so to the king," countered Will.

Lognion's eyes were moving quickly between the two of them, and his face was full of suspicion. Will understood why. *He's trying to figure out how we could both believe we were telling the truth when the facts should be obvious to both of us.*

Tintabel moved to stand protectively in front of the king. "Careful, Your Majesty. The vampire rumored to be leading them may have the ability to disguise his form."

Will smiled. "Funny. That's what I was just about to say. Instead, maybe I should point out that your entire family died in a fire a few days ago, but somehow you alone miraculously survived. Would that be because you couldn't fool them into believing you were the real Lord Tintabel?"

The king acted suddenly and without hesitation. Taking two steps back, he raised a force-dome around himself. "The question is easily solved. Let me see which of you bleeds." An earth elemental manifested by the archway leading to the stairs, and stone flowed up to block the exit. "Neither of you will leave this place until I am sure that the one who lies is the one who dies." More elementals began to appear around the edges of the room.

Tintabel laughed and raised one hand. A beam of gray light shot from one of his fingers and played over the king's force-dome, eating holes in the protective field.

Will was stunned. He'd never encountered a magic that could do that. He fired a force-lance at the vampire, then cast his blur spell. His attack went to waste, though, for a split second before he acted, Tintabel's body exploded into a cloud of gray dust, expanding to fill the entire room. A voice began to laugh, echoing through the chamber, and he recognized it as Androv. "It's a shame you ruined my fun, but it changes nothing."

The king's elementals were helpless to find a target, and Lognion himself was attempting to repair his defense to no avail. He dismissed it so he could cast another, but it was too late. The dust swarmed toward him, covering his body and filling his mouth and nose. The sovereign of Terabinia didn't even have a chance to scream before the air was taken from him as his lungs filled with gray powder.

Will was dumbfounded. He couldn't attack the dust without killing the king, but the king would soon suffocate if he couldn't do something. *And should I do something? If the king dies during this fight, is it really so bad?*

Still unsure whether Androv had hidden himself while controlling the dust, or whether Androv *was* the dust, Will used the rod to send out another chime. The return tone indicated that the room was clear of hidden foes. *Is he really the dust itself?*

Lacking a better option, Will activated the rod's iron-body transformation, then summoned his falchion and used the silver-sword spell to cover it with argent flames. Last but not least, he sent another thread of turyn into the rod and cast another of the new spells Ethelgren had showed him, a water-breathing spell.

The name was something of a misnomer though, for the spell did nothing of the sort. Instead, it created a highly concentrated zone of air within the caster's throat while simultaneously sealing the mouth and nose. The end result was that the caster could survive for up to thirty minutes without air, while the main drawback was that it made it impossible to speak. *But that's an acceptable problem if you're dealing with poison gases,* Ethelgren had told him.

Will didn't know if the gray dust was poisonous, but he definitely didn't want it in his lungs.

Chapter 56

The king was on his knees, clutching at his throat, and as Will watched he sagged to the floor, his chest heaving and moving, though nothing entered or exited his mouth but more gray powder. His hands tensed into claws and then relaxed as he finally lost consciousness.

Will had been preparing a spell while he watched, and when the king passed out he released it, surrounding the body with a force-dome barely large enough for two men. The dust exploded up and out of Lognion's mouth, swirling around the inside of the makeshift cage. Will moved closer, readying his burning sword.

His plan was simple, force Androv to resume his human form, then strike him down with the sword. He didn't know if it would work, but it was the best he could come up with. According to Ethelgren, the argent flames could destroy almost anything, vampire, human, or even tree, as Tiny had demonstrated.

After a moment, Androv's body reformed from the dust, and he stood smiling at Will with naked fangs that lent an entirely different feeling to the expression. "Please let me out, William. I'm dying to give you something."

Will could have dismissed the force-dome and then struck, but he wanted Androv kept busy. Sure enough, a second later, the vampire pointed one finger at Will and released another gray bolt of power. It struck the inside of the dome and began devouring the force-wall, crawling around the edges of it like acid on burning flesh. Will stepped to one side and swung the sword. It passed through the fresh opening and completely bisected the pompous wizard.

The flames guttered, and smoke billowed out as Androv screamed and collapsed on the floor in two large and very separate pieces. He glared hatefully at Will.

Dismissing the force-dome, Will swung again, hoping to end the master vampire completely, but the fiend smiled and exploded outward, blinding Will with a thick, gray cloud that swirled around him as it expanded. He could hear Androv laughing in his ears, and seconds later the vampire reformed several feet away. "Did Ethelgren tell you to try the sword? It almost worked, once. Surely, he knew that after that I would find a way to protect myself? Once burned, twice shy, that's what I always say."

Will noticed a band of burned flesh at Androv's midsection. He pointed at it and smiled.

"You think you've done me some harm?" A force-dome appeared around Will in the blink of an eye, and then the vampire bent down to lift Lognion's wrist to his mouth. With a flash of yellow teeth, he tore into the flesh and began to suckle on the wound, lapping at the red blood with a tongue that appeared black whenever it darted out from his lips.

Will was sickened by the sight, and it reminded him of the moments that he'd endured while the vampires had briefly fed on him. He tried to think of a way to escape the force-dome, but unlike Androv, he didn't know a spell that would destroy force effects. He couldn't steal it either, for unlike most spells, force effects were intimately tied to their caster—they couldn't be wrested away.

Androv dropped the king's still-bleeding wrist and stood up once more, his mouth stained crimson. The scarred flesh at his waist was gone. "See? Good as new. You're going to love it."

That sent a cold chill down his spine. Will lifted one hand and made a gesture that was easy to understand.

The master vampire nodded. "Did you know that of all the vampires you've met in this precious city, none of them were whole?"

Chapter 56

Will frowned.

"Except for me, of course," said Androv. "All the others are what they used to call 'lesser vampires.' Poor, sad creatures created accidentally, either through a botched feeding or an accidental cut or scratch. But you're worthy of more than that. I will make you my true child."

Will shook his head.

"That's too bad. I wasn't asking. Of all the people in this city, even your sad, centuries-old king, you're the only one I would consider granting such a boon to. Do you know why?"

Centuries old? That wasn't possible, not unless the king was a wizard, or was there some other way?

"Because you're a true wizard, like me. There aren't many of us left, so you're a rare find. Then there's also the fact that the extensive blood transfusion will give me even more control over your thoughts and actions than that pathetic heart-stone enchantment your king so favors. By making you my heir, I will double my strength on the council."

If that were his criteria, he'd do the same to Lognion. Will dismissed the water breathing spell and said, "You'll have to take this dome down first, and as soon as you do, I'll be all over you," threatened Will, waving the sword. He wished he could believe his own words. Using the rod, he replaced the spell as soon as he'd finished speaking.

"Oh! I forgot. You can't take it down yourself, can you? How rude of me." The force-dome vanished. "There. Now, by all means, vanquish me!"

He'd been waiting for that, and Will's turyn exploded through his body as he blurred to attack at the fastest speed he could manage. And missed. Androv neatly dodged the swing, and the next, and those that followed.

"Frustrating, isn't it? Here, let me help you." The vampire froze in place and as Will's sword swung in, Androv's body dissolved into dust just ahead of the flames, reforming behind it. "I let you cut me earlier. It's more fun giving people hope, then slowly crushing it."

Will felt despair, but not the sort his enemy wanted. *You were right, he found a way to defeat the flames.*

How?

He transforms freely back and forth to dust or ash. Can you think of a way to beat it?

No, sorry, just my final spell, the 'Last Resort.' I'll tell the next person to find me what a hero you were, though.

Just don't possess them.

No promises.

Will took a few more swings with the sword, then began firing force-lances at Androv at the same time. The vampire's body would explode into dust with each strike, only to reform a second later. "That tickles, William! Please don't stop!"

He knew the attacks wouldn't help, but he was gathering turyn while his enemy taunted him. As soon as he was almost full, he would feed it all into the rod, and then…

Androv reversed the game, sending a barrage of force-lances back at Will, forcing him to block them, but at the same time the vampire walked toward him. Will swung at him with the sword, while he continued to block the force-lances, but Androv ignored it, letting the blade pass through his torso. Then his clawed hand reached out to open Will's throat.

He frowned when the hardened skin prevented injury. "How annoying."

Now that Androv was right in front of him, it was time. Will slammed his turyn into the rod. In a second

Chapter 56

it would be over. *Sorry, Selene.* Pain shot down his arm, a wretched agony, but when Will's eyes opened it wasn't because of the spell effect he had attempted to activate.

Androv held his left wrist, and despite the hardened skin, he had crushed Will's wrist bones. The hand hung loosely without support while the rod had fallen to the ground. The vampire released him, sending more agony shooting up his wrist and arm, then he bent and retrieved the rod. "This little nuisance should have been eliminated a long time ago." Turyn whipped around the vampire's hand, and a red glow formed. The rod began to shift colors and soon it glowed as well, then it sagged, and molten metal dripped to the floor, sizzling on the stone.

Stunned by the pain, and the loss of his one useful tool, Will scarcely blinked when Androv exploded, flowed around him, and then reformed. He held Will's sword arm in an irresistible grip while his other hand clutched Will's throat. The vampire crooned in his ear, "Let me show you what the sword feels like." With a jerk and a twist, he pulled Will's arm out, back, and up until something popped and pain shot through him. The sword fell from his grip, but the hand at his throat vanished as Androv caught it with blinding speed.

Then he drove it into the center of Will's lower back. There was a moment of resistance, as the iron-body transformation tried to stop it, but the magic of Ethelgren's silver sword spell was too great, especially when combined with Androv's monstrous strength. The tip pierced his spine, then erupted from his belly.

Will screamed, while Androv levered the sword from side to side, opening a wide cut that caused his guts to spill out. The vampire lowered him slowly to the floor, then examined his belly. "What luck, William! I missed the hepatic artery and vein! It looks like it may take you a couple of minutes to bleed to death, rather than seconds. Aren't you lucky? Don't worry, though, I won't let you die all the way."

Androv exploded into dust and rushed at Will's face, but the water-breathing spell prevented him from entering. The vampire reformed with a look of frustration on his face. With one hand, he reached out and touched Will's lips. A war of wills ensued, and then Androv pulled the water-breathing spell away, flicking it into slivers of dissolving turyn with his fingertips. "Your will is *very* well developed for someone so young, William. Your teacher must be proud."

Despite the pain, or perhaps because of it, Will's mind felt clear, and sad. The faces of those he wouldn't see again flashed through his mind. His mother, Sammy, Tiny, Laina, Janice—and most of all Selene. *Selene!* In a moment of clarity, he realized there might be one last hope. Looking at his right palm, he began to form a spell.

"You still haven't given up? My word, William, you're a rare prize. What kind of spell is that? Not that it matters. Surely you realize nothing can kill me. Even Grim Talek would hesitate to try, for fear of earning my enmity for uncountable centuries. Go on. Let's see what it is. If it's something entertaining, I'll knock a decade off your punishment before I allow you some responsibility."

Ignoring the taunts, Will finished the construct, but he didn't put his turyn into it. Instead he activated one of his prepared spells, shoving half of his remaining power into the wind-wall spell. It exploded into violent fury, shredding the vampire's body, but only into dust, yet again.

Androv laughed as he swirled through the air, and as the spell faded, he started to taunt his victim once again. "I thought you might have something original. I'd never seen the other spell, but I suppose it was just a decoy—"

Chapter 56

His words cut off as Will pushed the rest of his power into the spell he had constructed and released it. Selene's Solution expanded to fill the room, sweeping up dust, dirt, trash, particles, and filth. It collected the spilled blood and the debris on the floor, it cleaned their clothes, and even their wounds. But most of all, it swept Androv up and gathered him in, inexorable in its pull.

In the past he had often wondered what her spell did with the dirt it collected, for it had to go somewhere. So, he had studied its inner workings, only to be amazed once again at the intricacy of her design. The dirt and dross were collected and converted into two opposing forms of turyn, then it was mixed and dispersed. The spell's organizing effect created a slight cooling effect in the area it cleaned, while the constructive destruction of the matter it collected created a warming effect that was dispersed widely at its boundaries.

Androv, master wizard and vampire, was converted into heat energy and absorbed by the cool earth that surrounded the chamber, and then he was no more.

CHAPTER 57

Will wished he couldn't feel his legs, but he could. If he closed his eyes it felt as though someone was holding him over an open fire, roasting his lower half in the flames, but when he looked at them, they were fine, except for the fact that he couldn't move them. By the same token, his entrails were a minor inconvenience, messy and sprawling across the floor, but they caused him little pain. *How odd,* observed the quiet voice in the back of his head. Maybe it was all relative and the pain in his lower body was so great that his brain simply had no time to process the pain from his other injuries.

He summoned the last regeneration potion from the limnthal and stared at it for a moment, his eyes going to the king. Selene's father had bled out slowly from the wound on his wrist, but the blood loss wasn't inconsiderable. Without prompt treatment, the man might die. If Lognion did die, the ramifications would be significant.

Still reeling from the damage to Cerria, Terabinia might fall victim to a fresh incursion from Darrow, especially if they were the ones who had sent the vampires in the first place. The nation would need a strong ruler to defeat such a powerful enemy. If Selene was back, she might take his place, but she wasn't. Without a king, Terabinia would collapse into chaos and civil war.

But if I save him, I'll die for certain. And that was ignoring the fact that he had sworn to kill the king eventually anyway.

He was fed up with stupid dilemmas. "To hell with all of it," said Will angrily. "I've done enough for this goddamned nation." Unstopping the vial, he drank its contents.

A new heat raced through him, and the burning in his legs changed to an intense sensation of electric pain. He cried out as it swept over him, and he felt the bones in his wrist and shoulder seek out their proper places and reunite. Glancing down, he saw his intestines snaking back into him, looking for all the world like parasitic worms racing to feast on his innards. Their movement was accompanied with a wave of nausea.

Once his bones were in place, Will scooted across the floor until he was beside the dying king. His healing was still intensely painful, but every minute counted. Summoning another spare tunic, he cut it into strips. *I need to store some damned linen bandages in there,* he thought, making a mental note. *I keep cutting up perfectly good clothes.* Will tightly wrapped the man's wrist, then tied off the bandage with a quick knot.

"There, maybe you won't die. Asshole," he announced faintly. His head felt dizzy, and he knew he was about to pass out. *Not yet.*

Will summoned two blood-cleanse potions and drank one. He poured the other in Lognion's mouth and held the man's mouth and nose shut. "I hope you fucking choke on it."

The king did choke a little, but he swallowed reflexively, and most of it went down. Will released him and lay back. *Damn, that was probably my last chance to get rid of him.* Then he closed his eyes and let the darkness take him.

***

When he woke again, he was still in the underground chamber and he could feel someone watching him. With a start, he realized that Lognion had propped himself up near the wall and was staring at him with baleful eyes.

"I see you're awake finally," said the king.

"You too, unfortunately," admitted Will.

Lognion laughed, but he lacked the energy to do it properly. "That's entirely your fault." He held up his bandaged wrist. "Does it feel good to be my savior?"

Will closed his eyes. "I was hoping I'd wake up in a soft bed with friends around me. How long have you been waiting just so you could irritate me? Couldn't you summon someone to get us out?"

"A few hours," admitted the king. "I thought we should talk first. Have a little father-to-son chat as it were."

"You aren't my father."

"You married Selene."

"She doesn't recognize you anymore."

The king shrugged. "Too bad. I don't give a damn what she thinks. You have to listen anyway."

"Just get it over with." Will sat up. He still felt drained, but he was no longer sleepy, just exhausted. The potion had had to heal a lot.

"I'm disappointed in you. You had your chance to be rid of me."

Will shrugged. "I thought about it."

"If you had killed me, Selene would have been crowned queen and you could have ruled by her side. I probably would have given you my blessing—"

"You'd have been dead," interjected Will.

"In a spiritual sense. I might have felt comfortable leaving it all to someone ruthless enough to save the capital

Chapter 57

and murder me at the same time. Instead, I find myself mildly disgusted by your weakness."

"I don't give a rat's ass what you think about me. Selene can't come back just because you're dead. I don't even know where she is. The kingdom might have fallen into civil war before she returned."

The king laughed again. "So you sacrificed your dream of freeing the elementals, the other wizards, your family—you sacrificed all that just so the kingdom would be safer? A stronger man might have taken the reins of power regardless of Selene's absence. You're powerful, William. You might have managed it."

"Someday. You'll be the first to know," said Will, miming the thrust of a dagger with one hand.

"You might just be the funniest man I've ever met. I'll regret killing you one day."

"That's where we're different."

"How so?"

Will grinned maliciously. "I'll be a happy man the day I put an end to you. I won't regret it at all."

"Work hard. If you can manage it, I'll cheer you on from the grave. No one has succeeded yet, though many have tried."

"Today would have been the day. Just remember that."

"Never fear, I've already got your reward in mind."

"Which is?"

"The Duchy of Arenata. The current heir is weak. I was planning to eliminate him anyway. The reward fits the deed, and I will gain a mighty vassal in the process," said the king.

"Piss off. I'm not swearing fealty to you."

"You've already given me more reason to trust you than any of the other vipers who have sworn their oaths. I won't ask for it."

Will frowned. "The ceremony will seem rather odd then."

"I'll confer the title in private. Decorum will be saved, and you will have a proper rank to merit Selene as your wife."

"Where's the catch? You never do anything that doesn't benefit you."

"The catch is your conscience. You never do anything that doesn't benefit the kingdom. So long as that aligns with what benefits me, you will be the finest of servants."

"Go fuck yourself."

"Say that in public and I'll have you flogged to death. Remember that. I'll tolerate your suicidal remarks only in private."

Wearily, Will got to his feet and walked over to the king, then held out his hand. Lognion took it, and Will helped him up. When the king staggered, Will slipped the man's arm over his shoulder. "Come on. Climbing the stairs is going to take forever. If we stay down here any longer, no good will come of it."

The journey up did take forever and there was no one in the house above. Will hoped to find assistance in the street, but while the sun was up and shining the street was empty. He resigned himself to a long walk. *Everyone must be sheltering at Wurthaven still,* he decided.

The half-hour walk took a full hour since they had to stop while Will gave the king some water to drink. Blood loss had rendered the king painfully weak and tired. They passed the gate to Wurthaven on their way to the palace, and Will saw that the bodies from the night before still lay scattered about. He could see the spot where he had left Tiny, but the big man was nowhere to be seen. *I hope he's somewhere safe.* There were no people to be seen anywhere.

Chapter 57

They continued on to the palace and found it similarly abandoned. Will helped the king into the palace and half-carried, half-dragged the man to his bedchamber. No servants appeared, and since Lognion looked pale and unwell, Will realized he couldn't simply leave.

He wound up helping the king remove his boots and then propped him up in bed before going downstairs to find the kitchen. An hour later, he returned with a pitcher of small beer and a platter full of sautéed sweetmeats, primarily liver and kidneys. His mother had always told him they were best for people who had suffered a lot of blood loss.

"Did you find anyone?" asked Lognion.

He shook his head. "Eat up."

They ate together in silence by mutual accord, and when the king was finally done he remarked, "That was well made. You cooked that?"

Will nodded, grunting around a mouthful of food.

"It wasn't bad. Not quite as good as some I've had but—"

Swallowing quickly, Will growled. "I was in a hurry. Nor did I feel like putting in my best effort, considering the patient."

The king nodded in acceptance. "I pity the cook that works for you then. For there's no worse critic of a man than someone else who has mastered his craft."

Will glared at him. "Do you even know what pity is?"

Lognion shrugged. "I understand it as a concept, though I've never felt it."

The day dragged on, and no one appeared. Eventually, Will left and went to Wurthaven, but the entire campus seemed to be deserted without a soul in sight. A quick walk through the city market yielded similar results.

The city was empty. Will couldn't help but wonder if he had somehow arrived at the ritual chamber *after* the ritual had been performed. *Maybe they already wiped everyone out?* He didn't know what sort of ritual had been planned. It was possible that it was designed only to destroy people while leaving the buildings unharmed.

But if that were the case, he would have died as well. *Unless they did it right after I entered the house and started down the stairs.*

Returning to the palace, he asked the king, who answered, "The ritual I had planned was destructive. The city would be rubble now. They must be alive somewhere."

Frustrated, Will stayed through the afternoon and cooked a second meal, this time with more thought and planning. Not because he wanted the king's approval, but simply because he couldn't bear mediocrity in food. This time the monarch was more plentiful with his praise, and Will refrained from any biting responses. Night fell, and though it was still early, the king fell asleep, victim to his recent frailty. Will needed rest too, so he retired to Selene's bedroom.

Using her signature spell once again, he cleaned the entire chamber, freshening both the pillows and blankets as well as cleaning himself. Then he stripped and climbed in between the sheets. Despite his anxiety over the vanishing populace, he was soon asleep.

EPILOGUE

Will slept like a rock, but since he had gone to bed early, he also woke early, sometime just before dawn. He didn't move at first, for there was something in the air that seemed different. Opening his eyes, he lay still, studying the room and trying to understand his strange intuition. The room looked the same, but then he heard a gentle sigh beside him.

Someone else was in the bed.

His heart leapt into his throat, and he suddenly wished he had kept his clothes on before he lay down. He could only see the back of his bedmate's head, and while his vision was sharp enough, the dim light made it difficult to discern the hair's true hue. He could only tell it was a very dark shade.

Not daring to move, he studied the invader, and after a brief while decided it was a woman. The shape of her hips and the slenderness of her shoulder made it plain. He quickly ran through the list of women he knew, trying to decide if one of them might suddenly leap over the bounds of propriety and do something so bold.

Laina had slept next to him once before, but this woman wasn't blond, and he suspected she was naked. Lowering his head, he lifted the comforter slightly to make sure his assumption was correct, and saw a quick glimpse of a shapely back and rounded derriere. *Definitely naked.* That ruled out his sister—she was no fool. *Tabitha?* Her hair was dark enough, and she presumably didn't know he was her brother, but that seemed too far-fetched.

Janice was the obvious candidate, since she had long had a crush on him, but given the way she had acted around Tiny, he thought she had already moved on. Then he remembered her white hair. It definitely wasn't her.

Darla? The Arkeshi had dark hair, but he suspected her back would carry more scars. He simply wasn't sure. Will decided it was time to evacuate the bed, but given how close they were, he decided to try one more thing out of curiosity. Craning his neck forward, he sniffed the woman's hair. His nose was filled with the scent of pines and fresh mountain grass. Will's eyes opened wide with disbelief, and then the woman sighed and scooted backward, bringing herself fully into contact with him.

"Selene?" It couldn't be.

She turned and looked at him, her eyes glittering in the darkness. "You woke up. You were sleeping so hard I thought you might never wake."

He kissed her, unable to do anything else. Clutching her in his arms, he held onto her for several minutes, hoping he wasn't still asleep. Eventually, he relaxed his grip so he could look at her face once more. "Is it really you?"

She nodded. "It seems like a dream, doesn't it?"

"How?"

"Your grandmother decided I had passed some milestone and brought me back, though I think it had more to do with the fact that my father's control enchantment vanished. Things were also getting difficult diplomatically."

"You can stay?" he asked.

She nodded. "You're in charge of the worst part of my training."

"What's that?"

"She said you'd understand. It's the first 'compression.' Do you know what that means?"

Epilogue

Will grimaced. "She would leave that to me. It's dangerous and painful. You're going to hate me before it's over."

"I would never hate you," she insisted.

"So you think. I nearly attacked Arrogan with an axe."

She laughed. "From what I've heard, your grandfather wasn't exactly brimming with warmth and human kindness." Her expression shifted, and her voice deepened. If she had been a cat, Will might have thought she was purring. "Say, I've noticed something since we're so close together." Her eyes drifted downward.

He flushed red. "Sorry, I have to pee."

She laughed. "Is that all? Then by all means take care of it!"

He slipped out of the bed, feeling self-conscious at his nudity. They hadn't seen each other in over a year, so it felt strange. Matters were made worse by the fact that he couldn't find the chamber pot. He scrambled all over the room on his hands and knees, but the vital receptacle was nowhere to be found. Unlikely as it was, he went to the front room to look but had no luck there either. *Ah well, the city is deserted, right?*

Walking to the window, he opened it and pushed the shutters apart before relieving himself on the rose bushes far below. A mad cackle rose in his throat as he enjoyed the sensation of doing something so obviously forbidden. Then he noticed a guardsman on the palace wall directly across from the window he stood at.

The two men locked eyes in a timeless moment. He was too far along to stop, and he certainly wasn't going to jump back and get urine in Selene's room. Despite his embarrassment, Will grinned sheepishly and lifted one hand to wave at the guard.

The other man smirked, nodded, then turned away, allowing Will to finish with a semblance of privacy. When he returned to the bedroom, Selene asked, "Did you just pee out the window?"

"I couldn't find the chamber pot."

Thankfully she had a sense of humor. "Did the guard see you?"

"Definitely, but I think we came to an understanding."

She gaped at him. "Oh, really?"

"He seemed to take it in stride, so I suppose he must see that sort of thing at your window quite often."

"What are you implying?"

He kissed her neck, then continued, "Well, since there's no chamber pot, I can only conclude you make a habit of using that window. The roses looked suspiciously healthy."

Selene pulled his arm out from under him and rolled over on top of him. "How on earth do you think I would manage that without falling to my death?"

Will shrugged. "Just stick your rear out and hang onto the edges of the window. If you're worried about falling, I could probably rig up a sling or something, maybe add a wooden bar to hold onto."

Selene was moving in a decidedly distracting fashion. "I think I've found something better to hold onto."

Will was in complete agreement, but he had two reservations. "What about your training?"

She leaned down and kissed his forehead. "She wouldn't have let me in here with you if that was a concern anymore. Personally, I think it had more to do with her testing me than it had to do with my training."

"Testing you how?"

"After," she breathed into his ear. "I've been waiting too long."

Epilogue

He never got around to asking her about his second concern, which was whether she needed to find a chamber pot for herself. The answer was definitely a no. A brief time later, they rested. "Testing you how?" asked Will again.

"I think she wanted to test my fidelity."

Will's stomach sank as he remembered his vision of her with another man. "You mean Sylandrea?"

Selene's head jerked back. "How did you know his name?"

"I saw you in a dream—together. You said his name then."

"Well, just so you know, *that* didn't happen, though I did have some dreams of my own. How could you have learned his name, though?"

Her manner was so relaxed and confident that Will believed her immediately. It took him a few minutes to explain the experience of astral projection, but apparently Selene had read up on it before, so the topic wasn't completely unfamiliar to her. "Is there anything that you haven't studied?" asked Will.

"Wizardry, apparently," she said sourly. "From the way you and Aislinn keep talking about it."

"So what was the test?" Will asked.

"I thought I explained that."

He shook his head. "Being alone for a year wouldn't be a problem. I know you better than that."

She sighed. "Sylandrea was in heat."

"Huh?"

"Elven males go into heat once every ten years or so. When they do, their urges become exceptionally strong, and they emit pheromones that tend to elicit a similar response in women around them. Unmarried men, like Sylandrea, are kept away from polite society during that period, but drabs like me don't count. I thought he was being nice, but in reality, he thought I would be a guilt-free outlet for his pent-up frustrations."

"That's awful—and don't ever call yourself a drab in front of me again."

She smiled. "Can I be honest?"

He nodded, but his stomach sank at the same time.

"I was sorely tempted, Will. I want to blame the pheromones. I've never been so frustrated in my life, but even so, I feel ashamed that it affected me so strongly. What you saw in your dream was probably what I was experiencing in *my* dream."

Will swallowed. "I trust you. I would trust you even if you made a mistake." He was struck by a sudden desire to tell her about his recent philosophical revelation. "Lies are like clothes, but trust is allowing your partner their privacy even when you know they need new clothes." He paused. "Wait, that's not it. Why can't I remember it right?"

Selene gave him a strange look, but her eyes were smiling. "Where did you come up with that bit of rubbish?"

"It wasn't rubbish," he insisted. "Even your father thought it was logical—I think."

"You've been talking to *him?*" She rolled her eyes. "I need to hear the story, but first, I think we need to remark our territories again."

"Territories?"

Her eyes were filled with hunger. "You've had enough time to rest."

It turned out he had, and their second dance was much longer than the first. The sun was approaching midmorning when they finally relented and gave in to the need for rest. They weren't sleepy, though, so the conversation continued.

Epilogue

"When did you get here?" asked Will.

"Yesterday afternoon," she told him. "Aislinn left me at our house, but there was no one there, so I went looking. I saw evidence of a lot of fighting, but there was no one around. So I went into the city, but it was also empty. Eventually I came here, but the palace was empty as well. Where were you?"

He laughed. "In all the same places. We must have missed each other at every stop."

"What about when you came here?" she asked.

"I was in your father's room until I came here to sleep."

She raised her brows in an unspoken question.

"He lost a lot of blood, so I fed him."

"You two seem to have gotten close," she observed, her tone suspicious.

A remark like that from most daughters might have been a joke, or a compliment, but Will knew otherwise. Selene feared and hated her father more than anyone living. "Trust me, we aren't. Far from it. In fact, if I had known you were coming back, I might not have kept him alive."

That led to a lengthy telling of what had occurred over the past week. Selene's reactions ranged from shock to anger at some of the things that had happened, but when Will referred to Mark Nerrow harshly, she stopped him. "That isn't fair," she said.

"I didn't mean he was *actually* as bad as your father, but he really is an ass."

She gave him a quick kiss, easing his frustration, then responded, "Don't judge him too harshly. He's a hundred times better than my father. He actually cares about his children, and that includes you too, even if he hurts you with his poor handling of the situation."

He could still hear his father's voice after their last fight, as he had walked away. *"It does matter if something happens to you."* Will shook his head to clear the memory. "He's still a jerk."

"He's human," corrected Selene. "I know he's hurt you, but remember this, not only did he raise Laina and Tabitha, but he's the only real father I've ever known. My time with that family is the only reason I'm not completely broken."

Will sighed. "I guess I can give him credit for a few things." Then he shifted the topic. "What did you mean by 'diplomatic tensions' earlier?"

She looked uncomfortable. "Well, I mentioned my problem with Sylandrea, but I didn't tell you the details of what happened." He waited, so she continued, "He came into my room one night and kissed me." Selene stopped. "No, that's not quite right. I kissed him, but that's why he was there. He knew what would happen. I realized my mistake almost immediately, but he wouldn't let me go, so…"

"So…?"

"I broke his nose—accidentally."

"You mean on purpose," said Will, feeling a small bit of satisfaction.

Selene frowned. "I hit him on purpose, but I didn't mean to break his nose, so it was an accident."

"What did you hit him with?"

"My forehead. I jerked away and headbutted him." Will began to laugh, but she went on, "Anyway, it turns out his uncle is rather important, so my stay there became something of a problem. Your bargain with my father to get rid of the heart-stone enchantment couldn't have come at a better time."

Will studied her for a moment, then spotted a small cut on her forehead. It looked to be just a few days old. "Is this from the headbutt?"

Epilogue

She nodded, with pouting lips and large, woeful eyes. "Think it will scar?"

He smiled, then kissed the wound. "I hope so. For me it will be a splendid reminder of your love. For others it can serve as a warning."

Selene rolled her eyes again. "No one will know what it's from."

"You can wear a sign," he suggested helpfully, laughing when she punched him.

"I don't want an ugly scar," she lamented. "At least not there, right in the middle of my forehead." Will pointed at his cheek, which still retained a long, silvery mark from a coachwhip in his childhood. "That's different. It's actually sort of dashing," she commented.

"Well, I've been thinking for a while that you needed to be uglied up a little bit anyway," said Will.

Her mouth went wide, into an 'o' of surprise. "What does that mean?" she demanded.

"You're too pretty. I was thinking you should start wearing sackcloth dresses, or maybe chop your hair up, but a scar would probably do just as well." He grinned. "We have to find some way to keep the men from chasing you constantly."

She growled. "Is that really what you think? And if I'm ugly, what's going to keep you chasing me then?"

"That's easy. I'm not after you for your looks." She smiled, but then he continued, "I'm actually after you for your money and the wild sex." Selene tackled him, and they wrestled for a moment before he cried uncle, laughing as he capitulated. "I repent, I repent! It's actually your inner beauty, your intelligence and personality."

"I'll show you some *personality*!" she warned.

He held up his arms. "Please, no. I surrender. I can't take any more personality. Maybe in a few hours."

She stood up and snatched the bedcovers away, exposing him to the air. "Weakling!" she declared imperiously, though her eyes were twinkling.

It was then that the door opened. Janice stood there, her expression blank, while Tiny stood behind her with a clear view over her head. Moving without haste, he put one hand over Janice's eyes, then helped her back out of the doorway. From behind them, Laina's voice called, "What is it? Is he in there?" Her head darted around the doorframe for a second, then her cheeks reddened, and she jerked back. Tiny's hand appeared—then slowly closed the door.

Will and Selene had remained frozen, but now they looked at one another, exchanging embarrassed looks. Through the door, Will could hear their friends talking. "I'm scarred for life. I'll never be able to unsee that," said Laina.

Janice's tone was calmer. "At least he didn't have to pee this time."

Tiny simply laughed.

A short while later, the married couple timidly emerged from Selene's bedroom. Laina hurried to give her best friend a long hug, while Will attempted to shift the focus elsewhere. "Is anyone hungry?"

Tiny's eyes lit up, but Laina had more pressing concerns. "Not anymore," she said harshly. "Where have you been?"

"Here. I couldn't find anyone after I sorted things out with the king," answered Will. "The entire city was deserted."

His sister glared at him, and he noticed that her eyes were red and swollen. "You told me to get them out of the city."

"But everyone was gone," he said, knowing he was missing some important clue.

Epilogue

Janice intervened. "After we got the students out, Laina insisted on coming back for the citizens, in spite of her father's objections. We found Tiny at the school entrance, along with all the bodies. You were nowhere to be found, and we couldn't wake him up."

"They had to use a cart to carry me out," Tiny boasted with a grin.

"And when he did finally wake up the next day, what he had to say…," Laina's voice tapered off as her throat closed up. She went to the window, facing away from them.

Janice helped once more. "His story wasn't very reassuring. So we spent the next day waiting miserably. It took everything we had to keep the people from returning to their homes, but fortunately Laina can be very persuasive when she puts her mind to it."

Selene smiled faintly. "Another speech? You really do have a gift, Laina."

Laina still wouldn't turn around, and she was busily rubbing her face with one sleeve.

Janice continued, "So the entire populace camped outside that day and the following night. We only returned this morning, when it was obvious that the city wasn't going to be destroyed. We've been trying to find you ever since."

"You could have left a note somewhere. Something!" exclaimed Laina, her composure crumbling again and angry tears falling to her cheeks.

Will crossed the room in two large strides and pulled her into a firm embrace. They stood that way for several minutes, and when he stepped back and looked at his friends, he saw an excess of moisture in everyone's eyes. More hugs were the only solution.

When things finally calmed down, Tiny brought up an urgent concern. "You asked if we were hungry a few minutes ago. I think we should revisit the topic."

Laina wasn't ready to let him off the hook, though. She shook her head. "He still hasn't told us what happened."

"We can talk *and* eat," suggested Tiny plaintively.

Laina threw up her hands. "Fine!"

They went to the palace kitchens and were promptly rushed out. While Selene's presence made a strong impression, they were told it would be some time. The forced evacuation and subsequent return had left the palace in a state of disarray. The returning soldiers and servants had wiped out the food that was already prepared, and it would take some time to get things back in order. Will suggested they return to Wurthaven. "I know my kitchen, and I can make a better meal anyway."

Selene lifted one brow. "Your kitchen?"

He refused to capitulate. "Your house, my kitchen."

"Our *home*," she corrected, leaning forward to rub noses with him.

Laina gagged. "There went my appetite again."

"I'm *still* hungry," Tiny insisted.

They left the palace and headed for Wurthaven. Will resumed telling his story. Earlier with Selene, he had ended at the point where he and Tiny separated, so he began with his entrance into the old Arenata residence. When it came to the point at which Androv had started inflicting terrible injuries, he tried to gloss over them with less dramatic phrasing. Selene's face went pale at those points, but Laina demanded more detail.

"Wait," said his sister, holding up one hand. "What do you mean he took the rod and broke your wrist? You had the iron-body transformation going, right?"

Will winced. "He just squeezed, and it sort of crushed all the bones." He watched Selene, carefully, noticing a pained look on her face.

Epilogue

Laina nodded, urging him to continue, but less than a minute later she interrupted again. "You said he ran you through with the sword. What does that mean? From behind?"

Will nodded.

"Where did it go in?"

He pointed to his spine.

"Ouch," said Laina, with a grimace. "What does that feel like?"

"Sort of like your lower body is being burned alive, but I think it's just the nerves, like a phantom pain, since I couldn't actually move my legs," he explained.

"If he stabbed you in the back, how did your guts come out?"

"He kept working the sword back and forth." Will demonstrated by moving his hand back and forth across his midsection. "That's when everything just sort of— spilled out."

Janice gagged and ran for the bushes. Meanwhile, Selene exclaimed, "Please stop. I can't bear thinking about it anymore."

Laina gave her friend an uncompromising look. "Don't be such a wilted flower. I want to know what happened. He's obviously fine now."

Will held up his hand. "It's all right. That's the worst of it. After that, I defeated him with a simple combination of spells."

"How?" demanded Laina incredulously. "One arm was broken, the other broken or dislocated, your spine was severed, and your guts were all over the floor! Not to mention this Androv was apparently immune to virtually every form of attack, magical or otherwise. There's no possible way you could have beaten him at that point."

Will couldn't help but embellish the story slightly. "I had a wind-wall spell prepared already, and since he didn't seem to care what I did, I readied another spell." He glanced at his wife so he could watch her reaction. "Selene's Solution."

Janice frowned, Laina blinked, and Selene gaped then said, "Tell the truth. What did you really do?"

Will drew an 'x' over his heart. "I swear to the Mother. That's what I did."

"Now I know he's full of shit," stated Laina, but Selene waved her to silence as her brain mulled over the possibility.

"Let him finish," said Selene.

Will smiled. "So, I was lying there, half dead and stricken with unbelievable pain, and I looked Androv right in the eye and told him, 'You may think you've beaten me, but you're about to make a clean exit from this world.' I cut loose with the wind-wall, and while he was still whirling around in dust form, I used Selene's spell to fatally tidy him right into oblivion." He stared at them to gauge their reactions, but no one said anything, so he added, "Get it? It was a tidy termination."

Selene groaned, and Tiny began chuckling.

"A clean kill?" suggested Will. "A hygienic homicide?"

Laina pointed at him accusingly. "I don't believe any of it, liar."

Selene broke in, "I think the spell would work, actually. But the rest..." She started shaking her head.

Janice returned, having recovered from her nausea. "He's terrible when he thinks he has an audience."

Laina agreed. "I'll believe the rest, but there's no way you said that bit about a 'clean exit.' You can barely think straight when you're *not* being tortured." Everyone nodded, seeming to come to a consensus. Then Laina

Epilogue

looked at the others. "Did he try to tell you about his philosophical revelation regarding lies and naked people? I've never heard anything so stupid in all my life."

Tiny and Will fell back slightly, letting the women take the lead while they began to enthusiastically discuss his flaws. The squire looked at him with pity. "It was a good story."

"You believed me though, right?"

Tiny draped a large arm over his shoulder. "Listen, Will. I *trust* you, and trust is something you give a friend even if you think they might be lying, because lies are like clothes…"

Will punched him in the side. "Let go of me, you traitor!" They laughed together the rest of the way home, where they found the remainder of the Nerrow family waiting with a big lunch already prepared, courtesy of Armand.

The powerful embraces he received from Tabitha and Agnes warmed him all the way through, and the final, unexpected hug from Mark Nerrow brought him almost to tears. After a year separated from Selene, it was the best day he could remember ever having.

Coming Soon:

Disciple of War

Conflict erupts between Terabinia and Darrow and Will is right in the middle of the fray.

Stay up to date with my releases by signing up for my newsletter at:

Magebornbooks.com

Books by Michael G. Manning

Mageborn Series:

The Blacksmith's Son
The Line of Illeniel
The Archmage Unbound
The God-Stone War
The Final Redemption

Embers of Illeniel (a prequel series):

The Mountains Rise
The Silent Tempest
Betrayer's Bane

Champions of the Dawning Dragons:

Thornbear
Centyr Dominance
Demonhome

The Riven Gates:

Mordecai
The Severed Realm
Transcendence and Rebellion

Standalone Novels:

Thomas

Made in the USA
Monee, IL
12 July 2021

73451043R00361